New World Order Underwater
The Nae-Née Inventors Strike Back

New World Order Underwater:
The Nae-Née Inventors Strike Back
By Stephanie C. Fox, J.D.

The world of Nae-Née has undergone a tremendous change. 6.8 billion human beings were Culled within the space of a year. Human beings – each one unique, many talented – have been erased.

The world has rebuilt itself, adjusting to the new reality of the damage wrought by human overpopulation and resource depletion. Most of the world is underwater, and a new order has been imposed with the old.

The old world order includes universal use of Nae-Née, the nanite birth control device, continues. Anyone wishing to reproduce must still get a license to do so. No license will be granted before a death has been recorded. However, thanks to Hamish's Regenics serum, some people are living extended lifespans, so fewer births are to be authorized.

Avril continues to be concerned by what she knows about the past year. The Cull was not a natural plague: it was genocide. The Farmers of the world – elites with access to the bulk of financial and other wealth – orchestrated the Cull. They are banksters, hedge fundsters, and corporatists. It is Avril who has dubbed them "Farmers" due to their treatment of humans as a crop to be managed.

She must find a way to make this crime transparent to all while remaining out of reach. The Farmers are a pernicious threat, one that must be addressed. Until then, the new world order will be one of fear and manipulation by the powerful few.

The conclusion to the Nae-Née series takes the reader to a Florida that is mostly underwater and to the International Criminal Court in The Hague, the Netherlands. A changed world that includes farms and orchards in every town, electric vehicles, and a currency that is created by the planet's governments instead of its banksters is shown.

New World Order Underwater

The Nae-Née Inventors Strike Back

Stephanie C. Fox, J.D.

QueenBeeBooks

Bloomfield, Connecticut, U.S.A.

Library of Congress Cataloging-in-Publication Data
Name: Fox, Stephanie C., author.
Title: New World Order Underwater: The Nae-Née Inventors Strike Back / Stephanie C. Fox.
Description: Connecticut: QueenBeeBooks, [2016].
Identifiers: ISBN: 978-0-9996395-3-5 (paperback)
Subjects: FICTION / Science Fiction / Hard Science Fiction. NATURE / Environmental Conservation & Protection. LAW / Government / General.

www.queenbeeedit.com

Cover design by Stephanie C. Fox
Cover Illustration by Steve Palmerton

This book is dedicated to my parents, Carole and Paul Fox.

This story is also dedicated to Earth's inhabitants,
both human and others.

I hope we can survive without a resource war.

It would be better if we voluntarily control our own numbers.

One can always dream…

Also by Stephanie C. Fox

Nae-Née
– Birth Control: Infallible,
With Nanites and Convenience for All

Vaccine: The Cull
– Nae-Née Wasn't Enough

What the Small Gray Visitor Said

Intrigue On a Longship Cruise

Scheherazade Cat – The Story of a War Hero

An American Woman in Kuwait

Hawai'i – Stolen Paradise:
A Travelogue

Hawai'i – Stolen Paradise:
A Brief History

The Book of Thieves

The Bear Guarding the Beehive

The Slamming Door:
Bone Cancer, Asperger's, and Loss

Elephant's Kitchen
– An Aspergirl's Study in Difference

Almost a Meal – A True Tale of Horror

The Visitor Experience at the Mark Twain House

This is story is a work of fiction.

Any similarity to persons living or dead is purely coincidental.

The places are real.

The Rome Statute is real, and served to develop the plot.

The world of *Nae-Née* aims to make the reader think.

The reader is encouraged to apply issues, problems,
and laws from reality to a hypothetical world,
and to consider their effect on our future.

Democracy cannot survive overpopulation.
Human dignity cannot survive it.
Convenience and decency cannot survive it.
As you put more and more people into the world,
the value of life not only declines, it disappears.
It doesn't matter if someone dies.
The more people there are, the less one individual matters.
- Isaac Asimov

Table of Contents

Earth's Ecological Bank Account

Before the Cull, think tanks that studied the annual ecological footprint of the human species calculated that we were consuming the equivalent of not one planet Earth, but exceeding it. Scientists (climatologists and ecologists) as well as Farmers (banksters, hedge fundsters, and corporatists) thought of it as the Earth's bank account. They weren't wrong.

In the year 2000, we exceeded that limit in October.

In the year 2015, we exceeded it on August 13th: lucky 13. That was when the Cull had gotten underway, though most people had no idea that the vaccination program that they would soon be required to participate in had just about cleared its final stage of development.

By the time of the Cull (might as well put a capital letter on that word, unofficial and unacknowledged though the event was in the history books!), humans numbered over 8.4 billion. 10 billion was the projected number for the mid-21st century.

Nae-Née, the birth control nanite of the planet's population policy, hadn't been enough.

It was not enough to require a strict licensing process before any pregnancy could be undertaken. The number of humans living on the Earth had stalled in most places, while drastically slowing in others, but the result was that that number had continued to grow.

Those of us who studied human overpopulation and its effect on the ecosystem were used to being maligned as cold, heartless, and worse. What we actually were was morbidly fascinated by the horrific situation that was unfolding. It was anthropogenic (human-caused) climate change and resource depletion, and it was killing the ecosystem along with the species that lived in it.

That included us – humans. Studying it and lapping up every last detail about it was what we did, because it fascinated us, and because we knew that what we studied was important. We needed the ecosystem to survive.

Intellectual curiosity is amoral. It is neither moral nor immoral; it simply is. The same is true of a mental assessment: it simply is. Debating its morality has no effect whatsoever on its correctness or truth. It simply is.

And unlike a financial bank, the resources in an ecosystem's bank account cannot be finessed. They are either there, being replenished at a rate that the Farmers termed "sustainable" – which simply means fast enough to maintain the ecosystem while also sustaining the living creatures who depend upon it.

Humans, cats, wild bears, foxes, hummingbirds, owls – they all depend upon it.

No ecological bankster could ever simply inflate the currency of the ecosystem, because that currency is measured in clean air, potable water, edible and oxygenating plants, and so on and so on. Unlike a financial bank, in which money could be created by fiat – by declaration – an ecosystem could not be managed that way.

No…an ecosystem functioned as banks used to function, before the banksters got greedy and did away with the gold standard in most nations, including the United States.

At that time, the Earth had just over 3 billion humans on it, which was 1 billion more than its carrying capacity for humans. Our species' ecological bank account was already in overdraft, but few of us were willing to notice it at the point, let alone actually do anything about it.

Worse yet, aquifers all over the planet were being depleted with no end in sight, while glacial melt had accelerated. Sea levels were up by 20 feet or so around the globe (oddly, levels varied from place to place, in part due to gravitational pressures). Fossil fuel use had spewed enough carbon into the atmosphere to raise temperatures by 8 degrees Fahrenheit, left unchecked by deforestation worldwide.

It had taken eons for glacial melt from the Ice Age to fill the aquifers, and in just 60 years, they were down 40 percent due to the combined effects of food production and home construction. Beef production was the toughest on water tables; cattle ate soybeans, corn, and alfalfa that had been grown with water. It was the highest water-consumer of all food crops. Replenishment of those aquifers would take centuries – centuries that population pressures wouldn't allow.

We were in a state of ecosystems collapse, with many humans in a state of denial.

Economists and politicians like to promote growth. Many of them talked of old-age caregivers continuing the species and maintaining a high level of comfort for the elderly. That, however, simply enabled a vicious cycle of resource consumption to continue.

That was not, unpopular though the word was, sustainable.

The Cull aimed at secretly reducing the number of humans pressuring the ecosystem of the entire planet Earth: aquifers, arable land, rainforests, fuels of every kind, breathable air, living space, you name it.

It was a covert resource war, waged from the top down on the vast human population.

I should add that the Cull was not disclosed to us. It was nothing that we approved of.

We figured out what was happening just in time to save ourselves, and most of our family and friends. We managed to circumvent our own attempted murders – our own Culling – and theirs. That accomplished, we had escaped to Switzerland and waited out the Cull under the guise of setting up a health clinic, and then come home.

We as a species went, in a year, from roughly 8.4 billion humans to half a billion.

Chapter 1

Home Again – To An Altered State

It felt as though I had swallowed a huge chunk of ice, even though I hadn't.

It was a vague sense of unease mixed with anxiety, and it didn't go away. It wasn't meant to go away, because something was very wrong, and I knew exactly what it was. The ice just wouldn't melt, it seemed – unlike that of the polar icecaps. Those were melting rapidly.

Damn!

This was what anxiety was like for someone in her forties who had Asperger's. I didn't know what it felt like for neurotypicals my age, but I wasn't likely to find out with any ease or convenience, and it really didn't matter. Perhaps this was just what it felt like for me.

We had been back for a week now from our year-long stay in Lausanne, Switzerland plus a stay in New York City (which was like Venice now, with its canals and waterways, but with all new granite curbing and bridges). We were home in Connecticut, back on Stoner Drive, and I was out in the back yard, looking at my top-frame beehive, checking on the honeybees inside it.

Amazingly, they were still there, not collapsed. How could this be so?

I lifted one of the wooden bars that the honeycomb hung off of, carefully inspecting what the bees had built. Odd…the wood was supposed to be replaced each spring, but we hadn't been here then. There were replacement bars – more than enough for a few years of replacements – but only a beekeeper could do this. Bees got used to the scent and presence of their keeper. It couldn't be done by just anyone.

We had left the bees so abruptly that I had not had time to seal it up properly for the winter. Not that it had been time to do so just yet, but still, I had fretted about that while we were docked on Lake Geneva in the *Shadowcat*, our yacht, safely away from the Cull that was taking place around the world with our extended family, as the weather turned colder.

Even though climate change was a reality, winters could still be horridly, intensely cold in some places, and Switzerland was one of them. I had read the art and art history and history books that I had bought in the Lausanne museums as we hibernated on our yacht much of the time, tucked away from the freezing cold. I hated the cold.

I studied my honeybees some more. Not collapsed – they were still buzzing around, building honeycomb, and I would have to harvest some of the honey just to give them room to live in there. Their numbers had definitely decreased since last year, but they were okay for now.

That meant that I would have to call a local beekeeper (a professional, full-time one) and ask to buy some more. If that meant getting another top-frame hive for them, so be it, I thought to myself, walking back into the house. At least that icy feeling had lessened with the activity.

I went inside. The news was on, and the anchor was saying, "Demographic studies have revealed the entire world population is now half a billion humans. That is just incredible! Isn't it, Lucy?" he asked his co-anchor.

"It is, Joe," she agreed. "Does the report say when humanity's numbers were last that low?"

He glanced up at the teleprompter. "1650. We were last at that number in 1650."

Lucy looked like she had been punched in the stomach. "How will we recover from this?"

I laughed mirthlessly, and said to her, addressing the TV screen, "We're not supposed to 'recover', Lucy. We're supposed to stay at this number. This IS the recovery – from overpopulating our planet."

The newscasters moved on to announce that beekeeping classes were being offered around the state. Courses would run for several weeks, and anyone interested should go to the website on the screen, or call the toll-free number.

Hamish was sitting in the kitchen, looking on his laptop at more specifications for the New York Regenics Clinic, plotting out the final touches. He laughed mirthlessly, and looked up as I spoke. "How are your bees?"

"Not collapsed, which is incredible considering the neglect they've just endured, but reduced in numbers. I'll have to find more, and I might get another top-frame hive for them all," I said. "What I don't understand is how they could not be collapsed. I'll just have to go exploring and get to know what's different around here, both in the ecosystem and with all of the deliberate changes to this area."

The icy feeling was back. I supposed it would stay like that until I had both explored the area and studied the situation online and in whatever books I could find…and had time to contemplate the implications of it all and plot my patterns of behavior to cope with it.

Or not. There might be other reasons for that feeling, and other remedies. We would see.

My husband looked at me for a moment. "You are not going out alone. We don't know how safe it is now, even though the 'plague' is over. Ed and Aaron are going wherever you go. Also, I might just come with you for some of that exploring. I'm as curious as you are," he said.

I gave him a wry smile. "I know it's not safe. It feels eerie. Things don't even sound the same. Sure, I hear Nature, but it sounds slightly different, and a bit louder. Perhaps that's only because the ambient noises of our own species are vastly reduced." I frowned at the table.

"Indeed," Hamish said. "You can have a hive of nanobees if you want," he added.

I looked up at him, suspicious now. "Is that why my hive isn't collapsed?"

He grinned mischievously. "Aye, it is. Those little demons are strong. I had them fly about in the spring, replacing the wooden bars of your hive. I knew you would be upset if we came back and the hive had collapsed simply because you hadn't been able to stay here and take care of it."

A slow smile spread across my face. "I hope you won't be upset if I want organic bees."

"No, of course not. Nanobotics are only a remedy, not a replacement for the real thing."

"Thank you!' I said. It was a quiet smile, though. That was the best I could do. This entire area – the yard, the neighborhood, the town, the county, the whole state, hell, the entire country! – felt like a pall was cast over it. It felt like we were at an extended wake or funeral, or as though one had just been held and the mood had not lifted yet. And why should it?!

The Cull had erased so many people.

I couldn't see a trace of them.

Our cars sat in the garage next to newly-installed electric charging stations. Mine was ready.

As I drove up Mountain Road toward the area where Aunt Zoe and Uncle Charlie's house used to be, I saw that the landscape had changed drastically. The roads had new, permeable pavement and, instead of the homes and subdivisions from the mid-twentieth century, there was now only farmland. Water could reach the ground via that pavement.

The only clues that demonstrated that this was, in fact, the same area were the fact that roads' names hadn't changed, and A German-style house that my mother and I had once toured when it was for sale – a farmhouse that was painted the palest pink at the time – plus some condominiums on the southeast corner of the intersection. Other than that, all human dwellings had been removed. It was eerie, to say the very least. And Hallowe'en was coming.

It was going to be a truly disturbing Hallowe'en this year, with so few people around.

For someone who didn't usually like to be around kids, I was an odd sort because I liked to wear my witch hat, a cape with a gold zodiac-on-black pattern that I had made, and answer the door and give out Hallowe'en candy. I doubted that I would be doing that this year.

The traffic lights were still working, but all around were trees, which had not been removed in the Cull, and fields, which had been the result of it. Soil had been trucked in and used to fill in former swimming pools and homes, the foundations of which had been completely removed. Food of all sorts was grown on those fields now, and some of it had been converted to fruit orchards. Good idea, but it was all possible due to a colossal crime.

Aaron sat in the front seat of my car and Ed in the back. Hamish had been startled when I announced that I intended to drive around the area and see what farms had what, and to learn how one acquired food from them. Was there any special system? Time to find out, I had said. With that, Hamish had called our friendly Blackout Security guys and told them to go with me.

Aaron and Ed felt more like family now than bodyguards, but that was what they were.

They had worked loosely with Hamish during his military past. Hamish had been in the British military and they had been in the U.S. military, but liaisons were not unusual, and people with an array of special skills tended to meet up sooner or later. There were other people with whom Hamish had maintained connections as well, but these were the guys whom I knew.

The founder of Blackout Security was another ex-military character, complete with stealth training, Navy SEAL experience, and whatever else might qualify him to organize this high-end, secretive service. He also had an excellent business sense. His name was Alan Myer Adams, and there had been an article about him once in *The New York Times*, but that was all. Hamish knew him, but said that we would likely never socialize with him. He was a recluse.

I didn't even know where he lived, but my mind was on other things. I knew that Hamish was nervous about me tooling around the neighborhood, exploring, and that he had likely shadowed this excursion with his flying nanobots, recording it all. Fine. I would review it all with him later, and look for any detail that I might have missed. Hamish would likely be able to fill in details that I had looked at and not understood the significance of, also. Those nanobots were how we knew so much about the Cull – the genocide – of the past year.

Ironic that I was being surveilled by my husband but not by the government, I thought with a wry grin. "What's funny?" Aaron asked, noticing that.

"Hamish is likely surveilling my activities today," I replied.

Aaron glanced in the back seat at Ed who, I noticed in the rearview mirror, raised his eyebrows. "Nothing gets by you," Ed remarked.

I relaxed slightly. The humor in this brief exchange was a welcome relief from the tension I was feeling. "At least you guys amused me for a moment. I feel somewhat short of breath – horrified by what all the changes we are seeing mean."

"What do they mean?" Aaron said, just to draw me out.

"They mean that all this was done to save the ecosystem and food supply. But the cost of that was mass murder, genocide, another holocaust, whatever you might choose to call it. It looks absolutely idyllic, lovely, peaceful, and yet…it's anything but that."

Another glance exchanged.

We were all still in a mild state of shock over something that had occurred just last week.

The President of the United States had died.

The announcement had come almost as soon as we had gotten home. We had spent just one night in Connecticut when it was all over the news. It was bizarre to think that he could have died of natural causes at the ripe young age of fifty-six, but he was dead nonetheless.

Several years earlier, he had had the lower half of a leg blown off in a failed assassination attempt on the steps of the U.S. Supreme Court building. He had seemed to make a complete recovery after that, and hadn't even shown a limp after receiving his prosthetic leg. It was a titanium one with a veneer that looked so much like a natural leg with a foot that, when he went barefoot on the beach with his family, photographers could not easily remember which leg was real and which was not.

The cause of his death was quickly determined to be an infection that had gone unnoticed, progressed rapidly, and gone into his heart. A puncture wound on his leg stump was discovered, and a sharp bit of his prosthetic, blamed on wear and tear, was reported as having had a build-up of necrotic tissue that had poisoned his blood. The excuse for his medical team having missed all this was that the president had been working nonstop, and had simply seemed overtired.

Granted, that was a hazard of the position, but Hamish wasn't convinced. "A likely story," was all that he had to say about that, and we all understood what he meant. Without a second glance at him, we had looked back at the television screen and listened to the next bits.

Those next bits were the most shocking: the vice president had died hours afterward.

Why?! He wasn't sick, he was only ten years older than the president, he had all of his limbs and other body parts (with the exception of some hair plugs, but that attracted no notice), and no cause was offered as an explanation. We had listened to that report in stunned silence, and gone to bed feeling confused and angry.

The next morning, an explanation was provided: The vice president had been assassinated by a renegade member of the Secret Service.

We waited for an explanation about that, but were quickly disappointed. In executing that assassination, the agent had been shot several times by other agents. That came as no surprise. We could easily imagine the vice president, newly sworn in as president, under attack and his guards therefore firing in unison at the threat, however useless their efforts.

Yet something about it all didn't ring true, and Jason had again assisted us in discovering the truth. The N.S.A., which stood for National Security Agency but was called No Such Agency by myself and anyone else who mistrusted it, had nothing on Jason…or Hamish. Jason had left swarms of Hamish's nanobotic cameras all over government premises during the past year, and now he came over to review the data with us. Hamish and I marched him down to the old basement den without ceremony when he arrived, waving off my mother's efforts to plie him with any drinks. Later for that!

After the Cull and the rise of the Orwellian police surveillance state, our trust in our own government's willingness to abide by and uphold the U.S. Constitution, particularly the Fourth Amendment, was completely vitiated. The Fourth Amendment guaranteed that U.S. citizens did not have to endure warrantless searches and seizures of our property. Hah! What a joke that seemed like now. So many people, along with their property, had been seized, searched, probed, sifted, and ultimately erased. If the absence of most Americans from their very existence wasn't a tip-off that the government was rotten, nothing would be.

In short, we had decided that if our government wouldn't uphold the law, it was up to us.

We were still in the data analysis phase, but we were almost ready to strike back.

The nano-cameras revealed that the president's infection had been contrived, not accidental. We carefully filed that information away for future use. What interested us next was motive. Why had the president been disposed of? It took us a few hours of searching, which meant more time shut away in the basement with Jason, but fortunately no one bothered us.

At last, there it was: the president had decided to shut down the N.S.A.'s warrantless wiretapping program, the Orwellian behemoth that was behind our every effort to live off the grid – the utilities grid, the data gathering and collection grid, and the surveillance grid. Not only that, but he had planned to overhaul the C.I.A. as well. His purpose was to weed out the Orwellian monster within both agencies. The vice president had planned to do the same.

"Well, that explains it," I said, sitting back for a moment and staring at the ceiling.

"What do you mean?" Hamish and Jason both asked me at once.

"No sitting president can just shut down the C.I.A. – and, now that the N.S.A. has grown to be a comparable monster, one that subverts the Foreign Intelligence Surveillance Act and turns its cyber-eyes inward, on its own citizens, the N.S.A. also – without risking death. It's been so since John F. Kennedy announced his intent to do that. He also wanted peace, and governments, particularly empire-governments, want to keep their military-industrial complexes in a state of constant war. That's what keeps the Farmers that fund and direct them happy."

My husband and our friend stared at me wordlessly. Hamish looked grim but unsurprised. Jason, who was in his mid-twenties, despite having survived the past year with us while remotely witnessing more dark secrets and crimes unfold than most people ever even hear about, was still capable of having his jaw drop and then gaping for a moment before snapping it shut.

It snapped shut a mere moment later, though. Jason had seen and understood too much.

"How do they usually control a president?" Jason asked me. "I mean, there have been several more since JFK, and none of them have done anything about this. All that time, the problem has obviously grown worse, or last year would have been very different."

"I suspect that, when they are briefing the winner of a presidential election, that candidate is hazed with a full disclosure, complete with graphic video and still photographs in vivid color and clarity, of the Kennedy assassination, plus the reasons behind it."

Now both of them gaped at me for a moment, brief though it was.

We looked at the vice president's assassination next, and it was more of the same stuff.

A hasty presidential election was being organized as a result, unprecedented in our nation's history. So many unprecedented events had taken place in the past several years that this did not induce much outrage, or even much emotion. I had commented that the world was probably feeling too emotionally drained to expend much mental or emotional energy on this. Meanwhile, the Speaker of the House of Representatives had been hastily sworn in as President of the United States, but he had indicated that he would not be running for that office.

We would review the candidates, choose one, and vote, simple as that. Claire, Fabian's new wife, had already gone to the town hall and registered to vote. The rest of us were already registered: myself, Hamish, my parents, Aunt Zoe and Uncle Charlie, Grandmère, and my cousins, Edgar, Fabian, and Jacques.

Focusing on the present again, I drove us on a grand tour of the town, looking at everything.

In the center of town, Whole Foods and the U.N. Agenda 21-style, mixed-use development remained, as did a lot of the homes nearby, but almost anything built post-World War II had been erased. In its place was acre upon acre of crops. At first, I had been amazed when I had checked the local grocery stores online and found that all of the ones I remembered were still there. But then it had occurred to me that consuming food was not the same as consumerism, and I had moved on to notice other things.

We saw cornfields where Elmwood, the working-class section of town, had once had homes. I slowed the car down and read the signs on the corners of the former streets, which had all been ripped up and then repaved. Different varieties of corn were listed under the street names.

The pavement was all exactly where the original streets had been. That land was basically ruined for cultivation, eviscerated of all nutrients, so it had made sense to keep the old street plans in place. It was eerie, though.

Where the industrial park had been, there were now a series of wind turbines. So that was where the town was getting a significant portion of its energy. "I read online that all new housing in rural and suburban areas will have solar panels – not placed too close together in case of fire – and that the power grid will also draw on wind turbines," I said.

Aaron grunted in agreement; he had seen that report too.

The town hall had a Three Sisters agricultural display on its front lawn. This meant that vines for squash and beans were wound up and around corn stalks, which was attractive and interesting, but more for show than for any serious volume of food supply. I parked by the library and we walked over to read the little plaques in front of them.

> *"This Three Sisters agricultural project is a cooperative endeavor by local schools. It teaches students how Native Americans grew their food, with varieties of corn, squash, and beans Connecticut tribes would have been raising at the time that English colonists joined them here."*

Sure enough, the varieties of each Three Sisters display were anything but the butter-and-sugar corns that I had been raised with each fall at roadside vegetable stands and farmers' markets. Instead, there were many others, and some were not historically accurate to the region, despite the claim on the plaque. It was kind of funny to see that claim next to the photographs of the varieties that were being grown. We saw variegated maize of all colors: red and blue, dark red to purple, pastels, some in the familiar yellow with white kernels, and yellow with red and black kernels.

"It would be fun to try the corn when it's ready, just to see what they all taste like," I said.

Ed rolled his eyes. Hamish had had to convert him to a (mostly) vegetarian diet and get him off of processed, convenience foods a couple of years ago when he began to feel the early signs of cancer. Once he understood that damage that GMOs (genetically modified organisms) were doing to his body, he changed, because he wanted to live longer and feel well. But it had been under protest. Some people just didn't like to pay attention to their food or try new things.

Aaron was just the opposite. He appreciated and liked to try new things. Whenever Ed complained about a new food experience, Aaron would grin at him and call him a Philistine.

The two were good friends, and had known Hamish for years.

Hamish, however, wanted to live on healthful, nutritious, organic foods, and he loved food adventures. As a physician, and one who had also developed both a nanobotic antidote to the covert destructive additive to the vaccines in the Cull and created an anti-aging serum called Regenics, he was someone to take seriously.

His advice was, in fact, taken very seriously. Our friends and family had all been vaccinated by Hamish, slowly, over a period of months, after he had extracted the nanites from the sera that had been shipped to his medical office.

Those nanites were the government's covert method of reducing the human population. They contained programming and needles that sought out and broke P53 proteins, which were the cancer tumor suppressors in our DNA. In addition, the vaccines that the government was using hit the human immune system with forty-plus disease preventions, which then crashed their systems. People had come in to see him with lesions, fatigue, and early signs of cancer. They weren't contagious, but they were dying.

Hamish had removed those nanites from people who came into his office as patients, then healed the damage by injecting them with his Regenics formula. After saving as many people as he could, and arranging for others to be out of town when the Cull came to our area, we had all left Connecticut for Manhattan and, ultimately, Switzerland, first by car and then by boat.

The Swiss Regenics clinic was ready to go by August last year, while the one in New York was just starting. The reconstruction and flood remediation, complete with dykes and dams, canals and waterways, and new, granite bridges and water taxis had put Manhattan's clinic behind. Lausanne, located on Lake Geneva, had not suffered the effects of sea level rising.

That had worked for us very nicely. Hamish had arranged for the purchase, outfitting, and supply of a huge yacht, which I had named the *Shadowcat*. Once it was ready, we had taken the entire family (and cats, Spock and Eowyn), plus a kid in his twenties named Jason Woodward, who had recently graduated from

M.I.T. and his parents, with us to Lausanne to wait out the Cull. Ostensibly, it was all about the Regenics clinic, but that was also a convenient cover.

On the way to Lake Geneva, we had stopped in Rosehearty, Scotland, to pick up Hamish's sister, Fiona, plus her fiancé and cat, Mallory. Then we had stayed away, keeping in touch with friends and business acquaintances and associates. Our new cousin-in-law, Claire, had married Fabian in Switzerland, and Fiona had married William shortly after that.

We tried to make the best of a terrifying time. Claire had lost her parents to the Cull, bakers who had a business outside Philadelphia. On the way back, we had paused offshore from Pennsylvania and sent Hamish's flying nanobotic cameras to show her the area and give her a sense of closure. Claire had looked, and she seemed to have worked her way past the immediate shock and grief of the loss to anger. I hoped she could use that to her benefit in some way, and planned to help her if I could.

The Regenics formula that Hamish had given us all had reversed the aging process. I was in my late forties but now appeared to be twenty years younger. Hamish looked to be in his mid-thirties. Grandmère was nearing one hundred years old, had ditched her cane, and her hair had thickened to a beautiful pouf of a snowy white mane. Her face was also fuller, and she walked steadily and faster. I hoped she didn't mind all that; the thought that she was benefitting from all this as a widow was why. She seemed to be enjoying life, though.

Aaron and Ed and I piled back into my car and I drove off, heading east, where we saw pear trees. Anjou, Bosc, and Bartlett pears were growing. The news reports had spent a lot of time online and on the air touting the wonders of how every town was growing its own food to reduce their dependency on trucking it in from elsewhere. Of course, there were greenhouses that produced food during the off seasons, to keep the grocery stores supplied, but this did go a long way toward reducing our carbon footprints.

An area of West Hartford that had been labeled "The Reservation" due to the Native American tribe names of all of its streets was now filled with raspberry, blackberry, and blueberry bushes. I was delighted to see it all, I had to admit, because raspberries were my favorite fruit. An area by the golf course was set aside for strawberries, but those only grew in June, so that field was lying fallow now.

"They didn't remove the golf course!" I said, surprised.

"Of course not," Ed said. "Banksters and other Farmers live around here. They like to golf."

"Oh, right," I said, understanding. The mansions near that golf course were still there, also.

I didn't want to drive all the way into Hartford, so I reversed course, turning back around toward Bishop's Corner. The other Whole Foods store, banks, restaurants, and the Big Y grocery store were still there, as was the U.S. Post Office. I drove through the back way around some of the stores and up Flagg Road. The beehives of Westmoor Park, a small farm that was open to public tours, had not been touched during the Cull. That was no surprise.

Turning right to head north on Mountain Road, I noticed that there was nothing to see, just idle land with fields where houses used to be. Only a few, colonial and historic homes remained. Also, the farmland that we had passed south of Albany Avenue was not producing anything right now. It was late September. "I wonder what they grow on the land by Mountain Road, south of Albany Avenue," I said aloud, to no one in particular.

Ed took out a pamphlet. He scanned it, then said, "Flowers."

"Flowers?" I said, incredulously. "All that land?"

"Yeah. Here – I got several of these this morning, just after Hamish called us and said you wanted to go out exploring."

I gaped at him in the rearview mirror for a second, impressed. Then I shut my mouth and laughed a brief laugh. "Of course you did. You Blackout guys excel at reconnaissance." I grinned at Ed, and pulled over by Gledhill Nursery. "Huh…this place is still here," I commented. Ed passed me one of the pamphlets.

"Oh, yeah," Aaron said. "Any business that dealt with growing plants was saved."

"Makes sense," I said, and looked at the pamphlet. It was from the West Hartford Town Hall. *West Hartford Guide to Farms and Orchards*, it was titled. It showed a smiling woman on the cover who looked like she was in her thirties, wearing jeans and a tee shirt. Her long, light-brown hair was up in a ponytail, and her gray-blue eyes stared into the camera lens as she held up a bouquet of purple-blue delphiniums, pink tea roses, blue hyacinths, and yellow-to-red parrot tulips. She was standing in front of a flower field of mixed items, leaning on a vendor's cart.

I opened it out and saw that the town was now in the business of growing all sorts of herbs, squash, beans, corns (multiple varieties!), and that the pamphlet boasted that the Native American method of Three Sisters was used to grow those things near the town hall. There were scallions, shallots, and other onion family plants, heirloom tomatoes, berries of all kinds. The town had planted orchards of apples (Golden Delicious, Granny Smith, Empire, and Macoun), peaches, pears, and apricots. Beehives were set up among each of the growing areas.

Crops were rotated, and each plot of land was given a chance to lay fallow every third season. All of it was organic – no insecticides. (At last, that was the standard!) The town even employed an entomologist to manage insects, which was done by sending natural predator insects to prey on unwanted ones.

The government had set up a credit and debit card system of purchase at each station.

Cash was accepted but not preferred, with no guarantee of exact change late in the day. Lovely…and a bit suspect. The Farmers (Hamish's and my private code for banksters and hedge fundsters, and corporatists) were trying to phase out cash from the economy, and thus track and control every financial transaction.

A police cruiser drove by, then did a U-turn and came back to pull up alongside us.

At least martial law was no longer in effect. I put my window down. So did he. The cop was in his mid-forties, I thought, with graying, thick, crew-cut hair, almost shaved on the sides, like a Marine. Dark brown eyes looked across at me, and a little camera was mounted onto his collar.

"Hello, Officer," I said, putting a pleasant expression on my face.

"Hello," he said. "Why have you stopped?"

I held up the pamphlet. "My friend just handed me this pamphlet, so I pulled over to look at it and see where I will go. I was just about to start driving again."

"Oh. Okay. Just checking to see what's going on. No problem then," he said with an equally pleasant smile. He drove off. Good.

I pulled out into the road again, checking all around before doing so, but there were no other cars out. It was late morning now, almost noon. "I'm used to seeing a lot more cars out and about – all day long, no matter what time it is. "We're going to have to get used to all new traffic patterns and intensities now…or the lack thereof," I commented.

"Yep, we are," Ed said, looking out the window.

Aaron had pulled the visor down in the front seat, and flipped open its mirror. "The cop is coming back," he said.

"Well, he was going this way before he talked to me," I said.

"Indeed," was all that Aaron said back. Blackout guys were trained to be suspicious.

The cop caught up with us, signaled that he wanted to pass us, and did so. "Good," I said. "He's not going to follow me around and watch me explore. That would take the fun out of it."

Ed snorted. "You don't seem to be enjoying this."

Funny how these guys could sense my mood, my plans, everything. Well, they were trained on stealth, reconnaissance, secret ops, and whatever else, and they were neurotypical. NTs could read people faster than anyone with Asperger's could, plus they knew me.

I drove up Mountain Road a bit more and turned down what used to be Lostbrook Road. The houses there had been built in the post-World War II boom of the 1940s. Now, they were just…gone. Instead, I found myself passing apple trees on gravel and dirt.

My heart was pounding again. This was scary, and I seriously doubted that I could pin this reaction on being an Aspie. Anyone who had lived here and known this area before the Cull who was seeing it again for the first time since then would react this way – especially knowing and having seen what I had: MRAPs and mobile crematoria camps and the residents of this area being rounded up and herded into military trucks, never to return.

Of course, few people had seen that.

Those few were limited to the people in this car, Hamish, the rest of my immediate and extended family, and a few friends (my parents, Grandmère, Aunt Zoe, Uncle Charlie, their three sons, Edgar, Fabian, and Jacques, Fabian's new wife Claire, Hamish's sister, Fiona, and her new husband William, plus our computer wizard, Jason, and his parents, Anne and Peter).

As the Cull came to our area, we had scooped up our family and friends and left to wait it out in safety. It was either that or lose most of them. Our house on Stoner Drive was still there, unmolested, as was Jason's, but Uncle Charlie's neighborhood was erased. We had watched it courtesy of Hamish's flying nanobots.

Uncle Charlie was in shock, but Aunt Zoe was taking it a bit more calmly. He had been a real estate developer, so his life's work had been erased along with the people he had lived near, many of whom had bought up the McMansions he had built. She had worked with him until he retired and wound up his business, just as they finished educating their kids.

Aunt Zoe's sister, Mindy, and brother-in-law had survived the Cull, so it was no wonder that she was handling this okay. Aunt Zoe was at our house, surfing the Internet, searching for a new home for them to buy. She and Uncle Charlie didn't want to stay with us forever, which was understandable. We were eleven people in one house and, big as it was, we were cramped.

It was probably just like the big extended American families of the nineteenth century and earlier, I mused. You could tell that farming families used to remain together working the land, generations all in one huge dwelling that had been expanded as needed, just by driving through the countryside. Pretty, rambling, clapboard farmhouses painted in reds, yellows, whites, blues, and even a pink one could be seen if one drove around Connecticut.

I hoped they were still there…

Glancing up at one of the street signs, I was startled to see another change: they each had been given new names in addition to the old ones. Lostbrook Road now sported a companion street sign just below its original one: Golden Delicious Apple Orchard. Hmm…at least people would know where to go for what food, but I doubted that the new names would catch on, and said so.

"Oh, they won't," Aaron said, "but the signs will likely stay."

I drove all the way down to the end of the road, to what had been Barksdale Road and was now Granny Smith Road as well, and turned left. The elementary school was – or had been – up on the left. "It's still there!" I said, surprised.

"Oh yeah," Ed said. "But it's closed for renovations. There are few enough kids now that they can improve each building and make sure that it is up to code and offers the latest and greatest bathrooms, theater and arts, and gymnasium facilities. Any contaminants like lead or asbestos are being removed by hazmat crews. They're probably almost done here," he summed up, peering across the playground at the equipment in the parking lot. It did look as though things were being packed up.

Across the street from the school was a small kiosk. It was a permanent structure with a series of barns lining the street up ahead of it. A parking area was just before the school, where two houses had been. I pulled in and parked next to another car. There were just four others.

We all got out and walked over to the kiosk, and as we drew closer, I saw that the barns were brand new, painted a nice dark red, and labeled. "Macoun Apples" read the first sign. Storage and processing, I realized.

We looked around as we walked, and I commented that this orchard had features that I had never seen before in any other orchard, but had read about online: sound-emitting equipment in flowering shrubs. The sound was of a low frequency, carefully calibrated by scientists and engineers to prevent insects that would have eaten away the leaves on the trees from mating.

The flowering shrubs were there to encourage honeybees to stick around without becoming malnourished from a monocrop. Bees, like other animals, needed variety in their diets. Small signs made of bronze set into granite explained this, with labels for the various plants, including honeysuckle, buckwheat, and gardenia, and herbs such as rosemary and lavender. Any that could be harvested would also be sold in the kiosk when ready, with seeds carefully reserved for the next growing season.

"Of course you've read that online," Ed said with a grin. "You're always researching stuff."

Aaron grinned. "That's what makes it interesting to guard her," he commented.

"True," Ed remarked. "And Hamish gets ideas for inventions from all that." He smiled.

As we entered the kiosk, I realized that it was more than that. It was a bakery and applesauce and cider production facility as well as a place to just buy apples. You could pick your own or not, as you wished. Teenagers who lived in the area picked the apples after school for pay.

That sounded like a good economic plan. Prior to the Cull, teenagers had been having a terrible time finding jobs, as had many other people. Picking fruit was an ideal job for a kid old enough to work. They would be out in the fresh air, and making money without being micromanaged.

We went inside and were immediately hit with the intense aromas of cider, cider donuts, and apple turnovers. I could make my own pies, but I loved cider donuts and cider, so I bought a bag of Golden Delicious apples, and one large and one small bag of donuts plus 2 jugs of cider. I handed one of the jugs to Aaron and the small bag of donuts to Ed. "These are for you guys," I said, careful not to say "for your guardhouse." That was no one else's business anyway.

I took out some cash to pay for the food, and it was promptly refused. "We only take credit or debit here," I was told. Of course, I thought…the better to be tracked. I paid with my Visa.

The woman in charge of the kiosk, which proved to be more like a small shop, handed us each a free sample of the cider, which was delicious. She pointed out the rest rooms off to the right, and left us to wander around the shop. A couple of men were also working in there, sorting fruit and sweeping the floor. I guessed that the teenagers would arrive a few hours later.

Next, the woman told us that the apple barns were not open to the public, as they were for storage and packaging only. The apples didn't just stay here; they were taken to Whole Foods, Big Y, The Fresh Market, and other area stores periodically. When the apple season was over, lots of apple products would be stored for sale during what was now winter: short but intense periods of icy cold, colder than what we who were in our thirties and forties had grown up with.

"But you won't necessarily remember that," she said, looking me over. "You're too young."

"Oh?" I said, looking back at her. "How old do we look?" I asked. It had been over a year since Hamish had injected me and the rest of our group with his Regenics formula.

The woman, whose hair was graying and had some lines and wrinkles here and there on her face, tucked a wisp of hair under her hat. She paused, then said, "You look like you're in your mid-twenties, and they look like they're in their late thirties," surveying Ed and Aaron with a practiced eye.

Wow. "I'm going to be forty-eight next year," I told her with a wry smile.

She stared at me. "I would love to try whatever you're doing," she said.

I smiled and took a card from the place, and she wrote her name on the back: Jenna Lane.

We thanked her and left, carrying our apples and other items.

Aaron waited until we were putting the stuff in the trunk before saying, "Don't tell everyone your real age…at least not just yet," he added.

"Okay." Telling people that did make us seem like science fiction characters with a secret.

I drove us back out to Mountain Road and headed north, heading automatically toward Aunt Zoe and Uncle Charlie's old neighborhood, more out of habit than conscious thought.

That ended when I turned onto Beacon Hill Drive, which led to their old cul-de-sac.

A feeling of panic settled in as I looked around. This was where the reality show that presented a massive crime had unfolded, courtesy of our flying nanobots. People had lived here in houses going up this hill. There had been yards with shrubbery, flowers, fences, swimming pools in some backyards, telephone poles, electricity wires, and driveways. It was all gone now, as were the people who had been called out of their homes, and dragged out by force if they didn't cooperate.

We had seen it all, and Hamish and I had watched it twice. The first time had been while aboard our yacht, the *Shadowcat*, once we had the family safely away and at sea, heading for Europe. The second time had been after we had picked up Fiona and William. We had to show them what was going on. Fiona had seen some vague signs of it, but nothing up close and personal. You usually only saw that if the military units were coming to take you away, never to return. You saw that if they were going to kill you.

The Cull had forced tainted vaccinations on almost everyone, and vaccinations of some sort on the rest. The result was that everyone remaining alive was properly vaccinated against 40 diseases, whereas a kill-shot had been inflicted on those who had been culled.

Hamish had protected us all by acquiring vaccines for all of the targeted diseases in the official vaccine months ahead of time, extracting any hidden nanites from them, and administering them slowly, over a period of months. He entered each record into a national database, as physicians were required to do, registering us all as having been taken care of, vaccinated as required by law.

The problem had been that the government might still try to pull anyone aside at work or visit them at their home and reinject them, thus introducing those damned nanites anyway. We had lost one of his Avon, Connecticut office employees this way, when they went away for a weekend to visit relatives out of state.

Claire had received an ominous letter from her mother just before it all started, along with a package containing the family photographs and all of her jewelry. Her parents had suspected that something was not right, but they had insisted upon staying in Philadelphia up until the very end. Hamish had been unable to persuade them to remain in Connecticut with us.

Hamish had saved some of our friends before we left the area by removing the nanites after the fact. And then we had escaped to Switzerland on the *Shadowcat* with our entire family.

We had contacted everyone that we knew while we were away, during the Cull and as it was winding down, and found out that they were still alive, no longer being pursued. Many of them didn't understand that it was a Cull, and we didn't dare tell them, at least not just now. What mattered for now was that they were okay.

"Breathe, Avril," Aaron said to me.

I turned to look at him, startled. Then I inhaled and exhaled a couple of times. I had been holding my breath, and then taking short, panting breaths. I was also stimming – tapping my fingers on the steering wheel and pursing my lips as they got dry – classic Aspie anxiety! Perhaps walking around would help.

Hollister Drive was the name of Aunt Zoe and Uncle Charlie's old street. Only the street itself seemed familiar now. I parked along it. New pavement marked it off, with new paint. There were green stripes of paints down each lane. I had seen that paint everywhere, and now I paused to stare at it. It seemed to glow.

Ed saw me staring intently at it. "That's solar energy paint. It stores whatever it picks up from sunlight and cars then pick it up as they drive near it. You have to drive right over them to get the benefit."

"Fascinating," I said, and meant it. "But we could have had it without the Cull."

"What I don't get is how the government justified taking all of this land. I know they had a legal device for doing so, but what was it?" Ed asked me. He was obviously trying to distract me.

"If an entire family dies and there are no legal heirs, the property escheats to the state," I told him. "But Uncle Charlie and Aunt Zoe are alive. Perhaps they'll get a letter from the state soon about this. If not, we will pursue other options. They're entitled to some money under eminent domain. It won't fully reimburse them for the value their house and property, but it will be something. They won't want to live with us forever."

I looked around us at what had been a neighborhood of homes. It was all squash fields now.

Butternut squash, acorn squash, turban squash, kabocha squash, blue and golden Hubbard squash, spaghetti squash, and even a few summer squash were visible, complete with edible squash blossoms. If I bought any, we would have to eat them that evening. Good thing we had some chèvre – goat cheese – to go with them, because that was exactly what I intended to do.

No sense in refusing to buy the food that grew at this crime scene. It wouldn't change a thing.

I walked toward the kiosk, which was across the street from the site of the house that we had visited our family at so often, and looked around. Sure enough, signs outside said that there were squash blossoms for sale, plus lots of different squash. No Three Sisters growing method here – just squash – fields of it.

It was neatly laid out around the trees that had stood around the homes that were now gone. I recognized these trees, and remembered how the houses, cars, gardens, and other details had been situated around them. The trees served as prompts to an open-book memory test.

Without thinking about it, I found myself wandering over to the site of Aunt Zoe and Uncle Charlie's house. A pumpkin patch covered most of it. Aaron silently followed me through one of the rows to the back. I walked through what had been the living and dining area, past where the deck had been, and across the former backyard. A patch of grass was untouched, and I walked onto it, and then stopped short. A big rock, rounded but with a slight depression that faced the patch, sat at the very back of what had been the backyard. It formed a natural seat.

I sat on it now, with my eyes on the ground, as they had been each time before. Everything felt the same as it always had as I did so…until I settled into place on the rock at the end of the former yard and looked up. Then I felt as if I had been punched in the stomach. Where the pumpkin patch ended, a narrow strip of grass grew, and then a field of butternut squash. That line of grass bisected the place where the swimming pool had been.

The view that I had expected to see in my moment of reverie was gone for good. In its place was just squash growing all around us, set against a background of trees. The neighborhood had been set against undeveloped woods, with the town's largest reservoir up the hill beyond them. That, of course, was still there.

I looked down at the soil and vines of the pumpkin patch. It was rather pretty.

Then I saw it: something gray and oddly shaped in the soil, something that had gone unnoticed throughout the planting season. This row hadn't been picked yet, which was probably why it hadn't been found by anyone else. I reached down and picked it up.

It wasn't a rock. It was a porous thing, slightly charred. I put it in my pocket quickly.

"Avril, are you okay?" Aaron asked me kindly.

"Yes, thank you," I lied to him.

"I know you sat on this rock often," he said.

I got up. "That was the last time," I replied, heading for the road.

Walking across to the kiosk, I saw Ed looking grimly at the pumpkin patch.

When I got inside, I did a double-take. Sophia was in there! She was working there, selling and organizing the harvest. It was a seasonal job, one that freed her up to write and draw and paint when the fields were fallow for the winter. We hugged and greeted each other, and the tremulous, anxious shortness of breath I had been feeling stopped, at least for now. "How are you?" we said both at once, then laughed.

Sophia and her daughter were fine. Catriona was studying at the University of Connecticut in Hartford, commuting back and forth on those eco-friendly buses, and studying during the commutes. She was still hoping to transfer to a coastal university and study marine biology, and I suspected that she would soon be able to do so. After all, the Cull – being called the Great Plague – was over now.

Sophia was busy with her pastel drawing and publishing her science fiction stories online. Her work was like vibrantly colored art – nothing like what I wrote, which dealt with science fiction becoming practical, science fact. She wrote beautiful imagery with a hint of terror that was pure fantasy and nothing that could get her noticed by any government radar. The surveillance machines that tracked leaks of secrets would not touch her.

We chatted briefly, caught up on basic news, and arranged to meet again soon.

I bought some squash blossoms, a couple of butternut squashes, and some acorn ones, and a pumpkin from the field where my family's home had been, for our doorstep. Odd shapes as well as familiar shapes of everything for sale – nothing was being wasted due to not being picture-perfect, and that was a good thing. When I was ready to pay, I found that this place insisted upon credit or debit payments also, but I tried to pay with cash, just to make sure.

Damn! Surveillance was built into the system. I wondered if it would follow me everywhere I tried to pay for anything now. The mere idea was making me angry. Was my cash now useless?! Clearly, the pamphlet had lied about the kiosks accepting cash.

Tomorrow would be October 1st. I didn't feel like carving a pumpkin this year, but I wanted to have one, just the same. It was a shred of normalcy in an otherwise contrived, abnormal scene. I was still here, able to enjoy the sights, smells, tastes, and other delights of the season – the fruits of fall. The people who had lived, and died, here in this ghost of a neighborhood, would never enjoy them again.

Damn the Farmers for that! Happy Hallowe'en, I thought with a bitter sense of irony.

I went home and unpacked the groceries, the result of shopping at farms rather than stores. Strange new world, I thought to myself, putting apples aside for sauce and a tart, squash on the counter, and then heading out to the back yard. I would plan my own garden, and not rely solely on the other ones. At least I could decide what to grow.

The conservatory was still in great shape, and Hamish admitted to having sent nanobots to tend its herbs and raspberries, blackberries, and strawberries. The berry bushes outside, which bordered the yard along its walls, were also in decent shape.

There wasn't really much decision-making to do, but I wanted to get everyone else into a home agronomy routine. This was to be an organic operation – no insecticides allowed. No one would challenge me on this, but I expected some resistance in the form of human laziness. Ours was not a culture that was used to farming. We were used to art, music, study, and letting other people – strangers in distant, rural areas – do the farming. No more.

The entire yard was not devoted to farming. Some was a lawn, which Hamish and I trimmed with an old-fashioned mower – no motor. It was a rolling cylinder that made no noise, and he loved it. It required no fossil fuels to run. The lawn was not a chemically treated monocrop of grass, but a miscellany of wildflowers with grass: clover, daisies, dandelion, and tiny violets. The bees loved it. This was another reason why our hives still had live honeybees.

The parts of the yard that were devoted to crops, aside from the berry bushes, were on either side. Heirloom tomatoes to the left (soil couldn't grow anything else once it had grown tomatoes, so there was no point in planning anything different in that area), and everything else on the right. The lawn stretched through the center in a wide swatch, plus around the rectangular crop areas, and around the house.

"Everything else" meant string beans, eggplants, purple and green asparagus, sweet potatoes, carrots, parsnips, and some red and orange pepper plants (no green – I didn't like their bitter taste). Right now, though, it was too late to plant anything. It was time to worry about the soil, and about maintaining it.

The world's topsoil layer, essential for agriculture, had been eroding away. Pastureland had been churned up for row planting, and it had gone from rich, dark brown to light brown to pale, sandy beige…until it actually was sand. This had actually happened in inland North America.

I had some hay to spread over the crop plots for the winter. That soil wasn't blowing anywhere – not if I could help it! Once we were ready to plant, it would not be via tilling the soil. No…we would be doing something else: gouging small slits into the soil though it and compost.

"Just wait until spring," I promised the four of them. "Hamish and I will train you to grow food on these plots. When Uncle Charlie and Aunt Zoe get a new house, we'll help you set up your own growing operation in the back yard. Then you'll have to keep it going."

Jacques had responded with a grim mumbling of "Dad'll never want to work on that."

My Dad, meanwhile, had come out and helped us pull apart the hay to spread over the plots.

My mother and Aunt Zoe had watched, looking serious. Aunt Zoe said, "I heard that. We'll see about that. Your father and I will adjust to composting, whether he wants to, or not."

My mother just laughed. "I'm with him. I don't want to, but I know I have to do it."

We adjourned to the kitchen to prepare dinner.

I was determined to create as much compost out of every last vegetable peel, fish skin, chicken or turkey bone, and whatever else I could get. I had bought a container for all of these rejects and lectured the entire family on its use, sternly decreeing that all plates were to be scraped into it after meals, and all food preparations were to contribute anything that didn't go into the meals for human consumption. I was anxious about maintaining our natural security.

The new regime ensued…with me policing every stroke across the cutting boards, directing traffic into the new compost can. The parents had looked like a deeply unpleasant chore was being foisted upon them. The cousins had listened with a bit more interest and, thus far, had not omitted a scrap for it.

Hamish got back from his office after we had the dinner cooking and the salads made.

It was then that I remembered what was in my pocket.

"Hi Hamish," I said, giving him a quick kiss on the cheek. "Come upstairs with me."

Intrigued, he followed me, stopping me at the foot of the stairs to say, "Wait – I want a kiss!"

I let him have one and then dragged him upstairs.

He came along willingly enough, wondering what I wanted. "This must be serious," he remarked. No way would I drag my husband upstairs in the middle of dinner preparations for sex; not with an extended family in the house! He knew it was about something secret.

We got into our room and I shut the door.

Hamish turned to look at me. "What is it?"

I had grabbed a ziplock bag on the way out of the kitchen. Now I opened it, held it wide, pulled the gray, porous object from the pumpkin patch from my pocket, and dropped it inside as my husband watched, open-mouthed. "So, Dr. MacDonall," I asked, handing him the bag, "is this thing what I think it is?"

"Aye," he said. "It's a bone fragment…possibly a knuckle. Where did you get it?"

"In the pumpkin patch soil in what used to be Aunt Zoe and Uncle Charlie's back yard."

"I see." He didn't say anything else, but stood there staring into the bag, which he held up.

"Do you think it might be a human bone fragment?" I couldn't help asking.

"Aye. I'll test it to make sure, but we saw what happened there on the nano-cam swarm."

Chapter 2

Cypherpunks and Bitcoins

One of the things that we had done during our time in Switzerland was to research bitcoins.

As long as we had been on a trip with a computer expert, I had not seen any reason not to ask Jason all about it. We would need a powerful computer with a cooling fan that wouldn't quit, he told us, and we would have to download bitcoin mining software to it.

Hamish had, clever as ever, engineered a special cooling system for it, complete with low energy use. The machine was in our basement, whirring away, and any excess heat was funneled into running the house's climate control system. After that, it was a simple matter of keeping the machine going. It was an experiment in accessing and using decentralized money.

Within a month we had put the plan into practice, and now about a tenth of our money was in bitcoins. I was amazed by how quickly we had amassed a fortune in them. The catch was that few people traded with them as yet, but that was changing every day. Each coin was encrypted in such a way as to be impossible to counterfeit, and the payer could not be identified, only the payee. There was just enough transparency involved to make it work without being tracked.

When we told the family about this, the reactions corresponded with the age of the individual: my cousins decided to invest, and my parents, aunt and uncle, and grandmother would not have anything to do with the idea.

Typical, I thought. Hamish had listened to what Jason had had to say and been sold, as had I.

"Tell us again what bitcoins are and how they work," Dad had said to me back in April, just after Jason had gotten around to teaching me about them and fully explaining the concept to me. "I just can't wrap my mind around this idea. It doesn't seem safe, real, or even tangible." This was the fifth time since the idea had first come up that he wanted to hear it. Dad just didn't like not understanding a thing, even if he wasn't going to join in.

We had been sitting on board the *Shadowcat* with our coffee and some madeleine cookies one afternoon, and he had caught me alone with my books. Everyone else, except for Grandmère, was out shopping, walking, working, or whatever they were doing. Grandmère had taken her drink and treat to the living room and tuned into French television. She had lost interest in bitcoins after hearing it for the first time. I hadn't actually expected her to buy into it at her age. She was in her late nineties, and she just wanted to relax. No one could blame her for that.

"And what's a Cypherpunk?" Dad asked just for good measure.

I smiled and bit into my cookie. "It's someone who knows how to manage bitcoins and digital data," I told him. "Jason is a Cypherpunk. It's a cool term for someone who works with cyphers – computer encryption for managing bitcoin tags. You get a string of code that is your own, unique key, keep it secret, and use it to trade digital money. Bitcoins can then be traded via a decentralized network of computers."

"I see. And what's so great about this?" Dad asked, still confused.

"I'm surprised you don't see it after last year's run on banks, with people unable to access funds, panicked when banks were bricked and boarded up, like the Panics that preceded the Great Depression. The point of bitcoins is to not be dependent on bankster-created funds. That way, when the banks collapse or fail for whatever other reason to back their currency, you still have access to money, and therefore to whatever goods or food you need."

"Oh. I think I see." David took a bite of his cookie and thought about that.

He had continued to think silently, and I had left him to it.

"What kind of car are you interested in?"

Jason was over, visiting Jacques. Claire, Fabian, and Edgar were in the living room with him.

I wandered in with my tea and cookies, curious to hear what he would tell them. All of my cousins were in the market for a car now that we were back to stay, as was Jason. He had said he was sick of taking public transportation and relying on rides from people. I didn't blame him.

"I'm looking at Tesla cars. I like the idea of a plug-in, battery-powered car that lasts all day on a charge," Jason replied. "I want one that Model Citizen can't surveil. That means tinkering, but it'll be worth it. What about you guys? Do you know what kind of car you want?"

Model Citizen was the N.S.A.'s warrantless spy program that watched us all.

"Probably a Tesla for me," Jacques said.

Everyone's eyes shifted to Edgar next. "Tesla, I think," he said.

Of course, this meant little in conversation. We would see what they actually bought.

Fabian said, "I might ask Hamish for some advice. A Tesla might be fun, though."

None of the guys looked at Claire, but she spoke up, oblivious to that fact. "I'm going to get an old Mercedes and have it converted to electricity, like Avril's car, and all surveillance crap removed from it." She looked rather pleased with herself as she added that last bit.

The guys all stared at her for a moment, and then Jacques said, "I'd better get that Tesla checked for surveillance tech, then."

Claire and I laughed, and Fabian did too. The others thought for a moment, then laughed.

Chapter 3

Wasi'chu

Uncle Charlie wasn't happy with our enforced vegetarian diet.

I had no sympathy for him. Meat and fish were very hard to find in supermarkets now. I had just paid forty dollars for a 2-pound bag of almonds, raw and unsalted, to be used sparingly as an ingredient in salads and cookies, and was in a mild state of sticker shock. What about other people, I wondered, with a much tighter food budge than myself?! I had put the almonds away in the back of the baker's pantry when I unpacked the groceries, and told everyone about the price.

Whole Foods was still stocking yogurts from Iceland, of all places, which amazed me. The prices had gone up by a dollar apiece, which wasn't much, all things considered. I had spent a long time in the store, just staring at the prices of everything most of the time, while also trying to take note of what was offered. Much of what I was used to eating was still there, but it was late summer. What would it be like in cold weather, I wondered?

Claire had come with me, and she had been a bit startled as well, but her main purpose was really to get out of the house and explore while seeing what I made of the changes. When I had realized that, I started telling her what I was looking for, and what impressed, disturbed, surprised, and otherwise jumped out at me.

Aaron and Ed appreciated that, too, because they were wondering why I was taking so long.

We as a species had been in overshoot for so long, caused in significant part by greedily consuming meat, that Uncle Charlie's seemed like a silly complaint. It was foolish to insist upon eating animals that consumed vegetables rather than those vegetables themselves. The hell with eating at the top of the food chain when there were so many great vegetables to enjoy anyway!

When that reasoning made no impression on him, I told him, as we ate yet another family dinner of imaginative and gourmet vegetarian fare, about the Native American attitude. It even had a word for the "greedy one" who wanted to eat meat: wasi'chu. It was a word from the Lakota and Dakota tribes.

"When Meriwether Lewis and William Clark went on their 1804 mapping expedition of the Louisiana Purchase, the Native Tribespeople called Lewis "Greedy One" in their own language because he would hunt birds and animals daily, eat what he wanted of the kills, and then discard the rest. They used the whole creature, and did not eat so much meat. They did not approve of killing so many creatures. It is not necessary. Good observation on their part," I summed up.

"Fine, Professor. Call me greedy," Uncle Charlie said. "I want a steak."

Aunt Zoe grinned at him. "You can have it in restaurants once in a while, and live on a healthier diet in between. Eat your quinoa-stuffed orange and red bell peppers and salad, drink up your butternut squash curry soup, and be quiet."

He grinned at her and spooned in a mouthful of it. "I should be so lucky," he quipped.

"You are so lucky," Hamish quipped back with a grin of his own, swirled some chèvre onto a leaf of Romaine lettuce, and forked it into his mouth.

"Too bad we can't have more fish," my mother remarked. "What did you say was wrong with most fish, Avril?"

"It's full of microbeads, plastic fibers, and other contaminants that are killing the fish and other endangered species. Pacific fish has cancer from radiation poisoning. We shouldn't ingest that, and the few fish that are deemed safe are super-expensive."

"Great," my mother said, in a glum tone. "Seems like everything is ruined."

"Yeah. Hamish should invent a nano-detox system for fish. You could make yet another fortune," I said, dreaming aloud.

Everyone stopped chewing and stared at me for a moment, including Hamish.

"I'll get right on it after dinner," he said.

"Is this how you two invent things?" Dad asked, grinning incredulously from ear to ear. "She muses about a seemingly fantastic solution to a problem, and then you make it real?"

"Aye, it is," my husband replied. "You have just stated our work method."

"Wow." Jacques said. "You're a dream team, pun intended. I have to do that with recycling."

"Aren't you and Jason working on that?" Claire asked him.

"We are. It's a bit slower going than it is for Avril and Hamish."

"You'll get there," Grandmère said, smiling encouragingly at him.

"Hey – here's a slogan for you," Claire said. "Don't throw it away – because there is no 'away'! What do you think?"

"It's perfect!" Fabian and Jacques said, both at once. Everyone laughed.

Uncle Charlie was still focused on steak. "If nanobots can get the pollutants out of fish, would it still be as expensive as steak?"

I looked up at him. "Most likely, the answer would be yes, because there still aren't enough fish to catch. The species we humans like to eat are still terribly depleted from overfishing, starting with the biggest of them, which were at the top of the food chain: salmon, tuna, halibut, etc. That means that large ones are fewer and fewer, and that the rest of the food chain on down is affected, with the numbers of each level out of balance."

"So what's wrong with eating steak?"

"It's a top-of-the-food-chain item. To produce it, cattle must be fed a lot of grains – grains that humans can't digest. That means that a lot of land that is geared toward agriculture gets allocated for cattle food rather than grains that humans can eat. This is not efficient, nor does it leave enough food for all humans and of the kinds that make a healthy diet. Thanks to droughts, you won't even see the breeds of cattle that you are used to eating – Angus, for example – being raised to become beef on your plate. Other, hardier species are taking their place. Add all that up, and you get other beef than you are used to tasting, and/or much more expensive beef."

"You don't need it, Charlie," Aunt Zoe said.

"I want it, though," he replied. "What was it that that makes me? Wasi'chu?"

"Yes."

"Don't be wasi'chu, Charlie. Eat your dinner," my aunt said with a grin. They were busy house-hunting, and she wanted Uncle Charlie to live in one with her for a long time. I didn't blame her. Regenics could only do so much. A healthy diet was also necessary.

There was a moratorium on any new development, and Uncle Charlie was not happy about it. He wanted to build a new house for himself and his family, to replace the one that he had built and lost, but the government wouldn't allow it.

"You're actually surprised?" I said to him.

"Well, no, but I am frustrated. We can't just stay here with you forever. You've been great, keeping us away from the chaos, protecting us from it and from my own impulse to run out there during it all and protest – I probably would have just gotten myself killed in the attempt – but we have to find another place to live."

"I have no plans to relocate," Grandmère interjected.

I looked up, startled. "You like it here? You want to be with us?"

She smiled at me. "Yes, I want to live with you now."

"Okay then, we'll renovate the upstairs so that you have your own bathroom," I said.

Pretty soon, we would have nothing but suites of rooms upstairs, but so be it. Sharing a bathroom down the hall among so many people could not go on forever. Grandmère gave me a big smile. "Thank you," she said.

It was tight in the Stoner Drive house, even though it already had two bedroom suites at either end of the house with their own bathrooms – occupied by my parents and by myself and Hamish – plus three more bedrooms and a full bathroom in the hall. Those three bedrooms were filled by Grandmère in the one next to my parents, Claire and Fabian next to us, and Aunt Zoe and Uncle Charlie in the middle, facing front, over the kitchen, across from them. Our bathroom was between our room and theirs, and I supposed Uncle Charlie could hear our shower running.

As if that weren't crowded enough, Jacques and Edgar lived in the attic now, which was, at least, finished. It had wood panels – cherry – and curtains, with beds that were low to the floors. At least they each had their own spaces up there, but the bathroom was down one level, shared with everyone else.

Aunt Zoe said, "We're hoping to find a house for sale with at least three bedrooms. We'll take Jacques and Edgar with us for now, but I doubt we'll be able to take Claire and Fabian."

"We don't expect you to worry about us, Mom," Fabian said.

"You two can live here as long as you want," I said to them immediately. "We love having you around. Besides, if you start law school, you won't want to be worrying about housing – just studying – and I'm looking forward to watching you two study and discussing the program with you sometimes." I smiled as I said this.

Claire smiled back. She was still in shock after seeing her old neighborhood outside Philadelphia erased, turned to grassland, parks, farms, orchards, and whatever else via our flying nanobot cameras on the way back from Europe. Her parents and their bakery had just disappeared. "We should start studying for the LSAT," she said. She was trying to move on.

I thought about finding a psychiatrist for her to visit, but worried about what she might feel safe confiding. She knew too much. There had to be a solution to that problem, I thought to myself, but I was still searching for it.

"I'll show you what you need, and help you with the arrangements," I said out loud. "You will need to learn the Princeton Review method, because they are the ones who make the standardized tests, and after that it's just a matter of practice, practice, practice, timing yourself with set after set of questions. You will need lots of sets so that you don't pick up speed for the wrong reason."

"What would be the wrong reason?" Fabian asked.

"If you use the same sets of questions, you start to remember them, which will give you a false increase in test-taking speed. That won't help you later, when the test is real."

"Oh…yeah. Thanks!" he said.

"You're welcome. We'll set you up with all the right tools, and leave you to practice in the den out back. We won't go out there. There's no need to walk through that room to get to another, so you can just take it over to practice."

My parents broke into grins. "You just practiced in your room."

"I did, but there's two of them in there, and no desk. There's a small table out on the porch."

There wasn't really enough extra space in Claire and Fabian's room for more furniture.

My mother nodded. She seemed fine with me and Hamish having control of the house, which we had after buying it from my parents. It still felt like ours – our collective territory – and I knew that she would be equally involved as we made whatever aesthetic and logistical changes here. We had to make those changes, take care of our family, and cope with all of the changes outside of the house and all around us without a lot of fuss. It seemed like the least we could do.

So many other families – Claire's included – had not had even that option.

They had not had any options at all, because they had not known what was happening.

We had had a Holocaust that was now being marketed as a plague.

I had taken to calling it a Cull while it was being perpetrated – with a capital "C".

Hamish had readily adopted that term, but we still weren't saying it when we went out.

I was not someone who could see ghosts, but Hamish had told me that, at various points in his life, he had. He had seen them in the war theater, which was not odd when one considered that battlegrounds tended to be littered with corpses when the fighting stopped. He had seen them when taking flying lessons and after that, over the southern part of the Atlantic Ocean off the Bahamas, including an entire ghost ship with a guy in rags running back and forth over the deck, waving for help…only to find that it was well-known and never showed up on radar.

That afternoon, before dinner, he had told me that he had seen some ghosts in our town.

He saw them when he and Ed had gone out for a quick reconnaissance tour of the town, the day after we all got back. When he told me about what he had seen, I was determined to go out the next day, and my farm, orchard, and berry tour had been the result. All I had seen were serious, stunned, living faces – no ghosts. I could feel cold spots all around, but I saw no ghosts.

Maybe it was just the cold feeling of knowing what had happened here and in many other places, I told myself. And yet, I knew what it meant to feel a cold spot. It was what a living person felt when a ghost walked near or through them.

And I knew Hamish could see ghosts. He had seen plenty of them in the war in Kuwait.

Hamish had wanted to check on things just as I had, see what was still there and what was not, and then go to Avon to see his office. They had done all of that, and it was as they drove around what used to be Elmwood, and around areas that had been developed into neighborhoods in the 1950s and 1960s, north of the center of West Hartford, that he saw the ghosts.

"Who did they look like?" I couldn't help asking. "I mean, I don't expect you to have known the ghosts personally, or even to have interacted with them much or at all while they were alive, but you may have gotten used to seeing them when they were alive, out and about, doing errands or eating in restaurants around here."

He and I were in the conservatory, and it was late in the afternoon. The rest of the family was home, but elsewhere in the house and on the property. We were alone together as I checked the herbs and strawberry plants, the fragrances of which mixed with moisture and potting soil in the small, round, glass-enclosed room.

He pinched a lavender plant, and then inhaled the scent on his forefinger and thumb. "There were some familiar faces. They looked like transparent PTSD cases. Some were in their underwear, and others in hospital pajamas, all barefoot."

"Were they in color, or whitish?" I couldn't help asking.

"Kind of in between…like with muted colors."

"Did they make eye contact with you? Did they talk to you…or seem to want anything?"

"Some did look at me, and acted surprised that I could see them, but they didn't really seem to expect anything from me. I just looked at them. They were walking all around, stunned and confused. Some looked angry. They weren't trying to go anywhere."

"Were there a lot of them?" I had to ask.

Hamish pinched a rosemary leaf and sniffed.

I did the same thing. The scent helped. I reminded me that I was alive.

He looked up and said, "Aye. Whole neighborhoods of them."

"Did you get out of the car at all?"

"Aye. I walked a bit away from Ed so that he wouldn't think I was daft – crazy…"

"Hamish, don't worry about lapsing into Britishisms with me," I said.

He gave me a wry grin and continued. "I spoke to a woman who looked to be about your age – the age you really are, not the age that you now appear to be – and asked her if she wanted anything from me."

"Can you hear ghosts talk?" I asked, surprised.

"Sometimes. But this one didn't make a sound. She just mouthed 'No' at me and shook her head. I nodded back, and she wandered off. But it was eerie seeing people in their underwear in late September, not shivering in the breeze, and not sweating in hot sun."

"You're just telling me this now, after I've been out and about?"

"I didn't want you to be thinking about it until after you had had your own tour," he said.

"Oh, thanks. Now I feel like an experiment!"

Another wry grin. "I guess you are. But…I didn't want you to be nervous when you went out for the first time since the Cull. I wanted to tell you now, so that you would know that you could go out without seeing the ghosts. You did tell me that you heard laughter in the Trinity Church graveyard on Broadway, remember? And that turned out to be a famous ghost, even though no one knows who that ghost is or what the joke is. So I know you can hear ghosts."

"Hmm…thank you. I did realize that they had to be there, though," I said.

He smiled. "You would. Funny that you are an atheist yet believe in ghosts."

"The Higgs-Bosun Particle ought to be called the celebrity particle. I wonder what they call the Asperger's particles – the ones that aren't attracted to it, as most particles are. Ghosts are just more 'magic' that hasn't yet been explained by science. Could you see any of them as we drove back from New York last week?"

"I thought I might have seen a few, but I was trying really hard not to," he said. "That takes some effort, though, so I went out to face them on purpose yesterday. Also, I figured I had to get on with it, because you would only stay home for so long, putting the house in order, before running out of certain everyday foods and go out yourself. And you did, today."

"Yeah, I did. I sat on that rock in the backyard of Aunt Zoe and Uncle Charlie's house, stared at the grass, and then looked up with a shock at the pumpkin patch that is now there instead," I told him. "I won't do that again. I managed to scare myself, and by accident."

But this wasn't about Hallowe'en, despite the spookiness.

Hamish looked as freaked out and unsettled as I had ever seen him, and he was generally unflappable, calm, and able to face anything. Knowing that he had seen war up close and personal, that had never surprised me about him. I had to do something for him.

"Hamish," I said, not sure just what that would be as yet, "I want to take you out with me to see the town…and the ghosts. I want you to tell me what you see when we go."

He looked at me, then said, "Be careful what you wish for."

"Oh, I know this will be seriously unsettling and all that, but I want to figure out what I might do for you…and perhaps them as well. Ghosts hang around because they have unfinished business. That's common knowledge even to people who don't see them or have issues with them," I replied.

"What do you have in mind?"

I gave him a mirthless grin. "You know what they say: the word processor is mightier than the MRAP – or the crematorium," I told him.

"Or something like that," he said with a wry grin back at me.

"We go tomorrow," I said. "And we can check on your office and the people in it."

The next day, we set out with Aaron and Ed following us, just like old times. Except that times were very different now.

Green buses went up and down Mountain Road, slowing traffic down.

We went all over town and beyond, and so did those infernal buses.

"What did they do, take away everyone's cars?!" Hamish said, outraged.

"Almost," I said. "Look – there's a few. And look at the models: Tesla, Mercedes converted to electric, like ours, and other brands, also converted. No more gas or diesel burners."

"Only the wealthy could hope to afford such vehicles," Hamish observed with disgust.

"Yeah…aren't we lucky." I said it without pleasure. Money was the new vehicle of independence and control of one's time, one's schedule, and a lot else.

We visited Nora and Ruby at the Canton mall. Nora had converted her car and used a hefty chunk of her savings to do it. Ruby lay quietly on her dog bed behind the counter as always, her eyes open, listening to the sounds around her. She wore her wide, embroidered greyhound collar.

Nora was delighted to see us. She came out from behind her counter and hugged me, and squeezed Hamish's hand. He seemed quite delighted and surprised. "I was worried about you two!" she told us.

"Worried?" I said. "We were fine, off in Switzerland. It was you who needed worrying about. How was that trip to Manhattan with Ruby, and how was it when you got back?"

Nora looked serious. "Eerie…VERY eerie. I left with everything looking like always – strip malls, lots of cars everywhere, and all of the same houses I knew along the way. I drove there and home again, with Ruby. On the way down, things looked different, and they got more so while we were gone. On the way back, everything looked…I don't know…erased, somehow."

Hamish and I exchanged glances. "'Erased' is the word we've been using too," he said.

Nora nodded. "My home was still there when I got back to it, but I saw so many that were simply…gone…and replaced with woods and open spaces that I didn't know whether or not to expect it to still be there. But, it was there."

"Good," I said.

She looked at us for a moment, and then said, "That convention you sent me to in Manhattan turned out to be a spa vacation and a tour of gift shops. The timing was perfect. I missed whatever went on here."

"Good," I said again.

"You set that up, didn't you?" Nora asked.

"Did we?" I smiled cryptically.

She smiled. She got it. "Well…thank you," she said. Neurotypicals caught on so fast. She wouldn't ask too many questions. She had to have known that something was up when Hamish and I had shown up in her shop for weeks to vaccinate her slowly, before the official vaccination policy had gone into effect. Yet she had not objected. She had simply thanked us very sweetly and let Hamish do his thing, registering her shots in the national database.

We stayed a little while longer, I bought some cards – done by a different photographer now, as some of the ones Nora had bought them from had not survived the Cull – and then we left.

On the way back, I deliberately turned in to the West Hartford Reservoir, the big one off of Albany Avenue. It was now guarded by a police officer, who stopped us as soon as we entered the parking lot. He let us park, but blocked our car in and ordered Ed and Aaron to wait for him to inspect theirs also.

I grabbed my handbag and took out my driver's license to show him.

His badge said Sorensen, and he was a big guy with a dark brown crew cut.

Hamish took out his I.D. also and passed it to him from the passenger seat.

The officer did a double-take when he saw our names. "You are the inventors of Nae-Née?"

I nodded, keeping my facial expression as neutral as I could (not difficult). Who knew how this guy felt about not being able to dictate whether or not to reproduce. He wore a wedding ring, I suddenly noticed, and he saw me look at it. Married people could get birth licenses.

He handed the I.D.s back. "You don't have a driver's license?" he asked Hamish, puzzled.

Hamish and I exchanged wry glances. "No," Hamish replied.

Officer Sorensen looked confused. "How come?"

This cop was nosy, but it seemed like he was just a curious guy, wondering for his own information about us, and that his curiosity was wholly separate from his duties. So, I said, "He let it lapse during graduate school, which was in Boston, conveniently located with lots of quick and efficient public transportation…and within walking distance of just about everything he needed. He just forgot about it. Then he met me, and I hadn't let mine lapse." I grinned.

Now the cop made a silent and long nod of understanding, and smiled. "I see. And you never wanted it back?" he asked Hamish.

"Not really. It was just another damned thing to think about," Hamish said.

I grinned. "I have the car keys, and if I need a bathroom stop, I'm in control – insert evil maniacal laughter here," I summed up.

Now the cop just started laughing. "You're funny. So…what are doing here, turning around? A lot of people come in here to do that."

"They do? Do any come in here to jog or walk dogs, or just enjoy the view of the water?"

"Well, yes, but since the incident a year ago, not so many, because they have to show their I.D. Most people out for recreational purposes don't want to go through all that," Sorensen said.

"What incident? We were away, setting up a clinic in Europe. We just got back a few days ago, and we're out to see what has changed, to learn about it, and get used whatever is new," I told him.

"Really? Well…terrorists poisoned the water. The MDC had a hell of time cleaning it up. The reservoir was shut down until the cyanide could be extracted, or whatever they did to get it out. It took a couple of weeks. We had to work overtime to block the entrance and secure the perimeter, so that no one could sneak in, and now it's all fenced and monitored with cameras. No one gets in or out anymore without our knowing about it."

Hamish and I had listened to all of this without saying anything. Now I had a question: "What was it like in this area outside of the reservoir during that time?"

"No showers, food had to be cooked with bottled water, paper plates only," he told us.

"Sounds miserable," I said.

"It was." The cop looked at us. "You really didn't know about this?"

"We heard one brief sound-bite about it, then nothing, which is why I pulled in here. I figured that if anyone would be able to fill in the gaps, a cop would. You were here, after all."

He nodded his head, shifting from one foot to the other. He was dressed in the standard dark blue of police officers, powerfully built, and equipped with a belt full of weapons. He also had a tiny camera strapped to his collar, I noticed just now. Well, fine – we were both being recorded and surveilled. So what? At least I was finding something out.

"So…can we go into the reservoir with our car and see it? Is that allowed?"

"Yeah, it's allowed, but first I have to check out these other people," Sorensen said.

"They're with us," I told him. "We'll just sit here and wait while you talk to them."

He nodded and approached Ed and Aaron's vehicle, his hand on his weapon, but smiling politely. I caught Aaron's eye and smiled, and he nodded and smiled back.

Hamish had his phone connected to Ed's, so we heard the whole exchange. Nothing disturbing; it was all just a quick repeat of the fact that they had been away with us, who they were, and that they were our bodyguards. "You follow them around wherever they go?"

"Yes, we do," Aaron said. "They're fascinating to work for."

"I'll be they are," Sorenson said, passing their I.D.s back to them. "Okay, I'll open the gate for you. The reservoir closes at dusk, as always, but you can leave whenever you want." With that, he went back to his cruiser, reached in, and pressed a button.

The gate swung open for us – just one side of it. A razor-wire topped fence extended from either side of it, on into the woods all around it. We saw cameras mounted on every third steel post, and they swiveled every which way. Some swiveled to watch us.

Sorensen waved us through, and we drove in, followed by Aaron and Ed in their SUV.

Once we were past the gate, everything looked the same as it always had. The water was pretty, the Canada geese and mallard ducks were there, and we even saw a couple of white swans and a grey heron. It was lovely.

We parked and sat down on one of the rough-hewn wooden benches. That was old, too.

Aaron and Ed got out and came over to us.

We smiled up at them, and they nodded, satisfied that we were okay.

Hamish had his arm across my shoulders, and he nodded to them to come back and chat.

"Hamish," I asked, "Do you think lip-readers are watching us on those cameras, or that they can hear us somehow?"

"Lip-readers, maybe, but that's all."

"Fine," I said. "I won't enunciate too clearly. So...was that attack on the water a hoax?"

"It was. The purpose was just to seal this place off in case of a real attack, to prevent one."

Somehow, I liked that better, but the lie and the inconvenience – the mind games played by our government – galled me. I said so.

Aaron seconded that sentiment, and Ed chimed in to agree with him.

We looked around a bit more at the wildlife, and I took a few photographs after getting my camera out of the trunk. They came out clear and sharp, so I put it away, and we drove all the way to the back, where the water treatment plant was.

When we got there, it was sealed off and heavily guarded by more cops, and an MRAP. The MRAP was painted with the symbols for both Homeland Security and the Metropolitan District Commission, and the cops carried assault rifles.

They were blocking access to the old footpath that Dad and I had walked on a few times. It was just to the left and behind the parking area, which was also sealed off. "I guess this security measure wouldn't work without cutting off access to the footpaths," I remarked.

"No, guess not," Hamish agreed, but he looked grim. "This is our brave new world."

"Indeed. Welcome to the New World Order...underwater," I quipped, turning the car around at the cul-de-sac while making sure to smile and wave to the cops who stood around, watching our every move. At least they smiled and waved back.

Looking in my rear-view mirror, I noticed that Ed and Aaron did the same thing as Ed steered around the curve to follow us.

"Let's get out of here," Hamish said. "I don't want them to detain us."

I looked over at him, vaguely alarmed, but decided to just drive calmly out without further ado. No reason to get panicky just because we saw law enforcement all around. As awful as the thought was, it still seemed reasonable to believe that white cops observing educated white people in cars would not lead to any kind of confrontation. And we kept pleasant, calm expressions on our faces at all times.

When we reached the pair of gates, the one on our side swung open as if on a sensor.

"That wasn't bad," I said, driving out. We waved to Officer Sorensen and drove out.

Hamish seemed to breathe a sigh of relief, though, and watched as Ed caught up with us.

I took us through the orchards, berry patches, and squash patch next, just to show what had been done to Aunt Zoe and Uncle Charlie's old neighborhood. Hamish got very quiet. His eyes went wide, and he looked around at everything very carefully. He had already toured this area, so I knew that his wide-eyed, tense aspect wasn't about new information.

He was seeing the ghosts.

"Are there a lot of them?" I asked.

"Aye. They're in shock, angry, and they're still in underwear or hospital pajamas. They are the people who lived in the neighborhoods that were erased from here. They look familiar, like people we used to see around town, in the grocery stores, in restaurants, and elsewhere."

"What can I do for you about them? Anything? I mean, you can't not go out anywhere, but can I help you with this at all?"

Hamish smiled at me. "No, you can't, but thank you. I'll just have to get used to this."

I didn't like that at all. "Maybe I'll think of something we can do for the ghosts, and maybe *that* will help you. Ghosts have unfinished business – issues that are unresolved. Maybe I can find a way to help them resolve those issues."

Hamish stared at me as I drove along, heading back down Mountain Road, toward home.

"What are you suggesting?"

"I don't know just yet, but I'm working on it."

When we got home, my parents and Grandmère were watching the news in the living room.

"Animal control authorities are asking people to please keep their small pets – lap dogs and cats, in particular – inside at all times," the newscaster was saying. This was the local news. It was Daniel Hauss, and he was looking very concerned as he announced this. "For reasons unknown, hawks, owls, and land predators such as coyotes are now very interested in small animals as prey, so take precautions to make sure that you don't lose your furry friends."

Hamish and I looked at each other, startled, and then at my parents and grandmother.

They looked knowingly out of the tops of their eyes at us. We knew why this was happening, thanks to the flying nanobotic cameras that Hamish had used to enable us all to watch the Cull. It was all saved as evidence, locked away until we figured out how to use it. The reason was related to how pets had been disposed of during the Cull.

At first, the mobile cremation units sent all over the country by the military had broken pets' necks and buried them. Then they had gotten lazy, and tossed the little corpses into the woods rather than bother with burying many of them. The bodies had become food for wild animals.

"Are Spock and Eowyn in?" I couldn't help asking.

"Of course. They're in their baskets on the porch, sleeping."

"Good." But I ran out there and checked anyway, and petted them. So did Hamish. He loved the cats as much as I did. Our cats never went out, but that announcement made me want to check everything about them immediately.

Anxiety thus allayed, I moved on to the next event.

The next event seemed to waste no time in appearing via the daily mail service.

It was an odd deluge of legal documents.

There was one for me and Hamish, and another for my parents, each assigning us portions of Aunt Zoe and Uncle Charlie's property, which the federal government had taken by eminent domain and then assigned to the State of Connecticut. Aunt Zoe and Uncle Charlie had a letter, as did Claire.

"Idiots!" I roared at no one in particular over the kitchen table. We were all in and out of there, eating lunch rather informally, as the kitchen table only seated eight if pulled away from the wall by the bay window. It looked out over the backyard. There wasn't room for another piece of furniture in there, so we tended to grab what we wanted at random times and carry it out to the porch, which was just across the hall, or into the living room.

But we were all in there at the moment. I could see that Dad had just opened his nearly identical set of legal documents and was staring at them with distaste, his lunch momentarily forgotten. His brother was right there in the room with us, and these papers talked of giving him money for the place where he used to live. What an outrage!

"Who are the idiots you are referring to?" Uncle Charlie asked me.

I looked up at him. "The Farmers' minions in the federal and state governments," I replied. "This is from the federal government, as it did the taking of your property. It seems to be laboring under several delusions. One is that we would leave you behind to get erased – murdered, ground-up, cremated, whatever – and not instead take you away with us during this Cull that they are marketing as a plague. Another is that you are dead, which you are not. The next is that they must then financially compensate the rest of us for your property."

"What?!" Uncle Charlie was stunned and outraged.

"What indeed. The government owes YOU money so that you can then buy another place to live, plus no obstacles in getting whatever style of home you wish to live in. I'm calling our attorney."

Before I could make another move, I noticed my cousins. They had, all four of them, been eating on the porch together and just brought back their dishes. Claire noticed the official-looking envelope that was addressed to her, picked it up, and started crying. That is, her facial expression showed almost no change other than a pronounced widening of the eyes, and tears rolled out. We Aspies didn't like to show any facial contortion when upset.

"I see you've gotten your eminent domain financial notice about your parents' estate," I said.

She looked up at me, too upset to speak for the moment, and nodded. Then she swallowed, recovered her voice, and said, "Guess so," quietly.

Fabian put his arm around her. "Shall I slit it open for you?" he asked.

"O-okay," she said, holding it out to him.

Hamish passed the letter-opener to him.

Fabian slit it open, and they stood there, reading through the pages gravely. Gravely was certainly the word for it; no one wanted to inherit their parents' property in their mid-twenties. Claire's parents had been lovely people. She would much rather have kept them!

At last, they looked up at us all. "My parents had a three-story Victorian house that I grew up in, and a store building in town that they owned and ran their bakery out of," she told us. "I've inherited the value of those properties, minus whatever bite the government takes out of that." She was turning red, but her facial expression stayed stubbornly flat.

Fabian was ready, though. We all knew, thanks to the fact that I had insisted, since being diagnosed myself with Asperger's, on educating the family about our traits, quirks, affects, and whatever else, what her next emotional response would be: she would need a way to completely hide her face as she cried, so that no screwed-up facial expressions would be visible.

We Aspies can be both frank about our emotions and determined to maintain our masks of dignity in facial expressions. If not too upset, we could just let tears stream out, but if very upset, as Claire was now, it was either bury one's face in one's husband's shoulder, or run for it.

Fabian was right there, so Claire availed herself of his shoulder.

Either way – Aspie meltdown or neurotypical – she was sobbing over being orphaned.

We all felt awful for her. A few tears leaked out of my eyes, but I kept it together. Hamish saw that and handed me a couple of tissues. I smiled weakly at him. Uncle Charlie was standing closest to her, and he actually put his hand on Claire's shoulders and gave her an awkward pat or two. He looked helplessly at Aunt Zoe, who moved closer, followed by my mother.

At least Claire had welcoming in-laws, I thought to myself. I hope her parents had realized that before they died, and I suspected that they had. I watched as my aunt and mother took turns wiping her face and talking to her soothingly.

After a few minutes, Claire was breathing calmly again, but Fabian wouldn't leave her. Good! I was quite impressed to observe how he was with her. When she wasn't sad, they had a good time together, and when she was, he was quietly there for her.

I had gone across to the dishwasher, where they were standing, and watched as she calmed down. She had so much attention that my efforts seemed superfluous in that area; even Grandmère had swooped in for a hug.

But my thoughts went back to dealing with the letters. "I'm going to call our lawyer now about the documents we just received. Would you like me to include yours when I ask for an appointment, so that he can handle whatever has to be done next?"

She looked at me like someone who had just come up for air from an underwater struggle, and with relief. "Yes, please! I'm sure I could figure it all out, but…"

"…but why upset yourself further when you can have legal help and focus on other efforts that life throws at you?" I said helpfully. "Being self-sufficient is good, but we're all more interested in helping you to feel better. Besides, anyone who aspires to attending law school won't be the sort of person who can't take care of life's logistics. You can do that later."

She smiled and handed me her documents.

With that, I took out my cell phone and called the lawyer.

Hamish picked up the documents that were addressed to me and him, looked them over briefly, then tossed them back onto the table as though they were contaminated. "Damn them. We'll at least arrange for you to get that money, Charlie, even though it's not all that you ought to get for the loss of your home. And Claire can get her money and be done with this."

Uncle Charlie and Claire both nodded with approval at this idea.

I was on hold for a moment with the paralegal, so I added, "Eminent domain won't give you the full value of the stolen property, but you must have that money. This is likely to take some time and aggravation—yes," I said, as she came back on the line, "I'm still here. Thanks."

Our attorney, one Mr. O'Shea, had just picked up and joined the phone call.

I outlined the problem, made an appointment to drop by with the letters and to bring Uncle Charlie and Aunt Zoe with me – Dad interrupted to say that he wanted to come along as well, to which my mother piled on that she too would come – and that was that. I thanked him and hung up. Done! For now…

"I may as well come along as well," Hamish said. "We will likely all have to sign something."

"Yes, I would expect so," I agreed.

Grandmère noticed that she had something from the government also, and showed it to me.

"Oh," I said. "Isn't this fascinating: apparently, the government knew that you went with us to Switzerland – why not the rest of the family?! – and is inquiring into the possibility that the military erasure squads might have either lost, destroyed, or stolen your Monet painting. How amusing…it's as if the Farmers knew damned well that you all came with us, and wanted to steal that land for itself, and pick up the awkward pieces of the situation when we all got back."

"Of course you can't accuse them of that," she remarked, "but I think you've got it right."

I took another look at the document, just because it was so intriguing. "This actually is fascinating," I went on. "It appears that the government has reconstituted and reinstituted the World War II Monuments Men, except that it is now called the Monuments Curators. It even says so in the information description. It's still called the MFAA – the Monuments, Fine Arts, and Archives Program, just as it was before."

"Well, my painting is here, they can't have it, and they don't have to pay me," Grandmère announced. "I won't be submitting any false claims for it. Maybe you should take this along to Mr. O'Shea, though, and tell him what's going on, just in case there is any action required."

I added that to the pile of documents.

The next afternoon, Hamish and I took all of those documents and went out to the garage to get into our car. I glanced around the garage at the other vehicles inside. My parents' cars were the other two vehicles present, with a line-up of four outside along the edge of the driveway for Aunt Zoe and Uncle Charlie's cars, plus a Blackout Security one for Edgar, and another shared by Fabian and Claire. Soon these would be replaced, and another would belong to Jacques, thanks to the money that the four of them had saved up while working in Switzerland last year.

Hamish noticed my gaze taking this in as the garage door opened and said, "We'll have to get all of their new cars either converted to electricity as your cousins buy them, or else persuade them to get electric ones."

I looked at him, realized something, and said, "Just don't get hydrogen fuel cells for the cars and/or the house and blow up the cars, the house, or both, with a car detonating inside the garage. I could just imagine that happening. Don't get some clever, fuel-efficient idea and implement as a surprise. The containment technology on those fuel cells is the problem still. It's not all worked out just yet."

He grinned and said, "Nothing slips by you. Okay – I won't sneak any in. But if that problem gets solved, we could all have clean energy that is independent of any power grid. And I will want to do that if it's possible. We shouldn't be stubbornly stuck in a state of asset inertia."

"No, we shouldn't, and that would be nice. Meanwhile, let's go see Attorney O'Shea and get these property problems dealt with. I want Uncle Charlie and Aunt Zoe to be able to start shopping for a new house – well, new to them, but a pre-existing structure, which is what they will likely prefer – without further ado. I wonder how much trouble they will have finding one that's available…"

Claire and Fabian appeared, rushing to catch up with us, and hopped into the backseat.

I looked at them, grinned, and said, "Don't worry – we wouldn't leave without you!"

They smiled back at me.

We got into the vehicle and I backed out, turned around, and moved into the street.

Aaron and Ed promptly appeared in our rearview mirror, like a roving security blanket.

"Those guys really make me feel safe," I commented, turning on the CD player. The music of John Williams' *Harry Potter and the Prisoner of Azkaban* filled the car.

Hamish smiled. "Good. I gave them a special background check, because I knew you would want shadows you could get to know and enjoy interacting with. Soon, we'll get to know a few more of them as they follow Claire and Fabian to work and school."

"Who follows my parents?" My parents had gotten into their car with Aunt Zoe, Uncle Charlie, and Grandmère, and were following us. It was a family caravan, and eerily reminiscent of our escape from the Cull, though without fewer cars, without two of our cousins, without our cats, and with no luggage. Still…it felt connected. This was, after all, about tying up loose ends associated with that experience.

"You've seen them. They check in with me and with Aaron and Ed every day. They stay in a house down the street, one that a couple who retired and moved to Montana sold us a few years ago. There's plenty of room in it for enough Blackout guards for our whole family."

"Wow. So much trouble."

"Aye, well, thanks to our smashing success with Nae-Née, it seems wise."

"Indeed."

Driving was easy, low-stress, and quick with so few cars on the road. We were in downtown Hartford, pulling up to CityPlace, the building where the law firm was, in less than twenty minutes, which was a record. I parked in the parking garage next to the skyscraper, and our shadows pulled into a space across from us. The garage wasn't full, so we had our pick of slots.

We all got out and waited for everyone else to join us, then went outside, in the front door, and through the lobby to the elevator. Grandmère was able to keep pace with my parents and aunt and uncle thanks to the Regenics formula that Hamish had developed, and she would soon be one hundred years old. I was awed by that revelation every time I thought about it.

Up and up we went to the firm's floors, which had a (to me) vertigo-inducing view of the Connecticut River. Pretty mahogany wood-trimmed furniture, bookcases, and moldings graced the library, and the carpet was a beautiful shade of forest green. Despite the stunning view, I clung whatever was closest in order to keep my balance. Damn the swaying that being high up caused! I knew I was standing still, but it just didn't feel that way.

I didn't have long to feel dizzy, though. The receptionist told us we could go in.

Aaron and Ed stayed in the library, watching us go. They could keep an eye on the door to our attorney's office from there.

When Dad had retired, he had handed our case files off to a middle-aged attorney whom he trusted with international patent work, an Irish-American one named Adrian O'Shea. We had liked the guy right away. He was straightforward to the point of being blunt, and had the necessary background in engineering to handle all of our inventions.

His steel-blue eyes and freckled face were framed by a thick head of reddish-brown hair, combed back sharply on the sides, and he wore a shirt with a white collar and blue-and-white stripes with red suspenders and a bright blue tie. He was a large guy with a wide frame.

He looked successful, that was for sure. And he loved us; Hamish had made sure to get him and his wife and teenaged son and daughter into his Avon office months before the Cull for carefully spaced-out vaccinations. Sean and Colleen had liked us, so Amy, their mother, did too, and felt comfortable with us. Amy was the quintessential soccer mom, ferrying her kids to play practices and sports matches.

When the Cull was over and we had returned from Switzerland, he had shown up at our house one evening, looking to talk with us privately. He wanted to know what the past year had really been about, and suspected that we knew more than we had ever said to him. After a brief glance at each other, we had then taken him downstairs to Hamish's basement lab and explained what had happened.

We had wanted to confide in someone like him – an attorney, to be precise – and one who was on our side. I had told Hamish that we might need advice at some point on how to handle what we knew, because we couldn't keep it to ourselves forever. He had agreed.

Thus, under the protection of attorney-client privilege, he was our partner in secrecy.

But that was not what we wanted to discuss with him right now.

As we all settled into seats on his chairs and sofas around the office, I took the letters, deeds, and other documents out of my bag and handed them to him.

He took them from me and we sat, twiddling our thumbs, waiting as he perused them.

After a few minutes, O'Shea looked up, inhaled deeply, gave a short sigh, and said, "I should be able to sort this out for you in a couple of weeks. It'll take some time to communicate with the government about all of these house and art mistakes, thefts, and whatever else, and to get your aunt and uncle's house money, and Claire's as well."

"Great!" I said. "Do we sign anything – letters, documents, whatever – or can that wait?"

"That can wait. I have to get those things ready first. If you want, I can swing by your house with them when they are ready. I'd call first, of course."

"Oh, yes, that would be very nice. Thank you." Most attorneys didn't make house calls, but we were a special case. Adrian didn't live that far from us. "If you wanted to stop by with them on your way home for the day on whatever day they are ready, that would be fine."

He smiled. Then he spoke again, to Claire. "Ms. Charbonneau," he began.

"You can call me Claire," she said.

He smiled again. "All right," but we noticed that he didn't use her name. It was awkward to call a client by her first name, young as she was, because she was just old enough to be an adult. Hmm…I remembered that feeling, when I was that age. "I did some checking into your case. You have inherited not only the value of your childhood home and the building where your parents' bakery was – minus the bite that eminent domain takes out of the transaction – but also their other assets. They left you over four hundred thousand dollars. Now, that would have been $640,000 if there hadn't been a government garnishment of every bank account in the nation, but that took forty percent of what everyone had."

We all took that in. There was a moment of silence as we thought about the legalized looting that had taken place just as the Cull had been getting underway. It had been caused by the debt-and-credit bubble bursting, deflation, and the economic crisis that had ensued. We were all remembering when banks had boarded up their windows and chaos had followed as people panicked, unable to access any of their money to pay bills or buy food. Good times…

But enough mental sarcasm; Claire was stunned. "So…how much is that altogether, and what should I do with it?" she asked.

"Well," Attorney O'Shea replied, "there will be an inheritance tax on it all, but it looks fairly neat and straightforward. Thanks to the evil events of the past year," and here Claire and Fabian did a small double-take as they realized that O'Shea understood that what had happened last year was a Cull and not a plague, "the government simply pays you money, minus inheritance taxes."

All told, with the four hundred thousand dollars, the value of the Victorian house, and that of the historic district store building, it came to a little under one and a half million dollars. That was the value of the life's work of two artisan bakers, reduced to a financial sum. It was so impersonal that I was glad that Claire's mother had sensed danger brewing and sent the family's personal effects to her daughter: jewelry, photographs, etc. Still, it was an account of another kind that remained to be settled, both to avenge Claire's parents, and the others.

Claire did not smile. She dragged her hand roughly across her eyes and said, "After the government is through taxing the proceeds of my parents' murders and its looting of their assets, I think it would be nice to just save the money. I can't think what to do with it just yet, and it's not like a law school has sent me an acceptance letter. It's too soon to decide. I wish I could just put it all in Switzerland, out of the thieves' reach."

O'Shea looked at her, considering. "Did you have an account in Switzerland while you were working there last year?"

"Well, yes, but…"

"Did you close it out?"

"No."

"Then you can put the money there if you wish."

At last, a slow, grim smile of satisfaction began to appear on Claire's face. "Okay. Good."

That took care of her business.

Uncle Charlie and Aunt Zoe had had all of their assets seized in the Cull, and now that they had turned up alive, the government owed them back. They would get their money – minus forty percent of everything – plus the value of their home, minus twenty percent. The cost of that house, previously valued at around four hundred and twenty-five thousand dollars, was refunded at the reduced sum of $340,000.

Uncle Charlie looked infuriated, but thanked Attorney O'Shea for his efforts. It wasn't O'Shea's fault, after all. He was just the messenger who was enforcing Uncle Charlie's rights to…a partial refund of a state-sanctioned robbery.

The check would likely be in the mail by next week.

As for Grandmère's Monet painting, the joke was on the government.

It was offering her the value of her "lost" art, minus forty percent.

"Write back to them and tell them to keep their money, that I have one hundred percent of my painting," she told the attorney with a smirk. "I wasn't so foolish as to take off and leave it unattended in a house that I had good reason to believe none of us would ever see again."

We all laughed, including Adrian O'Shea. "You people are fun clients. You're nobody's fools," he said.

With that, we thanked him and headed out.

It was almost dinnertime, so I took us to one of the Max restaurants. "Let's get Claire a chocoholic dessert," I said to them as we walked across the street. Luckily, that restaurant was still there. "You need one, and the rest of us might like something as well."

She smiled at me. She and Fabian had saved up a decent sum of money over the past year, enough that they could expect to pay for law school tuition – all three years' worth – in Connecticut. They would apply to Yale and the University of Connecticut, and then see what happened. Claire had quietly told me that she hoped it would be UConn so that they could stay close to home.

With any luck, that might just happen. Fabian, however, would have no qualms about commuting regularly to New Haven and back. The place had been reclaimed from the floods due to another huge engineering project by the U.S. Army Corps of Engineers, which had teamed up with a team of Dutch engineers. It was the same team that had worked on the Hudson River.

Yes…I could see the next few years unfolding, with Claire and Fabian studying hard, both working on law degrees while going about their academic and professional careers in their own ways. Claire would likely become an activist and an author, while Fabian would try to emulate Dad and Adrian O'Shea.

We all enjoyed a nice dinner at Max Downtown, and that included Aaron and Ed.

Sitting at the table with the two of them, we all felt an odd sense of nostalgia.

"Why does this feel so familiar?" Fabian said, smiling at the group. He knew why, though.

"It's just like we're back on the *Shadowcat*, but without stealth mode engaged," I replied.

Just when I thought that things were calming down, however, Farmers resurfaced.

A water war was unfolding in the eight towns that were served by our reservoirs.

A reservoir provides drinking water for its area with surface rainwater. That was how we got what we needed, for the most part, and it was managed by something called the Metropolitan District Commission (MDC).

Now, however, a water bottling corporation wanted to sink its pumps into some property in Bloomfield, one of those eight towns. The town council there had allowed this corporation to buy a piece of land in its industrial section without using its name, which meant that any residents who might possibly object had had no notice of this, nor any opportunity to make their objections heard before the deal was struck.

The corporation was based in California, but had recently relocated to Maryland.

That can happen when a place first gets sucked dry by overuse of water for cropland, combined with double the human population that the ecosystem there could support, water aquifers included, combined with water bottling corporations having the right to pump uninterrupted, regardless of a drought.

California had become a dry wasteland, cracked by earthquakes that had been caused by land recession (land sinks like a deflating sponge when its water is depleted). The final death knell had come with the influx of irradiated water from Fukushima, borne across the Pacific from Japan, when it had seeped into the groundwater there.

Now the water bottling corporation, called Angel Falls Bottling (love the name – there was nothing angelic about these demons!) wanted our water. It was even looking at sources of local spring water, which meant aquifers. Aquifers! I was outraged. Those were charged by ice ages, and we weren't going to have one of those anytime soon, not with a warming climate.

No…this was about sucking us dry and then walking away.

I was amazed, even though I shouldn't have been, at the short-term thinking about jobs without a thought devoted to our natural security. What would be left for future generations? We could easily have a drought here in Connecticut. We had had one every decade for my entire life, and earlier, so why wouldn't this just make it all worse?! We had "drought advisories" every summer now, too. That sounded suspiciously like an actual drought.

I looked into this mess and found that short-sightedness and a failure to self-educate was exactly what had happened. There was that, and a set of laws that had not been completed or expanded upon for almost ninety years.

The MDC had been created in the 1920s with "authority" over it to be held by the Connecticut State Legislature. And that was it! Nothing further had been enacted to guide lawmakers in governing the use of our water, a vital piece of our natural security.

If we had a drought, I could just imagine desperate wildlife, dehydrated, starving, and showing up in humans' back yards as they foraged for food. All we needed to do was let this bottling company in, and we would soon have a crashing ecosystem. No thanks!

The citizens' group that was protesting this was called the 8 Towns Water Warriors. Great name; it summed up who was affected by this invasion and what they were.

There had been no effort on the part of Angel Falls Bottling to interact with anyone other than the MDC officials and the government of the Town of Bloomfield. That had come as no surprise; Angel Falls Bottling knew that it wasn't wanted here, and it didn't care. It wanted our water, it wanted it at a huge discount, and that was that.

Claire and I went to a Water Warriors meeting, which was held in a Unitarian church on Fern Street in West Hartford. We both wanted to find out what we might be able to do to help, and we needed to know what had already been done.

There, we met the organizer, a nice woman from Bloomfield who was very angry, a Ms. Tollsen. She was a retired elementary school psychologist and amateur gardener who had her time volunteering as the town's gardener until this had come up. She wore a red fleece vest and slate blue cap. She had chin-length, wavy, white hair that came down on either side of her face, and bangs that peeked out from the brim of the hat. A huge, blue button on her vest said "Water Warriors – Save Our Water!"

We were quickly introduced to a plethora of her colleagues, and we sat down to read every handout that had been created, gathered, and otherwise prepared for the meeting. It took us about ten minutes, because we were fast readers.

"So, what do you suggest we do?" Ms. Tollsen asked when we looked up.

I smiled. "Don't bother with Angel Falls Bottling, because they haven't bothered with us, for one thing. For a few other things, contact our politicians – that means all of us writing our own letters to this effect – to say that we want old laws that provide loopholes that this and other raiding corporations can exploit repealed, and new, tighter ones enacted."

"Why would we want that?" asked another Water Warrior, a woman in jeans and a flowered blouse. She introduced herself as Beverly Greenwood from West Hartford.

"We would want that because of the Constitutional ban on ex post facto laws," I said. "No laws may be enacted that have an after-the-fact effect. We must get around that problem with laws that apply to all future raids on our natural security. A cease-and-desist order would be good. Also, anything that slows down the permitting process on any aspect of this deal, making it as unattractive as possible, would be worthwhile."

"We are very angry with our town attorney. He was working for both the town and the MDC, advising both, and he put together this deal with Angel Falls Bottling."

"Yes," I said. "I noticed that. A complaint should be filed with the Statewide Grievance Committee. Perhaps he could be disbarred for that, or at least get a blot on his record for unethical conduct due to a blatant conflict of interest."

"It has been filed," said a man who had appeared next to Ms. Tollsen. He was her husband, it turned out, a Mr. Jeppsen. He had thin, snowy white hair and a short beard, and a friendly expression. I wished we had more time to get to know all of these people, I thought to myself. They were interesting, and they were organized and determined. That may or may not be enough to keep this invading monster corporation out.

"Good!" Claire said, smiling.

He smiled back at her.

Next up, a woman from West Hartford, Sharon Lowenstein, said angrily, "What gives one town the right to make a decision that affects the water that supplies eight towns?!"

"Nothing!" we all chorused.

"Nothing," I said, "but ownership of a tract of land on which to do the deed, and a willingness to sell it for that purpose, even if that is unethical. This is coldly about what is legal, not what is justifiable or morally acceptable. We must treat this as a war of rules, of words, and of determination. Where is our state senator? I have met her, a couple of years ago. She seems like the sort who would help us fight."

"She is that sort," Beverly Greenwood said. "Here she comes now."

We looked, and saw an older woman, a retired kindergarten teacher with a short mop of curly hair, no makeup, and plain clothing in neutral hues walk in. She smiled and came over to greet us. Her name was Bess Blythe, and she was a Democrat. She liked to play basketball when she was in school, and now she and her wife (they had been the first lesbian couple to get married when it became legal in our state) took in teenage girls from the foster system to help them finish high school in a safe environment. They had helped four thus far.

Senator Blythe was outraged by this situation. The eight affected towns were her constituency, and she was prepared to go outside of those towns to meet with people elsewhere and spread the word about this. She encouraged us all to do the same, and stayed to hear our concerns, and emphasized that we were right to worry about what would happen in a drought.

"The MDC is wrong to say that there won't be a drought," said a woman from the Connecticut League of Conservation Voters. Her name was Lily Blue. "It is basing this claim on data that is over fifty years old." True; we had just read the data.

"What happens to our right to use the water during a drought versus that of Angel Falls Bottling?" a man from Avon wanted to know. "It seems that we the private citizens would be told, after conserving water, buying water-saving appliances and not running water while brushing our teeth, would be rationed, while this corporation would not."

I had a few cents to put in. "What about those of us who grow fruits, vegetables, and herbs in our yards? I'm not going to stop doing that for any corporation." People nodded vigorously at that. The mere idea of government interfering with private efforts to grow food was an outrage. Sure, growing lawns was superfluous, but food?! No.

We exchanged e-mails with people in surrounding towns. We would ask them to write to their local politicians, asking them to assist in putting a stop to this invasion and all future raids on our natural security in any way that they could. New laws were needed, and quickly. The legislative session was underway, and it promised to be a busy one.

We all felt very encouraged to see Senator Blythe in action, because she demonstrated a clear willingness to educate herself on topics that she had not previously had any knowledge of or experience with, and because she obviously saw it as her duty to connect and network with us.

"Please write to me at my office as much as you want," she said. "My assistant will show me everything you send – everything. Please come down to the legislative office building and watch us in session. You can sign up to speak for three minutes each and say your piece about this. Most importantly, please go online and file a public comment on each bill that comes up on this issue and any other that you care to make your views known about. All of them must and will be reviewed by the legislators."

People were very excited by all of this, and the room was soon abuzz with talk of how to do all this. In no time, I was surrounded by people who did not know how to find all of this data, but who wanted help accessing it.

I promised to go online when I got home and blog about this, posting how-to entries that would walk them through each step, complete with links to everything. The mood was one of hopefulness and excitement. It was good to see this after feeling that icy pall on the area when we had first come home. With that, Claire and I went home.

Wasi'chu wasn't just about individual eating preferences.

It was a trait of the Farmers.

Chapter 4

House-Hunting

"Hamish, do we need a neurotypical nanny to get through this?"

He looked at me, nonplussed, then said, "No." He was dreading this.

"Good." I had been joking, anyway. "Let's get everyone and talk – time to catch up."

We were at his office, meeting up with the people who ran it – at least, those who were still alive. One of them had been lost to the Cull on a trip to see her relatives last year, just before we left the area. We had managed to keep the others safe, but Leanne, our insurance claims handler, had been killed when she and her boyfriend had gone to Burlington, Vermont to see relatives.

Cara and Ellen were still there, though, running the office. They had managed to survive by staying in Cara's historic house. Ellen and her new husband had lost their apartment when the MRAPs had moved through their neighborhood, but Hamish had helped them find alternative housing after the fact.

They got all teary when we asked for details on the logistics of running the office.

"I take it our query brings up duties that used to belong to Leanne?" I said, keeping my expression flat and, I hoped, sympathetic. This was more facial contortion than came naturally to me. I was appalled by what had happened to Leanne, and at a loss for a way to avenge her. But there was no getting around the fact that we needed a new office insurance person.

"Yes," Ellen sniffed.

"If I can find a way to avenge her and whomever else the Cull got, I will," I said, "But—

"Cull?" Cara echoed, puzzled and still sniffling.

I handed them each a Kleenex (who knew when such things would revert to cloth hankies, to be laundered after every sneeze!). They knew how much sniffling bothered me and snoofed their noses quiet, then waited for me to go on.

"Yes, it was a population cull with a capital 'C', not a plague," I answered, "but don't go talking about that everywhere. Besides, you don't know enough details to explain it, and we don't want you attracting anyone's attention. But surely you didn't think it was an accident or a coincidence that our species was depleted to half a billion within the space of a year, did you?"

They gaped at me, open-mouthed, exchanged glances, and then looked at me and Hamish again. Ellen spoke first. "So that's why you were vaccinating everyone that you could way ahead of the government policy last year, and plotting to keep us…away from MRAPs."

"Aye." Hamish was standing against the counter in the back exam room. We had gone there to talk, away from the front desk, just to negate the possibility of some random patient walking in and hearing our conversation. He had taken the bone fragment here late at night the day after I had given it to him and confirmed that it was human…in this very room.

But our staff didn't need to know that. Ellen and Cara were okay, their husbands were okay, and as for myself and Hamish, we knew that Blackout Security was now covertly combing the countryside for bone dust and fragments in farmland everywhere.

Cara finally said, "I guess we have to face up to getting a new health insurance worker. I didn't want to touch Leanne's desk or anything in it. That means that we haven't done a thing about health claims since you left, but with no patients coming in, it hasn't been a problem."

"Until now," Ellen chimed in. "Now that you're back, we have to face it."

Hamish and I looked at each other. What the hell could we say?! It was horribly upsetting. "Well," I began, "I hope that we deadpan, flat-affect Aspies are conveying our own horror and outrage suitably about this situation, though I rather doubt that we can. I'm angry, and I don't know what to do about this…yet. I'll have to get back to everyone on that."

They looked at me. "That is a perfectly good thing to say, Avril," Ellen told me, giving me a kind smile of the sort that I was incapable of giving back. Cara said, "Yes, we appreciate that."

Hamish, eyes wide with discomfort, looked like he wanted to run out of here, but he stayed put. Men – and Aspie men being no exception – were, often, useless in such situations.

There was nothing for it but to say, "Do you two remember my oldest cousin, Edgar?"

They glanced at each other. "Yes…" they said in unison.

"Good. During our year in Switzerland, he learned a lot about running a health clinic. The patients were receiving elective treatment – Regenics – which no insurance plan covers. But he learned how to interact with everyone and run the business aspect of the practice fast. Now that we're back, we intend to put him to work here. He will start by learning how to process the insurance claims. I've warned him that he will have a lot to learn, and that he must defer to the two of you, both during and a long time after that learning process."

"Defer to us? How?" Cara asked.

"Seriously? You're older, more experienced, you're at home here, Ellen is a health care practitioner, and you are the manager. Edgar has an M.B.A. and a year's worth of experience. We don't want him to feel too comfortable just because his family put him here. But…I think he will do well here. He did well in Lausanne, because he is neurotypical and thus intuits his way through social interactions in an instant, and because he has already shown us that he feels the need to prove that he will work hard, and not rest on any imagined boss's family laurels."

They smiled.

"Okay," I said. "We are going to do two things now: 1. Go out to Leanne's desk and box up her personal effects no matter how much we hate it so that her work station can be Edgar's, and 2. See Edgar, who we left in the waiting area looking at magazines. We'll smile and wave at him while we do the desk, then go out and talk to him and bring him backstage."

Ellen and Cara looked shaky, and sounded it as they said, "Okay."

With that, I got up off of the stool I had been sitting on and opened the door. Everyone followed me out, including Hamish, who looked relieved that the meeting was over. "Not your usual staff meeting, was it, Hamish?" I said to him under my breath, as he caught up with me.

"Nae…and thanks. I couldn't have handled that well at all."

"Maybe you only think so," I said, grabbing a couple of flat, unused boxes and lids.

Cara and Ellen had reached the outer office area, and were smiling and greeting Edgar.

I joined them and we exchanged a few more pleasantries while they asked Edgar some polite questions about how he had liked living on a boat in Lausanne.

He said he had liked it well enough, and that it had been interesting. "It's a bit of shock to come home and see how different it is, though."

Sober nods were exchanged all around. Hmm…classic neurotypical behavior, I thought to myself. This ought to work out well enough. I didn't know what to do with the people next, so I went over to Leanne's desk and pressed the two boxes into shape, and then the lids for them. I put one on the side panel of the desk, the other on the floor, and collapsed into her chair to stare at what was in front of me: the remains of a working life.

Leanne was now ashes in the woods somewhere in Vermont, and her photographs and knick-knacks confronted me. She and Joe, her land surveyor boyfriend, smiling together as they held glasses of beer in some restaurant bar, stared back at me. Another image of her with her parents, who had lived in Worcester, Massachusetts, and another with her sister and brother-in-law, completed the collection.

I stared at them all for another moment, then suddenly grabbed them all and carried them to the work station in the corner where I often sat to read and take notes while waiting for Hamish. It had a desktop computer in it, and a scanner-copier-printer was connected to it. It was just a tiny alcove, but it had room to lay everything out. I turned on the computer and printer.

"What are you doing with her photographs?" Ellen asked me, looking around.

"I'm going to scan them and put them in a digital file, then reassemble them all in their picture frames the way she had them and wrap each one in cloth. They're all murder victims, so they ought to be remembered. You can help me label the digital files. We'll each have copies."

Ellen silently came over and helped me take the photographs out of their frames. The scanning took a few minutes, and she had them all back in their frames in no time flat. "Can we use some of the clean towels in the closet?" she asked me.

"Yeah, why not? No reason to get other ones. Leanne has a perfect right to that much."

Ellen was back in a flash with three of them, and we wound each framed image up.

"That looks well padded," I said, and laid the lot in a box back at her desk. The images still remained to be labelled, a thing I was saving for last, after it was all packed up. Leanne had a decent collection of junk on her desk – pretty things that she had liked to see during her work day – and I paused, puzzled over what was to be done with them later.

There was a snow globe that showed a shopping area in some quaint New England town. There was a little stuffed monkey with an insipid smile on its face, and a little rabbit, white, with a pretty floral pattern in its ears and on its paws.

Ellen came up behind me and stood there, staring at the desk. "Could I have her monkey?"

I turned to look at her, startled, and then said, "Of course. Take it! That feels a lot better than packing it in a box." I let out a big sigh of relief, and realized that I had been holding my breath.

Cara and Edgar were still chatting, but she was watching us. "Can I have the snow globe? I was with her when she bought that. She said it reminded her of her college days, and going out with her friends."

I held it out to her, and she took it. She went to her desk and put it there.

Suddenly, I picked up the cute little rabbit and said, "That little alcove where I sit is too bare. I want something of Leanne's too. Does anyone mind if take the rabbit? It's really cute."

Smiles all around, so I took it, felt how soft it was, and then saw the label. "Jellycat! No wonder it's so nice and soft," I commented. The floral fabric had a pretty red rose pattern on it. It looked nice in my alcove.

The rest of the job was easier. Leanne had the usual things that office staff people kept in their desks to make their time at work comfortable: aspirin, throat lozenges, individual-sized candy bars (Twix and Mounds), and a couple more odds and ends that were cute but little larger than coins. I gave them to Ellen and Cara, and they disappeared among the similar things in their desks. Leanne's sweater and spare sneakers went into the box with the photographs, and that was it. The desk was packed. The other box was not needed.

"The rest is just work materials," I said, surprised. "That's it."

"She was very efficient," Ellen said, by way of explanation.

"I knew she was a good person to hire," Hamish added, coming back out to us.

Well, I thought to myself, that awful task seems to have gone okay. I looked back at the others. "Okay, Edgar, I guess you should sit down and look through all of Leanne's work materials and get to know them really well. Once you've done that, you can get used to doing your job. And do whatever Cara and Ellen advise or flat out tell you to do."

He nodded and smiled. "Thank you." I nodded back. Edgar looked at his new co-workers. "I hope I won't get in your way or anything."

"We know you," Ellen said, giving him a playful tap on the shoulder. "You'll be fine."

That was easy, I thought, exchanging glances with Hamish. I went back to the alcove as Edgar sat down, arranged the image into a file with a label about Leanne and her family, and opened a Word document to go with it all.

Ellen came over to me and watched. "Pull up a chair," I said to her. "Let's label it all."

She did, and soon we had names with the faces. Ellen and Cara shared details of Leanne's life and family as they identified everyone, and I remembered a few things that she had told me herself a couple of years ago: Leanne and Joe. Parents Kevin and Linda. Sister Jennifer and brother-in-law Jeffrey. All gone. I wrote it all up in the Word document.

"Damn," I said, "it's her life, summed up in one page. I just realized we are composing her obituary. Maybe I should have it published. Look at this: birth date, death date, education, work, interests, all of it's here, in this one page." I saved the document and e-mailed it to myself.

Ellen and Cara had peered over my shoulder as I had written it all up. "It reads more like a pleasant biography than one of those bland, dry things in the paper," Cara said. "It makes her personality show. I like that part you included about how she loved to look for antiques and then research what they were used for online."

I said, "I hate those bland, dry obituaries. They seem utterly soulless and therefore insulting. Let's all go out to dinner in her honor later this week, when we can assemble a few more people. Hamish and I will throw her a memorial service. Everyone's invited. We will need to know how many people 'everyone' means, so that the reservation covers that."

On the way home, Hamish said, "You're not so bad at handling the death of an employee, you know that? And to think that you doubted you would know what to do."

"Yeah…I made it up as I went along. The stuff on her desk helped give me ideas."

"I thought you did great," Edgar added from the back seat.

We had spent the rest of the day at the office, with me calling and e-mailing invitees, sending the obituary to *The Hartford Courant*, and ordering a floral wreath with Leanne's favorites in it: daisies, cornflowers, and pale purple spray roses. The event would be on Friday, at Abigail's in Simsbury. Perfect – that place had had its own resident ghost for a couple of centuries.

For me, it was about plotting revenge for this death and more. For them, it was just grieving.

My mother and Aunt Zoe had made a nice dinner of wild mushroom soup and butternut squash ravioli with sage butter sauce. It smelled great.

Fabian and Claire had spent all day practicing for the LSATs on the porch. With very little effort, Claire was proving to be an expert at the Logic Games sections. Fabian was better at the Analytical Reasoning ones. They were both proficient with the Reading Comprehension.

Fabian was frustrated by this until I pointed out that Claire was a puzzle addict (as was I), whereas he was not. He disdained the time spent decrypting puzzles, but we loved it. We both loved it so much, in fact, that when we had come back to Connecticut, I had decided to order us each a subscription to *The New York Times* online crossword puzzle, plus the ones in *The Hartford Courant*.

Now Fabian was reconsidering his attitude. "We'll copy it for you too," I said, grinning.

"Just turn what you love into your work," I told her, "and don't worry about figuring out how to do that right this minute. It will fit into your life eventually…after you finish school."

Uncle Charlie and Dad had watched the news in the living room, with Dad getting up to pick herbs for dinner in the conservatory and pacing around the garden when a football game came on. He didn't like sports matches, but Uncle Charlie did.

Uncle Charlie and Jacques were watching the game, which was being broadcast from Dallas, Texas, when we walked in. Interesting to see that crowds could still be assembled for such activities, I thought to myself. I guessed that people who liked football still outnumbered those who didn't, and needed a distraction from the stressors of life.

Grandmère was sitting by her Monet painting near some of the museum books that we kept in the shelves there. She and I had often visited the Wadsworth Atheneum over the years, and we never came home without a book on whatever exhibit we had gone to see. Fabian and Claire had joined it with me and Hamish the week before, and we had brought back a jigsaw puzzle for Grandmère, who was having fun piecing together an image of an Edward Gorey montage. We had set up the card table for her, and she was quite happy.

Unfortunately, so were Spock and Eowyn. The two cats were fascinated by the puzzle. They were driving her crazy, leaping up onto her table and moving the pieces around. Finally, my mother found a puzzle cloth – a huge piece of green felt fabric with a black border. You just put all of the puzzle pieces onto it, rolled it up when you weren't working on the puzzle, and when you unrolled it, they were exactly where you had left them. It was great.

The door to the porch had been slid shut to block out the noise of the game. I grinned. Fabian had never liked the roar of a sports match of any kind; he would rather read. Claire was the same way, but even more so. They had loved visiting the museums of Lausanne with us, while the others had not cared one way or the other. Except for Fiona and William – they came with us.

But Fiona was back with her books, writing and reading and researching, safe with William and her beautiful cat, Mallory in Rosehearty, Scotland. We chatted almost daily on Facebook, sharing updates, photographs, and so on.

Jacques had been looking around for recycling work in town, but he hadn't been able to go out today. We had to get better organized with family security measures so that he could come and go as he pleased, and quickly. Hamish had gone outside to talk to Ed and Aaron about that as soon as we got home. My mother and Aunt Zoe had taken two Blackout guys to the grocery store while the others watched the house, but this couldn't go on.

Uncle Charlie got up and wandered into the kitchen during a commercial. He was restless and bored living in such close quarters. I knew he wanted out of here, and back into a home of his own, but that would take a little while. At least he was okay. That was the most important thing, and I think he realized that, because he had stopped complaining every five seconds.

Still, that didn't stop him from causing other trouble. Right in the middle of dinner, he asked Claire, "So, Claire, when are you going to give us our first grandkid?"

Claire stopped eating and looked up at him from across the table with huge, stunned eyes.

An awkward silence descended on us. Had Uncle Charlie forgotten about the birth control policy?! Nae-Née was still in force, and likely to remain so. C-SPAN and other political news outlets all indicated this in no uncertain terms. Besides, we knew that Claire wanted to go to law school and didn't particularly enjoy kids. Was this an attack of wishful thinking plus idiocy?!

Claire looked straight back at her father-in-law, and said, "Never." She looked angry now, like she was about to explode with emotion. Fabian, sitting right next to her, glared at his father.

"Never?" Uncle Charlie echoed. "Never?!"

Fabian looked angry now. "Yes – never! I told you that when we got married. We don't want kids. Not everyone wants kids. And Claire wants to go to graduate school. What's the matter with you, bothering her about that?"

Aunt Zoe turned to Uncle Charlie and fixed him with a pointed gaze. "Yes, Charlie, what IS the matter with you?"

He looked startled. "Just making conversation. I wonder whether or not any of my kids will have kids," he summed up in a self-pitying tone.

Dad said, "You don't have kids so that they can give you grandkids. You have kids so that they can live their lives as they want to and be happy."

Grandmère had a slight smile on her face. "Listen to your brother, Charles. This is not about you. Besides, you have two other kids. Wait and see what they want to do."

"I was just asking," Uncle Charlie said.

"Well, DON'T ask – ever again!" Claire roared at him, pushed her chair back, and raced out of the dining room. We heard her footsteps going rapidly upstairs, along with the sounds of crying as she went, followed by the door to her and Fabian's room closing with a slight bang.

I let out a mirthless, breathy, voiceless laugh, and said, "Wow. Good job, Uncle Charlie."

"What?!" he sounded really defensive.

Fabian got up and said, "You know exactly what." Then to the rest of us, "Save our food." He followed his wife upstairs, though not at the same speed as she had gone there.

I wasted no time in explaining this to my obtuse uncle. "I'm totally with Claire on the insistence that you never again bug her about reproducing. She really means it. As one female Aspie describing what it's like for another to do that, I can tell you that Claire will need zero distractions from other people in order to successfully complete law school. NO babies. Babies require constant attention, and law school will require intense focus without any distractions. As if she could get a birth license now! Claire has no parents, just us. Don't make her feel their absence even more by upsetting her. I'll bet she's wishing for her mother right now."

Uncle Charlie looked angry and resentful at being told this, but I wasn't a bit sorry.

Dad spoke up. "I'm sure that's exactly what she's sobbing about right now. I can't believe you just did that, Charlie. Come on – let's go for a walk around the block. Ed can watch us, but I doubt he'll have much to worry about."

Uncle Charlie pushed his chair back. "I'm done eating anyway. Vegetarian food is so quick and easy to eat."

"Stop griping about the vegetarian fare, Charles," Grandmère said sternly. "At least we're all okay. Who cares if the food is like this? It's delicious, healthy, and could be a lot worse – what if it had no vegetables or fruits?" She paused, then added, "Or we could be dead. But we're not."

"D'accord, Maman," he said, kissing her on the cheek and following Dad out.

They went straight for the guardhouse, and I saw Ed come out to walk with them. I knew he would hang back, just in earshot, trying not to listen, as he walked with them.

Hamish said, "Claire and Fabian weren't finished eating," as he looked at their plates.

"We can heat their food up when they come back," Aunt Zoe said. "And Charlie can apologize, or no dessert for him."

"You would do that?" My mother said.

"Yes, I would," she replied. "That was outrageous."

"What's for dessert?" I asked, scraping up the last of my food and putting it in my mouth.

"Rice pudding," Aunt Zoe said. "It has orange zest, vanilla bean, and a cinnamon stick."

"I thought you took that out," my mother said.

"I did, but it flavored the pudding, so I had to mention it," my aunt said. That was some of the last rice we had, but there was no point in saving it forever. Food just rotted if it wasn't eaten…except for honey, but that was beside the point.

"Why can't we eat rice much anymore?" Edgar asked.

"Because it's grown in Asia – in China, Japan, Vietnam, and India – and those areas are partially submerged, toxified by the Fukushima nuclear power plant leak, saturated with insecticides from decades of incessant spraying, littered with plastics, contaminated with runoff from mining operations, and flooded with water in every color of the rainbow," I told him. "Unless and until that gets remediated, not much rice will be grown."

I took a gulp of wine and another of water, and headed for the stairs.

"Where are you going?" my mother said.

"Upstairs. Claire has had several minutes with Fabian, and I am going to tell her what we are doing, that her food will be reheated for her, and give her as much empathy as I can, and sympathy for whatever I can't offer empathy about."

My mother nodded. "Okay. I'm glad you two are such good friends."

I smiled and went up there. No more sobbing sounds came from their room – just voices talking in somewhat calm tones. I knocked.

"Who is it?" Fabian called out.

"It's me – Avril. No one else."

The door opened. He waited, so I walked in and he closed it. "Hi Claire," I said.

She was red-faced and teary, but her eyes were calm. "I came to tell you that we saved your food, and will microwave it when you're ready, and that Aunt Zoe said she made a fancy spiced rice pudding. It smells like she used basmati rice. Also, she said that if Uncle Charlie doesn't apologize to you, he's not getting any. Dad and I scolded him, and Grandmère put her two cents in – twice – so I guess that's four cents. Then Dad took Uncle Charlie out for a walk."

"Really?" Claire was breathing more calmly now, sitting up on the quilt. Fabian sat down and stretched out behind her, close, with an arm around her. "What did you say to him?"

I repeated the entire conversation back to her, word for word.

"Are you psychic?" Fabian asked me.

"No. Why?"

"Because you guessed the general topics that we covered up here," Claire said. "I do want my own mother back, especially when something like that happens. She would never have bothered me about doing such a big thing as having kids just as I'm contemplating graduate school, and even so, knowing that I don't want any, neither she nor my father would have done it at all. You guessed the whole conversation."

"Well…you and I are a lot alike," I reminded her, "and I would be thinking and feeling those same things if I were you, including wanting my mother and blowing up at any idiot who expected me to do anything I didn't want to do."

She started crying again. "I don't want to be a mother. I want my mother. I can't be a parent while wanting my own mother so bad. Most people might feel better with a substitute – with a baby or with some other addition to their life like that – but not me."

"I don't know what's wrong with my father," Fabian said. "I don't want a baby either. I want to study and have a wife and go to museums, and he wants me to want football, noise, and whatever he likes. Sometimes I wish that my Uncle Henri were my father, too."

"Wow. You've never told me that before," I said.

"Yeah, well, don't tell anyone else. Except for Hamish – I know you tell him things."

I gave a wry grin. "Yes…I need someone to be able to tell anything to."

Claire seemed to be breathing much more calmly now. "Let's go downstairs. I want to finish my dinner before the dads get back."

We went back down, and Aunt Zoe gave Claire a big hug at the bottom of the stairs. "I'm sorry," she said to Claire. "I'll make sure that he doesn't upset you again. You deserve to be happy and have your life the way you want it. You do NOT owe us grandkids, and I don't expect them. I want you to go to law school if that's what you want."

Claire hugged her back. "Thank you. You're a really nice mother-in-law"

Aunt Zoe smiled. "You're a lovely daughter-in-law. We're all lucky Fabian found you."

Grandmère came out of the dining room, and Claire hugged her too. "Avril told me what you all said, word for word. She said you put your four cents in."

"Four cents?" Grandmère cracked a wide grin at that. "Yes, I did, didn't I…"

My mother had reheated Claire and Fabian's plates during this exchange. "Come on, you can finish your dinners before they come back in," she said. Claire hugged her too. She smiled and hugged back. She stroked Claire's hair, too. "We'll have a nice evening now. Maybe you don't need to practice any more LSAT stuff tonight."

Fabian said, "We could watch a movie," as he and Claire finished their food.

Jacques and Edgar had slipped into the living room to check the football scores, but Hamish had stayed. He hated football as much as I did. "I don't know what Charlie's problem is – he has two other sons to like football and do stuff that he likes."

Fabian smiled at him. No wonder my husband and Fabian were good friends. "Families are an awful lot of trouble," Fabian said. "Oh well."

"C'est la vie," Grandmère said.

"Indeed." I helped clear the table. I didn't care about the trouble as long as it all got talked out and resolved. I just wanted them all safe.

By the time Dad and Uncle Charlie came back, the table was set for dessert.

Aunt Zoe headed them off at the side door, and I heard her speak to Uncle Charlie in a warning tone. He nodded as they came back into view, walked up to Claire, hugged her, and said, "I'm sorry Claire. You don't owe me grandkids. I'm happy to have you as you are. You're just the right daughter-in-law; just the right wife for my son." Then he kissed her on the cheek.

She looked up at him from her seat, surprised to have gotten such a great apology. "Thank you," she replied. Then she got up and gave him a hug and a kiss back before sitting back in her chair. Classic Aspie – not much eye contact, but satisfied to accept and move on.

"Jacques, Edgar, get back in here," Uncle Charlie called. "Dessert!"

Dessert was delicious. Food always tasted better when no one was upset.

We watched a movie later. It was *Avatar*, a nice long one to give Claire and Fabian a change of pace and a good break from all of those test drills. They had been relentlessly practicing. Frankly, I doubted that they would have much trouble at all getting accepted to law school, and Claire wanted to go to the University of Connecticut, just ten minutes away.

For Aunt Zoe and Uncle Charlie, the task of finding a new house was proving to be a thoroughly elusive one. There just weren't any available. There were hardly any still standing, and most were either occupied, by owners or renters. Building a new home in a design that he would actually feel comfortable in was not an option for the foreseeable future. There were laws against putting up any new homes due to land trusts every which way we looked.

They spent the next day house-hunting, but got nowhere. When we got home, Uncle Charlie and Aunt Zoe were sitting in the kitchen with my parents, looking dejected and furious. My parents looked unhappy too – like they were in sympathy with my aunt and uncle. Grandmère looked displeased, too.

"What's going on?" I asked, pouring some tea for myself and Hamish and sitting down.

Without a word, Uncle Charlie turned a piece of paper that was in front him around and placed it in front of me. It was a legal notice that he and Aunt Zoe had picked up at a local real estate agency. It read:

> *"At this time, only apartments and condominiums are on offer for rent or purchase.*
>
> *Anyone wishing to become a homeowner will not be able to buy a detached house for the foreseeable future. All subsequent new home construction is being directed to green, eco-friendly, with urban and suburban options only. Land outside of these centers is being dedicated to land trusts.*
>
> *This notice has been issued to potential home buyers in response to repeated inquiries. The Department of Demographics, Department of Housing now considers this matter closed."*

I looked up from it, livid but not at all surprised. Hamish had been leaning in to read it, and he snorted in disgust. "Bastards!" was all he said.

I had a bit more to say. "That is the official equivalent of saying 'fuck you' to individual choice, liberty, and personal privacy! The hell with eco-friendly houses!"

Aunt Zoe was practically in tears. "I have tried not to complain, but I don't want to live in an apartment ever again! We're done with that. We're done with neighbors that we can hear, landlords, superintendents, rules, and being carefully quiet so as not to annoy the neighbors or let them hear our private business. We worked our whole lives to earn a house with a yard in a style of our own choosing, and it was stolen from us. I refuse to be content to be alive and leave it at that. I want my whole situation back, as it was before the Cull."

"Now you two know why I didn't want an apartment – same answers," I said, glaring at the piece of paper in front of me. "The next question is, what do we do next, because giving up isn't part of the plan. There are houses that still exist. The problem is acquiring one of them."

Uncle Charlie spoke at last. "None have been available yet."

"I know. Sooner or later, someone is likely to either die or relocate, and when they do, we must do our best to preempt any demolition plans. I pity the next generation," I said, "who have been raised with housing options that teased them with views of things that they won't have as independent adults. Scratch that – they won't really be independent adults on such terms."

Claire and Fabian had come in from the back porch in time to hear this, and they exchanged an unhappy look. Edgar and Jacques were right behind them. Happy times.

"Looks as though we're all in an enforced state of back-to-pre-Industrial-Revolution, multi-generational, family togetherness in our living arrangements,"

I said, looking up at them. "We'll figure something out to ease that a bit, but I'll be damned if I'll tell anyone to grow up, move out, and be more independent. This is a brave new world underwater, much as we dislike it."

Hamish and I decided to look into the problem and see what help we might be able to offer.

Any new construction, if by some miracle it could be approved, had to be eco-friendly. There was new construction of homes here and there, but it was expensive, and the design made us all feel very exposed. Modern architects were having a wonderful time with it, but Hamish and I had gotten curious enough to tour one, and we were appalled. They looked like see-through hobbit-holes, built into hillsides with walls of glass, or glass cubes, or glass other shapes.

They were also thoroughly equipped with every kind of home and appliance surveillance known to humankind. Hamish was outraged by it, and frankly, so was I. The mere idea of living in a fishbowl, which was what those glass houses essentially were, galled me. If I were to sit in my bedroom, I would not want it to have that much glass. My every move could be observed from a distance! The same went for the living room.

And what if someone rang the doorbell?! They would be able to see whether or not I was home. There would be no pretending not to be home, no making last-second adjustments to anything, because my every move or scratch would be visible to the visitor. For someone who didn't like to be observed, followed, watched, surprised, or otherwise monitored, these see-through hobbit-holes were a nightmare.

No wonder Uncle Charlie was so restless. He didn't even like the style of modern architecture that such designs entailed. He liked Country French, and so did Aunt Zoe. I didn't blame them. Our whole family liked that style. No…there was no way I would ever rush them to just buy a place already and move out. They could take their damned sweet time and get the kind of home that they felt comfortable in, I ranted over dinner after viewing the hobbit-hole.

Uncle Charlie was surprised. "I thought you would want us out, since I complain so much."

"Nope." I took another spoonful of curried spinach soup. "Not after seeing that. And to add insult to injury, when I told the real estate agent that we like Country French, not modern, she said, 'But this is French! The original design was created by French architects!' I told her not to try to sell me something that looked like a wide open, glass-walled, fish-bowl of a hobbit-hole. I distinctly saw Hamish grin at that moment, and then we said 'thank-you' and left."

Grandmère was listening to all of these with detached interest. It was detached because she had permanently moved in with us, so this was just a problem to observe. "Charles, that's absolutely true of you; I never saw anyone complain so much. You did it in Switzerland, too, instead of just accepting the adventure and enjoying the museums. Here you are, safe and well-nourished with your entire family still alive – a rare luxury in this world. Plus, the food you get is delicious and interesting, yet still you complain."

"I know, Maman. But I don't like being a guest, and the loss of control of so much."

"You and lots of others, but you are alive. This is my second holocaust. The first one wasn't nearly so easy. In Paris, we walked around daily past leering Nazis, terrified of being dragged into an alley and raped, starving every day as we struggled to stay alive on rations, and wondering whether our beautiful city would be razed any day. People in other places had all those worries PLUS the razing, and there were rapes all over the war theater. This holocaust was a lovely walk in the park thanks to Hamish and Avril. Great food, and watching it on Swiss TV."

"Oui, Maman. But we still have to figure something out."

"Oui, oui, oui. Stop worrying and griping. Just be patient, even if nothing presents itself for a while as a suitable answer. Accept long, boring periods of nothing happening. The alternative would be death and erasure, and no future at all for your children."

Aunt Zoe had calmed down considerably since we had seen the letter and talked. She said, "Listen to your mother, Charlie. I have cousins from Austria whom I never met because of the previous holocaust. They went into Auschwitz-Birkenau's ovens. We hit the ultimate lottery. So what if we are all jammed into a mansion with our extended family?! We're okay. My sister and her family made it. If our parents were alive, they would be saying the same thing and more."

He looked at her, then said, "I know. I just worry that we are in the way here. The holocaust is over, and we're still here." He turned to me and asked again, "Don't you want us out of here?"

I gave a mirthless laugh. "Maybe eventually, when you're ready to go and have a place you wish to go to, but really, I'm in no hurry. I trust no one with my family's safety now. This holocaust destroyed my confidence in strangers. Unless and until your next home is to your satisfaction and ours, vetted for surveillance, design, privacy, and you name it, I'm content for you to stay here. At least we can alter this place to our satisfaction. I'm not sure about others."

With that, we settled in to finish our dinner.

After dinner, I went outside to check on the bees, even though they were fine. Collapse still happened to some extent, but it was less each season, it seemed, likely due to the banning, at long last, of neonicotinoids. That left me just pacing around the hives, sniffing the sweet honey in the air, and listening to the buzz of the apiary. Funny; bees were deaf. I could hear them, but they sensed my presence through my scent.

Edgar appeared next to me as I sat on the lowest step, a huge piece of slate, looking out at the back yard, imagining improvements and a new layout to the garden. Maybe Claire would want to be in on planning that, I thought. This was her home too, now, and I wanted her to feel that way.

I looked up at my cousin. "Hey Edgar. What's up? I hope you're okay with your room here."

"What?" he said, surprised. "Oh, yeah, it's great. Thank you. No, I was wondering about something else."

"What's that?"

"How come you and Hamish haven't gotten your own windmill?"

I laughed. "Oh. I was wondering when someone would ask about that."

He grinned. "So? How come?"

"Well…those huge, white, windmills – which are actually called wind turbines – are usually put offshore or someplace on land far from any human development, they require rare earth elements to build them, which are more than just finite, as you might guess from their collective name, and I wouldn't want to have one close by when the next hurricane or other superstorm blows through. We could have a windmill blade through the roof – right in your room. Plus, those things are noisy to live near. The solar panels have the virtue of at least being silent."

I paused for a moment, then added:

"If you want to see windmills in Connecticut, you have to look in areas that don't have a lot of houses close by. They're great as long as they aren't right next to you. They also have to be placed away from migratory bird flight paths. If it weren't for those problems, I'd want one in this neighborhood. Also, we want to be off of the surveillance grid, and these solar panels achieve that. Wind energy would just put us back on it, exposing our proprietary data to more risks. Power-sharing systems are a great money-saver if you're on the grid, though."

He opened his mouth in an "O" of comprehension, nodded, and said, "I see." He grinned at me. "Avril, you know you talk like a book, right?"

"Oh, yeah – I know," I said. "I've heard that many times before." I grinned too.

The next day, Hamish hired someone from Blackout Security to scout out homes in the area – pre-existing ones – that were on the market, and to be on the constant lookout for any that became available for sale. There were none yet, though, so we settled for keeping Aunt Zoe and Uncle Charlie apprised of the scout's progress for the time being.

They appreciated it, and settled into life on Stoner Drive. Uncle Charlie got quieter. Aunt Zoe visited her sister, Mindy, and she enjoyed spending time with my mother and helping her sons and her new daughter-in-law with their daily routines.

Mindy and her husband and their kids were all okay. Hamish had seen to that by vaccinating them all himself and warning them, even if cryptically, that there was a dangerous plot going on with the official serum. He had had to scare Mindy by showing her what was happening to people who acquiesced to that serum, and show her the nanites, but it did the trick. Then he had left Blackout Security to do the rest while we were away.

Aunt Zoe was more concerned with Jacques' future. He was done with college, and wondering how to best use his environmental studies degree. Could he help with some eco-friendly program in town, perhaps? Town recycling programs had always left much to be desired. One would attempt to sort every plastic and paper and metal item, only to find out that most of it was rejected and tossed into the trash at the town processing facility.

Jacques knew all about this and was outraged. He wanted to go to the town hall and see what he could do to help. After a visit to the public works office, he had the contact information for the recycling company. He called nine times. At last, its director, a Mr. Andolini, talked to him.

Mr. Andolini confirmed all of Jacques' suspicions that vast amounts of plastic and other materials were going to waste. The machines that crushed and reprocessed it all were configured in such a way that only certain shapes went in without a hitch. The rest, he told my cousin, was just too much trouble to deal with, so it got thrown into the trash.

New regulations were being implemented, however, that would make this practice illegal. Mr. Andolini was at a loss as to how he was going to reconfigure his processing methods, so he agreed to accept some help from Jacques…on a trial basis, of course.

"Really? That would be great," Jacques said into his cell phone. "What would you like? Research? New ideas? A report detailing it all?"

After some quick discussion, Jacques spoke to Mr. Andolini again, and they agreed on a deadline for the report, and a fee. For $2,000, Jacques was going to prepare his research. He planned to pitch this deal to other trash companies and repeat this arrangement. Perhaps he would get a career going in renewable resources and help save the planet.

Jason was in on it with him, generating computer models of everything Jacques studied. My mother asked him about his parents. "They're fine, thanks for asking," he said. "They found jobs at Hartford Hospital. It seems that the place needs electricians and nurses thanks to the Cull. We're all still in my house, of course. I think we're a bit spooked by the idea of living apart."

Jacques looked up from his laptop at that remark. "So are we."

I gave a wry grin. "Indeed. We feel the same way. We are calmer living all together here, safe, despite the Cull. Uncle Charlie and Aunt Zoe are house-hunting."

Jason looked at Jacques. "Will you go with your parents?"

"Yeah, it's not like I have money on my own to go off and get my own place, and Avril's right: the idea holds a lot less appeal now than it did before the Cull. It's scary. Besides, I don't even have a girlfriend to go anywhere with, and neither does Edgar."

Jacques looked horrified at that moment; we hadn't spoken of Ellie, Edgar's girlfriend who had died in the Cull last year, since she had been taken. She had gone against all advice to Atlanta, Georgia, to meet college friends and protest the vaccination policy at CDC headquarters. They had been deliberately exposed to the illnesses that the serum was meant to target, then detained and forcibly vaccinated with the Cull serum, transported out of the city, and killed.

An awkward silence settled over us, and then Jason asked, "Where's Edgar right now?"

"At Hamish's office. He's the new insurance person there. Don't worry; we can talk."

We breathed a sigh of awkward relief, and then Jacques asked, "If you were to find a girlfriend, do you think she would move in with you, even though your parents are there?"

Jason laughed. "I don't know – I haven't met this hypothetical person yet, but I hope so. And who knows…maybe my parents would want to find another place. But if people really can't find other places right now, maybe we'll all have to get used to living with our extended families."

We all laughed – mirthlessly. That was already a reality for us. "Damn our cultural expectations that everyone move away from parents upon aging to adulthood," I remarked.

My cousin and our friend looked up at me, startled. "Yes, damn that," Jason said.

The next day, Hamish and I took a short tour of the area. What was still here, I wondered?

Out of nostalgia, I headed straight for Simsbury, to make sure that the Ethel Walker School was still intact. It was. "Amazing," I said, staring all around as I drove slowly around the campus, reminiscing about taking classes in the buildings, visiting classmates in the dormitories, participating in plays and concerts at the Ferguson Theater, and so on.

"What's amazing?" Hamish wanted to know.

"That my school is still here and not erased," I said. "Of course, I didn't know what would be saved and what would not. It was a bit overwhelming to try to anticipate or otherwise know it all," I explained. I had not wanted to look it all up, even if I had had access to the data.

But apparently, others had on both counts, because Ed said, "Schools, colleges, and universities were never going to be erased. Their faculty and most of their staff was also conveniently not erased, and never injected with the Cull formula. They were vaccinated slowly, ahead of time, as Hamish did for all of us."

"Look at that sign." Aaron said, pointing at a large one that had been driven into the grass.

Sure enough, a big sign in the school's colors, purple on white, read, "Classes will resume next fall, after families have had time to reorganize their affairs. Our profoundest sympathies to any of our students who have lost anyone to this terrible plague."

"Plague?!" I said in disgust. "If they only knew." I drove on.

Similar signs were on the lawns of the Norfeldt Elementary School, Conard High School, the University of Hartford, and Trinity College. That last one was a long jaunt from our usual stomping grounds, but I went there deliberately, so that we could see what the southern end of Hartford looked like.

We parked and walked around the campus of Trinity College, and wandered around the chapel with its famed organ that Professor Clarence Waters had designed. The whole place was open, which was not unusual, but it was eerily quiet, as if a funeral pall had been cast over it.

A man from the administration came out and spoke to us. He recognized us from news stories, so we didn't have to introduce ourselves. "Hello," he said, putting his hand out to shake. "I'm Charles Norcroft, the academic dean. Were you…curious to see what it's like here now, a year after the plague took hold?"

"You could say that," Hamish replied. "Is everyone gone until the next academic year?"

"Exactly. A skeleton academic crew is here for the planning and restructuring, as well as the staff, and we are working our way through college applications now. We expect to have a slightly larger student body for the next few years than we will in the future, due to survivors of the plague who were forced to withdraw from school until the danger passed. After that, we expect to be educating far fewer students each year. At least," Norcroft remarked ruefully, "no one will be likely to get shut out of a course that they want to take for the foreseeable future."

We all exchanged glances. The Cull had been about room in schools, among other things. Hamish was clearly having the same thoughts. We thanked Dean Norcroft and left.

The rest of the southern part of Hartford was a shock. Driving northward, we stared…and stared. I slowed down, rubbernecking at huge parks, lawns, gardens, greenhouses, and rest rooms. There were also orchards and crop fields, but all carefully tended by city staff. There was no traffic, and thus no horns honking at me to go faster.

"What the hell?!" I said, stunned. "It's beautiful, but completely redone!"

I pulled out to the left-most lane and saw a bus approaching. It was in a lane that was painted green, and labelled "GreenTransit" on the sides. It looked comfortable, and was about half the size of the ones we used to see. I stared at it carefully as it went by, off toward Hartford Hospital. Some of the passengers wore scrubs. I thought I saw Anne, Jason's mother, among them.

I stopped the car outside a public rest room and we got out. Inside, there were self-flushing toilets and what I jokingly called "Star Trek" sinks – because the first time I had ever seen one was in the television show *Star Trek: The Next Generation*, with Captain Jean-Luc Picard using one. Soap pumps, fully loaded with pink, creamy liquid soap, were next to each sink. Fancy air dryers blew the water off my hands.

Back outside, I said to Aaron, "Do tell what you read about Hartford."

"Okay. It said that it would look like this – like a huge park, partly devoted to growing food, part flower garden, part greenhouses for forcing plants into seedlings for distribution to the whole area, and with trees lining the streets. It will take a few years to grow them, so right now, they look rather small. See them, up on the grass past the sidewalks? They're all different species, but indigenous to this environment: oaks, maples, beech, etc."

"It certainly looks nice," Hamish commented. "And the air has never been so fresh around here. But the cultures of Hartford have been erased to make it all possible."

"Yeah…no more Frog Hollow, no more Jamaican or Puerto Rican groceries…no more crime, either," Ed said. "The bad is gone, so the good went too."

"There's something else," Aaron said. "There is actually an ordinance forbidding anyone on rented land to grow their own food. All rented land has been converted to land trusts. Few people can buy their own land now, so most live in apartments. Local food is all acquired via community efforts like this one."

That icy feeling of horror and outrage was back. "So…this is the damned New World Order," I said. "Nothing can be done to or with any land trust. It has to stay as is in perpetuity. Even buying land, if one manages to afford it, doesn't make it possible to grow one's own food. Only a few people will be able to do so from now on." It was infuriating.

There was nothing more to say about it right now, so we resumed our tour. Continuing north, toward the courthouses and Capitol, things began to look a bit more familiar. Those old buildings remained, as did the entire Institute of Living and the Hartford Hospital complex, complete with the children's hospital and the still-new Bone and Joint Institute. At least that hadn't changed, even though the run-down tenements that had surrounded them, along with the fast-food joints, convenience stores, and broken pavement were gone. It was pretty in its own poisonous way, tainted as it all was with genocide. Hamish and I stared at it, stunned into silence, as I drove us up Lafayette to Capitol Avenue, and I could see Ed and Aaron quietly staring behind us.

For lunch, I drove us up to the center of downtown Hartford, and parked in a special lot that looked like a small park with shade trees that appeared to have been planted for that exact purpose. "Wasn't there a huge parking garage here before?" Hamish asked.

"There was." I walked over to a vending machine by the entrance and paid for the parking space with my credit card. "Look, Hamish, the Agenda 21 surveillance mechanism now has a record of our presence here. No cash accepted."

I headed straight for the Wadsworth Atheneum, which was open. "We'll look around at the art and then eat lunch in their café," I said to the others. And so in we went, with me leading the way, to see something that hadn't been erased, altered, or otherwise indicative of the shock to the world around us.

The next day, I went out driving – with Aaron in the car, as I could forget about going anywhere alone – and put the windows down. Aaron wasn't pleased, but not because of the wind in his hair. "I love fresh air," he told me, "but using the air conditioning and having the windows up would be safer for you."

"Do you really think that some sniper is perched somewhere along my random, unplanned, undeclared route on the off chance I might happen to drive by?" I asked him.

"You're right. Let's enjoy the breeze."

I smiled and drove all over West Hartford, Avon, and Simsbury, exploring. Crops were being grown, rotated, and not grown to give farmland a rest. The whole area looked like a historic district. Historic districts were beautiful, but that beauty was a startling reminder of how the pressure that our species had exerted on the ecosystem had been so drastically eased. It was also a shocking and stark reminder of the Cull.

The one thing that stood out in the most startling way did not catch my attention until a couple of hours into the exploration. "I keep getting startled by the quiet," I said to Aaron. "It's almost silent here. I don't hear other cars, even when they are almost next to mine, until they pass by. The whole world has gotten quieter."

"That's because most of those cars are gone now, and the others are electric," he said.

Chapter 5

The Wildlands Map and Silviculture

The idea that humans could ever conquer Nature is an asinine one.

Nature doesn't need us. It will go on without us no matter what. It will adapt to anything.

We cannot.

We humans tend to be a short-sighted, foolish, invasive species. Over and over again, we fail to understand this and continue to try to conquer a force that is far more powerful than we could ever hope to be in its very effortlessness.

Nature simply exists, living and breathing, while we push and poke at it like fleas.

Yes, we must do some of that to survive, but we humans have done far more than that.

We have sought to use Nature for our own gain and convenience.

Look at what it had gotten us: collapse.

Nature would go on without acquiescing to our wishes, regardless of our efforts.

When he wasn't busy working with Jacques, Jason was available to us. He and Hamish and I still liked to look at the Earth from above, with our own personal version of Google Earth and Google Maps, using the flying nanobotic cameras.

It was no longer a horror show, at least not in the sense that it had been during this most recent holocaust. Instead, it was a shock of another kind. The Wildlands Map of U.N. Agenda 21 – which was now re-branded as U.N. Agenda 2030 – was now a reality…with some tweaks.

The tweaks were driven by anthropogenic climate change. Specifically, sea level rise had shrunk the continent of North America, changing its shape drastically. Nonetheless, using genocide, the plan for human compression into urban areas with very little suburban sprawl had been implemented. As a result, the Wildlands Map now reflected that.

Vast areas of the continent were now off limits to human settlement…and to humans at all.

No travel, no hiking, no camping – nothing in the way of human presence in those areas was permitted. Hence the impulse to send our nanobotic cameras flying over those places; even Connecticut had a few of them. They were the former National Park areas, plus other wooded and desert areas. Was this ban a cover for harvesting resources there, or to protect them?

I was really curious to see what was there.

Jason came over the next day to help Jacques with the computer modeling for their recycling report, and I asked him about the Wildlands Map sections that were in Connecticut. "What do think we will find that is different?"

"I think you will see bridges and underpasses devoted to wildlife use, smoothed over with grass and other vegetation. Eco-corridors, they are called. I can help you and Hamish find some before you go out driving, so that you can go within sight of them, if you want."

"Oh, yes please!" I said.

The scientists who devoted their careers to the ecosystem were at last being taken seriously.

It was time to do something different, and this measure of keeping humans out of the forests was part of that plan. We had to stop harvesting the forests as if they were infinite, or as if they would grow back quickly…or at all, if we took too much away. We also had to stop suppressing any and all forest fires, as if the slightest spark were a bad thing. Some forest fires were a natural part of the life cycle. The problem had been human settlements too close to wooded areas.

Silviculture, the art and science of growing and tending forest crops, was a practice used in Europe, Japan, and Papua New Guinea to control forests. Its main purpose was regeneration of the forest, as opposed to merely cutting it all down and then crying that there was no wood left to use. The United States still had time to save its forests, and it intended to do just that.

The trees could still be cut for wood – that wasn't precluded. But they must be grown back, and humans must learn to give up on instant or even seasonal gratification on that point. The trees were to be carefully tended so that they grew to desired and therefore useful shapes. The species cultivated were to be selected for future uses and then tended by educated growers.

A whole new industry was springing up along with these fabulous trees. Oak, cedar, pine, mahogany, and cherry – all of these prized trees were to be grown. Runoff would decrease, it was hoped, while nutrients in the soil would increase. I flew the nanobots over the forest and saw neat rows of saplings, then flew them downwards to read the labels. That's how I knew what species of trees were being grown.

Neither goats nor sheep would be allowed to graze anywhere near the forests, I read online, or they would never grow. Goats and sheep were organic brush-eating machines. Nothing could be expected to take hold as long as it had to contend with those animals.

This would take some serious effort and attention from humans, thus creating jobs, because goats and sheep were needed for other purposes. Goats were being let loose to eat the ever-growing kudzu plants that had been foolishly imported from Southeast Asia, and were now a persistent problem. The damned plant was smothering all other plants. Aside from that, goat milk made great cheese: the chèvre that my family loved, for example. Sheep were needed for wool.

Trees of varying ages would coexist in the forest, just as Nature grew them on its own, but directed by humans. Cutting of the trees would be done periodically to keep the growth from becoming too dense, and to prevent forest fires, it was hoped. One couldn't control everything, but one could still try. There was little choice in that: it was either try or die of resource depletion, and humans had never wanted that to happen.

It had nearly happened, and our government was at last wise to that danger, and doing what it could to prevent it from overtaking us or recurring. That was the carrot part of the equation. As for the stick: harsh rules to keep humans out and to force them into using harvested wood ONLY for approved purposes. We didn't have to build out of wood. We could use other materials. Wood was for furniture, for paper, for books, and for some tools.

It would be tricky to keep watch on all that wood, but our government congratulated itself on what was often called an Orwellian surveillance system. It would now be turned toward protecting the forests and maintaining a functional system of silviculture.

So, I thought to myself as I read this plan online: that is what the Wildlands Map was about.

How would this plan be carried out and maintained, I wondered? I kept reading. Surely, loggers would do whatever they could to loot the forests and ruin it all. Independent entrepreneurs would sneak in and do as they pleased, right? Marijuana growers would try to go in and grow some. Careless hikers would sneak in and leave campfires burning.

Wrong, and right: Wrong in that this would not be allowed, and right in that it would certainly be attempted. The U.S. Congress had passed a law – and here I sensed that some Farmers had bought themselves some politicians yet again – which enabled the plan to work.

The U.S. National Guard would be kept busy guarding the forests and evicting squatters, illegal loggers, and anyone else who lacked a permit to so much as be present in the Wildlands. What a joke of a name, I thought. The Wildlands would be part wild and part cultivated via this new policy of silviculture.

And what about responsible hikers and campers?! They were the losers in this plan. People ought to be allowed to enjoy the National Parks. Instead, we were losing them to the Farmers.

Who would be allowed in there legally?

The silviculturists would be on the list of legal invitees, of course, in order to cultivate, maintain, and oversee the forests. The National Guard was answerable to those scientists, which was nice to see. For once, I was seeing scientists in charge of the gun-wielders instead of the gun-wielders free to ignore them and screw things up further.

I wondered who had dreamed up this plan. Could it have been the environmentally educated offspring and heir of some wealthy Farmer? I could hardly wait to find out. And all I ever usually had to do was wait in order to find these things out. It would likely appear in the legislative history, if I cared to slog through that. But even more conveniently, it would probably appear on some news show such as *60 Minutes*.

For now, my guess was that this Farmer had seen the business opportunity in the heir's ideas, and the dwindling, soon-to-be-depleted and thus all gone trees out there. Something had to be done, or there would be nothing left for the future.

Funny…now that the world was flat – as in fully known thanks to satellites, scientific studies, the Internet, and whatever other modern data collection capabilities – anyone who cared to study a particular situation could know the scope of a problem, and thus suggest a solution. It took the financial resources of the Farmers to put solutions into action, however. That meant that a very wealthy few still controlled the Earth's resources. Some things never changed.

Or did they?

Congress had, astonishingly, just passed a new law about industry standards for certifying logged timber from felling to cutting into usable boards or milling into paper to market. The Forest Stewardship Council (FSC), an international group with an elected board made up of environmental, social, and industry interests, had been the official certifying authority for over two decades.

The entire industry had come to regard its assessment of whether or not a log had in fact originated from a carefully managed forest with sustainable practices. Customers and corporations all over the world looked for the FSC label on any wood-derived product, and were willing to pay the slightly higher cost to support it.

However, that label wasn't on more than 19% of all available products. What to do with the rest, to make it attractive to customers who cared about sustainable practices and proof of them? It was too much trouble to track it all, corporatists decided, so they had set up competing certification organizations with lower standards, and slapped those bullshit labels on the other wood products.

Therein lay the problem: how to put a stop to this and encourage stronger tracking efforts? This new law attempted to do just that. Whereas before it was legal to stamp wood with lies, now it was not. The FSC label was the only acceptable one now. It seemed that there was a lot more of a will to enact and enforce environmentally friendly laws now.

A sense of urgency had spread over after the Cull. A new environmental assessment of the Earth's resources was underway. This was to be permanent policy from now on. With silviculture underway and far fewer humans on the planet demanding or even needing any wood products, it was going to be a lot easier to meet the new requirements. Here was another hidden and ill-gotten gain that would be good for the ecosystem.

Chapter 6

Life in the Anthropocene Epoch

Welcome to the consequences of the Anthropocene epoch. It was the epoch of humans.

This term had been coined in 2002 by Paul Crutzen, a Dutch chemist. An epoch is part of a period, which is part of an era. We were living in the Anthropocene epoch of the Quaternary period of the Cenozoic era. "Anthropocene" was named for the human impact on the ecosystem. We had certainly had a significant enough one that the International Commission on Stratigraphy (I.C.S.) had seen fit to decree that the Holocene epoch had ended during the twentieth century. Thus, we were currently living in the Anthropocene epoch.

What did all this technical terminology mean? It meant that humans had shaped the Earth so significantly as to merit (though the word "merit" seemed too complimentary, nothing else quite fit) having it named for our species.

We had shaped continents, both by using fuel sources that heated the atmosphere to the point of melting icecaps and thus raising sea levels, and by holding that water back with dykes, levies, dams, and anything else that we could invent. We had even added land in some areas, such as Battery Park of Manhattan.

We had caused the extinction of so many species it was impossible to keep an accurate count of them all, while artificially seeking to keep others from going extinct via zoos, wildlife preserves, and captive breeding programs.

We had tinkered with the genetics of plants, animals, and ourselves for the purposes of breeding more food, hardier food, and healthier humans. We had done this for aesthetic reasons as well. We had done this for both ethical and unethical reasons.

The point was, we humans had done all of these things, and thus altered our planet.

The Lassiter Dam was a massive infrastructure project, a dam that held the Hudson River back at the point of the St. Lawrence Seaway. It was named for John K. Lassiter, the Secretary of Demographics. At the other end, the mouth of the Hudson River, there was a series of dykes designed by Dutch engineers. That wasn't enough to hold back the forces of Nature, however. Another series of dykes and a wall that stretched inland, into Rhode Island, closed off the other end of Long Island Sound.

And that was all that could be done to hold back the power of the ocean.

Newport, Rhode Island and all of its famed mansions, including such works of art as the Breakers, was underwater...gone. The History Channel and the Discovery Channel were full of stories of these lost places, with hour-long shows that lamented their loss.

I wondered at all that, with its omission of any of the cute little historic towns that had sat between Newport and Providence. They were beautiful shore-side places, with unique shops, franchise shops, fish restaurants (not that there was enough fish available to fuel them now), colonial-style houses, stone walls, gardens, and even an area with red-white-and-blue paint on its pavement instead of the usual yellow and white. All were gone with the relentlessly rising seas.

But back to Connecticut, where we were; I had such a knack for letting my mind wander off to some other geographic area. "It's a good thing that you have those flying nano-cameras, Hamish," I said. "You can endlessly satisfy our curiosity about the lay of the land."

He smiled. "What are you plotting this time?"

"Nothing too awful, I hope. The Cull is over, so this can't be all that horrific. I want to drive south as far as we can go with my old street atlas of Southern New England. The idea is to see how far we can go before the roads in it just aren't there – any of them. Then, you can release the nano-cameras and we can see what's different."

"I'm calling Jason, then. He can help us make a day of it," Hamish said.

"Really? You're all mine?" I asked, incredulous. "No work plans?"

"Nae. Just you and me."

"Great! When can we leave?"

"Is tomorrow at 10 a.m. soon enough?"

"Yes! We can't just go right now, with no prior notice. Jason could be working."

Hamish laughed. "Oh, he's working all right. Jacques and Jason are a recycling rehabilitation design team now. They're having a fine time."

The next morning, as I thought about the exploring we were about to do, I stared into my coffee cup. It was a Tuesday, and we were sitting in the kitchen, taking our time before we left. It was hard to believe that Hamish wasn't going to the office today, and that I wasn't in the throes of writing anything at the moment, even though I always had plans for some book project.

"Let's tour the area a bit farther from home. We have been so busy getting settled and used to the New World Order around here that we haven't gone very far."

"Fine." He smiled and gulped the last of his coffee. "Before we head out, though, I have something that Jason dropped off for our expedition." It was a tablet that I hadn't seen before.

"What's this?" I asked.

"It's a digital before-and-after map, completely up to date, showing the entire continent. Jason is still working on the rest of the planet. He's planning to sell his software to engineering and surveying firms, and offer it to city and town planners as well."

"That's brilliant! But why would he let us have this before he sells it?"

"He's filed the necessary copyright protections on this one, and he wants us to beta-test it. Any problems using it, understanding it, or whatever else, and we are to tell him so that he can fix the bugs in the system, if we can find any."

"Wow. If we find any, I'll be surprised."

"Me too," Hamish agreed.

As we headed out onto Mountain Road the next day and on toward Interstate-91 South, I realized something: "There is almost no traffic! All my life, I dreaded traffic, loathed the stress of it with its crowds and slow-downs, feared getting into a terrible crash, and now…well, look at it! There are hardly any cars or trucks on the highway."

Hamish nodded in the seat next to me. "It certainly is different now. I see a few cargo trucks and a car here and there, but nothing like the highway parking lots we used to face."

"It's nice. It's absolutely lovely. And it's a guilt-trip, because it took covert genocide to make it this way," I remarked. "It also took entrapment, what with emissions standards tightening so much. Did you know that the government processed every privately-owned vehicle in the nation at emissions stations, starting even before we left for Switzerland?! It was testing just to declare most of them illegal to drive on account of emitting too much fossil fuel. It made people sitting ducks for the mobile crematoria." I had just read that information the night before, thanks to Jason hacking some more Dark Net databases. It had made sleep fitful, I was so angry. "There's still tons of data to read and watch – the data that Jason helped us gather over the past year."

He looked at me, said, "Yes, it did, but guilt won't bring all those commuters, drivers, and other people back. Try to relax and find out whatever you are curious about."

I gave him a slight smile. "Okay, I will," I replied, and put a CD of a soundtrack from the Tolkien movie series *The Hobbit* on. Soon, the car filled with the pleasant sounds of the orchestra and the voices of the dwarf chorus as they ate up all of the food in Bilbo Baggins' larder. We hummed along to it.

Ed and Aaron were tailing us. "I wonder what our protectors listen to," I said.

"They like Johnny Cash, The Beatles, Duran Duran, Elvis Presley, Michael Jackson – that sort of thing," Hamish told me.

"Huh. I used to listen to those things when I was a teenager. Not Johnny Cash, though. I came across that later, when the biopic movie about him was out."

"I'm just glad you don't want to listen to that constantly now," Hamish informed me. "Too much noise! I prefer the operas, musicals, and movie scores you like. The stories are nice to follow, they have a point, and the songs are music rather than shouts in my ears."

"We think alike," I said, smiling for real now. "I love that…and you."

"I love you, too. Now tell me what we are looking for."

"Well, I was hoping to see how the land looks near what is now the shore, and where that is. Is there development there, or is it all removed? Can we even go there to look at it? If so, is it a pretty view, or an alarming one? Is it clean, or is there a lot of trash? If no trash, is that because of ocean currents not washing plastic and other crap up onshore, or because it gets picked up regularly by determined humans? Are there enough willing humans left to even do that?"

"I see. Quite a list, then."

"Indeed. Are you going to inform Aaron and Ed of these plans?"

He looked at me, doing a double-take, then said, "I guess I should." With that, he took out his phone and called them. A detailed conversation ensued in which he explained what I was up to – they were well used to me and my curiosity by now – and listened to what they had to say.

At last, he hung up. "What about lunch?"

I grinned. "Oh, I looked up a few places. Don't worry. You guys will get fed."

He grinned too. "I'm not worried, just curious. We'll probably get where you're taking us, find out about it, and then have time to tool around before lunchtime."

And we did. But first, we found the new shore, which was oddly receding back to its former extent. The southern part of the state was being reclaimed via a series of pumps that sent the unwanted water out to sea through the dykes at the eastern end of Long Island Sound. The idea was to save New Haven and its historic buildings, and to restore as many as possible.

Rhode Island had undertaken a similar and massive infrastructure project to save Newport.

It was all keeping the Army Corps of Engineers very busy.

For now, what was once suburbs, meadows, back country roads, strip malls with curb-cuts every few feet, cute little town shops, and whatever else – all erased during the Cull – had become new meadows, with tree seedlings starting to reclaim the land.

It was amazing to think that this land might ever, in the space of current human lifetimes, be usable again. As we had driven closer to the shore, the trees had gradually thinned out, and those closer to the new shore were drowning and dying if not already dead. If one looked inland, the same thing went in reverse, with trees living and sprouting up again.

Driving up the highway, I suddenly noticed something: we went over a small bridge that spanned a grass-covered area. "That's interesting," I commented, slowing down. There was no danger of getting rear-ended by strangers, and Ed slowed down, matching my speed. I stared, and so did Hamish. "Is that for the wildlife – a tunnel for them to cross the road with?"

"It must be," he said.

"Cool! I had read about those in bigger states with more wide open spaces. That is just what Connecticut and the rest of the Northeast needs. Wildlife have been losing habitat to overdevelopment and fragmentation by development for about a century, maybe longer. This should really help them."

"Maybe we'll see some black bears or foxes," Hamish said.

"Maybe. I hope so." I drove us to the marshland, as close to the shore as I could get.

As we walked around close to the new shore, our boots squished in mud and left footprints showing wherever we had been. "I'm glad you kept our boots from that trip to flooded Venice," Hamish said. "You are always prepared, it seems," he added with a grin.

"I try." I was looking around in disgust at what had once been a lovely New England town, with lots more houses. Now only the center of it remained, consisting of historic homes and public buildings. It was just past the wetlands, not currently threatened, and still beautiful with stone walls, colonial houses, and a coffee shop, a gift shop, and a pharmacy.

"What are you thinking about?" my husband wanted to know.

"I'm thinking that all the people who have been erased to return cute little towns to their eighteenth-century proportions, but with updated, reinforced construction plus electricity and plumbing for the few remaining people to enjoy."

"I want to know exactly who all of the Farmers are," I said. "I want to come at them with the same stealth with which they erased 6.8 billion people. They have earned that. They must not enjoy what they have wrought."

Hamish stood there, listening to me blandly, and I knew that his thoughts and feelings on this matter were anything but bland. "Is there a plan yet?" was all he asked.

"Not yet," I replied. "It may take us a while to figure out all of the details. Gathering information takes time, and you and I are not exactly subtle. We Aspies are like sledgehammers sometimes, so we will have to think about it and only talk about this in certain places. We must act as if we are under constant surveillance when inside any conveyance – airplanes, taxis, whatever, plus hotel rooms – and not talk about this unless we can be sure that our communications really are only between us. That's why I brought this up in a meadow."

He grinned at that. "I though as much."

Aaron and Ed had heard that much, and clearly agreed, because they grinned with approval.

"Let's get some lunch," I said, and headed for the car. "I have a nice place in mind."

It was in Glastonbury, and it served fish with imaginative vegetarian dishes. I was amazed that it was still there, but I didn't comment on that. Pulling up to it, I noticed that electrical charging stations stood in pairs between pairs of parking spaces. I pulled the car up to one of them and plugged it in. Ed did the same with the other vehicle, and we went in.

Lunch was delicious, and the guys happily forgot any complaints for a while, eating quietly.

I had brought all of our water bottles in from the car to refill in the rest room. Gone were the days when I would even consider using bottled water, produced by some hideous manufacturing plant. Why pay for a damned plastic bottle that would never break down, but would instead turn to flakes that choked the oceans and got eaten by plankton, which got eaten by fish, which got eaten by humans?! I hoped we hadn't just eaten plastic for lunch, I thought as I filled them all up.

We spent most of the rest of the afternoon driving around. "Hamish, have you noticed that anything labeled 'historic' is still here, but any unattractive and newer, clunkier structures are gone? I'll bet that the people who live in the pretty colonial houses are okay, too."

"Aye, I have noticed," he said, staring out the window. Much of the landscape was indeed swept clean of many buildings. "It's like the world is a Norman Rockwell painting again, but with more modern amenities hidden here and there."

"I wonder how long it will take people to realize that that is no coincidence, that they are still here and alive and okay, while their neighbors, whose homes were built in the ugly 1970s style, or in those Levittown trailer-taken-root style houses, are just erased."

"They'll catch on sooner or later, I'm sure."

"I want to help make it sooner. I'm still working on precisely how."

We heard the roar of a jet engine overhead and looked up. It was a military fighter jet.

I looked at Hamish, but he was staring steadily up at it, and then at a few more that had joined it to fly in formation. "Looks like a training exercise for the pilots," he said.

"So," I said, "all this fuss about clean energy and electric cars, and the government is still using oil to fuel its military machine." I had pulled the car over to look up and stretch a bit.

"Aye." The men all exchanged glances, but said nothing else.

We got back into the cars and drove off. I crossed the Connecticut River, going along I-84 all the way across West Hartford and into Farmington. "Where are you taking us?" Hamish asked.

"To the UConn Health Center," I told him. "I want to see how it looks. It was undergoing addition after renovation after expansion when we left."

"Huh." He was silent for a moment, and then he asked, "Are you hoping I will set up an official Regenics clinic around here – a satellite branch at Hartford Hospital or the UCHC?"

"What? No," I said. I just want to know what is still here. I'm curious, that's all. And I wonder how medicine and dentistry will be taught now that the human population is so drastically reduced."

"It will likely be different," Hamish said.

"Do tell," I said.

"Well…it will probably be less rushed, which means that interns will not have much opportunity to learn fast-paced, high-pressure emergency care, the trade-off being that they will be able to get enough sleep and pay much more individual attention to each patient. That will reduce human error significantly from day to day."

"Interesting. That's mostly good," I commented.

The reservoir was still frequented by Canada geese, plus a few Mallard ducks. I even saw a grey heron as it flew across the water and into the woods. "Maybe we'll see more swans from now on," Hamish remarked.

"Maybe…or maybe not, depending on biodiversity loss. But I hope so."

At last we arrived at the Health Center. It was a surprise: all finished. No renovations were in progress. The place looked almost unrecognizable until we drove up to it, and then little details began to pop out at us, things that we remembered from before all of the changes had started in the 1990s. Down the hill toward Farmington Avenue, the pond with the geese was the only familiar part. The rest was the new Jackson Institute.

The trouble with that place was its rigid schedule and opening and closing times: 9 a.m. to 5 p.m. Everyone had to leave by early evening – no staying late, which Hamish sometimes liked to do. He would just get really caught up in his work, and he wouldn't want to stop until he was finished with whatever phase he was working on.

"No thank you," he said. "Too many rules, too much regimentation to worry about."

"Right. Creators and inventors don't function on a standard schedule anyway. What are the people with the Mercedes SUVs who occupy these labs, then?" I asked.

"Corporate scientists," my husband told me. "I would stand out among them socially, and they would not just accept that and let it go. Nae…I'll work out of my present office for now."

We had seen enough, so I drove us home. Ed and Aaron looked relieved when they realized I was heading for Mountain Road, and they actually sat back in their car seats and smiled when I turned left to go north, toward Stoner Drive. I looked pointedly into the rearview mirror when we came to a stoplight and grinned at them.

When we got home, Jason was there, visiting Jacques. After they had discussed recycling for a while and written up some ideas on their laptops, they took a break and came outside, where I was checking my beehives. The hives were fine; I just wanted to hang around outside for a while. Hamish was hanging around with me.

Jason looked up at the roof, studying our solar panels, which were spaced apart neatly on the slate shingles, in brackets. Hamish had done a good job installing them, I thought, glancing up there also. I turned my attention back to securing the hives. "How did you get solar panels onto a slate roof?" Jason asked. "I thought it couldn't be done."

Hamish grinned. "It can be done with nanites. I had the nanites install the brackets, then climbed up there with the panels, placed them on the brackets, and had the nanites secure them."

"Awesome!" Jason said. "That sounds like the sort of thing that Ant-Man could do."

I looked up at him. "That's terrific! He could." Never mind that Ant-Man was a fictional character from the Marvel universe. I could just image the nanites working like the ants, forming tiny swarms that did Hamish's bidding as he guided them via his computer, moving the mouse, pointing and clicking as if playing a virtual game. But this was not a game – it had a purpose.

Later that day, back at home in the living room, I decided to listen to some music on the CD player. Looking through Dad's collection, I chose *Stabat Mater* by Giovanni Battista Pergolesi, because I liked the sound of the boy in the choir singing his solo. Dad would not approve of how I came to like it, but I didn't care: it was because of a scene in *The Talented Mr. Ripley*, which took place in St. Mark's Cathedral in Venice.

Dad had a huge music library that he had compiled over the years, one that made the prospect of buying him any new stuff intimidating. I mean, what if he already had it?! Lately, I had managed to win by going for medieval stuff. Anything really eclectic that he might not have discovered seemed to pleasantly surprise him. As for me, I liked it if it had been a in movie.

He liked classical, romantic, baroque, Medieval, European, American, orchestra and chamber music…and organ music, which meant listening to recordings and visiting the Trinity College Chapel. Secular or Christian, he liked his sophisticated music, and the Christian could be either Catholic or Protestant. He jokingly called himself a Huguenot heretic, which I found amusing.

As I looked at the data jacket, I studied the information on the performers and looked at the art and photographs on it, and the date it was recorded. It occurred to me that the boy who sang in it would, if he were alive now, be of age to attend college or university. But was he still alive, or had he been deemed "extraneous" by the Farmers, I wondered?

"Damned Farmers," I muttered angrily.

"I take it you aren't talking about people who work in agriculture," Claire said, coming in from the den just in time to hear me. Fabian was right behind her.

I looked up, nonplussed, and then said, "Well…there could be a few among them. They acted in concert as a gang of elitist monsters to decide who lived and who died. I want to figure out who they are, exactly how they did it, and compile all necessary evidence to bury them in their own evil New World Order…and sink the damned 'Order'," I said.

Claire and Fabian exchanged glances. "Who would judge them?" Fabian asked.

"Have you heard of the International Criminal Court yet?" I asked him.

"Maybe…I guess I've just been buried in U.S. law to write my admissions essays," he replied. "Where is it, and how does it work?"

"It's in The Hague, in the Netherlands."

"Can we help you bury them?" Claire asked. "Law school won't start for another year."

She was looking eager, and I knew she wanted blood on behalf of her parents. She had plenty of company…or would, once I wrote and released an unsanitized history of the Cull onto the Internet. Damn – I had a lot to do! "Quite possibly. This may involve some travel…and a lot more research into how the Court works, and who to send to it. We still need to find out precisely who the Farmers are, and gather enough evidence to bury them."

"Count me in too," Fabian said. "I'll even learn to use a nanite gun, or whatever weapon."

Hamish laughed. "And here you are applying to go to law school to use words as weapons."

Fabian shrugged. "So? By the time lawyers are using those words, the cops have rounded up the criminals. It would be good to experience that part of the process, at least once, in some way, don't you think?"

"Sure. I'll show you both how to use the nanite guns. If we actually visit the Netherlands at some point – and we are a ways off from being ready for all that – you should definitely be packing, in addition to having Aaron and Ed with us."

Hamish looked pleased, like he was spoiling for a fight. I knew that the complete lack of honor shown by the Farmers galled him.

"You too are going to have to think of this as on the back burner for months, at least," I warned. It's going to take a while to gather the data that we need. I might as well tell you future lawyers that this process is not merely called 'research'. It's called 'discovery'. It means gathering evidence and making sure that it is gathered in such a way as to be legally admissible."

They nodded. "We can wait," Claire said. "It'll be worth it."

With that, I put the music on.

My cousins and Jacques had made their choices and gotten cars.

Claire now owned a pale, steely blue Mercedes sedan from the late 1980s that was in great condition, but she hadn't yet taken possession of it. As soon as she had closed the deal, escorted by Aaron, she had sent it off per Hamish's instructions to be converted to electricity and to have all surveillance equipment removed. It would be off the grid.

She was quite pleased with herself, to say the least.

"But you will have to wait for it for a while," Jacques had protested when she announced it.

"So? I've already lived without a car for a while now. I'm sure that the one I had in Philadelphia is long gone anyway, so this doesn't change my life. The change will be when the car is ready, and I'd rather have it done right. It was weird registering it, though," she added.

Claire had been given a form at the Department of Motor Vehicles, which she had quietly stuffed into her handbag to look at later. It was to be turned in separately – and voluntarily – at a different window from the one where the registration forms were dealt with, or mailed in later. She had registered the car, gotten license plates, and left.

It was only when she had gotten home that she had remembered that form and taken it out.

"Look at this!" she had exclaimed, outraged. "It wants to know whether or not I live with relatives who can share a vehicle with me, and strongly encourages me to use public transportation or share rides rather than drive myself wherever I want to go, whenever I want to go anywhere!"

"Really!" I had immediately walked around the other side of the kitchen table to see it. Sure enough, the government was making its wish known that individual citizens not have their own cars. The rest of the family crowded around to look, so Claire passed the form around. We ended up saving it carefully, scanning and backing it up. Getting another copy from the Department of Big Brother's Motor Vehicles just as a souvenir seemed like an unlikely proposition.

"Have you seen the prices for a new electric vehicle, or what Claire had to pay to get her car converted to electricity?" Fabian asked. "They make owning one's own, individual car out of the reach of most people. What with the pay that most people can expect, they can never hope to own their own car. It's disgusting.

The economy has been rigged to foreclose independence via motor vehicle. Gone are the days of exploring in a car, it seems."

"That explains why we see so few vehicles on the road now," I mused.

"Jason bought a Tesla and removed the surveillance tech himself," Jacques told us. "He said he saved a lot of money doing that. He also did it to his parents' car, all inside his garage, while they were asleep." Jason's parents were sharing a Tesla. They couldn't afford another one right now, but Jason was going to surprise his mother with her own car soon. "He was spooked into doing it by what happened to you…or almost happened to you…on Route 44 in Avon before we all left for Switzerland."

"That wouldn't have happened to us," I told my cousins. "Our car couldn't be hacked. It was that other couple – the dead couple – who had a hackable car. I just swore as the guy behind me honked at me to drive into the intersection, and didn't move into the path of that oncoming black tractor-trailer truck."

Edgar looked up at me critically. "Most people would have moved and died."

"I'm not most people," I replied.

"We know," my cousins said, grinning at me.

I grinned back.

Hamish walked into the room in time to hear that. "No, she's not," he said, grinning too. Then he looked serious. "We're lucky that guy behind us didn't slam on the accelerator and force us into its path. That driver wasn't stopping or slowing for anything."

"Of course not," I said. "It was probably being driven remotely, by a drone driver."

Hamish did a double-take. "I should have thought of that."

"Don't worry; I just figured it out recently from some SmartTech reading."

"Huh."

Fabian ended up buying an old black Audi and having it fixed up like Claire's car. Jacques and Edgar got Tesla cars, red and blue, respectively. Jason pulled the surveillance gear out of them for a small fee – smaller than it might otherwise have been. With that, all of them had cars, all were registered, and all were hassled over the registration. All of them had refused to listen to a word of admonishment by the government officials about ride-sharing, disgusted with the attempted interference in their lives.

Our parents were amazed by it all. "Good for you for not cooperating with their survey-surveillance," Dad had said.

Another day, I took Claire with me on one of those exploratory drives.

We went – without informing Hamish or Fabian, but with Aaron and Ed in the backseat – all the way to New York State. It wasn't all that far, really. Just up Route 44 through Avon, a half-hour drive along the old state highway, and soon we were crossing the state line. The roads were newly repaved with that amazing, recycled plastic, plus they had electricity-storing-and-sharing painted lines in green.

I had looked up a nice place to eat lunch, and planned to look around an area with castles, mansions, and other palatial homes built of both stone and wood over a century ago, or slightly later. The highway had cut through that area, and many of those homes had fallen out of favor. After the Great Depression, the area had taken a downturn, many had gone to seed.

The plan was to see how many, if any, were still there.

Aaron and Ed had given up their protest about our destination, which they had kept up for the first half-hour of the ride. When they had realized that they were captive passengers, Ed had called Hamish to inform him of our plans, and that was that.

Hamish had told them to take care of us and stop worrying. The Cull was over, he had said.

That quieted them down, if nothing else.

Hamish was working in his office for the day, and the LSAT was over with. Dad had gone to see Attorney O'Shea with Fabian, to settle him into an internship. There was no reason not to give Claire a field trip while taking one myself.

We left late in the morning, and by half past noon were approaching the restaurant. We enjoyed a pleasant lunch of hand-cut fries with cayenne pepper and rosemary and turkey burgers with goat cheese, heirloom tomato, baby spinach, and pickles. There were mocha milkshakes for dessert, and then it was off to conduct our self-guided tour.

After I had paid the bill, I suddenly remembered the water, which we had been drinking along the way. "Come on, Claire, we need to refill our reusable water bottles."

Aaron and Ed paced around impatiently while we toted two each into the rest room, filled them, and returned to the car. "Don't look at me like that," I said to Ed. "No more plastic bottles of water pumped from elsewhere when the tap water is perfectly good."

"Yes, ma'am," he said wearily. I knew he thought of my every exit from the car as a security risk, but I had no sympathy. I wasn't some high-ranking political official, so he couldn't stop me.

Claire just laughed and handed Aaron his water bottle, and got back into the car.

Aaron said, "Did you know that plastic is made of petroleum – fossil fuel? We don't need to use any more of it."

Ed rolled his eyes and took a sip of water from his reusable, metal container.

To our pleasant surprise, we found lots of aging edifices that could have starred in many a horror, mystery, or vampire movie. "These places are beautiful!" Claire exclaimed, staring out at them. She asked me to explain the history of the area again, and I did. "Cool! Thanks for bringing me."

I pulled up to house after castle after mansion, some of which were on sprawling properties, and all in varying states of decay. Some had brambles growing all the way up their walls. Others were falling down here and there. Still others looked like they could be fixed up and lived in.

Some of them had explanations about their past posted out front. We found one that had been a hotel, and another a boarding school for high school girls, but most had just been private residences for wealthy New Yorkers who wanted country homes to stay at during the summers.

I photographed them just for fun, to show to the family later. My mother loved to see such things. She and Dad had gone on many such excursions. Now I was following in their footsteps.

Aaron and Ed began fretting that I might try to go inside some of these buildings, but I told them to cool it. "No, I may be on an adventure, but I'm not crazy," I said.

Claire laughed.

We got back into the car and went down the road, an old state highway that had just one lane going in each direction. "Is that a wildlife tunnel that we just went over?" Claire asked at one point, craning her neck back at a bridge with grass under it.

"Most likely," I said. "Too bad we can't look at it more closely."

She looked at me. "Is there a road that goes down anywhere near it?"

"I don't know…" I turned right, heading down a dirt road that would take us back there. Soon we ran out of road, but could see the tunnel off in the distance. All was quiet, except for birds chirping.

Aaron, catching on to what I was up to, protested. "Don't do it, Avril! What will we tell Hamish and Fabian if you two get mauled by a bear?"

I picked up my camera bag, grinned at him, and said, "Don't tell me you guys don't carry tranquilizer guns. I've read the Blackout Security data. I know you do that."

Ed and Aaron rolled their eyes and groaned, then got out of the car and followed us.

"This is great," Claire said. "I've read about these, and wanted to look at one for a while."

"I hope that once we've looked at one, you won't want to look this closely at another," I said to her. "Once is an adventure. Any more than that is tempting fate."

"Agreed," she said.

We walked noisily so that any nearby bears, lynxes, bobcats, or coyotes would hear us coming and stay clear of us. I felt a bit guilty, invading their territory just to satisfy our curiosity. Our species was the ultimate invasive species, the dominant one on the planet. "I'm going to shoot a few photographs, and then we really ought to leave," I said.

Claire took some photographs, too.

After about five minutes, during which Aaron and Ed deliberately chatted loudly, we left.

Back on the road, they visibly relaxed, happy that we had resumed our original field trip.

"You guys aren't complaining about the risks of this trip at all now," I teased them.

"After that little excursion, no," Aaron said. Ed just gave us an exasperated stare.

We walked around the grounds of a rambling, ivy-covered Victorian mansion a bit, leaving Ed at the car while Aaron accompanied us and vice versa at the next place. "I wonder why they didn't tear these places down last year?" Claire mused. "They certainly went to a huge effort to tear down almost everything else."

"Two guesses," I said. "One is that they weren't focused on these places because they weren't inhabited. The other is that they make great curiosities. These houses and castles could be put to all sorts of uses: movie sets, historical or ghost tours, or secret government murders."

She and Aaron paused and stared at me. "Always the conspiracy theorist, aren't you?" Claire said after a moment. "Except that your theories are usually right on the mark."

"Yeah, unfortunately," I replied. "It's after three. Let's go home."

The ride back was quiet, uneventful, and pleasant enough, though we did see a fighter jet fly overhead once. That was getting to be a regular occurrence.

We picked up Hamish at the office and took him to Max a Mia for dinner, and called Fabian to meet us there.

It was the perfect end to the day – something normal and familiar amidst all this change.

Chapter 7

Sanitized History Books

There are lots of things that you can scrub, sanitize, and otherwise alter.
Missions to outer space can be scrubbed.
Bathtubs and toilets can be scrubbed.
Accounts of history can be sanitized.
I was curious to see what, if anything, of the Cull could be found in the latest history textbooks, so I had bought some at the Barnes & Noble academic bookstore on 5th Avenue. Oh, wait…no…I bought them at the store on the 5th Avenue Canal. That was just after we had returned from our year in Switzerland.

There were three titles that stood out, and I had bought them all. There was a children's book called *Vaccine: The Plague – Prevention Wasn't Enough*; another for tweens and teens called *The Great Dying of Our Species*; and a college text entitled *Near Extinction: What Humans Can Learn From It*.

Now I could read the official narrative, and see what lies the Farmers were selling as the truth to the gullible public. Or maybe not so gullible – maybe there were some people who were at least skeptical, even if not in the know, like me.

I started off with the children's book. It seemed like a quick, straightforward, efficient narrative. That is, it was efficient in telling the lie that had been perpetrated and perpetuated. It seemed like a simple enough proposition to retell it with the truth about the Cull. All I would have to do, I thought to myself as an evil grin spread across my face, would be to load my metaphorical syringe of a tale with all of the germs (and nanites) of the truth.

I would do just that, I decided. That would be a lot better than simply releasing all of our flying nanite view videos of the Cull. How would we explain our possession of those away? It would be obvious to many that we could have been and most likely were the ones who had acquired all that footage. I mean, we were the nanite couple. I was the one who thought of jobs for nanites, and Hamish was the one who made those jobs happen.

Still, I wanted those videos released…anonymously. I would have to discuss that with Hamish…and Jason. Meanwhile, I got busy reading through *Vaccine: The Plague* and plotting out my own version, which I would call *Vaccine: The Cull*.

Writing alone for long stretches can feel both good and intense. After a while, one needs to take a break, stretch, and sit back and space out for a while. If you don't relax and zone out sometimes, you will just get burned out to no useful end. I sat back and thought for a while.

Luck counts for so much in life that it is amazing when people get blamed for any failures.

No one succeeds without help; no one makes it on their own. Hamish and I had been lucky.

We had made money, survived the Cull on our money and wits, and helped others to do that.

Those others could so easily have died in the Cull without that help. It would not have been their fault. There had been so little that any of the ghosts who walked around our town, ripped away from the lives that they had thought that they would live, could have done to protect themselves that it was unreasonable to ever think of blaming any of them for their fate.

Claire was doing some writing of her own. Law school applications were in. Time for fun!

As it turned out, once the LSATs were over with, she and Fabian could not go to law school next year, because the schools were all on hiatus. The Cull had caused the deaths of some professors, and colleges, universities, and graduate and professional schools around the world were still scrambling to hire replacements and successors.

Claire and Fabian had secured decent LSAT scores, written excellent, insightful essays and personal statements, and their college had kept pre-written recommendations on file for them. Their applications had been sent in, and acceptances had come back without a hitch.

Fabian had applied to Yale and Claire to the University of Connecticut. Claire loved the beautiful campus on the western edge of Hartford, a former seminary. It was conveniently located next door to the Connecticut Historical Society, too. They were waiting to hear back.

Claire had already looked up the professors who remained there, and was excited to study with them. Fabian just wanted to earn a spot on the law review and make money. He was a workhorse if ever there was one, while Claire loved the process of it all. She was in it to learn as much as she could about whatever fascinated her, and he admired that.

It was such a change from the way it was before the Cull. Now applicants seemed to have a much simpler, less stressful time of it once their paperwork was filed. Plus, it was all filed online. That was different from when I had done it, and it was intriguing to see just how streamlined it made the entire process.

With that dealt with, Claire turned her attention to honing her writing skills – both legal and creative. She wanted to have a little fun with this, so she joined a writers group at the Noah Webster Public Library. "I remember that group," I said to her. "I went to it for a while. Let me know what genres of writing you find people doing there."

She promised to do so, and soon reported that it was science fiction, short story, mystery, and forensic crimes, with an occasional romance story. Writing skills and attention to the story lines varied. Details counted for a lot, especially consistency, but not everyone was careful.

"Sounds familiar," I said. "Everyone wants to write, but not everyone cares about perfection and getting published. If you want to get published, or plan to self-publish, you need to care, of course. The benefit of this is the feedback – getting people's impressions of what you write can be very useful. It's like a mirror, showing you what they see and reflecting it back to you. When can you submit your work? That is, if you want to do that."

"Oh, I already sent something in. You have to hurry and do it the moment you leave a meeting. The queue of three stories fills up almost instantly," she told me.

"It was like that when I did it too," I told her. "What did you send in?"

"A short story. It's about a girl who sees ghosts. Also, she's an Aspie, like us."

"Of course she is," I said with a grin. "Mark Twain did advise people to write what they know. Can I read your story?"

"Sure." She gave me a printed copy. We were in her and Fabian's room, sitting on the bed.

It was about thirty-four pages long, single-spaced, and a quick glance showed that it was neatly aligned, proof-read, and had a catchy title: *The Cold Spots*. The protagonist was named Chloe, and she could both see and feel the ghosts. They were eerily just like the ones that I felt and Hamish saw. Had she heard us talking about them, I wondered? I didn't ask.

"When's the next meeting?" was all I wanted to know for now.

"Tomorrow night at eight o'clock. I wonder what people will make of it."

"Tune in tomorrow. I'll wait up for you so you can tell me what they say."

"Thanks!" she smiled as she said it.

The next evening, I made some rosewater almond madeleine cookies while I waited. I really wanted to know what kind of feedback she would get. I remembered the kind I had gotten, and I was curious to see if hers would be in any way similar.

I put the kettle on for tea and sat down at the kitchen table to wait.

Soon I saw Aaron driving up to the house with Claire in the front seat. She got out, thanked him, and walked inside, looking a bit confused. I watched her put her book-bag on the table and take out a sheaf of papers – printed copies of her story with written comments here and there, plus a little note at the end if the reader had bothered to write one.

"So – how was it? Was it helpful?"

She paused, looking like someone with mixed feelings on the matter, and said, "It was."

"Can you be more specific?" I asked, pouring some lavender chamomile tea and putting the plate of madeleines on the table.

She plopped herself into the chair opposite mine and said, "They called Chloe selfish. They said that she didn't emote enough, and that she should conform more to the people around her, interact more, show a greater range of emotion, and behave more 'appropriately' around others." She looked dejected…and insulted.

I let out a sigh of accustomed disgust. "Oh really?!" I said, without an uptick in volume.

Claire looked at me. "You don't agree?" She had a vague smile on her face.

"Hell, no!" I said. "Those are the exact same stupid remarks and insults that I got when I first submitted a story. It was still useful, mind you. And the readers revised their opinions when I disclosed that I have Asperger's and explained what that is. That's when it got even more helpful, because they told me to put more of those traits into the story, and hint to the reader that that was what was going on with my character. I did, and it made the story much better."

Claire looked amazed. "So that's what just happened to me tonight!"

I was so pleased that I let out a slight shriek of delight – a rare thing for me – and got up from my seat, walked around the table and hugged her. She stood up and squeezed me back, hard, just as delighted. "I'm going to revise it tonight and include all that. Chloe's going to have a detailed personality, and the reader will get an education in what an Aspie is like AND a scary story!"

"Excellent!" I said. We settled down to our tea and cookies, quite satisfied over this.

Grandmère walked in from the living room, where she was doing yet another intricate puzzle. "What was all that fuss about?" she wanted to know.

We told her, and I poured her some tea and got her a plate for some madeleines.

"Sounds about right," she nodded, biting into one.

We all settled in for more treats, and I said to Claire, "Let me tell you a musical tale of something a bit similar. You know that Wolfgang Amadeus Mozart, the genius 18th century composer, was quite likely an Aspie, right?"

"Yes…"

"And do you know how his 40th Symphony goes?" I sang a few bars for her.

"Yes! I know that one."

"Okay. Well, a long time ago – I think when I was your age – my father got tickets to hear it at Tanglewood. He thought it was going to be so great, because a French conductor whose recordings he liked was doing the performance, but it was terrible! The piece was eviscerated of its force, smoothed over, softened, and just awful. Having those sharp edges in it is what gives me a thrill when I listen to it. I was so appalled that I turned to my father and said, 'he took all the sharp edges out of Mozart,' and my father agreed that it had ruined it."

"Why would someone do that?" Claire asked, open-mouthed.

"Artists like to show what they can do," Grandmère said. "That doesn't mean that they should actually go ahead and do it. Music ought to be played as the composer intended it."

"Exactly!" I said. "This was years before I was diagnosed with Asperger's, and it was a few years after that before I even learned what that is. I now realize that this conductor, whose name I have since forgotten, had neurotypicalized Mozart. What I remember most about that performance, aside from how it sounded, was how it made me feel: angry! It felt like someone was insulting Mozart's very essence, dissing what made him unique…like scratching their fingernails across a chalkboard. It really bothered me, and that was before I fully understood the situation. That's why, whenever I get the sort of insults to my personality, my quirks, or my creative work, I have learned to turn around and educate the narrow-minded twit who fires them off. We don't have to take it, or conform to someone else's formula of how to be. We're cool as we are." I summed this up with a grin.

Claire grinned back.

Grandmère smiled and ate another madeleine. "I'm glad I know what Asperger's is now. Too many Aspies get dismissed, and their contributions to the world overlooked."

The next day, I sat down to think about what I would be writing into my version of history, my unsanitized account of the Cull. It would have to be coldly objective, seeing the side of those who would not accept migrants, not accept the so-called "excess" of humanity.

Reading articles on migrants to Europe, and how they are being repelled because, with the borders between Europeans nations opened to Europeans for inter-member-state travel, migrants are finding it easier to move through.

We had lived in crazy times, some said. Indeed.

This was one of the issues that I would deal with in *Vaccine: The Cull*, my tell-all history.

The influx of people from conflict zones had been relentless. My unsanitized history would show illegal ways to stem the tide – by making people sick in both zones, and thus exterminating the "overpopulation" in each one – as well as legal ones, which kept everyone alive. It was the illegal methods of handling human overpopulation that killed people.

This was the Cull: the vaccine with the deliberate taint of crashing the human immune system by going after too many diseases at once combined with nanites that would break its cancer tumor suppressor mechanism, thus guaranteeing death from it.

It didn't even have to be contagious, which was the terrifying beauty of it. Only those who were injected with it became sick. Those who were not were okay. It was like a poisonous flower to those who were lied to; they believed that taking it would keep them healthy, and so they accepted the injections and got horribly sick.

It was tested in Africa, which started the process of the Cull by killing off millions, then marketed world-wide with a lie. The lie was that it would protect against all of the illnesses that it claimed to have incorporated into its one serum.

Early tests had also been conducted in remote labs in the United States, close to the where the Farmers operated. Subjects were homeless kidnappees and migrants who had been captured en route to what they had hoped would be a better life. Those individuals had been contagious, but the Farmers had kept them under wraps, with one controlled exception in Georgia, which Hamish and I had almost gotten too close to.

The Farmers – a combination of banksters, hedge fundsters, and corporatists who controlled most of the planet's assets through possession of its fiat money and control of the four pharmaceutical companies that tested and manufactured vaccines – had arranged all this, aided and abetted by certain members of the world's governments.

This was about the Earth's bank account, which was not backed by gold but by the ecosystem and what it could produce: food, water, minerals, energy, space, fresh air, beauty, and other things that made life healthy and worth living.

One could not simply create resources and space that did exist. This was not like the world of the banksters of Wall Street who, colluding with their country's Federal Reserve Board, simply had it declare more money to exist, by fiat. Fiat money is virtual money, not anything backed up by gold or platinum or even silver. It's basically nothing. Our greenback dollars really ought to have Farmers' portraits on them instead Founders. J.P. Morgan could be on the thousand, John D. Rockefeller on the five hundred, Andrew Carnegie on the hundred, and so on. But no…that would be a dead giveaway, and they couldn't have that.

Banksters could arrange for more resources, imaginary though they were, the fiction of which would put minds at ease for a while – a short while. This had been done for decades since the gold standard had been abolished in 1972. It had gone on long enough that, by the time of the Cull, this complacency had spread like the untreated infection that it was, inducing more people to buy more property and goods than the Earth could support even in non-conflict zones.

Complacency had been seeded in the minds of common citizens, who bought houses, furniture, electronics, jewelry (including wedding items), and educations. They had then gotten married and reproduced, thus creating more humans to continue this cycle.

Growth rates slowed down as people became comfortable and healthy enough that they realized that it was not necessary to have many more children than they actually wanted in order to end up with that number of adult children. Diseases had been conquered to make this possible. Birth control also made it possible. Parents knew that they could keep their children healthy and see them survive to adulthood, so they only had one, or two, or three, if that was the family size that they wanted.

However…the overall numbers of the human species, once at a certain critical mass, continued to increase, birth control or no birth control. There were simply too many. Nae-Née slowed the process significantly, but it did not halt it. The Earth's bank account, however, was contracting under the pressure of so many humans placing so much demand on its resources.

It couldn't accommodate even those who already existed in the non-conflict zones, and yet those in the conflict zones were trying to relocate to be in the temperate, less-populated, resource-solvent zones. That would collapse those zones as well.

Migrants, they were called, would try to enter non-conflict zones because their own nations are overpopulated and in a state of eco-collapse, and in economic collapse. There was no hope of earning a living at home, so they would try to move.

The problem with that was that if all or even many who wish to move do so, there would not be a way to earn a living income in non-conflict zones.

This was a resource war.

We in non-conflict zones had enough.

Add more people, and we wouldn't have enough.

So that made any of us who realized that and repelled them the proverbial bad guys. But there it was: we had to be the bad guys and repel them in order to protect and take care of ourselves. Just imagine these struggling crowds of fluctuating sizes teeming at our borders: the U.S. border, and European borders, and off the shores of Australia and New Zealand. Then imagine our guards repelling them and getting charged with felonies when they were inevitably overwhelmed. They couldn't win.

Neither could the migrants.

But what about the vilification of those who worked on our side of the border? They were like soldiers on our side. Shouldn't we back them up?

We certainly should not have been required to agree to let more people in.

Well, that was what had been decided: to take them right back through when they get to our side, and put them directly back on the opposite side, do not pass Go, do not collect $200, as the *Monopoly* game instruction said.

They had had no realistic or reasonable hope of ever earning a living, no matter how honestly they intended to earn it, no matter how willing they had been to study or train for whatever skills were necessary to qualify for a given career. That being the reality of the situation, the Farmers had sought to erase them from the planet. But first, the Farmers shut down international travel, just to keep things neater.

The plan was simple enough: Make people sick, keep them in place while they are ailing, and then make sure that they stay sick and get worse and worse until they can barely move, let alone put up any resistance. Control their movements, keep them under the illusion that the authorities are helping them, and document them all so that no one goes unvaccinated.

Once the general population was weakened, the next phase was put into effect: Send the military around to neighborhoods designed as "excess" with more vaccines doses. Have them announce that anyone living there is to be given another dose on top of whatever they have already received. Anyone refusing to accept this will be dragged outside, strip-searched, and cavity-searched. Make sure that all residents are brought outside in their underwear and injected with this noxious serum. Rape a few random women to make sure that everyone complies.

After that, put them in camps, herd the staggering, weakened, exhausted sick into ovens that look like transportation vehicles, and turn on the sleeping gas. Then…turn up the heat, up and up and up until the crematorium has reduced them to ash.

Next step: Send the military through their neighborhoods to remove all traces of human settlement. Tell the military units that this is for sanitation purposes, and for recycling. Anything of value is to be saved, of course. Electronics were ripped apart, jewelry melted down, and art and artifacts sent off to museums.

After about a year of this, the Earth's bank account was very healthy indeed, with plenty of everything for the humans who remained on the planet. We no longer feasted upon the other creatures that dwelled here with such speed that they could not sustain their own populations. Our species was still using the Nae-Née birth control nanite and the policy of birth licensing was still in place, so our numbers would henceforth stay at roughly half a billion.

At last, due to an act of genocide on a scale that had decimated us, killing at least 6.8 billion of us, our population and consumption patterns were sustainable all over the planet. Almost no one lived in what had been called conflict zones and tropics of chaos. Those who did live there had Nae-Née and so little competition for resources that they felt less of an urge to relocate.

Some of them still wished to relocate, but it was illegal now. Happy New World Order!

There had been a cultural resource war in all this as well as an outright economic resource war, and that too was ended with the Cull and with the new non-relocation policies. These policies were put in place by the nations who had been called non-conflict zones. The people living there had become fearful and angry at the invasion from the Middle East and elsewhere by people who not only wanted their resources, but also to transplant their culture.

This was not the same thing as simply moving elsewhere – it was not mere immigration.

It was transplantation – the relocating of the bulk of their population to areas that had not gone into ecosystems collapse. The Middle Eastern men had gone to Europe first and made no secret of it. They would send for their families later, after getting settled. Once settled, they wanted Europe to accept them as the dominant, majority culture simply by overwhelming the indigenous European population with their own numbers.

When the Europeans had first accepted migrants, they had thought that they were being good neighbors, helping people escape from the destruction of their homelands by dictators, and by those radicals who had opposed the dictators. Both factions had committed horrific atrocities which were grist for the International Criminal Court: kidnapping, rape, mutilation, murder – and some murders by torture, recorded and released onto the Internet for the world to see.

Then more migrants had come, not interested in fighting to retake their own homelands.

The Europeans and the Americans (and soon also the Australians and New Zealanders) had woken up, after a year or so of taking in migrants, to the fact that this was a cultural invasion that would not stop. They were angry. Why should they destroy their own security to help this many people? It was not feasible! They could not afford it.

It was not their fault. It was simply not possible to provide space, goods, and services to a relocation of another culture, and one that was so completely opposite to their own. If that sounded nasty, so be it. That was simply what was. It was time to speak that taboo reality.

What pushed them to do so was what the Middle Eastern men had said on the Internet and how they had behaved once in Europe and Britain and Scandinavia. Those men had said that they wanted all of Europe, and America too, to become Muslim, to adopt Sharia law (that was what Islamic law was known as), for all European and American women to dress in hejab (a veil and cloth covering from head to toe), and for crimes to be punished according to that law (complete with stonings for adulterers and thieves' thumbs or even whole hands to be cut off).

Not only did they say this, but they menaced European women wherever they went, hissing at them as they went about their routines and normal lives, shouting at women who jogged or rode bicycles in shorts and tee shirts (normal attire for such activities!), and sending the Muslim women already resided in Europe to beat up women sunbathers in the summertime, shouting that they ought to cover themselves up, until they needed to go to the hospital for their injuries.

Worst of all, there were repeated incidents of male migrants from the Middle East raping and gang-raping women and girls of any age. This included girls who were under 10 years old. Women in Europe lost their way of life and basic freedoms before any legal changes could even be enacted to this invasion. An Islamic ambush, called Taharrush, was a threat to women in Europe. It meant being surrounded and raped, and it was an unreasonable situation.

I had wondered why, when our flying nanobotic cameras recorded the Cull of Europe, the demographics of the individuals being erased seemed to be predominantly from the Middle East, although there had been a significant distribution of some from other places such as Africa. No Europeans! It was only while in Switzerland, once we were all safely away from the Cull in our own part of the world, that I had been able to discover the reason why.

The news was full of stories and videos about this.

At first, I had found them in right-wing outlets – journals and websites that seemed like those that would have made Hitler and Himmler and Goebbels proud. The writers and announcers had come across as monstrously strident. I was horrified by how they sounded, and by their words. Oddly, most of them did not shout or spit, unlike Hitler had. It was only their overall tone and message that had been disturbing.

Nothing that they had said had impressed me.

Nothing, that was, until I found out what the cultural invaders had had to say.

One thing that I came across had been a complete deal-breaker in terms of accepting this cultural invasion, and it was said over and over again by the Muslim males: "Women are not halal (not clean), not human. Women are filthy animals not fit for human consumption or entrance into any sacred site."

Journalists, in disbelief that such attitudes could actually be held by any men in the present time, had posed a question about women to one male after another: Why do Muslims give the impression that they hate women?

The answer had been the same from one Muslim male migrant after another: "We don't. We own women. It's perfectly 'legal' to beat, rape, sell, trade, or misuse women as any man pleases."

Finally, the journalists had asked if it was a man's right to kill a woman. The reply: "Yes."

That was when I understood what the problem was.

It was so strange. All my life, I had sought out people from other cultures to get to know them and to learn about their mores, customs, beliefs, attitudes, dress, cuisine, music, literature, you name it. I had made friends from these other cultures from the time I had attended an international, secular girls' high school. This continued in college, graduate school, and after I had married Hamish and traveled the world with him.

Then this had happened in Europe…and it was not included in the history of the Cull.

I thought again about those friendships that I had sought out and established. I had no second thoughts about having established any of them, not even now. Why?

None of those people sought to disturb my culture – only to interact with us and go home.

This was an entirely different equation, and it did not compute.

Now that I had seen what it was that was being taught in schools, I was not pleased. Lies were being taught and believed, because governments have agendas and kids are gullible. Their parents were either gullible or scared. This was no way to live.

As I was complaining about this to my parents – I was finished reading through all this material and outlining what was wrong about it – the phone rang. "Shut up!" I said to it, because I hated the interruption and the startling sound of it ringing. But I looked at the display on its little computer screen anyway, because I had to know who was calling.

Not a solicitor, I hoped.

It was the West Hartford school board. Hmm…sort of a solicitor, I thought.

I picked up the phone, on edge at having to take a call rather than make one, nervous about interacting with anyone on a phone while my parents could hear me. This was a lifelong hang-up of mine, caused by constant coaching about phone etiquette and social interaction.

Aspies had to either live with this or else never learn to interact with others, I figured, so I had let them coach me. But no more! As I said "Hello," I took off, running up the stairs and into my room to shut the door.

It was Natasha Foley, who handled donations to the school board. I had donated money and musical instruments to the music programs of several area public schools several years ago. "Hello Professor Châtelet," she said. "How are you today?"

"Fine, but call me Avril," I said. If I could call her Natasha, she ought to be call me Avril.

"Oh! Okay," she said.

"So…what can I do for you?" I asked her. I barely knew her. We had handled the arrangements of getting the violins, flutes, French horns, oboes, clarinets, and so on, plus the money, and then I hadn't heard from her again beyond a heartfelt "thank-you" that had made me feel more than a little uncomfortable. Really, all I had wanted was to give the stuff and make sure that kids near me had the chances I had had, not deal with the fuss that ensued.

"Well, Avril, the school board was wondering whether you might be interested in allocating funds for anything other than music, art, drama, and things like that. We're coming up short on some other items this year."

Were they? I thought to myself. "And what might those things be?" I asked, suspicious.

"Well…" and here Natasha paused for a moment. "The school board wants me to ask you for funds for certain sporting programs."

"Oh really…" I said, allowing a flat tone of displeasure into my reply. "Do get specific."

She sounded like a person who did not want to do something that she had been ordered to do.

I was having fun now.

"They were hoping for a football field…the bleachers are old, the lights need replacing, and the turf needs work." She sounded almost apologetic. Apparently, she remembered my outright disdain for team sports and the injuries and culture that went with it, and my flat refusal to fund any of them.

"Were they?" I said, without any up-talk to that question, even though it was a question. "How amusing. I hope they use real grass, and not toxic astro-turf, but I won't fund sports."

There was an awkward pause, and then Natasha said, "I did tell them, but…"

I laughed. "It sounded as though you might have done so. I think I like you."

"Thank you," she said, sounding pleased. "What should I tell them?"

"You can tell them that you did as they required of you and asked me, and that I said no. I shall also say that my offer to fund musical instruments, the upkeep and bells and whistles of the theater, field trips to art museums and science museums, and the salaries of qualified teachers to instruct the students in those fields, stands."

Natasha sounded as though she was smiling, and I was sure she was. "I will. And I just want to say thank you for all of that, and it is appreciated by me, and by many who understand the value of it."

"You're very welcome. I'm sure that football and team sports will survive without me."

"Somehow, I think they will too," she said.

We ended the call on that note, and I felt a rather wicked and grim sense of satisfaction.

That was fun!

Chapter 8

We Are Invited on a Corporate Retreat

It was a big business now to gather old clothing, appliances, unwanted books – you name the product, really – convert it to its raw form as much as possible, and then create a new product out of that material. This meant that at last, corporations were devoted to combing landfills, consignment stores, thrift shops, and whatever else to find cast-offs and make pristine products that people from developed nations would want.

Jacques was determined to make a career out of doing that.

Another cleanup ambition of these corporations was aimed at the Earth's oceans and waters.

This was why Hamish and I were invited on a corporate retreat by a hedge fund called The Molech Group. Well, that and the fact that it wanted a small Regenics clinic set up alongside a spa at a hotel in Florida. We were sitting in the kitchen, having mocha java coffee and cookies because I had been baking. The aroma of chocolate chips and almonds filled the room.

"Wait, did you say Florida?" I asked Hamish, puzzled. "Isn't it pretty much underwater?"

"Well, yes, but Miami isn't completely underwater, and this group has spent gazillions on reinforcing some hotels and creating an ecotourism business there."

"An ecotourism business? What are they touring, the horror of an ecological catastrophe?"

"You got it."

"Huh. Interesting. No, make that fascinating."

My husband laughed. "Are you sure that it's a cat in this house that's named Spock?"

"Ha, ha, ha. Show me that letter of invitation."

"Okay, here." Hamish spun his laptop around to face me, revealing that he had opened an attachment from The Molech Group, complete with fancy letterhead – a virtual, formal, letter of invitation. The logo for the group looked like a naked man with a bull's head, and the outline of an "M" was worked into the bone structure of the bull's face.

I decided to read the letter first, and then look up the term "Molech" on the Internet.

Here is what the letter said:

Dear Dr. MacDonall and Professor Châtelet:

We at The Molech Group are pleased to invite you, and your family, on a corporate retreat at the famous Fontainebleau Hotel in Miami, Florida. The hotel and a small portion of Miami have been saved from the rising seas, and recently renovated by the renowned architecture and design firm of Llewellyn, Waters, & Van der Veen.

Four of our jets have been reserved to fly our guests to and from this retreat.

Our purpose in inviting you is to ask for your input in remediating the damage to the planet's ecosystems: water, air, and land. We are most particularly concerned with the water and air at this time, because it circulates constantly and quickly, bringing faraway castoffs to our shores.

There seems to be no way to solve this problem without inviting the best minds to share their input, and you have both proven yourselves to be among them. We at The Molech Group have followed your work in the journal Nanotech *with interest and attention.*

Our jets will take off from John F. Kennedy Airport on November 20th at 11 a.m. with the invitees and their families, to land in Miami at approximately 2 p.m. The crew will provide a guided mid-air tour of spots on the ground below that are famously in a state of eco-collapse. The guests will then spend 3 weeks at the Fontainebleau Hotel enjoying the creations of the world's finest chefs, swimming in the hotel's infinity pools, and touring the sunken city.

While the guests relax during the retreat's downtime – and this is meant in part as a vacation – The Molech Group will hold meetings in which each of its illustrious guests has a chance to present his or her ideas for solving the problems of ecological collapse. We expect that this will take about half of the time spent there, while the remainder of it will deal with consideration of each proposal, and possible deal-making.

The retreat will end with a flight back to JFK Airport on December 10th at 11 a.m.

We hope to see you there on November 20th, and we thank you for your attention.

Sincerely,
Mr. Jefferson Pierce, Director

"Wow," I said, looking up from the computer screen. "Let's do it. We won't miss voting in the presidential election, so that's no problem. Even if we have no plan to suggest right this second, I'm sure we'll come up with something, and I want to see who these people are. They've got to include a lot of Farmers."

Hamish stared at me, open-mouthed, and then said, "You're right. I was going to say that I don't know what to suggest, but so what? Let's take a risk and see what's going on. We should definitely get to know them face-to-face. It will at least be an intriguing adventure."

I smiled a slow, pleased smile. "Excellent. Now I'm going to look up 'Molech' online."

"Why?" Hamish didn't usually care about every last detail, but I was curious.

"Oh, you know how I write and research. I have to know every little thing. It may be significant in some way. It may reveal something about their character. I'm hoping," I went on as I went to the Wikipedia site and typed in the term, "that I will be able to guess whether or not these guys are Farmers, so I shall check both their website and their name."

"Won't their website just tell you about their name?"

"Maybe it will, or maybe it won't, but the problem with only looking there is that, whatever it says will just be what they want us to see and know, not what some outside source says. Aha! Here it is…" I read for a moment.

Hamish watched me and waited while I did so, but got impatient after a moment. "Well?"

"This is interesting, and that's putting it mildly. Molech, also spelled 'Molekh', 'Moloch', and 'Molok', means 'king'. It is also the name of an ancient type of sacrifice, or of a god."

"What was the sacrifice?"

I scanned the page. "Oh! It's appalling: it's child sacrifice, by fire, with the child still alive."

"What?! That's sick!"

"Yes…the idea was for the sacrifice to be a very demanding one, and it was done in several ancient cultures that predated the Bible. Losers of a war had to do it, and the Bible condemned it. So…this hedge fundster group has taken it as its name. Charming."

I started clicking away again.

"What are you looking up now?" Hamish wanted to know.

"The hedge fundsters themselves, at www.molechgroup.com, of course," I replied. "Here they are…that bull's head logo is there, as a shadowy backdrop on every page behind the text of a huge Molech god with a hollow body that contains flames. I guess that's where they burn the babies and children. Lovely people, these Farmers…"

I fell silent as I read for a moment, then starting reading off the facts again. "Founded in 1933, right after the passage of the Glass-Steagall Act, in protest of that law…" I glanced up at my husband, who looked confused. "The Glass-Steagall Act was passed by two members of Congress, one Representative and one Senator, who wanted to repair the damage done to the economy in the Stock Market Crash of 1929. It was Senator Carter Glass from Virginia and Henry B. Steagall of Alabama. Both were Democrats."

"What did that law do to repair the damage?" he asked.

"It forced a divorce of investment and commercial banking. Mixing the two makes banksters very happy by taking away the line between them. It leaves the system ripe for abuse by taking away crucial protections against a financial meltdown."

"Such as?"

"Glass-Steagall prohibited commercial banks from dealing in non-governmental securities for customers, from investing in non-investment grade securities for themselves, from underwriting or distributing non-governmental securities, or from affiliating (or sharing employees) with companies involved in such activities. On the opposite side of the equation, it prevented securities firms and investment banks from taking deposits."

"How did the Federal Reserve Board fit into this?"

"The Federal Reserve System was created in secret, at a resort island off the coast of Georgia – Jekyll Island – by a group of Farmers that included J.P. Morgan, in 1910, which became the Federal Reserve Act of 1913, which instituted the Federal Income Tax. It insures commercial banks. Imagine what happens when investment banks gain access to the bank accounts of every citizen who deposits what they have in a commercial bank, without the Glass-Steagall protections: failed investments, Ponzi schemes, and the use of that money to hide losses."

"Jekyll Island – same name as Robert Louis Stevenson's irresponsible scientist. I love it," Hamish said wryly. "So…anyone who puts most of their money in a bank could lose it to irresponsible, greedy banking practices that way? That's the perfect crime."

"Oh yeah, it's a monster, all right. Banksters and hedge fundsters immediately set about blurring the lines of Glass-Steagall via their highly-paid lobbyists. After sixty-six years, they finally managed it, and the economic collapse from the housing bubble and penny stock Ponzi schemes that ensued came in time to prevent us from earning a living in the several years after we got married. Remember that? No investors would take a chance on any of our ideas. Unknowns could just forget it."

Hamish sat back, stunned. "So that was it. It all traces back to Farmers like our prospective hosts. Wonderful." He stared off into space. "And now they are interested, now that your father got us going and we had some success. I don't trust them as far as I can throw them. We'll have to watch and listen carefully."

"Yes, we will. It will be a cautious, tense adventure to some extent, and we won't be able to talk completely without fear of being eavesdropped upon in our hotel room. It will be as much of a data-gathering expedition for us as it will be for them, and whatever they offer us – assuming that we come up with some great, useful idea to pitch – we will run by our attorney first. We don't owe anyone an instant, fawning, yes to any offer. Keep that in mind."

He smiled. "I will."

"Good. So…the next question is, what family shall we bring with us? We must reply."

Hamish looked back at the invitation. "Who did you have in mind, your parents?"

"No. They will be overseeing the renovation anyway. I want to have the plans all set, and the renovation taking place while we're away. That way, both Grandmère's room and Claire and Fabian's will get adjacent bathrooms installed while we're away, which will be very efficient. They are the people who will live here long-term, and having a shared bathroom for six out of eleven people is a recipe for chaos, so I want another bathroom off their room also."

"So who do you want to take with us, Claire and Fabian?"

"Yes. What do you think? Can Blackout handle four of us on a retreat, plus watch the rest of the family at home?"

"Definitely," and Hamish smiled as he said so. "I don't know if you realize it, but Aaron and Ed are only the most visible of the agents who tail us and look out for us. There are others watching, and enough of them for each family member. You and Claire and Fabian may be meeting another one on this trip, though," he added. "Aaron and Ed can't watch all four of us on their own."

"Interesting, though not surprising," I commented. "Let's tell Claire and Fabian."

"Can they come with us?"

"Oh yes. They'll have a fascinating time, and they really ought to see this ecological catastrophe. Florida looks like a reef around a sunken marsh here and there, and the rest of it looks like *Waterworld* just off the part that is still a recognizable bit of Miami."

"I'll have to pitch an invention," Hamish said.

"Something to clean up the oceans would be good," I said.

"Oh yeah…you suggested one a while ago…" he trailed off, thinking.

"I'm going to tell Claire and Fabian. They've been studying like crazy, and when they haven't been doing that, they've been panicking about getting accepted to the same law school, wondering whether or not they ought to go one at a time just to stay together. I can't say that I blame them, but they deserve a break."

Hamish grinned. "You and I were lucky that way – both in graduate school already when we met, in the same city."

"Indeed." I went out of the kitchen and into the porch.

Claire and Fabian looked up from their books.

"What are you reading?" I asked.

Claire said. "*Brave New World*. I like dystopian novels. It has similarities to the world we live in – this New World Order Underwater, as I keep thinking of it. I used it for my application essay, the one that had to be about a book."

"Cool. What about you, Fabian? Is that *Nineteen Eighty-Four*?" I grinned.

"Yeah. It seemed like a good one to write about for a personal statement."

"Who wrote in this genre first – science fiction?" Claire asked.

"Voltaire did," I said. "He wrote *Micromégas*, a short story about giant aliens who came to Earth on a survey trip, just to see what was here. The title character's feet were so big that he couldn't even see the humans aboard a wooden sailing ship. His foot sank right into the ocean, and his smaller friend had to show him the little ship full of philosophers. Then he laughed at them for overestimating their own significance in the universe. It was pretty good."

Fabian grinned. "You would know that. Sounds like a story about Farmers being ridiculed."

"Which brings me to my reason for coming in here to see you two," I said.

Two pairs of eyes turned to look at me.

I grinned. "Congratulations! You two are invited to come with me and Hamish on an all-expenses paid corporate retreat to underwater Miami, Florida! We shall stay at the luxurious Fontainebleau Hotel, hobnob with Farmers, and see the ecological catastrophe that is underwater Florida, up close and firsthand." I deliberately tried to sound like a game show hostess.

They gaped at me for a moment, stunned. Then Fabian spoke. "When is this? And why us?"

"It is for three weeks, from November 20th to December 10th. We'll go a couple of days early to Manhattan, and come home a couple of days after the corporate jets bring us all back. They've reserved four of them to take us there and back again. This is a chance for you both to learn through personal experience about the ecological upheavals that our planet has undergone."

Claire and Fabian looked excited now. "Thank you!" They said in unison.

"By the way," I said, "did you write anything about that in your personal statements, anything about what you saw when we went to Switzerland? We saw a lot of things on that trip that you could write about – not the Cull, but dykes, the canals and waterways of Manhattan, and so on. I'm just curious."

Claire said, "Yes."

Fabian said, "Yes."

I nodded. "Cool. So – are you coming with us on this trip?"

Fabian laughed. "Yes, they do. Thank you. I accept your offer."

"Me too," Claire said.

Fabian smiled. "So you want us to have a learning experience before we attend law school."

"That, and to be out of my parents' way while they supervise this big renovation. You too – hmm…homonym here: you two – are also getting a new bathroom, and it should be completed when we all return."

"What!" Fabian said. "You shouldn't go to all that trouble for us."

"No, you shouldn't," Claire said.

"Oh yes, we should," I told them. "This is as much for the logistical functioning of this house and this family as it is for your convenience," I explained. "Think about it. There are now eleven of us here. Even after Aunt Zoe, Uncle Charlie, Edgar, and Jacques move out to another house – and we don't know when that will be – it will still be crowded if we ever have overnight guests again, and count on it, sooner or later we will. There are cousins from France who could come, or Fiona and William could come. We need more bathrooms."

They looked at each other as if just realizing that. "I see," Fabian said.

"Okay then, and thank you," Claire insisted upon saying. "It will be nice to have our own bathroom to share privately. Meanwhile," she said to Fabian, "your parents and brothers will like it better with less competition for the bathroom that already exists."

"Exactly," I said. "It's a nice, big one, and I'm glad my parents had it redone several years ago, but it's not enough anymore. This house will be much more comfortable after that. Grandmère is already excited to have her own bathroom, all to herself. But she wouldn't really have it to herself if people need to pee and that one other one is constantly in use."

They nodded.

"That's settled then. Come and have a break. I made cookies."

"Avril," Claire asked, "what book did you choose for your essay, when you applied?"

"*I, Robot*," I replied. "I liked the idea of science fiction becoming science fact, and looking at all of the consequences of that."

A little while later, Claire came and found me at my computer with another question.

I could tell something was on her mind. "What's the matter?"

"I'm worried that I will mess things up for you on this retreat," she told me.

"How so?" I asked.

"With some Aspie social awkwardness," she replied. "I'll offend someone, somehow."

I laughed. "Oh, don't worry. Hamish and I are both sharp, definite Aspies ourselves. We can mess things up without any assistance from you."

Claire did a double-take, then burst out laughing.

"See?" I grinned. "It's time you learned this about life as an Aspie. Hiding it is fantasy. You can't conceal it. We have definite opinions and likes and dislikes. We don't like what most people like. We like things that don't interest most people. Our opinions about the world and what matters diverge from theirs also. That is what disconnects us from them, enabling us to think, focus, create, innovate, and invent. People are going to dislike us for all of those reasons. We might as well count on that, accept it, and stop caring about it."

"So we are inevitably going to offend someone every so often?"

"Exactly! Might as well get used to the idea and stop caring about that."

"Huh…okay. That sounds kind of liberating, in a way."

"It is."

"But I still care about other people."

"So do I. I don't want horrible things to happen to good people. I intend to go through life making an effort to be polite and not to offend them merely for the sake of offending them. But if they find me to be intrinsically offensive, I will resent that, and will not change for them. That's all I mean by all this."

Claire smiled. "That is a great philosophy of life."

"It's also good for a lawyer. We must not fear to offend, to be different, or to fight…with words. This is the life we have been dealt by the way our brains are wired up. We should embrace that and enjoy it."

"I'm going to tell Fabian all this. He worries about me in social situations."

"Tell him all this. Definitely tell him all this. He must understand you. He will."

"Thanks. Thank you for all of it – this vacation will be different from Switzerland."

"It will, in that a Cull is not going on, but bear in mind that these are quite probably the Farmers who perpetrated it. We are going to watch them carefully, to listen and observe. If we can do anything about them, we will…sometime after this trip, after gathering the necessary damning data."

She nodded, looking grave.

I changed the subject. "On that note, have a look at these swatches of cloth. The curtains and bedding in your room is too old, and that space is yours now for the foreseeable future. We'll change it all."

Claire gave me another shocked look. "Oh no…please don't do all that…"

"Okay then…you do it."

She did a slight double-take, realizing that this change was inevitable, and a fun one. "Okay." She grinned and chose a pretty floral pattern with pink roses, blue delphinium, and pale purple lilacs on green with dragonflies, bees, butterflies, and ladybugs. "This is fun. I'll come back to a whole new room. Maybe I won't tell Fabian about this detail. Let him be surprised by it."

We laughed.

With that, she went to talk to Fabian. He was nice to worry, but he shouldn't try to edit her.

Later, Hamish and I thought of something to add, something that needed to be said to both of them. "It is crucial that you not let on what you are thinking at any time, neither by word nor by facial expression. This is one area where Claire and Hamish and I may have the advantage," I cautioned Fabian.

"How so?" he asked.

"We Aspies have a natural tendency to keep our facial expressions neutral and not to gesture much, plus we are educated Aspies, which gives us a background in cultures, both our own and foreign ones. Even more useful, when we do show any facial expressions, it isn't done the way that neurotypicals express themselves, which means that reading us is difficult for those who know us and nearly impossible for those who don't. It's you who have to control your facial expressions on this trip. Not saying what you're thinking will be the easy part."

"Point taken," Fabian said, nodding thoughtfully.

"Once we don't have to be so covert and careful, however, you can go back to having an edge over us, though," Hamish said to him with a grin and a wink.

Fabian laughed.

We Aspies were guaranteed to come across as sharp and even oblivious to social niceties.

I knew it, Hamish knew it, and now we needed to teach that to both cousins.

Life was going to do it in the cruelest way if we didn't make the effort.

It would still do that, but it wouldn't hurt nearly as much if Claire and Fabian knew what to expect in advance. Claire showed plenty of promise about not letting the majority model of normal human – neurotypicals – bully us, a minority model of normal human – Aspies.

Fabian had chosen her as his wife knowing something about Asperger's, and that she was an Aspie, and now he had to become comfortable with that and proud of her. He was well on his way to that, but the idea of sitting back and saying nothing to back Claire up, while not helping to teach him just how cool our ability to walk, often unnoticed, on the perimeter while taking in details that most people routinely missed, was unconscionable.

Why not share and speed up the process of becoming comfortable?

Life was short, even with Regenics in the mix.

Sure, it extended our healthy lives, giving us more time, but it didn't cover the unknowns.

You never knew when an accident or other event might shorten your life.

That was why living it to the fullest counted for so much.

We were going to have fun while we could – as much as we could – and do what we could.

The presidential election came, and we were reminded of the shortness of life again.

We had studied the issues, checked what the candidates promised to do, listened to their stances on various things such as natural security, finance, and population – all related issues – and the choice had seemed obvious.

The two-party system was alive and well, despite perennial misgivings about it.

We had a female candidate who saw and accepted the clear link and interdependence of those issues, and a male candidate who did not. He wanted to end the population policy and build up the numbers of humans again. He also wanted to mine and drill as much of whatever resource as any corporation wished, regardless of the environmental impact.

"Why worry about the impact with so few of us making it?" he had asked, rhetorically.

But the question did not seem rhetorical to voters.

The female candidate had been quick to point out that, however awful it was to have lost so many people in the plague (I still couldn't bear to hear that misnomer, which was the most forgiving word choice for the Cull I had yet heard!), it made no sense to squander the opportunity to embrace new energy sources and to not do our utmost to heal the planet.

Why add more toxins to the planet when our invasive species had at last engineered viable alternatives to fossil fuels and nuclear energy? It was wiser to use wind, solar, hydroelectric fuel, and any other clean energy source, and to recycle all of the plastic we could recapture.

I voted for the female candidate. My family all said that they did the same except for Uncle Charlie, who almost didn't vote. He didn't like change, however good or good-intentioned it might be.

"People who don't vote are not to be taken seriously when they complain about their politicians," I said. "I'm sure there's something wrong with all of them, but not opting for anyone is giving up on one's duty to at least try to affect the outcome."

Uncle Charlie went out and voted…for the guy who promoted big business interests.

The female candidate must have convinced most of Americans, because she won.

She seemed like she would do.

Our new president was about to turn sixty, and she was married to a professor of international law and diplomacy. She herself had been an attorney before going into politics. They were from New York, and they had one daughter who was studying for a graduate degree in environmental economics. We would have a First Husband who would commute to the White House for events, but the party planning would be handled by a staff member.

The president would wear brightly colored pants suits with her brooch collection, which had been commented upon as a recurring human-interest sidebar by the press during the election. The brooches represented various extinct or endangered species of plants and animals.

Chapter 9

A Ride on a Luxury Corporate Jet

Aaron and Ed came with us. They packed extremely light.

We packed a bit more, bringing plenty of books to read. As we had done so, I had warned Claire that we were likely to interact with some very spoiled, entitled people.

"Some of the first signs will likely be the ridiculous luggage they bring," Claire had agreed. "It will be high-end, brand-name, and there will be way more of it than necessary per person."

I gave her a rather impressed and pleased smile. "Yes! I don't like those over-the-top, expensive-just-to-be-expensive brands." We were packing wheeled suitcases with collapsible handles. Mine was made of rough, durable, flexible, pink cloth. I had a similar one of navy-blue cloth for Hamish. There were no-name brands, and I liked them that way.

Claire had a pastel blue one like mine, and a black one for Fabian. We were packing for our husbands. "The perks of being married, for a guy," she remarked. "I hope we are remembering everything that they will need."

"If not, they have no right to complain. I will make Hamish look at everything before we go. We can make up the difference in the hotel shops," I said. "I used to panic and hyperventilate over travel, see a white haze in front of me, and carry too much stuff. I'm sick of doing that, of living like that."

"Huh. Me too…on both counts," she told me. "I would get anxious each time a school break ended and we had to go back to college. I like your method. I'll make Fabian review this bag."

"That's life and anxiety as an Aspie," I said. "It gets better with age, plus answering life's questions helps, such as 'who will I spend my life with' and 'what will I do with my life'."

Claire and I both laughed at that. It was true.

My mother came in and looked at what I was packing, asked if I needed any help putting it all together, and did the same for Claire. "She got me through some terrific, crushing bouts of travel anxiety," I told Claire, as she accepted my mother's efficient perusal of her and Fabian's bags. "It helped a lot. My mother always knows what to take and how best to pack it."

And she did: my mother had brought in clear, plastic, zip-closure bags to hold small amounts of toiletries. Claire and I organized all four bags with these. We had sarongs and bathing suits, not that either of us liked to swim that much, even though we knew how to do it. We had evening clothes, casual and dressy sandals, evening wraps, sunglasses, summer linen pants and cute tops to go with them…and a lot less complicated clothing for our husbands.

"Men don't need much," my mother said with a wry smile.

We put our laptops into our carry-on bags, plus cell phones, and plenty of paperback books.

"I know digital is more compact," Claire said, "but I like to flip back and forth when I read."

"Me too," I said.

Fabian and Hamish were made to stand over their bags and watch as we each showed them what we had packed for them, which they did reluctantly and with limited interest. When it was over, they thanked us nicely, though. "That's the least you could do," we told them. They grinned and thanked us again.

We left for Manhattan a couple of days early, and my mother said not to worry about the renovation of Grandmère's rooms. "It's not my first remodeling project, don't forget," my mother said. I could tell that she was looking forward to this. "We'll have it all done when you get back," she promised. "If not, if something delays it, we'll cope."

Manhattan seemed somehow less intimidating this time. I guess we were used to the idea of its canals and waterways and new granite footbridges. Hamish wanted to check on the Regenics clinic at Rockefeller University, to make sure that all was in perfect order, to see Dr. Nurse, and to go over some details for the new clinic in Miami.

Claire and Fabian came with us to see it all. "It looks a lot like the one in Lausanne," Fabian said. "Yes," Claire added, "It's just as pretty, and the people running it seem pleasant and competent." It was. It was decorated in warm pastel tones of rose and lavender.

What stood out most to us all was that this was the first time that we had seen it fully up and running while also conveying a sense of dull, routine existence in it. People were used to working there now. It had been working for just over a year. The patients still seemed to be only the most wealthy, privileged people, I noticed. When would other people be able to access this?!

Hamish told us the answer to that was we walked away, followed by Aaron and Ed. "We're having some trouble with that, actually. It's about prices. I think that the prices are being kept artificially high to limit access to an elite few. This has got to be linked to the birth licensing policy. Each new birth must be paid for in advance with a death. If more people get to live longer, then others must wait if they want to be parents."

"Boo-hoo," Claire said. "If I had my parents still living, I would pump them full of Regenics, prospective parents be damned. So would anyone else who could. Do you mean to say that the option of living longer, healthier lives is still not open to everyone?"

"Yeah, is that what's going on?" Fabian asked.

"It seems so," Hamish said.

"Why?" Fabian pressed on. "Is this about getting expendable workers?"

"It must be," Hamish said. "Looks like we're still living in a dystopian world."

"Of course we are," I said. We were walking toward the Metropolitan Museum of Art. "If we don't like it, and it is obvious that we don't, we must observe everything we can about this disturbing new world order, and then see what we can do about it. This trip is about reconnaissance…and a bit about enjoyment."

"Yes," Hamish agreed. "Learn all that you can about everything and everyone around us, remember it, and we can talk about it when we get back. Remember, our rooms could be bugged, so don't speak freely. Just try to listen and observe it all, and have a good time. Relax. You deserve it – you both study constantly, and you worked hard all last year in Lausanne."

They smiled and thanked us, and we went into the museum to eat lunch and see some art.

The next morning, we got up, ate a pre-arranged breakfast that Claire and I had set up the night before, and headed out. "No, there will be no rushing about at a café and hoping we make it on time," I said to Hamish. Breakfast was quick and efficient: juice, coffee, croissants, done. A Blackout Security vehicle rolled up to our door shortly after we were all assembled and ready.

We got into the van and rode off, looking around at the cityscape as we went along. The dykes and higher water levels fascinated us. When we had left the city the previous year, it had been under cover of darkness and by helicopter. It had been a close escape: the next morning, a travel ban had gone into effect, and all pretense of freedom dropped in the United States.

The Cull had intensified, though under the guise of fighting its fictitious plague.

That was all over now. Travel by plane, boat, train, bus, you name it, was all back in play.

And the world looked different.

It had looked messier last year. There had been far more people using far more resources last year – riding in more vehicles, buying more clothing and electronics, eating more food – and now most of them were gone. The detritus of their lives was gone, too.

The air was already cleaner, but the damage done by emitting fossil fuels since the mid-nineteenth century was irreversible. It was late November, and it felt like a very warm summer day. We carried our jackets, and stared at the towering levy that held the Atlantic Ocean back from obliterating John F. Kennedy International Airport.

After a brief view of that, we were moving rapidly down the ramp and up to the entrance.

We flew out of JFK International Airport shortly after 11:30 a.m. with a full crew and thirty or so passengers of various ages, interests, and descriptions. It was a fancy corporate jet, and full of executives, hedge fundsters, and their families.

We all duly arrived by 11 a.m., as the invitation had indicated. Actually, I insisted on getting there by 10 a.m. so that we could find the right place to wait and sit with our bags and coffee, not worrying about running late and missing our flight. It was a good thing, too, because neither of us had ever flown on a corporate jet before, and we didn't know what to expect.

We went to the information desk and explained the invitation, and were told where we were supposed to go. Not only that, but our hosts sent two of those funny little airport golf carts to collect us and our luggage, and we rode through the terminal to our meeting point, feeling somewhat dazed as the world around us went through a subtle but noticeable social change.

That change was evidenced by the way we were treated: waited on, fawned over, smiled at, greeted, ferried about, and otherwise fussed over. Our reputation had preceded us, it seemed.

A short while later, we were in a private corporate lounge, by our departure gate. Staff walked around offering drinks: coffee, tea, bottled water, fruit juice…and cocktails. Our hosts had spared no expense, obviously. Claire and I looked at each other when we heard the offer of cocktails, having trouble with the idea of drinking anything with alcohol in the morning.

We accepted cups of Mocha Java coffee with milk. So did Hamish and Fabian.

Some of the people there looked familiar, and I realized that I had seen them at the fundraiser in Manhattan the year before for the Regenics clinic at the Rockefeller Institute. I went across to the floor-to-ceiling windows and stared out at the rather startling view. It faced south, where the massive levees held back the Atlantic Ocean. They looked like they were over two stories high. We were three stories up. It did no good to contemplate the situation too deeply. It was silly…feeling anxious while viewing the levees would not cause them to burst.

"What, no cappuccinos for you?" came a voice behind us.

We turned around to find Mr. Jefferson Pierce himself smiling congenially. Green, slitted eyes stared at us with a cool, appraising, steely smile. His hair was graying at the temples, and the rest was thick, dark brown. He was dressed in a green polo shirt, khaki pants, and a navy blue blazer, looking as though he had escaped from some prep school. "I'm kidding," he went on. "Have anything you want. Our planes will take off in another hour or so. People are still arriving and having their bags loaded on."

We introduced ourselves to him, and he looked Aaron and Ed up and down carefully. Both were dressed in their usual plain, nondescript, dark but casual clothing.

"Can we all ride on the same plane together?" Claire asked.

"Of course!" Mr. Pierce said. "We wouldn't dream of separating you. We want you to meet new people, but not lose each other." With another smile, he drifted off to welcome a couple with a young daughter who had just walked into the room.

We took our coffees and wandered over to a set of cushy lounge chairs. All we had with us now were our small carry-on bags with laptops, personal documents, and books. Hamish and Fabian sipped their coffee, and Fabian took out his cell phone and began surfing the Internet.

Claire and I wanted to people-watch. This trip promised to offer us chances to watch the sort of people we were not used to, which made us both nervous and fascinated. It was too interesting a prospect to bury our noses in any reading material right now.

Perhaps later, when we were on sensory overload and needed to escape, we would read.

A woman in snakeskin heels and a leather skirt with heavy makeup and huge, gaudy jewelry was going around to all of the women with packages, smiling as though she were doling out the greatest treats. Judging by the responses of the recipients, we thought it must be something nice…until our turn came.

"This is a gift to each of the ladies on this corporate retreat from Lizz Designs," she said, handing Claire and me each a large package. "I'm Lizz Evans," she added, though the name meant nothing to us. Few brand names did, though.

We smiled politely and took them, and then Claire opened hers. She let out a slight shriek, turned pale, and dropped the whole package. Fabian rushed over to her and took her coffee from her, which he set down on the table next to her. Hamish walked over and watched, curious.

Aaron and Ed looked askance at what was poking out of Claire's package, but it posed no threat to us, so they just stood nearby, watching to see what would happen next.

Suspicious of what was inside, and half expecting to see a corpse of some kind, I cautiously opened my package and looked in. Scales! I could feel my ears go back, and even though my hair was down long, my ears showed; my sunglasses were perched on my head, holding my hair back. Lizz Evans looked dismayed as I dumped the contents of the package onto the floor and stepped back to look at everything from a foot away.

If only I could have gotten farther away than that…

…but no. The stuff was now all around us, being oohed and aahed at by other women.

"It's a huge tote bag made of snakeskin," I said, "and another, slightly smaller one that appears to be made of some Jurassic creature." No way was I using these!

Claire had dumped her package out to reveal the same things. Each product was slightly unique, which meant that it was fabricated using real snakes and…what, alligators?

We looked up at Lizz, hoping for some sort of explanation.

She was looking back at us as if we were the most ridiculous philistines. We didn't care.

When no further explanation seemed to be forthcoming, I asked for one. "Umm…who are you, and what is this about? Could you please tell us something about these items? They appear to be made of dead snakes and Jurassic creatures."

"You haven't heard of me?" Lizz Evans looked scandalized.

I was starting to enjoy this. She must be some fashion-monger. I loathed fashion.

Now I smiled at her, not bothering to hide my amusement. "No. Do tell us about yourself."

"Okay, then. I started my own company a few years ago, when the icecaps melted and Florida went underwater. As you must know, that meant that Florida's alligators – and the crocodiles that lived at its southernmost points –fled north, but many couldn't make it that far. Perhaps you remember the Army shooting them as people drove out of the state?"

"How could we forget," I said. "Go on." I thought I knew where she was going with this.

"Well, I had anticipated this, and as I love all things reptilian in clothing and bags, I sent my team south to collect as many dead alligators and crocodiles as we could get our hands on."

"Very clever. Good business move," I congratulated her. I made no move to pick the bags up.

"Thank you. Also, the Burmese pythons and boa constrictors that people had released when they grew too big to keep as pets were available for the taking. My company found itself well supplied for the foreseeable future. It's called Lizz Designs."

Claire and I exchanged glances. "Interesting," she said. "But no thank you. I don't like reptiles. I like cloth…florals…no dead things." She looked freaked out, and actually shuddered. Fabian shoved the tote bags back into their package and handed it to Ms. Evans.

She took the bag, looking offended, but quickly recovered and said, "No problem."

I gave a brief laugh at that, put my stuff back into its bag, and said, "Sorry, but I feel the same way. I can't stand snakes, and don't really want a Jurassic bag either. It's bad to waste resources, so this ought to go to someone who is excited to have it." I handed the package back to her. "It really is a clever business plan you came up with, though, making fashions out of something that you like," I said, smiling politely, with emphasis on the word "you".

Lizz looked a bit taken aback. "Are you sure you don't want to take it for someone else back at home?" she asked.

"Yes – I can't have that stuff around. When I was in grade school, if I came across a *National Geographic* photograph of any snake, or some other publication with glossy, color photos of snakes, I would involuntarily slam the book or magazine shut. I'm calmer now, but still want nothing to do with reptiles."

"I see. Well then, I'll just have to take them back." She smiled tightly.

"It was very interesting to meet you," I said. "Congratulations on your business."

She looked mollified at that, and moved on.

The next woman to receive her packages gave us a simultaneously puzzled and disapproving look, and then proceeded to fuss and fawn over her new gifts.

Claire and I just looked exhausted by that encounter, sharing a long look of joint exasperation and relief at our escape from snakeskins. "I hate snakes," she said, leaning back in her chair.

I laughed. "Me too…"

Hamish was shaking with mirth, and so was Fabian. "Claire, now I know to never, ever buy you anything like that!" he told her.

"Thank you," she said, and sipped her latte.

Hamish said, "I already knew Avril wouldn't like that stuff. Ugh. I love your aesthetic sense," he said to me.

"What, florals?" I said with a grin. "They aren't always in fashion."

"That makes it even better," he said. "Fashion is just marketing, to induce people to buy more stuff."

"You took the words right out of my mouth," I said. "I hate fashion. I like what I like, and the damned fashion industry teases me by making it briefly, then making it super-hard to find ever after. Plus, I have to have pockets installed in every dress or skirt I buy, because the idiots who make them think that women don't need or want pockets! That's how we get locked out of cars and homes," I said bitterly, "by not having pockets. Not me – I shall have pockets, damn it!"

Claire looked up at me. "You have pockets installed in your clothes?"

"Yes," I said, looking and sounding quite righteous over it.

"I do that too," she said. "Not always, but often. I think I'll do it to all of them now."

"I'll just bet that if you have anything that needs pockets, some craftsperson on this trip can help you out with that," I said. "If we buy any clothes, I will make sure to have it done."

A quietly dressed and more subdued-looking woman approached us with another gift package. "Hi. I'm Annie. The Molech Group is giving away tote bags with eco-friendly themes. Perhaps you'll like these. They're made of recycled cloth and hemp, and they show a new map of the world."

"Thank you!" I said to her, taking the package. Claire did the same, with enthusiasm.

Just like Lizz's gift, there were two bags in each package. These bags were a different but palatable kind of scary: they showed what was now underwater with startling, NASA-imaging accuracy. They had beautiful blue-green maps, one hemisphere on each side. The other bags showed plants that produced many of our favorite but endangered beverages: coffee, tea, wine, beer, chocolate. There were words around each plant telling us where these plants had been growing, and how far away from the equator they were being moved to remain viable.

We looked them over quietly, and then sat back with our coffee to people-watch.

A little while later, we boarded the planes. I felt like a movie character, staring around at the luxurious interior. It had carpeting that smelled new, teak wood paneling, and palomino leather seats that swiveled and reclined. The seats were clustered in groups around the windows.

Among the passengers on this plane were corporate responsibility officers – an oxymoronic job title if there ever was one – plus corporate attorneys, and other contractors besides Hamish, who had been invited to discuss methods of removing plastic and chemicals from the oceans.

I had been reading and enjoying the ride with Hamish when I overheard a woman scolding someone. Looking up, I realized that it was a little girl. The woman was scolding her 10-year-old daughter for reading and showing no interest in the other six kids on the plane! Damn...I was the same way when I was a kid. I hadn't even realized that this girl was on the plane thanks to the fact that she was so quiet.

The mother looked like she had just stepped out of Bloomingdale's. She was about four months pregnant. I put my book down and chatted with them. Soon it became obvious that the mother was neurotypical, and the little girl was on the autism spectrum. The mother wanted the girl to act "normal". The girl couldn't and wouldn't, and she was distressed by this demand. It represented rejection of who she was, and she knew it.

After watching this nonsense from the cranky mother, I pointed out that the girl's intellectual abilities, which were obvious to anyone who looked at her reading material and games (language and science toys), were being interfered with by this demand. "It stresses her out and distracts her. Nothing is going to make her neurotypical – ever. And the word is not 'normal' but 'neurotypical' – we on the spectrum are normal. We're a minority model of a normal human."

The cranky woman looked at me irritably, but listened.

I told her that a neurotypicalist attitude would not empower her daughter for success, but instead only doom her to failure socially, professionally, and emotionally. "It is pointless."

"I suppose," she said, "but she's so antisocial that it just drives me crazy!"

"She's actually just asocial, and there's nothing inherently wrong with that." I couldn't keep quiet. I had to do what I could to help this kid by showing the mother what she was missing and not perceiving about her daughter.

"I thought you didn't like kids," the mother said.

"Usually, I don't," I admitted. "But I like the introspective, quiet, intelligent, and different ones. The neurotypical ones are often bullies who don't think. That's what I don't like. Granted, there are some lovely neurotypical kids who do think, and I have liked them, but as a rule, I am too asocial to have much interest in kids. It's only when I see a misunderstood kid that I can identify with that I engage…and then I want to help her, or him." I smiled as I said this.

She looked at me, and then at her daughter. The girl had just taken a drink of cranberry juice from the stewardess and thanked her without making eye contact. "Lucy!" she said, still sounding petulant and disgusted. "Why can't you remember to look at people?!"

"I did look at her, and I said 'thank you,' which I thought was the most important thing," she replied, looking unhappy, and harassed as well.

The mother looked back at me. "She remembers everything she reads or hears, but not that."

"Of course," I said. "We Aspies are not wired to remember 'that' – it's extraneous nonsense to us. We learn just enough social niceties to get by. Our focus is on our interests, which become our work later on. Having a brainstem that is not wired for all those distractions, which you value and we see as just so much nonsense, is how we focus intensely and become successful at whatever we do. If it weren't for that, we would not have computers, great novels, or many scientific discoveries that our species can't live without."

Lucy was listening. Now she spoke up. "That's why I tell you that I don't want a sibling, too," she said to her mother. "I don't want some annoying baby that you like better than me, that will make constant noise, or to help you take care of it. I want you to be satisfied with ME as I am, and like me. But no…you are trying to get someone else. You don't want me."

The mother was pregnant, and I could relate to the fact that the daughter didn't want a younger sibling. She was happy alone, with the peace and quiet, and books and adults. I listened to her make it quite clear that she would never change even one shitty diaper…or other diaper.

Her mother said, "Be quiet! I do want you. I just want you to get along with people."

The girl looked miserable. I didn't blame her. "I hope it's another Aspie," she said.

I found that I liked this kid more by the minute, probably because I felt empathy for her. I smiled. "You're a lot like me. There's nothing wrong with you. It's very nice to meet you."

She looked at me. "Thank you. I'm Lucy."

"Hi. I'm Avril." We smiled at each other, Lucy a bit warily, but I think her mood lifted.

The mother scowled. Then she said to her daughter, "You don't like anything – not football, not shopping, not babies – nothing. Just books." Then to me, "I can't understand where she gets it from."

I looked up Asperger's on WebMD and showed them the markers for the condition in childhood, adolescence, and adulthood. "Do you have any relatives like this?"

The woman found the link on her iPhone, looked through them, and then said, "Yeah…my uncle and my brother! They are just like this!"

"Well," I said. "There you have it, then."

"I wish she didn't," the mother sulked.

"Well, aren't you insulting, to both your daughter and to me. And did you know that many famous inventors and authors were Aspies? We are designed to stand out and be independent of what most people like, NOT fit in."

"I like fitting in. I wanted a daughter who would go shopping with me and enjoy it. Lucy won't wear most clothes. The color is wrong, the style is weird, there are no pockets, the fabric feels funny, and on and on and on. I wish I could have known when we were conceiving her, so that we could have edited her DNA for that."

This woman had now made herself eminently dislikeable. "*Gattaca* all the way for you, huh?" I quipped, with a flat, not-amused, smile on my face.

"What's *Gattaca*?" she asked.

"It's a movie – dystopian science fiction. Babies born in it either have their DNA edited before going in utero or they don't, but it's those who do that get the cool careers and everything else in life, while those who don't get to scrub toilets and mop floors."

"Sounds about right. Too bad we can't control things for our kids, and give them the best chances. No gay kids, no disabled ones, and no…well, now this one doesn't seem so bad when I think about what else might have gone wrong."

"Yeah, reproduction is gambling with someone else's future," I replied. "With DNA editing, you neurotypicals can't be trusted not to edit us all out of existence and thus cripple our species, eviscerating humanity of its innovators. Nature just keeps on randomly making more of every type of human. There will still be more Aspies, gays, and whatever else. But good luck with the next human you are breeding. Perhaps you will get a high school and college quarterback who will then go on to be a Senator. Nature is like a box of chocolates: you never know what you're going to get…said the Aspie with the diabolical grin, paraphrasing *Forrest Gump*."

"You sound like Forrest Gump," the mother said.

I just gave her an evil grin.

After one quick glance around at the children on the plane, we realized that there were more than six other kids on the plane. There were even babies on it, born during the Cull! They had all been born to wealthy parents who had clearly had no difficulty in getting birth licenses.

The human tendency to continue increasing beyond available resources, i.e. food sufficient for all, was barely in check, despite Nae-Née. Malthus was right. A study would have to be carried out – and quickly – by independent ecological and demographical economists to determine just how many humans the Earth could now support. And then the Nae-Née policy would have to be adjusted to keep our species within that limit.

It was that, or another resource war, and more misery. That would mean some restrictions on personal liberties, but so be it. That would still be an improvement over humans killing each other to get whatever they needed. Would they stop, or would they covertly murder each other to make more openings for birth licenses, I wondered?

Even Malthus had seen this, and he had shown it when he was applying his skills as a preacher to the economics of the matter. He pointed out that one cannot have the good without the bad, nor appreciate virtue without knowing vice, nor comprehend benevolent deeds without experiencing or learning of evil ones.

After living through the Cull, I could certainly appreciate that, I thought to myself.

Hamish and Fabian had relocated themselves about fifteen minutes after takeoff. They were sitting with a group of men who were avoiding the noise of their kids, leaving them to their wives to deal with. Our Farmer hosts, I guessed to myself. Claire and I sat looking out the window for about a half hour, mesmerized by the changed shape of the East Coast.

"I still can't get the previous shape, the one that we grew up with and memorized on every school and book map throughout our educations, out of my mind," Claire remarked.

"Me neither," I agreed.

We were startled out of our reverie when a stewardess spoke to us, offering drinks.

"Would you like us to mix something for you in our blender?" she asked. She was a very elegant woman who smelled strongly of perfume (as if she had just walked through an army of scent-spraying department store employees) and artfully painted with cosmetics. Claire and I looked at her eye makeup with envy for a moment or two: she had pinks and mauves and purples shaded and faded to perfection. We were hopeless at doing that.

"Oh, yes please," Claire said, "as long as it is just fruit juice. No alcohol this early for me."

"Same here," I said. "I wish I could do my eye shadow as beautifully as yours."

The woman smiled and said "Thank you!" She took our requests, and left. We watched where she went. Her work station was a tiny kitchen near the control room, and we could hear the blender running. She came back about five minutes later. Fast! I couldn't have produced such a pretty and delicious drink so quickly. We smiled and thanked her.

Claire and I sat quietly with fancy juice bar concoctions, eating the fresh fruit on huge toothpicks first, listening. The chatter among the adult passengers revealed that they knew all about surveillance in Smart technology, and were savvy enough to avoid it or to pay to have it removed. No hackable cars, no self-driving cars, no entertainment systems that could be turned against them as listening and/or recording devices. The wives seemed to find this to be a nuisance, but the husbands had had this done to their phones.

And yet…they had every toy, including a drone for their kids to play with. One could buy them from various companies for a couple thousand dollars, and they did it. They spoiled their kids. Even the Aspergirl's parents did that. She had a laptop for playing STEM puzzle games.

As we sat there, looking around at everyone, taking in every detail, a man with loafers but no socks on who was wearing an ivory-hued linen pants suit and a bright blue silk shirt plopped himself down into Hamish's empty seat.

"Hello Avril," he said. "My name's Jackson Lionel Spades, but you can call me Jackson. Or Ace if you wish; people call me that because I tend to have one up my sleeve." With that, he grinned at me and gave a little laugh at his own joke. He spoke in a smooth, silver-tongued stream.

I never knew quite how to respond to such pomposity, and Claire gave me an amused smile. She looked as though she were squelching a laugh. I looked at Spades and said, "Well, I just met you, so I'll call you Jackson." I put my hand out, and he shook it with a smile. "This is my cousin-in-law, Claire."

"Charmed," he said, giving her a smile and a handshake. He sat back and sighed. "Pierce's had me running around nonstop this morning, greeting, meeting, and seating everyone." Suddenly he seemed like a tired host, pleasant and sincere. Like a switch had been flipped.

"Are you done with that yet?" I asked, smiling. "Can you relax at last?" It was kind of funny.

"Oh yeah. Now that we're underway, I can sit back and enjoy the ride for a while. Hey Katie—" he flagged down another stewardess, who was decked out in haute couture similar to the one who had brought our drinks, "bring me a Scotch and soda, would you?" He didn't even wait to see her acknowledgement of his order. He just turned back to us, smile re-plastered on.

"How are you enjoying the trip so far?" Without waiting for our replies, he continued, "You're going to love the Fontainebleau. It's been completed renovated and redecorated, and there are several new restaurants. I expect we'll be tired of it halfway through the retreat, but this is business."

Claire laughed. "That doesn't sound like something to get tired of in a mere three weeks."

Spades looked her up and down, still wearing his smile. "Right. Unlike most of us, you're not spoiled." He grinned and sipped his drink, which had arrived a moment ago. A kid ran by and he grabbed him, saying, "Slow down! Be careful – it isn't safe to run on a plane. It could lurch suddenly." With that, he waved at a stewardess and asked her to get the kid some fruit juice.

Claire looked intrigued. "I wouldn't say that. You just met me. My cousin here spoils me constantly. I'm very lucky to have her." She grinned. "You're nice."

My jaw dropped slightly for an instant, but I shut my mouth and smiled. "If we weren't airborne, I'd cross this space and hug you for that," I said.

As for Spades, he looked like he was at a loss for words. But not for long! He recovered and said, "I like kids, and so does my wife, but we don't want any. Drove my father nuts, but there it is. We're happy with each other." Switching topics, he glanced down and said, "Looks as though the two of you have brought a small library with you," peering into our bags. "And I saw you with the Lizz Designs. That was hilarious!"

Claire stared at him for a moment. "You try being surprised with snake bags!"

"Yeah!" I chimed in. "I hate fashion. It keeps changing for women. What a waste of resources! I want what I like, not what some self-appointed guru tells me to like, easily available at all times, and it had better be comfortable. Show me anything else and I won't so much as allow myself to be photographed while wearing it, let alone accept and wear it."

Spades gulped his drink with a start, then laughed. "Huh. Take that, Lizz," he muttered. "Actually, I think her designs are horrid." He grinned and got up with his drink, moving across the plane to chat up some other guests.

Claire and I laughed. "Well, he's not evil," she said to me quietly.

"No, he's not," I agreed, intrigued. Apparently, we were meeting a mix of personalities.

As we flew over Georgia, the pilot's voice came over the intercom. "Ladies and gentlemen, if you look out the windows now at the land below, you will see the effect of unchecked kudzu growth over the southeastern part of the United States."

That was all he said. But I knew what was happening to the other plant life in that region. Humans had not been removing it regularly, so it had been choking off all other plant life. It could grow as much as a foot in one day, completely covering and thus blocking all light to any other plants. No photosynthesis, no nutrients for those plants.

Kudzu was a vine from Southeast Asia that had been imported to the southeastern part of North America as a shade bush. It had beautiful purple-to-blue flowers that grew upwards to a tapering and arcing point. Here, it was a damned weed that had done its job all too well.

When the announcement was finished, our host stood up, picked up the intercom from the wall, and spoke into it. "The reason why we just had the pilot show you that is that one of our latest initiatives involves using kudzu and other weeds as biofuel. Cars and trucks can run on electricity in cities and towns, but out farther from built-up areas with complete infrastructures, we need alternatives. This one shows great potential, and we hope to develop it into a viable source within the next year or so."

Huh. We shall see, I thought to myself, staring down at the now-sunken, former coastline.

I was looking for Jekyll Island, Georgia, the birth of the Federal Reserve System.

After some searching, I saw the outline of it, and did a double-take. It wasn't underwater!

Then I laughed to myself. Of course it wasn't. Of course the Farmers would have funded the preservation of this resort island, with its golf course, huge conference center, and other one-percenter amenities. It was walled off from the ocean, in what looked like a colossal folly of expenditure, both of resources and human effort.

Well, that was that, I thought. Of course they treasured their secret meeting place.

I turned back to look at the people inside the jet and sipped my drink.

Everyone else had already gone back to their conversations, oblivious to the air tour.

There was one more announcement that counted as ecological education. It concerned the Turkey Point Nuclear Power Plant, which was actually well south of Miami. It was underwater, along with the original airport. We would be landing at a much smaller one that had been built on some land that was cleared of older, less-desirable high-rise apartment buildings, just north of the area where we would stay for the next three weeks.

The captain's voice suddenly announced this, and the following: "We are diverting our flightpath slightly south before landing to show you the site of the former Turkey Point Nuclear Power Plant, which was shut down by the U.S. Army Corps of Engineers and the Nuclear Regulatory Commission when sea levels rose several years ago. All nuclear materials were extracted and taken inland to safe sites for storage, and the plant was decommissioned. There is no threat of contamination from it now, but our hosts wanted to show you this before landing."

We all stopped whatever we were doing to peer out the windows at it.

To the northeast of the site, which had not been torn down (merely abandoned after all hazardous materials were removed), we could see two huge, round towers with slightly domed tops. To the west of them was another, smaller one, plus two more to the south of that one. All around it, submerged and just barely visible from above, were long, rectangular structures. It was a ghost complex of poison power, hopefully no longer a threat.

I could never understand what the appeal of nuclear power was. It had too great a risk of meltdown and leakage to seem worth the effort and expense of installation. All I could think of was the meltdown disasters at Three Mile Island, Chernobyl, and Fukushima, and wonder why anyone would continue to insist that using nuclear power was in any way wise.

Apparently, it took a worldwide flood of such stations to shut them down.

Humans could be such fools, I thought in disgust.

Beside me, Claire echoed my thoughts aloud.

I turned and looked at her, startled. "Are you a telepath?"

She looked at me the same way, and then we both burst out laughing, but only briefly.

Such thoughts weren't that difficult to anticipate.

As the plane was on its final approach, the captain's voice came over the public address system: "Just as a reminder, ladies and gentlemen, please be extremely careful not to have any contact with the water in Florida, other than that from the tap or in swimming pools, and do not drink from the tap. Pathogens, radiation, and other contaminants have been brought to this area by ocean currents. Thank you for flying with us, and enjoy your stay in Miami."

Chapter 10

Overhead View of Miami

We humans are an invasive species, I thought as the plane made its final approach.

The view of Florida from overhead was frightening; it showed the familiar outside, sunken.

We take for granted our assumed preeminence, using land, water, air, and any other resource we can acquire until it is either gone or utterly destroyed. Only then do we pause, but still we do not see our own similarity to locusts as we seek yet another commodity to feast upon with reckless abandon. All we ever seem to want is more, more, more…

Which is why, several years ago, the Nae-Née device that I imagined and my husband had made a reality become the population policy enforcement mechanism that the planet's governments agreed to use in order to check our insatiable predilections.

Still, the damage had already been done.

One example was that most of Florida, including the bulk of Miami, had been subsumed under the rising sea level. What remained was now a travesty of a tourist amusement park, a destination for scientists and vacationers alike.

When I had found out that we were headed there for a corporate "vacation", I had gone online once more to do some research on it. I wanted to get a sense of the area that we would visit, partly because the prospect of spending an extended period of time in a part of the planet that was now hostile to humans terrified me, and partly because I wanted to learn what I could about it prior to going there. In short, the usual reasons for research motivated me.

This was an ecosystem that showed in the most obvious and sinister of ways what humans had done to ruin it: Obvious in that it was flooded to the point of having put most of Miami underwater; Sinister in that there were other hidden dangers to be aware of.

The Earth was paying us back for our wasteful, selfish past.

Life is unfair, and Nature is indifferent.

At home, I no longer enjoyed drinking hot tea or coffee out of my global warming mug, the one that I had bought from the Unemployed Philosopher's Guild. The coastlines and sea changes that it depicted had become too real for anyone's taste. Better to wake up to coffee in my French farmers' market mug, or the I Love Cats one.

The sea levels were depressing just to contemplate, let alone prohibitively expensive to combat. Nations everywhere seemed to be putting up a heroic but probably futile resistance. The problem had become the Borg of our reality, and there was no stopping it, despite massive public works construction projects around the globe. Dykes, levies, walls, barriers of every kind that engineers could imagine were going up.

Paris was inundated with water, building dykes, and putting up with canals meanwhile. The Métro was ruined. On the mug, it was just gone, with nature having taken its simulated course. The coastline of northern France had nearly been shockingly reduced, receded to the department of Orne (France didn't have counties; it had departments), until a massive infrastructure project rescued part of it. Bordeaux was underwater, but work was being done to save it.

Giverny had almost been lost, along with Monet's gardens, and Paris was hastily surrounded by levies that leaked while more permanent structures were being built as rapidly as human labor and machinery would allow. I had been afraid to look at the area of Provence where my mother had grown up, fearing that it was inundated, until I read about the dam across Gibraltar.

The Netherlands was shielded by a fortress of half-mile-high dykes. The International Court of Justice and the International Criminal Court had both been hastily (though temporarily) reassembled in Geneva, Switzerland while the Dutch had built their new dykes. We hoped to visit that area soon, and I looked forward to seeing Bethany again…plus this new engineering endeavor. The World Courts were being moved back to The Hague now.

Many other places were simply gone, both on the mug and in reality, including much of Norway, a chunk of southern England, just about all of Ireland, and a small part of Scotland. A lot of Indonesia and Southeast Asia was lost, along with many South Pacific Island nations.

Ironically, thanks to the Gibraltar Dam, Cleopatra's Alexandria despite having been submerged and barely accessible except to scuba divers for millennia, was now easier to access. But Liberia had disappeared, and the coastlines of Nigeria, Togo, Benin, Ghana and the Ivory Coast had receded. Eastern Africa's coastline had receded by a hundred miles or so, as had western Madagascar. Somehow, vanilla farming continued.

Iran's coastline had shrunk, taking with it the oil fields of Abadan in the south. Pakistan and western India had lost a huge chunk of territory, and Bangladesh had at last succumbed to the inevitable. It was now a horrendously crowded, tiny, waterlogged nation, full of people who had rushed inland over a period of weeks. There had been a lot of outright murders by its militia as the crowds surged relentlessly forward out of desperate need to stay on what passed for land.

Singapore was gone, but that nation had been prepared with floating homes and engineers who were scuba diving and building dykes with water pumps. There was nowhere else to go, so that country's leaders were determined to reclaim their city-state with technology. People called it the Venice of Asia now.

Australia and New Zealand had suffered minor territory losses by comparison, but Australia had the unenviable condition of a large desert area over most of its territory, so it was struggling with the problem of smaller farmland areas.

Oddly, a few of the coral reefs of the planet seemed to be benefitting from all this. With higher water levels, some of them appeared to be recovering. But most were lost, dead from warming oceans. Marine biologists were having a fascinating time monitoring temperature levels around them, watching as the rate of die-offs slowed. Time would tell what effect on that ecosystem all of this change would have.

South Korea had shrunk, and China had lost a huge amount of its eastern coastline. Japan had gotten off rather easy by comparison, with only a slight shrinkage on its western coastlines. Northern Asia, including Russia, was nearly gone. The former Soviet republics, happy to have said good-bye to the Russians, were unhappily greeting them in huge numbers as people rushed away from a submerged St. Petersburg, while Moscow scrambled to build levies against the incoming and relentlessly forming peat.

In South America, Brazil had taken the biggest hit of all. At least they had gotten to host the Olympics first, journalists kept saying. The Amazon River had expanded and been renamed the Amazon bay. That wasn't all: the continent now had a Bay of Uruguay, which was an epitaph for that nation when it went entirely underwater. If only the sewage had been dealt with sooner...

And then there was North America. Florida was gone.

Most of Louisiana, much of Georgia, the Carolinas, Delaware, New Jersey, Cape Cod of Massachusetts, and of course Manhattan were underwater. Washington D.C. was just barely hanging on due to some hastily installed barriers. More were going up in cities elsewhere, similar to the ones built for New York City. But it no longer contained five boroughs. Staten Island – gone. Brooklyn – gone with Long Island. Somehow, the Cold Springs Harbor laboratories had been evacuated in time, all the way up to Cooperstown, New York, so now that town boasted more than baseball memories and a graduate program for museum curators.

Cuba was gone, too.

That hadn't been pretty. The U.S. Navy had hastily withdrawn its personnel and jihad prisoners from the base at Guantanamo and sailed away, leaving behind a humanitarian crisis of epic proportions. Hollywood was already hard at work on an equally epic series of movies about this, plus the other crises around the globe, with Hollywood itself relocated far inland.

When Cuba went under, so did Cuban communism, which may have been part of the reason why so little assistance was forthcoming from the U.S. government until it was too late. The government had said, in response to criticism about failing to come to its neighbor's aid, that it was busy trying to save and relocate the Cuban Americans – and many other Americans – whose habitat in Florida had disappeared.

It had been terrible to watch the reports, gathered by journalists via aircraft, of flotillas of Cuban, Jamaican, Haitian, Dominican and other refugees as they were forced to avoid people and pets in the water. Those with life jackets had a fighting chance, but many got attacked by sharks as they pleaded with people in boats to pull them aboard. Many other people – both in boats and in life-jackets – died from drinking saltwater, not realizing that it would kill them.

So many others simply drowned.

Central America was suddenly inundated with crocodiles that had fled the Caribbean Islands. It was an ecological disaster as pumas and Jurassic creatures battled for territory, competing with humans who, more than occasionally, got eaten in their sleep along with the big cats. Insects were another problem, and mosquito netting was in short supply.

Hawai'i was still there, though some of its territory on the coastline was gone. Waikiki Beach was no longer a vacation mecca because its hotels were no longer the coastline; instead, the coastline consisted of those hotels. Ni'ihau, the island that was populated almost entirely by indigenous Hawaiians, had lost the most territory, but it was still functioning as before. It was amazing to see which parts of the planet were affected most and which were affected least by rising sea levels.

That was another odd facet of the problem: sea levels did not rise evenly all over the planet.

Perhaps that was what made the job of the engineers easier as they prepared dykes and dams.

Regardless, the news that the public had seen had been horrific enough.

And that was without the secret Cull of the planet's human population.

Only those of us with nanobotic surveillance technology knew about that, in all of its monstrous detail, and ours was not sanctioned by any government. We had to conceal the fact that we knew what we knew.

The view of Miami from overhead was a scary enough one, and that was without knowing what dangers lurked and roiled in the waters that surrounded and covered most of it. Where once there had been a sprawling metropolis along the southeastern coast of Florida, now only a few small islands remained.

This included an airport, a few luxury hotels (one of which included The Fontainebleau, where we would stay on this trip), and little else. It was a small resort village now for indifferent one-percenters – those of the U.S. population who controlled an inordinately disproportionate amount of the nation's wealth, and thus its resources.

One could see the pinks, yellows, whites, and turquoise hues of the stucco veneers of its buildings, its old streets and the tips of its skyscrapers, and – if one felt like going on a longer boat adventure – the submerged mansions that had dotted the outskirts of the city.

Those were typically white with vermillion-hued, brick roofs, reminiscent of Spain.

They had been very attractive residences, often serving as locations for scenes in such television shows as *CSI: Miami* and *Magic City*.

Not anymore; now they were an elaborate aquarium for ocean life, such as it was.

Miami underwater remained, though it was expected to decay and crumble away soon.

As such, tours in glass-bottomed boats were part of the experience of visiting this resort.

Still, the lights were kept working by an ambitious tourism company, just to make things interesting on those boats, and perhaps to keep people from getting lost.

The company, Miami Underwater Tours, online at www.miamiunderwater.com, was backed by the hedge fund group that was sponsoring this trip, the Molech Group. With Disneyworld moved to central Georgia, they had had to come up with a new attraction, and the sunken landscape had readily presented this idea. The investors had immediately seized upon it as a viable ecotourism destination.

For now, only the wealthiest could afford to experience this, but that was expected to change.

I had my doubts. After all, *Jurassic Park* had done plenty to illustrate the point that just because one could do something, it didn't necessarily follow that one should do it. What were the risks? How could this possibly be safe?

A lot of money had been spent on this project. Glass enclosed each and every light, keeping the water out of the wiring and bulbs. Changing dead bulbs was just one perilous proposition.

That warning from the captain of the jet that had brought us to Miami was another.

In my online research, I had seen videographics of pollutants carried by ocean currents, and waves of them came through submerged Florida. They brought radiation, microbes, microbeads, algae blooms, and too-warm temperatures to Miami and its surrounding areas.

Hamish would see what he could dream up to mitigate this situation, but it seemed like both a Herculean and a Sisyphean task. After all, it was connected to the waters of the entire planet.

Of course, Hamish had proven before that he was not to be underestimated, so I waited.

Maybe I could help him along. I had before, after all.

Chapter 11

The Fontainebleau Hotel

I had been to Florida as a teenager with my parents, before the Sixth Mass Extinction.

That Florida had been a thriving ecosystem, far different from the one I called home back in New England. It was tropical, with moist, warm breezes, palm trees, small lizards hopping around, birds chirping, lush, green lawns, and vibrantly colored flowers.

The Florida I was looking at now was like an alien landscape…and seascape.

I didn't recognize the place, other than the famous outline of the Fontainebleau Hotel.

The ecosystem was silent, and nothing moved in it. Nothing alive flew, crawled, or hopped.

There were a few palm trees and patches of lush, green lawn, but they looked as though they had been freshly planted and installed. The overall effect was eerie. The water even smelled different. Instead of a pleasant whiff of seafoam in the distance, I smelled something sharp. Was that what ocean acidification smelled like?

I glanced at my family, and they too seemed to be smelling, seeing, and sensing it. Claire and I exchanged shocked glances. Hamish looked wide-eyed. Even Fabian looked unsettled. Granted, people with Asperger's feel as though every sense is on all of the time, which gives us a heightened, acute perception of our surroundings, one that feels intense and even alarming whenever we transition abruptly to a new place. But Fabian, the one neurotypical relative with us, the standard against which to measure our own reactions to this place, clearly perceived the change as well.

"Haven't you been to Florida in the past, Fabian?" I asked.

He looked at me, snapping out of his reverie. "Yes – we went to Disneyworld when I was 8."

"Claire, what about you?" I had to ask.

"We went when I was 10. This feels, smells, looks, and sounds shockingly different."

It certainly was.

Hamish had been to Florida on a conference several years before it flooded, so he nodded.

I had been to Disneyworld as a child, and then again as a teenager to see EPCOT and to practice my French in the international section adjacent to it. Also, my mother had brought us to a few other places around Florida when she attended some nursing conferences, so I remembered the former ecosystem well. Taking in this changed land- and seascape, I was already nostalgic for it, with all of its insects, Jurassic threats in ponds, and whatever else was now lost.

We were reminded once again, immediately upon being dropped off at our hotel, not to have any contact with any water other than tap or swimming pool water. This was announced in the bus that brought us there over the address system, with the warning to parents to emphasize this danger to children – repeatedly, if necessary.

Lucy, I noticed, had listened in silence and with rapt attention each time this was said.

Her parents noted that, tapping her to make eye contact, exchanging nods with her, smiling at her in approval, and then leaving it at that. Ah, the perks of having a kid on the autism spectrum, I thought to myself. Hamish noticed this too, and exchanged a grin of approval with me.

She paused as the guide talked about acidification of oceans, and asked, "What causes that?"

The guide looked stumped, so I said, "It's caused when carbon dioxide is absorbed into the water. It dissolves to form an acid. If enough of that happens, the balance is thrown off, and the life in the water can't adapt. That's ocean acidification, with species die-offs."

She listened with interest, and so did her parents. Then we all went inside.

The other kids on this trip were paying absolutely no attention to anything that did not amuse them, and their parents had to shake them, grip them by the upper arms, and bore this dangerous situation into their brains. If that actually worked, I would be very surprised. I hoped we wouldn't have any horrific tragedies on this trip.

As a history junkie, I was already loving this. The Fontainebleau Hotel had been designed by modernist architect Morris Lapidus and completed in 1954, and had hosted such movie productions as *Goldfinger* and *Scarface*.

Although it had originally been decorated to mimic the opulence of Versailles, its recent overhaul and update focused on ocean themes with clean, simple lines. Today, the hotel was spectacularly redone in hues of blue and seafoam green on white marble. The patterns in the fabrics depicted starfish, coral, and various tropical finfish in contrasting colors of reds, oranges, and yellows, plus darker green seaweed. It was beautiful.

The artwork that was hung all over the public areas of the hotel featured movie art from the 1950s, 1960s, and even the 2000s. It was all about the period pieces that had been set in Miami, complete with kissing couples frozen in time, dressed for starlit, starlet-attended parties.

There was a juice bar as part of its cocktail lounge, several gourmet restaurants, a poolside grill and bar, a café run by Chez Bon Bon, and room service. Fabian and Claire were enjoying a quick perusal of the juice bar offerings as we all stood in the lobby waiting for our room assignments, and I was starting to peer at the menu with them, when Hamish warned, "Don't drink too many of those. Smoothies break down fiber, which means too much sugar and less protection against cancer. They're fine as a treat once in a while, though."

Fabian looked up him, surprised. "But you have injected us all with Regenics," he said.

"That will only get you so far," Hamish replied. "You still have to eat a healthy diet. Regenics gives you a huge boost, but it's not a magic elixir. Nothing is protection against irresponsible, unhealthy eating habits. Think of the immortal elves in *Lord of the Rings*. They eat salads and other healthy things. They don't just rely on their genetic makeup."

Claire laughed. "You knew that, Fabian!"

"Yes, dear," he said.

While we waited for our room assignment, we continued to look around.

The swimming pool wound around the courtyard longer than any of the snakes that had been turned into Lizz Designs, a beautiful curve of blue set against a white background. Cabanas of rattan furniture arranged under small tents dotted the perimeter. There was a kiddie pool and a lap pool as well, with more seating around them. I realized that we would be expected to spend a significant amount of our time at these spots, and took a good look, calculating how much reading material I had, and how likely it would be that people would actually let me read it.

After about ten minutes of this, we were each given key cards and told that our room was actually a suite that included two large bedrooms with a full bath each, plus another, smaller room for our "guards" that had two double beds and a day bed." We got into the elevator and went up to the tenth floor.

Once we were alone in our suite with our Blackout shadows, Hamish let loose the nanite scanners, checking for surveillance devices of any kind. He found one in the living room, hidden behind a picture frame, in the lower left corner. It blended in with the design of the frame.

"I'll just make the reception go to static noises," he said. "All they'll get is crackling."

"Won't they just switch it out for another one when we leave the room?" Fabian asked.

"Probably," he said. "I'll leave this system in the wall right next to it, and have it seek out any others each time. These nanites move around on the walls, invisible to the naked eyes, and I watch them on my phone. It'll be entertaining to watch the Farmers go crazy trying to find the source of the interference with their…interference with our privacy."

"Fine way to treat a guest," Claire griped.

"Oh, we're not exactly guests," I told her. "We're business invitees, and this is a bit of corporate espionage at work. If they can steal our efforts and avoid paying for them, or at least anticipate them, they will. Any information at all is something. And remember – don't talk about this outside of our rooms."

She and Fabian nodded.

Hamish changed the subject. "The Ace of Spades enjoyed meeting you. He thought you were very forceful, definite, and unconcerned with appearances."

I laughed. "He's a caricature of himself."

"Which one was he?" Fabian asked.

"Jackson Lionel Spades," I told him. "The one whose voice has the most beautiful, insidious, and mellifluent tones of entitlement to it."

Everyone laughed. "Oh. Him," Fabian said.

We looked around the place, chose our rooms, and then went to balcony to look out.

Our suite faced the Atlantic Ocean, with no hint of the submerged state of Florida, which was behind us. "Is it possible to look out in the opposite direction from some viewing deck?" Claire asked. "I think it might be scary, but I'm too curious not to ask about it."

"It is possible," Fabian told her, and us. We were all listening. "The hotel anticipated people's curiosity, and designed a lounge on the roof for that, plus another elevator with a water fountain that runs from the lobby to the roof, and filters through an infinity pool up there."

Wow. We would definitely be going up there to take a look. In fact, we decided to eat dinner up there, away from any social obligations. We were just too tired from the activity, noise, excitement, and incessant interactions of the journey to seek out the rest of the group tonight.

The food was typical Florida fare: chicken gumbo soup, crab cakes, spicy curly fries, and key lime pie, and we wondered how the restaurant had gotten the ingredients. "Probably flown in," I said. The view was anything but normal: as the light faded, we stared in shock out at the submerged landscape – er, cityscape. Streets, broken skyscrapers, high-rise apartment and condominium complexes, and a distant shopping mall, many with parking garages, all showed just barely under the surface of the water.

We were relieved when the sun went down, until we got a shock: the street lights under the water still worked! They lit up all at once like an underwater Christmas tree, delineating the grid of the lost city as if by magic.

In the first few days spent on this luxurious working vacation, I listened to the people around me – all of them, of every age, background, and education attainment – with a view toward understanding what they were capable of doing and had done.

Why? I was looking for something.

We were among the Farmers of our species – a smattering of the elite, evil cabal of selfish, super-wealthy, banksters, hedge fundsters, and corporatists. The business elite who had invited us along on this trip, replete with agendas of their own, were among those who had perpetrated the Cull on the rest of the human species while protecting themselves from its effects. Their goal had been to survive what they had wrought so as to enjoy the spoils among themselves, plus whomever they deemed useful enough – to them – to be left alive.

And then there was us. We had foiled them to some extent by enabling people whom we had both chosen and simply been able to help. We strongly suspected that we had been targeted for death in the Cull, but had been successful in eluding and sidestepping it.

Now, here we were, apparently deemed useful to the Farmers after the fact.

I was determined to gain an understanding of who among the Farmers was actually guilty of perpetrating the Cull and who was merely a protected family member of a Farmer. The point of that was to know who would inherit each Farmer's little empire of money and influence, and thus continue that empire, and to see wasn't evil. One couldn't shut it all down, but it would be good to know who was merely shockingly lucky by birth and who was a monster.

That was not all.

If we were able to find all this out, and remove the monster Farmers from the equation, thus getting the ghosts of the Cull some measure of justice, history would not only reflect that, but the Farmers' heirs could be made useful to the rest of our species.

What I had in mind was exactly what was planned by the monster Farmers who had invited us on this trip: cleanup. The planet was filthy, contaminated, befouled, polluted…well, you get the general idea. Someone with money and influence – no, a whole of someones – would still be necessary in order to clean that up.

Ingenuity alone had never been sufficient to any massive undertaking, and we were all contemplating the mother of all undertakings. No one succeeds on their own. Hamish and I certainly knew that from our own success with Nae-Née. We had had help.

Therefore, the Farmers' heirs – any who were innocent of perpetrating the Cull – must help.

And this cleanup and remediation plan must be put in motion before rounding up the monster Farmers, because once that was done, the heirs would hate us. Family loyalties run deeper than ethics, and even if those heirs were sickened and horrified beyond acceptance of their progenitors, they would still not want anything to do with whoever rounded them up.

No…there was serious business of two kinds to see to.

At first, I had trouble reading while surreptitiously watching and listening to people.

Kids kept grabbing my bag and running off with it, which meant that I had to get up, chase the stupid toddlers, and snatch the bags back while ignoring their shrieks of protest. I did glare at their stupid parents for not preventing this as they looked up at me, startled.

It was fun for a moment to tell one mother, "You aren't watching your kid enough, or that wouldn't have happened. I shouldn't have to watch my bag while reading my books. That's your job." She looked outraged that she couldn't just zone out and chat with her friend, until some older people sitting nearby agreed with me out loud.

Tough.

But it was more than that. Kids who were old enough to talk coherently would walk up to me and ask me about my books, why I wasn't chatting about fashion like the other women present (strange children!), why I wasn't wearing similar clothing to theirs (where were these kids raised, I wondered, that they were impertinent enough to ask and that this seemed noteworthy to them?), and so on.

Claire came and sat with me and got those questions too, until one of the mothers withdrew her daughter and told them that they weren't being polite. Finally! Claire and I were in plain, Lands' End bathing suits, not Chanel or Yves

Saint Laurent ones, and we didn't care. What mattered was they were comfortable tankini-style suits – easy to wear.

We slathered on some sunscreen lotion, and took out books on ecosystems collapse, banksters, history, and complex novels that taught something while telling an engaging story. Why this would induce kids to come over and be puzzled that we did not have beat-up romance novels, fashion magazines, or some other dull thing, we did not know, but it happened.

Claire and I spent a day and a half like this until I had an idea. "Claire, please stay here and guard our stuff. I'm going back to our suite to get us something…something that may stop this nonsense." Aaron got up to follow me.

She looked up at me, one eyebrow raised, and said, "Okay. I'll be here."

I took off for our room, walking fast, passing our hosts and a bunch of other people, including a guy in a wheelchair who was having no trouble reading a pile of medical journals. Easy for him, I thought! Maybe he just looked unapproachable…or maybe I hadn't seen the kids bugging him for attention at the moment that they had. He looked oddly familiar.

Up the elevator, down the hall, key-card in the slot, in the door, over to the stack of books…and there it was! The pile of books I had brought on serial killers, history's megalomaniacs, banksters who had gotten caught (one was a good contrast between Charles Ponzi and Bernie Madoff), and a good one with gory images about Jack the Ripper.

I grabbed the lot of them, returned to the pool, and placed them on the table between my lounge chair and Claire's. When Ed saw what I had brought, he started laughing.

"Why did you bring so many more books down here?" she asked me.

"Look at them."

She did, and then got it. "What are they, kid repellents?"

"I sure hope so." I picked up the book I had been reading and opened it again.

It wasn't long before the same girl who had come over to criticize our reading material was back. She grabbed the book on Jack the Ripper off the top of the pile and started looking through it. Normally, I hated to have my books handled roughly, because I liked to keep them in as pristine condition as possible, but this was worth it.

"What is this?" she asked, her eyes wide. The girl was perhaps nine years old, and she had proven herself to be very emotional, very rude, and very nosy. She liked to play loud games with the other kids, running around with them, shrieking, and often, but not always, taking a leading role in the games. She did play well with others, we had noticed, but she was annoying.

"What is what?" I asked, looking up.

She thrust the book at me, open to a particularly gruesome photograph of Catherine Eddowes' face, which was all cut up by the damned Ripper.

"Oh. That's one of a serial killer's murder victims on the forensic pathologist's table. Jack the Ripper cut her corpse up. He did that to all of his victims."

"He was a murderer?"

"Yes. But don't worry. He lived over a century ago. He's won't kill anyone else."

She stared at me, still looking horrified, and put the book down. Then she ran over to her mother. The girl was pointing at me as she talked to her mother. I went back to reading, but glanced over at them. So did Claire. "Looks like she's telling on you now," Claire observed.

"Yeah, it does."

The mother came over to us. "What have you been showing my daughter?" she demanded.

"Showing her? Not a thing. Your daughter came over here not once, but twice, picked up my books without asking permission, and leafed through them. She also criticized my choice of reading material, and that of my cousin, as well as our attire." With that, I gazed back calmly at my interrogator.

The woman looked a bit taken aback at that. "I see."

I decided to be friendly and introduce myself, so I smiled in what I hoped was a pleasant manner and spoke again. "I'm Avril Châtelet, and this is my cousin, Claire Charbonneau. I'm a professor from the Rockefeller Institute, and she's a future law student. What's your name?"

The woman looked at bit surprised by this change of tone and subject. She was clad in one of those fashionable bathing suits with all of the right accessories, while I had old sunglasses perched on the top of my head (and I was sure that there were a couple of scratches on the earpieces), with a plain white linen lounge coat over my bathing suit. Claire's was similar, except that it depicted sand dollars. We were quite the unfashionable, didn't-give-a-damn, pair.

"I'm Angeline Travers," she replied. "I'm a wife and mother."

"Nice to meet you," I said, and I shook her hand. "So…what are you interested in, and what does your husband do?" I might as well ask, since I was bound to run into him at some meeting. Claire dragged another lounge chair over for her. Angeline sat down, looking out of her element.

Angeline glanced back at the place where she had been sitting, but her friend just glanced back, looking up from her magazine. They shrugged at each other. "We won't keep you from going back there. It just seems like we ought to chat more than we already have. We're all going to be here for three weeks, after all. Might as well introduce ourselves and talk a little," I said.

She looked completely nonplussed by my questions, while I was having fun…finally.

At last, she decided she had to come up with something. "I'm interested in reality TV, celebrity biographies, child nutrition, and my husband is a managing partner of a corporation."

"Really?" I said, intrigued. "What corporation?"

"It's called the Axis Plastics." She looked at me steadily, as if she really wanted to ask me something, but wasn't sure that it was a good idea, then decided to go for it anyway. "Aren't you the inventor of Nae-Née?"

"Co-inventor. I thought of the concept and the name, and my husband, Hamish MacDonall, who is a physician and a nanobotic engineer, made it a reality. The Orwellian use to which it was put, as a mechanism for social control, was not our idea. Yes, the Earth was grossly overpopulated, but I don't know who in the government thought of doing that."

Angeline was listening to this with rapt attention. I hoped she would remember all that, and not twist my words later to all of her friends, whom I suspected were other corporate wives who wanted babies. "I thought so. I had my kids before that happened. And I actually like the convenience of the device. It's nice not to have to worry about getting pregnant, or to have to worry about getting more birth control or running out of it."

I nodded and smiled, taking that in. "So…what biographies have you read recently?"

She looked uncertain, though I wasn't sure what about. "Nothing high-brow," she said, sounding almost apologetic. What did she think I expected, that everyone else on the planet read the sorts of things that I did?! Apparently…

"Well, what was it? I'm curious. I like meeting people who are interested in things that I would not gravitate toward on my own," I said, hoping to reassure her.

I guess that did the trick, because she breathed a bit easier and said, "I read one on James Gandolfini over the summer."

"Oh! I loved his movies, and he was fun to watch in *The Sopranos*," I told her.

Now she looked really surprised. "You did?"

I grinned. "Yeah, I did. I don't just read this academic stuff all of the time. I have some fun books," and here I pointed out the historical fiction and a science fiction book, "and I love movies and television. It's also fun to look up actors and actresses on Wikipedia and the Internet Movie Database, just to see what in their personal experience helped them to portray which character or historic figures, and how much research they did for the roles."

Angeline looked at me like I was a puzzle. I smiled. I was well used to that look at this point in my life, and I had always reveled in it. It was entertaining, and standing out was something that I had accepted as a normal way of life for me ever since I was a little girl.

She told me as much, so I told her that.

"Huh." She broke eye contact, which was a relief, because maintaining was starting to get a bit painful.

"I hope you realize that I don't expect everyone I meet to be much like me at all," I told her.

She smiled now. "That's a relief. I saw you over here with your books, and your cousin, and didn't know how to talk to you."

I laughed. "That's okay. I don't know how to talk to people sometimes, either. It's the human condition."

She laughed, and she sounded more relaxed now. I didn't trust her not to be rude to me later in a future social interaction, but we could interact well enough for the duration of the trip, which was all I wanted.

"Did the biography you read talk much about James Gandolfini's health, or did it just suddenly spring the death by heart attack on the reader with a shock? I mean, we knew how he died anyway, but some biographies milk the emotional suspense factor for all it's worth in the telling of the story." I was hoping to find out more about the book, and see if Angeline would relax some more.

"It did spring it on you somewhat." She paused to consider that. "Yes, it did. It helped that I already knew what happened to him, because it made me feel so sorry for his family."

I nodded. "So what are you reading now?"

"Nothing – just the magazines. I didn't want to carry a book with me, and I don't really like digital readers. I figured I would just relax and watch my kids."

"Kids?" I asked, looking around. "I saw your daughter. What other kids do you have?"

"I have Tilly, whom you saw, and she's nine, and a son who is twelve, Walton. He's around here somewhere, probably playing with water pistols with his friends. I told them not to shoot anyone who is reading, or to bother people."

I looked around the enormous expanse that was the pool area, which seemed to stretch well over an acre, and finally spotted a group of boys running around the potted palm trees far down the curving area, near the giant rock that was a water slide. "There they are," I said.

Angeline looked and said, "Yes – he's the one in the red-and-light-blue swimming trunks."

Walton looked a lot like his mother, with blond hair, light brown eyes, and a water pistol that would have vaporized a foe (or 20) if it had been a ray gun in a science fiction flick. It looked like one, anyway.

"Nice water pistol," I said, grinning.

His mother smiled.

Claire had been watching this exchange over her science fiction novel. It was *I, Robot* by Isaac Asimov, who was thought of as the father of science fiction. Odd…H.G. Wells had written in that genre before him, and Voltaire had done it first. Whatever…

Angeline now turned to Claire and asked, "What will you study in law school?"

Claire smiled and said, "Oh, the usual required courses like torts, criminal law, civil procedure, property, and then I can pick what I want after that. I'm interested in a lot of the things that my cousin studied: international and environmental law. She wrote her thesis on outer space law. I still have to figure out what I want mine to be on." Turning to me, she asked, "You went into law school knowing what you wanted to write your thesis on, didn't you?"

"Yes, I did. But don't worry. By the time the law school is up and running again, you'll have it figured out. And don't worry too much about getting permission for the topic: professors tend to prefer students who are genuinely enthused about a topic on their own, rather than students who just write about whatever they're told to write about."

Claire looked very happy about that.

Angeline stood up. "Well, it was nice talking to you. I guess we'll see each other soon at the next event that's planned. I think we have a nice dinner tonight in the main restaurant. Nice meeting you too, Claire," she said.

"Nice meeting you, Angeline," we both said, picking up our books again.

The quiet did not last long.

The kids had been looking at the ocean, and suddenly a collective shriek issued from them.

"What now?!" I said, putting my book down.

More shrieks, pointing, and generally anxious behavior from the kids caused me to get up, walk over to where they were standing, and take a look. A huge, nearly transparent, grayish mass floated on the waves, and it was getting closer. It wasn't moving, however, so it hardly posed a threat. Nevertheless, the kids continued to make an irritating and needless fuss.

"Whatever that is, it's dead. It's not going to bother anyone," I told them.

A group of unhappy little faces stared back at me, with screwed up expressions of horror.

Strange creatures; I had never worn such expressions on my face, nor had I panicked over the sight of a dead thing. I may have been disgusted by sights and smells – especially smells – but I would have been far more interested in knowing what I had encountered than in screaming.

I realized I was regarding them all with an impassive gaze, and that I was likely moments away from being scolded by one of their equally emotional mothers. How tedious. I turned and waved at one of the lounge waiters, who had just served drinks at a nearby table.

"Yes, ma'am? Can I help you?" he said, coming right over. He was in his late twenties, and wore a white polo shirt, shorts, knee-high socks and white sneakers, and a serious expression.

"Yes, please. Could go inside the hotel and find a Dr. Charlie Sabin? He's a cetologist – an expert in whales. He has sandy-blond hair, brown eyes, and is just under six feet tall. Sorry, I don't know where he might be; I just know he's among our group on this trip."

"Yes ma'am," the waiter said, and went inside.

Some of the mothers had appeared just in time to hear this request.

"Why did you ask him to bring that Dr. What's-His-Name?" asked one of them.

I turned to look at her. "Because I think that's a dead whale that the kids are screaming about, and he can explain it to them. If they understand exactly what it is and how it got that way, they are likely to calm down and not worry about it anymore," I told her.

"Sometimes it's better to just soothe and distract them," she said. "Tell them…"

"I'm not going to tell any kids any lies or made-up nonsense. You do that if you want, but I won't. Oh good – here he comes," I said, as the waiter reappeared with Dr. Sabin and pointed me out. I smiled politely as the scientist approached. Fabian was with him.

"Professor Chatelet! How nice to meet you," said Charlie Sabin, putting out his hand.

"It's nice to meet you too," I said, shaking it. "Call me Avril." I glanced over the wall into the ocean waters. Good; the dead gray mass had floated even closer. "The reason why I asked for you is that I know you are a cetologist, and this huge, gray, decaying something-or-other has floated close to the hotel. The kids all screamed their heads off when they saw it. I think it might be a dead whale, and was hoping that if you could explain this to us all, we would both learn something and be…calm."

"Okay, but only if you call me Charlie," he said.

I smiled and agreed to do that.

With that, Charlie Sabin stepped up to the wall, looked out, and said, "Yes, that's definitely a dead sperm whale. It likely died far out to sea and the currents have been bringing it closer and closer to land. When a whale dies, it usually sinks to the ocean floor. As whales decompose, sharks, other sea creatures, bacteria, and other microbes feast on their carcasses, eating everything under the skin, which floats away. This is nothing to be afraid of," he told the kids. "Death and decomposition are just normal ends to a long life. Whales can live over 100 years."

The kids looked fascinated as they listened with rapt attention. The mothers looked impressed. I was having a good time just hearing the most likely, reasonable explanation of what had happened.

Dr. Sabin joined me and my family for dinner that evening by the pool. He was a fascinating conversationalist, and we all had a good time plying him with questions.

"Could radiation and dead zones have any effect on the whales?" Claire asked him.

"They could," he said. "We're just starting to study how radiation affects them now. There are a lot of questions to be answered. But ocean acidification is what causes dead zones, and I can already tell you what effect that has on whales: their song is amplified over much great distances, typically up to 70 percent farther than in healthy zones. Plus, their hearing is affected in that they can hear everything in that range. It can be very confusing and distressing for them."

"Will that damage their hearing?" Fabian asked. "I know sonar blasts do that."

"It might, be we're more concerned about them getting separated from their pods, lost and confused, and dying that way. Whales are extremely intelligent, like humans are, and they could be despondent over the loss."

We all looked at each other, appalled.

The rest of the discussion was about efforts to clean the ocean of toxins and debris.

We exchanged e-mails and other contact data, and agreed to keep in touch.

A couple of evenings after that, after a nice dinner, there was a cocktail party.

Claire and I dressed in our flat, rubber-soled sandals and breezy dresses. I had my Hawaiian one, which depicted pink hibiscus blossoms on a pastel blue background. Claire's dress was all about seashells: conch shells, scallop shells, oyster shells. It was in pinks, blues, grays, blacks, ivory, and a little sand.

"You look beautiful!" Hamish and Fabian chorused at us as we came out to meet them. We had gotten them both ready first, and then booted them out while we primped. Guys were easy to prepare for a party – just hand them a pre-selected outfit, check that their hair was combed, and send them on their way. They both looked good in their cotton shirts and chinos. Their shoes were clean, new sneakers, plain, just as they ought to be.

We had gone down to dinner together, sat quietly at a table on the side of the room. It was a booth that curved around in a half-circle, which allowed us to people-watch during dinner. "I hope we don't get fat eating like this every day for three weeks," Claire said as she enjoyed a halibut steak in a citrus-butter sauce. "This is a predator fish. I shouldn't be eating it."

"We'll just have to get back to yoga when we get home," I told her, eating the same thing.

Our shadows sat at a table just off to our left, with a good view of the entire room.

We really weren't expecting to be attacked. This was a business trip, not a military op.

It was after dinner that we were expected to mingle and interact with people, and I was dreading it. What could we possibly talk about with people? Social interaction meant not discussing anything work-related, and that bored and frustrated me.

Well, I would just have to try it.

We moved on to the lounge and scoped out the room. On stage was a small troupe of acrobats in colorful costumes from, of all groups, Cirque du Soleil. Wow…the Molech Group had really spared no expense! People could either sit at tables or go up to the bar and hang out, leaning against it or sitting on one of its high, wooden stools.

Hamish and Fabian got a Scotch and a Belgian beer with an orange, respectively, and vanished into the crowded room, with Ed following them. I spotted them a moment later, chatting with Andrew Ellsworth, whose engineering company built water purification systems. Good – pick their brains until you see what sorts of problems the Farmers want to fund solutions to, I thought. No point chatting up other scientists until after our presentations; they would see it as a competition, and clam up.

Aaron followed us to the bar, where I ordered a raspberry margarita with about three-quarters of the usual amount of ice (those were difficult to drink when they were so cold!) and waited for it, watching the acrobats. He didn't order anything; he was on duty.

Claire got a glass of fresh-squeezed orange juice with peach schnapps in it. It smelled good. "I don't want to get too drunk," she said. "I've never been into heavy drinking."

"Neither have I," I said. "If it doesn't taste good – like raspberries or some other great fruit – I don't like it and can't drink it. I don't like Scotch, and that makes me feel just a bit guilty, because I'm married to a Scot. Hamish thinks that's hilarious – that I feel obligated to like Scotch."

"Me too," Claire said.

We settled onto some stools, insisted that Aaron take one, and watched the show. It was really good. "Maybe we ought to go see this group perform in Manhattan sometime," I said.

"You'd have to order tickets way in advance," Claire said.

"Not anymore," said a voice behind me. I turned and saw a man in a blue blazer and khakis sidling up to the bar. He had blond hair that was combed sharply back, greenish-yellow eyes with a reptilian aspect to them, and he ordered a whiskey sour before taking the stool next to mine. "I'm Rob Danforth," he said, holding his hand out to me.

I shook it and smiled, and introduced myself and Claire. Aaron had instructed me not to draw attention to him with introductions, so I omitted him, but Danforth's eyes coolly took him in also. The raspberry margarita was starting to make me feel very relaxed. Damn – I couldn't possibly keep drinking such things just because we were on a luxury retreat!

"Oh, I know who you are, Professor," he said. "You're famous. You're the genius inventor of Nae-Née and an author. And who did you say this lovely young lady is?" he asked, giving Claire a rather disturbing once-over from head to chest to hips to toes. She looked disturbed by it, too.

With a forced laugh, I said, "It's my husband who is the genius. I just tell him my science fiction fantasy, and he makes it real."

"Don't give me that, Avril – can I call you Avril? You get the creative process going."

"Yes, if I can call you Rob. Tell me what you do."

"I'm in gene-splicing. My company employs scientists to study DNA, take apart its strands, put them back together, and hopefully, someday, edit them. Perhaps you've heard of us: Tacttag. I'm the C.E.O."

"Oh yeah – I have. I guess you couldn't use 'Gattaca' after the movie was made, but I see: you wanted a name made up of only the first letters of DNA components." Claire looked at me questioningly, so I added, "Thymine, adenine, cytosine, thymine, thymine, adenine, guanine. Put them all together by first letter and you get the company name. 'Gattaca' was the same idea."

"Oh, right," she said, nodding in recognition. She smiled. "I'm learning science constantly, either by reading it or talking with you. It's fun." She sipped her drink and watched me with Danforth.

"So…" I was curious about his corporate motives. "What sorts of things would you want to edit out of DNA? Heredity illnesses, such as Huntington's disease, Addington's, Parkinson's, Tay-Sachs, multiple sclerosis, lupus, and so on?"

"Exactly," Danforth said. He had just been joined by another man in similar clothing. Did these guys have an unspoken uniform, I wondered? I was no fashion expert, but I knew what wealthy, old-guard American males wore, and I was seeing this getup at every formal occasion. It was almost funny, but I wasn't going to openly laugh at them about it.

He turned to his companion, and I worried momentarily that Claire and I were about to get hit on until I noticed wedding rings on each man. This guy had very short brown hair and blue-gray eyes. "Hi, I'm Bob Dillion," he said, and spelled it for me. "I'm the C.S.O. – Chief Science Officer, except it's for a corporation, not Starfleet," he joked.

I grinned and shook his hand. "Nice to meet you. This is my cousin-in-law, Claire Charbonneau." He shook her hand.

"You were asking about our corporate mission?" he said rather than asked. "It really is one of genetic empowerment. There are so many contaminants in the environment now, and in foods, that it seems prudent to help human reproduction along a little by removing potential damage before it strikes. We hope to eliminate all sorts of undesirable conditions with Tacttag's technologies, including the diseases you just mentioned and others, such as autism and other mental disabilities. Homosexuality, too, since those people have such a disadvantage in life."

I had been waiting for him to say that.

"Really?" I said in a low, menacing tone. The margarita was doing its job on me, and I was glad. I had drunk about two-thirds of it by now, and welcomed the loss of inhibition at this precise moment. "I have autism – it's Asperger's. So does my cousin, and so does my husband. It is not a disability. As for homosexuals, you sound like Nazis when you suggest that."

Danforth and Dillion looked a bit confused and uncomfortable. Good.

"Surely you have heard of Asperger's, the talkative form of autism?" I said, not really meaning it as a question, nor expecting an answer. "Mark Twain, the greatest American humorist had it. Jane Austen, who wrote the most perfect novels of all time, had it. Wolfgang Amadeus Mozart had it. Thomas Jefferson and Nikola Tesla were Aspies. Would you have what made them unique and able to give society and culture and science what they gave it edited out?"

Claire was looking at them steadily, daring them to say yes right along with me. Just say it, I thought, and we'll both make you regret you brought this up.

"Uh, no, but autism can be caused by vaccines and water impurities…"

"Is that what the pseudoscientists in your company's employ told you? Because if you pay someone who wants money but who doesn't care how they get it, they will tell you whatever you want to hear. What independent scientists have you listened to? Have you asked for any outside opinions? Can't you get some college professors who have no financial stake in the answer to give you some answers?"

The two exchanged awkward glances, but seemed at a loss for words.

"Most of your company's goals sound great, but not that one."

At last, Danforth found his voice. "I didn't mean to offend you, Avril, but a lot of parents want kids who are not on the autism spectrum."

Claire and I exchanged a collectively offended glance, then fixed our gazes on them again. "Well, too late, and too bad. You've offended us both. Parents ought to want people like us."

"You two don't seem autistic at all," Dillion commented, futilely backpedaling.

Now I gave a mirthless grin. "We get that a lot. That's because we were both raised with neurotypical mothers who taught us social skills. And we're female, so it Asperger's presents differently with us. That doesn't mean that eye contact isn't a bit painful to maintain. I tend to make eye contact when I finish making my point, at the end of a statement."

With that, I looked them both pointedly in the eye, and then looked at my drink for a moment. Then I was off again, on a roll. "It seems to me that 'a lot of parents' are lazy and selfish and therefore unfit to be parents if they only want a conventional, easy-to-raise, boring child. We are the quiet, introspective, obsessed-with-learning ones as children. We listen to warnings like the one about the water here. No one can tell us what to be fascinated by, either, which it why our innovations and creations are unique and memorable and useful."

"That may be true, but children with Asperger's have problems fitting in." Danforth said.

"As if that's all that life is about! We Aspies are designed to stand out, NOT fit in. Look at what people who are different have done for the world – Aspie or not. The price of getting those leaps forward is uniqueness. You ought to value it, not seek to erase it."

"Exactly!" Claire said. "Would you wish that Virginia Woolf, or Adam Smith, or any of history's other great writers had never produced what we have today? Isaac Newton was quite likely an Aspie. He was an irascible guy with very few friends, but it is his work that really matters to us all. I want to be like them – to leave something behind that will be memorable and useful to our species long after my life is over. That's what I dream of, not of fitting in."

"Have you two always prized fitting in no matter where you have gone in life?" I asked.

"Uh…" The two corporatists looked a bit sheepish. The effect was one of disingenuousness.

"And about homosexuals: did you know that the British destroyed Alan M. Turing, the father of the modern computer, the man who broke Enigma, the German coding machine, because he was gay? What a waste! He never fit in socially. He stood out. The jury is out on whether or not he was on the autism spectrum, but he was clearly different. Nature does not care what we want or one whit for our stupid human prejudices. It parks genius and innovation at random, and we must take it as we find it – where we find it – in whom we find it."

Dillion gave me a long, steady look. "Thank you for sharing your thoughts with us," he said.

Danforth exchanged glances with him, and then nodded at me. "We will definitely take what you have said under advisement. I think we could counsel parents in the future against trying to stop an Aspie from being born."

Dillion nodded to him. "Let's put that in our mission statement: that we will not splice out Asperger's or high-functioning autism." He turned to face me and Claire and said, "We'll write a new mission statement up tomorrow and find you. Please let us know what you think of it."

Claire and I looked at each other. This sounded promising, though we weren't going to get too terribly overjoyed by this fairy-tale promise just yet. "Okay," I said cautiously. "We'll see what you come up with."

"Yes, please – we would like Claire's input also." Danforth smiled at her.

"You should see all that Claire is capable of," I told them. "She is an amazing cake artist whose work tastes absolutely delectable, plus she's a voracious, intellectually curious reader, an excellent writer, and a prospective law student."

They both looked very impressed, with elaborately emotive facial expressions to convey that.

Claire and I smiled broad smiles when we saw their faces contort to communicate their understanding and appreciation of that information.

"Can we get you refills on your drinks?" Dillion asked, trying to relax the mood a bit.

Claire and I looked at each other, startled, and then into our now empty glasses. "Um…thanks," I said, "but one of these alcoholic treats is quite enough. Do you think this place would do what a juice bar does, and just skip the booze?"

Claire chimed in, "Yes – that would be great. Same flavor, no alcohol."

Dillion gave a flick of his chin at the bartender, who appeared in a flash and offered just that.

I ended up with a mix of freshly squeezed orange juice and crushed raspberries, and Claire had the same with crushed peaches in hers. "Thanks – this is delicious," she said, and I echoed that appreciation to the bartender, and smiled at our drinking buddies. They got refills of their alcoholic drinks.

We sat back and watched the rest of the acrobat show onstage.

After a few more minutes, the Farmers took their leave of us.

"Good – they're gone, damn them," I muttered, the sound no doubt lost in the loudness of the lounge. "You know why they want to edit us Aspies out of existence, don't you?" I asked Claire. "We aren't controllable, not by social cues, and not by that Common Core crap in the latest education curricula. We only accept and cooperate with those cues if we see some strategic value to complying. As for Common Core, we are too inquisitive to accept some truncated method of non-reasoning in mathematics. We need to see what's going on in each equation in order to fully understand it. No…we shall not study to be good little drones to serve the corporatist Farmers."

I was furious, and Claire saw it. "Sip your drink, Avril. You're right, but calm down."

The drink was delicious. I sipped it, and took a couple of deep breaths.

After double-checking that they were really gone, Aaron leaned over to us and said quietly, "That was awesome of you."

We both smiled at him. I said, "If they actually come back to us with a new mission statement that impresses us, I will faint." But I was enjoying myself nonetheless.

Claire grinned. "I just want to thank you again for inviting me. This is a fun trip."

Chapter 12

Fashion Victims

The "fun" was to continue a couple of evenings later at a party that was to be held in the grand ballroom by the pool – for adults only. Somehow, babysitters had been found to watch all of the corporate and Farmer kids. We adults were to report to the ballroom at eight o'clock for enough snacks to constitute dinner plus cocktails. We were also expected to be dressed up, and even more so than before.

Groan...Claire and I had unhappily set out on a dress shopping excursion the morning following the party in the lounge, wondering how we were going to find anything comfortable, either with pockets or that could have pockets built in by the next day, that we actually liked.

We dreaded it, but out we went into the sunshine to at least try to find something that we might be willing to wear. If we found something almost like that, we would have it altered, though we knew not where. "There must be a way," Claire said. "This is a place where over-the-top-wealthy one-percenters party, after all, so there must be something and someone around here who could help us if we hate everything the shops are selling."

I smiled wryly. "Sounds like you and I have had similar shopping experiences and frustrations with the fashion industry."

"I think so," she agreed. "I hate shopping for clothes. The stupid styles keep changing."

A mall had been built several blocks down from the Fontainebleau Hotel and across a footbridge, inland...or, what used to be inland. The hotel was actually on an atoll that had always been an atoll, and it and the land nearby just happened to be of a high enough elevation that they had remained above the water when sea levels rose. We skulked off to it, with Ed in tow. A new Blackout Security guy had joined us early this morning, a tall, thin, gray-haired guy named Lionel with steely, bemused, gray eyes.

The first shop we happened upon was full of customers who were pawing through racks of Lizz Designs. We did a U-turn when we realized what was in there, waving dismissively as the shopkeeper called out to us, and ignoring the efforts of some of the women who now knew us by name to induce us to stay for so much as another moment.

"No snakes for us, thanks!" I said, bolting from the place. "Damn...doesn't this little islet have any shops with dresses made out of cloth?!" I griped, walking away as fast as I could.

Claire was just as fast on her feet, no surprise since we had been confronted by more snakeskin – and close-up – than at the airport. "I don't know, but if not, I'm rebelling and wearing my shell-patterned dress again." She looked angry.

"I wish fashion weren't so changeable and important socially for us women," I griped.

"Me too."

"It feels better to bitch about it – a LOT – than to just look around."

"Indeed it does."

Ed was doing his best to keep his facial expression neutral. He didn't have such problems.

We walked around what proved to be an absurdly upscale mall, the kind that required one to go outside into the fresh air in order to leave one shop and enter another, trying to relax. Lionel followed us, bemused. "I've never met women who shop like you two do before," he said.

I turned around, glaring. "Well, now you have. Men get pockets in everything and the colors and styles don't change too much, which doesn't impose upon your time and attention much. Women get just the opposite, which sucks for those of us who hate change, like what we like and nothing else, don't want to look ridiculous, and insist upon being as comfortable and free to move, unrestricted by weird styles, as men are." Claire was looking just as ill-tempered at him.

He had stopped short, looking like we would bite if he so much as twitched, and was listening to us. "Okay. You'll get no argument from me. I'm just here to watch out for you while you…can't find what you need."

"Hmm…let's take a break," I said.

"There's a coffee shop," Claire said.

"Good. Let's sit there and drink cappuccinos and look at the map of the mall."

We did that. Ed and Lionel got coffees and sat with us, their eyes on the doors.

While we sat there, Jill DuFour, one of the women on the trip whose husband owned a company that manufactured genetically modified seeds, walked in. She was very chic, fitted in well with the others, and favored a strong, heavy scent. I was fairly certain that she was one of the people who had called out to us; she was carrying a Lizz Designs bag.

"Avril! Claire! Didn't you see us in the Lizz Designs store? I was trying to get you to come in!" she said, walking up to us.

"That was you?" I asked, keeping my tone rhetorical. "We definitely heard someone calling to us, but our hasty about-face departure was about putting some immediate distance between ourselves and those hideous, disturbing reptilian materials. We hate snakes, and it felt as though we had walked right into a nest of them. We're happy to talk to you here."

Jill looked taken aback. "Oh. I see." She paused. "But the snakes are dead. They won't bite you." She paused again. "I guess I shouldn't show you what I bought, then."

"No!" Claire said, rather emphatically. "No…no thank you," she said.

I shook my head also. "We can definitely handle the suspense until tomorrow evening. You're out shopping for tomorrow evening, aren't you?"

"Yes," Jill said. "And who is this with you?" she asked, eying Lionel.

"I'm Lionel," he said, smiling politely.

"Lionel is our private security guard," I told her. "And this is Ed," I said, introducing him.

"Oh! Of course," she said. "A famous inventor like you can't just walk around on your own. It wouldn't be safe. I have a shadow too," she said, as if having one put her in a club. "There he is," and she gestured to a guy in a tropical shirt who looked like he lifted weights in his spare time. The guy was perusing the shelves, trying and failing to look like some random shopper.

"Do you want to get a cappuccino and sit with us for a few minutes?" I asked.

"Okay," she said, and sat down, waving to the barista, who came over and took her order. "So…where will you two get your dresses, then?" she asked.

I sighed; so much for taking my mind off of this stupid errand. "We're still trying to figure that out. Do you happen to know where we could get something loose, comfortable, made of actual cloth, that either has pockets or could have them installed by tomorrow, and in pinks and floral patterns?"

Jill sipped her coffee and stared at us. "That's really specific. I don't know…it's all about what's in fashion now with stores, so you might have a hard time."

"We know," Claire said, sounding unhappy.

"We could be reading, but no…we have to waste our time on looking at ugly clothes that the fashion industry has decreed shall be the only things available, and expects and requires us to like, buy, and wear, whether we want to, or not," I said bitterly.

"Wow." Jill said. "You are definite."

Lionel smiled. "As I just found out when they left that snakeskin dress shop," he said.

Jill shot him a disapproving look. Evidently, her bodyguard never voiced an opinion.

I glanced around the small table, realizing that Jill, Claire, and I each had long hair that was held back with our sunglasses, and that we each wore comfortable blouses and casual pants, and carried handbags.

And I realized that that was where the similarities ended. Subtle differences set us apart.

Claire and I used no hairsprays or gels in our hair. We brushed our hair back, sort of parted on the side, and let it fall in waves to our shoulders. Our sunglasses were not the most expensive brand known to womankind; they were just basic black, and if someone had asked what designer or brand they were, we would have had to take them off and check. We wore linen pants with deep pockets, and cotton shirts. Mine was a very thin, white peasant-style with loose, three-quarter sleeves and a pink rose pattern. Claire's blouse was a lot like it, but with little embroidery – more roses, in white. My bag was a nice cloth one, black with pink florals. So was hers.

Jill was very different. Her hair looked dyed, ironed flat and stick-straight, and it was sharply parted in the middle. Her sunglasses were by Chanel, with its large, double-C logo on the sides. She carried a Hermes handbag. Her pants were tight – too tight for usable pockets – and her blouse was a snug, sleeveless one. She seemed comfortable in her outfit, but I wouldn't have been. What a difference the details made!

But who cared? She spoke in complete sentences, and she wasn't pushing us to just buy and wear something that we hated. She was looking at the map of the mall, and now she pointed out two different stores that sold dresses made of fabric rather than of dead creatures. Claire started to look a little happier, and I know I was feeling better, too.

"Why don't you try this place," Jill was saying, pointing at a shop that was around the bend from the coffee shop. "If they don't have pockets in the clothes, the hotel tailor could fix that for you. I'm told he's very good and very fast. I think Annabeth said that he's Italian, so you can't go wrong with him. Luca – that was his name. Yes, he's got to be Italian."

Claire and I exchanged glances, looking more upbeat. "Thank you!" we said.

"No problem." Jill smiled sweetly.

We picked up our spoons and scooped up the foamed milk that remained in our cups. "This shopping trip just might prove to be fun after all," I said, "and it might end soon, too," I added, smiling to myself.

Claire looked very happy when she heard that.

"Okay then. I hope you find something you like," Jill said, looking glad to have helped us. She took out her phone and paid her bill with it. "Well, I should be going now. Bella and Annabeth weren't finished yet when I left, so I said I would go back for them."

"Oh! Well, thank you very much for checking on us and helping us," I said.

Jill smiled nicely at us. "See you!" she said, giving a wave. "Can't wait to see what you find tomorrow night!" and she walked out of the shop.

Claire and I finished up, and I put a ten- and a five-dollar bill on the table under our saucers.

"Okay, we're going to give this another try," I said, and out we went. It was a beautiful, sunny day in what remained of Florida, and the breeze belied the ecological catastrophe that could be seen just beyond the shops. I figured I ought to at least try to enjoy being here.

Claire looked around and said, "Look at the way this mall is designed. There is a place to stand and look out at the ocean, but none for looking at where the rest of Florida used to be. Only the employees can see it from the backs of the stores, as they take out the garbage and lock up."

She was astute. "You'll do well as a law student and after that," I said.

She smiled.

We walked around the curve of the courtyard, past the water fountain and koi pool, past palm trees, and found the store we were looking for. Jill had directed us to a cute little boutique with lots of handmade, unique items called Evelyn Designs. Loose, flowing dresses with the potential for pockets to be added were in fact on offer.

Claire and I both relaxed. I could feel myself doing that, breathing easier and my mind turning happily to thoughts of lunch, reading, and escape to the pool with my books. Claire looked like a kid in a candy shop when she saw the color palette: pink, blue, lilac – pastels!

The woman whose shop it was lived in one of the few McMansions that hadn't been subsumed during the deluge that had swallowed up most of the state. Her husband owned this mall. She smiled when we walked in, got up, and introduced herself. "Hello! I'm Evelyn Ames. I make most of the dresses that I sell, and I design them all," she told us.

Evelyn was an elegant woman who looked to be in her fifties, chic but a natural beauty, with thick, wavy, graying hair loosely tied back from her face. She kept pushing little wisps of it out of her way. Her dress was a long, loose ivory-hued one with a coral pattern in various hues, complete with some tropical fish swimming around the shapes. To complete the ensemble, she wore a long, thin necklace of shells.

We chatted for a few minutes, and she told us all about how her husband had been quick to buy this acre of land when the condominium complex that was there got damaged in hurricane. He had razed the structure and built this one-store shopping center.

Interesting…it looked like it might actually be able to withstand high winds. "There are outer window covers that slide into place when we get a hurricane warning," Evelyn pointed out, watching my eyes go over the walls and general construction of the building rather than her dresses. She walked over to the window and pressed a button.

Claire and I watched as a huge panel slid out of the stucco exterior, across the window, and locked into place. The panel was the same color and material as the wall it protected. "Clever," I said. "It even looks nice."

"Thank you. John was very careful to hire an engineer who designed for the weather here. He designed the complex himself, though; he's an architect," she said proudly. "We have no basement, only a large storage area and sorting room in the back. There is also a nice rest room, if you need it. Every shop has one," she added.

"Really? That's impressive."

"Yes – we wanted customers to be able to count on them. It's better than a big public rest room," she told us.

"How long have you lived in this area?" I asked her.

"Oh, twenty or so years. We were among the lucky ones whose homes weren't washed away when the sea level rose. We still have our same house. It's a large, white, stucco one with terra cotta tiles on the roof."

Claire looked intrigued. "But didn't you have to leave for a while? Wasn't this area evacuated for a while?"

Evelyn looked serious at this subject change, "Well, yes, this whole area was evacuated. John had our house boarded up before it got too high, and yes, we did leave."

"Where did you go?" Claire asked her.

"We have friends whose luxury homes John has designed. They live all over the world. We stayed with people at a ranch in Montana for a few months, then another few in Colorado…" she was thinking back. "Let's see…where else…it wasn't bad for us, really, we were very, very lucky…we went to the new Hollywood studios for a couple of weeks, then to Maine for a summer. Lots of places. Our friends were very good to us."

"Interesting," I said. "You must have a lot of accommodating friends who like you a lot."

"We do. Some of them come to the Fontainebleau often now, so we see them still."

"What was it like when you finally came back here? And why did you want to live here after all that happened here?" I asked, curious. "We saw the news reports and videos that showed the area being evacuated by the Coast Guard, and it being overrun by alligators, crocodiles, and snakes. And we saw the U.S. Marines shooting them and hauling them away. It was incredible."

"Oh, it was," Evelyn said, shaking her head. "John wanted us to be far away from that before it got too chaotic. He anticipated all this. So did our friends, who insisted we get away quickly. When we came back here, there were still some reptiles around. John had a crew go in and clean out any that remained. Then we had to renovate our home a bit, due to some minor damage. We didn't come back until the Fontainebleau renovated, though. It was safer then, with some of our friends in charge of that. At last, we got to reciprocate for their wonderful hospitality."

So that was why this couple had been helped out so much, I thought to myself. Of course, they could actually be well-loved friends to those Farmers, but I saw an exchange of sorts in it. Still, being friends with a Farmer didn't make one a Farmer. She looked healthy; she had to have been inoculated with every last vaccine the slow, careful way, rather than with the Cull serum.

"And after all that happened, you and a few other people still wanted to live here?" I couldn't help wondering about it. "You didn't want to leave now that so few people live here permanently? I'm just trying to imagine how lonely and isolated I would feel, if most of my state sunk under the ocean and almost everyone else had had to move out."

Evelyn smiled at that. "Oh, we're not lonely. We travel and still see people, and the big danger is past. And there are plenty of people to keep us company most of the time. Our neighbors travel and then return to their homes, just like we do, so it's fine."

"I see. Well, thank you for accepting our nosy questions," I said to her. "We don't mean it as nosiness; we're just fascinated to learn how people coped with such a tremendous change."

"It's perfectly fine," Evelyn said, smiling sweetly. "To tell you the truth, it feels good to talk about it. Now, why don't you have a look around, and we can talk more if you want later."

With that, Claire and I smiled and turned our attention to the merchandise. It was all made of soft, natural fibers – silk and cotton. Clair and I couldn't help commenting happily about this to Evelyn, who said that she wouldn't work with anything else. We loved natural cloth. It was easy to take care of and comfortable. "That's exactly why I only work with natural materials," she told us with a smile.

We chose a few things each and went into the fitting rooms, with Evelyn available to look us over in each dress. In a few minutes, the deed was done: we had chosen two dresses, sans pockets, but with seams where pockets could be added.

Evelyn insisted upon adding the pockets herself. "Luca is very good, but I made these dresses." We didn't mind in the least. She had us demonstrate how deep we wanted the pockets first. "Oh – you have a pocket watch! How interesting. I see what you mean now," she said, observing that I kept keys and tissues in my pockets as well. Claire did the same. Evelyn asked us to put our hands out, traced a piece of fabric up past our wrists, and then took the dresses into her back room.

"You can come in if you want," she said. "Perhaps I ought to make all of my clothes with pockets from now on…"

"Oh…I wish every designer would do that," Claire said wistfully.

"Me too," I said. We chatted with her about the shock of walking into the Lizz Designs store, and our frustration with shopping in general.

"That's why I make dresses," Evelyn told us, laughing. "I don't like that high-end, trendy junk. Don't tell the other shopkeepers I said that," she concluded in a stage whisper with a conspiratorial smile.

We said we wouldn't.

After about twenty minutes, our dresses had lovely, soft, deep pockets. Evelyn refused to charge us extra for them, which sweetened the deal. "That's terrific!" I said. "They're perfect! I haven't enjoyed buying a dress in years, but I have today."

"I can't remember when I've liked something this much," Claire said. "Thank you!"

Evelyn beamed at us delightedly. "You two would have loved the clothes of the 1980s."

"I did!" I told her. She looked at me for a moment, startled. "You don't look old enough to remember that decade," she said, confused.

I smiled. "I'm in my forties. I was an 80s teenager. I loved the beautiful, loose, floral dresses and other clothes with pockets, and have bitterly resented their disappearance from the market ever since then," I said.

"You're lucky you were a teenager at that time," Claire said. "I couldn't even find any."

Evelyn was starting to put things to together. "You're Avril Châtelet!" she said.

"Yes, I am."

"It's nice to meet you," she said. "I'm so glad you like what I make! May I tell people about this? Would you be willing to write me a recommendation?"

"Definitely," I said. "Maybe it will encourage more designs like yours to inundate the market. No…I'm getting carried away with wishful thinking. I don't like what the proverbial group of 'most people' likes. But it's worth a try!" With that, I went to the computer and wrote on the Evelyn Designs website a review about why I loved her work. Claire did so too, and then she and I each took two of her business cards.

She was quite delighted, and smiled happily as we paid for our dresses. She wrapped them up in pink and blue tissue paper, put them into our shopping bags (we had each brought a large tote bag – stores no longer gave out one-use packaging materials), and walked with us to the door.

We waved good-bye, still smiling, and walked off toward the footbridge. It was shaded by palm trees that had been brought in fully grown, and pink granite flamingos graced either end of it. Lionel walked with us, offering his congratulations on the expedition. Ed lagged behind.

"Thank you," I said. "And best of all – we're done! You can get back to watching us at the hotel, where every vantage point has already been scoped out, studied, and logged, however it is that you do that. I hope we seem easy to watch this way."

He laughed. "There is less running around."

Claire burst out laughing. "Wait."

Lionel looked at her. "What for?"

"Wait for Avril to go exploring the ecosystem. Wait for us to find a museum."

"Oh. Yes, I know what I'm in for. I've heard about all that."

I laughed. "Oh course you have." I grinned at Claire. "He wouldn't have come here without knowing what to expect of us."

She smiled. "I do feel bad about you having us watched constantly by private security. It's a huge expense. I mean, I don't know what it costs, but I can guess that it's expensive."

I looked at her seriously. "It's worth every penny. We're famous inventors, and that's just the way it is. Private security must follow the whole family around for the rest of our lives. Some ransoming kidnapper would love to extort a mint of money from us, and they could kill the kidnappee if their faces are seen. So don't feel bad about being shadowed. We want you alive."

She stared. "Okay then. I can live with it." To Lionel, she said, "You Blackout guys are all very nice. It's fine going wherever we go with you. You never judge us for whatever opinions we have, or if we get upset about something and express that."

Lionel said, "Of course not! People get upset. That's life. You're fine, and we intend to keep you all that way." We had gotten back to the hotel in record time, and he suddenly glanced up at the building. "You two walk fast."

"Yeah…we like to get where we're going. A year in Switzerland, using our own two feet most of the time as transportation, will do that to you," I said. "However, I always liked to walk fast, all through school. Finishing it and sitting still, researching and writing is a bit too sedentary a life to be healthy."

The next evening, Claire and I were very happy in our new dresses. Our husbands thought we looked beautiful, and we could move and breathe in them. Even better, we each had another one for whatever other formal party came up next. "There's bound to be another – and we won't have to go shopping!" I said gleefully.

"Hurray for that!" Claire said.

Fabian and Hamish laughed. "You too are fun to be married to – not too much shopping," Fabian said. "One thing I expected to have to endure, not merely experience, when I got married was lengthy and tedious shopping trips. Guess not," he summed up.

"Aye – not with Avril, either. Though it is fun to bug her sometimes," Hamish added. "If it's not about clothing, Avril can get interested, and then I will whine, "Can we go?"

"Yeah…you do that sometimes. Usually it's in a shop with puzzles, knick-knacks, or other curiosities in it."

We checked ourselves over, combed our husbands' hair again (they had missed a couple of spots), and decided that we were ready to go. The guys were dressed in linen suits this time, with beautiful shirts in contrasting, solid colors: Hamish wore a navy blue one with a bright blue shirt, and Fabian wore a slightly lighter hue with a white shirt.

Claire's dress was long with a peasant blouse of a top, as was mine. We had chosen very similar styles, but the truth was that Evelyn didn't vary them a whole lot…and we didn't care! Claire's dress had a pattern of orange blossoms on pastel blue, complete with some fruit here and there. My dress was white with cacao blossoms, with some cacao pods worked in here and there.

Hamish and Fabian paused to ask what they were, so intrigued were they by the artistry.

"Wait until you see our other dresses from that shop," Claire said.

We got those out and laid them across the sofa. Why not? We were ready early, and this was fun. "That place is amazing," I said. "The woman designs both fabric patterns and dresses, and makes most of them herself. She even installed pockets for us on the spot."

"Nice, deep pockets," Claire said. She had a new pocket watch that Fabian had given her for her dress, and was very pleased. It was her birthday, and they had spent the day out together, eating lunch alone in a restaurant nearby. Aaron had followed them at a discreet distance.

The other dresses depicted an iris garden in pinks, blues, and lavenders with bees and dragonflies in them…and one hummingbird (mine), and a rose garden with pinks of several hues and honeybees flying over them (hers.) Both had ivory backgrounds.

"We have to go back there one more time," Claire told me.

"You read my mind," I said. "There's a dress with raspberries and honeybees that I want."

She smiled. "I saw that one and thought so. The berries look striking against the black."

"Which one do you want?"

"The almond tree one."

"Oh yeah…that was a great one – it showed almonds in various phases of growth, and blossoms on the trees, and butterflies." It was also against a sky blue background, with an edge of green grass around the hemline.

That was enough fun with dresses for now. We went to the party, where the food was delicious – like something out of a magazine to look at and a gastronomic fantasy to taste, complete with cocktails in every flavor.

Jill came up to us as we walked in, seeming to slither across the room to meet us.

I grinned, and Claire faced her calmly enough, trying not to look at her dress much.

"You found that store!" Jill said.

"Yes, and we can't thank you enough," I said. "We're going back for more – we loved it!"

"That woman is very nice, and talented," Claire told her. "She even installed pockets for us!"

"Really? Well, you two look beautiful. Don't mind the rest of us here. We're still caught up in the latest fashions, but to tell you the truth, I think I miss cloth. Next time, we're going to abandon Lizz." Jill leaned over to us, swirling her tiny straw in her drink, and whispered, "She's leaving tomorrow – she'll never know!"

Claire laughed out loud at that.

"You two are brave enough to tell her immediately that you won't wear her clothes," Jill said, sounding a bit wistful.

We looked at her, incredulous. "We are too freaked out by reptiles, and we're just stubborn."

"Well, good for you!" Jill said, and disappeared into the crowd…of walking snakes and Jurassic creatures, we noticed.

The guys had taken glasses of champagne while we chatted with Jill. Hamish nudged Fabian and said, sotto voce, "Aren't you glad not to be married to a snake or a crocodile?" Fabian snarfed his drink, swallowed the rest of his mouthful, and cracked up.

Our Blackout guys were having serious trouble maintaining neutral expressions.

We walked into the room, eating what the waitstaff offered, and worked our way up to the bar. On the way, we watched the women in the snakeskins greeting each other. "You look amaze!" one of them said. Claire started laughing and couldn't stop.

Fabian took her arm and said, grinning, "Wait, you haven't had a cocktail yet!"

"I don't need a drink to get silly in this room," she said. "This place is hilarious!"

Hamish and I laughed too, though not quite as deeply. Claire and Fabian knew that those outfits had been born of an ecological catastrophe, but there was comedy in this aspect of it. And yet, my mind wandered to the news clips of the U.S. Marines shooting snakes and Jurassic creatures as people fled the onslaught in their cars, SUVs, and on foot, screaming.

It was good that someone could see the comedy in this situation, years later.

The ballroom was predictably full of people who were dressed to the nines and milling about with drinks, mingling, hobnobbing, and otherwise schmoozing. It looked like we were in for a night of tedious social interactions relieved by the fun of eating gourmet goodies, which were being toted repeatedly across the room on trays and proffered by hotel waitstaff. At least there was that part to look forward to, I thought to myself.

With polite smiles affixed to our faces, the four of us entered the room.

Ed, Aaron, and Lionel followed, spreading out among us, watching.

I seriously doubted that anyone would try to poison us or otherwise injure us, but so be it. This was our chance to observe human behavior. Never mind that Aspies didn't see what neurotypicals saw, or understand it as they did. If it was really that important, we could always ask Fabian what he thought of something later. He had laughed when I had suggested that, but agreed to do his best to explain who knew what later on.

The music was soft jazz, reminiscent of New Orleans, another lovely city salvaged by the U.S. Army Corps of Engineers…but only the French Quarter and other historic, wealthier areas of it, of course. The other areas were both submerged and erased, with all traces of human settlement and development having been removed.

It was quite the opposite of Miami, I mused, ordering a strawberry daiquiri and admiring the pretty strawberry on a long toothpick before plucking it off and eating it. Miami had become submerged before the Cull, and the ecological and human disaster that had so publicly ensued had led to the decision to make what remained of it an underwater museum. It was to be a historical and environmental showcase of what had been, and how it was lost.

We were going to see that, our hosts had promised. I dreaded it, but was curious to see it.

Our group had broken up into four individuals silently wandering through the room with cocktails, eating gourmet food, listening to the jazz band, and people-watching. The music was very good, as was the smoked salmon, the avocado slices, and everything else.

Alistair Bosch, one of the Farmers who had organized this retreat, was enjoying himself. He was thin, with wavy silver hair, and the blasé demeanor of a man who took life's enjoyments for granted. I wondered what he was involved in – what kind of Farmer he was. I would find out soon enough, I told myself.

He was chatting with the Ace of Spades, the drunken Farmer who had plopped himself into the seat next to mine on the plane. Spades was a bit shorter, his hair looked like he kept it deliberately longish, preferring the look of someone who needed a trim – in contrast to Bosch, who had not a hair out of place, nor too long – and his clothes, though high-end, were just slightly loose on him. Spades seemed to like comfort and a touch of disarray as a matter of personal style.

Spades was, as usual, drunk already. He seemed to have a knack for staying perpetually buzzed without feeling ill. Hamish had told me that Spades was a Regenics client, and that he had warned him that Regenics would only repair some of the damage inflicted on his liver, but that the trade-off would be considerably less life-extension. Spades had just laughed and said, "You gotta die sometime, and as long as I can have fun until then, that's a trade-off I don't mind!" Well, good for him.

Spades wasn't making any effort to keep himself clean, though, and his wife was clearly irritated by that. She was wearing (no surprise there) a Lizz sheath dress, and her hair was a mane of honey brown, much like his, only about a foot longer. They were quite a pair to look at. She clearly cared about him, because she kept turning away from her friend to brush crumbs off of his shirt. Her name was Deanna, and he smiled at her every so often. She smiled back.

After a few minutes of this, Spades moved off to refill his martini, twirling its olive on a toothpick, moving carelessly across the room toward the bar. His glass was about three-quarters empty. I caught Claire's eye and she turned to see what I was amused by. She smiled, then stepped out of his way just he nearly dropped his olive but caught it.

I took a stuffed jalapeño pepper popper and looked away, watching what looked like a river of reptiles slithering through the room. Were Claire and I the only ones in florals? Probably.

"Avril!" I jumped, midway into biting into the pepper. It was Mel, one the wives who had liked the creepy snake dresses. She was wearing a green version of one, and I looked at it with detached interest. The strawberry daiquiri was working on me.

"Hi Mel," I said. "Are you having a good time?" I tried to smile pleasantly, and I guess I managed a passable effort.

"Yes, and you?" she looked my dress up and down. "No Lizz designs for you?"

I could tell that she didn't approve of my choice, which only entertained me. I grinned. "No. The hell with the fashion industry. It really has some nerve, telling me to like whatever it cranks out, buy it, and wear it, even those I don't and won't. I like what I bought across the walkway from the Lizz store. So tell me…does she tint those snakeskins different colors? I thought I saw a couple of red and blue reptile dresses."

For barely a second, Mel looked a bit offended, but then that mien disappeared without a trace. A smile plastered itself onto her face. "Yes, she does. This green is not the original color of the snake." She gestured at her dress like a runway model parading her wares.

"Is it comfortable?" I asked.

Mel looked startled. "Does that matter?"

"Yes, it does."

Looking me up and down like I was an alien who had just gotten off a U.F.O., she finally said, "Somewhat, but that is not what's most important."

"What is most important?" I wanted to know.

"Style, the latest fashion, and promoting the eco-friendly message of my husband's company." She turned and glanced across the room at one of the Farmers. She was married to one Livingston Carlisle, who had arranged a big meeting that Hamish was fretting over. He was still determined to have some great nanobotic blueprint to present, something aimed at cleaning up the oceans, rivers, and other waterways. I wasn't worried. We would think of something.

"An eco-friendly message in fashion?" I said, delighted. "So we are both dressed with that in mind. Your outfit sends a message that we must never forget depleted or endangered species, as does mine. I love beautiful plants and the insects that help them to grow, and my husband has designed nanobotic bees. Meanwhile, I keep top-bar beehives at home." I smiled at her.

Mel looked startled, and then she smiled again – genuinely this time.

She looked like the sort of person who enjoyed bullying people, leading cliques, and having a small crowd to run with. She also could see that I had been the girl who was apart from that bunch in high school and wherever else, and that I had not cared.

She saw me smiling at her, barely blinking as Aspies do (we did that a lot less – only to keep our eyes moist), and neither caring about fitting in nor meeting with her approval. She could see me appraising her, and was a little unnerved by it. The tables were turned…

I was there as an environmental consultant, not merely as a wife of one.

She took that in and gave me another smile. "So we are. Your dress is beautiful."

"Thank you."

The rest of the evening passed similarly, and I enjoyed the food and the fruity buzz of my drink, along with the buzz of conversation. It was good to stand out rather than to fit in, and it was fun – especially knowing that we were not fashion victims.

Chapter 13

An Accident…or Two

It happened when we were on a lazy, relaxing night tour of underwater, downtown, Miami, just as one would expect an accident to take place: without warning, while caught unawares.

There were twenty or so of us in a glass-bottomed boat, and it was evening.

The city lights were on – underwater. The effect was dramatic and beautifully backlit.

Also for dramatic effect, the theme music to an elegant crime show about a luxury hotel that was set in the late 1950s or early 1960s, *Magic City*, was being played as our guide pointed out submerged city landmarks.

Then, just as the tour moved out over the main strip of historic Miami, a young woman clad in a string bikini swam gracefully underwater, her long, lithe body undulating in the currents below us. She had been hired to do this, and we all got the dramatic point of it, having been shown the pilot episode of the show in the waiting area before we boarded the tour boat. To make a short story long, she was acting out the opening credits of the show.

Well, isn't that lovely, we all thought, until something seemed…off.

We knew she could breathe, because she wore a tiny oxygen mask. The little tanks were hidden under her hair, just behind her ears. Her hair was long and waved prettily out around her face as she moved.

No…she could breathe. It was something else that wasn't right with her.

Then we saw it, just as that girl did. She swiped at her leg as if to scratch an itch, and a huge piece of skin – and underlying tissue – came off as her nail scraped over her leg. The look of horror on her face matched those on ours in the boat.

The guide and the boat's pilot saw it too. The boat was stopped, and the girl was gingerly hauled aboard. Overhead lights were dim, but they provided plenty of illumination for her predicament. She was quite literally melting without losing her shape.

Hamish ordered everyone back, and pulled a pair of surgical gloves out of his cargo pants (which he insisted upon wearing almost everywhere). Suddenly I was glad he dressed like that! He touched the girl's forearm, and a dent appeared where he did so, probing with two fingers. He withdrew.

The girl could not speak, and looked up at me as she lay on the glass bottom of the boat, terrified. Claire reached out to her in sympathy and I gripped her hand, holding her back. "You'll just hurt her some more. All we can do is stay with her."

I turned to the girl and said, "We won't leave you."

It was all the comfort we could offer her.

She stared at me like she was clinging to me, and I forced myself to maintain eye contact and a facial expression that would not scare her. I even tried a vague smile, and may have pulled it off. The girl relaxed a bit from exhaustion a moment or two later, and her eyes closed.

Another moment passed, and she ceased to breathe.

I looked up at Hamish. "What just happened? It reminded me of those purple jellyfish off the coast of the Pacific Northwest, disintegrating. It looked like her body turned to gelatin from the outside in…sort of like those quack abortion potions that were sold, unlicensed, in the later nineteenth century, which did that to women's organs from the inside."

He looked back at me, expressionless, listening, and then said, "It's exactly like that."

Doctors tended to let shocked and horrified people talk a bit, but I was calming down a bit now, having said my piece. "What could have caused that? What is in the water below us? Radiation? Chemical contamination? Both? More horrible stuff?"

"Something like that." And he took out a small tube from one of his many pants pockets, unstoppered it, and scooped some of the water from over the side of the boat into it. He replaced the stopper and tucked it into his pocket before anything else could happen, and took off the gloves, pulling them inside out as he did so.

I glanced around. Everyone was too stunned to say anything, and I realized that their attention was back on the dead girl, Hamish's action with the water sample now forgotten.

There weren't many places at the hotel from which to easily take a sample of the ocean's waters in this area. I wondered what the tests on that sample would reveal. They couldn't be anything good, that was for sure.

The tour guide had switched the music off as the girl was dying, and the pilot was taking us back to the hotel. They both seemed to be in shock, and then I noticed the pilot.

He looked like he knew the girl. Was he her brother? He was crying silently. I nudged Hamish and nodded at the crying guy. Hamish did a double-take when it hit him. "I think he's her fiancé," he told me.

The boat pulled up to the Fontainebleau dock and we all moved back as a crew with a stretcher rushed forward to take the girl's body away. I saw the tour guide push the pilot to go with them, saying that he would moor the boat and take care of everything else.

We got out next, walking quietly back toward the pool, and then sat down.

We felt terrible, but also terrified. No wonder we had been told to swim in the hotel pool and nowhere else. I felt sorry for that girl and her fiancé. They were probably just trying to earn some money, and had gotten far more than they had bargained for.

The next day, I was sitting at the pool with a book when I got thirsty. Hamish was alternately sitting with me and chatting with people all around the pool, moving from group to group. I flagged down a passing waiter and asked, "Could you bring us some water?" He nodded, so I said, "Thanks," and looked at my book again.

I knew it wouldn't be tap water; Florida was a peninsula of limestone that had been fracked with acid injection to get at shale oil before sea level had covered the entire state. Any groundwater would be brackish and therefore undrinkable. Shale oil drillers had sworn that they would be careful, as they always did, and then they hadn't been. Consequently, all water that we drank on this trip was bottled. It was beyond a nuisance for the chefs and baristas; all cooking water had to be brought in daily. A special filtration system took care of the bathwater.

What I hadn't considered was my own personal security. The anonymity of eating out at a local restaurant in New York City or West Hartford, Connecticut was gone as long as we were here. A couple of minutes later, he came back, carrying two glasses of water on a tray. There were slices of orange floating in each glass among ice cubes, which made it look really enticing. I put my book down and sat up, smiling politely at him, and reached for one.

"Take that away!" Ed said, appearing at my elbow out of nowhere.

Aaron was just as quick to appear. "Yes. Bring out two glasses with unopened bottles of water. You like flat, not carbonated water, right?" I nodded, wondering what this was about.

The waiter paused, startled, and glanced around. A couple of tables away, Lucy's mother, who was about five months pregnant called over, "I'll take those – I like orange slices." He walked over to her table, put the glasses of water next to her, and went back inside.

I looked at Aaron and Ed, still wondering why the show of plastic bottles was necessary.

Ed spoke to me in a whisper. "You're famous, Avril, and so is Hamish. You'll just have to waste some plastic bottles every time you order anything from now on."

Aaron added, "Yeah, if you think it was bad before, it's even worse now that Hamish is ready with Regenics. The Farmers may want to get rid of you. You're both too clever to be left undisturbed."

"They're probably hoping that you don't have your affairs in order, so that your billions can escheat to the government – and them, ultimately, as many of them have connections to the Federal Reserve Board," Ed put in.

"I see," I whispered back. "The Federal Farmers would jigger things so that our money would get siphoned wherever and into whatever government projects they want. Uh-uh."

"Exactly," Aaron said. "I knew you'd catch on. You always do."

"We made our wills before we left on this trip," I told them with a grin. "No escheating."

They grinned at each other. "I knew she'd be a step ahead of them," Ed commented.

"Yeah, but you're even quicker on the draw. I don't want the wills to be necessary."

The waiter was back with our water. He had a plate of orange slices, two empty glasses, and two plastic bottles of Evian water – my favorite. He put everything down on the patio table next to me, one by one. "Should I open the bottles for you?" he asked.

"That's okay, I'll do it," I said. "Thank you." I smiled sweetly at him, then reached for a glass. He nodded and smiled, and I held out a five-dollar-bill as a tip. He pocketed it with a "thank you" and walked off.

I looked at Aaron – he was the foodie of the two bodyguards – and asked, "Can I have the orange slices, or is that dangerous?"

He held up the plate and sniffed, then said, "It's okay."

With that, I cracked open a bottle of water, poured it into a glass, and squeezed in some of an orange slice. I put the expended bit of fruit on the plate again, and had a sip. Finally! I had been getting thirsty. It was hot and humid here.

The woman who had taken the glasses of water sat up and drank the contents of one of them. She put the glass down, settled back onto her lounge chair, and picked up her magazine again.

I picked up my book again.

Aaron and Ed sat back down at the next pair of chairs, watching everyone. I glanced over at them and realized that they were just sitting there, not relaxing, and that they had not put their sunglasses back on, either. Odd; they usually sat back, feigning enjoyment of the sunshine while actually staying alert. This was different. They had dropped all pretense.

Hamish came back over to me and picked up the other bottle of water and an orange slice. "Thank you for this," he said, and upended the bottle into his mouth. He bit into the orange slice and sucked the juice out of the pulp.

"You're welcome. Our guardians made me get it like this – unopened."

Hamish grinned and raised his bottle of Evian to them in a toast, then took another sip.

Suddenly, I heard a strange gurgling-choke of a sound from the woman with the magazine.

She was flailing around, foaming at the mouth, her magazine sliding off of her lap. She smacked the air around her, and the remaining glass went smashing to the concrete, spilling water every which way.

Hamish rushed over to her, flipped her over, and yelled for an ambulance. Meanwhile, he gripped her from behind and pushed, attempting to use the Heimlich maneuver to empty her stomach. It would be too late, I knew.

Regardless, he kept working, unwilling to give up hope. Blood started coursing out from between her legs. A team of EMTs appeared, racing toward her with a stretcher. Hamish let them put her onto it, shouting orders at them. They nodded, followed a few of his instructions (what few could be acted upon away from an ambulance or, better yet, a hospital), and then raced off, wheeling the stretcher.

I walked over, stunned, and told Hamish what had happened a few minutes before his return.

He listened, grim-faced, and said, "Aaron and Ed just saved your life. That woman might not make it, and it's over for her pregnancy."

"They saved both of us. And yeah…I saw all that blood come out. She won't be pregnant for long. Where is her husband?"

Hamish glanced around. "I think he was in the gym, running on a treadmill. Someone will tell him what happened." Sure enough, we saw the husband through the glass, racing through the lobby, looking panicked. He just made it into the ambulance before the doors shut and it rushed off, siren blaring. Lucy stood inside by the glass doors, looking horrified. Mel and Spades appeared and took charge of her.

"The hospital is just a block away, right?" I asked.

"Aye – it has all of the bells and whistles, plus the Regenics clinic, a spa, a health club attached…and a forensics lab. The police department is across the street from it. Not that they'll necessarily be able to prove who did this."

"You never know. Can you find out what happens next, using your medical credentials?"

"I'll try."

"We ought to confirm our suspicions. I think that was tap water…meant for me to drink."

"Indeed." He had looked shaky from the uproar already, then horrified.

Aaron and Ed had come over to stand with us and listen to this exchange. They nodded.

After a long pause, I said, "This means that another opening for a birth license has come up."

"That's a definite motive," Ed said, "but likely not the only one."

I wondered about these so-called "accidents" some more. The population policy required a strict balance sheet of debits before credits now. That meant that until a death in one's area was recorded, no new birth licenses would be granted to any applicants, regardless of how wealthy they were or how mentally balanced they could convince an examiner that they were.

So…were these deaths really accidents, or were they murder? I was no detective, but this thought was no great leap of logic.

Since the Cull, the United Nations had created a World Population Bank Account, complete with a website with which to track its subject matter. One could visit it at www.un.populationaccount.org to see how many humans existed, where on the planet they lived, and even watch deaths and births being subtracted and then added.

No new deposit, i.e. birth, would be allowed unless and until a debit, i.e. death, occurred.

Every birth was now tracked and registered. There could be no mistake.

I didn't believe that – no system was ever perfect – but it seemed fairly airtight.

Hamish had designed each Nae-Née device to do one thing and one thing only: ensure that the woman in whom it resided did not gestate a new human being. It did not inform the Operator of her location. It was not to be a surveillance device beyond its original purpose.

He had even gone beyond that directive, not trusting the government, and made sure of that.

Jason had been happy to help him subvert any further Orwellian plans.

Now that I thought about that again, and the potential for murder that a Nae-Née device with a GPS signal would entail, I was relieved. Our paranoia and determination had not been quite that focused at the time that we had decided to do this. We had not thought of the device as a tracker for an assassin, or for a simple murder to make room for another birth license.

The effect was the same. We had done all we could to block that possibility.

Meanwhile, Lionel had done his own detective work. "It was definitely an attempt to kill Avril," he told us that evening, back in our suite. "Jason is still checking to see who did it, but the motive is just as Avril thought, which was to get both her death and an opening for a birth license. Looks like the opening was achieved anyway," he added.

Lucy's mother was going to live, but her pregnancy was over, just as Hamish had said.

The next day, I couldn't stop thinking about being in a huge hotel with a homicidal maniac.

I had to remind myself that I was likely there with many genocidal maniacs.

"No matter what you or any of your 'friends' have to say about this, unless and until your parents are dead and buried – and yes, we intend to be buried, not cremated – and unless and until you are not merely heirs but actually in control of our operations, tar sands will be churned up in Canada for fuel, fracking will continue in the Midwest, or whatever they're calling that region now, and in Pennsylvania, West Virginia, and anywhere else we can find it, and for-profit resource mining will continue to be the order of the day." The speaker sounded snippy.

There was a pause. "Remember this, Junior: we are in this to make money. This entire retreat is about making us look good, first and foremost. Anything after that that helps clean up the ecosystem happens only if it makes money, and by 'money' I mean a lot of it."

The voice that I heard as I came out of the stairwell and toward the hallway that led to our suite was annoyed, as if bothered by some misbehaving pet. It was also mellifluous and self-entitled: clearly, one of the Farmers who had organized this retreat was telling off his son.

Who could it be? I wasn't very good at processing sounds – not to the point of being readily able to recognize individual voices. It was a constant source of frustration to me, but there it was.

Aaron was right behind me. We had left the poolside because I had forgotten a book, and I was just intending to get it and return to sit with Claire. We had only taken the stairs because I felt the need for some exercise, and climbing stairs was a good way to get some.

Cautiously, I crept out of the stairwell, making no noise as I moved the door aside. I hoped I hadn't clicked the door handle too loudly as I opened it, but it seemed not; the speaker and his son were still in the hallway.

Their backs were turned to us as they stuck their key cards into the slot of their suite door.

They were still bickering. The son sounded resentful and like he disagreed with theft.

Several of the Farmers on this trip had brought their college-age and older children with them, and this was one such family. I wasn't very good with discerning ages from looking at people, either, another frustration. For an Aspie who lived for information, not being able to get it just be observing people was maddening. And this was spying. No future in covert ops for me!

As Aaron and I approached the suite door, I had just about given up on knowing who these people were when they glanced up at us. I smiled one of those polite, social nicety smiles at them and stuck my key card into our door's slot. They smiled and nodded back.

Aaron nudged me, prodding me to get in quick, keeping his expression professional and neutral; bodyguards were expected not to smile at the people that their clients mingled with.

We went into the suite and I shut the door behind us. Aaron looked grim, but he wasn't glaring at me. Was that because he wouldn't scold a client, or because of what he had seen?

"Who was that, Aaron?" I said.

He looked at me. "Oil barons. Well, one of them and his son. He Culled off the residents of farms in Pennsylvania and Canada so that fracking and tar sands could be mined. Apparently, his son doesn't approve. The son doesn't know the half of it."

"Huh. Good to hear that the next generation isn't evil, I guess." And I guessed that I would have to comb through all of our stash of footage and other data that our nanobotic spy swarms had gathered last year. It was time to memorize who was who.

Although…not knowing that yet, while we were on this trip, likely served another purpose.

It was safer to be able to look at the Farmers with ignorance of their crimes as long as we were face to face with them. It wouldn't do to stare at them, wide-eyed with horror and disgust, while we were essentially in their clutches.

There would be plenty of time to fully understand who and what they were later on.

Later on came sooner than I thought it would.

That evening, dinner was on the rooftop lounge. At least it wasn't littered with background noise from some loud form of entertainment. People milled around, sampling gourmet goodies on trays and sipping cocktails until we all sat down.

We found ourselves at a long table facing the ocean…and the Farmer that Aaron and I had seen in the hall earlier. Next to him was another. They didn't seem too interested in us at first, just impressed that we had Aaron and Ed guarding us. The Farmers all had security people following them around, though none were quite so obvious as ours. (Hamish had assured me that they were not from Blackout Security. Good.)

A few minutes after we had all sat down together, the men across from us paused in their banter to introduce themselves to us. "You must be Avril and Hamish, the famous Nae-Née inventors!" This was the ominous oil baron. When we nodded and smiled, he continued, "And who do you have with you?" He looked between us. Claire was next to me; Hamish and I flanked her and Fabian.

I made the introductions. "And you are?"

"Darren Winkle," he said, smiling. "Perhaps you've heard of Shale-Hale Corp.? That's us."

"Oh – yes, I have," I replied. "Nice to meet you."

He introduced his wife, Lenore, and son, Derek, who nodded and smiled, then turned back to talk to the people sitting closer to them. I didn't care; it would have been too much effort to try to hear whatever they were saying diagonally across the table.

I looked at the other Farmer, who promptly introduced himself. "Hi! I'm Anthony Bane."

"Hello. It's nice to meet you, too," I said. "What do you do?"

"I'm in weapons manufacturing and transportation. My company designs and makes most of the military's weaponry and equipment, plus it devises systems for moving it around rapidly."

Like mobile crematoria, MRAPs, and assault rifles, I thought to myself.

Claire had turned to look at him, wide-eyed with shock.

I hastily smiled and said, "So you're like Tony Stark. Cool!"

Bane grinned delightedly, and Winkle elbowed him playfully. "We make a great team," he said, laughing. These two Farmers were certainly insufferably pleased with themselves. "We power the entire military-industrial complex."

I smiled and glanced at Claire, and saw that Aaron had gripped the back of her dress and tugged ever so slightly. She broke her gaze to glance up at him. He was smiling kindly at her, as if to say, 'Wait. They won't be happy like this forever.' That just made me determined to come up with a way to make that a reality. I didn't yet know how I would do that, but it had to happen.

Fabian grabbed her hand under the table and squeezed it.

The bread arrived, and Claire recovered enough to focus on taking and buttering some.

I joined in, hoping that I looked convincing caught up in Marvel Comics allegory rather than fully cognizant that I was sitting across the table from some of the primary architects of the Cull. These bastards had manufactured and developed the method and some of the materials used for murdering Claire's parents and billions of others.

We were glad when they lost interest in us and went back to bantering and drinking.

Chapter 14

Oh, So NOW All Lives Matter

It was interesting to see the change in attitude by our government now that the Cull was over.

Suddenly they were chiming in with those Whatever-the-Description Life Matters campaigns, simply saying "All Lives Matter" – a thing that we all should have be able to say even before the Cull. But no…instead, we had heard things like "Black Lives Matter", and "Other Specific People's Lives Matter" rather than "All Lives Matter". I had previously checked for "Women's Lives Matter" and found occasional mention of that.

Now that there weren't so many humans that the Earth couldn't comfortably provide for them all, things were different. The fewer people there were, the more each one mattered. This, of course, was the obverse: the more people there were, the less each one mattered, because of resource depletion. There hadn't been enough to go around in comfort. The Cull had just graphically demonstrated that.

Talk of a high-quality college education for all had resumed, too. Colleges and universities would be back up and running by the next academic year. Because of that, it was back to the same old discussions of a bachelor's degree for all, and there was no more worry about insufficient space for all applicants, nor was there any concern about finding a slot in prerequisite classes in order to graduate on time, i.e. in four years.

Not only that, but discussions of overflow having to settle for online universities or community college had ceased. Those had never been even close in quality to face-to-face, in-person colleges and universities anyway. Vocational, trade, and technical schools were still in demand, because they taught specific skills that some people wanted to learn and society needed.

In short, the competition caused by human overpopulation that had shut so many people out of achieving their academic goals and pursuing life-long aspirations had been removed. Things had calmed down to levels of competition not seen since my parents' generation.

I was torn between anger at the hypocrisy of it all while thinking of those who had been killed and awareness of the reason for the Cull: to make all this possible. It was hideously inescapable. But now that it was over, we had comfort, security of a sort, and fewer people.

We had less freedom and more surveillance. It was worse than George Orwell's Oceania.

It was the exact situation I had griped about well in advance of its reality: we were facing the question of wondering if and when the Farmers of the New World Order would ever put back our civil liberties once the threat of human overpopulation had been neutralized.

I was going with never for my guesstimate.

The only way to get our liberty and freedoms back would be a revolution. For that, all humans would need full awareness of the situation. The only way for that to work would be a full disclosure. It was time to write and release an unsanitized history.

Hamish and Jason and I could arrange that. It would have to be anonymous.

Unfortunately, the actual writing would have to wait until after we got back.

As I sat reading and watching the goings on at the Fontainebleau Hotel, these were the things that I thought about. Well, those things and when the right to habeas corpus would be reinstated. Specifics about that question, once civil liberties were suspended for martial law, when would they ever be put back in place, nagged at me relentlessly.

It was time to answer that question, and it had better be in the affirmative.

How would that come about? I thought about it, and thought about it. What could possibly induce the politicians to put back our civil liberties? Suspending them had been done with the only legal excuse allowed by the U.S. Constitution, which was instability. Instability caused by the economy, which was caused by ecosystems collapse, which it would not come right out and say was caused by human overpopulation.

Perhaps our government could be made to realize that since we were living in a Post-Growth Age, the Farmers could no longer count on being able to buy politicians. The idea had some merit and hope to it; if no one could buy a politician any longer, then perhaps, at last, they would truly become responsive out of necessity to all citizens.

Democracy took stability and resources. If our government could be persuaded that those conditions were met, we could have it back. That was my hope, anyway.

And then there were the other nations of the world. They had never all had civil society.

The idea that they might now all have it smacked of utopian fantasizing, but with a stabilized population worldwide and a reorganized, non-growth economy, perhaps civil society might eventually spread. One could hope, and take action in that direction, just to get things going.

Sigh…more work to do after writing that history.

The next day, just like most days spent at this retreat, we sat by the pool reading. I looked at news reports on my laptop for a while, reading article after article about the water wars that had plagued India, South America, and other regions that had been turning to desert due to drought, runoff of soil nutrients, deforestation, and pollution.

People had still been killing each other and taking each other hostage and claiming it was about religion. It wasn't. It was really about each group doing its utmost to claim control of a crucial resource for itself – by denying it to the other. The Cull was over, yet all was not well.

I got up and wandered over to the retaining wall that separated this luxury hotel from the reality that was an ecological catastrophe in the ocean beyond it. Trash made largely of plastic, both hard and soft, floated with the currents, collecting in a corner. It was a softly bouncing cluster of pretty colors…and all rubbish that could choke or strangle any sea creature that was unfortunate enough to swim close to it.

Oddly, there had been a news report on television about a missing boy, 5 years old. He was from a rural area in Georgia, where the peach orchards were. In fact, his family owned and operated one. How could a child still go missing now, with so few people in the world, I wondered? Well…there were always monsters. I should know; I was on a trip hosted by some.

After staring out at the empty Atlantic Ocean for a few minutes, I went back to my seat with Claire, picked up a novel, and tried to take my mind off of such things. The novel was engaging enough, full of detail, and it took me back to a time when no plastic existed, let alone filled the seas. It was a nice escape.

Too bad it couldn't last.

"I dare you!" said a child's voice.

I tried to focus on the plot of the novel.

"We're not supposed to!" came the reply.

"So what? No one's watching. Go get that big yellow piece. It looks like a rubber duck."

I looked up and watched for a moment. I couldn't help it. It was too hard to ignore what sounded like trouble brewing. Six kids, all around nine or ten years old, were standing by the retaining wall, climbing up on the lounge furniture to take a look over the top at the ocean.

Glancing around at the kids' mothers, I was disgusted to see that none of them were taking the slightest notice of this. They were engrossed in their reading and chatting with their friends. It was unbelievable, yet I was not surprised in the least.

Claire's eyes moved up from her book toward the kids.

"Go on, get it! If you don't get it, I'll tell everyone back at school that you're a wuss!"

That did it. A boy in a pair of blue swimming trunks put his leg up to the edge of the wall.

With one last look at the inert mothers, I put my book down and raced over there.

"Put your leg down and all of you get away from this wall right now!" I said loudly.

They did as I told them, staring at me wide-eyed. Hmm…maybe it wouldn't be difficult to prevent a death or two after all.

"You were going to jump over the wall into that polluted water and get some of that plastic?! Did you have a plan for getting back up here? There's no ladder or steps." This was directed to the kid who had almost leaped over the side.

I looked at the bullying brat who had goaded him to do so. "Did you give any thought to what that water is like? It's full of poisons and microorganisms that would make your friend very sick immediately."

Claire had gotten up and come over to stand nearby.

"Go back to the pool where it's safe, and stay with your mothers," I said to the kids. With that, I turned to go back to my seat. The kids took a couple of steps toward the pool, making me think that the incident was over.

No such luck. The mothers had finally noticed that something was going on.

A few of them had thrown their magazines and cocktails aside and gotten up.

One of the mothers was irate. "You were very inappropriate with them!" she told me.

The others chimed in, agreeing. It was just a lot of noise to me.

Claire looked like she was about to start shouting at them.

That was it. I told them all off for that. "Don't instruct me in how to deal with kids!"

"What…?! I'll tell you whatever I want about how to interact with my kids!"

"NO, you won't. I don't care. I will not learn it. I have no interest in learning it. Either you keep your kids from leaping to their horrid deaths by warning them in advance of the danger and paying attention to them, or take the consequences! Those could come either in the completely unacceptable outcome of their actual melting deaths in the acidified and irradiated swale that the currents have brought here, or in a very specific and unsettling lecture to them from a professor."

The women looked outraged at being told off. I was enjoying this.

"Next time it may not be me, but your kids will live to learn from this. Either that, or pay full attention at all times to your own kids and protect them YOURSELF. It's completely your fault that someone else dealt with this. Now get away from me and watch them yourselves, even if that means no time to relax for you! I should not have had to do anything about this!"

I went to sit down again with my books, shaking with rage and upset at being scolded.

As I turned my back on them, I heard a few choruses of "Arrogant bitch!" but no one followed me to continue the interaction. I may have been an asocial person most of the time, but they were blatantly anti-social.

Really, I should not have had to stop someone else's kids from leaping into the Atlantic.

Idiots! A dare to see what would happen…how stupid kids could be! I wasn't like that as a kid. I was different. I thought things through even as a kid. I knew I stood out, and I never cared. I would silently watch the others doing stupid things, not joining in. But the dangers were different then, and less…horrific.

And the parents were idiots too! Relying on chance to keep their kids safe from something preventable…how stupid! Better to tell them not to do something, and why. My parents always did that. The kids would have understood and been scared by the danger, enough to avoid it.

Claire had appeared, silently, stealthily, and headed off the stupid, inattentive, defensive, angry mothers. I hadn't noticed her until now, but she was telling them not to bother me, and to go back to their fashion magazines (she diplomatically called it "reading material"). It didn't matter; we both sounded cold, distant, and arrogant, I realized, but I laughed just a little.

I stared at the scene in my half-stupor of shock from that most unwelcome and anti-social interaction, feeling its unpleasantness wear off. It was wearing off because of the delight that was spreading over me at seeing her in action.

At last, it took effect: the mothers, offended beyond their range of belief, subsided and sat down to their…I checked to see what reading material they sullenly raised to eye level…yes! They really were fashion magazines, and some soppy novels.

Claire came over and sat down in the cabana with me. "Yes, I did check first. They really are reading *Elle*, *Marie Claire*, *Glamour*, and romance novels."

I realized I was staring at her with an amused smile on my face, and broke into a full grin. "I love it. And you. That was awesome."

"Thanks, I love you too," she said. "I've never liked babysitting. I must be missing a gene."

"So am I, but I don't miss it."

"Ha, ha, ha. What is it with us? When I get really involved in studying or writing or whatever – creating a showcase cake, it doesn't matter what creative activity – I yell at anyone who distracts me. I was outlining a story about eco-disaster when that ruckus started."

"Were you? That's terrific." I smiled and sat back in my seat, feeling calmer.

Claire looked at me. "You don't care, do you?"

"About what?"

"About being thought of by those neurotypicals as 'inappropriate' and whatever else they called you – all those judgmental terms they used on you."

"Oh. No, I don't. I used to feel like someone had punched me in the stomach when that bullying term was used, until I realized something, and gradually, as I conditioned myself to remember something really useful, that feeling ceased."

"What was that something?" Claire wanted to know.

"It was that no one died and made the neurotypicals the final arbiters of what is and is not correct for an attitude or behavior. Just because they are the majority model of human, that does not entitle them to instruct me. Also, as an Aspie, even though I am willing to do my best to interact with other people reasonably, thoughtfully, and politely, things will still go wrong from time to time. This means that I will still get funny looks or judgmental comments, even though I have done my best. I won't accept or put up with that any longer. When I got to that point, I ceased to care about the judgments of others about those times when it goes wrong."

Claire was intrigued, and a little frustrated. "How come I still care…"

"You still care because you are young, and you need more interactions before you become inured to that nonsense. Don't worry. You'll get there, and probably faster than I did, thanks to having an older Asperwoman to ask about all this. You seem determined to do so."

She grinned. "I hope so. Thank you."

"You're welcome."

"Avril?"

"Yes?"

"What is it with us? What annoys us about slow, stupid people, and so we don't join them?"

I rolled my head sideways and looked at her. "We are disconnected from caregiving. That focuses our attention and efforts far more acutely on whatever it is that we seek to excel at. And it's not a trait unique to Aspies. It's one that anyone who is an expert in their field or skill or both, or anyone who is well on their way to being one, expresses. Just think of a Michelin star-rated chef. They scream and yell at their staff and don't care who thinks they are rude, arrogant, or horrible, and all the while, they are absolutely right about whatever it is that they are yelling. And then they get the Michelin stars."

"So we are in the right? But we won't be liked."

"Mark Twain used sincere sarcasm when he said, 'It is better to be popular than right.'"

Claire considered that. "So we can't be both."

"Not with our irascible, Aspie quirks and personalities, no."

"Hmm…I don't care, then. I don't need people like these for friends. They won't ever read what either of us write, will they?"

I stared off into space, not seeing the scene in front of me. "Only in college."

"Damn. Well, so be it, then."

"Indeed. Some others may read our stuff out of college, but not many. Not unless it is news."

"Huh." She picked up her laptop and resumed what she said she had been writing.

A moment later, she stopped working and starting laughing to herself.

"What?"

"'We are disconnected from caregiving,' says the woman who just stopped a bunch of kids from leaping to their deaths," she replied with a guffaw.

"Oh. That. I'm not going to just sit here sipping my cocktail. That's what psychopaths do."

"Right." She gave me another grin and resumed typing.

I picked up my book, broke my rule about booze during the day, and ordered a cocktail. Raspberry. Soon the day felt calmer, and I relaxed into a happy mood of reading.

The kids stayed in the swimming pool. I vaguely heard one of them bitterly chastising her mother for not having warned about the radiation swales. "You should have scared me. It would have been better to hear a real story and be scared by it than to almost jump in and die!"

I sipped my margarita and smiled.

A little while later, Mel came over and sat down in our cabana. The relaxation evaporated.

"Hi Mel. Come to tell me not to be an arrogant bitch, and to play nice? I was happy not playing at all, and then those kids almost died, forcing me to interact. I'll be damned if I'll apologize for the way I handled something under pressure of imminent death."

She smiled. "No, I'm not here to do any of that. I told those mothers that they were the unreasonable ones. Some of their kids did that, too, which was funny to watch."

Claire and I looked at her, nonplussed.

A moment later, Claire asked, "Do you have kids?"

"Yes, one son and one daughter, but they're in school, in Switzerland. Teenagers."

Claire and I exchanged glances.

I asked Mel, "Would you have warned them about the radioactive swales when they were little kids, or not?"

"Yes, I would have."

I stared at her.

She laughed. "We're not all clueless, self-absorbed parents," she told me. "I studied psychology. I know what Asperger's is, even if some fools removed it from the DSM manual."

I smiled, but among the Farmers on this trip, it was always a mirthless, guarded smile.

Mel went on, "You Aspies are different. You don't stay in your ivory towers. When you chat at a party, it's always to share your research – whatever it is that you've been working on. I think you are also measuring people's responses to it."

"Oh. Well, yes. We do that. We want to know whether or not the world around us, outside of academia, has any idea of what we are working on, and not because it's about us. It's because we care about the impact of the work, and what good it may do in the world. Locking it up among academics makes it pointless. It must leave the metaphorical ivory tower, and go out into the world. If that means that an asocial person such as myself must chat awkwardly with neurotypicals who find it difficult to connect to the data, we must still get them to try."

"Yes, you are right. Do you worry that fights such as the one you just had will close them off to your message?"

"I do, but those fights are inevitable – guaranteed, in fact. That is why I write my books, and why, although they have lengthy bibliographies at the ends, they are not presented in dull, dry, inaccessible academic form. Most people don't even want to read something like that. If all that people see of me is a piece of writing in a catchy, clever format, and no interaction such as the one I was just forced to engage in, I think the work has a far better chance of reaching them."

Mel nodded, thinking that over. "So you keep to yourself most of the time, writing."

"Yes. It's fun, and calming."

"But isn't it lonely?"

"No. I have my husband, and my family. One of my cousins married an Asperwoman – Claire – so I have a good friend for a cousin-in-law. It's nice to have a family member with whom I have something in common, who is my friend. Plus, I have a few other friends. It's a common misconception that we Aspies have no friends. What we have are a few close ones."

Claire nodded. "That's true. Though I lost most of my friends over the past year…"

Mel looked sober at that. "You'll make new ones."

"Perhaps. Avril didn't make friends in law school. Lawyers are too competitive."

I agreed. "My other friends are all from situations outside of law school, such as college." I was thinking of Bethany, my friend who was in Amsterdam, where I had sent her to escape the Cull. Claire's friends…who had they been?

Claire seemed to know what I was wondering about. "I had some friends from summer trips with my family, but we only connected at Lake Champlain, where we would stay. I never knew how to get in touch with them."

"We should check to see what happened to them. Maybe they are alive."

"Maybe." She looked back at her laptop, and I could see her focus on her outline.

Mel stood up. "Well, it was nice talking to you. I'm going to read my book now."

"What are you reading?" I asked, sincerely curious.

She smiled. "*House Rules* – about an Aspie teenage boy. I've read *Elephant's Kitchen – an Aspergirl's Study in Difference*. Next, I'll read *Look Me in the Eye*, and *The Curious Incident of the Dog in the Night-Time*."

Of course; she was into psychology. I smiled. "Those are good ones," I said. "I think so too."

"Just remember that *Look Me in the Eye* and *Elephant's Kitchen* are the only ones of those that were written by real Aspies. The others were written by neurotypicals who were straining to get into our heads."

Mel smiled. "I will."

With that, we all went back to our own reading material.

I was taking a break from reality – a much needed break – with the *Outlander* series.

That break was punctuated by searches on the Internet for whatever piqued my interest, so it usually didn't last for more than a few hours. This time, reading about human developments from European settlers slowly spreading around North Carolina in the eighteenth century was what did it. I ended up online, looking at Google Maps with my laptop. But I got distracted and looked up more than just the places in the novel.

"I thought you wanted to read for fun," Claire said, looking up at me. "What are you looking up now?"

"Places in this novel, but then I moved on to current human settlements all over the planet. I used to look on Google Maps for things like solar panels on rooftops, or historic sights, or whatever, and I still do that, but now it's to see where people still live, and to get a sense of how many are left as I do so. Before and After Maps are included."

She stared at me. "I think I'd be afraid to look."

I looked up at her. "I can understand that." I paused, then said, "Right now I'm checking Tornado Alley, that area where houses got erased by Nature every year. It always amazed me that insurance companies would pay for rebuilding, or that people would insist upon rebuilding there. I guess it was all about owning the land, and being among familiar people and places."

Claire looked interested. She asked, "And? What's there now?"

"Nothing. I think those people are all gone now."

"I can't say I'm really surprised to hear that. What else are you looking at?"

"Native American areas. They've put up lots of wind turbines, which is really cool."

"Wow! That is cool. Maybe I'll surf the Google Maps site later after all."

She picked up her book and started reading, though. Maybe later, I thought…when she could think of something other than Philadelphia. It was fine for me to look wherever my curiosity took me, but not so easy for her. I wasn't about to suggest that she look at anything upsetting. We couldn't speak freely about it among the Farmers anyway.

The next day, we were again sitting by the pool with our books, as were the mothers, and the kids were again playing nearby. The mothers glanced up at us as we arrived, set up our things, and settled in, then quickly looked away as I met their gazes with a look that I hoped said, "What nonsense are you going to try to bother me with today?!" Hah…that took care of that.

Claire smiled and opened her book, but I could see she was trying to keep a straight face.

A little while later, one of the kids decided to come over and see us.

Without moving my head, I moved my eyes up and to the side in the direction where I sensed movement. What trouble was in store for us next, I wondered, feeling a bit worried. Then I saw who this kid was and relaxed. I put a bookmark where I had stopped reading and sat up.

"Hi Lucy," I said, smiling. "How's it going? How's your mother?"

"Fine," she said. "I've been reading." She showed me an issue of *National Geographic*. It was the standard version, not the one for kids. The featured article dealt with extinctions, and showed the great auk, the last of which had been bludgeoned to death on Eldey Island off of Iceland in 1844. "My mother's going to be okay," she added.

"Good! I'm glad to hear it."

"Yeah. I want my mother."

"Of course you do. The great auk," I said, taking the magazine and staring sadly at the cover. My expression didn't really change much; it was just my tone and a wistful look in my eyes that gave away my mood. Lucy wore the same one, though. It occurred to me that this was an intellectually curious child whose curiosity would likely go largely unsatisfied, teased by the awareness of what was now lost to the Sixth Mass Extinction.

"I was wondering about something," Lucy said to me.

"What's that?" I asked.

She relaxed by taking a deep breath and looking mildly pleased. "I was wondering how to watch for extinctions. Aren't they still happening? I keep asking my parents to take me to museums that show extinct species."

"Oh." I was intrigued. "You would want to visit the Smithsonian Institution in Washington, D.C., the branch called the National Museum of Natural History, and the American Museum of Natural History in Manhattan, New York City. As for ways of studying species depletions, there is something called a 'species-area relationship' – also known as a SAR – expressed by a formula, which is $S = cA^z$. But there's more to it than that." I paused to let all this sink in.

Lucy stood there for a moment, thinking. After a moment or two, she asked, "What else?"

"You would have to decide which species interest you most, if you want to be a scientist. If it's birds, study ornithology. If it's insect, then entomology. And so on. After you have done your Ph.D. and worked as a post-doctoral assistant, you can go off on your own and widen or narrow your focus as you wish. Or you could be a traveling journalist, like the authors of the articles in that magazine. That's the fun of completing graduate school; once you're done, you can do something unique with the credential, if you want to. Some of the most amazing, intriguing things have come from people who do that."

Lucy listened, and then said, "What did you study?"

"I studied the history of medicine, and then law. Claire is going to study law, too."

Lucy looked at her, smiled politely, and looked back at me. "I thought you were older than her, but it was just an idea. People call you 'Professor' and you know things, plus you seem like you have already done things, like you don't have anything to prove. You don't look old at all."

I grinned. "Thanks. You've hit upon one of the reasons why we are here. I'm actually 48 years old, and Claire is only 26. My husband is a physician and scientist who has developed a formula that slows down the aging process. That's why you don't see any gray hairs on me."

"Why would you want to slow it down? To live longer and look prettier longer?"

I laughed. "You guessed it – mostly. Another reason is to have more time to do more. The world is still a fascinating place. We want to see what happens in it. So much has happened so fast in the past few years, and more will follow. We intend to see it all, for as long as we can."

"That's neat," Lucy commented. She looked as though she were thinking about something.

"What are you thinking about?" I asked. "Is it what you will study eventually?"

She smiled. "Yes. I think I want to learn about plants. I've been looking at our food, and at the flowers in the hotel, and I stop to smell and touch plants in gardens all the time. My mother says it drives her crazy – that I should just keep going and not stop constantly. It makes it hard to see everything that I want to see."

"So you want to study botany," I said. "Cool."

Claire spoke up. "Take at least one class in paleobotany. That's like archaeology for plants. We're in the midst of the Sixth Mass Extinction, so many plants will be like animals in zoos – extinct in their natural habitats, yet still alive in controlled conditions."

"Yes!" I said. "Tell your parents all that, and that you won't stop stopping to scrutinize whatever fascinates you," I added with a big grin.

Lucy grinned too. "I will," she said, and then asked, "Do you have any advice for a kid like me – a kid with Asperger's?"

"You mean for getting through school and to the finish line of your academic credentials, including a Ph.D.?" I asked with a smile.

"Yes."

My smile widened. I couldn't help it. This kid was great. "Okay. Avoid any and all special needs classes. If you can do regular ones, and I'm sure you can, do them. You are likely to excel at them. A lot of this nonsense about special education for people on the autism spectrum is more about holding us back than about helping us. We don't need it. The idea is to keep us from pulling ahead, because we are different, more focused, and thus more likely to excel. In fact, this started as humans became overpopulated. The idea was to decrease competition and make things more homogeneous – the same – for all. But we're no longer overpopulated." I paused.

Lucy looked as though she were memorizing all this. Good.

"But enough digression…I get sidetracked when I get going because I have a lot to say." I looked at Lucy. "Avoid anything labeled Common Core. That is what a lot of that nonsense is called. It can badly confuse you about math, and that's the last thing you need. Look up the previous teaching methods and use those to learn the math."

"So…I should avoid whatever they try to push on me that would stick me into a group on the edge, and just study with the others?"

"Yes. There's nothing wrong with you. You have a minority model of what is a normal human brainstem. You belong in the regular classes, and sometimes in the advanced placement classes. You are designed to stand out, not fit in, so that is how it will go for you. You won't have a lot of friends – just a few good ones – and you won't fit in until you are older, so don't waste your life trying to fit in with people with whom you have almost nothing in common."

"So I shouldn't try to have friends?" she asked.

"I don't mean that at all. I mean that you will be the different one in any group with other kids while growing up, and that that is just fine. Study the differences, revel in them, and study whatever fascinates you. Get the best grades you can, but if they are not all As, don't panic. They won't be all As anyway. But they will be good overall. Being unique, focused, and working hard will go a long way toward acceptance to college and graduate school."

"I think I see. Thank you." She smiled at me, and then went over to her mother.

"I think her mother could hear this whole conversation," Claire told me.

"Yes," I replied, watching them. Her mother looked pale, but like she would be okay.

A little while later, the mother came over to talk to us. "My daughter enjoyed talking with you," she began. "My name's Lynn," she said a moment later.

I smiled politely. "That's nice. I'm glad, and it's nice to meet you," I said, addressing each point in order. Then I asked, "Are you going to be okay?" I couldn't bring myself to say I was sorry about the lost pregnancy, and I doubt she would have found me sincere if I had. I had heard her fail to appreciate Lucy too much already for that.

"Yes, thank you. And please thank your husband for me. He was quick to figure out what I needed and order it." She paused, and then said, "Lucy says she doesn't want to have kids. She wants to study and be a scientist."

"Oh? It sounds like she is thinking about her future, and how she wants it to be, rather than just letting life happen." I smiled politely again, and waited.

"I want grandkids!" the mother said, sounding like she was wailing a bit.

"So…you want her to reproduce, whether she wants to do so or not?" Claire asked.

I smiled for real now. "People call child-free women selfish for not wanting to have kids, for doing what we want to do instead. But really, it would be selfish to avoid the criticism by having kids we don't want and then making them unhappy. Our kind of selfishness is a good kind. It thinks ahead to the effects on other people."

Lynn glared at us for a moment. "I don't think Lucy is going to have a sibling now."

I added, "Maybe you'll appreciate Lucy as she is, and see her fulfill her aspirations, whatever they prove to be. Don't you want to see your daughter happy that way?"

"Well…yes, but…" the mother said uncertainly.

"Then think carefully about her life. It's HER life to live."

She nodded, sighed, and went back to her seat. We watched her pick up her magazine and stare at the pages, not seeing what was on them, lost in thought. She glanced up at Lucy. After a moment, we exchanged glances and smiled at each other. Maybe Lucy and her mother would be okay together. Maybe.

"My mother never failed to give me acceptance as I am," I said, disgusted.

"Neither did mine," Claire said, watching them.

Thanksgiving came, as we knew it would during this trip, and a dinner was held.

I dreaded it on Claire's behalf.

Last year, in Lausanne, we had found a turkey and cooked a nice, traditional Thanksgiving dinner, but we had foregone our usual rendition around the table of what we were thankful for. We were thankful to have escaped the Cull. We were thankful to have Claire. But Claire's parents had been killed in the Cull, and we didn't want to upset her with a litany of thankfulness when her thoughts would be of the nice parents that she no longer had. Those parents did not get to see their daughter married to her college sweetheart, nor to enjoy anything else.

This year, we knew that we were eating that meal with their killers.

I had called home to see how the holiday preparations were going, and my mother had said that she and Aunt Zoe had had a difficult time locating a turkey for sale, but at last had managed it. It wasn't very big, but it was big enough for everyone present. "I'm sorry you won't be here for it," she added.

"Me too, but I'm glad you found everything for the feast," I had replied.

That turkey had come from a farm in Massachusetts, and she and Dad and Aunt Zoe and Uncle Charlie had made a day trip of going there to get it, complete with a cooler to take it home in. Well, at least they had enjoyed a nice day out together, complete with a farm restaurant lunch.

News reports across the nation featured families serving vegetarian meals for Thanksgiving – no turkey – and not by choice. "If we had had our way, we would be eating a traditional turkey dinner with all of the usual dishes, not a dinner with a piece missing," one woman said, "but we don't have a car to drive to a poultry farm in the country and buy one." Few people in cities did.

As for us, we had a gourmet catered meal.

Every plate looked the same: a couple of slices of turkey breast meat with gravy, laid neatly over garlic mashed potatoes with a spring of rosemary sticking up out of it, some cranberry dressing on the side, and some haricot verts. This was preceded by a bowl of butternut squash puree soup with chopped fresh sage in it. The meal was concluded by pumpkin pie with fresh whipped cream, dotted with candied cranberries and pecans.

Very pretty, we all thought. I imagined that the hotel staff got the legs, thighs, and other turkey parts that didn't look so uniform on the plate…and that acquiring these turkeys had not taken a grand search and tour of the area. It must have simply been flown in.

Claire sat with Fabian and they both did their best to ignore the trite little speeches that several of our illustrious hosts stood up to make. Fabian was whispering to her that he was thankful to have her. Smart; he managed to keep his wife distracted enough that she could stay calm and eat her dinner. But she knew what was going on.

I sat on the other side of her at a long table, listening to the nonsense. It was more rubbish about how all lives mattered…and gloating that they had help to save – even "pardon" lots of turkeys – by helping to change the food system across the nation. Of course; one of the corporations present was a huge agribusiness. TownFarmUSA had overseen the reorganization of food production and distribution, planning and implementing town orchards, berry patches, corn and wheat fields, squash patches, vegetable farms, and dairies in town after town.

While the Farmers feasted on every sort of food that they could desire, with no difficulty acquiring it, the rest of the nation was regulated and farmed. All this was done to enable the Farmers to remain wealthy and powerful. Happy Orwellian Thanksgiving, I thought to myself.

Oh yeah…all lives mattered, as cogs in their political and economic machines.

Chapter 15

"How Did You Know?"

Demographics Secretary John Lassiter was among the people at the hotel.

At one point, he caught me sitting alone, enjoying a book by the pool, and sat down in what had been Hamish's seat. Hamish was at the bar, showing the video presentation of his nanobot scrubbers to the corporate investors on his tablet.

Lassiter gazed at me for a long moment.

I looked up at him, annoyed, wanting to read. "What is it?" I asked, hoping he would go away again and leave me alone. The people on this trip were getting to be pests, with constant demands for social interaction. Some was all right, but this was too much. It was like they wanted me to say something foolish, and were daring me to do so.

Lassiter continued to stare a moment longer.

"If I have bits of lettuce in my teeth or a smear of chocolate on the corner of my mouth from lunch, just tell me and get on with it," I said, getting really annoyed.

Finally, he seemed to realize that I wasn't going to be able to read an exact message on his tiresome face, because he said, "How did you know?"

"Know what?" I said. Perfect, I thought to myself. This idiot wants to play guessing games.

"You know." That stupid stare reappeared.

"No, I don't know whatever neurotypical message you are trying to convey with your eyes and weird facial contortions. Just ask me whatever it is that you want to know." I actually glared at him, this government official who knew terrible secrets. He was that annoying.

He looked taken aback.

I spoke again. "You don't interact with many people on the autism spectrum, do you?"

His eyes widened for a moment, then relaxed. "No, that's true. I don't."

"Well, THAT is something that your question would fit, even if it wasn't about that," I said with a wry twist of my mouth. But I couldn't hold facial expressions for more than a moment. They were too odd a language to me to use much. "Your behavior for this entire social interaction and your expectations of it give that away. Just be direct with me."

He smiled. "Okay, Professor Châtelet. How did you know to save your extended family from the…plague? Your neighborhood was unaffected. How did you know that your uncle's area wouldn't be unaffected?"

"Oh, that," I said. "Finally, a question that I can process. Okay, Mr. Lassiter: I didn't know. What I knew was that I didn't know and was unwilling to leave them all behind and take the risk that anything bad might happen to them, so Hamish and I took them all with us. That way, we wouldn't have to worry about them. Instead, we could relax, and focus on our work."

"And your family just agreed to up and leave with you – for a whole year?"

"Well, yeah! It was a luxury yacht trip to the French part of Switzerland, and several of them had jobs in the Lausanne clinic. The others were retired, and free to come along."

He stared at me. "That's your position on this?"

"Of course that's my position on this, as you phrase it. How ridiculous! Why would we, who have the resources and a place to go to, and who plan ahead and think long-term, do anything else? That's just what Aspies are like. If you didn't know that about people on the spectrum, you should learn it. We are planners, we study, and we don't do or like what most people do or like."

"You don't follow the crowd then."

"No."

"You are different."

"Yes."

"But doesn't it bother you not to fit in?"

"No. I take pride in standing out and not fitting in. I have all my life. So does Hamish."

Lassiter stared at me again, and it seemed that I might have actually blown his mind. Or was he just a good actor? Regardless, he knew he wasn't going to get any more out of me on how I "knew" about the Cull and kept my whole family alive. It didn't matter. I could see that I was being tested on many levels, and had likely been tested every step of the way from the time the vaccinations had begun. Well, I was still alive, and so was my family, so I must be acing my way through it all. That, and Blackout Security must be reliable and happy with its pay.

I smiled again. "What did you get to drink? I got a strawberry orange purée."

I looked at Lassiter to see if he would accept the change of topic.

He seemed to understand that the interrogation was over. "A Bloody Mary."

"Is it a virgin one, or one with alcohol in it?" I asked.

"It has vodka in it." He had another unreadable expression in his eyes, but I had seen that one before on many people all my life. "Don't you want a margarita? Why are you staying sober on a vacation?"

Actually, I might...if I weren't reading a book. Also, I might if I weren't anywhere near this guy. "I'm reading now, and I really like this book, so I don't want alcohol, but I might want it later, with Hamish and when I feel like sitting here to people-watch."

"You do that? Even if you can't read people?" Lassiter actually seemed curious.

"Yes, I do that. Some are quite entertaining...characters. Those are the ones I watch."

"I see. Anyone in particular you want to watch?"

"I don't know yet. We've only been here for a few days, and we'll be here for a few weeks, so I'll have to observe people a bit more before I decide. Meanwhile, I'm getting tired from an overload of social interaction, so I brought this novel with me to escape from it for a while." With that, I gave him a toothy grin, deliberately naughty but not meant to be malicious.

He grinned. "You want me to let you alone with your book."

"Well, yeah, but it's nothing personal. It wouldn't have mattered who sat down across from me and tried to talk. I would still have explained the situation after giving whomever it was a couple of polite minutes of attention."

Lassiter laughed. "You're blunt. I like that. You're honest and don't care what people think."

"Caring uses up way too much emotional energy, and I learned sometime in college that it's just not worth it to obsess over such things. People don't really care. Social niceties are about social control. I'm too recalcitrant for those after a point." I really just wanted him to leave.

We grinned a knowing grin at each other, at last connecting.

With that, Lassiter at last left me to enjoy my drink and my novel.

A few minutes later, Hamish came back to check on me. "Everything okay?"

"Yeah." I knew he had seen Lassiter drop by for a chat.

"What did he want?"

I told him.

Hamish looked grim, but was keeping his face away from Lassiter, who was at the bar now, getting another drink. He glanced back at him, and then made me recount the entire conversation. When I was done, he grinned. "I love you. I knew I married the right person!"

I grinned back, and he kissed me.

That evening, at a dinner in the ballroom, I was not grinning.

I was thinking, and thinking fast.

The problem was that Leo Uberfein was in the room, sipping a Scotch-and-soda while laughing uproariously at some joke that the person across from him had just made. I couldn't hear any of it; they were all the way across the room, which was full of background noise.

If Uberfein was here, on a retreat for families, then his son might be here.

Claire and Fabian had met him in Switzerland, but I had not run into him, nor had Hamish.

I pulled my husband close for a kiss and whispered, "Stay close as if we're making out slightly so we can whisper."

Without missing a beat, he smiled, kissed me on the cheek, and said, "What's going on?"

"Leo Uberfein is here, which means that his wife is likely here, and possibly his son, Jacob, whom we haven't met. If we recognize him, we must not show it."

"Understood." Hamish glanced around the room as he sat up. "I see them."

"All of them?" I asked.

Claire and Fabian turned to look at us, and Aaron and Ed perked up. Those agents had excellent hearing. It must have been difficult for Aaron not to turn around and look. He was sitting across from Ed at our round table, with his back to that part of the room.

A moment later, Fabian saw Jacob sitting with his parents and another couple, who had their son with them as well. Fabian sipped his beer and leaned back, then passed the bread to Claire. She took some and smiled at her husband, then concentrated on buttering it. Now everyone had seen Jacob Uberfein.

Jacob looked very different from the way that he had looked in the video that our nanobotic spy-cameras had taken in Atlanta, Georgia, just before we had all fled to Switzerland. That video chronicled the last weekend of the life of Edgar's girlfriend, Ellie, who had not taken Hamish's warnings seriously. It had not been safe to go to the headquarters of the Center for Disease Control with her college friends and protest the vaccine policy, but she had gone, unable to resist a chance to get together with all of her old friends again.

Jacob Uberfein had been one of those friends, and now he was the only one left of that group.

The group had had a lovely weekend together, reliving old times, sharing a couple of apartments, ordering takeout, and even going on a drive outside the city to nearby Elberton, to view the Georgia Guidestones.

Hamish and I had seen them the previous fall, and nearly gotten ourselves killed. We had encountered a runaway patient from a CDC facility, or so we thought. It was actually a controlled experiment of public exposure to a virus. We had managed to stay out of range and get away, but everyone else at the convenience store and gas station in question had died.

A year later, the vaccine had been fully operational, the virus and nanite serum in use for the Cull, and mobile crematoria teams were moving throughout the nation as people fell ill within days of being injected. These teams were run by military units which traveled around, followed by military infrastructure and housing removal teams. It was eminent domain perverted into an eminent removal policy, erasing all trace of neighborhoods and even whole towns.

It had been no accident that a sick escapee, similar to the one that Hamish and I had gotten close enough to see, was allowed to stumble right up to Ellie and her group. At the airport, as the group tried to leave, they were detained and forcibly injected with the Cull serum.

We had watched it all, powerless to do anything about it. The group of friends had been marched into a back ballroom of an airport hotel which was sectioned off in plastic and met by military medical teams in environmental suits. They were fed GMO foods to activate the serum as quickly as possible, and we saw it start to work.

Then we had seen Jacob Uberfein identify himself, scolding the soldiers, trying out the "Do you know who my father is?!" line on them in an effort to save his friends.

He was the only person it had saved.

He was abruptly injected with another serum, a nanite gun was held up to his neck and the swarm of P53 nanites withdrawn from his body, and he was forcibly marched away from the area, protesting about his friends to no avail.

We hadn't seen him again until his bankster father and socialite mother had turned up in Lausanne at the Regenics clinic there, and then it was only Edgar, Fabian, Claire, and Jacques who had run into him.

Edgar had known Jacob from photographs only. He and Ellie had gone to the same high school, and reconnected after finishing college. That meant that he did not know her college friends, and thus had not been invited – thankfully for his family – on that fateful trip of hers.

But Edgar recognized Jacob, and had asked him about Ellie. He couldn't resist.

From what Claire had told me, however, it was Jacob who had had the most awkward time of it during that encounter, struggling for a suitable explanation to offer. We all knew the real story, having seen Ellie and her friends weaken and suffer until they walked into the mobile crematorium that had gassed and incinerated them, but Jacob didn't know that.

All Jacob knew was whatever he had been told, and whatever he had been warned.

Clearly, he had been warned not to reveal the circumstances of his very narrow escape.

Now it was up to us, and particularly Fabian and Claire, to play dumb with him.

Were the Farmers on this trip still watching to see how much we knew, and how we knew it? If so, we intended to stonewall them. As far as we were concerned, we were just on a pleasant trip, invited to relax here.

But Jacob Uberfein didn't come over to talk to us. He saw us, looked very upset, and pushed his food around his plate, not eating. We didn't see much of him for the rest of the trip, and when we did, he didn't talk to us.

I guessed that he didn't want to risk slipping up and revealing anything.

We looked confused that he wouldn't talk to us, and did so deliberately.

We kept that up and enjoyed our trip, and watched everyone carefully.

There was plenty to observe.

Chapter 16

Growth is Over – A New Normal

How would the Farmers stay rich beyond the vacuous paroxysms of avarice without growth?

Hmm…the new normal did not encourage more of the same thing that had collapsed the ecosystems of the entire planet, from its drinking water to its oceans to its air to its land.

They would have to reengineer the economy to make it about repairing and sustaining the ecosystems. They would have to make it all about creating one's living by keeping the Earth healthy. They would have to break many of the habits that they had taken for granted.

They would have to start listening to and reading the works of other economists.

What?! Yes…there were other economists than the ones that we usually heard from.

For too long, as if growth were a party that its revelers were determined should go on forever – a fantasy world if ever there was one – the economy had been in a state of either "growth" or "stagnation". It was in a state of growth if all was going well, complete with consumerism and resource depletion, operating on the absurdly fictitious notion that the Earth and its resources were either not finite, or else replacement technologies could be made to stretch them out.

But all things eventually end, and this absurd game was nothing but entropy in action.

It was time to face up to those facts.

It was time to say that an economy that was not in a state of growth was in "equilibrium".

Stability was another great term for it.

We needed a realistic attitude, and to think of growth in other areas: innovation, invention, creativity, and so on. If we were ever to mold our society in the style of *Star Trek* rather than in Oceania, we would have to get going on that immediately.

I was ever the optimist, looking for hope that human society could do well, and be good.

As long as humanity still existed, why not?

All we needed to do was get those damned Farmers out of the way, because they would never rejigger the economy to be about anything other than growth and resource consumption. This whole convention was nothing more than a pretense.

We had law courts for that, and the U.S. Constitution.

It was time to find a way to revive the best of that, to throw off martial law entirely, and to get on with the business of living life, of advancing technology, and of having goals far more worthwhile than merely to acquire more clutter.

The Large Hadron Collider hinted at the beginnings of warp drive.

Organic farming, soil conservation, and suggested that we could feed the people who existed.

The fact universities all over our planet still existed, still had most of their faculty members, and would soon open for academic programs announced that. Ivory tower mentalities could be attacked as exercises in futility soon enough. For now, the world needed to be brought back online. The Internet had stayed online, but many vital systems had been offline during the Cull.

Democracy was one of them.

I kept saying that democracy required money, breathing room for humanity, and security.

Well, we had those ingredients now, however abominably they had been provided.

It was time to prove who had provided it, how, and to do something about that.

Once those balance sheets were rectified, the economy could be put in order.

When that was done, we could get on with the business of stability.

It would be great, if we could do that.

After this trip, I thought we could.

Chapter 17

Sustainability for Non-Renewables – A Joke

There was much talk at this retreat of sustainability.

Sustainable this and sustainable that: it was all about conservation and judicious use.

It was also a joke, though neither a humorous nor an intended one.

The idea of sustainable policies, habits, practices, whatever for anything that was finite, be it rare Earth elements, water, fossil fuels, or anything else was ludicrous.

It was not possible.

It was all about slowing down and postponing the inevitable: resource scarcity, or depletion.

What then?

The Farmers had rigged the situation to enable themselves and some company for themselves to survive beyond most of the humans who had shared the planet with them. That number had been far more than all combined who had ever previously lived on the Earth. Now it was down to half a billion. Good job, Farmers…but what benefit would there ultimately be for us?

It was just a matter of time before crunch time, no matter how careful the last of us were.

It was down to a question of how much more time we had to enjoy life before then.

As soon as I had the chance to tell one of them what I thought about it all, I would.

That chance came when Spades plunked himself down on an extra lounge chair at the pool a week into the retreat, drink in hand per usual, startling Claire and me out of our books. "Hi ladies! Enjoying our little getaway?" he asked, breathing a fire of martini.

Claire could barely keep a straight face, and I would have lost it if I hadn't had something to say that I had been saving up for just such a moment…when one of our hosts invited it. "Yeah, it's great! All the berry-orange puree drinks we could possibly want, an occasional buzz, sea breezes, and recreational reading time, complete with people-watching opportunities. Thank you very much for this," I replied.

"You're very welcome," he said, grinning. "Are you sure you don't want anything stiffer?"

I grinned. "No, I just wanted to say something stiffer to one of our hosts, since this trip is all about eco-friendly sustainability, and you'll do nicely. You seem ready, too, with a good, stiff drink to fortify yourself with as you hear it."

"Lay it on me!" Spades practically shouted, smiling and sitting back in his chair.

I refrained from shaking my head. The fact was that this Farmer had a strong element of likeability. He seemed faithful to his wife and basically good, despite his love of alcohol. Smiling, I told him, "Okay, here it is: I think about how things are set up and why constantly, and this trip has me focused on corporations. A corporation should be about sustaining the people in it, NOT about extracting the maximum amount of wealth and then abandoning the people and the ecosystem to live on nothing, impoverished and depleted. We're heading toward our own extinction otherwise."

Spades had stopped smiling and was listening to me with steady, polite attention.

Had he actually taken that in?

A moment later, I had my answer.

"I agree with you," he said. "It should not be all about a running start-up, to make a play on the concept of I.P.O, sell-off, or bust. But what about the shareholders?"

"Buy them out and dump them," I said. "That's the only way you'll ever succeed at ditching the fantasy that they want, which is endless growth in a world of finite resources."

He sat there, listening. "I so want to do that," he said, a tone of listlessness in his voice.

"Why don't you start plotting to do so then?" I asked him.

He rolled his head slightly to the side to face me. "I should. I might just do that."

Claire chimed in, "If you plot secretly, you could pull it off without warning."

"That may be the only way," he said. Then he smiled at her and excused himself.

Well, it was worth a try, I thought to myself, picking my book up again.

Chapter 18

Greenwashing

"Damn!"

Hamish's expletive startled me. I had been reading. "What?" I asked.

"It was a lot easier to dump all that shite into the oceans and spew it into the air than it will ever be to remove it," he said bitterly, "microbeads and other plastics, cesium-129, runoff from fertilizers, oil spills, algae blooms, you name it, that rubbish is in there, keeping fish and coral and everything else from growing or ever being healthy again!" He sat there, staring at his laptop screen. He looked as though he were daring it to present a solution.

"Yeah, it's always easier to destroy than it is to create…or to heal," I agreed.

His eyes moved up to glare at me briefly, then back to the screen. His head hadn't moved.

"Have you decided how you might clean that mess up?" I asked.

"Nae…not yet."

Hamish was anxious because the meeting in which we were to present whatever knowledge and ideas we had to contribute to remediating the pollution of the planet's ecosystems – the very purpose for which we had been invited on this retreat – was in two days, and he wasn't ready.

All I had to do was back him up and chat up the Farmers who had invited us while imparting useful knowledge. I was to point out ways in which they could both profit from remediating pollution and reasons why it was important. I was always ready with plenty of that, but Hamish needed an exciting nanobotic solution to present. I thought he had one, so I tried to remind him.

I tried to be reassuring. "Oh well. It'll come to you. You created the Nae-Née nanite without any more input from me than a general idea. You created nanobees. I thought you were planning to create a nice swarm of microscopic, unwanted-atom herders," I said, picking up my novel. "Environmental insecurity concerns galore can be swept up by those and filtered out."

I was still tired from constant academic reading – or at least, my mind was. Time for more novels, I had been telling myself for months on end. Frankly, I didn't care when I might stop this. Eventually could come at some random time, when I felt good and rested. The hell with everything for now, I kept thinking. I felt starved for frivolity after the horrors of the past year.

Hamish, however, could not stop working, could not relax and enjoy himself. He felt the need to wipe his slate clean to atone for a military past. He often said so to me, in private. My view was that he could never wipe it clean, not ever, but that atonement was still good.

I felt his eyes on me and looked up, startled. "What?" I said, nonplussed.

"That's it! You're a genius!" he shouted.

"What did I inadvertently do now?" I asked, puzzled.

"You've solved it! I'll create swarms of nanites with feathers – not wings, but sets of rotating feathers that can move in any direction – that move together at subsonic and supersonic speeds, gathering toxins at the atomic level! The very toxins they seek will fuel them!" He looked really excited now – gleeful, even. "A collector ship can follow it, to gather the rubbish."

"That's awesome, and it sounds like a great plan, but I don't see how I solved it for you."

"You did what you always do: you treated it like a science fiction question, not concerning yourself with reality so much that you would limit your ideas to current, existing technology. It's that kind of insight that leaps us forward. You relaxed and applied your mind to the problem. You're a genius!" He jumped up and kissed me.

I kissed him back, stunned. "Huh. Well, now you have to do the work of making it real."

He sat down on the big, comfortable, poufy ottoman in front of me, put my feet in his lap, and grinned at me. "THAT is why we are an inventor team. You are co-inventor again. Your name is going on all of the legal documents for this as co-inventor, and don't you say no to me!"

I looked at him, pleased but cool. "Okay, I won't, but you do realize that I won't understand the blueprints much, don't you?"

"Aye, but that's so beside the point that it isn't even worth mentioning. I'll be telling the lawyers how we came up with this when the time comes to draw up the patent."

I smiled. "Okay. That'll be great...awesome...perfect – and all that good stuff."

Hamish gave me a really great kiss and went back to his computer.

I had to order us room service that night, because he wouldn't leave his laptop for hours – not until he had completed every last one of the specs for the new idea. The only time he moved was to use the bathroom or to accept a memory stick from me to back everything up.

He seemed annoyed when I distracted him to insist that he save his work every few minutes, but I noticed him pausing after that, every ten or fifteen minutes, to do just that.

When the food arrived, I laid it all out and wondered when he would touch it.

No sale; he was still working, four and a half hours after he had started.

I walked over to him with the asparagus purée soup and spooned some into his mouth, but he wasn't interested and waved a second spoonful away. "Come on, when will you eat?" I asked. "That laptop will be still be here."

"I know, I know! Give me another hour or so." He was impatient to keep going.

"Fine. This hotel suite has a microwave oven," I said, and ate my food. An hour! What did he think this was, my first spec write-up? Besides, I was an author who would not leave a computer when I had a flow of ideas going. I could relate to what he was doing.

It turned out to be an hour and a half later. He heated up his own soup and crab cakes, and sat next to me on the sofa, happy now, eating it all.

"I saved the key lime pie," I said. "We can eat that together."

He kissed me on the cheek and finished his dinner, smiling like the Cheshire Cat.

A while later – quite a while – we got out of bed.

Hamish was a bit slow to let me get up, but I needed to stretch.

Since he couldn't keep me there, his mind went straight back to the nanite swarms he had just written code for. "It will be very important not to lose any of them in the oceans, or rivers. I had to give them all codes, and group codes, and build tracker nanite swarms to retrieve any that fail to return. But – and this is the beauty of your idea – they can stay out there a good long time, cleaning and clearing up microbeads and whatever else."

"Cool – tiny maelstroms of pollutant sweepers," I remarked. "You always create just the right thing. You get obsessed and just go for it," I summed up with a grin.

"Aye." He grinned back.

"It's nice to see you successful now. That means I get some of your attention."

He grinned again.

We needed a good night's rest after all that excitement, but the next day, we were very busy working, and so we made ourselves scarce. Our host actually called the room to see if we were okay. We assured him that we were fine, but working on our presentation for the following day.

In reality, we were madly drawing up the document for the patent. I edited it in a couple of hours, and Hamish backed the whole thing up on three different memory sticks. The next issue was deciding how to get it to our attorney, who was aware of what we were doing, but not yet in possession of any documents with which to prepare a patent filing.

We wanted that underway when we walked into tomorrow's meeting.

"No problem," Hamish told me. "I'll have Aaron take on a special flight, and then he can come back. Since Blackout will sent us Lionel, we should be okay. I know him and trust him to watch us. But I want to share five percent of the profits from this invention with Aaron and Ed, and I'm going to tell them so. That will make Aaron the ideal person to entrust with this data."

"Excellent. They're like family to us now. They can retire wealthy, whenever they do so. Though I hope they don't do so for a while…I've gotten comfortable with them…"

My husband grinned. "Don't worry. They'd both be too bored if they stopped now."

He called Aaron and gave him the memory stick a couple of minutes later. A Blackout plane was waiting at the tarmac where we had landed a few days earlier.

"I'll be back tonight," Aaron promised as he left.

Lionel was proving to be a serious but friendly guy. When he came in to eat lunch with us, Hamish immediately sat him down in the living room and began a medical examination, which concluded with an injection of Regenics serum.

"Is that what I think it is?" Lionel asked.

"Aye – it is. Just what I've been promising you for a while now." It was actually an additional shot, because his previous one had counteracted the Cull serum. This time, Lionel was in for the life extension treatment. He had already gotten it for his fiancée months earlier, but had been too busy until now for his own. We felt a pleasant sense of closure about this.

Lionel was a comforting and reassuring bodyguard.

Ed was with Claire and Fabian. When they heard what we were doing, they wanted to eat a room service dinner with us, and we acquiesced. "It's a lot easier to reveal absolutely nothing if we're not in the dining room with other people," Claire said, and Fabian nodded.

It was a nice meal, shared with our guards.

The next day, Hamish was ready to meet with The Molech Group. So was I.

Aaron was back, and he and Ed followed us to the meeting. They stopped at the conference room doors and took seats in the lounge nearby. Lionel would follow Claire and Fabian around.

Hamish had written a PowerPoint presentation, let me edit it the night before, and was up bright and early to go over it all. He had been warned severely not to make the slightest change to it – neither a space nor a punctuation mark was to be changed.

He was true to his word, and by lunchtime, we were installed in one of the hotel meeting rooms, dark with walnut wood paneling (I hoped it was a veneer – how could they cut down any more of that rare tree just to decorate walls, I wondered?!). Lunch was brought in from one of the Fontainebleau restaurants.

Arthur Cantilever, who was launching a start-up company to handle ecosystems remediation, leaned over to me, wanting to say something, so I leaned in. He had organized this meeting.

"We know you won't eat steak, Professor Châtelet, so we ordered a variety of dishes for you. There are fish plates, salads, fruits, and other things we hope you will like," he said.

Wow…they seemed to be alternately trying to woo us or kill us. I smiled and said, "Thank you! I'm looking forward to eating it all." And I was.

We started eating, and someone across the table and down a few seats from me said, "I wonder how big the Pacific Garbage Patch is. Maybe we could go for a walk on it and try to measure it."

"The term 'Great Pacific Garbage Patch' does NOT mean a literal continent of trash."

Heads turned to look at me, so I continued, "Instead of a solid mass, it's more like a soup, with bottle caps, scraps, flakes, and other debris floating around an area the size of Australia. There are five such areas, not just one. Imagine a soup with chopped herbs and then see them as interchangeable with plastic flakes and nurdles, carrot slices with bottle caps, and so on. Then imagine unwanted bones and gristle - things that a human would pick out of the mix – garbage!"

Now they were all listening, and Hamish looked amused as he clicked on the file he needed.

"Throw in a few ghost nets made of plastic that wrap themselves around seals, add the plastic soda can holders (for 6-packs) that get around sea turtles, and you'll be infuriated with our throw-away culture and the laziness of our species in general. We ought to go back to using hemp nets and glass bottles with metal caps that must be returned for reuse. It would be great to collect all that bigger stuff, in addition what Hamish is proposing to sweep up at nano-levels, get it out of the waters and shore areas, and recycle it all," I summed up.

The Farmers nodded, no doubt already imagining ways to turn that crap into money. Good. Whatever it took to fix things was fine with me.

I heard a few remarks around the room about how, now that the problem of billions of humans producing waste and pollution had been mitigated – awful though the roughly 6.8 billion deaths that that represented was – it ought to be a lot easier to remediate that damage.

True, but it was shocking and appalling to hear it iterated by the Farmers themselves.

I turned to Mr. Cantilever again and said, "I have been wondering about something related to this meeting since we received our invitation to it."

He smiled politely. "What is that, Professor?"

I smiled back, mirroring the phoney warmth he conveyed, or at least trying to. "Have you invited anyone from China, India, or another nation with a heavy ecological mess to deal with? This meeting is meant to cover water pollution, is it not? China has water in all other colors besides blue and green, the only natural hues, and even those may be as vivid as their red, orange, yellow, purple, and pink waters. A quick Google Image Search would show photographs of water in those colors, complete with lots of floating plastic trash. Eventually, that water circulates around the globe. It's coming here to be our problem."

Mr. Cantilever actually looked unhappy, and not at me. "No…but we will rectify that shortly. This is not the only meeting we intend to have while we're here. We'll have someone flown in within the next day or so. Who would you suggest?" he asked me.

"A scientist would be good, preferably one dispatched by the Chinese government, since that's how they work. They don't just have private businesspeople get together and then present their government with a plan like Americans do."

Mr. Cantilever nodded. "That's what I suspected. Thank you." With that, he turned around and motioned to a younger man in a casual suit with a polo shirt on under his linen jacket. The man had been steadily tapping away at his electronic device. He nodded to Mr. Cantilever now, and started tapping even more furiously at it. Then he lifted it to his ear and started a phone call, and left the room to continue it.

Hamish had finished setting up and adjusting the equipment, and now he cleared his throat loudly. When that failed to get people's attention, he tapped the microphone that was clipped to his shirt and did it again, which caused it to make a loud squeak and puff. People looked up.

"Good afternoon," he began, and with a grin. "What we have in our planet's oceans right now is a state of environmental insecurity – a term coined by my lovely and clever wife."

I had started grinning when I saw the gleam in his eyes. He loved to mess with rich people who thought that they were in control of everything. Now all of those eyes turned to regard me with interest for a moment. I glanced at them, still with a ghost of a smile on my face, and then turned back to Hamish. They turned to listen to him also.

The term that scholars had long preferred was "environmental security" – but mine was more on point by its unsettling tone.

These Farmers hoped to use that wealth to remediate the damage. It was a tall order, and one that they could not hope to fill without a genius such as my husband. They were used to being in control of everything, and using money to solve any problem.

The fact was that these rich people weren't in control of the environmental damage that their businesses had done, and they knew it. None of them had a clue as to how to clean up the mess that was our planet's oceans, and much of their decision-making had led to the pollutants getting in there in the first place. And Hamish was no minion. They would have to be polite to him.

I loved it.

Granted, there were other Farmers elsewhere who had done plenty of damage, but they weren't all here right now, and it was time to get going on this. Nuclear power plants in Japan, manufacturing in China, and ship scrapping in Bangladesh were partly to blame also. So were oil spills in Nigeria that had leaked into the ocean after oozing down its rivers. So was the lack of sanitation in Sao Paulo, Brazil.

Decades of cruise ships spewing sewage in international waters hadn't helped, either.

Temperatures had risen in waters worldwide, and coral reefs had bleached in tropical zones. The oceans and seas were full of dead zones, and there was no going back from that. The oceans were a cesspool of death, it was our species' fault, and on and on and on.

Hamish managed to calmly present these facts in a succinct, dry way that refrained from assigning blame to anyone in this room.

This room was currently populated by the owners of huge corporations: cruise lines (guilty), insecticide manufacturers (guilty as hell), oil companies (love those offshore drilling platforms with all of their accidental fires and spills), soda companies (thanks for all those plastic bottles and aluminum cans floating out there), and more.

I glanced around at these guys, and detected no signs of guilt on their faces. Instead, it was like this cleanup meeting was just the next big money-making operation in the history of capitalism. There was finally no way to put it off, so they were turning it into a business investment opportunity.

Okay. Hamish and I could profit from doing something to help the planet. Why not? This was a good idea, after all, not an evil one.

There was one guy here from a pharmaceutical corporation. Him I watched with more interest. He certainly looked like all he cared about was profit. He was the owner of two of the four companies that remained in the U.S. Back in the 1950s, there had been a lot more of them, and competition among them. Well before the Cull, those corporations had merged, repeatedly swallowing each other up until just four monster companies remained.

Alistair Bosch controlled the two who had manufactured the serum used in the Cull.

I wondered which one had handled the nanobots that had ripped apart P53 proteins, the cancer tumor suppressors. Shut those off, and you're doomed. Of course, the serum itself was pretty nasty also. It was a cocktail of forty or so vaccines that, one at a time, administered slowly by a responsible physician, would provide immunity against whatever disease or virus the vaccine was designed to protect against. But, hit a person's immune system with all of those at once (or even just several, let alone forty), and it crashes.

It was amazing to realize that I was sitting in the same room with one of humanity's mass murderers. I took another bite of sushi, followed it up with some red and yellow cherry tomatoes with watercress, and sneaked another glance at the guy.

Bosch was silver-haired, sleek, and fit. He was about Hamish's height, green-eyed, and slightly tanned. He wore khakis and a lime-green Izod polo shirt with a brown belt and brown loafers (I had seen his feet as I walked in). It was only now that I had been sitting still for a while that I had started to memorize faces and match them up to name plates, which were on the table in front of each of us.

The guy had a lot of mannerisms that I found to be both smug and irritating, such as the way he swallowed and then looked up from time to time, closing his eyes, moving his head up to face Hamish, and then opening them. How neurotypical of him, I thought, and that's rather mean to neurotypicals as a group. I mean, they don't all have arrogant demeanors, as if they consider themselves to be above, well, you name it.

I couldn't watch Bosch for long though. For one thing, it would be too obvious, and for another, I wanted to pay attention to what Hamish was saying. He was talking about what was in the ocean and what effect it had on human health.

That, after all, was what The Molech Group cared about. There was money to be made in restoring the health of the oceans and thus the health of the half a billion humans who remained after the Cull. Economies wouldn't run well with either too many or too few of us.

"The first thing that all of these pollutants do on their way to making us humans sick," Hamish was saying, "is to get into marine life far down in our food chain: fertilizers and insecticides run off from land during rainstorms and into rivers and oceans (insects now digest and excrete them, having evolved to cope with the threat posed by those poisons, thus making them worse than useless), microbeads get washed down the drain with cosmetics, lead and other heavy metals get into the mix the same way, and then we eat and drink it all after a while. Fish eat plankton that ate microbeads and methylmercury. That's what mercury runoff turns into. That's why you hear that it's bad to eat swordfish, especially for pregnant women," he added.

"But all kinds of fish are affected now, including salmon, oysters, and starfish – I know, we don't eat those, but other creatures do, and when they die, the checks that they provide on other life forms go away, causing population explosions and imbalances, which can further reduce the populations of the fish that we want."

"As if that weren't enough, fisheries are collapsing due to discarded nets, which snare huge schools of cod, tuna, salmon, and other species that we humans like and drag them down, immobilizing them. They can't swim for food or to spawn, so they die."

"They're just part of the oceanic ecosystem, which needs every species for the food chain to be healthy and to continue to produce. Plastic bits permeate the entire ocean – not just the surface, which we humans can see – right down to the sea bed, which is coated with plastic nurdles and other rubbish that washed from factory lots as surface runoff during rainstorms, into rivers, and out to sea."

"What about that rubbish we see on the surface of the sea when we go out cruising around the Caribbean?" Mr. Carlisle asked. "What are those things called…"

"Windrows," I said. "It's foam and seaweed, which the wind and water currents push into long rows. They blow and drift out of those long rows and back into them again, over and over. Plastic gets attached to the seaweed, which grows around it, and even though it breaks down far more slowly in water than on land in the hot sun, it does break down."

A glance around the table showed a lot of grossed-out and intrigued faces. Good.

"Doesn't biodegradable plastic take care of the problem of toxins being released into the oceans and elsewhere?" Mr. Carlisle wanted to know.

"Actually, no, it doesn't," Hamish replied. "That stuff contains bisphenol-A, known by the acronym BPA, which is made from petroleum. It still contains toxins. There is another kind of plastic that breaks down another way, called polyethylene terephthalate (PET) plastic. It goes with and high-density polyethylene (HDPE) chemicals, by-products of plastic production. This breakdown process involves photodegradation rather than biodegradation. They turn into flakes, which still get into the ecosystem, just at a lower level than the BPA. That stuff could be in the fish that we eat. So, all that the greenwashing by marketers accomplishes is to induce people to buy and throw away yet more plastic, even though there is no such thing as 'away'."

An awkward pause ensued.

"But you know that," Hamish said to the room at large. "You knew when you asked me to talk to you about this that I would have to speak frankly about pollutants and toxins in order to explain it all. Let's face it: you formulate, manufacture, and sell what then becomes a problem for the ecosystem. It has long since proliferated exponentially to the gazillionth power. We might as well get that out there, and address the elephant or gorilla or whatever outsized, metaphoric creature that is sitting in this room, staring at us all."

Rueful grins all around. At least these Farmers wanted to go through with this.

Mr. Carlisle spoke again. "I think I saw some foil balloons in windrows in the Sargasso Sea."

Hamish said, "You definitely did. People release them at birthday parties, even though it's against the law, or they just lose their grips on them. Those balloons ought to be banned. I realize that there are people at this table who make hefty profits from manufacturing them, but killing the ecosystem will ultimately kill humans. If you take Regenics, you can count on living to see that happen, and living long enough to starve with the last of us humans."

"So how long will it take to remove the plastic?" Mr. Cantilever asked.

"Getting it out could take decades, and how many decades depends on how many swarms of nano-scrubbers we humans choose to deploy. That's what this meeting is about, among other things, so it's good that we discussed all of this. If you're serious about removing plastics and other pollutants from the oceans, that's great, but you need to prepare a place to receive the mess, and then you can decide what to do with it all."

Puzzled looks around the room.

I spoke up again. "Come on, you guys. You're geniuses at finding a way to make money out of petroleum products. You're about to retrieve gazillions of tons of them, because that's what plastics are made from. There must be something you can do with them – melt them down, extract certain materials from them, store the slag until you figure out how to reuse it – and make something else out of it. Who knows…maybe you can build spacecraft with it."

Laughter around the table. "Maybe," said a guy far down the table. He looked familiar.

"Don't you have an aerospace business?" I asked him with a grin. He had been interviewed on *60 Minutes*, appeared in lots of magazines, and we all knew it. His name was Moshe Elon.

"I do," he said, grinning back. "I'll get right on that."

Now people all around the room were grinning.

It occurred to me that the Farmers were concerned about keeping satellites running.

Good. I realized that the cost of that was downsizing by erasure of billions, but keeping the GPS systems and other space-dependent technologies of our infrastructure functioning was not a bad thing. Nothing, not mass genocide, nor moralizing, would change that.

I lapsed into thought about other infrastructure. Aging infrastructure, in the form of water delivery systems, sewage removal, electricity, and roads would have cost between half a trillion dollars to a full trillion before then. Still, there was a lot less of it to replace and maintain, and it had to be done.

"Another problem is viruses, which is why I mentioned starfish," Hamish went on, bringing back to the business at hand. Good! I had insisted that he include that point, because it offered the most graphic example of the threat to fish from warming oceans. They can be transported in huge balls of tangled, discarded fishing nets, which become little – well, 500 pounds isn't really 'little' – biomes full of fish, sea anemones, and whatever else. That's how viruses get brought to shore when they would normally remain out at sea."

"As oceans warm up – and here is where oil well fires and sewage dumps from cruise ships come in, among other things – viruses that have existed in

Nature for eons suddenly thrive. They migrate away from equatorial waters and affect sea creatures that never had any contact with them before. This is why starfish were turning to goo in the waters off of the Pacific Northwest a few years ago. There are almost none left now. Nature does evolve, but not that fast."

Mr. Cantilever spoke up. "How fast can Nature cope with change?"

I spoke up. "Not fast enough to benefit humans. Nature is utterly indifferent to what we want. Just think of the second *X-Men* movie, which had Dr. Jean Grey explain it at the end: 'Mutation. It is the key to our evolution. It is how we have evolved from a single-cell organism into the dominant species on the planet. This process is slow, normally taking thousands and thousands of years. But every few millennia, evolution leaps forward'," I summed up.

"How do you remember such a long quote?" Mr. Cantilever asked me, looking amazed.

"It's fun to me, so it comes easily. I love any quote that makes its point eloquently, and I commit them to memory because sooner or later, they are useful. Quotes are a fun way to make a point, and fun makes a thing memorable. But keep in mind that we are not mutants, are only making nanobotic leaps forward."

Everyone was listening closely, and I realized that I had been enjoying myself…perhaps too much. I had to say something else and quick. "Has anyone thought about the fact that coral reefs all over the tropics have pretty much bleached and died? Those reefs were huge, living ecosystems that supported many other crucial life forms. It all kept the fisheries going. That's a huge part of the reason why we no longer have much wild fish to eat."

"Perhaps new coral reefs will form in what used to be cooler areas," Cantilever said.

I looked at him for a moment, taking in the intensity of his cognitive dissonance, and then said, "Yeah, maybe…after an ice age and several millennia. Formation of a coral reef takes so long that it won't help the human species, or many others any time soon. The Earth will do just fine with or without us. We ruined too much of its resources without thinking, and we did it fast. But! Back to Hamish," I said, as if announcing the main act of a show, and looked at him.

The faces obligingly moved with mine. The nanobotic scrubbers would gather radioactive atoms and herd them into waiting containers, shear seaweed off of plastic, and gather that plastic together, pushing it into larger waiting containers. It might actually remove the bulk of the plastic from the oceans, and the radiation also, if enough of them were deployed.

"How will these nanobots run? I mean, with what as a power source in the cold of the oceans?" Jack Enright wanted to know. He ran a nuclear engineering company that was busy taking plants offline, and he was concerned with storage of nuclear waste. I wondered what he was doing with that waste, and whether or not he was storing it safely.

"That's the beauty of it," Hamish said. "The very material that they seek deep underwater, where it's dark – radioactive pollutants – will fuel them. Closer to the surface, solar energy will do that. Either way, plastic and cesium-129 and cesium-137 will be gathered, herded into clusters for removal."

Bosch had a question. "What are the…health effects on humans of these pollutants?" He asked it partly while looking down at his plate, then, batting his eyelids as if he couldn't quite marshall his thoughts to ask it on that pause, and finally making eye contact with Hamish at the end of his question. Fingernails on a chalkboard to me…that was how it felt to watch him!

"The health effects on humans include stomach cramps, diarrhea, and rash," Hamish responded, "with possible further complications from any radiation, such as the cesium-129 and cesium-137 from Fukushima, Japan, cyanide from sunken and rusting canisters, or viruses that are brought in by whatever currents move through a given area of the sea."

"So," Bosch followed up, eyelids aflutter, "Could someone get as sick as that?"

"Indeed, yes they could. Granted, a swimmer would have to have repeated exposures to such contaminated waters without knowing what they were risking. With all that in the mix, humans risk quite the cocktail of horrors just to go swimming, let alone fishing or eating anything from most areas now. That's why we're eating farmed fish, raised in carefully shielded pools by experts in aquaculture." Hamish smiled as he said this, seeing doubtful glances at lunch plates.

"What I can do for you depends a great deal on whether or not you first have the sources of their pollutants removed from the planet's oceans and sea beds, and from its riverbeds. I mentioned just now that there are sunken canisters of cyanide that are rusting and leaking. These are from hardrock mining operations, when a boat carrying them sank. There are lots of rejected metals that occur in the tailings of that kind of mining: cadmium, mercury, lead, zinc, copper, arsenic, antimony, selenium. I can remove the tiny particles that have escaped, but you need to remove the causes and larger deposits of those things, or it's just a Sisyphean game."

With that, Hamish proceeded to show them his plan to create swarms of flying and swimming nanites, complete with a radio-camera attachment. The swarms would generate an electro-magnetized field to collect microbeads and molecules of contaminants such as methylmercury. "I can't yet promise to be able to clear the oceans of radiation, but I'll see what I can figure out as time goes on," he told us.

I was sure that he would. Hamish could do quite a lot, and had proven it many times.

With that, the tone of the meeting changed. It was time for Hamish to sit down and eat while the investors took in what they had just heard. A contract for work wouldn't be pushed under our noses just yet anyway; we were just sharing and collecting information on both sides at this point in time. There was no way that we would sign without running the document by our attorney.

Adrian O'Shea was back in Hartford (he had an office in Manhattan also), and on call.

"The patent on this nanite swarm is being filed as we speak," Hamish added.

Cantilever had one statement to make. "What we're doing is a pragmatic response to a new business reality," he said. "That does not mean that we believe in human-caused climate change. Change happens. It has happened before. The fact that it is happening now does not automatically justify labelling it 'anthropogenic'," he summed up.

I listened to this articulated statement of denial with one eyebrow slightly raised, in silence.

When he was finished, Cantilever pointedly looked at me.

I gave him the faintest of smiles and said, "Okay. What really matters is getting the mess that is our planet's ecosystem cleaned up so that it stops leaching money into oblivion, and starts being profitable again. Only a clean, healthy ecosystem has any hope of doing that."

He let the matter drop at that. Clearly, neither of us would yield any further on this point. He easily agreed with me on that last point, and said so. That congenial smile that he habitually wore reappeared as he nodded, as he happily forgot our political divergence for the moment.

Bosch had one final comment to make. It was more like a silvery threat than a comment, though: "We can develop and release an antidote to any ocean-borne pathogen that comes along once we capture some of the affected organisms and study them. It shouldn't take too much time for our zoologists and bacteriologists to come up with something. It shouldn't take much to get it past the FDA. We have enough senators and congressional representatives on our side."

Great…more tampering with the ecosystem was in our planet's future. When Bosch's order was up, more half-baked toxins were likely to further ruin the ecosystem. Something, though I didn't know what just yet, had to be done about these damned Farmers.

Next up: a presentation by an ecologist-engineer on discarded ghost nets, trawl nets, and other fishing gear that now choked the oceans. In flagrant disregard for international law, so many nets had been dumped overboard by fishers that they scarred pinnipeds such as seals and walruses for life – or simply strangled them to death. The engineer, Scott MacKinnon, discussed a plan for retrieving them.

"The poor seals," Carlisle said. But that wasn't why these Farmers cared about this.

Oh no. Their reasons were purely selfish. Their yachts had stalled when the damned things had wrapped themselves around their ships' propellers on the way to Hawai'i. A hired captain of one of those yachts (owned by Carlisle) had gotten a near-fatal gash in his shoulder cutting them off. Several surgeries later, he was still unable to move his arm fully.

He was only alive because he had worn scuba gear to do the job, and by some stroke of luck – if you can call the stroke of a blade hitting his shoulder but not his oxygen line – he had been able to breathe. Carlisle's son had managed to pull him out of the water before a shark got him.

The discussion had turned to other environmental problems once Hamish was finished with his presentation, such as invasive species of plants, animals, and insects. Gone were the days when simply using more poison on said species seemed to do any good. Instead, insecticides had only caused the targeted species to develop an immunity to them.

So how could one hope to do anything about an insect that relentlessly feasted on valuable trees and crops? "Get an entomologist to help you identify and deploy insects that prey on those insects, or whatever creature might help without consuming the surrounding ecosystem," I piped up again. What was with me? I had a lot to say today, it seemed.

But that was apparently what was wanted of me, because Carlisle smiled and wrote it down.

Another scientist at the meeting was an ecological ornithologist who brought a sampling of the plastic objects that birds had eaten. His name was Andrew Kalakaua Koa, Ph.D., and he looked more like a champion surfer and beach bum than a scientist, which gave him an aura of coolness. He was from the University of Hawaii at Manoa, and he had traveled the world to collect this stuff. He emptied a bag full of it out onto a tray that he had abruptly taken from a waiter, and started pawing through it all, holding up one item after another.

Holding up a rainbow of bottle caps, he said, "Birds are attracted to these reds and blues. They eat them, they feed them to their chicks, and then they starve to death. The chicks die a horrible death, feeling full but getting no nutrients out of the process. I can't tell you how many albatross carcasses I've found with their stomachs full of these things. If clear plastic packaging could be replaced with clear edible products that contain nutrients for sea birds and marine life, they could eat it instead of choking on it."

I seriously doubted that this was making much of an impression on the Farmers assembled here. Dr. Koa was going to have to explain how they could profit from cleaning this up, and how this was harming humans. Then he [pleasantly] surprised me by saying, "Like Dr. MacDonall said, this stuff breaks down and gets into the seafood that we eat. Plankton and other sea vegetation carry BPAs, PETs, HDPEs, and get eaten by larger sea life, such as the fish we eat. That's why I wanted him to do his presentation before I did mine."

With that, he held up another object, one that resembled a thimble, except for the fact that it was made of pastel blue plastic. "Anyone know what this is?" Dr. Koa waited. "No one?"

I had waited long enough. I put up my hand and said, "It's a tampon applicator. They're unnecessary bits of plastic. No one needs a tampon applicator when they can wash their hands before and after inserting one, and if they don't have access to clean water for that, there are always cardboard applicators. As long as we have reliable sanitation services, it's better to just get the kind of tampons that come with no applicators."

Dr. Koa smiled. "Exactly! Thank you, Professor Chatelet. I knew I would have to wait for a woman to identify this, but think about it, guys," he said to the Farmers, "do you really want your kids finding these and playing with them?! They're known as Jersey beach whistles."

A collective moan of disgust went around the table as the fathers took that in.

"That's really gross," Spades said, wincing. "My nephew did find one once, when he was five. I snatched it from him and told him not to touch garbage."

People all around the table looked revolted by that imagery. Good.

Dr. Koa showed us a few more things that he had gathered from various beaches: the contents of cargo shipping containers that had gotten lost at sea, including plastic bath toys, toothbrushes, children's toy cars and dolls, and so on and on. Nurdles, too. What a sewer we humans had unleashed on our oceans, the incubators of much of our own food, and the habitat of so many other species that didn't deserve this!

Lunch concluded on a pleasant note with various sorbets, and I downed a scoop of raspberry, another of mango, and one more of huckleberry. Where had all these fruits been flown in from, I wondered idly, but I had to pay attention to the present scene.

Mr. Cantilever approached me one more time on the way out. "What do you think the Chinese scientist ought to bring with him?"

"Bring with him?" I asked. "It's a 'him' already? You've got someone on the way?"

He nodded and smiled. "Yes. He'll be arriving in a couple of days. So, what do you think?"

"Well…" I thought for a moment. "You could have him bring several vials of that tainted water to show people. I can just see the advertisement now: 'Get your Chinese water! We have all the colors of the rainbow here! Beijing Red, Shanghai Pink, Nanking Yellow…' and so on."

Hamish had turned to put his arm around my shoulder on the way out. He caught the last of that exchange and laughed. So did the Farmers who were gathered near us. They were actually amused! Huh…I never seemed to realize it when I was funny.

Mr. Cantilever thanked me with a smile, said he would ask for that, and waved as we left.

We made a Skype phone call to O'Shea when we got back to our room, and he answered immediately. His cheerful face came onto the screen on my laptop after a couple of rings, grinning from ear to ear. "So, I take it you had a successful presentation, and duly impressed those hedge fundsters?" Adrian had adopted my terminology, and I grinned back.

"Yes, it certainly did," I said. "They love Hamish's new nanobotic swarm."

"Excellent. I'm not surprised," O'Shea said. "Our patent attorneys, under my supervision, have been working since yesterday afternoon on the application. It should be ready to file in a couple more hours, before the end of the business day today."

"Terrific!" Hamish said, smiling. "I knew we could count on you."

Adrian O'Shea looked very pleased with himself. Why not? He had things under control.

He would also be handling our contract negotiations with them. We might as well take the bastards for all that we could. They deserved it. I intended to get them to arrange and finance the cleanup of the Earth's oceans, and then…

…well, let's just say that I had an "and then" in mind for them.

A few days later, we sat in on another meeting, one that was mostly attended by Farmers.

Few scientists or professors chose to attend. They preferred to spend their time fine-tuning their proposals on their own, but Hamish had finished his patent documents and designs for his atom-scrubbing nanobot swarms, so we attended…and watched. It was intriguing.

Despite the fact that the Earth now had 6.8 billion less potential resource consumers on it, and despite the fact that the Nae-Née policy was still in place, the Farmers persisted in discussing growth. Just who did they imagine was going to swell the world economy?!

It was a buffet lunch meeting, a casual one in which we all sat with our plates, enjoying the food in lounge chairs inside the hotel. I just listened for a while, exchanging glances with Hamish as we ate our ahi tuna in silence, and wondering how much longer that fish would exist.

Hamish was watching me, no doubt wondering how soon I would say something.

He had to wait until dessert, which was little macaron cookies and lattes, but I said something. "Well, thank you for inviting me to sit in on this," I said to Jack Enright. "Lunch and a show! This certainly is fun, watching you guys discuss plans for living a fairy tale. It won't come true, but it's entertaining."

Enright looked at me, startled. "How is economic growth a 'fairy tale'?"

I smiled. "I mean that growth is over, that there aren't enough humans left on this planet to fuel it, nor does the Earth's Bank Account contain enough material resources with which to grow an economy. It is time for downsizing and equilibrium. If you can aim for and achieve that, the economy will be healthy. Too many economists fail to link the proverbial 'economy' – the stock markets, currencies of nations, and so on – to actual wealth, which is not money but land, resources, and education. That's the fantasy: that endless growth can happen. It can't, because no matter how one jiggers the numbers, the Earth's resources are finite. They have shrunk, along with the available land masses."

Sober faces – even Spades' face – stared back at me.

Carlisle looked at me unhappily. "Are you saying that we must face a contracting economy, with no further hope of growth, ever?"

"I'm saying that there will be small ups and downs, slight fluctuations from quarter to quarter, from now on, but no more growth that surges up and up and up. The Industrial Revolution is past, and the Earth's resources are just about used up. We have to budget ourselves for the rest of the time that our species inhabits this planet. Space travel is not yet an option, and I'm always betting that any Earth-like planet we ever find will already be occupied by other people with a prior claim and the biological immunity there to enforce it."

"Budget?!" Bosch was actually staring at me steadily, as though he had just noticed me. "There are only half a billion of us now. We ought to be able to use what we want now, and to stop worrying."

"Funny you should say that after the previous meeting, which was all about cleaning up the ecological catastrophe that we now have. The Earth is no longer a garden of delights. We have to grow those delights under carefully controlled conditions rather than relying on Nature to just make it happen. If toxins don't preempt that kind of growth, a superstorm might. No, we don't have much time, nor any surplus, with which to be careless. That is over."

"So what is this 'equilibrium' you speak of?" Carlisle asked me. "How come I have never heard of it? I've gone to the best schools, and I've never heard of it."

I smiled again. "Of course you've never heard of it. The Wharton School sold you what you and your family wanted to buy: a recipe for promoting a growth economy. If I were you, I would check back now and see what its professors are offering. You may just find that they are at last promoting equilibrium and stability rather than growth, which will lead to stagnation and collapse. I am not an economist, but I like to read what they write, and my favorites are the ones that most people don't listen to – or haven't been listening to – because they skip the fairy tale."

Enright wanted to know: "Who are they?"

"They are the ones you need to consult, and not out of any other instinct than survival. This is not the world that you were raised and educated in. Your heirs will have to deal with this changed world, and you need to prepare them for it, starting now. I'll e-mail all of you a list of their names and tell you what they have been writing – book titles, I mean, not just what I said here." With that, I took a small pad of paper out of my handbag, and said, "Write down your e-mail accounts here, and I'll send that data to you later this afternoon."

The Farmers grabbed it and passed it around, scribbling down their names and addresses.

Huh. Not only were they listening, but I had just acquired their top-secret e-mails. I loved it.

A little while later, I sat with my laptop in our suite, entering all of that data into my files and e-mail account, and preparing a Word file with a list of what I had promised. It was easy; every time I wrote a book, I kept a detailed bibliography of sources. All I had to do now was copy-paste the relevant data into another file, touch it up, and send it off.

In short order, I had sent the Farmers a list of academic and financial world experts, a trove of economists who would not humor them, not lie to them, and not feed them any fairy tales to make it easier for them to sleep at night. The Farmers had heirs, as I had pointed out, and those heirs needed to be prepared for the new reality. The younger generation would learn it all and use it to their own advantage, and the by-product of all that would benefit other people.

At least, that was the hope.

Otherwise, what was the point of our nanobotic attempts to heal the damage to the Earth?!

Oceans, air…all to be scrubbed. Plastic bits – nurdles and whatever else – that coated the ocean floor would have to be removed, vacuumed up, and otherwise taken off of the seabed. Otherwise, the ecosystem would be choked of nutrients and die. It was already close to death.

The Farmers were ready with a plethora of silly words aimed at selling everyone on the idea because, let's face it, money and influence on their own wouldn't get the rest of the world to help. People had to be convinced to help. (Well, I supposed that they could be forced, but no one wanted to work that hard at it).

Accordingly, "sustainability" was joined by yet more meaningless drivel such as "watershed protection" (to keep future plastic from being added to the waters of the planet), along with corporatist nonsense like "collaboration," "stewardship," and "partnering".

This meant that foodservice disposables – polystyrene plastic cutlery, styrofoam insulated clamshell boxes, and polystyrene-coated paper drink cartons and cups, plus plastic ketchup and other condiment packets – had to go.

The only solution was to return to glass milk bottles with metal caps, to be rinsed out by customers daily and returned when the next delivery arrived. Hurray for the return of the milkman! My mother and father would be very pleased. They still reminisced about such things.

People who ate in fast-food joints would have to settle for real paper containers, and damn the inconvenience if the sauces seeped through! Want ketchup with that? Pump it onto your fries before you leave the counter, because that's the only chance to do it. And so on.

Was all this effort an act of human arrogance that we could actually repair the damage of past gluttony, waste, and carelessness, was it desperation, or both?

I came out of that greenwashed meeting feeling rather depressed and hopeless.

Still, it was better to have found out what was happening than not, I thought to myself.

Chapter 19

I Think I Met the Operator

The man in the wheelchair rolled over to a stop at the seat across from me.

I knew, from overheard conversations around the poolside and elsewhere in the hotel, that he was a physician, and that he did not actively practice medicine.

I was sitting at a table by the pool with a novel, reading, and sipping a cocktail, trying to forget the horrific scene of the evening before. It was midafternoon, and it had taken me most of the night before and half of the novel to calm down and fall asleep. Now I was continuing my escape from reality, or trying to.

The man in the wheelchair was determined to converse with me. "That girl wouldn't have felt much. I'm a doctor. Trust me, she would have felt like she was very drunk, and falling rapidly into a deep sleep," he said. His gaze shifted to me. He knew I was listening.

Without moving a muscle, I moved my gaze from the text of the story and over the top of my novel, staring directly and rather steadily back at him.

His face had a Roman nose with a slightly simian aspect to it (due to the deep lines that ran from just over his nostrils and on down around his mouth to his chin), with a sallow complexion and dyed, short, wavy dark hair to go with it. He wore a white polo shirt and khaki pants, neatly belted, and a straw hat. His cold, dark brown eyes stared…bored…into my blue ones.

I did my best to bore my gaze right back at him, whoever he was. "She looked at me. She seemed fully aware that she was dying, and terrified," I replied.

"Be that as it may, it was very quick."

"Tell that to her brother, or whoever the pilot of the boat was. He was crying."

"That was her boyfriend. No legal ties for the hotel to worry about."

"How horrifically convenient," I said with a glare, and moved my gaze back to the novel.

The simian in the wheelchair paused for a moment, and then rolled himself away.

I glanced up at him, thinking that he seemed very familiar.

Well…I could look him up on my laptop later.

I went back to my novel and did my best to get lost in eighteenth century Scotland.

But before I had the chance to do that, I overheard another conversation between that man and one of the corporate wives who had come with us on this trip. Her name was Jennifer. She was talking about the possibility of having another baby, and he was telling her that it was unlikely that she would be able to get a birth license.

"You know how it works, Jenn. Even though you and your husband qualify – and I've seen your applications, you check out financially and psychologically – the system works like an inverse checkbook. There must first be a death to balance the account. Only then can there be a birth. The Earth shall never again have too many humans on it for its ecosystem to service."

Jenn looked decidedly petulant at this. "But there was just a death yesterday," she said. "Who – what prospective parent – benefits from that?"

The doctor laughed a mirthless laugh. "Why, Jenn, how mercenary of you! Be careful, or you will make yourself a suspect in that death."

She looked affronted. "I had nothing to do with it! I thought it was an accident. So sue me for looking for a way to have a kid. I want one. We've been married for about five years, and if that stupid nanite hadn't been invented, we would have had at least two by now."

"That nanite being invented is not why you haven't had kids. The U.N. population policy is the reason why, and you know the reason for it. Everyone who wanted kids before that policy was free to have them, regardless of the fact – and don't bother to argue that it isn't so – that the Earth is still in the sixth mass extinction since life began on it. I don't see why people like you are so determined to have what you want, when your offspring will inherit such a world."

"Whatever. I want a family. I want someone to be there for me in my old age, and having only one child seems like a poor bet for that. I want to see that someone as a baby and a tween and a teenager, and then as an adult, knowing that I have helped her or him to grow up. I've always wanted it. It's a deep, instinctive longing. Why can't you understand that?!"

"Oh, I understand it perfectly well – all too well. That's not the point. My wife and I had one child, before my accident. He grew up and is fine. But we never intended to have more. I read *The Population Bomb*, you see. Even if Ehrlich's timetable was off, it still made valid points, and the predictions he made still came true, and horrifically so."

"But what about that death? Who benefits? I didn't cause it, but it's still a 'debit', as you say. I want to know whether or not it means that I can have another baby."

"You are persistent. No, my dear Jenn, I'm afraid that that particular debit was already spoken for, by an earlier birth license application that had had to be put on hold for a while."

Jenn regarded him with a gaze that was both angry and suspicious.

I quickly moved my eyes to the pages of my novel, but I wasn't seeing the words on the page. Instead, I was wondering whether that so-called accident really had been one.

And I knew that this was the Operator.

And I saw that this vampire-like, predatory hunting for a death to exchange for a life was part of the new world order. To keep our species at half a billion, each new life that was made must be made deliberately, and only after a death had paid for it.

I had no intention of rolling over and dying so that some breeder could selfishly reproduce.

No. I wanted to stick around and observe some more. Why should I leave this life before I wanted to? No reason at all – I shouldn't, and I wouldn't. I wanted more time. I wanted to see what was going to become of us all.

What we were experiencing now was not yet over. The transformation was not complete.

I thought I wouldn't interact with him again on this trip, but even a luxury hotel isn't that big when the ecosystem around it is so hostile as to preclude most excursions. Within a couple of days, he was rolling up to me in his top-of-the-line, fit-into-any-tight-space wheelchair.

This time, I was sitting inside, in the café, enjoying a cappuccino and a raspberry-orange treat with my novel on the side. Funny…I wasn't reading any heavy research on this trip – nothing that would require such deep concentration as to make observing my surroundings difficult.

"Professor Châtelet! How are you this morning?" he asked, inviting himself to my table.

I put the novel down with some reluctance, then decided it was unavoidable and stuck the bookmark in it. "Okay, how are you? And what is your name? If we're going to interact, I might as well know your name, too." It wasn't like I was about to call him 'Operator' and let on that I knew he was the trigger-switch guy of the nation's Nae-Née devices.

He gave me a serpentine smile and replied, "It's Dr. Richtermetz. It's German, and it means 'judge' and 'knife'."

"It's always good to know what one's name means," I said amiably. "My last name means something like 'chateau' – one that's more like the size of a large house than one of the ones from the Loire River area."

He nodded politely.

Damn…this conversation was strained. What did he come over here for?!

The silence dragged out, so I said, "Do you want a cup of coffee? I was taking my sweet time with mine." He nodded, so I caught the waiter's eye (amazing that that didn't take much time – I usually had a lot of trouble doing that) and waved him over.

Dr. Richtermetz's order was soon placed, so I asked him, "So…what's your first name? And do you know what that means, also?" And I grinned at him.

Now he smiled. "You ask a lot of questions."

"Well, you sought me out. We have to talk about something."

"True. It's Kurt. I think it means 'brave counsel' – or something like that."

I smiled politely. "'Avril' is an obvious one, and my middle name, Antoinette, means 'priceless'. I like them all well enough."

"Clearly. You didn't take your husband's name."

I grinned, but with a 'challenge-me, I dare you' tinge to it. "No, I didn't. I knew when I was eight years old that I could never bear to change my name. Then I saw the courtesy title 'Ms.' in my third grade textbook, asked about it, was told that it was for women who wanted a title that merely indicated gender, and thought, 'Problem solved!' Later, I read about Lucy Stone, the first woman to keep her own last name when she got married – in 1850 – and that was that."

Dr. Richtermetz smiled again. "My wife kept her name too – it's Needham – but I don't think she put so much thought and planning into it. She just told me that she wanted to do that."

"Is she here?" I asked.

"No, Shari didn't have time. She's busy in D.C. She's a lobbyist."

"I see." I could just imagine her siphoning off data from him over the phone while he was here, learning what the Farmers on this trip wanted, and then rushing off to Capitol Hill to make sure that it was duly voted for.

After watching him carefully, I finally decided to just go for it and ask. "Several years ago, when the population policy was first formulated, promulgated, announced, and implemented, I saw a doctor who looked just like you – same face, slightly different model of wheelchair – on television, discussing it. His name was Maxwell R. Kramer, M.D."

A grin spread across his face. "There's no fooling you, Professor. That was me. I've upgraded my wheelchair since then. We circulated a fake story about me having no family so that my wife and family wouldn't be targeted."

I nodded. "Good move. I remember some lunatic shot another physician you worked with."

"That was sad. She had a family who missed her."

His cappuccino arrived, and an apple turnover. I watched him taste his coffee, then asked him, "So, have you checked out the hospital and my husband's Regenics clinic?"

"I have. It's excellent – very calming and efficient."

I smiled. "Thank you – I'll tell him you said so."

"Do."

What did this guy want from me? Just to observe me a little? Okay...

He spoke again. "It's ironic to see the inventors of Nae-Née with a life-extension therapy. You prevent more lives from coming into existence, yet offer a way to prolong existing ones."

At last we were getting to it. He wanted to figure us out. Fine. I didn't care about concealing such things. "Yes...we wanted to be married with no kids, and no worry of accidental kids coming into existence. Every child born ought to be wanted, and no mistakes allowed, and so on and so on. But...usually, by the time you earn enough money to have fun in life, your body has most annoyingly aged to point of no longer being pretty, no longer being healthy, and no longer being limber and able to move comfortably and quickly. How can one travel and see the world like that? It's too late. Hence these inventions. We invent what we feel is missing in life."

"I see. That's quite a thing to do – very impressive. But, if everyone lives an extended lifespan, that means that fewer people who want to have babies can do so. Have you thought about that since the birth licensing policy came out?"

"Of course." I grinned at him.

"And?"

"And that's too damned bad. I'm with the people who already exist, not babies, not people who want more babies, and I don't care if they don't like that. They will just have to take their chances. After all that our species has done to crash the planet's ecosystem, I have no sympathy for those who just don't care and who want more babies to keep on doing damage to it."

"So you overheard my conversation the other day at the pool, with that would-be mother."

"Yes, I did. And how do you feel about those wishes of hers? I thought she seemed like an anthropomorphized vulture, circling human corpses, waiting for her opportunity to get what she wants, regardless of the cost to others."

Now he grinned. "Yes, she is such a creature. I can't say I feel a lot of sympathy for her, either. She can take her chances for all I care, too."

"Huh…" I sipped my cappuccino. "So many dead so fast, within the space of a year or so, and people know that our species is watching its eco-bank account now, expecting to balance the checkbook, a death before another new life can be created…it's a macabre situation, yet I don't see any other way. Have you seen the Georgia Guidestones, and what's written on them?"

He looked at me carefully. "Keep humanity at under half a billion, in perpetual balance with Nature, or something like that, yes."

"Well…we're more or less there, and yet I keep wondering: what if we had been able to beat the plague and just let Nae-Née get us there? Wouldn't that have helped the ecosystem? Wouldn't we have been able to do it – bring our numbers down while we all coped with ecological collapse, sharing resources carefully, cooling it with the insane consumerism? It's just something that I wonder about."

Now Dr. Richtermetz laughed. "That view represents wishful thinking. I thought you of all people knew that everyone never does what they ought to do. I've read your work, so I know that you know it. No…nothing short of an Orwellian society would get that job done, and even so, there would be revolutions against green policymaking. No. Nae-Née is necessary, but its true value is in maintaining a status quo of our species' numbers, and enforcing that status quo."

"Yes, I do know. I just wanted to talk it out with you and hear you outright say it."

"I can appreciate that. Does it ever weigh on you, the fact that you thought up the idea for Nae-Née, and now it has morphed into an Orwellian tool for saving the planet? I know you meant is as a voluntary device, to be available on demand. The very way that you and your husband designed it is ingenious in that it doesn't break any part of the reproductive system; it merely puts it on hold, until it is wanted for use."

"No, it doesn't. The Orwellian use to which it was put was not our idea, and we were never asked for permission about that. No…people who just don't care about the impact they have on the world as they consume it, as long as they are able to do that, don't concern me at all. They disgust me. I think of them when I think of the birth licensing policy. The only thing that I object to is the murder of someone who already exists. Nixing a pregnancy to prevent another human from existing has never bothered me."

"You don't like babies, either, do you?" He ate some of his apple turnover.

"No – not most of them. Reproduction is gambling. You have to accept whatever you get, even if it's a loud, neurotypical, annoying person rather than a quiet, introspective, studious kid. I would want the introspective studious kid, so I should not be a parent. I'm too picky, and I want quiet too much to like most kids. I want my husband and other family, and that's enough."

"There's nothing wrong with that."

"Exactly." I ate the next to last bite of my tart.

"But don't you think life is much nicer now, with the plague behind us, and far fewer humans in existence? Now the Earth can heal, and it's less crowded." He was creepy, watching me carefully, gauging my responses. Well, I was doing that right back.

"Nicer?! The Earth's ecosystems are so thoroughly polluted now that they won't recover any time soon, and not without some really clever technology combined with complete changes in the behaviors of the humans who still exist. Yes, I hate crowds, but this is ridiculous. Billions of people had to die just to shut off many of the spigots of pollution production, and I'm willing to bet that most of them were not evil people, and that they didn't deserve to die."

He smiled as I said this, as one who is indulging a child does. "That's true," he said.

"Got any more interview questions for me?" I asked, disgusted.

"Nope." Dr. Richtermetz swallowed the last of his cappuccino with the last of his treat, and excused himself. "It was nice visiting with you, Professor. I'll see you around the hotel, and the clinic, I expect. Have a nice day."

"You too – good talk. Thanks for the visit." I smiled politely at him.

He smiled and waved, and then I watched him wheel himself away, out of the café. He obviously had more appointments on his agenda.

I ordered another cappuccino and picked up my book.

Chapter 20

Hamish is Inducted Into the Molech Group

The way that I expected to spend my evening of eavesdropping via techno-telepathy was by listening to a bunch of hedge fundsters talk about a mysterious plot to ruin everyone else's lives. What I wanted was to gather enough damning data to legally bury them.

Well, that and a few other juicy details. The devil tends to be in those.

It was those juicy details that I had been expecting, and therefore had focused my attention, but when it was all over, I found myself reconsidering that first bit very carefully. Hamish had been promised that secrets would be revealed at this meeting – secrets that explained how the words on America's Stonehenge were made a reality. That henge could be none other than the Georgia Guidestones.

The evening before, Hamish had set up the flying, microscopic nanobots with me.

We would have three swarms moving about the meeting, audio- and video-recording it all.

I would remain in our suite, as women were not members. The sexism involved galled me, but something else nagged at me: an inkling that I wouldn't have wanted to be there in person. Besides, literally becoming a fly on any wall I chose held considerable appeal.

We ate in the suite that night, going over the last few details. Claire and Fabian had been told to eat in one of the hotel's restaurants. If they came back early, I expected to be in our bedroom with the door closed and locked, watching the feed. They were not to know about this.

At last, at five minutes before nine, Hamish kissed me good-bye and walked out with Aaron. The meeting was in a large hotel suite on the top floor, he had told me. The nanobot swarms were in his right pants pocket. Once he arrived, he would let them loose by pulling a handkerchief out and brushing his nose with it. All three swarms would then disperse.

There was no problem with his technology, which was par for the course with him.

Off he went, into an elevator, up several floors, and out on the side that faced the ocean.

He was greeted at the suite door by a smiling Jefferson Pierce and Carlisle, who ushered him inside and pressed a glass with two neat fingers of Scotch whiskey into his hand. "Come on in, Dr. MacDonall! You're one of us!" True; Hamish's net worth, thanks to Nae-Née alone, was easily competitive with any of theirs. That did not, however, make him one of them.

Hamish paused at the door, looking at the group assembled within.

I looked too. The gathering could have been an aging Hasty Pudding Club at Harvard, or any other group of privileged ivy leaguers. They were preppie, flawlessly groomed, and their ages ranged from forties on up. With Regenics in their systems, some of the men who looked to be in their forties could have been much, much older, I reminded myself. An aura of creepiness hung oppressively over them all.

They moved a few paces in, at which point Hamish found himself confronted with a massive metal statue of a bull. Flames flickered beneath it. "What's this?" he asked.

"A German founder of our group used to arrange the entertainment at our secret meetings," Carlisle told Hamish. "He had a life-size bull, and would make sure that a street boy had been captured in time for the meeting. The child would be drugged, but the timing for the sedative to wear off always coincided with being shown to the group, confused as to how he had wound up next to a huge metal bull. No sooner would he wake up and take notice of his surroundings than he would be forced inside, and the fires lit. Drinks would be served as he roasted and screamed."

As the origins of the Molech Group were explained to Hamish, he had listened quietly. It was only when shown a small bull-cauldron statuette with a trap-door bottom that he spoke. "What is it with Germans and ovens?" he asked mildly.

The room burst into laughter. These fiends didn't take themselves too seriously, it seemed.

The introductions resumed in a whirlwind of names and faces. Hamish looked as though he were certain never to remember them all. I felt the same way, until I reminded myself that I was watching it all via nanite spy-swarm, and that it was being recorded. We could review it later, and memorize all names and faces at our leisure.

More banter ensured, along with more introductions. Hamish met all of the Farmers we had seen on the plane, in the hotel, and around it, minus the men and women who worked for them. He also met many of the people he had treated with Regenics in Lausanne, banksters who had gone there with their families (their families were not present), including Leo Uberfein. "Dr. MacDonall! Nice to see you again! I knew I'd be seeing you at one of these meeting sooner or later," he said with a grin and a wink. Hamish smiled and shook his hand.

The Farmers were getting their own drinks tonight, and eating from a buffet. No witnesses would see or hear any of this…or so they thought.

I smiled to myself as I thought about that. But I didn't smile again for quite a while.

Spades lumbered by, half-drunk as usual, and poured more whiskey into Hamish's glass. No matter how entitled and blasé the guy seemed, I couldn't hate him. If he actually knew what was going on with the others, I would be very surprised.

He came across as a deep-down, intrinsically good person who happened to have been born into a wealthy family. He also fell asleep a lot after drinking, and several times, I had seen the other Farmers wait until he was passed out in a drunken stupor before quietly sharing secrets, not that I had been able to hear any. It looked like the same thing was going to happen tonight.

Anyway…Hamish had noticed something odd about the flames under the bull. "Are those flames getting hotter?"

"Yes, they are," Dillion replied. "The occupant should be coming around right about now."

Hamish gaped at him, horrified. "Occupant? You've actually got a person in there?"

Enright appeared on his other side and laughed. "No – it's just a recording. We don't actually roast a real human child in this thing. It's just symbolic now. But we do turn up the heat as part of the show." With that, he actually glanced at Spades, who was awake still, and in earshot.

A voice howled, seemingly from inside the bull. Was he kidding?!

"Where is that sound coming from then, if not inside the bull?" Hamish had to ask.

"The flames don't heat the center," Pierce told him, sipping his drink. "It's kept cool there. The audio speaker plays the recording from that spot."

I directed a nanobot swarm closer, to get a view in between the flames. There was almost no space for any such thing, nor could I see anything dead center other than ash. No uniform set of holes, no mesh grille, nothing. Hamish couldn't get that close, so he had to just nod.

The men moved over to the buffet, chatting.

Suddenly, the screams reached a crescendo, and those sounds were joined by pounding.

It sounded authentic enough to me.

Hamish stopped eating his caviar and looked over there as the flames roared up.

"It's always a shock the first time someone sees and hears this," Carlisle said, smiling. "But don't worry – it really is all fake. Some Hollywood, special effects guy set it up for us." He patted Hamish on the shoulder and wandered off with his drink, flopped into a poufy chair by the windows, and was soon chatting with someone else.

A few minutes later, the bull-cauldron got quiet, and the flames went down.

It was possible that the flames were controlled by a machine, but those sounds…no way!

Bosch came over to the feast of delights on the buffet table, took some shrimp and avocado snacks, refilled his martini glass, and waved Hamish over to a pair of poufy chairs all the way across from it. "I don't want to sit too near the food, or I'll overindulge," he admitted.

Hamish smiled politely and settled in across from him with his own snacks. I knew he wasn't particularly hungry, but he ate a couple of things, just for appearances' sake.

Bosch looked at him steadily, sipped his martini, ate the olive off of its toothpick, and finally said, "I've been following your work with the vaccine serum, along with that of various other physicians, of course. There was no fooling any of you, we knew. We're all great admirers of your canniness, stealth, and careful protection of a few well-chosen individuals."

My stomach turned over. Were they planning to roast Hamish in that horrid bull?!

But no…Bosch went on, "You protected your family – naturally – and people around you on whom you rely. But you left a few people exposed, which had us confused for a while. We weren't sure, when that girl – what was her name Ellie? – got lost in Georgia, and Claire's parents in Philadelphia, whether or not you were fully aware of what the serum contained."

Hamish stared at him, staying silent, waiting for him to talk a bit more.

"Oh yes, we were keeping track. We wondered whether or not you might make a nice new member of our group. We finally decided, when you got your entire family out of the United States right under our noses, that you were clever enough to join us. Any new member to the Molech Group must pass certain litmus tests, if you'll pardon the scientific joke. There are, of course, hereditary members, like Spades, but they aren't kept fully in the loop."

They glanced over at Spades, who was snoring loudly next to his empty glass.

Enright and Dillion opened the bull-cauldron, poked around inside with a long-handled metal pitchfork of sorts, closed it, and then Dillion turned the heat back up.

Hamish stared.

"Yes, it's real," Bosch informed him. "We found an orphan from the plague who had gotten separated from his family, about six years old, we think, in southern Alabama. I don't know what we'll do for future gatherings as everyone gets settled…" he trailed off.

Oh…I felt sick as the air rushed out of my lungs. Hamish forced a deep breath in and out.

"Anyway," Bosch abruptly resumed speaking, "we always wait for Spades to nod off before turning up the heat. He loves kids, no matter where they come from." He sipped his drink with a long-suffering roll of his eyes, and continued, "We kept a lot of unwanted kids for this. We'll run out of them soon, though. It always amazed me when the anti-abortionists claimed that 'every child was wanted' even though they're not. People want to pass on their own DNA, and they want a kid with no past and, therefore, hopefully no problems. Granted, that doesn't always work, but that's what people say."

Whoa…! NO kid should be disappeared and murdered, let alone tortured to death! I sat back in front of my laptop, stretching low over the bed as I crouched there, watching helplessly. The kid in that bronze bull was past saving. Damn…we had enough right now to go to The Hague, but it had to be organized. There was no getting around that, damn it. I was going to have to move fast, or at least fast enough, if we were going to prevent this from happening at another meeting. When was the next one? Maybe Blackout Security could find and rescue them.

Dillion came over and sat down across from Hamish and Bosch. "We meet twice a year, so be sure and bring your wife and cousins to our retreat next spring. It's at a hunting lodge."

Hamish nodded at him speechlessly. He was obviously in shock. He sipped his whiskey.

Dillion smiled. "If you enjoyed that show, don't worry – we have one every time."

"Great," Hamish said. I wondered whether or not they picked up on his lack of enthusiasm.

Bosch spoke up. "Getting back to the plague…we were very impressed that you found the nanites in the vaccine serum, although we weren't really surprised. We were even more impressed when you managed to extract them and reverse their ill effects. "

Hamish nodded. "Thank you. It was a fascinating puzzle to unravel."

"I'll bet it was a neat little game to a genius like you." Dillion smiled over his screwdriver.

Hamish smiled politely. Yeah, I thought…to a non-evil genius, it was.

"So," Hamish asked, "how did you decide what to do, to whom to do it, and so on?"

He was being careful to keep his tone one of mild interest rather than of fascination.

Enright and Bosch laughed. "We focused on the useless eaters," Bosch said.

"Ah," was all that Hamish said. Then he smiled back and sipped his drink.

As for myself, I was torn between being sickened by the Farmers' talk and elation at having definitively identified them. Pay dirt! At last, we were sure that we had found them. That was the difficult part, it had seemed. I checked that the nanobots were indeed recording this. They were.

Bane sat down with them. He was quite delighted with himself. He said, "Now all we have to do is pay the lobbyists to make sure that a state of war continues. So far, so good: we are still at war with many African nations, and several in the Middle East. Our military-industrial ATM is still churning out money. War pays, and we mean for it to keep on paying." Winkle turned around and nodded, then took a swig of his whiskey. Bastard.

Dillion got up and poured them each another round of drinks, and Hamish decided to follow him and get some more food. He was obviously determined to stay completely sober. That seemed wise for an evening spent among a group of secret genocidal maniacs.

I wondered what their next scheme might be, so I kept the nanobot swarm trained on Dillion. After his introduction of the gene-splicing scheme, I figured he had to be the brains behind the deeds. Bosch was the silent partner, directing the crimes but fuzzy on precisely how to execute, er, commit them. I now understood that he ran both Tacttag and the vaccine company. He did understand the general idea enough to enjoy them, though, sick bastard that he was.

I didn't have to wait long.

Dillion sat back down and outlined his next scheme. It was exactly as I had thought: editing all forms of autism out of human DNA, along with any genetic illnesses such as Tay-Sachs, spina bifida, and whatever else their scientists might target. "So many parents complain about having kids on the autism spectrum that we're keeping that on the gene-editing list."

What he failed to notice was that he was sharing his plan for eradicating Asperger's with a genius who had it. I had told Hamish about this in advance, so now my husband just let Dillion talk, nodding and taking it all in as Bosch looked smug.

Better to let them spill their guts, I supposed, but wasn't this plan illegal? It seemed to me that it smacked of a crime against humanity. When I had first told Hamish about it, he had immediately confirmed my suspicion that tampering with DNA on this scale could do little good and much harm to the future health of the human species.

Enright came over and sat down next to Hamish with his drink. The Farmers were all grouped around Hamish. "We've been wanting to induct you into our group for a while now."

Hamish raised an eyebrow at this. After all, he and I had almost gotten Farmed on our way back from a restaurant last year, and watched as another couple had been successfully Farmed. "Really?" was his only reply.

"Oh yes," Pierce said, pouring another few fingers of vodka. "Thanks to you and your Regenics formula, we can indulge ourselves in sex, booze – not cigarettes, but one can't have everything – and still live a long time. And not worry about surprise pregnancies. Life is great thanks to you." He sat down in the wing chair opposite Hamish, raised his glass, and sipped his drink.

Hamish just listened, intrigued. He did sip his Scotch, but that was all.

Pierce was really getting into his rhythm now. "Yes, thanks to you and to Bosch, here, the world isn't too crowded anymore. Our Peg-Leg Prez didn't object after he was made to understand that next time, it would be his wife, or perhaps one of his kids with a missing limb."

Bosch looked a bit annoyed at Pierce for letting this slip. "Really, Pierce, that isn't something we mention in polite company."

"I thought this was where we could mention any secret, and relax!" Pierce said, downing his vodka and getting up for more. "What does it matter?"

Bosch rolled his eyes, closing them perfunctorily at the end of the roll, and shook his head.

"I thought you and MacDonall might like to compare notes on nanites, that's all!" Pierce said, still swigging his drink around in its glass.

"I could hardly do that," Bosch said. "unlike Dr. MacDonall, I am a businessman, not a nanobotic scientist." He turned to Hamish. "If you're that interested, I could send you a file. It would have to be off the grid, of course, a flash drive delivered by courier. The scientist who developed it died in the, er, plague."

Hamish gave him a vague smile with a devilish gleam. "Of course."

Bosch was so arrogantly confident in his own untouchability that he soon forgot all about that, comfortable as he was at this party. He was enjoying his drink and the repartee too much.

As if all this weren't outrageous enough, the Farmers next informed Hamish that they had the ideal method of tampering with human DNA to make a sub-race of drones who could be easily controlled and made to do society's grunt work: the Zika virus. It took almost no effort.

"It's spread by infecting the water worldwide and transmitting it via mosquitoes," Bosch told him. "We have agents who go to tropical Africa, which is the planet's incubator of deadly viruses, research lethal ones, and bring whatever biological matter transmits it back as "research material" for our laboratories. Next, we arrange for its accidental deposit into tropical waters elsewhere around the globe – wherever sanitation infrastructure is weakest. Then we quietly ensure that scientists do not get enough funding to work on a cure, watching the mayhem."

Enright chimed in, "Once lots of people are sick and lose interest in reproducing – thus keeping our species' overall numbers down – we'll claim that withholding insecticides was what enabled it to spread. This'll lead to politicians and government agencies reauthorizing their use, a win-win for us! Not only that, but all those microcephaly babies will grow up to be factory worker drones, perfectly happy to spend their lives doing repetitive tasks."

"So, Hamish," Carlisle asked, "can you help us to get the waters clear of radiation, plastic, and other contaminants so that the oceans and rivers will still grow safe fish to eat, while leaving this scheme in place?"

"I'll see what I can do," Hamish lied to them.

He'd see, all right. He'd see them cleaning that mess up and then rounded up before they could commit any more crimes. I knew he was already plotting his next op with Blackout Security even as he listened to this plan for another crime against humanity.

Pierce gloated about GMO seeds being free and clear for sale. "No more pesticide use was the trade-off for getting that approved, but it was worth it," he said.

So that was what was likely growing in towns and cities around the globe now.

Bosch commented, in an insufferably smug tone, "With fewer humans on the planet, there are fewer plagues to worry about, too. People spread them around so fast when there are more of them in existence."

Hamish actually turned around in his seat to look at Bosch at that point. "That is not true. There are always viruses and bacteria. It is only human contact that brings them to our attention. Meanwhile, they continue to exist and mutate. We can never simply sit back and relax, imagining that we are safe merely because of geography or economic advantage."

Bosch, Enright, and Carlisle paused in their nodding, smiling, imbibing, and glass-clinking, then shrugged. "C'est la vie. We'll just have to take our chances. We've done what we could."

They certainly had.

I left the nano-swarm to record all of those details, since Dillion was obliging with them, and followed other conversations. Switching between different windows on my computer, I listened in on schemes to control the world's remaining oil and natural gas supplies, its arable lands, and its potable water.

Some of the members spent some time bragging over drinks that they had quietly bought water-rich land in South America for use wherever they wanted it. Enright said with a hopeful tone in his voice, "We haven't been able to get into Bolivia, but maybe now that there are fewer Bolivians, we will be able to do that soon."

Another swarm caught Farmers discussing how the mobile crematoria that had disposed of Cull victims, whom they called plague victims, had been broken down and retooled for other uses, such as melting down plastic. How convenient, I thought – great way to hide evidence!

On and on it went. I wondered how Aaron was doing, out in the conference room across the hall, or pacing up and down outside this huge lounge from time to time.

I clicked another window on my computer to hear about Africa and China.

It seemed that those places were being used by the Farmers as well. The American and European Farmers were sharing Africa with the Chinese Farmers, which took some coordination. Bosch's corporation was busy moving nearly uncontested through the jungles of the Congo and the Amazon, searching for plants and insects that might yield useful medicines. I hoped they got Marburg and Ebola viruses for their troubles.

Somehow, I doubted that, as they moved through those rainforests, their scientists and handlers were taking care not to deplete it all. To these fools, Nature was still something merely to be harvested and used up, like there was no future to be concerned about.

That wasn't all. I checked on Hamish again in time to see another guy plop himself down on the chair next to him. "Hi," he said, holding his hand out to shake Hamish's. "I've been wanting to meet you. I'm Alex Ballmer. I run the mainframe computers that make up the Creative Cloud." He smiled ingratiatingly, and I turned the nanobotic camera swarm to face Hamish. "We help Big Brother to watch everything, both in and out of the country. Nothing gets past us."

His control on his facial expressions was admirable even for an Aspie. I say that because even an Aspie would be expected to have some noticeable reaction to meeting someone with control over the world's data. This guy had access to all of our secrets and copyrightable materials…if we upgraded to the latest software and allowed that insidious program in.

We didn't. But Hamish didn't discuss that with him. He just smiled and shook hands.

There was always some possibility that this guy knew about Jason and our practice of thwarting the intrusion of the Creative Cloud into our lives, but Hamish just listened politely while revealing nothing. I moved the swarm out into the room again.

It was more of the same, in a perverted sense of the message on the Guidestones.

Essentially, the Molech Group had spent the last few decades making that list of ten pieces of guidance a reality since one of its members – and they had no idea which one – had quietly arranged for the construction of that mysterious edifice. They did not, however, know who the Henge Donor had been. That story really had died with the donor, burned in a barrel by a local banker who had agreed to cremate the story. How apt, considering the mobile crematoria.

This group had actually taken that list to be a set of instructions rather than mere advice!

It was beyond appalling, and yet…it was deeply satisfying to hear on another, perverse level: it was the final bit of evidence that crowned the collection that we and Jason had compiled over the past couple of years. It proved that the events of the Cull had in fact been a deliberate, premeditated set of acts, a crime against humanity, a war crime, genocide even, with full mens rea (criminal intent) to go along with it.

I hit "Save" on the recordings, backed them up, and called Jason as soon as Hamish left the Molech meeting. We spoke in a guarded way, but he would meet us at home when we got back. Another basement meeting was in order. I had also spoken to Aaron and Ed, and they had put the word out among Blackout Security to find the orphans and rescue them.

A couple of hours later, Hamish came back to our room, red-faced and furious. He had done an admirable job of keeping his emotions under control and concealed, but at last he was free to talk…and explode. Guesstimating about a five-minute delay between that and his arrival in our suite had been simple enough, so I was ready for him when he walked in.

"Hi Hamish," I said, getting up and giving him a hug. "You did it. You got the evidence."

"Aye." He hugged me back, but said nothing else.

I waited a moment, then stood back, looked at him, and said, "Yell! Do something. You just heard and saw and were told about lots of crimes. One was over with by the time they told you. I believe them – they are kidnappers and murderers. They're probably pedophiles, too."

"Bastards!" he roared. "I would have torn that thing open if I could have. But I couldn't do anything to save that kid by the time I understood that it was for real. After that, several times, I wanted to throw my drink at those Farmers, or better yet, light it after dousing them with it."

"But you didn't, and if you had, you wouldn't have been able to destroy more than one monster, if even that. You kept your cool, and now we have a shot at getting the lot of them."

He looked at me, and took a deep breath. "That's what I kept telling myself."

"Keep doing that. We'll see them in a courtroom yet, and then…who knows."

"The law likely won't punish them properly." Hamish still looked furious.

"No, it won't. But it will ruin their chances of ever enjoying life again."

"That I can accept," he said, and hugged me again.

It was enough to prove what had been done, how it had been done, and who had done it.

It was enough to organize into a solid body of evidence, write up as a truthful history of the past year, complete with an explanation of the evil reasoning behind it, and to present to a prosecutor.

That was where my ideas fell apart.

I was going to have to do some more research: this meant reading the treaty called the Rome Statute, which laid out the details of and governed the International Criminal Court. I would have to fully understand how the Court worked and what it could do before approaching anyone there.

Damn! I would have to continue my poker face until we went home, which would not be for another couple of weeks. We were only one week into this retreat. Fine. So be it. I would wait. This would be worth it.

It would mean vindication, justice, and closure for the dead and for their survivors. My thoughts went right to Claire, of course, but then to the hundreds of millions of strangers still left without the people whom they had been deprived of by the Cull.

Chapter 21

Superstorm – Water, Water Everywhere

This trip was proving to be unsettling in every way that it could.

A Category 5 hurricane was suddenly announced, and it was headed our way.

"Oh, yay," I said, using a flat, sarcastic tone. "Should we barricade ourselves somewhere else in this illustrious hotel, or is the place sufficiently reinforced against such assaults by Nature?"

Hamish looked unsure. He hadn't engineered the building.

Fabian looked horrified, and put his arm around Claire, who looked oddly calm.

He did a double-take when he saw the look on his wife's face. "You're not scared?"

"No," she told him. "We'll either survive it okay, survive it at great inconvenience and with quite a soggy mess to contend with, or not at all, in which case it won't matter. The only thing that bothers me is having to survive it as a widow," she said in a rather thoughtful yet detached tone. "I am not interested in figuring out how to cope with that outcome, so let's stay together."

Fabian gave her a long look, hugged her, and said, "Okay."

As it turned out, we needn't have worried. The building was engineered strongly enough against the onslaught of winds, rain, and tidal waves, and we ended up watching a rather terrifying show all day and into the night out our suite's floor-to-ceiling windows, which stretched around the outer walls of it.

I inquired about the people who lived nearby, and was told that they had boarded up their homes and gotten rooms at the hotel. "What about the staff?" Them too, I was assured.

When I double-checked this by asking the people who brought our meals up from room service, each one told me that it really was true. "Thank you for asking," a man named Carlos said, "but it really is true. We'd all go on strike – or quit – if they expected us to leave our families out in storms like this. We get them here every year, and stronger than ever now."

Hamish stayed close to me as I stared at it from the sofa, too stressed to eat, keeping his arm around me. "If you weren't here to watch this with, I might be scared to look," he told me.

That broke my gaze. "You would? I thought nothing scared you."

"You're wrong. Why do you think I vaccinated the family so carefully, all spaced out, and took you all away via such a circuitous route? I don't want to be alone any more than you do."

I hugged him and curled up closer to him.

Claire and Fabian were curled up on the other end of it. It was a long sofa.

Our Blackout guys were sitting in the suite with us, keeping a polite distance, but we knew that they needed company as much as we did, and were glad to give it to them. Their military training, weaponry, and protective instincts were useless against Nature, and we all knew it.

Sometimes, it was just better to stick together.

When the storm finally ended, I called home and told our family that we were okay.

My mother had a fit, of course, but what could we do?

"We're due to go home in a couple of days anyway, so you'll see us shortly, Mommy," I said to her, hoping I sounded reassuring. She had once told me that I sounded sharp no matter what I said. I resorted to words. "I love you, Mommy."

That seemed to work. She calmed down and chatted about the rain that was coming their way, "Though it'll be nothing like what you just experienced. I can't believe you all sat there and watched it through a huge glass window. I'd have been too scared to look at it."

Yes, we were a bit crazy. But…it had felt right to stare Nature in the proverbial face rather than cower from it in terror. The past year or so had taught us all that humans were scarier than most of what Nature could throw at us. We had stayed dry, so there was no reason to look back at the memory in fear.

Our Farmer hosts, of course, met the conclusion of the storm with arrogant smugness.

"This is how it is when one prepares for the assaults of Nature with engineering, foresight, and human ingenuity," Enright announced in the hotel's main ballroom the next evening. We were all assembled there to share one last dinner as a group, and to talk about the storm.

My family and I exchanged incredulous glances, and dug into the appetizers without a word.

As soon as I could say what I wanted to say on my blog, however, I would. For now, I wrote it and saved it for later. I noted the irony of writing about the fact that we had just visited a place with water all around us that was undrinkable, useless to us due to its toxicity. We couldn't even swim in it without a lethal injury, and I disclosed the horrific, gruesome details of the "accident" that we had witnessed, leaving out speculations about murder.

The main point that I sought to make was that water misuse and abuse had done more to cause desertification all over our planet – including underwater ones – than fossil fuel use had. Granted, fossil fuels had done plenty to alter the biosphere and kill a huge chunk of the ecosystem, but sucking the planet dry on land while allowing wastewater to run off into the rivers and oceans, had been fatal to many ecosystems.

It was amazing that we had any usable arable land left. Now we saw frantic efforts to plant trees just to retain what little water remained far inland. It was insane. The comparisons to the once Fertile Crescent of the Middle East were inescapable: that area was now a total desert, and it had been for several millennia due to water use and abuse, without a thought for the future.

Our planet was a grand-scale version of Rapa Nui – Easter Island – right now.

We couldn't move to Mars, and what would be the point of doing that?!

Mars was a crashed ecosystem. Our sun had burned hotter in the past, making Earth inhospitable to humans when humans did not yet exist. Mars had been the place to be then, and now that the sun had cooled enough that the Earth was the place to be, humans existed…and we were still killing our only home. Going to Mars, a planet that was about a quarter the size of Earth, one that was desert all over, was lunacy.

But that blogging was later. We had a bit more time before our departure for home, and I would have to conceal my true opinions of many things a bit longer. That meant another day of enduring bickering mothers, screaming kids, and phoniness. Sigh. Poor us! Surely ours was the saddest story, slumming it in a resort hotel, my own snarky thoughts chided me.

At least the orphans got rescued. Blackout Security had used the cover of the superstorm. They were all being held at a resort hotel near Disneyworld, in Georgia, the new location, and the Molech Group didn't know…yet. We breathed a major sigh of relief and resumed the trip.

Once again, I found myself by the pool for another day, with everything back in place as if there had been no hurricane. Claire was walking around the hotel, looking at the artwork and photographing it with her camera to show Grandmère when we got home. I was alone, reading.

"Lucy! Why can't you just play with the other girls and let me alone?!"

Oh, great. That awful woman was picking on her Aspergirl yet again. I looked up.

Lucy was sitting next to her mother, surrounded by books on plants and dinosaurs, bothering no one, while her mother chatted with her friends. It looked as if the girl's mother simply wanted to chat about things that children should not hear, and wished to be temporarily rid of her.

I was about to invite Lucy to bring her stuff over to sit with me and read when the Operator, Dr. Richtermetz, rolled up to my lounge chair. Damn! I put my book down and sat up. It seemed only polite, since he couldn't flop into the next lounge chair.

"Hi, Dr. Richtermetz. How are you?" I said.

"Fine. How are you? Looking forward to returning home?"

I gave him a careful smile. "Yes, I am. Lots of people to see, writing to do, and so on."

"I suppose you are looking forward to leaving these people."

"What makes you say that?" I asked.

"The look on your face when that woman is mean to her daughter. I know that you and Lucy both have Asperger's, and that Lucy will quite likely grow up to be the scientist she wants to be. And I see how unappreciative her mother is of how intelligent and introspective she is. You are disgusted with the mother, frustrated that you can't help the girl more, and you hate to see that."

Huh. Maybe the Operator had some good in him. Of course, no one was all good or all bad. "Yes, that's true," I said.

"Not all parents are good at it, or should even be parents," Dr. Richtermetz said. "Tests and forms cannot prevent every problem."

"No, they can't. They can only screen for the most glaringly obvious difficulties. The subtleties are left to chance. At least Aspies are still being brought into existence. We will always be better off with more Jeffersons, Austens, Twains, and Madame Curies."

"Yes. But what do you think about parents? I only ask because you obviously don't want to become a parent, yet you seem to understand the value of a good one versus the detriment of a substandard one."

"Oh…you mean the difference between a zygote donor or incubator, versus a father or mother, versus a dad or mom?" I asked.

"I think so," Dr. Richtermetz replied. "Please elaborate on that." He smiled indulgently.

"A zygote donor impregnates a woman and walks away, doing nothing more for a future child, and an incubator of a woman brings a child into existence without feeling obligated to care about it or bother to make sure that it is okay. The Nae-Née policy seems to have done away with those, as far as I can see. But after that, it can't fix every other problem."

"Such as the ones you see around you."

"Exactly. I see a lot of mothers and fathers here, but very few moms and dads. The mothers and father make sure that their kids are well fed, properly nourished and in perfect health. They make sure that their offspring have every educational and other opportunity in life. But appreciating their kids as individual people and taking a real interest in getting to know them, and accepting them as parents who play the reproduction lottery by having kids at all…I don't see such parents – parents like mine. Those are the moms and dads."

Dr. Richtermetz smiled. "That's what I thought you meant: those last titles are honors."

Chapter 22

I Pledge Allegiance to the Untied States

What was the real oath of allegiance now?

What was the one that the Farmers of the New World Order really want to hear, now that they have coerced and lied their way into getting people to compromise, surrender, sacrifice, and otherwise cede their civil liberties and freedoms in order to safeguard their security?

Not that it actually got them much security, when the Cull was added to the equation, but what is it that those bastards really wanted from the rest of us? We were, after all, mere fodder, seed, and worst of all, fertilizer to them.

It seemed to me that the treasonous spirit of what they wanted was this:

"I pledge allegiance, to the Banksters, of the Untied States of America, and to the New World Order for which it Falls, One Nation, Divisible, and Subject to the United Nations."

That really sucked. That "Untied States" thing was just me being sarcastic, not a typographical error. I couldn't resist switching that around. It deserved to be mocked.

We got back to Manhattan at last and headed straight for the firehouse.

The flight hadn't been long, but it felt like an eternity. The obnoxious, spoiled brats of all ages had made it feel that way. Mothers with their Lizz Designs, competing for Best Dressed Bitch Award all the way to JFK Airport, and kids screaming the rest of the way, bored by their electronic games, had tired the four of us out. Aaron, Ed, and Lionel didn't look so good, either.

At last, we all stood in front of the terminal at JFK Airport, pausing before heaving our bags into waiting Blackout Security vehicles. Three black SUVs had pulled up to take us back to the firehouse in Manhattan for a few days.

"It feels like mid-summer," Claire said. "It's not as humid, but I don't even need a jacket."

Once in the vehicle, I noticed the temperature: 82 degrees Fahrenheit. That explained it. Was fall cancelled? No…the ride into the city revealed trees in the final stages of shedding leaves.

"Let's stay here for a couple of days," I said. "We can rest, speak freely amongst ourselves, enjoy Manhattan, and then go home."

"Good idea," Hamish said. "We can swing by the Rockefeller Institute and check out the Regenics clinic there again without being in a hurry. Plus we can see who we know that is still alive and teaching and researching there."

Claire and Fabian looked pleased with this plan. They gave us tired smiles.

"I didn't realize it was possible to feel so tired after a flight," Claire said, "but all that noise and bickering was exhausting. My parents never acted like that. They got along…and quietly."

"Same here," Fabian said. "I've never seen married couples act like that – not in person."

Hamish cracked up. "They're just wealthy and clueless. It's good that that seems abnormal to you. It bodes well for your future."

They smiled.

We all retired to our rooms upstairs to space out for a couple of hours, then regrouped for dinner. We ended up at a Belgian place nearby, eating mussels and fries – "moules et frites" on its menu – and I got a raspberry beer. After that, we went walking to a chocolate shop and got dessert, with Aaron, Ed, and Lionel watching everything and everyone as they ate. Lionel was going to live in the Blackout Security house on our street when we got back.

It was a good evening, and it felt like home, even though the real one was in Connecticut.

That feeling likely came from not having to watch ourselves for slip-ups in conversation any longer, and from being alone together as a family. We were back in our own familiar territory, and starting to relax.

The next day, Hamish had to visit Dr. Nurse and update him on the details of setting up the Miami Regenics clinic, so the rest of us went to the Museum of Natural History to see what was new there. The answer: Plenty.

We spent over two hours studying exhibits on the Sixth Mass Extinction and the new map of the Earth. It was presented as a computer-generated, interactive display, sponsored by Google Earth, and it was an unnerving thing to behold, because it was reminiscent of an art show that I had seen in Soho several years earlier with Hamish. It had shown Antarctica with all of its ice melted away, and now that was almost a reality.

I told Claire and Fabian about it while we were looking at it.

"Seems like the artist knew what was going to happen," Fabian said.

"She or he must have been studying that along with art," Claire added.

"Indeed." I bought a book and a DVD documentary on this exhibit to show Hamish.

We found that the whole exhibit was a touch-screen computer display, a huge wall of glass that responded when we tapped certain spots. "I wonder what happened to Louisiana," I said, tapping New Orleans.

The scene zoomed in slowly and showed us. New Orleans was still there, but just barely.

It was another Miami, but with some dykes to hold the water back. That mostly helped the people farther up the Mississippi River, though. New Orleans had been reduced to a series of islands connected by bridges. The bridges and everything else had already been photographed, and we could see that someone had gone to a lot of trouble to maintain the eighteenth-century French character of the place, because the bridges reflected the aesthetic style of that time, except for the materials, which were brand new.

The French Quarter remained, as had famous cafés and restaurants such as The Café Du Monde. The place had suffered minimal wear and tear thanks to constant vigilance, but the Ninth Ward was now permanently underwater. I suspected that it had been wiped clean of human traces during the Cull, or just before, as sea levels had risen.

"Look, you can tap here and a voice will talk about the place," Fabian said. He tapped it.

A woman's recorded voice softly informed us:

"New Orleans is now a historic resort vacation site. Only the French Quarter and the historic areas remain, many dating back to the eighteenth century. The beauty of the place has been carefully preserved, with much of the run-down twentieth century development, which had been in the areas that were flooded, removed. This was done first by Nature, then by the U.S. Army Corps of Engineers.

"Unfortunately, many of the ancient graves were damaged in the floods. As a result, the appearance of the famous New Orleans cemeteries is maintained, but any below-ground burials had to be exhumed. Those bodies were cremated and the ashes scattered over their graves. Relatives and tourists may visit the graves, but the occupants are gone, unless they were in above-ground mausoleums, of which that cemetery has many.

"New Orleans maintains all of its old traditions, including funerals with bands marching, Mardi Gras, crawfish, beignets, and all of the familiar Cajun and Creole cuisine that goes with it – plus the people who speak those dialects."

We looked at each other when the voice stopped.

"All of those traditions, the cuisine, and those dialects?!" Claire said in disbelief. "Sure."

"It's turned into another Colonial Williamsburg, except that it's Old New Orleans," I said.

Fabian looked both appalled and intrigued. "Smart way to save it – turn it into a money-making machine. I'd go there just out of morbid curiosity, to learn about it."

"Me too," Claire and I chorused.

But it would be a very different experience than the one we had always anticipated.

None of us had ever visited New Orleans before the rise in sea levels, before the Cull, or before this reclaiming of the place. We had always talked about it, wanting to go, but one can't go everywhere and do and see everything at once. If we went now, we would see something far different: a ghost town with a different history lesson than the one we had come to expect.

We read some more about the salvaged city on the poster boards.

"That's odd," Fabian remarked. "It says here that Tulane University and other institutions have been salvaged. I wonder why the voice didn't talk about that."

Claire leaned over and read off the names. "They saved Tulane, the University of New Orleans, Louisiana State University Health Sciences Center, and the New Orleans Culinary Institute. Huh…I guess they want gourmet food available in the cafeterias at those other places," she said with a wry smile.

"Why save schools there, of all places?" Fabian wondered, staring at the board.

"Think about the geography involved, think about the climate and the ecosystem there, and think about the viruses and other airborne, waterborne, insect-borne, and other problems associated with a tropical area. The Big Easy is conveniently located to deal with the Zika virus, and it was at Tulane that it was proven that mosquitoes transmit malaria. Also, if there is anything funny going on – anything secret to be researched – an isolated place in that region is ideal for further research. Not too many residents are around to talk about it."

My cousins gave me one open-mouthed look, shut their mouths, and turned back to the display. They gave it another careful look, considering that information, and said nothing further.

We didn't like to talk about the strategic value of anything in public, so that was all we said.

We went home, met Hamish, dumped our bags, and headed out to the nearest of our favorite restaurants, a café that served omelets, salads, and crepes. On the way, I ducked into a diner to grab a copy of *The Onion*, the free satire newspaper of New York City.

I unfolded it and read the headline out loud: "'Superstorm Uncovers Secret Laboratory in Georgia – Plot to Reduce Resource Use Via Plague Uncovered.' What'?!" I said a moment later. "I've been scooped by *The Onion*!" I said, in mock outrage, keeping my voice low.

The others gave grim smiles. "That headline sounds about right," Fabian said. Claire nodded.

"Actually," Hamish said, "that story got the location of the facility wrong, but it's fiction."

Claire rolled her eyes. "Who cares? That story is disturbingly close to the mark."

"A lot of the stories in *The Onion* are," Fabian told her.

The next day, Claire and Fabian took off together for the Cloisters, a reproduction of a Medieval European castle, and a branch of the Metropolitan Museum of Art. Claire wanted to see the gardens and tapestries, and they would eat in the café. That meant that another pair of Blackout Security agents appeared to accompany them there, plus Lionel. "I still don't feel used to this," Fabian remarked, but he escorted Claire with their shadows without objection.

"They're going to have to stick with Blackout Security until they are used to it, and then keep on using it," Hamish said, as we got into a cab with Aaron and Ed.

We found the Rockefeller Institute and the Regenics clinic running smoothly, and our old office suite still functioning as well. Our offices looked the same as they had when we had left them, and even our secretary, Kay, was still there. She said that her family was mostly okay, except for some cousins from Ohio who had disappeared. Hamish and I looked grimly at each other when we heard that, but made no comment about it. There was no point.

The multi-cultural, international academic faculty had survived the Cull.

It took a quick tour of the premises to confirm this, but it was the first thing I did. Aaron paced behind me as I walked all around the campus, glancing into offices, seeing their occupants inside, and pausing for greetings and hugs. Judging from Aaron's behavior, I suspected that he already knew all this, but I wanted to see it for myself.

Dr. Mohsen Mahmoud came out of his office and chatted with me for several minutes. "Yes, Allah be praised, my parents are still in Alexandria, still alive. They are retired from their medical practices, and they keep asking when I will give up teaching and practice myself, but I love this, and my wife is happy practicing." His wife, Dr. Haleh Khashnood, worked as a surgeon at Cornell University Hospital nearby. Both of them were fine, as was their little girl.

Professor Leila Azadeh looked up from her electron microscope and stared at me for a moment, confused. I realized that she was thinking about her work and mentally switching over to the face in front of her, so I waited. Then she smiled and walked around to hug me. "How are you? How was your time in Switzerland?"

"Fine," I said. "We set the clinic up, got it up and running, and saw lots of museums there. Also, my cousin and his fiancée got married, which was fun, and so did Hamish's sister and her fiancé. It was a year of touring and family events."

"That's wonderful! That's so nice." She smiled happily.

"How are you? How did your year here go? And how is your family?"

"Not bad, not bad. My mother arrived here just before the travel ban, and she is still here. My husband is used to having her here now, and he loves her food. He doesn't want her to go back to Shiraz!" Leila giggled at that. "She makes these wonderful cookies, you see, with a paste of rosewater, pistachio, and almond pressed between two wafers. He's addicted!"

"Oh, you gave me some of those once! I love those," I said. "What about the rest of your family? Are they okay?"

"Well…we have lost contact with some uncles and aunts in Mashhad, and a cousin who was studying in Esfahan, but everyone else is okay. The cousin was their son. We weren't close, but my mother keeps hoping to find out something. At least she isn't asking to go back there. Iran is a bit disorganized since the plague."

I expressed sympathy and agreed that her mother should remain with her, in New York.

One person who came out to greet me was Dr. Mohana Avninder. She taught robotic surgery and practiced it, so I was surprised to find her in her office. "Oh, I keep my practice from taking over so that I have time to share what I know with students," she said, smiling, in her musical Hindi accent. "How was your trip to Florida – or, what's left of Florida?"

I told her about the eerie seascape of the place, and the toxic water, and the odd death.

She listened soberly. "Horrible. The world is so changed. When the travel ban was lifted, I persuaded Rajiv to go with me back to Mumbai. It was like another world there – one that I did not know. So few people! I grew up there, and it was always teeming with people. Now traffic is calm, and the population is…well…vastly less. Our parents were relieved to see us. They were scared by the plague, and puzzled at first by the sickness…" she trailed off.

"What kind of medicine do they practice?" I asked, wondering how much she knew.

"My father is an immunologist, and Rajiv's father is a virologist. Our mothers are gynecologists."

"I see. Why do you say that they were puzzled at first?"

Mohana looked furtively down the hall, then pulled me into her office. I hoped it wasn't bugged, I thought to myself. Aaron followed us in. "Who is this with you?" Mohana asked nervously.

"Mohana, you know I am followed by private security wherever I go, and have been for years. This is Aaron. He's like family now. He won't tell anyone anything that you say."

She breathed a sigh of relief. "Okay. Our fathers showed us something. They were administering the vaccine doses as they received them, until their patients started showing up in their offices with many of the disease symptoms that the vaccine was supposed to prevent. That was when they met to take a look at the serum. What they found frightened them more than anything else ever has."

With that, she looked at me, almost accusingly, and waited.

"Did they get it out and go right on with the doses, and were they able to draw what they found out of the sick patients?" I asked her.

"Yes, they did, and they were, but they had a tough time helping the sick ones."

"Get in touch with Hamish for them. In fact, he's in his office now."

"Thank you!" she said, looking relieved. "Thank you."

"You're quite welcome," I said, and we hugged.

She knew. She knew, and she had guessed that Hamish and I knew. She also trusted us enough to speak cryptically and seek our help. Of course we would help. Damn the Cull! We had done plenty of covert resistance, and it looked as though that sort of thing wasn't over yet.

Fine.

When I met up with Hamish an hour or so later, having completed the rounds, seen Dr. Nurse and visited him in his office, and gotten coffee with Aaron at the cafeteria, Dr. Avninder was in his office. She was looking a lot more relaxed, like someone who had gotten answers.

"Hello, Avril," she said. "Thank you again. Your husband showed me a few things on his laptop, and it all looks just like what I saw in India."

Hamish looked at me with grim satisfaction. "I'm sending a shipment of Regenics serum to counteract the damage. It should arrive in Mumbai in a few days." He looked at Aaron. "Was everyone careful as they talked about this?"

Aaron nodded. "Yes. At least this office checks out. Hers," and he glanced at Mohana, "we hadn't checked. We're doing that right now."

"Thanks." Hamish looked pleased with all of this.

I was rather pleased with myself for managing that conversation with Mohana back there.

We came home and saw everyone, and found out that the remodeling of Grandmère's bedroom and bathroom was completed to her satisfaction. Good – a thing done. Claire and Fabian were delighted with their bathroom as well. The work was beautiful, and we all had more breathing room and privacy now that we were all back together in the huge house.

There remained just one more thing to do, which we ought to have anticipated.

Grandmère had bought herself a brand-new television so that she could fall asleep watching old black-and-white movies, but it wasn't installed yet. The fact that Hamish was the only sufficiently savvy person in the family when it came to electronics was serendipitous, because if anyone else was, it might have been installed as is.

We couldn't let that happen; if it were turned on without modifications, Grandmère would have been watched as she watched television. Her every remark in earshot of that pernicious device would also have been listened to and recorded by some remote server. Such was life in the Orwellian police surveillance state.

"What are you doing?!" she asked as Hamish unpacked it and pried it open with his tools.

"Removing the surveillance hardware," he replied calmly. "Also, I've called Jason. He's on his way over to hack the surveillance software out of it. After that, we'll hang it up across from your bed and hook it up."

She stared him for a moment, incredulous, then seemed to catch on. She went downstairs, shaking her head. "Avril, let's make some tea and have some madeleines. I can't watch him take apart that new television. I know it will work when he's done, but I can't watch."

I followed her, laughing softly. "Don't worry, Grandmère. My parents experienced this same thing before we all went to Switzerland. They replaced the televisions all over the house, and Hamish did this to those devices also. You know they work – we can watch anything we want."

She turned back to look at me at the bottom of the stairs and smiled. "All right, then."

We had a nice forty-five minutes in the kitchen, and then her TV was ready.

Jason had hacked every TV in our house, and each one was informing our computer, a Dark Net one, of what data was sought. It blocked all efforts to access it while sending bogus data back to the Farmers. I loved it.

A house on Stoner Drive had come up for sale, and Uncle Charlie was interested.

We were interested too – in combing it for surveillance technology and eradicating it before letting the family move in. Spooked by his experiences of the past year and a half, Uncle Charlie let us do that. He was just happy that it was nearby and attractive, meaning not modern. We were, as an entire family, damned if we would accept anything that didn't meet our own standards. The hell with whatever the new world order wanted to foist on anyone!

The occupants wanted to move to Chicago, where they had a son and daughter-in-law who lived and worked. That was why the house was suddenly available. Attorney O'Shea had the deal sewn up in no time, and the mood in our house lifted immediately.

The place was a sprawling Dutch colonial house, partly covered with stone and partly white clapboard, with two stories above ground, plus an attic and a basement. The garage held two cars, but there was plenty of room for two more in the turnaround of the driveway. It was ideal.

Blackout Security was promptly turned loose on it, with periodic nanobotic check-ups by Hamish. After that, solar panels went up, and all electronics that the family wanted were installed: television, phone, internet, and so on. It wasn't long before Aunt Zoe was decorating.

Satisfaction to all at last! My aunt had it painted a shade darker than periwinkle blue. It was very pretty, and soon my mother was having a lovely time shopping with her for furniture, curtains, knick-knacks, carpets, tiles, and so on. The kitchen and bathrooms all had pretty granite countertops, just like the ones in our house, and everyone liked the grays and whites.

My mother was home now, cleaning up after lunch, having left Aunt Zoe there.

"Mommy! Don't put any plastic containers in the dishwasher!" I sounded really frustrated as I said this, having said it many times. She just didn't like to wash anything by hand if she could possibly avoid it.

"What was the reason why again?" She sounded bored with it.

"The heat of the dishwasher makes the plastic release lots of BPAs – bisphenol-As – which contain synthetic estrogens, which causes cancer. If you wash them by hand, they aren't so risky. Look," I showed her how to do it fast, "just get a little bit of water on them, then a drop of dishwashing liquid, scrub with mostly soap to get the grease off quickly, then rinse. If you really hate drying plastic containers by hand, leave them on a towel to dry and get them later."

"Or let you scold me and explain it and watch you do the deed," she said with a mischievous grin on her face.

"That works, too…this time," I said.

A little while later, in mid-afternoon, not two hours after I had fed both cats, they were pestering my mother for food. "Damn! I just fed them," I said. "They do NOT need to eat again. What's the matter with you, Spock?"

He was the more aggressive of the two. Eowyn was just sitting at the cats' placemat on the kitchen floor, calmly watching. She figured that if more cat food was served, that would be nice, but she was neither counting on it nor pushing her luck.

My mother laughed. "He's hoping I don't know that you fed them."

"Spock," I informed him, "Humans tell each other when we've fed you! You can't fool us."

Dad walked by and laughed. "He's gambling."

I took my tea and left the room. Spock followed me, still staring at me. Eowyn flashed past me, down to the basement to see Hamish. Well, at least they wanted us around. It was nice to have been missed.

Fabian and Claire were out on the back porch as usual, looking at their books. I had heard them come in from a walk around the neighborhood. They were rosy-cheeked and cheerful, which was nice. Claire was smiling, and flipping through a book I had brought back on red algae and the fate of Miami's ecosystem since sea level had risen. Soon, though, as she saw the photographs, her expression changed and got serious. The topic was anything but uplifting.

"What's going on?" Fabian asked.

"The cats were lobbying my mother for more food. It's way too early for more," I replied.

"Do they think they live on K Street?" he asked wryly.

"Guess so."

Grandmère asked, "What is K Street?"

I looked at her, nonplussed, and then grinned. "Oh! It's that street in Washington, D.C., where the lobbyists have their offices."

"Oh, right. That city named its streets after letters and states. Funny cats."

Funny cats...not-so-funny fatcats on Wall Street...

That wasn't, however, the only thing wrong with the financial system. There were far too many regulations attached to the federal tax code, as well as to the banking system, and they ripened the financial system for abuse by riddling it with loopholes. It was time to wipe the slate clean and start over, but the Farmers would have none of that, so the politicians did nothing.

The empire that Western civilization had built had risen quickly – in just a few centuries – and it had only taken a couple of decades to collapse it by collapsing its economy. It was morbidly fascinating to realize that the same fatcats who had crashed the economy were now seeking to rehabilitate it by recycling the rubbish that they had dumped into the ecosystem.

The repeal of the Glass-Steagall Act had opened the Pandora's Box of Farmers.

They had gone ahead with every money-making scheme that occurred to them, mining, logging, and fishing. They had sold genetically altered seeds which the winds carried across property lines and into organic farms, seeds which were both genetically spliced with neonicotinoids that poisoned bees.

When they encountered a plant that wasn't liked, they sought to make money from its eradication. Never mind the damage inflicted upon the ecosystem: poison made money, and greed was good. Instead of getting entomologists to decide which insects could best attack invading pests, a shower of toxins was released, poisoning every form of life it touched: plant, insect (including the beneficial ones, like bees), and humans who worked on the farms.

And now the Farmers were afraid that they had irreparably harmed the ecosystem's ability to produce food for the future. They were the sons and daughters of the previous Farmers, coming of age, ready to inherit what their parents had done.

What good was an empire of money that couldn't buy any safe, edible food?!

They would not be pleased to find that they had inherited a wasteland, a radioactive and toxic soup with no oxygen or life in it, and slag rather than air.

How odd it was to realize that we had seen the Farmer's children and heirs in Miami, Florida, a generation of angry Farmers who looked at their parents as the perpetrators of their ruined inheritance rather than cash cows who would pass on a fortune to them.

Things had changed, yet they had remained the same.

Yes, these young adults were Farmers, just like their parents, but they offered some hope.

They hadn't engineered the deaths of 6.8 billion human beings.

They hadn't poisoned the planet.

And they would be the next people to hold a hugely imbalanced portion of the world's wealth, thanks both to the removal of the Glass-Steagall Act and a tangled web of unnecessarily complex banking regulations. We needed financial rules – laws – but they must be simple rather than complex, and they must emphasize individual and corporate responsibility. No more Farming! That was killing us, even now, even after the Cull.

Would they let go, enable once more the non-Farmers – the rest of the human species who needed to work – to hold steady jobs with benefits and a realistic chance at a livable income, or not? Or would they only allow more precariat jobs – those unstable ones that came and went with no benefits and low pay? At last accounting, that was all that roughly three-quarters of the world could hope to get.

Something significant had to change.

History had repeated itself many times, but that was usually because it wasn't studied.

The Farmers, the politicians, and the ninety-nine-percenters needed to study financial history. They also needed to know that theft would be punished. No more Ponzi schemes, no more Farming, and no more acting with an impunity that comes from a sense that crime will go unpunished. It must go punished, with prison time, or complacency and theft will continue.

Theft was part of the problem: untraceable, incremental theft. Jiggering and triggering of loopholes and the rest of the world's financial system to put the vast majority of the wealth into their own pockets was theft. It was what had led to revolution in France over two hundred years ago, and the Farmers had sought to cover up their crime via the Cull. Both needed exposure.

What then? Prison sentences for theft? Okay, but what about the Cull? Death sentences for that would be nice, but the International Criminal Court didn't hand those out. It all needed to go on the public record, to be noted by historians ever after. It would be sloppy to merely skip over the theft and go straight to the Cull. That would enable the next generation of Farmers to proceed as their parents had before them. No – no more of that!

The Farmers were still vastly outnumbered by the rest of humanity. They were still one-percenters, as the rest of society thought of them: a tiny minority who controlled an absurdly greater proportion of the world's wealth compared with everyone else.

To understand just how much this was, graphs existed that depicted the disparity: an astonishingly lengthy horizontal line hugged the bottom of one that focused on working class, middle class, and wealthy individuals, and that was just for our glorious Untied States. At the far right, which was a small section for wealthy citizens, the line spiked sharply upwards, hugging the side, and went up and up, seemingly without end. It was reminiscent of eighteenth-century France just before the guillotine corrected that disparity.

People who had that wouldn't just give it up.

The economy needed to be rejiggered to spread wealth out among most of society. Government spending had to be reapportioned and vastly reduced. War budgets had to shrink. Health care and education needed more resources. Ninety-nine percenters needed some assurance of a good life.

Relying on the younger Farmers to simply have a crisis of conscience and an overriding concern for the good of society would not do the trick. No…something more would be necessary. It would have to be something that scared them into good behavior, just as the banksters of France had learned that lesson.

The guillotine was gone, but the international courts of law could help. As I read about the International Criminal Court, I realized that all it needed was the right evidence, and enough of it. I started going through the mass of data, sorting it and preparing it. It was huge.

The discovery process, which was what lawyers called the seeking, finding, and gathering of legally actionable evidence of a civil or a criminal wrong, was crucial to bringing about the necessary changes to human society's remaining half billion members. I hoped to assist the Prosecutor of the I.C.C. by organizing as much of it as possible, to save her some time.

I wanted to avoid the problem of cherry-picked evidence, ill-gotten evidence, and of the appearance of simply having handed a huge body of evidence to the Court. Who was to say where it had all come from? A chain of custody had to be established. It would do no good to have it all thrown out as the "fruit of the poisoned tree" – a legal term that meant that the proffered evidence was illicitly acquired and thus worthless.

Jason and I had our work cut out for us, it seemed. More data was still coming in.

When I explained what I was doing, Hamish, Claire, and Fabian insisted upon helping.

"Great," I said. "It'll be us, the nanite guns, the memory sticks, and Blackout Security."

Fabian just had one question. "How come people didn't see this coming, and just obediently went along with the vaccinations, without kicking up a fuss and questioning authority?"

I laughed, but mirthlessly. "Schools. Our school system – the public one – is why. It was set up according to the model of the Prussian system a little over a century ago to train kids not to think but to obey authority figures. Rote memorization without connecting the dots was the goal so that a vast majority of Americans would acquiesce to dull lives of labor and service jobs."

Fabian looked appalled, but Claire just looked introspective. "That makes sense," she said.

I went on, "Banks, the stock market, and corporations are not set up to benefit anyone other than those who run them. Education is aimed at making us all good drones to serve the banksters, hedge fundsters, and corporatists."

"Clearly, they didn't get to you," Claire remarked.

"We Aspies are too independent for that. We are a threat to them, so they keep us economically weak as much as they possibly can. Its objectives failed to ruin me because I was safe at a private school. My cousins excelled and so made it past the filter in public schools. How did you get through it?" I asked her.

"Private school. It was an Episcopal one, but it was nice. We were encouraged to connect the dots. I distinctly remember enjoying the experience on many occasions. Creativity and original thought were allowed and encouraged." She grinned.

So did I. "Let's subvert the Farmers with what we've got, then."

"This is one of those times to say, 'insert evil grin here'," Claire said.

Chapter 23

The Recycling Age

Jacques was having a fine time when we got home.

He had prepared a system of classification of plastic waste, with credit given to the discovery of the Great Pacific Garbage Patch for a list of considerations. He was quite delighted with it now that he was in full swing with this fabulous system, and we found ourselves just as delighted for him. It was a great way to track and manage everything.

"We live in the Plastic Age," Jacques wrote on his newly created website, with a rhyme of a URL: www.PlasticSpastic.com. We laughed at the name, but he stuck to it. Why not – it was catchy, and that would draw attention to it.

"There are plastics every which way we look. Human consumerism has led to a throwaway culture that must be reversed, because there really is no such thing as 'away' in the ecosystem."

A list of classifications for plastic discards followed:

1. Closed-Loop Recyclability Index (CLRI): Ease to recycle for a given product.
2. Extended Replacement Time Rating (ERTR): Length of time a product lasts.
3. Reduced Maintenance Time Rating (RMTR): Whether or not a product needs maintaining.
4. Potential Number of Products Replaced/Obsolete (PNPRO): Whether or not a product eliminates the need for other products.
5. Raw Material Extraction Stress Index (RMESI): Whether or not the product is made of 100% post-consumer material.
6. Non-Toxic Status (NTS): Whether or not the components of the product are benign to the ecosystem.

This list was the blueprint for the new recycling plan.

All plastic packaging products must be taken out of service and no longer produced.

I thought he needed his own lobbyist and politician to make this a reality.

"We looked at a pair of students who are developing bacteria that will eat plastic pollution in the oceans and other waterways, but that's their business model, their patent, their invention. We intend to deal with the plastic pollution that already exists, and clean that up while making money," Jacques told me, full of enthusiasm. "We have to collect as much plastic as we can get and sell it. If we can grind or melt it for reuse, we could corner the market."

"That sounds great!" I said, smiling back.

He was off to a great start with the substance of the idea, and Jason, in on it to handle the computer modeling, had set up their website. Their ultimate plan was to have a corporation that handled recycling, which was great. Perhaps if Aunt Zoe and Uncle Charlie got too bored with retirement – especially now that they had a longer one due to the life-extension of Regenics – they would want to get involved. It could be a brisk family business, and do a lot of good.

As I thought about that, I wandered outside to check my beehives. The bees were okay.

While I stood over the hive, holding one of the top-frames, staring at the honeycomb and inhaling its lovely, sweet scent, it occurred to me that the State Apiary Inspector would have to visit to make sure that I was doing everything correctly, and that my bees were healthy.

He was a nice man, a former military nurse turned beekeeping cop and instructor.

He was the one who had taught me how to help the bees get rid of mites, which they got on their own, not because of any irresponsible practices on the part of humans. What you had to do was pour an entire package of confectioners' sugar over the hive and let the bees eat it off of each other. In the process, they ate the mites off, cleaning each other. The inspector called them "ghost bees" during this process.

My bees looked okay for now. Mites were visible to the naked human eye, and there were none on them. Good. I put the hive back together and stepped back. The bees knew me, of course, and my pheromones, so I hardly ever got stung now. They could smell fear, and were deaf, despite the steady humming sound that they made. I thought they were beautiful.

Fabian had taken an interest in them, so I had had to check his immunity to stings – ironically, by having a bee sting him. No problem. It hurt, and the unfortunate worker bee died, but she had demonstrated that he could be a beekeeper and help me out. That was great, because now I had an assistant who could gather honeycomb and fill jars with lovely, berry-infused honey. With so many kinds of berries in our yard, I couldn't call it any particular flavor.

Looking happily and calmly at the hives – all four of them – a thought occurred to me: What needed to happen was not just recycling EVERYTHING for profit, but also a law that imposed a moratorium on making new plastic bottles, and an army of inspectors at the state and federal levels to police the system.

We would need to lobby (oh, joy) politicians to get that done, and hire consultants to help.

I didn't know how to set all this up, but Jacques and Jason had an awesome idea, and it was one that needed developing. The two had become great friends over the year we had all spent in Switzerland, and they had come up with a viable idea for a joint career.

Their friendship extended to video gaming as a pair in the den, which meant that Claire and Fabian needed to keep the door to the porch shut or else study elsewhere. But that would end soon, when Aunt Zoe and Uncle Charlie moved with Jacques and Edgar. Meanwhile, they would game at Jason's house sometimes. Jacques was hesitant about impromptu invitations to dinner for Jason, but I invited him often enough to make up for that. Jacques thanked me each time.

I had walked in on them to get DVDs a couple of times and found out that they were frustrated about meeting women. They had abruptly stopped discussing this when I went in there, but I had asked them about it, curious.

"There are too few women to meet now," Jason said.

Jacques nodded. "I should have met someone in college, but I always figured I had time."

I stood there for a moment, not knowing what to say. The fact was that it was entirely possible that they might not find anyone for their entire lives. I couldn't possibly tell them that it would work out without sounding offhand and selfishly unconcerned. I had my soul mate!

"Damn," I had said instead. "Don't give up hope. You don't know what situations you may end up in that might lead to meeting someone. If you don't play, you don't win, and all that. The Cull can't have killed off everyone…"

I trailed off, thinking. All they needed were girlfriends, or even wives – not kids.

But that didn't seem to make the search any easier.

Claire had lost her parents, and these two had lost a chance to find a soul mate…maybe.

Edgar seemed similarly discouraged about his future happiness in that area.

Only time would tell how they would do. I couldn't solve every problem.

But…I did have an idea for a more immediate one: investing in a new business model: "Why don't you make a business out of mining electronic discards – phones, televisions, computers, whatever – for rare earth elements?"

Jacques and Jason looked at me, looked at each other, and then back at me. "How?"

"Well, you figure that out. The problem would be getting investors. I could be an investor, and have Attorney O'Shea set up the legal documents, stocks, etc. for you. After that, you guys would know better than I would how to gather the elements and process them. I mean, you know what those things are, how they are used, and how hard to acquire they are if they have to be mined from their sources, which are running out because they are…rare. Why not just do an end run around that problem by getting what doesn't need to be mined?"

"Yes, we get that part," Jason said. "Thank you – having an investor, especially one like you, would make it all possible. This is exactly the sort of thing that we wished we could do in the first place."

Claire and Fabian had just walked in; they had gone out to lunch together, and just come back. "I'll invest too," Claire said. "Fabian can be your attorney when he finishes law school, and I'll help in other ways when I'm done, also."

"Thanks!" Jacques said. "Edgar can get in on it too – he'll manage things. I know he isn't busy enough at Hamish's office. Let's have the whole family get in on it."

"What's this?" Edgar said, coming into the room.

We told him.

"Great! I'll do it." Hamish's office wasn't keeping him busy enough.

I hoped that this would make things easier for my unattached cousins, and Jason. Having a cool career and financial resources tended to make it easier to find someone sometimes. Money might not buy happiness, but it certainly bought opportunity.

I smiled and went off to call Adrian O'Shea.

Later, Hamish came home, and I told him what was in the works.

He was quite pleased to hear it. "Perfect! Now all we have to do is wait for Charlie and Zoe to finish settling into their new house, and the whole family will be happy."

"Happy?!" I said with a laugh. "It'll take more than to stop his complaining."

"Aye, well…we can't have everything."

True. Personalities were what they were. Perhaps Uncle Charlie would get bored with his enforced retirement and lend his experience to the business, just for something to do.

Chapter 24

A Constitutional Amendment

Some junior senators and representatives who had been elected just before the Cull (er, plague – it still wasn't quite time yet to call it what it really was) had decided that they had nothing to lose by actually serving the interests of their constituents.

When had that last happened?

Not for quite a while, I thought, mentally reviewing United States political history. To be precise, this group of junior politicians had drafted an amendment to the U.S. Constitution. They were determined to make a dent in the continuous damage that the political process as it was did to the ecosystem, the economy, and the people who had to live with it. They had even, astonishingly, gotten the required two-thirds of both Houses of Congress to propose it.

Funny…we had just had another amendment passed a few years ago, establishing a mechanism for our nation's population policy. That one was still in force, and was working by keeping our population stable. The Cull had given it a major boost, of course, by whittling down that number considerably.

But this one was different. It was about natural security, and it involved independent experts. I thought it was a clever idea, and worth a try. Who knows, I thought? I might actually pass…and save our water. Here was the text of the drafted law:

Amendment XXIX [2018]

Section 1. The right of present and of future generations of human beings who are U.S. citizens to Natural Security, which shall be defined as the health and stability of ecosystems responsible for generating life-sustaining functions, shall be inalienable.

Section 2. The President of the United States shall appoint a Panel of Experts to assist the Congress in its deliberations on and for the writing of such laws as may affect the ecosystems of the United States, its economy, its finances, and its population. Each Expert must be a well-known, oft-cited author, professor, scientist, economist, engineer, jurist, or combination thereof in his or her field. Additionally, each Expert must have no financial stake outside of their government salary in the outcome of any legislation resulting from their advice.

Section 3. An Expert must be present when either the House of Representatives or the Senate is voting on a bill, and shall have the power of veto over said law. If the vote is tied, the Expert shall cast the tie-breaking vote.

That was it, and it was incredible. I had never seen anything like it before, and wondered whether or not it would pass. Now all we had to do was see if three-fourths of the legislatures of the United States liked this idea. If so, we would have ourselves another amendment.

Chapter 25

Environmental Insecurity

Claire and Fabian were very interested in environmental law and toxic torts, which came as no great surprise. I was delighted. Hamish was intrigued. They kept telling us what they were studying, though Claire did it more than Fabian did.

"So," I said, "you are interested in environmental insecurity."

She looked startled, but then grinned at me. "Yes! That's the ideal term for it. I want to learn what's damaged, and what laws already exist to remedy that damage – and what others need to be enacted."

"You do realize that it's the polluters and the big corporations – the Farmers – that pay, not the do-gooders. Often, the philanthropists want attorneys who know how the bad guys think and operate, with work experience helping them get away with stuff, before they will hire you."

Claire looked frustrated. "I know," she said.

"Yeah," I said, "I didn't want to help them either. Don't worry about it. We can't all dance with the devil, walk on the dark side, and whatever other silly metaphors you want to throw in."

She smiled. "I hope I can find something to do with the degree. But you have, so I guess it'll all work out eventually. Meanwhile, I intend to read ahead as much as possible before law school starts."

"That's the spirit," Hamish said.

Fabian was more interested in how he would make that branch of law pay – also good. "I'll help the Farmers for a while. I want to earn money. Claire can do whatever she wants, but one of us has to make money, so I'll pick something that's a sure thing."

"The Farmers are starting to look into ways to clean up the ecosystem and make money doing so," I told him. "So maybe you won't feel like you're doing something unethical in order to earn a living."

He actually looked considerably more cheerful at that thought. "Let's face it," he said, "even people who can make themselves do whatever comes along would prefer to do something that makes the world a better place."

As I had observed both of them over the past year or so, it had become more and more apparent that he was more or less a neurotypical, and an easy-going one at that, who loved intelligent women – particularly if they were on the autism spectrum. That was perfect, because he had one in Claire, who was a polymath with a very straightforward, honest personality.

No wonder I liked her so much.

It was funny to see what was happening, my mother and Aunt Zoe had said to me one day.

"What's happening?" I asked.

"You and Hamish are drawn to Claire and Fabian in a big way. They are a lot like the two of you, yet they are their own people," my mother said.

Aunt Zoe agreed. "You and Claire are Aspies, and you both have guys who adore you."

"Yes, it's perfect," my mother said. "No wonder you are such great friends. It's good to see that you each have such nice marriages and friendships with the other couple. It's also rather hilarious to see the effects of Regenics. You all look so close in age now. Well, Hamish looks a few years older because he is, but you basically look like people in the same age group hanging around together…and yet, you two are mentoring the younger two."

Aunt Zoe had nodded.

It was a pleasant surprise when Claire announced that, to celebrate their acceptances to law school, she and Fabian were going to prepare a gourmet dinner party for me and Hamish. She intended to make a showcase cake to go with it, too.

"Did you learn how to decorate them from your parents?" I had to ask.

"Yes, I did," she told me. "My mother was the artist in the operation. My father was the business end of the bargain, though he could bake the cakes and mix up the icings. He was hopeless at decorating. I had fun learning how to do all of that by spending my free time in their bakery kitchen. Other kids were out playing, socializing and texting, and I didn't care about that. I wanted to be with my mother, and I wanted to learn from her."

Her eyes suddenly got huge, and she stared at nothing in particular. I knew what that meant: she looked like she might cry, and I felt that anxious feeling one gets when one does not want to leap across the small gap of space between people too soon for a hug, yet must do something to help. "You preferred to hang out with your mother rather than other kids?" I asked.

Claire seemed to recover her composure somewhat. "Yes."

"Classic Aspergirl," I said with a grin.

Suddenly, she grinned too. Aspie pride and finding little things in common always worked.

The dinner was amazing, the cake looked like it was in a magazine, and it was delectable.

We had herbed mushroom risotto, sweet potato and russet potato fries (hand cut and homemade), warm pistachio-crusted goat cheese in a mixed greens salad, and butternut squash bisque with apricot beer.

The cake was a white chocolate one with black raspberry filling and white chocolate buttercream frosting and fresh black raspberries on the side. Claire said that we could thank my bees for that. I said that we could thank her artistry for the rest.

It was amazing: vines of fondant cradled fondant black raspberries, which crept around open law books and closed ones. The closed ones were impressive enough to look at. They depicted U.S. Supreme Court reports. But the open ones actually had text! Claire had written, in blackberry coulis sauce, she informed me, several case citations, including *Griswold v. Connecticut, Eisenstadt v. Baird, Roe v. Wade*, the Dredd Scott case, and the *Amistad* decision.

Hamish took one amazed look and said, "If a career in law doesn't work out, you could always make cakes."

Fabian looked proud of Claire, put his arm around her waist, and said, "She could."

As for me, I insisted that no one touch it until I had photographed it from every angle.

That done, we settled in to enjoy our feast. "Next time you decorate a cake, I want to watch," I told her. "It would be fascinating to learn a bit about how you do this. It's incredible, both to look at and then to eat."

Claire smiled happily, and we chose from a variety of teas to have with that fabulous cake.

"It's a shame to cut into it," Hamish said.

"It would be a shame to let it rot by forgetting that it is food art," I told him.

With that, he stopped worrying about decimating it and enjoyed two pieces.

"I'll go for a run tomorrow," he said. "Ed can come with me. He needs a run."

I laughed. "Claire and I might check out the yoga schedule at the health club."

As we sat there, just the four of us (the others had gone off to bed and left us to chat), Claire stared into the distance, thinking.

Hoping that she wasn't getting sad again, I asked, "What are you thinking about?"

She looked up. "All those people that Hamish vaccinated. I know you saved a lot of them," she said to him. "But," and this was to both of us, "you could only save some people from the Cull. Does that bother you?"

We glanced at each other, and then he told her, "Yes and no. There is the urge to save everyone, but you just can't. The Cull was too big of a problem for the two of us to completely stop, and we knew it. You can only save the people you have in front of you, and as long as you do that, it should be okay to live with one's efforts without guilt. However…now that the Cull is over, there may be other things that can be done for those other, lost people."

She looked at me, confused. "Like what?"

I gave her a slightly cryptic but bemused look. "We shall see. Laws can be used. Vengeance and justice have yet to be meted out. Just remember: no one does anything big alone. No one becomes a success without help, and no one's big plan happens without collaboration. This will take a while, but we have a while. My plan is coming together nicely."

Claire and Fabian we listening with rapt interest as well as attention.

Hamish, sitting next to me, was looking at me with the same expression I had.

"What?" I asked him.

"Nothing."

"It's not nothing."

"Okay, it's not. I'll just say that you can consider me on standby for your plan. Let me know when you've got it fully formed."

"I may need your advice and input as I formulate it," I told him.

"That's fine." He smiled.

I changed the subject. "Interesting – and great – choices of law cases on this cake," I said.

Claire smiled. "Birth control rights for married couples, then birth control rights for anyone, abortion rights, slavery cases…they seemed like the right ones, about privacy and liberty."

"Indeed," I said. "The right to privacy was in the birth control cases," and here I was thinking of *Griswold v. Connecticut* and *Eisenstadt v. Baird*, "and in the abortion case of *Roe v. Wade*, and liberty in the slavery cases." With that, I ate a frosted case citation. It tasted really good.

"I thought *Roe v. Wade* was about privacy," Fabian said, sounding confused.

"Yes and no." I explained that it was about freedom from eighteen or more years of being figuratively handcuffed to unwanted offspring.

Comprehension dawned on his face. "I'd better get all this straight. Thanks," he said.

"No problem. The use of Nae-Née involves both privacy and liberty…or did until the population policy," I thought aloud. "But, that's fine. We can't just reproduce and insist upon access to resources as if they were infinite even though they're just…not."

The others nodded. On that note, dessert ended, and we cleaned everything up.

Claire and Fabian attempted to send us off and do the entire cleanup themselves, but we insisted that we needed to move about. It was still early when we finished, so we decided to watch a Marvel Comics movie, and chose *Captain America: The Winter Soldier*. The part about the New World Order, and Arnim Zola's remarks about how people would be so terrorized as to be willing to sacrifice their liberty to safeguard their security, was our favorite.

We had wanted to keep the mood light, but that movie was about an ongoing struggle between a secret, sleeper cell villainous organization and the good guys. Oh well. The good guys did come out okay in the end, even if not exactly on top, so it was fun to watch.

Christmas was coming, and my mother was suffering from a frustrating change:

She could no longer go shopping as a form of entertainment.

Aunt Zoe didn't like that, either. The two of them had formerly enjoyed trolling the malls of central Connecticut and beyond, having Dad and Uncle Charlie drive them to places such as Wrentham, Massachusetts, Burlington, Massachusetts, Clinton, Connecticut, and elsewhere just to visit outlet malls. Amazingly, Evergreen Walk remained in South Windsor, but the industrial-scale shopping developments of the Buckland Hills that had overlooked them were now gone.

I wasn't going to miss them.

Westfarms Mall in Farmington and West Hartford was gone, too, as was the sprawl around it. The Berlin Turnpike, once infamous for its incessant curb cuts for a plethora of shopping establishments, was now transformed. Town after town was completely changed.

Of course, the consumers had nearly been erased from existence, so there was no longer much purpose to shopping centers. It was a strange thing to realize, and a thing that one realized over and over again, whenever one went out driving.

Many of the old thrift shops were gone, too. My mother had combed through those that remained. She needed a new pastime. Aunt Zoe suggested that they take up a craft.

But what craft, and who would teach it to them? Drawing? Knitting? Tatting? Pottery? Shouldn't it be a useful craft, as crafts used to be before one could just go out and buy whatever goods were needed or desired? So many questions presented themselves.

My mother also fretted over how to celebrate Christmas. Aunt Zoe wondered about Hanukah, too. Eight days of presents, not to be shopped for or given out. Frankly, I wasn't upset about it at all. What did we need all that for?! It just cluttered up the house with stuff.

"What do you mean, how to celebrate it, Mommy?" I asked. "We don't really need yet more stuff. Getting more feels like a kind of sickening gluttony. Can't we just bake all sorts of cookies and a nice cake, and make some special dishes for Christmas breakfast and dinner? What do we need shopping for, anyway?"

I was actually relieved to stop with all of the shopping and buying and…consumption.

Consumption of resources was what had gotten our species into ecology arrears in the first place. It was actually a good thing to change our habits, our thinking, and our compulsions. It was a compulsion, really, this urge to shop.

"Maybe shopping is the modern-day woman's gatherer instinct at play," I mused aloud.

My mother and Aunt Zoe stared at me.

"So we are primitive to want to go shopping?" Aunt Zoe asked.

I grinned, snapping out of my train of thought. "Yes…and no. It's still useful, to a point. But you can't shop like you used to in malls that no longer exist. There must be some other ways to enjoy the holidays. I mentioned a few, and we all like those. It's the actual holidays that are fun to me, not the hunt for gifts to wrap up. I'm perfectly happy to dispense with shopping for the people who are so taciturn that guessing what inanimate object would deliver the most thrill value to them is next to impossible. Every family has at least one such person in it."

"You mean Edgar and Fabian," my aunt said.

I grinned. "I do. They always either found whatever they liked on their own, or not, meaning that they didn't care about the presents. We shouldn't waste money and resources giving each other junk that no one likes, wants, or even needs. It's insane. Why can't we just relax and eat and visit with each other? Can't we tell stories of Christmas and Hanukah, learn something, or relearn it, and sing a few songs, even if our voices aren't show-quality? That could be fun."

My mother sighed, then smiled. "I guess we'll have to do that." Aunt Zoe agreed.

We got out the recipe books and started planning.

For Hanukah, Aunt Zoe took the lead, announcing that we would do pretty much what we did last year, which had been spent docked at the shore of Lausanne, Switzerland aboard the *Shadowcat*. We would light the menorah, using the one she had bought in Geneva (Hamish had forgotten to pack one), and sing and hear Hanukah stories for eight days.

We would also have potato latkes and salads for dinner on the first and eighth nights.

When the time came, she also wrote checks for each of her sons, plus one for Claire, and put them in cards. The checks were small, just fifty bucks apiece, but that wasn't the point. The point was to remember everyone.

Hanukah was really for kids anyway, she added. To that end, we all went online to shop for gifts for Mindy's kids. "Do we need eight gifts for each one?" I asked, logging into my Amazon account and clicking on a few links.

Aunt Zoe laughed. "No. Let their mother worry about that. Between Christmas and Hanukah, those kids are going to be thoroughly spoiled. I was thinking that one thing each would be enough from everyone. We're only going over there once, anyway, not every single day of Hanukah."

"Okay." With that, I decided to get them all books, considering their ages and what stories I had loved at different times in my life. That meant a Dr. Seuss book (*The Lorax*), *Cheaper by the Dozen*, *Nineteen Eighty-Four*, *Sense and Sensibility*, and *To Kill a Mockingbird*. Those choices seemed safe; school had been suspended for a year, and Mindy had been struggling to home-school the kids. She was doing English, and Jack was doing math. I hadn't kept track of whatever else they were trying to teach the kids.

My parents got toys for all of them, and so did Aunt Zoe and Uncle Charlie. They did not buy any that required electricity, however, and I was glad about that. "We'll leave it to you to educate them," Dad said to me with a grin. But he had chosen puzzles and puzzle toys, which were guaranteed to make the kids think and develop problem-solving skills.

Claire decided to give them books, too. *The Butter-Battle Book* by Dr. Seuss got into the mix, along with *The Good Earth*, *The Giver*, *Little Women*, and *I, Robot*. Fabian and Hamish got to sign their names to what we bought, and were quite delighted about escaping shopping.

Jacques and Edgar, however, had no such out, and ended up with more toys for them. Aunt Zoe reviewed their choices carefully, and approved some Minecraft games and other virtual Avatar software. They were dismayed when they found out that Mindy had banned all such toys, and went back online, dejectedly, searching for alternatives. After a while, they too bought puzzles and puzzle toys, checking with Dad to avoid duplicating his efforts.

When we went over to Mindy's house, on the eighth day of Hanukah, the visit went well. Mindy lived five minutes away with her husband, who still worked in Hartford as an insurance executive, and their kids...all five of them. It was bedlam, with screams, shrieks, and running, and it never stopped.

I was stunned to silence, backed into walls most of the time, watchful and anxious.

So was Claire.

My mother and Aunt Zoe were perfectly calm, of course.

The guys were all calm, too – there was no pressure on them to take care of the kids.

We were there to chat and eat snacks – that was the agenda. In other words, we were there to socialize. I talked like a book, people said, so I wasn't looking forward to this, but I made the best of it.

We ate another dinner of latkes with salads, which Mindy had been creative with (poached apricots, chevre, scallions, and white balsamic vinaigrette). The kids seemed quite pleased with everything, said "thank-you" to us all very nicely, and then we watched them spin the dreidel, which fascinated Claire. Watching it felt new every time. I had only seen it done a few times, due to being away at graduate school or traveling when my cousins were of age to spin it.

The evening was over before we knew it, and it was fun for everyone.

In the very brief interval that ensued between Hanukah and Christmas, Claire and I turned our attention to cookie-baking. We had about a week and a half for all of this.

Jacques was having a fine time creating his environmental reports for the recycling companies. Each one covered a different topic as it related to processing synthetic materials. Toxic molecules in the synthetic chemical structure of plastic seeped out into the foods that they contained, and continued to do so once discarded.

"It seems like one just can't win," Jacques said in disgust as he rattled off these facts over dinner one night. "We are the poisons that we eat, which we eat because our food is packaged in them. I hope that we are working our way toward reconstituting all of this rubbish, turning it into something useful – NOT food packaging – and then rebuilding our food packaging system to use something else. Otherwise, we're just killing off our own species, not really nourishing it."

I didn't have much better news to share. It was a rare evening with fish for dinner: cod. Fisheries were collapsing due to overfishing, pollution in the oceans every which way we looked, and continued competition for it from corporations and the last few private boats still in operation. It was amazing that any remained.

Aquaculture – fish farming – was another food supply option, but we had tried some of that and it tasted…flat. It wasn't very good. What it lacked was flavor, and the texture was awful. Tilapia was the worst, of course, but farmed salmon didn't taste right. It was dyed pink, and it was fed in filthy tanks that weren't filtered often enough to get rid of fish excrement.

We were eating wild cod, and our food budget (well, let's face it – we were so solvent from Nae-Née profits that a "budget" wasn't an issue), or more accurately, our food expenditures, were absurdly high whenever we ate fish. Sometimes, we just couldn't resist buying fish, because we missed it. We liked salmon, cod, halibut, trout, hake, and shellfish such as mussels, clams, shrimp and, occasionally, lobster.

Who didn't? But at $22 a pound, wild-caught halibut was a luxury.

Steak cost much, much more, and even Uncle Charlie passed it up when we ate out. At $60 per entrée, he said he would choke on it. We were all amazed to hear this. Nevertheless, Aunt Zoe and I each bought a pound of it and put it away for his next birthday, as a surprise.

It was mid-December, and too warm to justify adding blankets to our bed. I had put on the flannel sheets in October, but with those and the quilt, we didn't want anything more on the bed.

"Our bed is the same way," Claire told me. "We don't want to add a blanket. It doesn't feel like December at all. Weird…and it's even weirder that we're getting used to this as the proverbial new normal." We were making tree-shaped butter cookies while watching TV and sitting at the kitchen table. I was pressing them out through the battery-powered gadget, and she was putting green sugar on every other one, and red sugar on the rest. It was an old family recipe from my Nana. "This is a great recipe you have," she added.

Tomorrow we would be making another recipe from Claire's family, one that I was very grateful to know that she would be shaping, because it had to be done all by hand: Viennese crescents. I would only be responsible for scraping real vanilla bean into the confectioner's sugar. Evil grin in my mind as I thought of that…

Even Grandmère didn't want a blanket on her bed. She came into the kitchen to watch us and told us so. "Joyeux Noël," she said. "It feels like Indian summer, not December. I know I should say 'climate change' and not 'global warming', but it is odd to feel how warm the temperature is while smelling these cookies baking."

Christmas came and went very nicely.

On Christmas Eve, we ate a light dinner of salad with toasted almonds, orange wedges, dried cranberries, and mixed greens, and mussels cooked in a curried white wine butter sauce. We had plenty of baguette slices on the side. For dessert, we ate chocolates and Christmas cookies.

When we were finished eating all that, I made a chocolate orange cake with grated bittersweet chocolate on top, to eat the next day. It was beautiful, with marbled layers and fresh-squeezed orange juice and pulp frosting on top of the layers and chocolate added to the remaining half of the frosting, which went around the side.

The odd part about making that cake was that before I had done more than grease and flour the pans for it and laid out all of the equipment and ingredients, I was roasting. "What's the temperature out?" I asked.

My mother peered at the thermometer, which was affixed to the outside of the kitchen window. "68°Fahrenheit," she announced. Then, "Wow. That must be some kind of record."

The news was on, and Aunt Zoe turned up the sound slightly in time to hear that it was in fact a record…of having been this warm for the past four Christmas Eves. The weather report was doing its usual run-down of how often this exact temperature had been recorded on this date.

"I'll be back in a few minutes," I told them. "I have to change my shirt and put my hair up."

I went upstairs and tore off my shirt, paused a moment, and tore off my bra as well.

The door opened and closed, and Hamish appeared. He grinned, then said, "I thought you were making a cake now. But if you aren't in a hurry to go back downstairs yet..."

"Oh, very funny," I said. "Hold that urge until later, and we'll definitely do something. I'm overheated from moving around to cook dinner. It feels really lucky that I don't have to clean every last dish, pan, and cooking tool. But did you hear how warm it is? I was dressed in a three-quarter-sleeve shirt, and suddenly I was miserable. Open the windows."

He did that, on each side of our room, and the cross-ventilation of fresh air felt good.

I grabbed, stopping to stare at it in slight disbelief, a pale pink camisole with a built-in bra, and then shrugged and put it on. Next, I picked up my gold matte curve of a hair clip and tied my hair up off my shoulders, leaving the barrette with the dragonfly motif in place. "That feels much better. If I don't do this cake early, it's going to start feeling like a chore rather than fun, and if I don't make it at all, I'm just going to feel bad about it."

Hamish came over and gave me a quick hug and kiss. "Later, then," he said, smiling.

I went back downstairs and found another delay waiting: the cats wanted more food.

At last, I was working on the cake, with everyone out of the kitchen but Hamish, Claire, and Fabian. Grandmère appeared once after about an hour to get some tea, and I insisted on making that for her. Claire gave her a couple more Christmas cookies.

"You're lucky, Grandmère – you don't seem to need to go for walks or to exercise, but you're perfectly shaped and sized," she remarked.

Grandmère smiled. "Part of being a frail old lady pumped up on Regenics, I guess," she said.

The cake took me a couple of hours, and then I sat down for tea and relaxation, too. The others had watched some interesting shows on the Animal Planet channel while I worked, with me looking at the most interesting parts. It was about unusual pairs of animal friends, usually in captivity and well fed, but a couple of instances of inter-species friendship in the wild.

Claire kept cleaning up the tools as I went along. "I've never felt so spoiled while baking," I said to her. "Thank you." She smiled. "It's working out well for me, too. This is how my mother and I spent Christmas Eve: she would make a cake for the family, and I would help by washing everything for her as she did it."

At last, there was nothing left to do, and we all went up to bed.

The next day was still warm, but I was able to dress nicely without overheating. Open windows helped. "This feels like early summer," Claire said, amazed. We all nodded. The news reported that the cherry blossoms in Washington, D.C. were starting to bloom. So strange...

Gifts were all handmade. I did calligraphy for everyone, using my fountain pen and some antique-hued parchment paper to make name signs for doors for my cousins and Hamish (for their future workplaces), and some pretty framed art for my aunt, uncle, parents, and Grandmère.

My mother had decided to surprise everyone by learning to make lace, so we each got a beautifully patterned circle. Mine was in a lovely heart pattern, like the engagement ring that Hamish had given me so long ago. Claire's was a pear shape, following the same theme. Fabian's looked like scrolls. Hamish's was the most intriguing: it looked like nanobots.

"These are amazing, Mommy! How did you learn so many twists and shapes so fast?"

"I had nothing to do. Shopping is gone, so I was bored enough to learn a craft."

"It looks more like you became an artisan than a mere craftsperson," I said, impressed.

She smiled happily.

Aunt Zoe had made small throws in pretty colors for the foots of our beds: lavender for Grandmère, heather pink for me and Claire, light blue for Hamish and her sons, and a forest green for my parents and Uncle Charlie.

The guys had all bought their gifts, and they looked a bit abashed at our efforts.

"Don't be silly!" we all said. "The books are great!"

And they were: Hamish had found some new ones that described dyke and dam projects around the planet, complete with photographs. Fabian had found others that showed satellite images of the planet's ecosystems, complete with forests (tropical and temperate), deserts, and everything in between. It was completely up to date.

Dad had found the most fascinating one of all, a NASA infrared study of the Earth's aquifers, showing how much remained plus how depleted they were counting from the Industrial Revolution, and studies of the oceans, complete with dead zones, irradiated zones, coral reefs, both bleached to death and still alive, and fisheries that were still healthy.

We also had a fun Skype call with Fiona and William in Scotland, during which her cat, Mallory, and our cats climbed up onto the keyboards and touched noses to each other during the call. Merry Christmas, cats!

Then Hamish had a surprise for me. He brought out a box with a familiar shape, and said, "I got you a better one."

"I thought we agreed that we had enough stuff," I said, protesting feebly. I didn't want to spoil his enjoyment of the moment, though.

"One more thing and I'll stop for a while," he said with a smile. "Open it."

I did. Then I stared in shock as realization hit. It was a Stradivarius violin.

"Wow." I was stunned. "These are…rare and irreplaceable."

"I know. One came up for sale and I had to get it for you."

I looked up at him, gaping. "Thank you! It's amazing…but I hope its former owner didn't meet a Farmed end. I hope it won't prove to have a nefarious history behind it, at least with the owner immediately preceding me."

"I checked that!" Hamish said. "Don't you think I know enough to check that?!"

"Well, yeah…I just can't help thinking of the looting that went on last year."

"Don't worry," he assured me. "You're covered. I had Blackout make sure."

"Okay then." I smiled at him and gave him a kiss and a hug. The papers that came with the Strad showed that the previous owner had been the Julliard School, and that the violin had been at Christie's for a few years, unsold. "Oh…I see. They were trying to sell it for a while."

Hamish grinned. "See? It's okay. It was part of the estate of some wealthy investor who had lived a long, comfortable life and wanted the thing sold to benefit her heirs, who didn't play an instrument." He showed me the history of ownership on the deed. "We have enough security at home that you can keep it here, and I've had a special safe made for our room, for you to keep it in. I know you like to keep your violin in there when you're not playing it."

"Excellent! I'll donate this one to someone who wants to learn to play it," I said.

"What is it about those violins that's so special?" Claire asked. "I know it's something."

"The wood that they were made from is really flawless – no knots, nothing that impede the resonation of the sound that the instrument makes. It's something about the climate. Antonio Stradivarius used wood that was denser than most, due to the Little Ice Age of 1645 to 1750. That Little Ice Age was caused by the unusually low solar activity of the Maunder Minimum."

Claire looked fascinated, listening to every word. Fabian looked politely interested. The rest of the family looked indulgently bored. Sigh. "Well, at least we're interested in this," I said.

Hamish kissed me and laughed. "I'm interested. I looked that up before buying that Strad."

Hamish and I went out to the little guardhouse to get Aaron and Ed. "Come on, you too," Hamish said. "No one's coming to murder us today. We haven't stirred up any trouble lately. Come back with us and eat dinner." Lionel's fiancée had moved in with him down the street. What about these two? They ought to be in with us, we thought.

"You can't spend Christmas here," I added. "You're family. Come and eat with us!"

"Just a minute," Aaron said, and made a phone call. He hung up a moment later. "Okay. Good to go. Merry Christmas!" They had looked really pleased at my comment, and Hamish smiled and shook their hands.

There were only with us for forty-five minutes, but the thought of not having them come in and eat with us had been, quite frankly, unpalatable. These guys had been with us for a lot of adventures, and likely would go through a few more. I would not have enjoyed my dinner knowing that they were out at the guardhouse, eating nothing special, with no family around.

We had a lovely meal. I had sprung for a serving of halibut for everyone. My mother had cooked it in an orange-butter sauce. Aunt Zoe had made chèvre mashed potatoes with fresh rosemary and a side of asparagus. Claire had made a nice, smooth, carrot and parsnip purée soup. Grandmère had even gotten in on the preparations a bit by laying out smoked salmon, cream cheese, whole wheat crackers, and wine glasses.

This was followed by the cake. Not surprisingly, we were all happily sated.

Best of all, the men cleaned up the mess – as we cooked and baked, and after dinner.

The whole family was glad to have Aaron and Ed there, and Grandmère said that it felt as though we were back on the *Shadowcat*, all together again. "I mean that in a good, nostalgic way. Everything that happens in a holocaust isn't bad. Sometimes, friendships get stronger."

We all nodded, and my mother poured the eggnog, sprinkled in some nutmeg, and I sliced the cake. We were going to watch reruns of Christmas movies after that, no matter how many times we had seen them before, and sit around the living room, looking at books.

So, we did that, and all in all, it was a successful holiday.

The next day, we went to see Aunt Zoe's sister, Mindy, and her family. This was their Christmas visit with us. We brought food with us – fruits, chevre, crackers – laid it out, and then tried to stay out of the zones of demolition…but they were fluid, not fixed.

Hamish ended up with chevre and strawberries on his pants after half an hour. Dad managed to sidestep Sam, who was now about six years old and oblivious to how noisy and messy he was, but it was close. I let him stumble into a doorframe when he came at me with jam on his hands. He fell and screamed, and I just glared at Mindy and Aunt Zoe when they looked up at me.

"He's fine," Jack said. "That's what you get for not keeping your hands clean, Sam."

Mindy rushed over and doted on him, cooing and fussing.

Claire and I looked at each other and headed for a sofa on the far side of the room. We sat down together, alert and tense. "How much longer do we have to stay here?" she asked me.

"I don't know. It's been an hour so far," I replied.

"What are you thinking about, Avril?" Claire asked me. She looked a bit red and wide-eyed, and the thought suddenly occurred to me that she might be watching the way Mindy talked to her kids and missing her own mother.

I arched an eyebrow, then said, wryly, "I'm just watching Mindy's I.Q. points fly out the window with every word she coos," hoping to make Claire smile.

It worked. Claire laughed, then chimed in: "No, wait…it's closed. They went *splat* onto it."

Now I was laughing, and so were Fabian and Hamish, who had come over to sit on the arm of the sofa on my end (It only held two people). Fabian recovered first. He sat on the other sofa arm and leaned down to kiss his wife on the cheek. "That's hilarious," he said to her. "I've married my best friend." He whispered to us, "Babies look like little aliens – creepy and hairless and puffed up. You can't talk to them, only babble, and I don't babble."

"Fabian, you never mentioned that," I said. "You were always the nicest and most introspective kid I knew, but I did not know that you were thinking and feeling all that."

He grinned. "I think I just prefer women with Asperger's. The ones I have been happiest interacting with have had all of those traits, or most of them. It's only recently that I found out that those traits are on the autism spectrum. Besides…if I were with a woman like that," he gestured at Mindy, who was washing her son's sticky hands with a wet towel now, "it would feel like I was with my mother, and no guy wants that." He looked at Hamish for agreement.

I turned to look at Hamish, who grinned. "Aye. That's the truth. You're nothing like my mum, Avril. She was insipidly sweet – cloying, almost. That's why I left home early. Fiona coped with it much better. My mother did insist that we both study our way to the top of academia, though, like my dad had before he died."

Hamish's father had been killed when he was eight years old, in some oil fields in Iran. He didn't talk about his parents much, but I had known these things. I realized that he was bonding with Claire and Fabian by sharing this, and leaned against him with a smile.

Claire was getting red-faced again, though. I looked around. Mindy was cooing and fussing over her daughter Leah now, hugging her and smiling. The jokes and memory-sharing hadn't helped for long.

"Time to go home!" I said. "Hamish, get our coats. You and I and Claire and Fabian are bailing out of this party early. We can go home and watch some movies together, until this party is over and the others come back. If they don't approve, we don't care!"

"Yes, dear," my husband said, and disappeared into the front hall. He came back with our coats a minute later and handed them around.

"You're leaving?!" Mindy said, outraged. "But you just got here!" She had no idea why we needed to get out of here, and I had no intention of enlightening her.

"We've been here for over an hour," I corrected her. "It was very nice to see you, but we have something we planned to do, and I drove us here separately with that in mind." With that, I hugged her quickly good-bye, and turned to go, waving at Jack. He waved back, unconcerned.

We all filed out without further ado, and before anyone else could object.

Once in the car, I said, "We've escaped! What will we watch?"

Claire said, "I'd like to see some romance story. What have we got?"

"Jane Austen movies, Diana Gabaldon stories…I forget what else right now, but more."

"Perfect. We'll have leftover soup and crackers and watch that, and forget about reality."

"Sounds like a plan." That came from the back seat, where the guys had piled in.

Claire and I looked at each other, startled. I suddenly realized that I had dragged her out of the house by the sleeve and seat-belted her into the front seat.

I had hugged her, too. Then I said, "You guys actually want to sit with us and watch romance stories?"

"Aye."

"Yeah."

"Okay, then." And off we went, with Aaron and Ed tailing us as usual, down Fern Street.

We had a lovely afternoon at home with the guys, eating Christmas cookies, drinking fancy teas, and watching two long movies. Why couldn't we have more days like this, I thought to myself? Because having fewer of them makes them feel more special.

Chapter 26

Damning Data

Some people liked to call them flash drives, but I preferred to think of them as memory sticks. Memories were what made us unique. Memories were what we had to share. Memories were what remained of the people whose lives were documented on the ones I had hidden.

We were in yet another one of those in-between eras of history, between conflicts, collapses, and monstrosities. It was easy to look back at the previous upheaval and sit in smug, armchair judgment of those who had made the decisions and done the deeds that had to be condemned.

But those deeds were so terrible that condemnation could be the only response to them.

That was why I wanted to release the data on the Cull that we had archived.

"I've gone over those memory sticks and put it all together," I said to Hamish.

Hamish looked alarmed, but agreed. "It must be anonymous," was all he would say.

Of course, it had to be stealthy and not open with our identities. I wasn't willing to be a martyr, dead and thus unable to do anything else, nor to have my husband dead. I started reviewing all of the data we had compiled. It was a massive amount of video, secretly obtained text files, and so on. Jason had kept records of where he had found all this stuff, too. We kept it hidden, but accessible.

It was going to take me a while to decide what to say and how to say it, but I started in on it.

The Cull had not ground up ALL of the Earth's best, brightest, or most talented.

I suspected that that had been by design, but there it was.

Meanwhile, my family wanted to do fun things, and to include me in them.

My father loved classical music, and he had instilled that love in me.

I still played my violin, listened to CDs of whatever orchestra pieces I liked, and attended concerts again, now that the curfew associated with the Cull had been lifted. We could go out after dark and not worry about when we had to be back home. Funny that I was thinking about that months after getting back to our old life in the United States; it was over a month or so before we came home! But…I still thought of it from time to time.

Now that we were back, my father had looked up the organ recital series at Trinity College Chapel in Hartford. This series ran every fall, and every spring. A music professor named Clarence Waters had designed the organ, and a planner he knew had told him about Waters.

Waters had been choirmaster to the boys' choir in West Hartford at St. John's Episcopal Church in the 1950s. This planner had been the soloist, a boy with perfect pitch and a great voice. He was paid, too, so no paper route. When his voice began to change, the boy had to quit the choir. Waters told the boy to look him up when he was getting married, and he would play at his wedding, so the boy did that. The church where that wedding was held was a converted Catholic gymnasium with a crappy electric organ – but you wouldn't have known it when Professor Waters played it.

This Friday, we were attending a concert by a Québécois organist, a Professor Isabelle Demers, who had an impressive set of credentials. Hamish and I were going, my parents were going, Fabian and Claire were going, and Grandmère announced that she was going.

We ate at A.C. Petersen's before the concert because we thought it would be a quick and efficient place to go, and it was on the way. It was very good, with spicy curly fries, coconut chocolate chip almond ice cream, and all. Ed and Aaron seemed to enjoy it, too.

And then there was the chapel. I brought my camera and took photographs of the carved pews first, and the pipe organ. The carvings included firefighters, Native American warriors and other tribespeople, Medieval and twentieth century scholars, dragons, trees, and more. That was as much fun as the concert, and Claire had fun looking at all of the images when we got home.

As for the concert, we were treated to several pieces from various time periods, and it started with John Williams' *Harry Potter* music. I loved it! I could hear magic wands being wielded, Harry Potter and his friends arriving at Hogwarts, a Quidditch match, Voldemort doing some dastardly deeds, and Hermione and Hagrid arriving in the Great Hall at the end.

There were some pieces related to the 1,001 tales told by Scheherazade in the Arabian Nights, and then some fascinating "short studies" by Professor Demers' friend, Rachel Laurin. These depicted the movements of a hummingbird and an exchange between two mockingbirds. The first bird would sing a tune, and then the second, who was a smart-ass, would embellish it. Mockingbirds, the professor explained with a mischievous grin, usually repeated tunes back verbatim, not with any changes.

The last piece would have been more appropriately titled *Look Ma, No Hands!* At least, I thought so. It was actually *Variations on a Theme by Paganini*, and had a signature tune that I had heard in a funeral piece for violin by Wagner and in a keyboard piece by Andrew Lloyd Weber. It was too much fun to think of as a funeral piece. Demers played almost all of it with her feet, and fast. She only touched the upper part of the instrument to adjust the settings, which she did several times, until the last bit, which she played with her fingers.

The program said that she was often recalled for encores, so it was no surprise that she was called back a few times just for applause. After that, she said that she would do a one-minute piece as an encore, so that we could get home safely (it was January and quite windy out, with lots of leaves blowing about, and it did start to rain as we drove). The piece was from Tchaikovsky's *Sleeping Beauty*.

Now that it was January, the odd warmth that had persisted through December and beyond was finally fading away. That night out at the organ recital had been the last of the comfortable temperatures we were to enjoy for a while. A cold wind came on abruptly, and the weather did not warm up again for a few months.

It was time to face being snowed in much of the time. This was life in the changed climate: shorter, colder, and more intense winters. We would have to stock up on milk, coffee, orange juice, and whatever else, and stay in as much as possible.

Hamish called his office staff in advance of any major snowstorm and told them that the office would be closed. A voice mail system was set up by Jason that enabled Edgar to record announcements to any patients or other callers that the office was closed. He promptly re-recorded a replacement greeting as soon as it was safe to go out again.

The first snowstorm came on a Wednesday after that concert, and dropped forty-eight inches on Connecticut, western Massachusetts, and part of New York State. Rhode Island and the partially submerged Boston area got thirty inches, and New York City, Pennsylvania, New Jersey, Delaware, Maryland, and Virginia were buried in at least thirty-six inches of snow.

Washington, D.C. was now used to budgeting for several huge snowstorms, to shutting down most of its traffic for a couple of days at a time, and to lots of snow games. The national news showed people of various ages playing on huge snowdrifts, throwing snowballs, making snow angels, and building snow-sculptures of all kinds (art schools were a regular feature for news crews, it seemed, which was always fun to watch).

People were not allowed out in their vehicles during these storms, and no one particularly missed the fatal accidents of years past. Police drove up and down highways, avenues, and other roads, ordering people to go home. Work was telecommuted as much as possible.

Runs on grocery stores still happened, but not with crowds. There were no crowds, I had to remind myself, as I shopped in ease and disbelief at the ease of movement through the aisles just before each snowstorm. I bought cookie-baking ingredients and soup-making supplies without thinking about the ingredients anymore. It was second nature now to toss them into my cart.

In between snowstorms, I would get more jigsaw and other puzzles to surprise Grandmère with. These I brought out when the snow started up again, to her great delight. We had to pay for longer, warmer, more comfortable springs, summers, and autumns with monster snowstorms, she said, but it was great to sit inside, cozy and able to ignore them as they blanketed everything.

Snowmaggedon after Snowmaggedon soon felt routine, and I intended to make the most of it by writing. I had gotten through the memory sticks with the data on the Cull, reviewed them all, and was composing a truthful history of that crime.

Our cache of memory sticks likely contained the only evidence of the Cull that the public would ever see: mobile cremation camps, military units, kidnappings, beatings, robberies, rapes, torture, and murder of millions of Americans. They also contained some recordings of murders on cremation ships, of immigrants to Europe, and even a few, smuggled via Blackout Security from around the world, showing more in Asia, Australia, and the Pacific.

How would I share this data with the world? Very carefully. I didn't want to put my family at risk in the process. But history should not be allowed to be scrubbed of these bloodstains. People should know how the Earth's bank accounts were balanced.

They should know why the small number of humans on the planet were so numbered – at just under half a billion – and why they no longer had to concern themselves with short showers or insufficient food. Now all they needed to do (not that it's a minor project by any means) was clean up the ecosystem.

Finally, I decided to write the story, keep it simple and horrifying, and leave it at that.

The truth was, after all, horrific enough on its own. Once it was out, it could be backed up with public access to what I was now thinking of as Damning Data. It could also be backed up with some arrests and convictions…but first things first: I had to get this written.

One afternoon – a drizzly, gray, overcast one – I found Claire in a mood that matched the sky. She was morose but calm, with her head down on her books, sitting at the table out on the porch. She had obviously gone out there to study, but wasn't doing that.

"Where's Fabian?" I asked.

"At the law firm, interning," she said. "He fits in well there. Law school will be the same."

"You're going to love it," I told her. "I would make my outlines and read them over and over, alone. As soon as I could arrange it, I took classes that were seminars so that I had to write papers instead of taking exams, because I learned more that way and got better grades."

"Really?" Claire sat up. "I want to do that after my first year."

"You won't be able to do that with all of your classes, but you will with many of them."

"Good." She stared off into the distance.

"What are you thinking about?" I asked her.

"My parents, and all of the people who studied, got jobs, worked hard, got houses or apartments or condominiums, commuted to work, took care of their homes and families, and got murdered and disappeared anyway. It's like doing that did not protect them against anything."

"Oh. Yeah. It didn't, and it didn't in earlier holocausts."

Claire looked up at me. "You mean World War II and what happened to people then."

"Yes. What you're pointing out makes me feel less bad about how my life was before you knew me, before the world had heard of me. It often takes a chaos event – that's a math term – to have the clout and money and resources to protect oneself and one's family."

"What was it like before you were famous?" She waited for me to tell the story.

"Hamish and I had a spotty record of barely making any money at all. We worked constantly, but it didn't make us a living, no matter how much we did to earn it. We traveled to Kuwait and Hungary to work, and I wrote and he did his science. He has no idea how to handle a business deal, so things kept falling through. What he needed was a successful invention with someone else to handle the business arrangements. So, we kept ending up back here, with my parents."

Claire was listening, wide-eyed. "How did things change?"

"One day – you've probably come across this story in some newspaper by now, online of course," I added with a wry grin, "I thought of the birth control nanite idea. I was just walking around the neighborhood here, back in my anonymous days when no one would have had me on their radar. That's how it is when you haven't done or written anything that would raise a red flag to the powers that run things."

"And?"

"And I came back inside, went down to the basement, where I had set up Hamish with whatever nanobotic tools that he and I had scraped together money for, and told him. He thought it could make money, so he got going immediately on the prototype…which is still working in me today. Later, at dinner, I thought of the name for it when I asked Hamish to help. He said, 'Nae, I shall not,' and with that, I had the idea."

Claire smiled. "I think I remember reading that story in *The New York Times*," she said.

"It took him a short time to create the prototype, and then we arranged a clinical trial with my gynecologist. She was very helpful. Before we knew it, Dad was involved, filing the patent and arranging for an investor, which was very nice of him. I think he was our chaos event. No one becomes a success without help, you know. No one. We all have help."

"So you keep telling me," Claire said. "What else did your father do?"

"For one thing, he paid what it cost to cover the government filing fees. It's disgusting what it costs. In the nineteenth century, when it was a new legal protection, it didn't cost much at all. Anyone could become an inventor. Not anymore! You need a few hundred dollars for a preliminary patent, which lasts a couple of years, then thousands and even a million more."

"That makes it out of reach for most people…"

"Exactly! You have to pay a patent attorney, and that's where inventors get shut out of the business, or have to cede profits to a big investor. Patent attorneys have engineering backgrounds and cost millions of dollars before long, and millions more when an invention is registered for the long term. Dad is a patent attorney – both international and in the U.S. – and he took care of all that. He also negotiated our deal with the corporation that manufactured and marketed Nae-Née, which put us in a much stronger position that we could ever have been otherwise."

"So that's how it became a marketable product for sale as a voluntary device?"

"Yes. Dad was our chaos event. We paid him back, of course, and now we take care of the family. Nae-Née paid us a lot, and we have used it to protect ourselves. Without it, we would have had to spend the Cull here, not aware of what was happening, surveilled, and likely with Hamish struggling to keep the Cull's monster nanobots out of us, without access to all of the lab equipment that enabled him to help a lot of other people to avoid it."

Claire stared at me. "I would have died. Fabian and his brothers and parents would have died. Grandmère would have died."

"Yes. We would never have been able to convince them to leave the area and come with us. They would not have listened to us, nor taken anything we said seriously. No matter how many graduate degrees someone has, if they are an outlier – someone with knowledge and expertise but on the sidelines of society – they aren't taken seriously. It's our success that makes the family and other people look at us the way that they do, and act on what we say."

"That's rather depressing." Claire sat back on the sofa, slumped, and stared listlessly at her books. They were laid out on the table in front of her. She put her head back and stared up at the ceiling. "Even without a chaos event, you were doing some fascinating things."

"I was scraping along. You too will find your niche and be okay. Don't worry about how long it takes. Just focus on the process and it will work. You and Fabian may feel the anxiety of being young and not 'there yet' too, but just tell him that. Tell him that no one makes it without help, and no one makes it right away…usually." I grinned.

"You kept coming back here anyway, even after you had money," Claire observed.

"Yes. I wanted to. I don't like change. I love this place, and I want my family. But it feels very different now that we've bought this place and are in charge, so to speak. The feeling of dependency is gone. Still, it's the entire family's house, not just mine and Hamish's. It's my parents' house, and Grandmère's house, and yours and Fabian's for as long as you want to be here with us…and I hope that's for quite a while. It's a nasty world out there. Climate change is moving lots of extended families in together, and I don't even mind."

Claire lifted her head up and smiled. "Me neither. I want a cup of tea."

"Let's go make some. I made cranberry-orange scones, too."

We got up and went into the kitchen.

I thought of that time in Lausanne that the cousins had encountered Jacob Uberfein, and was glad that I had had my double-take after rounding a corner, out of his and anyone else's sight. Damn! I was going to have to be a very, very good actress forever after. I would have to lie by my very behavior, seeming never to have seen Jacob until we were in Switzerland.

Just possessing a memory, let alone a memory stick, was a very risky business. Silly me; I had thought that once the Cull was over, it would not be dangerous anymore. Wrong!

I hated being overly careful. It took so much mental energy!

No wonder Mark Twain had said that if you tell the truth you don't have to remember anything. I had lived by that rule all my life, even before I learned that axiom/quote. Now I didn't dare keep that up. Damn!

In college, I had been a liberal. I still was one, but only to the point that cultural inclusiveness didn't threaten a woman's freedom of movement and personal security. When I looked at the opposite end of the political spectrum, at the libertarian and conservative end, I found them downright nasty and malicious.

They had wanted to keep Nae-Née from becoming a matter of policy, abortion to be illegal, miscarriages to be prosecuted as if deliberate, and birth control extremely difficult to access. They wanted these conditions in place even though the planet was alarmingly overpopulated. They wanted to constrain women's personal liberty and choice about reproduction, while complaining bitterly about every constraint on their own choices where space and resource use were concerned, yet they failed to see the irony in that.

But…the planet couldn't support any more humans, and it couldn't even handle those who already existed. Something had to be done without murdering anyone who already existed, anyone who was a citizen of the nation that they were sworn to serve, and so they had finally acceded to the idea of the Nae-Née treaty.

What convinced them was the scarcity and insecurity they faced as the people from the conflict zones of the planet, from the nations with collapsing ecosystems and economies, began to flood into the cooler, still functional non-conflict zones. They were fleeing wars – resource wars – at home.

Add to all that the fact that there were so many young people, educated and with unreachable career aspirations, from those nations – a number equal to the populations of the United States, Canada, and Britain – and you had a recipe for trouble. Rather than stay and fight and die, they left, wanting a better life that they could access at home.

Well, therein lay the problem: there wasn't enough of that life to share with the exodus of nations and cultures whose customs were the opposite of those in the non-conflict zones.

The politicians of the non-conflict zones were having none of that.

At first, the liberal politicians were, and their rhetoric was full of humanitarianism for the unfortunate people who were fleeing strife back home. But then they began to realize that if they extended that attitude long enough – and "long enough" was actually just a year or more – they would be inundated.

Belatedly and regretfully, seeming to feel as though they were reprehensible for doing so, they were willing to close the borders to their nations and make some effort to keep the influx out. The public saw that much, at least, through the media before the flow of information was clamped down to hide the truth.

There had to be a way to keep more people out. But it was not feasible to simply put up a solid wall sealing off the entire border of any area. Borders were just too porous what with rivers, train rides, and hills and fields to walk over.

Only the Swiss had had the financial resources and the foresight – as well as the independence due to not having joined the European Union – to keep the influx of migrants out. They had drones flying over their borders, cameras in camouflaged trees, and robotic machine guns that could be triggered at a moment's notice of a migrant. Neutrality requires money to enforce it, which was why the Swiss kept themselves solvent above all, and at all costs. There is no other reason why others would ever respect it and keep out otherwise.

That sounded like pure evil, but at least that gave migrants the option of not going to the Swiss border. What the U.S. and the E.U. did when they realized that they had waited too long and were overwhelmed was far worse: the Cull. They got rid of those who were not "wanted". Every life did not "matter" to them, and they proved it. The Swiss had always known that.

They weren't the only ones who did it. Australia, New Zealand, China, India, and Brazil were just as ruthless in disposing of immigrants. Then, when they realized that their own numbers, apart from the immigrants, were in overshoot, they went after the morbidly obese, the sick, and the chronically poor. Lives deemed to be "in excess" were being erased.

"Sorry, but there are just too many of you, and you are blocking access to a comfortable, prosperous, pleasant life for the rest of us," went the rationale. It was all behind closed doors, spoken in secret by cabals of banksters, hedged fundsters, and the like, but it was said, planned, and, ultimately, done. We now had proof of the Farmers of the Molech Group saying all this.

I thought about Anne Frank, Miep Gies, and the rest of the people whom she hid during World War II...not that it had worked. Well, it worked for Otto Frank, but only for him. He came home alone from the concentration camps, with no family but Miep and her husband Jan.

The other Franks – his wife and his daughters Margot and Anne – lost their cat, their home, and their lives in that holocaust. They were more than excess to the Nazis. They were Jews, a group who had been deemed usurpers of much of the wealth of Germany. It didn't matter that they had done it by excelling at academics and business. What had mattered to the angry Germans was that they had done it at all. While they were at it, the German Nazis had taken out their resentment on the Romani people, homosexuals, and anyone who resisted their regime.

Germany had been impoverished and humiliated by loss from World War I, and they were angry. Germany, like various other European nations, had always had repressive laws on Jews. The Rothschilds, that wealthy banking family of German Jews, had risen from a situation in the eighteenth century in which they were not allowed to use a surname, though they had one in mind just in case things improved...and they did, for a while.

But that was the problem: things improved...until the next resource war, and the next.

This cycle had repeated for millennia over human history: humans in a particular area would prosper, use vast amounts of resources, reproduce as much as they wished, and then there would be a crash. It had happened millennia ago with the Anasazi tribe in the Southwest. The crash could come from a war, a collapsing ecosystem, or both. The war could come from a neighboring group that wasn't so well off. The failed ecosystem could be caused by Nature, by human activity, or both.

Anthropogenic ecosystems collapse was nothing new. What was new was the scale of it.

I thought again of Anne Frank and her family.

All that they had done was to run a business successfully in Amsterdam, in the Netherlands, having fled a repressive, hostile Germany. The business had sold fruit pectin for making strawberry jam (that was the flavor that Miep had tested in the company's kitchen). Miep's job had been to field phone calls from customers with questions on how to successfully use the product and make their own jam. There was nothing sinister in that.

And yet…any human effort that does well can and will become the victim of its own success.

Overshoot. Overdevelopment. Overpopulation. I had a book lying around somewhere that explained that in graphic and disturbing detail. Too many people using too many resources led to scarcity, destruction begot more and more depletion of resources, and on and on.

A resource war was inevitable, and we had just had a massive, albeit covert, one.

Now things were lovely and quiet…for those of us who hadn't been targeted for erasure.

The next generation of children – those who would all be born after the Cull – would know nothing of the previous world without being told. I was determined that it not be forgotten. The simplest way to let a history and the people in it die forever was to suppress any mention of their existence, thus erasing their memory along with them.

Those kids ought to know how crowded the world used to be, what that was like, the resource consumption and ecological damage done by so many humans and, most importantly, their mass murder. They had to know that a crime on a scale never committed before in human history had in fact been committed, no matter how dangerous it might be to tell about it.

Of course, I had no intention of paying any price for telling it.

We would release it all onto the Internet AND submit it to the I.C.C. judges.

With that accomplished, going after us after the fact would achieve nothing in the way of concealment. Well, it might achieve vengeance, but we planned to be a bit quicker on the draw. We would help capture the Farmers and beat them to the punch…and let the Court punch them.

Now to successfully execute that plan…

My family could see what I was up: another book. That much was obvious. But it wasn't long before Grandmère figured out exactly what this one was about. My unnatural secretiveness was what gave it away. "Avril, I know what you are working on," she said to me one afternoon as I paused in the middle of work to get a mug of tea and some cookies.

"Really?" I said. "How do you know it, and what is it that you think you know?"

She grinned. "You are writing a history, unvarnished with official lies, of what happened last year – of how billions of people were murdered in the most massive cover-up ever, disguised as a plague. I know this because you usually bore us all with detailed lectures on your projects."

I let out a long breath. "Damn. That's true." I stared off into space.

"Don't worry about it," she told me. "We're on your side and we won't tell anyone."

Hamish appeared just then, back from his office. "Where's Benjamin Franklin when you need him?" he asked.

Grandmère looked at him. "Ah. Oui…his observation on secret-keeping. We aren't going to drop dead in order to keep secret what we have figured out. But I'll let the rest of the family figure it out on their own," she promised. With that, she turned around and headed back to the den to work on her latest puzzle.

Claire was the next to comment what I was up to. "You're writing about the Cull, aren't you?" she said a day later. "You are obsessed with something, and you keep writing things on post-it notes, stuffing them into your pockets, and disappearing into your room to type them up."

"Yes," I said. I waited to see what else she would say.

We were eating lunch in the kitchen. Fabian was sitting with us, and he nodded. "The game is afoot, and we are on to you," he informed me. "We knew you would do this eventually."

"Okay, fine. You're on to me. But you seriously must tell no one. This could be very dangerous, and it really would be nice to survive long enough to release this work, completed, to the world and see how it is received."

"You can count on us not to tell," they said in unison. I smiled incredulously and nodded.

As for my parents, they had caught on just like Grandmère had and said nothing. But…they walked in on the tail end of that conversation and grinned at me. They had gone out to lunch with Grandmère, and the three of them gave me knowing smiles. "Good. At last we can stop tiptoeing around this topic," Dad said, grinning broadly.

There was an insufferable amount of grinning going on, it seemed.

My mother was just as bad. "I thought at first that you were becoming more mature, but that didn't seem quite right. No…that couldn't be it, I realized. This is about secrecy, and security. And 'mature' isn't the right word to describe it." She looked at me carefully, sizing me up as she stood over the kitchen table. "Aspies are what, stealthy?"

"Sometimes," I said, starting to smile again. "But I guess stealth with one's family is a fantasy. I'll have to settle for stealth with those outside it. Wish me luck pulling it off."

"Good luck," she and Dad said.

"Bonne chance," Grandmère chimed in. "You'll pull it off. This is important."

Hamish said, "Now that that's out of the way, it will be easier to act natural around here. But let's not invite any strangers into the house, or anyone outside of the family, while she's working on this. It's too dangerous. I know the Cull is over, but it is still a very sensitive topic."

Dad nodded, looking deadly serious. "You don't have to tell a lawyer twice." Then he looked sternly at Claire and Fabian. "Got that, future lawyers?"

They both grinned. "We know what attorney-client privilege is," Fabian told him.

Claire did add, though, "We can't claim that, though – we'll just have to lie for now, and claim total ignorance. It'll be easier for me. I'll just say I'm on the autism spectrum and can't read people who don't tell me things." And she smiled a smile like a cat who had swallowed the canary, or some such forbidden thing.

Later that afternoon, as I sat back at my desk, writing up bits and pieces of this history, she came up to my door and knocked. "Can I come in and visit?" she asked.

"Okay. No point in keeping people out now, I guess," I said, letting her in.

She sat down on the chair next to my desk. "How are you presenting this one?"

"What do you mean?"

"I mean, what style, length, etc. are you using to tell the tale?"

"Oh. Funny you should ask it like that. I'm going to make it a straightforward children's book style, but without bothering with anything more than a photograph on the cover that I took at the Georgia Guidestones. Remember them?"

"Oh yeah – I remember them all right. Is the children's story style supposed to save time?"

"Yes – exactly. It is meant to move things along, so that the story can be read and absorbed and shared as fast as possible. I don't even care about copyrighting it and making money on this one. That's not the point, since I shall be releasing it anonymously. Anonymous is the way to go when you want to sit back and watch the reaction."

She nodded. "Good plan. So…how did you get into the writing business, anyway?"

"That was an abrupt topic change."

"I know. I'm just curious."

"Okay…well…let's see…no cubicle job would ever accept me, nor would I do well attempting one. I have tried retail jobs, but arriving on time was something I always failed at, even though I was quite willing to stay overtime to make it up. But no…that wasn't good enough. And once at those service jobs, it made little difference how competent or knowledgeable I was. It was always about social interaction and displaying a demeanor that pleased the boss. I don't have that demeanor. Putting one on is phoney and repugnant to me."

"I can certainly relate to that. In our bakery, I always preferred to hone my skills backstage in the kitchen with my mother, working on the cakes, than to interact with the public at the counter out front, with my father." Claire reminisced.

I smiled. "You get it, then. Did your parents make you stay out at the counter much?"

"Some. They wanted me to understand that part of the business and to gain some experience dealing with the public, but the public didn't like me much. Only when they saw and knew my cake art did they smile at me. My tone wasn't…I don't know…fawning enough, or something, and I gave forced smiles with little eye contact."

I gave a laugh and a grin in one whoop. "Oh…I can totally relate. I once had the owner of a gourmet breakfast and lunch take-out scold and lecture me in front of a customer about dropping everything, leaning on the counter, making eye contact with him, saying 'yes, I will get you that,' and so on, even though I had just listened to his order, committed it to memory, and begun to prepare it. I lasted three weeks in that job before quitting that summer, and Dad said that he would have taken off his apron then and there, said 'fuck you,' and walked out."

"I love it!" Claire said. "So what did you do next?"

"I went back to library work, and to graduate school, where I realized that I could not help clients because I can't tell when people are messing with me – teasing, or whatever – and that I love to edit and write, and to research new things. I just got into the groove of finding topics that intrigue me, gathering research, and writing it up in a way that non-experts can follow and learn from. I love it, and learning other skills along the way, whatever they may prove to be. That's the beauty of a law degree: the topics can keep changing. You will never get bored because of that."

She looked both delighted and fascinated. "That's what I'm hoping I can do with mine."

"You will. Don't worry, don't rush, just enjoy the process and you will get there."

"Thanks. I hope you're right. I still get anxious about it – because I'm not there yet."

"Hmm…that is maddening. Come talk to me and Fabian and Hamish and the rest of us when that feeling hits. Do that to take a break, then go back to whatever you're working on. At least you know you're going to law school. Enjoy the free time to read whatever fascinates you, and do that for your law thesis. The world will always have plenty of people to do typical legal work. Don't make yourself write a typical boring insurance paper for a thesis, or whatever seems most likely to get you a job after graduation. It won't."

"Aspie empathy…I'll leave you to your outlining," she said with a grin, and left the room.

A couple of days later, Aunt Zoe was over for coffee and cupcakes. She and Uncle Charlie were happily settled into their new house down the street, but they still liked to come over a lot to visit. I guess a year and a half of enforced togetherness can bring people closer. Families have blow-ups and arguments, but if they're basically good people, as mine were, they like to visit.

Claire and I were home, but Hamish was out, and so were Dad and Fabian.

Hamish was at his office, working on getting more people access to Regenics.

Dad was "Of Counsel" on his firm's letterhead, officially retired, but he was back there today, coaching Fabian in legal research. Fabian was determined to spend the time leading up to attending law school doing something to prepare himself for the legal profession. Good. He would learn about the various practices of law: patents, corporations, tax (he was good at math).

I was starting to draft random bits of the truthful history of the Cull, but after a couple of hours' worth of work, I was hungry. I knocked on Claire's door and suggested we get in on the cupcakes and coffee. She had made them last night, and suddenly I couldn't stop thinking about them. They were almond with rosewater buttercream, pink-tinted, and the icing was swirled artfully (how else with Claire doing it?) to look like roses on top of each one.

We went down to the kitchen and greeted my mother and Aunt Zoe. Grandmère joined us as soon as she realized we were having an impromptu party. My mother laid out the cupcakes, and I poured the coffee and set out the creamer and raw sugar.

Once we were settled, Aunt Zoe asked me, "So – how goes the writing?" She had a devilish gleam in her eye. She didn't know what I was writing, just that I was writing again.

"Good. There's always plenty of data out there on ecosystems collapse."

That had satisfied her. We enjoyed the cupcakes and tea, and conversation turned to other topics. I hoped it merely seemed as though I was less boring, holding forth less.

When she had gone home, my mother asked, "What sort of data?"

With a mischievous gleam, I replied, "Oh, it's the same damning data that you've all seen some of, and I'm using it to write a truthful history. The format is going to be more of a short, dark, metaphoric fairy tale than a dull, dry history book. It has to be when one is forced to rely on secretly acquired videos and other Dark Net data. It includes motives for murder – er, genocide on the most massive scale ever," I replied. "Everybody gets damned by this data – damned if they did, damned if they didn't."

"At the risk of sounding naïve," Grandmère said, "what motives? I mean, I'm expecting to find out similar things to what went on when the Marais section of Paris was emptied into the Vélodrome d'Hiver, things like, people were angry with the victims."

"That's exactly what I'm finding," I told them all. "People were angry with the victims, though only in some cases, such as migrants. They are in Europe and in the southern part of this country. It is all about economics – because it was a resource war – just as in the Second World War. The motives are all accounted for in the damning data – and stated outright."

"Sounds like you have compiled an airtight case," Grandmère said. "I still remember my Jewish friends who disappeared from Paris. There was nothing wrong with them – nothing at all. They didn't expect us to change our culture to be like their own. It was live and let live."

"Indeed," I said. "In that holocaust, openly hateful Nazis went after quiet, unobtrusive Jews. In this one, a secret cabal of Farmers went after an openly hateful horde of Islamic invaders, and after a heedlessly growing invasion of Catholics. All were from collapsed ecosystems, brought on by human overpopulation, fleeing that and economic collapse. Something was bound to happen. The non-collapsed, non-chaos zones of the planet were under no duty to collapse by altruism. Help a few, yes, but all?! It was more than anyone could hope to do."

"It does seem as though this resource war was more desperate than the last," Grandmère said.

"That's how one forgets one's own security and that of the people who share it. No one has the right to give it away – as some liberal leaders offered to do. That, too, increased the speed of the invasion. It made it much, much more intense. I'm writing about the fact that there was no perfect, morally and ethically correct solution in this holocaust."

Claire asked, "But what about the people who were already here, citizens who were Culled?"

"You mean people like your parents." It was not a question from me.

"Yes," she said, "and others. I wonder about people on welfare, people who were homeless, disabled, and those who lived ordinary lives, not standing out in any way, not doing anything remarkable with their lives, and just…stagnating while playing by the rules. Why kill them?"

"They were deemed 'useless eaters' by the Farmers. That is the answer for the 'others' you asked about. As for many other hard-working, middle class Americans, they were pushed out of the middle class by economic manipulation. The economy was deliberately crashed by the banksters and hedge fundsters of Wall Street, and it restructured American society. The American Dream was made unaffordable. You made it through college before that became apparent to the general public. But even people without loans were deemed to be in excess as the Farmers aimed to Cull us all down to that magic number of half a billion human beings."

She looked a bit confused. "My parents paid for me to attend college, and I didn't need loans. They said that they were determined that I wouldn't have a life of debt slavery. They hadn't had that burden, but they did have college educations, they told me. They were determined to give me the same thing that they had, and so they had only had one child."

"They sound a lot like me and Avril's father," my mother said.

Claire smiled. "They were. What?" She asked, looking at me. I was staring at my plate.

"Anyone with loans was Culled." I looked at her. "Hamish and I tried to warn them and to get them to come north and join us here, and we secretly paid off the loans that they had. They had some on their business, loans which they could handle thanks to steady showcase cake orders. It wasn't enough to protect them. Now I think we should have had them kidnapped and brought with us, but your father actually anticipated that and told us to leave them be, that they could take care of themselves."

Claire – and everyone else – was staring at me, horrified. After a few moments, Claire got up, came over to me, and hugged me. "Thanks. I know you tried. They were like that, though – convinced that their government wouldn't do anything underhanded, and determined to manage on their own."

She stood back, and said, "No one makes it alone. You keep telling me so. It's true."

That was no consolation.

Chapter 27

An Unsanitized History Book

It was written: a different history of our depopulation, one that told the truth.

It told the story of another resource war, one that hadn't targeted any particular ethnic, religious, or racial group. It hadn't targeted people by sexual orientation, either. This time it had been preemptive, a war by the Haves on the Have-Nots, to remove them from the game before they could attack. The foresight involved, the planning, the strategy, and the actual strike, had been excellent. It was stealthy, that was for sure. But every crime has its errors of execution. The criminals are always noticed by someone and unmasked.

That unmasking was unfinished business.

Now I would be stealthy.

As I had drafted my unsanitized history book, I showed the holocaust that was visited upon the Islamic world and Africa – the whole planet, not just the areas that I was familiar with. The Cull was perpetrated there with particular cunning and ruthlessness, leaving very few individuals remaining to either practice Islam, that most vicious of religions, nor to need food, water, or space. The Nae-Née policy remained, further keeping numbers way down.

Imams preached against it to no avail. The area was still considered a threatening conflict zone, one that could always cause yet more trouble. Its governments were not trusted to remain peaceful, nor were its people. Too many instances of jihad – Islamic holy wars – peppered recent history for it to be otherwise.

Even without the Cull, the Yazidi, a peaceful group of Iraqi Christians, had been nearly decimated while being raped, tortured, and killed just a few years earlier. It was amazing that any Yazidi people were left, but there were, and the idea was to keep it that way.

Taken together, this data suggested that the Farmers of the entire planet, from its various nations, had colluded to reduce humanity's overall numbers. They were co-conspirators in the most colossal genocide of all time. They had to know who each other all were.

As this alluded to the previous holocaust, this bit should function as a teaser to attract readers.

I thought about the fate of people's pets.

Cats and small dogs had been summarily executed by having their necks broken, while large dogs were shot. Other pets, such as reptiles, rabbits, guinea pigs, and the like, had also been killed, but the methods were not easily discoverable. There was only so much that cyberspying could reveal, it seemed, before it was both too much data and too upsetting to continue.

It was enough to know that innocent pets, who had never done anything to so much as annoy their humans, had been murdered without the slightest warning, nor any chance to defend themselves. It seemed even sneakier and more sinister than the fate that their human companions had met. At least the humans had sensed danger.

I picked up Spock and cuddled him as I thought about all this, kissing and petting him. "You're a purrfect cat," I told him. He smiled at me, and I settled him back onto his bed. He purred, clueless as to the reason behind this sudden affection, and it didn't matter. He got affection like that from me without any reason behind a love of the cat and a desire for feline affection, as did Eowyn. I picked her up next and gave her the same treatment. She purred but, being a girl cat, stiffened after a moment or two, so I put her down.

The two cats settled onto the bed, curled up into cute little fur balls, and stared at me.

Lots of cats, dogs, and humans to avenge with this effort…and their humans.

Why else had the Farmers wanted to erase so many of their fellow citizens? Too much had become automated, thus eliminating job after skill after avenue of employment. People had worked to develop a skill, be it data entry, customer service, or even driving. They were eventually forced out by robots and computers that were retooled to replace them. They were treated as an excess to be deleted, like so much unwanted software.

One afternoon, as I was editing the fully drafted book up in my room, Claire came in to visit me. I had the door closed, so I got up and opened it to see who was knocking, and was actually glad to take a break. "Hi Claire! Come on in. I need a break. What's up?"

She smiled and came in, then looked around, unsure as to where to sit.

"Just flop on my bed. I read there all the time," I said. I also made the bed every day, so the room looked presentable and comfortable enough. "I've always treated beds like sofas in rooms where I can shut the door to keep distracting sounds out – and every sound distracts me." I grinned as I said that last bit.

"I got curious about something. What I'm wondering is, how is it that humans got so overpopulated? Our species has been around for eons, and suddenly we were just eating up every last bit of the planet's resources. How did it get so tight, and what was it like before? I mean for individual families, not our species as a whole. Well, no…I mean both!"

"Well, it's a long story. Have you heard of Thomas Robert Malthus, or Paul R. Ehrlich?"

"No. Who are they?"

"Malthus was a late eighteenth and early nineteenth century Cambridge-educated economist who studied demographics, and a British cleric. He didn't believe in birth control, the silly, unreasonable, unrealistic guy that he was, but he was right about what drives human overpopulation and how plagues, wars, and famines act as checks upon it."

"And Ehrlich?"

"He's still around. He's an entomologist – American – who wrote *The Population Bomb* in 1968, which has a famous equation that illustrates how the impact of a population is equal to its size. Multiply that by our per-capita consumption, then by the energy use of the technologies to drive that consumption, and you've got our species' impact on the planet. He has written and co-authored a bunch of other books since then on both topics, several with his wife, Anne H. Ehrlich. She can draw, and she studied biology. One of their more recent books is *The Dominant Animal*. Guess which one that is?"

"Us?"

"You got it. We can fly higher, kill anything, and control much of the ecosystem."

"So what about how humans lived in the past versus how we have lived that led to overshoot and overconsumption and all of the other conditions that led to the Farmers wanting to do a Cull on everyone…except, of course, for themselves?"

"Well…in Malthus's day, extended families lived together if they were middle to upper (read, wealthy) class, as we are doing now, or got servant jobs or agricultural jobs. What the members who could not afford to marry did not do was reproduce. They just did without sex and they stayed single, for the most part. Religions had a big business that way, too."

Claire was listening intently, and then she said, "Maids, cooks, butlers, valets, footmen, groomsmen, chauffeurs, secretaries, nuns, priests, field hands…maiden aunts and bachelor uncles…all celibate due to financial constraints, then."

"Pretty much. Plus prostitutes, starving kids in streets and workhouses – that was after the Poor Laws that Malthus disapproved of on the grounds that they just made more poor people come into existence – what else…career soldiers…you get the idea. I have absolutely no interest in reverting to that era. Women couldn't get an education unless they were in line to become reigning queens of nations."

"And we live in a big house now with Aaron and Ed in the guardhouse. And sometimes other guards are around. I'm glad we don't have servants for everything. Too many strangers watching us, judging us when we have the slightest disagreement, as all families do, plus I would feel guilty having someone do all my housework for me. At least people don't have to be celibate."

"I'm sure Aaron and Ed haven't lived a life of celibacy. Thanks to birth control, they can have lives. They have had girlfriends, just no one current, that I'm aware of."

"They have? Who? Do you know?" Claire was curious.

"One might have been an F.B.I. agent. But they broke up. Long distance was a problem, I guess, plus they don't want to change careers."

"Oh. I don't want a commuter marriage."

"Neither do I. That's how I got malnourished and seriously unhappy in Hungary," I told her. "There was nothing to do there but work with little kids, which I did not do, and the food was just awful. They use lard instead of butter and olive oil, and have mostly beef and pork dishes."

"Yuck! Remind me not to go there." Claire grinned.

"Okay. Stay away from Eastern Europe because of the food…and women's pigeon-holing."

She laughed. "Okay…thanks for the break. I want to go read tort law some more. Fabian and I are reading the Larry Flint case, which is fun." She got up and headed for the door.

"Oh, I loved that one, and it wasn't even assigned for some strange reason, but I found it in the book and read it anyway. The movie about him was pretty good, too. Here…" I got up and found it on a shelf. "…you and Fabian can watch it, but read and outline that case first!"

She laughed, took the DVD, and said, "Actually, I've already outlined it."

I grinned and went back to work.

Before she left, Claire said, "You certainly have a huge collection of DVDs. Why did you buy so many when you can just watch movies on cable TV, or download or stream them? I mean, they take up a lot of shelf space."

"True," I said, "but they came in handy last year. If the internet fails, and cable TV stops, I'll still possess copies of my favorite movies and documentaries. I like to collect them to save the points that they make, or just because they're pure fun. No apocalypse is getting in my way!"

Now Claire grinned. "I see. Good idea." With that, she left with the DVD.

"Dad, how come you don't say much about the holocaust we just lived through, and the problems we are still dealing with?" I asked.

We were eating cookies in the kitchen one afternoon. My mother and Aunt Zoe had gone out, Uncle Charlie was sitting in their newly bought but old house down the street, and everyone else was out, working at jobs or studying in the law library.

"I was born in 1943, right in the middle of the war, and I lived for a while in a France that was still recovering from it. My sister and your Uncle Charlie were born later, when the economy eased up. By the time they were little, there was money for all sorts of good food, nice clothes, toys, jewelry for your grandmother, and so on. Uncle Charlie never got a taste of difficulty until this past year or so."

"Tell me again about your parents – where Grandpère was during the war, and so on."

"I've told you before, but I'll tell you again: he was in the French Foreign Legion, running an espionage operation against Rommel. That's why he was away. Your grandmother had to lie to the Nazis about him, saying that he was away in Indochina, so that they wouldn't get too interested and check on him. After I was born, she said he was dead, which was a lie, of course, but it kept them off her back."

The door opened, and my mother walked in. "What are you two doing?" she asked.

"Eating these delicious cardamom butter cookies," Dad said. "Have some."

"So, Mommy," I asked, "tell me more about Nana and Grampy during World War II."

"What's to tell?" she said. "They were in the Resistance, passing messages around secretly in the night, or in baskets of eggs, and they hid a little Jewish girl in their loft – successfully. They never got caught, and the girl, Rachelle, grew up and became an attorney with the United Nations. Later, she left and helped to recover stolen art. I'll have to check on her. She should still be around, possibly living in Arles now, retired."

"Interesting," I said. "Let me know what you find out."

"I will."

Claire asked me how I had been able to write the unsanitized history book.

"Think about it coldly, because you want to be a lawyer. We lawyers analyze situations from a cold, dispassionate point of view, sort of like detectives, but applying law and reality to them, because emotions do not change what is. Facts simply are."

She thought about that. "How did the government cover its tracks so well?"

"By lying, for one thing, and by preying upon people's gullibility for another. It assumed that people would be obediently distracted by its falsified news reports and by whatever pastimes they enjoyed. It also banked on the idea that no one would believe that it could betray them to the extent that it did. This was rather different from the previous holocaust in that many people simply did not know what was going on, while the few that did tacitly agreed with it."

"Agreed with genocide?!" Claire was in disbelief.

"Yes. They didn't want to get killed themselves, and they didn't want a crowded world with so much competition for resources that, when they understood what was happening, even if only in a vague sense, they did nothing. They gambled on the idea that they would be the ones around to enjoy the end result. Many lost that bet, but some won it."

I went on, "Even many of those people could not believe that the plague was actually a cull. It just seemed too incredible to them – like paranoia. But you know the saying: 'Just because you're paranoid, it doesn't mean that they're not out to get you."

At last she said, "You have got to release this, no matter what the reaction to it," and left.

Winter was ending, and as Jason and I put the final touches on the video files that would be released with the unsanitized history, we started making our plans for a trip to the International Criminal Court at last. But we would have an Easter dinner before that.

During warm weather, we had made jars of jam – raspberry, blackberry, strawberry jams – and applesauce, which I insisted upon flavoring with cinnamon and varying with apricots and peaches. We had canned green beans and boiled pumpkin, and stored it in glass jars in the pantry. No more cans – they were full of chemicals, just like plastics – and worked those chores into our warm-weather routines.

Gone were the days of simply treating a grocery store like a pantry and just proceeding to recipe preparation. Now there was a lot of advance work. It was good exercise, going out to pumpkin patches or farmers' markets and picking stuff straight from the patch, or just buying it from the stand and hauling it all home. It was also satisfying to prepare it at home.

The Easter feast turned out to be a duck dinner. It had included a curried carrot purée soup, scalloped russet potatoes with rosemary and garlic, and snap peas. As we ate, my mother suddenly noticed something that I was surprised never to have spotted before: both Hamish and my father were eating their food section by section. Dad ate his snap peas, then his potatoes, and then his duck. Hamish ate his potatoes last.

"You're not supposed to eat your food that way," my mother said, disapproving.

Grandmère sighed, "I never could get him to eat his food in random order."

I laughed. "That's a classic Aspie male trait," I told her. "It's not even important."

They both looked at me, nonplussed. "Really?" my mother said, amazed.

"Yes. Aspies males do that a lot. It's funny, but I never noticed Dad doing that before. I guess I just don't watch him eating. Hamish does it – I've noticed him doing it. But who cares? As long as they're not slorfing and slobbing their food all over the place, it doesn't matter. They're enjoying their food the way they eat it. Besides, there's no such thing as the Enjoyment Police, nor should there be."

Aunt Zoe, Uncle Charlie, Edgar, and Jacques just watched it all like a tennis match.

Dad and Hamish suddenly had to stop eating because they couldn't stop laughing.

Dessert was a pear and almond tart – Grandmère's recipe. She had actually made it herself. There was no commentary on the way that anyone ingested that. We just ate it. Fabian and Claire were in stitches by the time dinner was over, so that was good.

We had been headed for a collapse with or without the Cull, I mused as I compiled my notes and thoughts on the matter. It was just a matter of how much still-fertile topsoil and aquifer reserves remained and where on the planet they were that determined our diet now. Thanks to NASA and the imaging apparatus of NOAA, humans could track and plan it all.

There was a lot to say, and a lot to explain. I had begun the history with the Georgia Guidestones. People reading this ought to understand what had been planned and why – what the planners – the Farmers – had considered when they plotted the largest scale of genocide in human history. The Georgia Guidestones practically wrote their agenda for them.

The next time I took a break to get some coffee and cookies in the kitchen, Dad said to me, "Don't forget all those news clips and YouTube videos of migrants in Europe. I hope you're mentioning what those showed: rapes, looting, beatings, and the rest of it."

"Oh, I am, Dad," I said. "Don't worry. I'm including it all. 'Rapefugees Not Welcome' about sums up the problem. I mean, if being a nice humanitarian means that hordes of misogynist, military-age males are going to tromp in, refuse to assimilate, consider women to be loot for the taking and raping, and announce in video after video that their intent is to change the culture of Europe…all because their own ecosystem has collapsed…then the hell with the humanitarian assistance. That assistance must be conditional upon decent behavior and a willingness to assimilate, or no deal! They wouldn't go back to their collapsed hell-hole of a desertified land, so they could just face the consequences."

Dad smiled. "So you aren't a total liberal, then."

"Not totally, no. Yes, I want abortion on demand, birth control access, freedom of speech – that can serve very nicely as a warning to someone's evil intentions – you know: the freedoms that an ecologically and economically non-collapsed society can afford. But after a collapse, my view changes to one of protecting ourselves. That's why you and the rest of the family were quietly slipped across the ocean, under the radar, and into Switzerland."

"Indeed. I knew that much. I just wanted to make sure that you were fully aware of it."

"I am. I am and I'm angry about a lot of things: about collapse, about human overpopulation that was left unchecked until we were facing total collapse and chaos, with no more safety, about that loss of safety from hordes of migrants flooding into what used to be calm territories, and about the Farmers who helped crash the system to get us all to that point."

"What's this?" my mother said, coming into the kitchen with her tea mug.

"We're taking about migrants and the reign of terror they brought to Europe," Dad said.

"Oh, right. I know this is terrible of me to say, but I hope that they went into the mobile ovens of Europe first. The ones that did the rapes, I mean. I don't wish terror on the women and children, or any men who didn't commit those crimes, of course." With that, she put her mug in the dishwasher and shut it.

"Well, Mommy, you're in luck, because they did. It wasn't just that one clip you saw on the way past France aboard the *Shadowcat*. I have checked lots of videos until I have gotten dizzy from watching them. It's a definite thing: the migrants went in first, and only when they were all reduced to ash did the Cull turn to the indigenous population of Europe. But…that population was stable, so there wasn't much to do to reduce it. That's why our relatives in France weren't carrying the nasty nanites in their blood."

She was listening to me with interest. Her only comment was, "Wow."

With that, I went back upstairs with my cookies and coffee. This would be a short, succinct, terse, and otherwise not-lengthy history. Why? Most people were not like me: they didn't like to read heavy detail. I would include a few carefully chosen videos in the bibliography – both of migrant criminal behavior and migrant demise – and then just provide our vast trove of video as links at the end.

The remaining general public was about to find out the entire truth of the Cull. They would have everything that I could see, and had seen. And then…the Farmers could face the music at The Hague. That would require some logistics, but it would all be worth it.

The Farmers who had orchestrated and perpetrated the Cull should not enjoy its result: a less crowded planet. Let their heirs live to clean it up instead. That was likely the best outcome that we could hope to achieve, but it was one that I could live with.

No doubt, the Farmers would not let their vast fortunes escheat to the government via a criminal conviction. No…they would sign it all over to their children first if it was their act of freedom. That was just how those demons operated. Perhaps their assets could be seized…

I intended to sink that New World Order – underwater, where it belonged. The next day, Jason came over and we released *Vaccine: The Cull* onto the Internet. Bitcoins paid all of the publicity costs involved, making the origins both digitally and financially nearly untraceable.

The only thing that might nix that would be a No Such Agency supercomputer, but Jason was on that, too. "No way they'll know it was you," he assured me. "It'll be all supposition. Besides, too many people will have read it and downloaded it by the time they ever hack it."

Yes, the New World Order was going underwater.

Vaccine: The Cull
A Population Policy Wasn't Enough

It is quite likely that you won't want to know what I am about to tell you.
It is also entirely possible that you won't believe it when you read it.
Neither of those possibilities, however, makes it any less true.
Who am I?
I am an observer. I am an intellectually curious person who watches trends, who doesn't follow crowds, who notices things that most people consider unimportant or else are too busy going about their everyday business of living to focus on them, and I am one who questions authority. I take nothing that it presents for granted, but instead research and verify it, or research and disprove it.

America's Stonehenge

In Elberton, Georgia, on a remote farmland out in the countryside, is a stone monument.

It has four tall monoliths of granite that point out like a ceiling fan in four different directions from a center slab, topped by a capstone.

No one knows who had it built – only that its construction was handled by a local banker on behalf of the secretive, anonymous donor, and that the job was completed in 1982. He burned all of the correspondence a few years before his death to make sure that the secret died with him.

But that's not the most interesting thing about the Georgia Guidestones, as they're called.

What is most interesting is what's written on them in eight languages. It's a list of advice for the human species after an apocalypse:

1. Maintain humanity under 500,000,000 in perpetual balance with nature.
2. Guide reproduction wisely — improving fitness and diversity.
3. Unite humanity with a living new language.
4. Rule passion — faith — tradition — and all things with tempered reason.
5. Protect people and nations with fair laws and just courts.
6. Let all nations rule internally resolving external disputes in a world court.
7. Avoid petty laws and useless officials.
8. Balance personal rights with social duties.
9. Prize truth — beauty — love — seeking harmony with the infinite.
10. Be not a cancer on the earth — Leave room for nature — Leave room for nature.

We have just experienced that apocalypse.
The Earth's human population is now at half a billion, just as these stones suggest.
How did we get there?

Some want you to believe that it was from a plague, one caused by a vaccine went wrong.

But it didn't go wrong. It went exactly according to plan. Whose plan was it?

The Farmers

I call them the Farmers. They are a mix of Banksters, Hedge Fundsters, and Corporatists.

They control the world's banking system and financial resources, which means that they also control its other resources. Wealth, after all, is not merely money. It is tangible resources that back up money, such as natural resources (land, water, minerals, and so on), and human capital (education and skills).

How much of the resources did they gain control of? By the time the apocalypse took place, one percent of the human population had acquired 40 percent of everything – and I mean wealth: money, land, resources. Included in that one percent were the wealthiest ten percent, who controlled 85 percent of everything. The poorest half of humanity owned one percent of everything.

That is quite an awesome power to wield in what is the Sixth Mass Extinction in the Earth's natural history. The Earth's ecosystem – Nature – also known as its carrying capacity for life – was, and still is, in a state of collapse. The ecosystem is the Earth's Bank Account.

The Draining of Earth's Bank Account

Ecosystems all over the Earth were collapsing. (And they continue to collapse.)

Temperatures were rising due to excessive fossil fuel use, icecaps were melting and causing sea levels to rise, species depletions were occurring at all levels and threatening fisheries, nuclear accidents were irradiating oceans, waters all over the planet were full of plastic and other trash, which was being ingested at all levels of the food chain, overuse of antibiotics was causing medicines to be less effective, desertification was happening between the Tropics of Cancer and Capricorn, making agriculture less viable there, floods were washing away the topsoil layer, which was also being depleted of nutrients by wasteful farming practices, and so on and on.

Societies saw a breakdown in civil order wherever people could not grow food.

Nations like China, whose people had depleted the fisheries in their oceans, sent illegal trawlers to rob other nations of their fish, which they sent home. This meant that people in Africa or South America starved because there were not enough fish for them to pull from the ocean.

This was what it meant to drain the Earth's Bank Account of resources. It meant war.

The areas where this happened came to be known as the Tropics of Chaos, or conflict zones.

Human overpopulation was the root cause of the collapse of the ecosystem, and the Farmers intended to not only stop that process – if they could – but also to ensure that they survived it and remained in control of the world's resources.

Economic Warfare

For the Farmers, this was a secret war, conducted on paper and with computers.

It was the same thing that had happened with the banking system and the tax code: laws that made the playing field level and fair were chipped and whittled away at over the past century by amendments, addendums, regulations, and whatever other degradations could be hammered onto them. Politicians did this, directed by the Farmers, who had paid for their campaigns.

We can't all buy ourselves a politician.

If you can't buy one, your vote is but a tiny jab of direction to any politician who represents you in government. The real influence comes from those who have the attention of and steady access to the politicians.

Farmers don't show up personally to demand this or that of politicians.

That would be too obvious.

Instead, they send lobbyists, who are highly-paid attorneys, to instruct the politicians.

The banking system became rigged this way as well.

Debt and credit became a way of life as everyone else in Earth's developed nations – the ordinary, private citizens – assumed that there would always be more growth, and thus the ability at some unspecified time in the future to pay off all debts.

Meanwhile, there was no reason to worry about the future, because it was assumed by the majority of economists that growth would never cease. There were a minority of economists who knew that this was a fantasy, and they knew it because they took into account the fact that the Earth's resources are not infinite.

Money must be based on something that actually exists, such as gold. But the gold standard had been done away with during the previous century, and after that, money was created by fiat. A fiat, it should be pointed out, is a fictitious thing. It means "declaration" – but one can't declare a resource of any kind into existence.

This is how debt and ultimately unpayable credit ballooned larger and larger, until…

…the planet's population was living on a lie, lost in a fantasy that it could have whatever it needed or wanted and live that way happily ever after. People bought houses, food, goods, and cars in the developed nations with this money, and real resources went into producing them, while those people remained, for the most part, blissfully oblivious to the ecosystems damage being done in faraway nations in order to produce whatever they wished to buy.

It was the Farmers in the developed nations who were benefitting from the interest payments on credit card and other debt taken out by middle- and working-class people, who leveraged their debts with more credit. It was not possible in contracting economies for non-Farmers to acquire enough money to pay off all debts and free themselves from them. Debt slavery had thus become a way of life for most people, while the Farmers had no incentive to change anything.

The Farmers had all of the information about any trade in the stock market, which made any deal a guaranteed moneymaker. They were the only ones with this advantage, and that was by design. Sixty-six years after the previous major economic depression, they had caused U.S. politicians to allow commercial and investment banking to reunite. This undid a crucial protection against future economic crashes.

Farmers could now dip into pension funds and private bank accounts to fund trades in the stock market. Essentially, they were gambling in the national casino with other people's money. As long as account holders didn't all try to access their money at once, or in significant numbers, this worked. But economic bubbles eventually pop, and when they do, economies crash. That means that when enough people are in debt at once, they will try to take out their savings and use it to pay debts.

Casinos Masquerading as Banks

The Farmers also controlled the world's currencies – each nation's money – by owning their banks. They concealed the inner workings of the banks, driving up more and more debt to keep the system going. Above them all, the Farmers controlled a World Bank, which constituted a New World Order of financial control.

This is what was happening with the economies of developed nations between the wealthy and the non-wealthy – the haves and have-nots. That microcosmic situation was amplified on a global scale between the developed nations and the non-developed ones, with the economies of the chaos zone nations financially beholden to those of the nations in ecologically stable nations.

In the undeveloped nations, nations with extractable resources such as oil or minable ones such as heavy metals, landscapes were ruined. Life there was overcrowded, hot, and unhealthy, food was insecure, water was depleted, and the people there were without hope of a good future, but they knew that it was better elsewhere.

Still, the people in the developed part of the world didn't care, and borrowed against time.

Time ran out, and this continued.

The financial model of continually generating more debt, perpetrated by the banksters, all with fictitious loans that were repeatedly resold to create fictitious money, ballooned at last to the point of an explosion. Millions were made homeless in the developed world, while millions were unable to make a living in the undeveloped world.

In each place, they were left bankrupt, holding the proverbial bags, while the World Bank bailed out the preferred parties: The Farmers, who owned the banks. The Farmers had treated the planet's economies as one huge international casino. They were addicted to gambling with other people's money, and when that hadn't been enough for them, they had gambled with fake money that they had conjured into existence for the express purpose of keeping the game going.

There were too many people living on borrowed money and time.

Debts could not possibly be repaid, nor could resources be expected to service everyone.

By "everyone" I mean all human beings, not just the Farmers who gambled.

Neither the Earth's bank account nor any conjured by the Farmers could keep up with the collective pressure that the human population and a few greedy gamblers were exerting.

Something had to give, and soon.

Demographic Damage Control

There were too many of us, however wonderful, innovative, and fascinating we were.

There were too many of us in the settled, calm, developed part of the world, and even more than that in the undeveloped part. There were too many problems facing us, threatening war, famine, and horrid death: debt, resource depletion, ecosystems collapse, food insecurity, rapidly falling water tables, and so on and on. For those in the conflict zones, war, famine, and horrific tortures were already a way of life…and death.

With all of these mechanisms in place, and with power concentrated in the hands of just a few, the stage was set for what I call the Cull: a covert resource war via a vaccine.

I mentioned a mass extinction and human overpopulation.

Here are some numbers to illustrate that point: the Earth's carrying capacity for humans was measured many decades ago, before the ecosystem had reached a critical state of collapse, at 2 billion. Our planet had that many humans on it in the year 1930.

By the start of the 21st century, we had 6.9 billion humans, with no sign of slowing down.

Soon after that, we reached 8.4 billion, which was when a population policy was instituted by the United Nations treaty of 2012, but it didn't stop it from being discussed. That policy had required that everyone on the planet get a birth license before reproducing, and it was enforced by a nanite that did not cause injury: Nae-Née was its name.

With the Nae-Née nanite, our numbers seemed to stabilize…but not for long.

Soon there was concern among the world's scientists and economists about having enough food, water, land, clean air, and other resources for all of the humans in existence, let alone future humans.

It was clear that water tables – underground aquifers – were diminishing.

In fact, they had been depleted by 40 percent in just 60 years, and it would take another ice age to replenish them. But the planet's temperatures were warming up, so no ice age was coming any time soon. Besides, ice ages last eons. Clearly, this lack of water was a problem that was only getting worse, and it wouldn't be solved in time to do several billion humans any good.

Not only that, but sea levels were rising, which meant less land to occupy, yet more people wanted to spread out on it. People didn't want to live pressed tightly together with no privacy, always aware of what the others were doing and saying. Humans like independence and room to move and breathe, and that was another resource that was in short supply.

There was more bad news: the topsoil on that land was being depleted of nutrients from a combination of wasteful and inefficient farming practices, and would not be able to grow enough food for everyone in a few more decades.

Honeybees and wild bees, butterflies, and other pollinators, all essential to agriculture, were also dying off. Corporations that made insecticides were to blame, both for selling their poisons, and for pushing politicians to enable that. The regulatory agencies responsible for stopping this were disarmed of any enforcement authority by these lobbyists.

But wait – weren't the oceans getting deeper, and thus having more room for fish? Don't make me laugh. The oceans were full of plastic debris from human manufacturing and wasteful behavior. They were also warming up, which was killing coral reefs, the primary breeding grounds for fisheries. There were dead zones in the oceans where nothing could grow. Worse yet, the oceans were acidifying. Shellfish near shorelines died in oil spills and choked on plastic, as did fin-fish farther out to sea.

The air was difficult to breathe, and it was warming up due to all of the fossil fuels humans burned for transportation and electricity. This caused health problems and violent storms that destroyed human settlements and vital ecosystems, and it sped up the warming of the oceans.

Antibiotics lost their effectiveness from overuse in factory farms.

That ought to paint a sufficient picture for you of what a collapsing ecosystem is like.

Several regions around the world faced collapsing ecosystems, and could not grow sufficient food to feed the people who lived there. Land that had been used for millennia as farmland became desert as its topsoil lost its nutrients from being overworked. Famines ensued. People left the countryside for cities, which were the political centers of nations often run by repressive, undemocratic regimes. With increased pressure for resources on those governments, their economies collapsed. In response, the people protested, whereupon the governments repressed them, often brutally.

What was not understood was that human overpopulation was the force that drove all that.

Migrants

These places included the Middle East, South America, Central America, much of Africa, and parts of Southeast Asia. Also, because sea level was rising, it included many tropical islands in Oceania, the Indian Ocean, and elsewhere. These were the Tropics of Chaos I mentioned.

The Middle East presented its own particular set of problems associated with human overpopulation, which had caused the ecosystem there to crash long ago.

The Fertile Crescent was no longer fertile, and hadn't been for many millennia. Other areas, such as that to the north, in Syria, had more recently crashed and given way to desertification.

When that happened, it was promptly deserted for cities.

These cities became overcrowded.

The people who both governed and lived in the Middle East were unhappy with the resulting resource crunch, and soon they were at war. The war was fought from within, as governments cracked down on citizens, making harsh laws to control the people under their rule, and as the people resisted.

That wasn't all. The Middle East had vast reservoirs of fossil fuels underground, which were far easier to burn than to seek other sources of energy. This led to war being waged upon the area by empires in other regions of the world.

At the same time, and for decades leading up to the war over oil, Middle Eastern nations had fought each other over access to water. They had dammed up rivers to keep what little water the region had for whichever country was upstream. They had forced cultures with less funding and modern weaponry into the least desirable areas, and remained at war with them ever after.

All the while, no one had paid the slightest attention to the threat that unchecked human reproduction posed to their natural security. Natural security is the safety that one enjoys when there is enough food, water, space, and other resources to make everyone comfortable.

The people in the Middle East, and in other areas such as Equatorial Africa, did not have enough food, clean water, or work to live comfortably. They thought that leaving and looking for a better situation elsewhere might help.

Things got worse and worse, until mass migration from war-torn areas to neighboring countries led to huge camps there. These camps were quickly filled with people who were not allowed to enter those countries and live fully in their societies. The reason was that host nations could not afford to share all that they had with the migrants: education, health care, jobs, and so on. This meant that migrants stayed trapped in camps for decades.

Some left, heading north, risking arduous and dangerous treks back through the war-torn area. The motivation was to reach the nations beyond: Turkey and, if one was able to migrate there, Europe. Turkey had its own share of migrants, and it too found that it could not afford to share its benefits with the newcomers.

Even before all this had happened, vast numbers of people from the Middle East had walked out, heading north, into Europe. They had chosen not to go south, where there were more countries run by Muslims, who shared their cultural and religious identities. This was because those nations held territory that had also become desertified, and was thus barren of resources.

When they got to Europe, they set up homes together, in communities that were small at first but quickly grew larger and larger, until whole sectors of European cities were inhabited by Muslims. Next, they insisted that the indigenous population of Europe change to suit them.

What they wanted was a replacement of secular law, law which could be shared by everyone, regardless of what religion they followed (Europe had many different religions: Catholic, Protestant – both of which included many sects – Judaism, and even Hinduism. It also had Wicca, an ancient, pre-Christian, Nature-worshipping religion.). All of the previously established religions in Europe had taught the people who lived there that secular law worked best. People got along when they assimilated and did not insist that others do as they did.

When they had insisted that everyone adopt the same religion, those times were called first the Dark Ages or the Burning Times, when Wiccans were murdered, and then the Middle Ages or Medieval Times. But that was long past, and the Europeans lived peacefully together. They wanted it to stay that way.

Now the people in Europe, both past and present migrants and the indigenous population, faced a tense, crowded situation and a culture clash. (More on this soon...)

That happened often all over the planet: nations ignored the threat of unchecked human reproduction, and then found that they could not cope with the needs of its results. More people meant the need for more space, more food, more jobs, and it didn't matter how willing those people were to study and train and work. The economies and the ecosystems that they lived in could only produce a finite – limited – amount of what was needed.

The rest of the people were, to be honest, in excess of the Earth's capacity.

It was happening everywhere on the globe that societies were not thriving.

It was also happening where societies were still functioning. This seemed strange, because Europe, Scandinavia, and Japan had long since stabilized their populations naturally. Their people had learned to have only as many children as they could afford to feed and educate by adjusting to food prices and other costs of living, long before the population policy was instituted. Top-down governments, which have monarchs or shoguns, can simply institute resource-conserving policies and enforce them. So can socialist governments.

Politically stable nations included those of Europe, Scandinavia, Japan, Australia, New Zealand, certain parts of Oceania, and the United States. Australia, New Zealand, some parts of Oceania, and the United States had needed a population policy to stabilize, but each was still over their territory's ecological capacity.

The problem was that they either would not or could not assess the carrying capacity of their lands. Having a large territory can have that affect, as can certain forms of government. Democracies work when there are plenty of resources, but not so well when those are dwindling. To preserve that way of life, strong measures are needed: population stability and resource preservation, protection, and sustainability.

None of that is as much fun as using as much of whatever one wishes, but it works.

Human overpopulation had happened in those nations because the people who lived with such comforts had seen no reason not to have as many children as they wished to have. It should be noted that those people did choose to have far fewer children than those in poorer nations, but the total numbers of humans had continued to grow anyway, before the population policy.

The people in these nations had access to abortion and birth control, but no population policy. This had caused their numbers to grow, and their appetite for resources to increase. This was what led to the depletion of fossil fuels, and eventually of water aquifers. And that, in turn, was what led to attacks on the Middle East, already a region in collapse and chaos, for oil.

The people in solvent nations lived temperate zones – areas where the climate was cooler and where the ecosystem was still capable of growing things. They did import many goods from other nations, but they could grow food, and they had, for a longer time than the people in the Middle East did, enough water.

Because of this, the people in these temperate zones also consumed far more resources than those who lived in the conflict zones. And why not? They could just import whatever they didn't have right at home.

But the migrant newcomers walked in, and many arrived and got settled beyond the camps and fences before those things existed, which greatly increased the numbers of people already living in Muslim sectors of European cities. Soon, they wanted European ways replaced with their own, and said so. They wanted all of Europe to be just like the home that they had left.

The problem was, as mentioned earlier, not only one of resources, but of culture.

The people who tried to move from Africa and the Middle East had a religion and a culture that was quite the opposite of that of their hosts. The people in the host countries were willing, at first, to politely welcome the newcomers and offer them the food that they had, a place to sleep, and to meet with them to see whether or not they might be able to accommodate them for the long-term as well as the short. But the migrants kept coming, with no end in sight.

Warehouses became refugee centers, as did empty hotels, palaces, and cruise ships.

As more people kept coming, camps were set up for them.

Even before the camps were set up, however, complaints began to be made by the migrants.

They didn't like it in the planet's temperate zones.

The food, the weather, the overall temperature, the culture – it was all different!

Really?! What did they expect to find, that everything was the same as at home?!

Their complaints were mildly amusing at first, but not for long.

Pretty soon, videos showed what the migrants were like, and newscasts showed interviews with them. Demographic studies were done, which meant that numbers of every aspect of the migrants – ages, genders, cultures, and attitudes – were tallied up. Most of them were military-age males, away from their families. The others included women, children, and elderly people.

The migrants were not accepting of the differences between themselves and the Europeans and Scandinavians. They became hostile, belligerent, and demanding. Soon, the Europeans were afraid of them, and very sorry that they had invited the migrants to come to their countries.

What did the newcomers want secularism replaced with? The law of Islam, of course: Sharia.

Just what was it that the migrants did that first offended and soon frightened their hosts?

It was most particularly about a difference of religion, and one of opinion as to the priority of law versus religion. The Muslim migrants considered the laws of their religion to be the most important thing not only in their lives, but in those of everyone around them. This, unfortunately, included non-Muslims, whom they called names such as "infidel" and "gaffer".

The Europeans believed in keeping law and religion separate, with law above religion at all times. The vast majority of Europe and Scandinavia were Christians with a Muslim minority but to them all, religion was culture, not a law unto itself to be obeyed.

These hosts therefore maintained a strict, legal separation of religion and state. That, they believed, was the way to maintain respect for others, freedom, and safety for all. The people in Europe and Scandinavia were friendly, accepting of differences, and they lived together without fighting. The women had equal rights with men.

That did not sit well with the newcomers.

Women Lose First…to Superstition

The Muslim newcomers wanted women covered from head to toe in cloth whenever they went out, and accompanied by men. They called European women rude names such as "whore" for wearing tee shirts and showing their hair, and objected during the summertime when they sunbathed in skimpy swimwear.

The women walked and bicycled wherever and whenever they wished to go, wearing colorful and imaginative clothing, cosmetics, and shoes of all sorts. They wore lighter clothing in warm weather, and less of it. They also showed their hair, and enjoyed the wind in it and the sunlight on it. They sung and spoke in public. The men did not feel entitled to make decisions for them.

The migrants – the vast majority of whom were Muslims – were different. Their way of life and of thinking was just the opposite. This is not to say that the migrants were not an educated or trained lot, because many of them had university educations. But that is not enough. Their culture and its attitudes about life in general was essentially frozen in what, to their hosts, was the Medieval Era…which the Europeans had passed several centuries earlier.

It is when one looks at how a culture views and treats women that this is clearest.

The Muslims required women to wear cloaks over their entire bodies to conceal their shapes, and scarves over their heads. Some even insisted upon face veils for women. Women were not to sing where men who were not their family members might hear their voices, because this might seem sexually attractive to strangers, and that was forbidden.

European and Scandinavian women wore bathing suits in warm weather that covered no more of their bodies than underwear did, and even in cooler weather, they wore no cloaks. The shapes of their bodies did show, they were attractive to look at, and they laughed and spoke and sung in public!

It was not long before attitudes clashed and there was serious and even horrific trouble.

That trouble was rape. Mass rapes, gang rapes, and rapes of little girls were committed. Migrant males would surround women and attack them in a practice known in the Islamic world as "taharrush" – and laugh as they took what they thought they were entitled to – women who were not Muslim. They also raped little boys when they could find no other victims.

At first, none of this was reported openly.

The Europeans and Scandinavians were shocked and stunned by this behavior. They shouldn't have been so surprised. A study of the new arrivals' culture and religion might have warned them. Soon, women in Europe and Scandinavia found that the assistance to the migrants was coming at their own expense. They were losing their safety, security, and sanity. Some lost their health, and a few were burned with fireworks in public.

They found out, too late, that some Muslim males will injure a woman who refuses them.

Muslim males were used to having access to sex often and from their late teen years, because of arranged marriages. This was not available to them once they had left their nations of origin. One of them, unaware of how bizarre and absurd he seemed to the Europeans, allowed a video of himself to be recorded in which he told his interviewer about a hospital stay he had just had due to a lack of sex.

It got worse when another interview showed these men saying that European women were "trash" and "war booty" – and that they were there for the taking.

What was this talk of war booty about?

Resource War is Recognized at Last

It was becoming clear at last that this was, in fact, a resource war.

Some Muslims, called Islamists (those who wanted to force it on others), actually said so. They said that they wanted to turn Europe Muslim, and make Muslim babies with European women. Of course, the wishes of the women were not even considered.

The European women soon found that they had a difficult time riding bicycles or walking alone because groups of Muslim males would shout insults at them. Soon it escalated to physical attacks, and the European nations with the most social services became known as the rape capitals of Europe, and even of the world.

Governments did not know how to handle this. The police, journalists, and politicians of these countries had been taught not to point out physical, cultural, or religious differences when handling a rape case. Their laws were so inclusive and careful not to discriminate against those who differed from them that they could not point out those differences. To do so would be "culturally insensitive" – another term for bigoted.

But that attitude went too far when it discounted the loss of personal freedoms, safety, sanity, and security of the indigenous European women. It forgot that crime was supposed to be fought, and fought effectively, not with handicaps. "Political correctness" was backfiring.

The Europeans wanted the Americans to take some of these migrants, but enough was enough. The Americans had seen enough, and were disgusted by the foolish attitude and self-destructive handling of the influx of migrants. Already, the migrants and the Muslims whom they joined marched in the streets of Europe loudly chanting the mantras of Islam, threatening, harassing, and intimidating observers.

What was next, destruction of the beautiful, world-famous art, antiquities, and architecture of Europe?! No. That must not be allowed. Europeans began to come to their senses, late as they were to do so.

Militant Muslims had destroyed ancient wonders in their own part of the world, including monolithic statues carved into mountains millennia ago. They had done so because their religion forbade depictions of the human form…or so the fundamentalists said.

This was a religion that had not progressed beyond its Medieval phase. The most aggressive of them picked and chose whatever bits of their religious text, the Quran, that they liked best, and used its words to try to control others. This was a people with Medieval attitudes who had access to modern weaponry and other technology, such as the Internet.

Growth Ends

Even as the migrants destabilized life in the non-conflict zones, there was still the problem of excessive debt in most of the nations there. That debt was not going to be repaid. It would just grow and grow due to interest on loans, and the economy had gone into a depression.

The Farmers insisted that it was only a recession, but a recession is a term for an economic downturn that lasts several months to a year at most. In it, employment, gross domestic product, and trade all decline, but hope remains for a recovery.

A depression lasts years, and this one wasn't going to end.

Growth was over.

Certainly, an economy could, if stabilized, fluctuate from time to time without truly growing or crashing. Nothing stays absolutely stationary, a straight line with no change at all for months or years on end.

But a major downsizing was underway. This depression wasn't going away. The global economy was contracting without a concomitant contraction of resource consumers. Consumerism had gotten humanity there, as had religious superstition about abortion, birth control use and access, and an economic model built on falsehood and fantasy.

You can't lie to yourself forever about debt.

Eventually, it comes back to bite you.

That bite could mean repossession of a car, filing for personal bankruptcy, losing your home, and worse: starvation. It could happen anywhere on the planet due to simply running out of time to put off payment time, and then…famine hits.

Then the excess of humanity becomes obvious to all.

Keeping that from happening had always been the goal of political and economic elites.

In theory, the Ponzi scheme of debt that the Farmers were carrying on could continue forever…as long as everyone continued to participate, and as long as there were always more participants. But that was just a fantasy, and they knew it.

First, there was the world-wide population policy using the nanite called Nae-Née.

Next, there was the realization that, with or without Nae-Née, Nature would limit growth. It would do this because the Earth's Bank Account was finite. It became clear that Nae-Née on its own would not reduce humanity's numbers. Finally – and this was the worst realization – it was understood that Nature would not reduce humanity's numbers in time to avoid a resource war.

Not Our First Holocaust

This was not humanity's first resource war. We had had many others.

The most recent Holocaust was what our history books term World War II, in which specific groups were targeted: Jews, Romani people (also called gypsies – they are the nomadic people of Europe), homosexuals, those with birth defects and mental deficiencies…and anyone else whom that war's aggressors wanted to snatch space and resources away from, or to deny resources to.

Humanity's Latest and Greatest Holocaust

This resource war differed in that it didn't seek to eradicate particular groups or cultures.

Why not?

Well, the problem wasn't that humans were culturally diverse. That was an asset, after all. It meant innovation, invention, creativity, and other wonderful things. These ought to remain, the Farmers reasoned.

The problem was simply that there were too many of us.

Therefore, some of every group would have to go, plus the sick and abnormal, because taking care of them drained resources. First, of course, they would be squeezed for all of the money they could be drained of with hospital bills, prescription drugs, radiation, and chemotherapy. After that, it would be open season on them.

Genetic abnormalities could be detected in uteri – before a fetus was fully developed. That meant that there would be far fewer abnormal humans to begin with. Likely, the Farmers calculated, they would be eliminated in the Cull, along with many normal ones, simply to get our numbers way, way down.

As the collapse of the Earth's Bank Account unfolded, questions of ethics were asked.

As huge numbers of people – in the tens of millions at first, and later in the hundreds of millions – tried to relocate from their ruined ecosystems to areas that were still functional, some fleeing war-torn areas, while others simply sought a better, more abundant, life, the ethical questions included this one: Couldn't the people with enough just share?

Well…no. Not for long, and not amicably.

Of course, the migrants were coming anyway, with or without an invitation, but now the Europeans talked of sending them back. There were immigrant detention centers and airplanes for that, and boats, if that wasn't enough. But…land connected Africa to the Middle East, and the Middle East to Europe.

Razor-wire fences went up at most European borders. Switzerland added cameras and automated machine-guns. The war was on, but something more needed to be done about this problem. After all, that was just one part of the world. The pressure was global.

The Australians and New Zealanders were greeted with boat-loads of migrants. Many were from the Middle East, but many more were from Oceania – the islands of the Pacific Ocean that were sinking as sea levels rose. They were both climate refugees and economic refugees.

Rather than simply accept them (Australia was already overpopulated by its own people) the refugees were put on islands offshore, and housed in detention centers. They remained there for years while their applications were processed.

This delay was a problem wherever migrants and refugees went, because there were just so many of them. They all had to be identified, registered, and their cases examined.

Why not just let them in and share?

There wasn't enough of everything, and as the reader can see from the situation in Europe and Scandinavia, it isn't advisable to let in criminals. If they could possibly be identified and sent back or at least locked up, that ought to be done, people insisted. One can't blame them.

Now on to the Americas, where migrants had been coming across national borders for decades: in recent years, as ecosystems collapsed, the pace and their number had increased dramatically. The Americas were dealing with their own resource wars.

Gang violence in Central American nations along with floods and droughts made life both dangerous and famine-ridden there. South America was busy destroying its rain forests, and Brazil's human population had grown much faster than its sanitation infrastructure.

This led to both water-borne and climate-driven diseases, and birth defects…which included babies born with abnormally small brains. Those brains would never grow to a normal size, a condition called microcephaly. Mosquitoes with viruses were blamed, but it was also related to the stagnant water in the favelas – the slums of Brazil's big cities.

The United States was where people wanted to go, but like Europe, it was not the haven that they imagined it would be. Culture clashes weren't as threatening for migrants and U.S. citizens, but there were some obstacles to observe.

One of them was about religion: Catholicism. That religion competed with Islam for the largest share of the planet's human population. It was a close race, not that it was official, but it was on. Occasionally, it was discussed by Catholic and Muslim religious leaders as they expressed a wish for more babies to be born to their followers.

This, despite the Nae-Née policy; if only that had been enough for the Farmers!

The Population Policy Wasn't Enough

But they weren't willing to wait the few decades that Nae-Née would require to bring the numbers of humans down to a sustainable level on Earth. They wanted to reduce our species' numbers faster.

They were convinced that waiting for the humans who were still alive to live out their natural life spans and die of natural causes would mean that too much food and too many resources would be consumed before the Earth could recover.

Recover?! The Earth's ecosystems – Nature – would go on with or without us humans.

But so what, they said?! They wanted it to go on WITH us humans, not without.

And they wanted to be among those who lived to enjoy that.

They wanted long lives with good food and plenty of room and clean air and clean water.

Don't we all?

And so it began.

The Farmers hatched a plan to "solve" the world's problems.

They intended to reduce humanity's numbers and with that, the pressure on the Earth's Bank Account, and reset the economic systems to reflect less of everything, including debt. That would hide their Ponzi scheme by stopping it, they reasoned, and keep them out of trouble yet still wealthy and in control of resources.

That motive did not, of course, give them the right to end another person's life.

I just thought I would throw that thought out there: what the Farmers did was unethical.

It was immoral.

It was also the sneakiest, stealthiest, and most insidious way to wage a resource war.

For that is what the Cull really was: a covert resource war.

The Covert Resource War

The Farmers had joked that we needed a new plague, but plagues don't kill more than a few hundred million people at a time, and there were billions to be killed. So, they did it with vaccines. Well, one super-vaccine, to be precise.

This vaccine claimed to target at least forty diseases with one serum. This was guaranteed to crash the human immune system, because the proper way to administer a vaccine is to give a dose that targets just one disease at a time, spaced apart over a few months. However, the purpose was not to preserve human life, so it aimed at many illnesses, plus it contained a secret ingredient to assure its success as a murder weapon: a nanite.

This nanite, a microscopic robot, was injected into the human bloodstream in the vaccine. It then traveled into the brain and sought out a part of the patient's DNA (deoxyribonucleic acid – the genetic code that serves as the biological blueprint for an individual life form). It was looking for something called a P53 protein, which is a cancer tumor suppressor. Without this protein functioning properly, a human body cannot heal itself. Once the nanite found this part of the genetic code, it broke it. Thus, the vaccine was a guaranteed kill-shot.

Vaccines are supposed to prevent whatever illnesses they are created against.

This one did the opposite: it caused a plague. It was an insidious one that manifested the symptoms of multiple diseases, and it was caused deliberately. A naturally-occurring plague does not kill a huge percentage of the population. It kills what feels like very, very many to those who lose loved ones, but when it is over, it barely makes a dent in overall numbers.

This "plague" was different. It decimated the human population.

In other words, it did its job, and it did it well.

Farmers had been running a brisk business of drug development for decades. Some of these drugs helped, but most just made money. Any that actually helped would cure disease, which meant less money for the corporations, which was bad for business. Illness pays, so the Farmers liked illness. They preferred to bleed sick patients' bank accounts dry by selling them useless drugs for as long as possible. They had no intention of dispensing medicine that actually healed, thus enabling long, happy lives, and the ability of those patients to leave some money to their heirs. Instead, anything inexpensive and helpful got patented and locked away in a safe.

It took the Farmers several decades to whittle the playing field down to the point that it was tight enough to control like this. There used to be many corporations – pharmaceutical companies – in the 1950s, all in competition with one another. They manufactured vaccines, prescription drugs, and other treatments that physicians and surgeons used to fight disease.

Gradually, however, these corporations dwindled to just four.

The Farmers had executed their plan – the Cull – with great foresight and efficiency. It had started with gaining control of the pharmaceutical industry, continued with absurdly high salaries for the scientists whom they employed in that industry, and been sealed by making those scientists sign confidentiality and non-disclosure agreements as a term of employment. Any whistle-blower who dared to disclose the truth was to be arrested, prosecuted, and imprisoned.

Scientists with advanced academic degrees toiled in laboratories to develop the vaccine, which meant wearing elaborate protective suits just to handle and experiment with the viruses and bacteria. Physicians then tested the medicines that the scientists develop on their patients, both in and out of hospitals, but most intensively in secret laboratories in rural areas.

The Farmers had arranged it all with the assistance of military physicians and scientists.

It had started as a secret program in which "volunteers" were invited to participate – usually drug addicts who wanted to detoxify. As payment, they agreed to let the government test early versions of the serum on them, with a promise that they would be cured at the end of the tests.

They were not cured, of course. They were killed.

So were the scientists after the serum was developed.

Infomercials warning of the dangers of whooping cough, for just one example, were broadcast repeatedly. They urged everyone to get vaccinated, regardless of whether or not they ever came in contact with anyone whose immune system wasn't strong enough to resist that pathogen.

Soon, however, the vaccines were all simply required by law – for everyone, everywhere.

Settled residents couldn't escape them, migrants couldn't escape them – no one could.

To get the process started, national databases were prepared to register each vaccination given. Doctors were required to enter each vaccination into them. Anyone who wished to get vaccinated ahead of the crowds could do so at their physician's office.

Once the injections were legally required, long lines formed in shopping malls and other public places as people obediently reported for them. Medical teams, unaware that the sera contained nanites that violated their oaths to do no harm, administered the vaccine. Police officers kept everyone in line and assisted with the registration process.

This took care of most people's injections, but not all.

Roadblocks were set up. Police and military physicians were everywhere. Anyone driving on the road was checked on the government database, and often injected on the spot. This didn't always happen, but it usually did. It depended on who one knew, and one's vaccination record.

Every U.S. water reservoir became a razor-wire fenced, surveillance zone with MRAPs, guarded by cops with assault rifles. A lie was broadcast, informing the public that terrorists had poisoned the water. Wherever the Cull was taking place, the water was abruptly shut off. This stressed out households full of people who were feeling the ill effects of the vaccines, making them more compliant. It was tougher to store rations and wait things out without water.

Next, homeless people were rounded up under false pretenses and taken to remote facilities, where they were injected with the first doses of the fully formulated serum. They were not seen again. These homeless people came at first from the streets of cities around the United States, but soon the country's own climate refugees, displaced by ecosystems collapse, were taken away.

Yes – the United States had climate refugees from floods, earthquakes, and droughts.

At the same time, the prisons were being emptied out. Inmates, whether convicted rightly or wrongly (errors do happen from time to time), were summarily injected with the serum. No further analysis of any individual's guilt was made. They were simply dispatched – end of discussion. The prison guards were sent home, replaced by military vaccination units to administer the serum. From there, the rest was easy, with the general prison population weakened. The United States was over its ecological capacity, and that was that.

It had no room for more people, as the migrants from Central and South America found out. They went into detention facilities to wait, and wait, and wait. If they managed to slip past border patrols, they were found later on, and imprisoned. They were to meet a mysterious fate, which came not long after that of the convicts. The migrants disposed of along with the homeless and displaced citizens of the United States.

How were they "disposed of"? I'll get to that shortly.

If anyone resisted, they would be dragged outside and clubbed.

All pretenses of individual rights had been dropped.

The military units had been primed for this the year before the vaccine was released with training exercises that taught them to pretend that all civil liberties were suspended. It was war on the populace, a state of martial law, and it became a reality the following year.

So what happened next, once people were outside with the mobile military units?

They received additional injections of the vaccine. The point of this was to sicken and kill any who had not yet had the serum. Some people, you see, had gone to their physicians in advance of all this, and received vaccines that did not contain anything that was meant to harm them. These physicians had figured out what was going on and tried to save their patients by spacing out the vaccine doses, serum by serum, over a period of months. This dose aimed to cancel that effort out.

Many people were already feeling ill, however, because they had not had physicians who sought to save them. Their physicians had followed the rules, else those people had been injected at malls and other public places. Consequently, they were tired, fatigued, exhausted – it varied by individual due to age or infirmity – with lesions and sores from the first doses.

This was about managing health, not preserving it. People were being Farmed.

The Farmers were conducting a Cull, and they meant to reduce our species numbers.

By the time people realized this, they were usually in their underwear.

In Europe, it was decided that all of the Muslims would have to go.

The Europeans also targeted their continent's nomadic group, the Romani people.

Any not living in settled area, in homes of their own, were Culled.

Migrants were lied to so as keep them from panicking or fighting. They were told that, if vaccinated, they could more freely around Europe. This was just a ruse to catalog the ones who had avoiding registering in a particular country, which they did because they hoped to register in the wealthiest nations of Europe rather than the poorest.

One way of fooling migrants into believing that they had secure passage wherever they wished to go was to issue them a World Passport. These documents were created by the World Service Organization, which honestly thought that it was helping people.

Soon, merely by existing, these passports marked migrants as such, tagging them to the government officials all over Europe and anywhere else. This made the migrants very easy to round up and inject with the Cull serum.

At first, the European Farmers had offered something else, the idea being to let migrants face the Cull back home. This was in the early days, while the vaccine was not quite ready, or still being prepared in sufficient quantities.

Migrants were taken straight back to the border and given two options. One of them was to start walking toward their home countries, conflict zones though they were, and if they stepped on a land mine or got killed, too bad.

The other was far more sinister: they could go to a holding camp and remain there, in limbo, until the European Union figured out how to handle the massive influx of them. Those who chose the latter were vaccinated and, when they began to get sick, they were taken into converted cruise ships.

The Middle East and Africa became peppered with U.S. and Chinese military outposts.

China had solved its problem of a vastly disproportionate number of marriageable men to marriageable women by culling those men once they had taken care of their elderly parents. Any men who were not married and whose parents had died, for example, were culled. This left an open question as to what it would do in the future with the remaining unmarried men once their parents died...but it also culled many of those families altogether, as it turned out. Military units in China were kept busy burning human corpses and cleaning up rivers.

As the planet's other empire, China had its own Farmers, though they were government officials with their hands in the cookie jar more than independent hedge fundsters. That didn't make what they did any less heinous. They had murdered – erased – the population of most of Africa, working village by village, then town by town, and finally gotten to the cities. The U.S. Farmers had sent in military units as well, so the genocide was carried out by both. China's Farmers were as bad as the Farmers of the United States.

They did it by putting tranquilizers into food that they "donated" as relief packages. Once the people they intended to kill were sufficiently loopy from the drugs, the Chinese medical teams had moved in, injecting Africans with the Cull serum. Often, they didn't even wait for people to be at death's door, or even confirm that they were fully unconscious, before escorting them into "disinfectant chambers" to kill them. They just got them inside and turned up the heat. The result was that Africa still had people – indigenous people of every culture – living in cities and in some small towns, but most towns and villages were simply erased.

South America and Central America met a similar fate, with the exception of uncontacted, indigenous tribes. They were left alone. The Farmers there had no regard for their own people once their numbers had exploded past a tipping point set by some nameless, faceless officials.

Japan had another dilemma: how to solve the problem of Fukushima without any help.

In Japan, the disaster at the nuclear power plant in Fukushima was a convenient Cull pretext. People were brought back to live in the area, to clean it up, and lied to. They quickly got sick on both the vaccine and the radiation in the area. The Farmers of both of those nations had no trouble later claiming that there was an environmental toxin putting everyone at risk.

The problem with its culture was its absolute determination to save face, as it put it, by insisting upon doing what could not be done: take that destroyed reactor offline and get rid of the hazardous material that was leaking into the Pacific Ocean. Too little too late, it decided to do what it had previously thought impossible by doing the unthinkable. It forced its nuclear power company officials to don radiation suits and do the job, assisted by robots.

In short, it sent them to their deaths, and then burned the evidence.

But there were still many Japanese people in existence over and above the number recommended in the Cull plan, and so they were recruited to handle the stockpiles of still-hot fuel rods that were being stored in barrels near the site of the ill-fated nuclear power plant.

All spent fuel rods were taken to a special laboratory underground to be reprocessed. If that didn't work, the whole mess was destined for the nearest obliging volcano. The planet Earth could incinerate the problem, it was hoped. This only further reduced Japan's numbers.

India had always had a cremation practice for its dead, but now it used ovens instead of piles of wood for funerals. It couldn't afford to expend the wood to make enough funeral pyres for everyone anymore.

All the while, newscasters announced that a mysterious plague was causing severe illness, with lesions, intense fatigue, and often death. The announcements did not say that death was always the result of the plague, because some hope was to be left.

Hope made people easier to manage. Without it, people become more difficult to deal with.

Always, these newscasts would be framed carefully, so as to show only what the Farmers wanted the viewing public to see: the military units with their MRAPs and physicians in decontamination suits. No neighborhood-removal equipment was shown, no dead pets, and no mobile crematoria. Those followed later, after the news crews had been escorted away.

In a year's time, the process was complete: we were only half a billion humans on Earth.

Concealing the Evidence

What happened to all of those people? Why don't we see cemeteries full of them?

For that matter, why don't we now see the homes where they used to live?

Well, the Farmers had thought of everything.

The mobile military units erased all traces of those murder victims – for that is what they were. They did so by waiting until they were almost dead of the forty-odd diseases in the vaccine, then escorting them into a huge truck for a cleansing shower.

It wasn't a shower.

It was an anesthetic gas that flooded the enclosed chamber.

You know how when a pet is dying, and the veterinarian puts it to "sleep"? That is done with an overdose of anaesthesia. It kills the pet, gently. It is a kind way to end a sick and hopefully elderly companion's life.

That is how 6.8 billion humans died.

But where did their bodies and things go?

Cleverly devised concentration camps – mobile ones – were created. The camps left no trace of themselves, nor of their operations, that way. They really were operations – military ones. Each "op" was conducted by a mobile military unit which roved around whichever region of the country it had been assigned to. Soon they finished with the homeless – and moved on.

As it moved, each unit would visit neighborhoods in the suburbs of cities. The unit commander would announce that they would be administering additional doses of the vaccine to all residents, and to report outside in their underwear or nightwear, bringing nothing with them.

The answer is that those trucks not only functioned as quiet killing chambers, but also as mobile crematoria. Once they were dead, those people were burned up, at high temperatures and for long enough to turn them to ash. Any materials such as jewelry or dental fillings and implants fell into traps to be collected and removed.

What about their homes, vehicles, and whole neighborhoods?

All removed by the military units, as part of their ops. Paved streets, utility poles, underground plumbing lines, sewage ducts, and all, all gone! It was all torn up and carted away. Homes were looted for valuables, and then emptied for recycling of any materials that could be reused. Pets were killed, necks broken by the military units.

How could the soldiers do that, you might ask?

Training, repetition, drilling, indoctrination, and threats, that's how.

What happened to the soldiers later?

They met the same fate as that of their victims which, just as it was for the civilians whom they killed, came without warning. It was delivered via an aerosolized dose of the vaccine, until one or two elite units remained in reserve, at the beck and call of the Farmers. They may still be around as if this writing, but rest assured, they won't be there forever if you are reading this.

What about the people who were "erased" from existence elsewhere?

The Europeans converted cruise ships to other things besides migrant detention centers.

Many ships became mobile crematoria.

The Farmers had recruited vast numbers of soldiers in every nation with false promises of free educations, health care, and jobs after a tour of duty subduing the "unruly" civilian population. All they had to do was spend a year wherever they were sent, doing an op there.

It was only after the people in those places got seriously ill that the Cull was declared a plague, and the military units were required to "disinfect" the areas. It took a while, but those areas became mostly depopulated, with the exception of their own Farmers.

There weren't many left, however. This "vaccination program" left no one undiscovered and undisturbed. Once the military missions of genocide were complete, other units came in to administer health checks – and the vaccine serum – to the soldiers. Thus, those who had been instruments of the Cull were erased.

Medical and Financial Terrorism

This holocaust differed from the previous one in its covertness. The plan was not admitted to be so even to those who were about to die. Instead, its victims were stubbornly lied to up until the last moment, told that they were sick and being cared for by government physicians who needed the assistance of the military for logistics. There were no blatantly cruel, aberrant experiments conducted on knowing victims, as with the notorious butcher physician at the concentration camps in World War II.

No...but this was a holocaust, just the same. It was marketed as a plague. It was committed in an attempt to reverse, or at least halt, the Sixth Mass Extinction of the Earth. It was done with great deliberation, stealth, and forethought – all of the elements required for the commission of a crime. The only things missing, as of this writing, are its inquest, arrests, and prosecutions.

The Farmers surpassed Hitler's crimes against Jews, Romani people, homosexuals, mentally retarded people, Churchill's against India during 1942-1943, Tojo in Nanking and elsewhere in Asia, Pol Pot, Genghis Khan, and just about any other monster in history one might name. For all of those murder victims combined cannot equal the number erased in the Cull.

So...this is the price that we paid as a species to save our planet's ecosystem and to preserve our species. The question as to whether or not it has actually worked is still an open one. What we now have is a perversion of Charles Darwin's "survival of the fittest" theory. It is not a natural, unconscious result of honest competition for resources. Instead, it is the result of stealth and genocidal mania. No plague would kill so many!

But what of those who survived due to no fault of their own, merely to some great, good luck of circumstances? There are those who lived in non-conflict zones, non-flood zones, non-drought zones, without being culled. They knew nothing of the secret plan to reduce our numbers, yet they survived.

How are they the fittest? And don't they deserve to know what really happened?

Do they suspect what really happened? It is, after all, oddly convenient, and too convenient.

Look, after all, at who did not die in the Cull: scientists, engineers, the most famous authors, musicians, celebrities of various kinds, physicians…in short, the wealthiest and most privileged members of all of the societies on the planet, and their friends and families.

It makes for a convenient way of keeping people from noticing or questioning things.

That can't be an accident of Nature, nor of any vaccination policy.

New World Order Underwater

So now you know why there are only half a billion human beings alive today.

Much of our planet has gone underwater, both ecologically and financially.

The Farmers thought that they would reset the slot machines in their casino with the Cull.

Now you know why the news analysts say that the economy is in a state of equilibrium.

Now you know why you can earn a comfortable living, why there is room for us all to live without being close up against one another, why the topsoil layer has more fertile time left to provide fresh fruits and vegetables for us all, and why colleges and universities are able to accommodate most applicants.

The only question that remains is, how long have we got before time runs out again?

Why Have I Told You This?

Hopefully, because you have read this, you will join in a revolt against the Farmers.

Revolt against the New World Order and put it underwater.

We have gained a reset of the Earth's Bank Account and of the financial playing field at the hideous and heinous cost of a covert holocaust. We have been treated as a crop to be farmed so that the casino may continue to operate. We must wake up and refuse to cooperate, refuse to be surveilled, controlled, herded, limited, silenced, and short-sold as commodities.

We all matter.

If the Farmers won't acknowledge that, we must force them to do so.

They certainly won't do it on their own…ever.

Chapter 28

Farming the Farmers

"Claire and Fabian, as long as you're both waiting for law school to start, the two of you are coming with us on this expedition. You asked for it, you got it. The law firm won't object, Fabian," I told him, seeing his worried look. "You work there for free anyway. Imagine what being there for what promises to be an historic event will do for your future law careers. Even without that, think of the beneficial impact that the perspective of seeing a branch of the World Court will have on your educations."

We were eating dinner when I had broken the companionable silence of the meal with this pronouncement. With Uncle Charlie, Aunt Zoe, Edgar, and Jacques now in their own house down the street, our remaining group was a lot calmer and quiet. Perhaps it was the satisfaction of an issue resolved. Of course, life has a penchant for throwing more issues at us, but that was probably what it was.

Fabian grinned. "Okay. I'm up for a little adventure and travel."

"Me too," said Claire. "Are we really going to tour the World Court?"

I grinned as I ate my salad, forking in heirloom tomatoes, and lettuce. "You bet – both civil and criminal branches. The civil court, called the International Court of Justice, is in a beautiful, ornate, old building. The criminal court, known as the International Criminal Court, has been around for a much shorter time, and is in a large, white, modern building that looks like two small slabs facing each other at an obtuse angle with a small section in the middle."

"And you want to send the Farmers to the I.C.C.?" Dad asked, rushing me to the point.

"Yes. This is a reconnaissance mission."

"So what do you hope to accomplish at the I.C.J., then?" he wanted to know.

"Maybe sue them for money, so that they can't afford to be Farmers anymore," I said. "It's disgusting that they have so much of the world's financial resources under their control and that they're still there, living as before the Cull after perpetrating it. The total federal estate tax exemption that one person can bequeath to another is $5.46 million. No taxes due on it, ever! There's a gift tax exclusion of $15,000. It doesn't stop there. All a Farmer has to do is set up a hedge fund and make the heirs managers of it, and they get around more taxes. There are trillions of dollars in these hedge funds. But, if all goes well, the I.C.C. can add that to their sentences."

Hamish asked, "How many trillions?"

"About 3, but that's pretty bad."

He stared off into space, looking dazed. "I thought it was more like a few hundred billion."

Dad laughed. "No. Worse. It's always worse. What do people do with that much money?!"

"They hoard it and use it to control politicians, the military, and corporations," I said.

My mother and grandmother exchanged amused glances.

A moment later, my mother said, "They ought to be arrested for that."

"They ought to be arrested for what they had the politicians do," Grandmère said.

"First, the Prosecutor needs to present proof to the I.C.C., show criminal acts and intent, and a trail of evidence that can be followed and discovered in a way that won't be thrown out."

Spring came, and some hedge fundster in the Netherlands wanted a Regenics clinic there, Hamish informed me. Bethany and her husband were still there, so I was excited to hear it. It meant that I could visit her and see the sights. Perfect – it would not be obvious that our trip was about the International Criminal Court!

By this time, *Vaccine: The Cull* had been out in the public domain for a couple of weeks. It was being read online and discussed in blogs, political news shows, and elsewhere. No one could be certain as to its authorship, thanks to Jason's clever cybercraft, but speculation online and on the air was rampant. We were all following this with rapt attention and some amusement.

Now that a trip to the Netherlands was in the offing, I had a wild idea.

"So you're actually pleased at the prospect of another adventure in the *Shadowcat*?" he asked. He looked happy. "This one won't be like the last one; we can just go directly there without worrying about encountering a cremation ship, hiding via radar and sonar."

"Good. And yes, it sounds fun, with less pressure, and it's a chance to see Bethany."

Hamish looked at me for a moment, which made me look at him carefully. Then he said, "I'm having some work done on the *Shadowcat*." He waited to see what I would say.

"What work are you having done?" I asked, suspicious, though I had an idea of what.

"Ultra-capacitor fuel cell installation," he said. "No more fossil fuels. That, and restocking the food, toilet paper, fresh water, soaps, lotions, shampoos, etc.," he summed up, clearly hoping to distract me from the power source change with that litany of supplies.

Seeing as it was a done deal and thus a moot point, and considering the fact that my husband was an engineer who would never endanger us with a poorly-researched, unsafe power sources, I simply said, "I see," and left it at that.

"You're not going to say anything else?" he asked, incredulous.

"No. You already changed the power sources of the cars and house, which neatly keeps us off the grid, so there's no point in freaking out over the yacht. Been there, done that," I summed up. "I'm more interested in what we might do about the Cull once we get to that country."

"Oh?" Hamish raised one eyebrow, imitating the Vulcan our cat was named for.

"I want to deliver our case file on the Cull to the Prosecutor of the International Criminal Court," I told him. "I've everything ready to give to her."

He looked at me, open-mouthed for a moment, then said, "Awesome. Let's do it."

"You are not taking either of those cats on that yacht again!" my mother said when she heard about our upcoming trip. "You're not fleeing danger this time. It's just a trip. I'll take care of them here, and they'll be perfectly happy. It was not so great for them, never able to enjoy the run of the ship, and us always worried that they might get out."

"We keep them indoors at home thanks to coyotes and hawks around here," I said, "but thanks. I didn't really want to drag Eowyn across the ocean again. This trip will be much more fun…no fears of genocide-in-progress, and all that."

My mother gave me a wry smile. "Indeed…mass murder does put a damper on things."

"Yeah…about that…I'm determined to see the World Court, both the civil and criminal branches of it. It's just a fantasy right now, but it would be great to round up the damned Farmers and try them there."

She looked up from her book at me. "Don't get into any trouble," she said.

"We'll try not to," I told her. "Why would you wonder whether I might get into trouble?"

She put her book down. "Well…you did get shot at by a lunatic in New York City, you did go on a dangerous reconnaissance trip and witness homeless and displaced people being rounded up throughout the Appalachian, Alleghany, and Blue Ridge Mountains – didn't you see a rape also? And you know much more than the average person. Now you want to tour the World Court. For all I know – and you tend to tell me these things after the fact, not before – you are plotting something else, perhaps concerning the 'Farmers' as you call them."

"What was I supposed to do, ignore all that when I realized it was likely happening and what it all meant?! I had to confirm it and then do something about it."

"Yes, but it was reckless and dangerous." My mother was still bothered about my next move.

"Reckless?! It was risky, yes, but worth it. It was about keeping the family safe, and gathering information so that we would understand the problem and how to respond to it. As for waiting to tell you about the dangers once you're safe, and once Hamish and I were out of danger, not before, so that you understand why we do what we do, that was just logical."

"Yes. But it was devious. I suppose you won't tell me about this latest plot – and don't tell me that there isn't one – until it's over. Whatever it is, don't lead Claire around with any illusions about it. It won't bring her parents back."

"Oh, now you think I'm plotting some necromancy?!" I said, annoyed. "That's absurd. Also, deviousness is what gets a job done successfully. Failure is not an option. We're going to see the Netherlands, visit Bethany, tour the museums and the Courts, and learn about the dykes and canals firsthand. I'll take lots of photographs to show you how they have walled the ocean off. It literally is a towering wall of transparent levees, but seeing it in person makes one understand it far better than seeing it on the Internet. This trip will look like art, law, and eco-tourism."

"What's necromancy?" my mother asked.

"Raising the dead. It's a branch of magic. It's not real, obviously. Just because I'm an Aspie and I keep learning things and checking to see what is possible in the world does not make me immature, or lacking in judgment, or heading into disaster! We're guarded by Blackout Security! How much trouble can we get into that our fame would not already have attracted right to us?!"

She signed and looked at me. "I suppose not much more. Have a good time. Say 'hi' to Bethany for me. I'll feed the cats, like I always do anyway."

"Do you want to come on this trip?" I suddenly wondered if that was what bothered her.

She looked surprised. "No. I think you and Hamish and Claire and Fabian should go."

"Okay." Damn. I really didn't know what she wanted of me. She had done a great job of being my ally and advocate while raising me and on into adulthood, but our brainstems were wired differently enough that we didn't understand each other. It could be frustrating.

With Sophia, I could ask all sorts of silly questions about idioms and colloquialisms that the neurotypical world used and enjoyed intuitively but confused the hell out of me. Not so with my mother. She treated me alternately like an encyclopedia and a child in an adult's body.

I didn't see that changing. But it didn't change something else: I had to have my mother around. I couldn't deal with the idea of not having her in the world, and easy to spend time with – logistically. I just wanted my mother, with an instinctive need.

So did Claire, and hers was gone. Perhaps that was why we were drawn to each other – Aspie empathy. We had both had neurotypical mothers who had raised us without knowing that we were Aspies, simply compensating bit by bit for whatever social intuitiveness we lacked by coaching us to make up the difference. With Claire's mother gone, she only remembered the good aspects of her, and that was fine.

I would accept the difficult aspects of mine along with the fun ones. She was alive, at least.

A couple of days later, Claire and I decided to plan out our garden, and to order seeds and seedlings for it. "We ought to have this taken care of before we leave," I said. "I'm sure we'll be home in time to plant everything."

She had nodded, and we had enjoyed plotting it all out.

We still had a few more days to go before it was time to leave, and we decided to go to some local nurseries to see what they were selling. It was fun, but something odd happened. A seed vendor was at Moscarillo's, and he tried to sell us some of his genetically modified organisms. All we had to do, he informed us, was sign a home gardener's contract at the time of purchase.

"What would be in this contract?" I asked, waiting to see what he would say.

Claire looked at the guy like she was watching a mandrill poking at a lioness – the lioness being me. She looked like she was enjoying the show, too. We had each taken a copy of the contract and were looking it over with interest. It was put out by the DuFour Corporation.

"You would have to agree to use all of your seeds, saving none for the next growing season," he replied, looking smugly self-satisfied at having remembered his rehearsed lines.

"Really?" I said, dragging that word out, and smiling dangerously.

Claire turned away and hid a smile behind the pages she was reading.

"Yes," the man said. He looked like he was in his thirties, and he wore a silly straw hat with a huge, wide brim. The rest of his outfit was straight out of an L.L. Bean catalog. I was sure he had never worked a day in his life on a garden, much less a farm.

"And why does your company not want any seeds saved for next year?" I had to ask.

"It's all in the contract. We formulate our seeds year after year to resist pests, so you wouldn't want to keep reusing the same genetic formula," he told me.

"And what happens if someone does save seeds and grow them another year?" I wanted to know. "People who know how to do that could grow everything and make their own private seed banks. How would you know? What about seeds that blow away in the wind and sprout elsewhere, on adjacent property?"

"We would visit your garden – that's in the contract – to make sure. This contract gives us the right to sue you if you breach that promise." He looked unhappy that I wasn't just taking one, signing, and going away; other customers were walking around in earshot, and they were looking up now and then, obviously listening to our conversation.

"I see. So…your company wants to come onto private property at will, then, and police what people grow. This is a clever marketing plan for people who don't do their own research. I'm sure lots of people will fall for it and be sorry later. It will also entrap neighbors of people who sign on, and force them to accept these seeds, whether they want to, or not."

The GMO vendor looked a bit angry now.

Ed was standing off to the side and endeavoring to maintain a straight face. The vendor noticed.

"You're too late," Claire told him after a moment. "We just ordered all organic plants and seeds. We have it all planned out. My cousin would never let strangers come onto her property and tell her how to run anything," she added, grinning from ear to ear.

"True," I said. "And this place offers plenty of organic growing supplies and plants." Turning to the owner of the business, who was lurking nearby, observing this exchange, I asked him, "You are going to continue to sell organic plants and supplies, aren't you?"

"Of course," he said. "This is just an experiment. He's here for a week, selling his wares on our premises. If he makes a sale, I'll be surprised."

"What do you get out of this?" I wondered. "Is his presence here benefitting you in some way, financially or otherwise?"

"His company is paying me a small fee to allow him to offer his seeds to private gardeners."

"Interesting. Will you do this every year?" Claire wanted to know.

"We'll see how it goes," the owner told her.

We thanked him and wandered around, looking at the forced bulbs that were in full bloom. The scent of hyacinths and lilies filled the greenhouse out back, and the pastel hues of those plants plus potted tulips, narcissus, daffodils, and other gorgeous blossoms stretched across row after row after row. We chose a few to bring home to my mother and grandmother, and a few more for Aunt Zoe's house.

As we moved our small cart up to the register in the greenhouse, we realized that the owner was there to ring us up. We were all out of earshot of the GMO vendor, so I asked him, "Do you have anything to say about that GMO vendor now that he can't hear you?" I hoped the guy hadn't bugged the place to eavesdrop.

The nurseryman looked up with a gleam in his eyes. "Yes. I was pressured with heavy sales tactics to let him come here. A lot of our town's plants are GMO crops, and these agribusinesses want to corner the market. Individual gardeners, people with their own homes and yards, don't necessarily want that."

Claire and I exchanged glances. Ed was listening, too. I asked, "Do you need a lawyer to keep them from bullying you?"

"No, I think we're okay for now,' he told us, "but I don't want that vendor back."

Huh. I gave him my business card and he took it. "Thank you," I said, paying for the plants.

"Thank you," the owner replied. "I'll call you if the seed company gets too pushy."

We rolled the cart out to the car and loaded the plants into it, carefully placing them on the sheet of plastic that I kept folded up in the trunk for that purpose. Glancing back, I could see the GMO seed vendor watching us while talking on his cell phone.

As we drove off, Ed said, "I could hear him mentioning your name."

"Thought so," I commented.

We couldn't get to The Hague with our evidence fast enough, I thought to myself.

DuFour and his crew had to be reined in. If only his corporation could be forced to respect individual consumer choice, this might stop. Legal bars to ownership of neighboring crops ought to be the law of the planet, not just Europe!

Claire asked me what I was thinking about. "You're awfully quiet. What are you plotting?"

I laughed. "You have gotten to know me well. I might ask you the same thing sometimes," I told her. "Okay...have you read my honeybee book?"

"Yes..." she dragged her answer out, clearly wanted me to go on, so I did.

"These agribusinesses have their scientists modify the DNA of crop seeds by splicing disease-resistant strands of code into a species that farmers want to grow, plus they engineer those seeds to resist insecticides. Insecticides are at last being banned, but there is a legal holdover that needs to be defeated: if seeds from one of their plants blow from the property of one farmer, a farmer who has bought those GMO seeds, onto the property of another farmer, one who is doing organic farming, they will, as will any seeds, take root."

Claire listened carefully, then said, "Oh...I see. The agribusiness will then claim ownership of whatever grows on that neighboring farmer's land, taking the profits from that other crop, forcing that farmer out of the organic crop business, and thus Farming that uncooperative farmer. Damn! How can that be stopped?"

"That is a question that has plagued U.S. organic farmers for a long time," I said. The Farmers have bought themselves politicians for decades to facilitate this, and there has been nothing that could be done to stop it. They pay for lobbyists and they hire attorneys with the highest-priced law degrees, often paying their tuition off in return for assistance with case law all the way up to the Supreme Court of the United States. It would be great to drag them into the World Court, but Americans are notorious for walking out of it and declaring that no law shall ever supersede our own. That sounds great, but only to a point."

"To what point would that be?" Claire asked.

"To the point of barring Orwellian surveillance, but not to theft and total control of all financial and other resources," I replied. "For several decades after World War II, the United Nations had only a civil court – the International Court of Justice. It handles civil matters only, but if nations didn't want to be bound by their rulings, they could just walk out. Individual corporations don't end up in that court – only attorneys who represent individual governments, who then agree, at least in theory, to be bound by the ruling of the I.C.J."

"So what can be done about those Farmers, then?" Claire asked, sounding unhappy.

I was unhappy too. "Well, there has been some frustration over that, and it was addressed over a decade ago. There had been no international criminal court since the Nuremberg Trials – no mechanism in place for crimes against humanity, Nature, or whatever else affects us on a planetary scale – until then. It was a mistake to assume that a special court just for the Nazis could be assembled, adjudicate one big trial, and then disbanded without ever being needed again. So...the International Criminal Court was created and assembled in 2005. We're going to see it when we go to The Hague. We'll visit both the I.C.J. and the I.C.C., but it's the I.C.C. that we want. That's what I want you and Fabian to see when you come with us."

Claire looked both amazed and delighted. "Thank you! If I can help, I will," she said.

"Help? We're just going to turn over our evidence," I told her.

"Oh," Claire said. "But maybe I can help. I found something and I've been saving it."

I almost drove into the car in front of me when she said that, but stepped on the brakes in time. We were on Mountain Road, waiting at the traffic light where Fern Street met it, and there was a car in front of us. "What do you mean, you found something?"

"I mean just that. I was afraid to think of what it might mean, or to distract you while you were writing this winter, but I asked Jason to look at it with me when he was visiting to work with Jacques just before Zoe and Charlie moved out with Edgar and Jacques in January. Fabian looked, too. It's definitely something that is for the future, not the past, so I just let you write your history of the Cull. When we get home, I'll show you and Hamish."

The light changed, and the car behind me beeped at me. I stopped staring into space and stepped on the accelerator, thoroughly distracted. "You're just telling me this now?! We have to visit Aunt Zoe next. This is going to drive me crazy for that visit. We can't explain to her why I will be in a huge rush to go home," I complained.

"Sorry," Claire said. "But you just finished writing, and you were so busy secretly releasing that history that I figured I ought to wait. Fabian was the one who suggested that I wait, actually. He knows how focused you get when you're about to release a new book, secret or not. And now you know…at least, you know there is something to know," she added cryptically.

I took a deep breath and gave her an annoyed but amused sidelong glance, and then drove us the rest of the way to Aunt Zoe's house. It was coming along nicely. She had settled everything that she had into it, and accepted my parents' gift of mattresses and sofas before the family had actually moved in. In the past couple of months, the place had been transformed into a fully furnished, comfortable home.

It was strange to see someone have to reconstitute their home almost from scratch, but they seemed to like it. Aunt Zoe had a few things that she had saved when we had frantically and covertly moved them all over to our house in the week before we had fled the Cull to Manhattan, and then onto the *Shadowcat*.

At least my aunt had plenty of her own personal mementoes, family heirlooms, photo albums, and framed photographs. Some favorites – prints of scenes from historical and archaeological sites around the world graced the hallways and living room. Aunt Zoe had bought these in earlier travels and from local artists whose work she had admired over the years.

"The house looks great," I told her. "Here are some sweet-scented bulb flowers for you. You can plant them in the yard in the spring."

"Oh, thank you! You know all of my favorite colors," she said, kissing me and smiling.

"So does Claire," I said. "She chose the red-and-yellow parrot tulips for you."

"They're my favorites!" Aunt Zoe said, kissing her as well. "Thank you very much!"

We stayed for just a few minutes, and then made our escape. I must have looked restless.

Aunt Zoe made it easy. "You look like you're up to something," she said to me. "I've seen that look on you a lot over the past year and a half, and after you whisked us away – and just in time – I know what that means. Will you be telling us what this is about in a little while?"

"Yes, but I don't even know what it is yet," I replied, looking at Claire.

Aunt Zoe looked intrigued. "Really…" She sized up Claire. "You're both in on it, and Claire is the ringleader this time?" She smiled. She knew we were about to go to the Netherlands.

Claire said, "Not a ringleader, exactly. Maybe 'instigator' is the better word for it. Avril can have the title of ringleader. I'm not ready for that just yet." She gave us a wry smile.

Aunt Zoe laughed. "Okay. Just don't let anyone say that this is deceitful or lying. You do what you have to do to pull whatever it is off, and it is okay to tell it later…just like that history book that, as far as we are all concerned, some anonymous person wrote and released. We don't know who gathered the information for it, how, or anything," and she grinned at us.

"Thank you," I said, and Claire nodded.

We left in a hurry, and found Ed pacing up and down by the car. Aaron and Hamish had pulled in behind us. "Let's go," Hamish said. "Ed called us. Lionel is bringing Fabian home right now, and they're picking up Jason on the way." He looked at Claire.

Claire looked both unnerved and pleased. "Good. I've wanted to show you this for a while."

Hamish only looked more intrigued, but said nothing. He got into the car with us, nearly kicking over the hyacinths, but righting them in a hurry as he hopped in and sat down. Ed rode down the street with Aaron.

At home, we each grabbed a plant and marched inside with it, putting them on the kitchen counter for my mother and grandmother to deal with, no longer really focused on them.

"What lovely plants!" my mother said. Then she saw our faces, and realized that Aaron and Ed had come in with us. "What's going on?"

"Claire has something to show us," I told her, "something that will likely involve Jason, a certain digitally isolated laptop, and some data that we haven't known about before. Lionel is bringing Fabian and Jason here now."

My mother arched an eyebrow at this. "Great. Deceit now, disclosure later."

Dad appeared and we told him what was up. He told my mother to stop it.

My parents said nothing else, so I made tea and we waited while Claire went upstairs to get something. She and Grandmère came into the kitchen at the same time, and Claire was now carrying a memory stick that we had never seen before. We all looked at it, and then at her.

Fabian and Jason arrived a moment later, followed by Lionel, who waved and then left.

We had settled into a practice of sharing secrets with Ed and Aaron, but Lionel and other Blackout Security people tended to hear them later, when it was time to make a plan of action on those secrets. Today was no different.

Leaving my parents and grandmother in the kitchen, we all marched into the hall, opened the door to the cellar stairs, and went down to the den where Hamish and I had first worked with Jason. Out came the laptop from the safe, and Claire handed over the memory stick.

"Where did you get that?" Hamish asked her.

"Spades dropped it at the Fontainebleau during the cocktail party. He was so drunk that he didn't see it fall out of his pocket. No sooner had Bosch handed it to him than he lost it. I saw it fall when he stumbled with his fourth martini and paused to catch his olive on a stick. He seemed so pleased with himself that he could catch it while drunk and not get any of the martini on him that he couldn't have noticed that. It fell right by a chair leg next to me, so I fumbled my canape or whatever we were eating, caught it, and scooped that stick up and put it into my own pocket."

Hamish and I were staring at her, slightly agape, and impressed.

Fabian looked delighted. "You didn't even tell me you got it until after the trip."

"Yeah, well, I didn't dare act like I had anything at the time, and I was afraid to talk about it all while we were on that trip. What if someone heard us, bugged our rooms again, or noticed us even thinking about whatever its secrets hold on the plane ride back to New York? I didn't want to risk it, so I just threw myself into enjoying the trip. Then we came home and we were so busy...at last, we can focus on this. I just know it's something important."

Jason had the laptop ready, so he clicked on the icon for this mystery data, and...wow.

"It's a gene-splicing plan, complete with research, development, and marketing," Hamish said, scrolling through it. There were files and files of data. All of them were peppered with the logo for the Tacttag corporation.

"I take it this is not about Regenics, or the Cull," I said, as Hamish bore the look of someone reading data that he had never seen before.

He straightened up and looked at me, furious. "No, it's not. It's as bad as the Cull for the future of humanity, though. It's a plan to edit anyone off the autism spectrum before they are fully formed and developing as a fetus. The plan is to create a race of all neurotypical humans."

"No more creators, inventors, innovators..." I was livid. "They were always going to go ahead with this, and now we have evidence of it. "Thank you, Claire – this is evidence of a crime against humanity in the making!"

Claire looked the same way that I felt, but also like someone whose suspicions had been confirmed. She said as much. "I knew it! I mean, I didn't know it for a fact, but I felt really, really sure that that was what it must be. Those guys from Tacttag didn't sound like they would take us seriously at all. They sounded like they were humoring us, remember?"

"Indeed I do," I said angrily. I quickly repeated the entire conversation to the group.

They all looked outraged. Claire asked, "Why can't they use genetic manipulation on people who already exist?! Can't they use it to reset DNA back to a healthy state when they get cancer?! That would be a good thing, but trying to homogenize the human species is asinine."

Hamish looked impressed. "For a non-scientist, you understand a lot," he told her.

"Yeah, well, I've been listening to you and Avril talk about it, and reading."

"It's a secret war on Aspies and on non-conformity," I said.

"Not if we have anything to say about it," Fabian said. "Right?" he looked at us.

"Right!" Hamish and I practically roared, and Claire gave a little hysterical shriek of delight.

"To war, then," Claire said. "Can we really show this to the I.C.C. too, and stop a future crime against humanity? I'm sure the Farmers will have some Orwellian excuse about how this is for the good of humanity, but it's really not that at all!"

"Oh yes, we shall, and the Prosecutor will argue that they are criminals. There are several co-conspirators to this one. Let's check and see whether or not they have anything to do with Autism $tates while we're at it," I said. "It certainly doesn't state anything for any of us!" I added angrily. That name had always grated on me.

Damn Autism $tates. That organization didn't let any of us who were on the spectrum do any speaking. The mere idea of neurotypicals running an organization with no one on the autism spectrum in a position of authority was outrageous. It was for parents of autistic children who wished not only that they had children who were not autistic – and the parents of silent children, children who could not express themselves or ever live independently were in need of a support system, it was true – but it was also for parents who didn't want any part of the autism spectrum.

That was really what galled me, and Hamish and Claire as well, about Autism $tates.

Those parents wanted ordinary, neurotypical, easy-to-raise children who fit in and did not stand out. They wanted kids who liked what most people liked: food, drink, pastimes like football and baseball, loud social gatherings, and no deep thinking. They wanted kids who would grow up and function independently according to some magically preordained schedule.

The whole thing was absurd. It reminded me of that scene in *Pride and Prejudice* (a book that was touted as the most perfect novel ever written and by an Asperwoman) in which Elizabeth mocked Mr. Darcy and Caroline Bingley for describing the ideal accomplished lady. She was an ideal, a paradigm, an impossibly unattainable dream. She could never be real.

That was what was so ludicrous about the fantasy that Autism $tates dreamed of, and which Tacttag proposed to make a reality. If it managed to do that, it could inflict permanent damage on the genetic health of the entire human species. It was insane, idiotic, and criminal.

The Cull had eliminated 6.8 billion human beings.

This would cause us to go extinct due to our own stupidity. It was genetic suicide.

We needed some humans to be different, to offset the others, and to offer advances.

The inventors of the spear and the discoverers of fire had been autistic, as one famous woman on the spectrum, Temple Grandin, Ph.D. had famously said. If that wasn't the ultimate argument for appreciating the wonderful things that autism had to offer, there were always Wolfgang Amadeus Mozart, Thomas Jefferson, Jane Austen, Mark Twain, Vincent Van Gogh, Marie Curie, Virginia Woolf, and plenty of others to illustrate that point.

A couple of hours later, I walked into the den in time to hear Hamish and Fabian discussing this planned crime, plus the general practices and policies of pharmaceutical corporations.

"So there are actually inexpensive cures in existence for many problems?!" Fabian asked.

"Aye, that there are," Hamish replied. "I had an inside track on this during medical school, thanks to an internship. Not many people wanted to learn about the research side of medicine up close and personal; I was the only one in my class. What I found was that these companies will hire scientists to do research, let them study wherever the data took them, and then – if the data took them to something that wouldn't make tons of money for the corporation – patent it and lock it in a safe. They also required non-disclosure agreements to be signed by those scientists. The whole idea was to make cheap cures and treatments inaccessible to the public."

"That's heinous!" Fabian said, sounding incredulous.

"Yeah, well, you're young and still shockable," Hamish replied.

Fabian sat there, appalled, staring into space, contemplating it all.

A few days later, our conversation turned back to the Rome Statute.

Claire was wondering what the chances were of an outcome that would feel like justice to the victims of the Cull, herself included.

"Well, that depends on your definition of justice," I said. "What are you hoping for?"

"Death, ideally, but the treaty only offers thirty years to life. It makes me wish that the United States would try the Farmers for their crimes."

"Indeed. I would prefer that too, but the I.C.C. would never choose death as a penalty. It can't. Also, once they try the case, whatever the result, just as in the U.S., that's it – no double jeopardy may attach."

"Yes, I know," Claire said, staring off into space, thinking.

Fabian asked, "But won't the U.S. insist on taking over adjudication of this case?"

"Complementarity is part of the deal, too…that means," here I looked at Hamish, who was looking lost as we launched into legalese, and explained further, "that any potential case that deals with crimes named in the Rome Statute, which the laws of the nation or nations involved also cover, may be adjudicated by either the I.C.C. or a court in that nation or nations."

"So why would any case go to the I.C.C. rather than to the courts of the nation of the defendants, and why would it go to the I.C.C. instead?" Hamish asked.

"It would go to the I.C.C. only if the nation of the defendants or nation where the crime occurred was not handling the case, and that nation might not do so because it was unwilling, which would mean the defendants would be literally getting away with murder, or because that nation was in such disarray that it could not handle the case even if it wanted to. The United States has spent the past couple of years both in such flux that it hasn't had its act together enough to prosecute the Farmers even if it wanted to, plus it has shown unwillingness to do so."

"How has it shown unwillingness?" Claire asked. "It seems more like its politicians have been hamstrung by being bought out by the Farmers. But what about the courts?"

"The courts were kept unaware of the crimes as part of the pattern of crime," I said, thinking aloud. "There was definite collusion by enough of the military and scientific sectors to enable this pattern to play out to its horrific conclusion. Our politicians have ratified the Rome Statute, but our police and courts are entirely suspect in light of the crimes of genocide, war crimes, crimes against humanity, and crimes of aggression. The ultimate question will be answered if they opt for cooperation by the U.S. in apprehending and handing over the Farmers to the I.C.C."

"That would suggest that the U.S. government would be turning on the Farmers, refusing to be their puppets anymore. No more funding, but no more manipulators," Fabian said.

"Exactly. That's what we must hope for," I said. "The idea is that they will find out the truth and decide that the I.C.C. is the way to clean our nation's slate and start over."

"That would be one way of attempting to wash the blood off of U.S. hands," Hamish said.

"It can't be washed off, only avenged," I said.

Chapter 29

Another Trip on the Shadowcat

This time, as we made our way to Europe aboard our yacht, my perception of our progress and surroundings was very different. Whereas before we had been intensely focused on not calling attention to ourselves, and on not letting the cats out the doors and onto the outer decks, this time we had left them home and were not avoiding notice by crematoria ships.

We felt reasonably safe from human predators.

As a result, we went outside a lot, stood on the deck of the ship, and looked around.

We also got there faster, seeing as we had no need of a circuitous, covert route.

I noticed many things. Well…I always noticed things when I felt free to look. What did I notice?

Not too many dolphins, which disappointed me, though we did see some near the end of the trip. What caught my attention more than anything else was the flotsam – the floating rubbish – that seemed to be every which way we looked. There were no icebergs, of course. They had all melted a long time ago.

"I never saw so many bottle caps and plastic flakes," Claire complained. "It's gross! If this were a soup, I would throw it away and start over. No…maybe I would get a skimmer and remove the obvious rubbish and rejects."

"So you would be ejecting the jetsam," Fabian joked, but we could tell he was disgusted.

"Oh, ha, ha, ha," she said. "Don't you think this is terrible? I mean, think of all the aquatic birds and fish and turtles that are dying of indigestion and intestinal blockages from this crap!"

They were standing on the rear deck, peering over the side, as we raced northeast, toward Halifax. Hamish and I were out there with them, listening. He laughed mirthlessly as Claire said this, and they looked in our direction.

"Nanites won't take care of everything. The Farmers have plans to get that bigger stuff out, and make a profit from doing so. If it takes years, they will turn it into a business venture and remediate this pollution," I told them.

"Come here," Hamish said. "I want to show you something."

We followed him to the very rear of the deck, and looked where he pointed. "See this tube-like, black contraption? It's called a sea-bin rubbish collector. Watch what happens as we move through the water; it sucks in every bit of large plastic it encounters."

We watched, and we were very pleased to see that it worked.

"What happens when it's full?" Claire asked.

"Ed has been lifting the net bag out, dumping it into a large, black plastic dumpster in the hold, and storing it to get rid of when we get across the ocean. See the chute opening next to it?" We looked and saw it, three feet above the water level. "There's a place waiting for this. If it gets too full, a barge will meet us midway, but hopefully we can make it across on our own and still have a lot of debris to get rid of."

Claire looked very impressed by this. "It's great, but no way will we not need to do that."

Fabian looked speculative.

"What?" I asked.

"What do we do if we encounter a turtle or some other creature with plastic stuck to it?" Fabian was looking at the small dingy tied to the back of the yacht, skeptical.

"We help it, I guess."

Hamish went back inside to look at some data on his laptop.

A few days later, we did encounter a creature in trouble. It was a whale, accompanied by her mate and calf, and we could see their pod up ahead. The members of the pod were swimming fast, as if they had given up on this slower member due to her lack of progress.

Claire wanted to help it, and so did I. Fabian and Hamish saw and wanted in on it, too.

Aaron and Ed were nervous. How would they pilot the yacht and take care of us?

"We'll all manage," I said, putting on a life jacket. All six of us put them on.

Hamish looked both excited by what we were about to do and like he wanted to keep me out of it. Fabian wore the same expression. Neither man dared tell his wife not to involve herself, however. Claire and I exchanged grins. Helping a huge mammal with a fishnet tangled onto its tail was risky, but none of us was willing to just leave her to her dismal fate.

Aaron brought out a huge pair of shears and assured us that it would cut through the plastic.

I took it and tried it out, manipulating the scissors. "I can handle this contraption," I said.

We – Claire, Fabian, Hamish and I – got into the dinghy, which was a bit large and likely could have held all six of us, and Hamish started up the motor. He maneuvered us up to the female humpback whale, keeping well clear of the long net, which trailed behind her.

"Ed's getting into the helicopter," Fabian said, looking back at the *Shadowcat*.

Claire and I looked too. Ed was in the pilot's seat of it, checking the controls.

"He's going to collect that net after we get it off of her," Hamish said. "The chopper has a mechanism for doing that. We'll have to get inside, out of the way when he's ready to drop it on the deck of the ship."

Good plan. We all turned our attention back to the whales. We were almost in position next to her...which would enable us to do nothing about cutting the net loose. I looked at Hamish. "I'm planning to greet her, and then gradually let us loose speed to get to the trailing net. It's the only safe way to approach," he explained.

I nodded and got the shears ready. "Yes…it's better to try to ask her if this is okay first," I commented, "not that she's likely to object to being helped." It would be possible to cut one-handed, big though they were, while holding onto the net with my other hand. "It looks like a discarded trawling net that didn't sink to the bottom of the ocean."

"Maybe it started to sink and the poor whale went by and got stuck in it," Claire suggested.

"Sounds likely," I agreed. Whales could stay underwater for up to an hour.

We were right alongside the whale, who sprayed a huge blast of water from her blowhole.

"Can we touch her?" Claire asked. "Is that safe?"

"I guess so," Hamish said. He was watching everything carefully, and I knew he would move us away immediately if he thought the whales were getting spooked.

Claire and I reached out and laid our hands on the whale's flank for a moment.

We all looked up into her face and saw her eye regarding us steadily.

"I think she realizes we want to help her," I said. "Let's try to cut this thing off of her."

Hamish nodded and dropped us back slightly, idling the small motor to keep us in place.

I grabbed for the net, and Fabian and Claire did also. After a few tries, we had it. Hamish had shut off the motor. I tugged on the net to get closer to the whale's tail, and saw that the damned thing was wrapped around the entire base of it plus one side of the fin. Without another word, I started cutting. It was exhausting work, but I figured that she was already even more exhausted.

I cut and cut and cut, and managed to get pretty far until I was panting. It was about twenty minutes into the cutting when I glanced up at the net. "Damn! Maybe a third of it is off now," I said. "At least this whale is holding steady. Of course, they're as intelligent as humans, so that's not surprising."

Indeed, she was staying as still as she could while letting us work, and her family had moved slightly ahead and to her other side to stay close but out of the way of the rescue operation. We could see a slight gash in the base of her tail, but it wasn't very deep. It seemed like just getting this thing off of her would do the trick, and it could heal up.

"Let me do some of it," Claire said, holding her hands out for the shears. I gave them to her and sat back to rest for a moment. Claire looked delighted to be doing this, and so was I, even if I had temporarily run out of energy. This was the sort of thing I had always wanted to help with.

Claire managed to cut more than a third of the net free before turning the shears over to Fabian, who finished the job. When he did, he quickly passed me the shears and pulled on the net to get it away from the whale.

"Don't let go of that net," Hamish said. "Let her take off first!"

Fabian hung on to the edge of the net, and we watched as the whale family swam away.

A minute or so after the whales knew that they were far enough away from us not to capsize us (I did mention how intelligent whales are) the female leaped up, completely out of the water. She was free, and she was elated! Her mate and calf started celebrating, too.

Hamish told Fabian to let go of the net, and we went back to the yacht. We stowed our lifejackets and went inside, where we watched Ed lower a mechanized hook into that net and lift it out of the water and onto the rear deck of the *Shadowcat*. It was huge.

"That thing looks like it's a mile long," Fabian said.

"It is," Aaron told him, joining us in the back living room to look out at it. "I've called that barge to pick up everything we've collected. This is just way more rubbish than we ought to be keeping with us."

The next morning, it appeared. It was a huge, ugly thing, but it relieved us of all plastic.

But before that happened, we were treated to an hour-long thank-you show by the whales.

We stood on the side deck, gripping the railings, so happy we could burst, grinning.

After about ten days at sea, we were approaching Europe. There was no particular due date for our arrival. That meant that we could take our time, looking around slowly at all of the changes to the area, and that we could see whatever we wanted, even if it meant a slight deviation from the most direct route. We were being eco-tourists, and it was a self-guided tour.

We saw a lot that was different: dykes, canals, and wind turbines headed the list.

Also, we saw The Ocean Cleanup, a contraption that was set up just past the coastline. It had been invented by a Dutch teenager named Boylan Slat, and it consisted of an anchored tower with long, flexible arms of moveable material that gathered plastic of various sizes and swept it up for collection and removal. There had been some concern about it harming sea life, but it was watched regularly. So far, so good.

We had wondered how much of the coastline of Europe would be gone due to rising sea levels, and were in for a surprise: the European engineers had fought it and won, beating it back significantly (most of Ireland, however, was underwater, as that nation had not had the funds to save the bulk of its territory).

Northern France, Belgium, the Netherlands, and parts of southern England were still above water. This was due to human engineering projects, and a steadfast refusal to cede the land to Nature, rising sea levels, the consequences of human fossil fuel use, or anything else.

We passed a massive structure which protected northern France and Belgium – including the Mont St. Michel, a small island that had graced postcards for a couple of centuries – and noted the wind turbines that both dotted and powered it. It was named for a Belgian engineer who had lived in both nations, Charles Joseph Van Depoele.

Gone was the familiar view that had spanned Dover, England and Calais, France for millennia, though the Chunnel that ran under the sea still connected the two locations. Instead, walls and dykes protected the land beyond. The one on the English side was named for an English civil engineer, William Jessop. There were no beaches to speak of anymore, though.

The Baltic Sea was dammed off. Denmark would have been completely underwater if not for another dam beyond that one, which was called the Nils Foss Dam. Each dam had a complex dyke in it, with canals from which ships could move between levels. We didn't explore far enough to learn the name of the dam that kept the Baltic Sea level from rising.

We detoured to see it. It was fascinating; even the Middelgrunden offshore wind farm remained, though the white posts on which the wind turbines whirled seemed shorter now. It was an optical illusion, of course. They were only another foot underwater.

"How could they succeed at holding back so much water?!" Claire said, astonished.

"It's incredible," I agreed. "The Europeans are clearly determined to keep life as they knew it before rising sea levels intact. Perhaps if we meet an engineer on this trip – one who works with dams, not a nanobotic one, like Hamish – we can find out more."

We turned back toward our destination, which was Amsterdam. Our itinerary would have us visiting Bethany there first, while Hamish planned the Regenics clinic in that city. The plan was to see Amsterdam, Delft, and to spend a week or so with her. We weren't on a fixed schedule. After that, we would go to The Hague and present our case files to the prosecutor of the International Criminal Court, and then tour the area before going home.

As we neared the Netherlands, we saw an awesome sight: a 100-meter-long floating barrier in the water that was cleaning plastic out of the North Sea as it drifted toward the land. This had been the first such barrier to be deployed, and it was working beautifully. Others had been built off the coasts of Japan, China, Bangladesh, and Nigeria.

We watched as small recycling scows collected debris for transport to land, where it would all be melted down. The plastic could be used to make new plastic objects or burned as energy. I thought of Jacques and Jason's work, and hoped it was going well.

Fabian was standing on the deck with us, staring out at the Cornelius Lely Dijks (*dijk* was Dutch for dyke), which protected the Netherlands. It was an incredible piece of engineering to behold, regardless of whether or not one knew much about the field.

The water between the floating barrier and the dykes of the Netherlands was relatively debris-free. We moved past the barrier and up to the entrance of a canal, and stayed on deck to watch the fascinating process of draining each level that we entered in order to lower our yacht, bit by bit, to the same level as the polder of the Amsterdam area. It was a monument to the human effort to negotiate with Nature. All it would accomplish, however, was to buy time.

Speaking of that, when it was time to leave the country and go home, the *Shadowcat* would be brought to The Hague to meet us, and we would repeat this process in reverse, south of this spot. We would be staying in hotels on land for the duration of our visit to the Netherlands. It was more convenient, and more interesting that way.

As we stood on the deck looking ahead, we saw an expanse of water that suddenly dropped off. Gone was the lovely view of the coastline that tourists of the past had enjoyed. We wouldn't see much until we were practically on top of the Netherlands, we realized.

With that, Fabian turned to ask me, "What makes you think that the evidence you have will be accepted by the Prosecutor? Will it be admissible?"

I looked at him. "You've been reading your law books on evidence for U.S. courts," I replied. "The International Criminal Court works differently. It allows the admission of all relevant and necessary evidence. It must be truthful and voluntary, but that is for witness testimony. Cyber-snooped evidence in which the accused are shown committing their crimes is acceptable. It has to be reliable evidence, or it's useless, but I think we're good on that point."

"Oh. Good." Fabian looked pleased. "I'd hate to think we came all this way for nothing."

I smiled. "I don't think we did."

"How will you approach this?" he asked.

"I will be presenting all of the accumulated data that we have and then asking the Prosecutor to initiate the case *proprio motu*, which is a Latin term that means on her own initiative. That is one of the three ways to pursue a case in the International Criminal Court. The other ways are for a nation to refer a case to the Prosecutor, or for the United Nations Security Council to do it."

"This is fascinating," Claire said. She had come out onto the deck in time to hear that.

"Aye, it is," Hamish added, joining us. "I was wondering how that would work."

"Is there any chance," Fabian asked, "that the I.C.C. might not accept this case?"

I smiled grimly. "I seriously doubt it. Granted, the Prosecutor has the option, should the Pre-Trial Chamber hear the request to prosecute a case and deny it, to come back later with more damning data, but I think we've got it all. This really looks like a slam-dunk of a case."

With that, we fell silent, watching the point at which the ocean seemed to drop off into nothing grow nearer and nearer, as we made our final approach to the Netherlands. Soon we saw the dykes that we would be lowered to the lowland nation through, and the Netherlands itself.

It was eerily fascinating to see the colors of a nation suddenly revealed, far below sea level.

Chapter 30

Dutch Ingenuity

Whoever said that the low-lying marshlands of the Netherlands couldn't be saved from rising sea levels hadn't bet on Dutch engineers. Their ingenuity and determination had led to the reinforcement of the existing set of dykes and canals, plus the huge levee wall that towered above the lowland nation. What they were stubbornly maintaining was known as a polder: a low-lying tract of land enclosed by embankments (dykes) that forms an artificial hydrological entity, with only a manually operated device for a connection with outside water.

The Dutch had lowered the elevation of slightly more than one quarter their territory centuries ago by digging up the peat from their land and selling it. That act of harvesting the land itself, had dropped the topographical reading by one meter below sea level.

Of course, that was before sea level had risen altogether.

Regardless, Dutch engineers had found themselves fighting incursions from the sea ever since then. They had put up one hell of a fight when the speed at which the polar icecaps melted had picked up. With similar speed and ruthless efficiency, they had built a wall to contain the sea, holding it back. They also had benefit of neighbors who were equally determined not to cede territory to the seas. Fortunately, their neighbors had higher ground on each of the Dutch coastal, international borders, and so the levee walls had a place to connect to land.

The levee walls presented a rather terrifying sight when viewed from the Netherlands.

They towered thirty feet high. Each panel was constructed of reinforced, transparent polymers, and held in place on either side of each block by a massive foundation of equally reinforced concrete with steel bars running up to the tops.

It was possible, if one cared to look that way and study the scene from land, to occasionally observe sea life of varying sizes passing by if they moved up against the levee, plus whatever plastic and other human-dumped trash came with them.

Bethany had gone to see her husband one day at his office, which faced that wall, armed with a pair of binoculars just to look. The view through that thick plexiglass was only an inch or so into the darkness beyond, yet she thought that she had seen a narwhal and a whale, though she hadn't been certain what species of whale. She also saw the trash, and had looked until the sight began to scare her. She hadn't gone back to do that again.

The awesome and terrifying power of Nature to smash through that wall was what had scared her off. How could this wall hold forever? But the Dutch engineers proudly assured everyone that it could last and be maintained for at least eight decades, and that it could withstand periodic, piecemeal replacements of its sections.

Well, that sounded a bit more reassuring.

No wonder New York and New Orleans had summoned them to help.

I had to admit that I had a reasonable amount of confidence in the dams and dykes that they had designed for us. The U.S. Army Corps of Engineers had actually built it precisely according to the Dutch specifications, and the U.S. Congress had funded it without more than a few hours' debate. That debate had come across more like a checking of facts followed by a decision to leave the problem to experts. It was clearly borne out of fear of the awesome and terrible power of Nature to wash away anyone and everything that got in its way.

So much the better; we humans weren't ready to give in and give up just yet.

To get from just about any Dutch city to the sea, one had to go to a dock along a river or canal, board a boat, and ride up to the dykes. The boat would then move into a section of dykes and wait for it to be filled up, which would then raise it up part of the way. Once up, it would move into the next level and repeat that process, and so on until it was all the way up.

At that point, it would be let out, and pumps would push the water back out and into the sea. There was no docking one's yacht out there, and cargo container ships had to unload to smaller ships. Those smaller ships would then bring the goods into Dutch cities, and out again.

The Dutch were thus, astonishingly, able to continue to produce tulips, beer, and Gouda cheese just as they always had, and to export it.

When I thought back to the ancient days of a far lower sea level, one in which a land known as Doggerland had existed, this amazed me even more. 12,000 years ago, Doggerland had stretched across the North Sea. There had been no aquatic delineation of the nations of England, Scotland, Norway, Belgium, Netherlands, France, or anything other than a continuity of land then. People had simply walked across it all, and lived and died and been buried there.

8,200 years ago, a glacier from North America finally finished the job that incremental melts had been doing to raise sea levels, pushing out the hunter-gatherer-fishers who lived there. Their remains, plus those of aurochs and other ancient creatures, were trawled to the surface by fishing boats in the nineteenth and twentieth centuries. At last, a scientist asked that a human skull with teeth be saved, at which point it was carbon-dated. It proved to be 9,500 years old.

Human remains were still buried under what humans used to think of as a shallow sea.

It was strange to think of now.

The Netherlands was a liberal country, politically, with over fifty percent atheists, legalized abortion and prostitution dating back into the late twentieth century, and a fascinating history. It was comprised of twelve provinces, only two of which were called Holland (North Holland and South Holland, to be precise), hence the reason for not calling the entire nation by that name.

The place had lots of art and culture to recommend it, plus law: two international courts, one civil and one criminal, were located in the Netherlands. The International Court of Justice was housed in a beautiful, Neo-Renaissance brick building called the Peace Palace. Actually, the I.C.J. had only existed since 1946, to coincide with the formation of the United Nations, but the building had been completed and inaugurated in 1913.

It also housed other courts, plus the Peace Palace Library of International Law, opened by Queen Beatrix as recently as 2007. The Dutch were an interesting people; they had a constitutional monarchy, and the monarch did not have to stay on the throne until death. She or he could retire, and Beatrix had, unlike the British.

The other major court, of course, was the International Criminal Court. It was housed in a tall, white with blue-hued windows, modern complex of buildings. The I.C.C. had existed since 2002, which was not very long, but it was something.

The I.C.C. had seen fit to judge and sentence a Dutch businessman for the sale of some of the chemicals that went into Saddam Hussein's lethal recipe of poisons. Those mixtures had been unleashed upon Iranians during the Iran-Iraq War (1980-1988), on Iraqi Kurds in Halabja, Iraq, and left unused in vats in Kuwait City, Kuwait, after the invasion there. This noxious stuff smelled faintly of garlic and apples. If you smelled it, you were pretty much doomed.

Conveniently, the huge corporation that had sold the other ingredients to Saddam had escaped any legal censure in the I.C.C. However, several of its top executives were convicted of criminal negligence and mass homicide due to an explosion of their chemical plant in Bhopal, India. They didn't dare set foot in that nation again. The scientist on staff who was in charge of monitoring factory conditions there had repeatedly warned them that safety precautions were inadequate. They had ignored him every time. There was no telling top-level executives anything; what mattered to them was shareholders and profits, and only that.

Both of these courts were in The Hague, which was along the coast, in South Holland, well southwest of Amsterdam. We were headed to Amsterdam first, to see Bethany and to give Hamish time to start another Regenics clinic.

We loved to visit museums, and we planned to tour the ones in Amsterdam, and to make a brief excursion to Delft, the hometown of the famous seventeenth century painter Johannes Vermeer, and from whence the famous blue tiles hailed. I really wanted to see that place, and Bethany was game.

Amsterdam had Anne Frank's The Secret Annex museum in it. It was actually called the Anne Frank House (online at http://www.annefrank.org/en/). That was definitely on the list. It was located along one of the city's famous canals, the Prinsengracht. This was where Miep Gies, along with a trusted few others, had cared for eight people, who had been hidden on the upper floors for three years behind a door with a bookcase for camouflage.

It hadn't worked. Some monster had betrayed them for five Dutch guilders apiece, and they were all taken away in August of 1944. Only Otto Frank, Anne's father, had come back. He had returned to stay with Miep and her husband Jan, and to run the business again that sold pectin and instructions for making strawberry jam. Eventually, he got married again, and published Anne's diary. That was the holocaust museum that we wanted to see on this trip.

Anne Frank's diary was assigned reading when I was entering junior high school, and yet, whenever I encountered someone who hadn't even heard of it let alone read it, I was always amazed. This had happened in America every so often. What happened to "never forget"? One ought to read and remember these things!

But…people didn't, and so the Cull had happened. Another holocaust had happened.

At least we had saved Bethany and many other people, but we couldn't stop it.

There was another museum worth seeing, one that would help with that just by being pure fun (well, my idea of fun!). It was full of art and historic artifacts, and it was called the Rijksmuseum (online at https://www.rijksmuseum.nl/en). A famous miniature house, sort of like a cabinet, was kept there. So were some of Vermeer's paintings, plus those of other painters of the same and earlier and later periods.

"Before last year, we had a really tough time finding places for the kids in good schools," Bethany was saying, "but since the plague, it's been really easy. It's amazing."

Bethany and I were in cat heaven. We were touring the cat-related attractions of Amsterdam.

She had found them all during the past year or so since Hamish had diverted her and her family away from the Cull. With her home back in Massachusetts effectively erased, they had no clear plans to return to the United States just yet. For now, her husband was working in Amsterdam at the job that her Bankster uncle had found for him, and she and their kids were enjoying her aunt and the city.

We visited the Kattenkabinet Cat Museum and a refuge for strays called The Catboat, shopped in a pet store called Cats & Things, ate at the Amsterdam Cat Café, and concluded the day with a drink at the Café de Prins, one of the many pubs around the city with at least one resident cat in it. This one had a nice, friendly, tiger-striped male that nuzzled us as we sat there, admiring the wood paneling and sipping our beers.

"Really?" I said, listening to my friend while feeling that now-familiar mixture of horror at the reason why this was so and happiness for her that something was falling nicely into place.

"Yes, the kids are really happy in their new schools. It's also oddly simple to find nice apartments that are empty and affordable, really close to my aunt and uncle's house, but my aunt is dead set against it. She doesn't want us to move out!"

"That may be because she is enjoying your company, and also because she is spooked by the events of the past year," I replied. Then I looked steadily at her, to capture and hold her full attention. "Bethany, there is something on the Internet that I want you to read – tonight. Would you be willing to do that?"

She looked at me skeptically. "Well…I do have to help the kids with their homework…"

"It's not that long. In fact, it's only about the length of a book chapter. It's a short history of what happened over the past year and why it did."

She looked up at me, wide-eyed. "You mean…"

"I mean…I can't and won't add to what I've said, but it's good that you're catching on."

"Okay. I'll read it. Tonight." She looked a bit stunned, having realized that she was about to receive some information that would shock her…and she seemed to realize that I had something to do with its existence. Little did she know…

We sat there, sipping our raspberry beers and petting cats, and Bethany told me what it had been like in the Netherlands for the past year, both during the Cull (which she still called a plague), and after. She had been more afraid during the early months of it than later on, which puzzled me.

"Why would your fear decrease? I mean, you must have realized what was going on. Still, this was the safest place I could think of to send you – your neighborhood in Massachusetts was getting erased, but your bankster uncle's place seemed like a good bet, and it was."

"Oh, no – it was – you did the right thing – it wasn't that," she said.

"So what was it?"

"It was the Muslim – Islamist – migrants. I know it's politically correct to differentiate between those who are just members of that religion and call them Muslim versus those who are militant and wanting to force it on others, which means they are Islamists, but they were so aggressive that I stopped after a while."

I stared at her. "They bothered you?!"

"Well…a little. Nothing like what you read about in the news, because you had me followed by Blackout Security agents, I realized. Some Islamists bothered me, hissing and surrounding me when I went out to buy groceries."

"Ah…that's called "taharrush" – surrounding a woman to sexually harass her, perhaps gang rape her with hands or worse, by penis – an Islamist practice. They will do it to any woman, Muslim or not. What happened next?"

"Those horrible men were quickly surrounded themselves. I didn't understand at the time who these guys were who were helping me, but they were Americans and Europeans. I could tell by their accents. They shot the migrants – well, Muslims – that was all I could be sure that they were when they were bothering me."

"They shot them?" I needed to hear more details.

"Yeah…that was the odd part. They didn't die. They writhed in agony, and then my rescuers leaned over them and pressed their guns, which were really small, to their faces and said some things that I didn't hear to them. They were speaking very softly, and on purpose. I just stood there, frozen."

"Then what happened?"

That's when it got weird. They seemed to shoot the Muslims again, except it was more like…un-shooting them. I don't know…the guys suddenly stopped struggling, like they were comfortable again, though some had peed their pants." She smiled at that memory.

"I see."

Bethany looked at me, confused. "What do you see?"

I gave her a mirthless smile. "I see what happened."

She looked at me, a partial comprehension dawning on her face. "Are you going to tell me?"

I glanced around.

Aaron and Ed were at the next table, sipping pale ales, watching us. Ed nodded at me.

"Okay," I said to Bethany. "The Blackout guys had Hamish's nanite weapons. Those don't kill. They attack the nervous system, making the one who is shot feel as if gazillions of fire ants are stinging…internally. You just aim the weapon at your opponent, and fire. To take them back, you have to press the weapon up to the person and hit the reverse switch. That's what they did."

She was gaping at me. "Wow…"

"Close your mouth and act like you're not stunned, even if you are still amazed," I told her.

She closed her mouth and stared into her beer. "That Hamish is amazing," she said.

"Yes, he is. The guns are now biometric, too, so that they can't be snatched and used against us," I added. "He just gets cleverer and cleverer."

"Do you have one?"

"Oh yeah…I'm armed and dangerous." I gave her an evil grin. "We all are."

"Cool." She smiled into her beer. "I still don't know whether or not to feel guilty about my changed attitude toward Muslims – the men, anyway."

"Guilty?!" I spat out in disgust. "Feel no apologies whatsoever. A Muslim woman is just a Muslim woman, and that religion won't let her switch to anything else, though some do anyway, and good for them. Ayaan Hirsi Ali dumped it flat. But a Muslim male who believes in the hadiths of the Quran, and who enjoys committing taharrush, is a piece of shit. They consider women to be chattel, and assign us the legal and moral importance of animals…and unlike people in our culture, they don't give animals any respect. No…be glad that they are gone."

She was listening to me soberly, despite our alcoholic drinks. "We are judging another culture by the standards of our own."

"Yes, we are," I agreed, "and as long as women's safety, sanity, and security is at stake, I shall continue to do so. As you well know, since we went to school together, I went through college agreeing with most politically correct viewpoints, but not all. If a culture clash meant a choice between acceptance of some other culture even if it had a misogynist practice or siding with women, I sided with women every time…and people knew it. So I will always do that, political correctness be damned."

"Me too," Bethany said a moment later.

A cat sidled up to our table and rubbed itself on my leg. Another approached Bethany. We paused in our discussion of heavy issues to pet them both. The cats in this place were very friendly, apparently used to strangers and able to enjoy them. "Not every cat likes to be touched and petted and otherwise interacted with by total strangers," I commented.

"No, that's true," Bethany said. "My cat, Teddy, doesn't. He just likes the family." Bethany had brought her huge, tiger-striped, Maine Coon cat to Amsterdam to live with her aunt and uncle when she and her family had fled Massachusetts.

We petted the cats until they walked off. One of them, a lithe, shorthair brown-and-black tiger, leaped onto the wooden bench next to me and started washing its hind legs, suddenly and deliberately oblivious to us. A guy at the next table saw this and laughed. We smiled back, then turned back to our beers.

"So," Bethany asked, "you saw the beautiful Peace Palace. I've been there, but I'm not sure what it is exactly that they do there now. I know it's a branch of the United Nations, but that's all. What kinds of cases do they deal with there?"

"Civil matters between nations who agree to be bound by the judgments of the International Court of Justice," I told her. "The United States won't be bound by it. Other nations have agreed to that, though, so it has cases on its docket."

"But if they did the Nuremberg Trials through that branch…"

"They did those trials in Nuremberg, Germany, back when the U.N. hadn't created a permanent international criminal tribunal. It was all ad hoc, a case-by-case creation of a court, which was really inefficient. The idea of creating a permanent criminal court as a branch of the U.N. got delayed until almost the end of the twentieth century."

"So what happened – how did one get created?" Bethany hadn't been to the new court building to look around, she had told me, so she hadn't toured it, and hadn't read about it, hence all the questions about it. That was fine. It was forcing me to review what I knew, and to explain it to a non-lawyer.

"In the summer of 1998, for five weeks, 162 nations met in Rome to discuss a treaty. That's what the Rome Statute is: a treaty. NGOs – 137 of them – were given one room to gather in. They could not attend the discussions, but they set up computers and shared data with the delegates and their legal advisors. This enabled everyone to keep track of which nations had agreed to what, and how many votes there were on each point from day to day. The United States had wanted this document and contributed heavily to its formation…and then it wouldn't sign."

Bethany looked at me open-mouthed. "Why wouldn't we sign?"

"The problem was really just about U.S. senators being unwilling to subject Americans to any international criminal court, which, if you've read the Rome Statute, seems absurd, because the United States legal system is compatible with it, and because it has a decent track record of handling monsters properly on its own. Monsters also tend to have a really hard time escaping from us, or evading us forever, so the failure to ratify this document just makes our government look…foolish. The U.S. pushed for this treaty, and helped write it, and then wasn't thrilled about actually applying it. There doesn't seem to be anything wrong with this thing – I've read it."

"So we've never signed it?"

"Not on July 17, 1998. We waited another year and a half. The United States had signed the Rome Statute on December 31, 2000. But then U.S. Senate refused to ratify it. This was a mistake; the International Criminal Court will exist and process cases regardless. It was really absurd. The treaty requires that any nation that is a party to it have laws on its books that complement it, including prohibitions on genocide, war crimes, and crimes against humanity. The U.S. has all of that. We even have what it takes to satisfy the I.C.C.'s need for complementary jurisdiction, which means that either the U.S. legal system or the I.C.C. could handle a criminal matter of that sort on its own, with legal justice, finality, precedent, and so on. Our government did ratify it eventually, though. That was a year and a half ago. I just found that out, after we got back and I started reading about the I.C.C."

"Why were they so reluctant to sign it, I wonder?" Bethany was still puzzled.

I smiled. "It does seem really weird of us, doesn't it? This is a bizarre case of an empire that, despite the absence of another empire challenging its hegemony on the world playing field, feared the slightest threat to that dominance. It didn't want to give an inch, which is usually how an empire that has peaked behaves just as it starts to decline."

She stared at me over her beer. "So our own government was suffering from fear itself?" she asked, echoing Franklin Delano Roosevelt's speech of long ago, just as the United States had faced a long-past crisis. "That's lame."

"Pretty much. We have nothing to fear from its application, especially since our own legal system usually handles monsters properly on its own, which would mean that this Court wouldn't have much reason to prosecute Americans anyway. But...we wanted the Rome Statute, we pushed for it, we helped author it, so we ought to join it. We did, though."

"Huh. It's like it wants an unfair advantage over everyone else on the international playing field, even though, just by being the only superpower and the wealthiest nation of all, it already has that unfair advantage."

"Exactly," I agreed. "They want to be Farmers, as I call the very criminals who should be in front of that Court, and they are from all over the planet, but many are from the United States."

"Farmers?"

"That's what I call banksters, hedge fundsters, and corporatists – unethical ones."

"Huh. That fits."

With that, we petted some cats.

Later that week, we made a special trip – with Bethany, her husband, and kids – all eight of us, in fact – to a place south of Amsterdam called Keukenhof. The purpose of the trip was to see the Dutch tulips in bloom. To get there, we took a public bus, which nearly gave Aaron and Ed heart attacks, but they handled it well in the end. I think they also enjoyed seeing the tulips.

The place was a beautiful profusion of vibrant color, a whole spectrum that we drank in.

We couldn't stare at it enough. Everyone was quiet, just wandering around, enjoying it.

"I read it," Bethany said suddenly as we walked along ahead of the others.

I smiled and nodded at her. "Good."

"That's why you're here, isn't it?" she asked. "You're here to do something else about that."

I just smiled at her, and suddenly smiled too. She had looked worried, but then pleased.

"Thank you for keeping us safe."

"You're welcome."

Our time in The Hague was both productive and instructive.

A case could be initiated in one of three ways: 1. By referral from a nation that was a party to the Rome Statute; 2. By a referral of the situation from the U.N. Security Council; or 3. By the initiation of the Prosecutor of the Court on her or his own authority.

By bringing our data as private citizens to the office of the Prosecutor, we were asking her to go with the third option.

We met with a law clerk at the International Criminal Court, one Mr. Jan van der Voort, a young clerk in the office of the Court's Prosecutor. Like most European attorneys, he had grown up in a privileged family of other lawyers, all well-connected. It took money to become an attorney, and tuition was not, as in the United States, the largest share of that endeavor. Instead, it was necessary to work for years after graduating from law school as an intern…which meant no salary. Only wealthy people could afford to do that, and only those with enough influential relations could hope to secure a paying position after that.

I had briefed Claire and Fabian on this before we left for the meeting. "It was something that I found out in law school," I told them, "by talking with foreign law students." Interacting with people from other nations was something I had always done, both because it fascinated me, and because I didn't fit in with the other Americans. Looking back, I knew that it had been an advantage that exposed me to ideas that some of my more typical classmates missed out on.

Jan was a thirtysomething Dutch hipster, which came as a mild surprise. He wore round, John-Lennon-style glasses which darkened on their own out in the sun and faded to clear inside. He led us into his office and invited the four of us to take seats on the sofas. He took an armchair, joining us around his coffee table once he had offered us tea, water, or whatever else his assistant might bring us. We declined; we were anxious to discuss the future of the case…if it even had one.

"Oh, it definitely has a future," Jan assured us. "The question before us is, how much transparency can the world bear from it?"

Fabian looked taken aback. "What are you saying, that this case must proceed in secret?"

"Yes, and no," Jan said cryptically. Then he said, "The Court works *in camera* a lot, to shield victims of atrocities from the perpetrators. That means recordings of testimony are heard."

Hamish, the only non-lawyer present (our cousins had now read through much of what I had suggested on various aspects of law, national and international law, and the history of it, making them pseudo-experts in advance of law school), was impatient to know whether or not we had come all this way for nothing. "Please elaborate," was all he said, however.

Jan smiled. "The case will proceed as long as the…what do you call them? 'Farmers'? – can be brought to justice. By that, I mean apprehended and transported here. This, forgive me, seems like the tallest order. These men are the wealthiest, most guarded and insulated on Earth. They shield themselves behind the U.S. government, which has notoriously walked out of the World Court, claiming itself subject to no authority other than its own."

Hamish and I exchanged glances. "We'll get them here," he told Jan.

"Intriguing," Jan said. "What do you have in mind?"

I spoke up. "Well, what we would need from the Court is a little sneakiness and subterfuge, so that the Farmers won't know that they're under arrest until they're actually under arrest."

"You expect the Court to issue arrest warrants without announcing it to the media, only quietly to the United States government, and then ask it to pick them up?" Jan looked doubtful.

"Not exactly. There's another entity that would be available and willing to make the arrests and transports. This Court has had repeated difficulty with criminals evading arrest, capture, you name it. And why wouldn't it? What's in it for a criminal if they surrender but trial, conviction, penalty, and universal condemnation? They have no motivation to cooperate. They must be arrested without warning, and handed over to the Court. Otherwise, it's just another escaped Yugoslavian or Nazi monster on the run, only this time it's Farmers. I don't know where they would hide this time, but they might."

Jan watched us. "Ah. I see. Well then, I suppose we are going to trial…whenever they arrive." With that, he launched into the particulars. "In that event, we want to see justice done, and to show the world that justice is done. Care must be taken not to cause the world to feel such wrath toward your country that peace is threatened. I say this because these 'Farmers' are the perpetrators of such horrific genocide on much of the rest of the human species, while it appears – and excuse me for saying so, as I realize that they did kill over three hundred million of their own citizens – that the United States came out of this better than any other nation did."

"Even Canada?" I couldn't help asking.

Jan laughed. "You're right – they didn't do much to Canada." He sobered a moment later. "Well…they did do away with the Muslim immigrants, and Asian immigrants. They exterminated anyone who was not a member of the indigenous population. Hindus were left by and large undisturbed, but others were not. Many nations have Farmers, not just yours."

We sat there, listening to him.

Finally, I said, "We did the best we could to find everyone. Have a look at the names."

"Oh, not to worry! You have done an enormous thing here. It is amazing."

I breathed a sigh of…not relief, exactly, but something in me eased.

"I must say," Jan added, lapsing into thought, "that whoever crafted that story that was released onto the Internet, *Vaccine: The Cull*, did an excellent job of it. It explains enough without revealing too much. It simply states the crime, the method, the conditions which gave rise to the motive – collapsing ecosystems brought on by human overpopulation – and wraps it up quickly and efficiently. The world will likely be content with the I.C.C.'s summation, and with that. We do wonder who wrote it, though," he added, with a gleam in his eye.

"Do you?" I said, with a gleam in my own.

Claire broke our pointed eye contract with a question. "I was wondering…if this Court was created so that the victors of a war – any war, including a resource war – would not judge the losers…"

"Yes?" Jan asked, waiting for her to go on.

"It's just that the losers are all over the world. There is no truly uninvolved, impartial nation in the mix this time. I have been reading about international law, tribunals, arbitration panels, and other courts formed by the United Nations or other international groups in history – outside reading at law school – and it seems that we are back to that again, just as with the Nuremberg Trial. Aren't we?"

"Ah, I see," Jan said. "Yes, that we are. But the Prosecutor will go ahead with this. We cannot let such things stop the wheels of justice from grinding out a decision. People need closure, don't they?"

"Yes, we do," Claire replied. "I do."

He looked at her sharply.

Fabian said, "My wife lost her parents in the Cull. My cousins tried to persuade them to stay with us in Connecticut, but they insisted upon returning to their business, which was just outside Philadelphia."

"I'm sorry," Jan said. "I cannot imagine what you are going through. I lost only a distant cousin, someone whom I knew only from a family tree. I won't pretend to be able to offer you empathy, but you have my sympathy."

Claire looked at him, intrigued with his insightful response. "Thank you."

Jan looked back at the pile of data in his lap, on the coffee table, and all around the room. His staff had been busily printing out all data files that it could, while also setting up audio-visual equipment on which to view the photographs and videos that we had gathered. It was already a shocking amount, considering the fact that this was evidence from the digital age. (The data from the Nuremberg Trial had been massive enough – all in paper – to fill up six freight train cars.)

"Professor Châtelet," he began.

"Call me Avril," I said.

That seemed difficult for him, but he did it. "All right. Avril…something else concerns me."

"Would it, by any chance, be logistics?" I asked.

"Yes, it would. I am wondering how we are to issue warrants for verification of this data, acquire the data, and then peruse the data, without tipping off potential defendants."

I smiled a little smile. "I thought you might. I suggest the following sneaky modus operandi: cybersnoop it ALL first – where it is, what it is, who has it, what it contains, how it proves the case, and so on. At the same time, keep secret tabs on where your quarries are at all times." When Jan looked shocked at the audacity of this idea, I said, "Why not? Dutch ingenuity has taken you pretty far already."

"How do you mean?" he asked, confused.

"Your country has plenty of adept people in it. Surely you must have a few virtuoso computer hackers who can access the Deep Net, the Dark Net, isolated computer databases, and so on. I mean, this is the culture that created a huge polder to keep itself from going underwater. New world order after new world has lived underwater without actually going under the water. Why let this stop you? What I am suggesting is that you get all of the means of both prosecuting this case and arresting its defendants in place simultaneously so that you can move by stealth. That way, when you are ready to pull that trigger, every gun is in place, trained on every target by an expert sniper. This is too important to miss."

"So…now I see why the United States has been the most powerful nation on the planet right for so long," said a female voice behind us.

Jan looked up, then stood abruptly.

We turned in our seats to see a calm, tall, thin, elegant African woman with long cornrows that were swept up into a bun standing just inside the room. She smiled at us serenely.

We all stood up to greet her. "Madam Prosecutor," I said. "It's very nice to meet you."

Aminata Diouf was from Senegal. She had grown up partly in Dakar, and partly at the various schools around the world where she had studied, thanks to a father who had insisted upon an international education for her. She had never married, though it was rumored that she was seeing someone now – something that was not done where she was from. Senegal was mostly Sufi and Sunni Muslim, with a small percentage of Catholics and an even smaller one of Protestants. Outwardly, it presented itself as a secular state, but where relationships were concerned, religion still held some sway.

The Prosecutor stepped forward to shake my hand. "It's very nice to meet you too," she said.

The Prosecutor wore a brilliantly purple skirt suit with a set of hand-carved wooden beads and some gold bangle bracelets. Her black robes hung over her arm, and she clutched the white frill of a bib that every member of the legal profession in Europe wore to court.

We looked at each other for a long moment, sizing each other up, with friendly, careful smiles on our faces. This was, after all, a friendly meeting. I suddenly wondered whether or not I was sufficiently dressed up to be here, and then felt ridiculous for worrying about it. I was wearing a pair of clean, black linen pants, a soft, cotton-silk blend shirt with three-quarter-length sleeves in the palest of pinks, and a scarf that depicted slightly darker pink peonies with black, flat, leather-strapped sandals. I had my pearl earrings on and my hair in a dragonfly barrette made of some sort of bronze-hued metal.

She must have been thinking about the strategy I had been suggesting. Perhaps it sounded absurdly naïve and unworkable to her, I thought to myself. At last, Ms. Diouf broke the silence. With a quiet smile, she said, "So you want us to sneak up on the defendants."

I raised one eyebrow and said, "Ideally, yes. There have been too many tales of them getting away, going into hiding, and enjoying the rest of their evil lives, penalty-free. Blackout Security is run and fully staffed by people who are very aware of and upset by what has happened. They value the United States Constitution and all it stands for, and want it restored. What has been done is a travesty and an end-run around the law and humanity."

"Indeed." Her voice was rich, melodious, and a bit mesmerizing to listen to, but I wasn't overly distracted by that.

"So," I said, "can you arrange to do that, or not? I'm just thinking of the victims and of their survivors. This is one of those survivors," and here I gestured at Claire, "my cousin's wife. No doubt you can find more. There are always more."

"Yes," Ms. Diouf said. "There always are." She shook Claire's hand and thought about this.

"Can you prosecute this case?" Claire asked her.

"From what I have seen and heard thus far, yes, I think I can," Ms. Diouf replied. "I will have to petition the Pre-Trial Chamber for permission to proceed, but I would be astonished if they did not grant it. As for maintaining the element of surprise, I would need special permission to move with the necessary stealth to allow for the successful arrests of each defendant. What bothers me is who to send those warrants to. With the recent assassination of a sitting U.S. President, I have doubts about sending them to the C.I.A., the N.S.A., or any other U.S. agency. A trial judge would do, however."

We just listened to her.

Ms. Diouf looked at Hamish. "Please tell me again shat sort of help can you offer. The International Criminal Court does get outside help for arrests, but with so many nations' political systems in a state of collapse and reconstruction, our usual avenues are closed right now."

"We can offer the assistance of a worldwide network of ex-military special ops members who believe in such principles as the United States Constitution – as originally written – and other stable government systems that are currently being reconstituted. It's called Blackout Security, and it has been protecting my family for years with great success. This is their website." With that, he went to the nearest computer terminal and entered it into a search engine.

She looked at the site, impressed. "With their help, this may all be possible."

Fabian breathed a sigh of relief and said, "Thank you."

"Don't thank me yet. Wait until the deed is done, and we know that those responsible for this 'Cull' are in custody. When the moment comes, those U.S. agencies may have to be present, but Blackout Security may be the answer to the need for both transparency and effectiveness."

Claire nodded, and so did Fabian. "We just want to see them punished and stopped, so that they can't do this again," Claire said.

"Oh, I doubt they can do this again," Fabian said to her. "Too many are dead."

I looked at him sharply. "Fabian, some of these Farmers are plotting to alter human DNA."

The prosecutor looked alarmed at that. "Two cases, then?"

"No...I think they can be linked," I replied.

"That would make it simpler." She paused, then asked, "Did you call them 'Farmers'?"

I had lapsed into thought for a moment, so I looked up at her, startled. "Oh. Yeah. It's a term I coined a long time ago, even before I understood who they all were and knew the scope of their activities…and crimes. It encompasses Banksters, Hedge Fundsters, and Corporatists. They're all Farmers in that they treat the rest of our species like a crop to be sown, grown, reaped, harvested or plucked, ground under, traded – whatever suits their purposes, and the hell with the rest of us. We only matter to them as a commodity to be used and profited from."

Ms. Diouf had listened to this with interest. "'Farmers'," she said. "It suits them."

We showed her the case of Dr. Anthony Warburg, the murdered oncologist and immunologist in Boston. He had been cracking the case of the vaccine Cull serum and P53-breaking nanite wide open. Our data, mined from the Dark Net, showed that he had also found evidence of Tacttag's DNA-editing scheme that was aimed at preventing Aspies and other autistic people from ever being brought into existence again.

Ms. Diouf actually showed some signs of fury when she saw that. "Yes, this definitely amounts to a scheme of genocide, both past and planned for the future, and a crime against humanity, by the same individuals. What you have shown me of the warrantless cyber-snooping by the N.S.A. points to the methods employed to commit these crimes. I think I have what I need here. It will take time to go through it all, but it will be worth it, and I think the Judges will allow this case to go forward."

"So…thirty years to life for the Farmers?" I asked.

She smiled. "Something like that, though there are almost always a few who get less."

I thought of Spades, who seemed not to be fully aware of what was happening around him. "Yes. I can think of some people who may deserve only a year or so, and then go home."

"It is a very complex case. Nothing is ever simple," she agreed. Then she said, "It is interesting that it is you, the inventors of a population control device, brought this data to me."

Hamish and I exchanged glances and smiled. I replied to her, "Interesting, yes. When I thought of Nae-Née – and it was the concept, because the name came to me a few hours later while joking around with Hamish, who did the actual inventing – what I wanted was a quiet, peaceful, non-violent way of coping with human overpopulation. It was realism about the human sex drive, disconnecting it from reproduction. I just wanted a voluntary, safe device."

Ms. Diouf nodded, smiling slightly. "Good to hear. Why did you gather all this information?"

"I sensed that something horrifying was going on. First, I saw that the American Dream was dead and gone. Then I began to understand that it was killed by human overpopulation and near-complete consumption of certain resources – they called it 'elbow room' during the time of mass immigration and settlement of the continental United States. It takes resources such as water and raw materials and space to fuel a dream. People want to own property and earn money with which to live comfortably and well on that property. Then they want to stay in the game with a great education. Well, the colleges and universities only have so much space. Bigger is not better with education; smaller is better in terms of quality and individual attention. After I appreciated all of those unpleasant truths, I realized what was coming and why, and saw some signs of it."

"Aha. I see." Ms. Diouf was certainly a good listener.

"This must sound strange to someone not from the United States. We have always had great aspirations, along with expectations of fulfilling those aspirations. The time came when that was no longer possible for most. It was only possible for the few who had amassed and hoarded the most wealth. For the rest, it was fattening GMO foods, and substandard education. Next it was overcrowding in cities with dwindling water supplies and fracked, poisoned water supplies."

"Yes."

"I want people to have those things: great educations, personal space, fresh fruits and vegetables and plenty of organic grains and whatever else to eat, and to have choices and be happy. It shouldn't be only for the privileged few whose families managed to grab it all. I knew something was rotten, so I kept watching. Hamish knew and helped to watch. He knew how to watch better than I did. What we saw was a horrific, Orwellian way of resetting the system."

"And you wanted to do something to redress this great wrong. I see. Well...good!"

I had a few more points to make before leaving. "What we have presented to you is more than mere supposition. It is evidence of a crime. No natural plague would kill so many humans. At most, only a few hundred thousand would die of such a thing, but you would need both an expert witness – a virologist or bacteriologist, perhaps – and this evidence. However..." and here I paused for dramatic effect, since I couldn't stop myself, "...there is a suspicious pattern to the deaths from the Cull. Perhaps you have noticed it."

She looked at me, questioningly. "I have thought I noticed something..." She trailed off.

"It is that those left alive are the intelligentsia of the human race," I explained. "The professors, physicians, scientists, engineers, lawyers, artists, musicians – all of the innovators and thinkers and creative minds – are still alive. It is the masses of people who had no opportunities to become a professional of any kind who are dead, regardless of whether or not they had the potential to do so. People who were treated as the proverbial 'useless eaters' of societies – people with no clout – those are the ones who were Culled."

"Ah...yes, you are right. That is something worth adding to closing arguments, I think."

We shook hands with her, left the material with her, and walked out. It was obvious from that conversation that she had read my anonymous, unsanitized history. She seemed to know that she had just met its author, but had kept silent about that, and that was how I wanted it.

There were just a few more days before we planned to go home, so we spent them enjoying The Hague. Bethany had checked up on the current location of Johannes Vermeer's painting *Girl With a Pearl Earring* for me; it was in the Mauritshuis in The Hague, its usual location. We went to see it and whatever else that museum had to offer. It was a small mansion, the former home of a 17th century prince who had ruled the area. It housed Dutch Golden Age paintings.

The guys seemed to enjoy the visit, but it was me and Claire who stood for long stretches staring happily at the vibrant hues in still lifes of irises, parrot tulips, roses, narcissus, and the vases they had been placed in centuries ago. We stared at fantastical scenes of peacocks, tigers, and white deer sharing a garden…or was it a forest? It looked like both, and the idea of them living peaceably together in it was simultaneously ludicrous and idyllic.

We saw scenes of Dutch people enjoying dinner parties together, listening to and playing lutes and piano fortes, carousing and laughing, or standing around together chatting. We saw the *Girl With a Pearl Earring* portrait and thought of the novel about her, the movie, and the fact that she was likely just one of the painter's daughters, not a maid, and laughed.

After a few hours of this, we took a walk in the city's Japanese Garden, which was in full bloom. Its red bridge and purple wisteria presented a striking color contrast. We wandered around the garden for over an hour before leaving for dinner.

That was just the day after our visit to the International Criminal Court.

We had a couple more lovely, leisurely days to explore the city before going home, during which time we scoped out its financial district, a thoroughly modern area, and the Noordeinde Palace, which was where the Dutch royal family spent most of its time. It was not open to the public, as it was the monarch's working residence. It wasn't a huge place, just a beautiful, elegant one that seemed sufficient for its purpose.

We celebrated Earth Day in The Hague, which was oddly satisfying. It was satisfying because we had come there to do something about the Farmers. It was also satisfying because saving the Earth from climate change was such a joke. It couldn't be prevented, only coped with.

We spent the day outside, buying picnic foods in paper wrapping and listening to talks on how to live in an eco-friendly way. There were a few new ideas that caught our attention, but we were also pleased to realize that we had already been doing many of those things.

Earth Day felt like an ecological awareness holiday that one didn't take a vacation on. Every day ought to be Earth Day. But killing most of us off to save the Earth was insanity. I hoped that the Farmers wouldn't get off on any such plea.

They deserved worse than what they had perpetrated on their own species…far worse.

Chapter 31

Discovery

Discovery is the process by which the evidence of a case is researched, read, investigated, and otherwise assembled and gone over with painstaking precision until the attorneys involved know every detail. It is done in advance of a trial, either civil or criminal.

The International Criminal Court called its discovery process an "investigation", but it was the same thing. With the months ticking slowly by, the Court's Prosecutor read what she already had from us. Even though the idea was to see whether or not an investigation was warranted, no one who was aware of what was happening actually doubted that.

The purpose of the investigation was to verify the allegations in the material it had.

We went home to wait and watch, and to be ready for whatever came next.

Quickly – about six weeks after we got home – the Rome Statute made a startling reappearance in the national and international news. Apparently, it was announced, the document had been on our government's docket in the days before the Cull had gotten underway, and the U.S. Senate had ratified it, and notified the United Nations. It was now reported that, during martial law, just before the Cull had taken off, the United States Senate had ratified the Rome Statute by a vote of 84 to 16. This put the crimes of the Farmers and any military officers who had perpetrated the Cull, complete with their plans and intentions to commit those crimes, squarely within the purview of the International Criminal Court.

During the Cull, that news had been suppressed. Now, the Farmers' preoccupation with decimating humanity's numbers, and their inattention to other matters during the imposition of martial law, was coming back to bite them. Only passing mention was made of this news, and then other items were discussed. It was convenient that this didn't get much attention. I hoped that the Farmers wouldn't be tipped off. We wanted them relaxed and oblivious to their fate.

My guess was that our politicians had wanted to free themselves from the influence and control of the Farmers who had bought them. They had paid for political campaigns for decades, and then hounded the politicians with lobbyists in between each election. The politicians were tired of going along with neonicotinoid use killing bees, fossil fuels and mining polluting waters and lands, and so on. This was their chance to get out from under all of that.

The Farmers could be prosecuted in The Hague. No ad hoc court would need to be assembled. No special declaration needed to be made by the United States government authorizing the I.C.C. to proceed with the case. As for other defendants, the United Nations Security Council could refer the case for prosecution. It was either that, or a declaration from any other nation that had Farmers to indict (actually, the I.C.C. called an indictment a "document containing the charges" instead). All this dealt with the matter of jurisdiction, and there was nowhere on the planet that the Farmers could realistically hide.

Blackout Security and Jason did some snooping, to be ready for the next move.

The Prosecutor took her time going over all of the data we had given her office.

It took her four months, in fact, which she had to do before initiating the discovery process. This was a source of frustration to Claire. She was eager see the Farmers prosecuted, and fast. Granted, she had read the entire Rome Statute, but that was no reason why she couldn't share her true feelings with her family. We did our best to be good listeners. People do have the right to vent and rant privately to their families.

"Just keep telling yourself that they'll get their days in court, and they'll get what they deserve," I told her. "The Nuremberg Trials took nearly twelve months, so this trial won't be over in mere days."

"I know," she said. "It's just that it sucks to have to wait after all this."

"The legal process is slow, careful, and detailed. But it can deliver justice," I added.

The Prosecutor concluded her review of the data we had delivered to her and presented her assessment to the Pre-Trial Chamber, which consisted of three judges. These judges, we found out after checking the I.C.C. website, were from Germany, Japan, and Costa Rica. They reviewed the evidence presented, and agreed that Prosecutor Diouf could and should proceed with an investigation. That would mean gathering evidence of bone dust in crematoria, both from ships and from cargo containers. These crematoria were currently afloat around the globe, and parked in shipping yards. Incredibly, no effort had been made to destroy them.

This, along with depositions of surviving witnesses, promised to take another four months.

"What's a deposition?" Jacques asked.

"It's when an attorney interviews someone about the events and subject matter of a case, and records it on video in and writing," Claire told him. "Prosecutor Diouf told me that I can expect a visit from a representative of the Victims and Witnesses Unit of the I.C.C. sometime during the winter…or spring. Apparently, my deposition is to be recorded, and my name not shared during the trial. What a joke; the Farmers met me already."

"Oh. Cool," Jacques said, "about the definition and the entire arrangement. There must be some defendants who don't know you. They shouldn't make it any easier to find you."

We could all appreciate that sentiment.

While the Court did its thing, we did ours.

Soon we would plant the spring crop, and I was determined not to have to worry about water.

Specifically, I was determined not to be cut off by a state or military rationing of the water supply and thus unable to irrigate our own crops. To be self-sufficient, we would need our own system, one that worked via rainfall and capture plus trickle, drip, and pour.

It had to work for the conservatory, too. No longer was I satisfied with mere watering cans.

What if water were ever rationed?! There wasn't much we could do to stop that.

We weren't in the business of buying politicians. We wanted that stopped.

Accordingly, I looked at drip kits from a company that sold them to small farmers, which was what we were when we sought to ambitiously grow a full salad and fruit bar's worth of food each year, plus the herbs to flavor it. Too bad we couldn't do wheat, oats, and rice, but one can't do everything, I told myself. But what about the conservatory?

"We'll hire someone to the do the work for you," Hamish said. "I can't wait to see this."

"You want to see what I've designed, plus watch it get built?" I asked.

"Aye. It sounds ingenious, and you know how I love ingenious creations."

"Okay."

We hired a local guy who enjoyed doing both engineering and sculpture, one Jack Garrett. He had studied engineering at California Technical University – the same CalTech that *The Big Bang Theory* took place at – and then abandoned the field after a decade. Next, he had gone to the Rhode Island School of Design to study sculpture.

At first, modern art had been his thing, but all of his work was both functional and attractive. Soon, he had found himself hired out to homeowners who wanted cat walkways that wound down to indoor fountains and pools with koi, and so on.

Now I called him – he lived in West Simsbury – and explained what I wanted done.

"Sure, I can help you out with that," he had said.

He came over and looked at the conservatory, which was designed much like that of the Mark Twain House, but with wrought iron that swept in graceful curlicues over the glass panels. I didn't want to sacrifice that style to modern plainness, I told him.

"This is a challenge, and a fun one," he replied. "Not to worry; I won't destroy the aesthetics that you love. I can drill through the metal and make drip-holes that carry water, in controlled amounts, from plant-shaped cisterns to the inside of the conservatory. You won't even have to water the plants when I'm done."

"Wow…what shapes can you make?" I asked.

"How about a pitcher plant?" Garrett suggested. "Those naturally store water."

"That's perfect!" I said. "Do it, please!"

He smiled. "If you want, and I realize that you didn't request it when you called me," he added, eying our drip system out in the gardens, "I could create some interesting shapes out of wrought iron to water those crops. It would be that same system, only decorative as well as capable of watering your garden." He paused. "They'll also make nice, low lightning rods."

I was intrigued, and so was Hamish. "What sorts of shapes?" Hamish asked.

"Anything you want," the sculptor promised.

I thought about this. "Can you do a huge strawberry with water coming out where the tiny seeds would normally be?"

He looked delighted. "I could. You want four of those? I'm guessing they should match."

"Yes, please," I said, smiling happily.

"It should take about two weeks to do the conservatory, which I'll do first, and then I'll replace these plain garden drippers over the next couple of weeks after that," he told us.

Excellent! We signed the work order and left him to his measurements.

Hamish hung around to chat and watch him with the work, while I visited the scene periodically just to see how it was coming along. It was fun to watch, and in what seemed like no time (time flies when you have a court case to watch on the news), the conservatory was a work of both art and engineering.

The sculptures of the strawberries proved a bit trickier. The giant strawberry was made detachable. Jack, as he insisted we call him, tinkered with the design, making it branch out in clusters of berries surrounded by leaves and blossoms, and low to the ground. It was beautiful, and it had plenty of room to both catch and hold water. Each sculpture connected to the parts that were designed to sprinkle water all over the garden, curving metal extensions with holes. The curlicues mimicked vines and wended their way through each section. Perfect.

Meanwhile, it was time to plant the crops in the back yard.

Claire and I had it all planned out: we would plant strawberries (how could we not have a strawberry patch with those sculptures?), spinach, green and purple asparagus, red, orange, yellow, and purple bell peppers (no green – they tasted bitter), several varieties of heirloom tomatoes, Bibb lettuce, Romaine lettuce, tomatillos, nasturtiums, sweet potatoes, blue potatoes, zucchini squash (we would eat some of the squash blossoms as well as the squash), butternut and acorn squash, pumpkins, snap peas, small eggplants in both dark purple and striped, "fairy tale" purple (Claire and I agreed that the big ones weren't as good), orange and rainbow carrots, parsnips, green beans, cucumbers, artichokes (Claire was going to teach me her family recipe for those), jalapeno peppers, some red, purple, and yellow corn, scallions, leeks, and elephant garlic.

"The yard itself is going to disappear under this garden," Fabian had said as we had placed our order for the seeds several weeks earlier. But he had looked eager to see that happen.

So was Hamish. When the stuff arrived, he and Ed and Aaron met the delivery truck at the end of the driveway, and I could hear hoots of excitement as they signed for it. It arrived on a Wednesday morning in early May.

Fabian was all dressed for the office in a nice shirt and chinos, but he seemed to know what was coming when he saw everything. "I'll call the firm and tell them I'm needed at home today, and go change my clothes," he said. After a quick call, he dashed upstairs to change.

Claire and I raced out back to meet the guys and started directing the placement of each plant according to the plan that we had worked out ahead of time. We had planted some things already using seeds that we had saved from the previous season, but we were also attempting an ambitious garden with plants that neither of us had grown previously.

"My mother grew artichokes every year," Claire told me. "Don't worry."

I wasn't worried. This was going to be both fun and great exercise.

At that point, as we started placing the plants according to Claire's diagram, I did a double-take. "Claire, you've re-done this thing since we laid it out!" But I thought it was great: it resembled a kaleidoscope in some places, laid out as it was according to a wild pattern. The corn, squash, and peas were to grow up together in a Three Sisters method, and a huge carrot patch in the shape of a carrot stretched across one of the plots, crossed by a parsnip patch. Lettuce and spinach made up the leaves.

She grinned. "I guess I missed decorating cakes."

Fabian burst out laughing. "You just don't want to make us all fat."

"You've got that right." With that, she got to work.

We joined her.

It was all organic, and we would weed and hoe the whole thing daily…and drag our husbands outside to help. "You too are going to get your share of exercise doing a fair share of the work for the family food," I had told them. They had just nodded and smiled, and then turned to us to say, "Yes, dear."

Ha, ha, ha…but they were helping. They patiently walked around with the seedling tomato plants, placing them where we told them to, and Ed and Aaron stood around watching us all pierce the compost layer of the soil to put the seeds deep down into it. We were referring the instructions on depth of planting and watering, looking back and forth at the plots and advice.

By lunch time, they had gone back to the guardhouse at the gate, to watch for intruders. None were expected, but we had rounded up quite a few Farmers, so it would be nice to do our own farming without being attacked in the process.

Also by lunch time, the four of us were a complete mess, but we felt good.

"Come in and eat lunch," my mother called from the back door. "I made panini sandwiches and blackberry milkshakes," she added. "You can finish after a nice rest and a meal."

She didn't have to ask twice. We were hungry. Dad and my mother were grinning as they watched us silently demolish sandwiches that contained cheddar cheese, roasted red bell peppers, fresh basil, and a mix of eggplant and sweet potato fries. My mother had been having some fun with her mandolin slicer, inspired by our industry in the back yard. Dessert was the milkshakes.

Grandmère enjoyed it all, even though she could only drink half of her milkshake. Fabian finished it for her. "Lunch and a show," she joked, smiling.

Claire said, "I hope the stuff we grow gives us a bit of a show all season. It's great fun to find oddly-shaped vegetables and then guess what they are shaped like. Carrots and parsnips shaped like scissors or protractors, twisted, curled-up sweet potatoes, tomatoes with pointy bits that look like faces or horses…"

Fabian laughed. "I didn't realize you were so fanciful."

"Well, now you know. It's fun sometimes to not grow up." She grinned, and he smiled.

Once again, we were all busy until dinnertime, planting the rest of the garden. By late afternoon, we were done with the heavy lifting and planting, but into the detail work of it all. Hamish and Fabian sat down on the benches near the house and watched as Claire and I fussed over everything, straightening stakes, propping little signs that identified plants, and so on.

The work spilled over into the conservatory, where the avocado plant was bearing fruit again, the herbs were always growing and needing weeding and plucking, and the berry vines were being pollinated by our honeybees. The top-frame hives were just outside the conservatory, and our illustrious sculptor had ingeniously created an opening in the decorative metalwork that served as a bee door.

"This is going to be great," Claire said, and I agreed.

Aaron and Ed came out to see what was going on. "Looks great," Aaron said.

Ed leaned against the wall, resting his hand on it as he looked around. Suddenly, he jumped away and yelled, grabbing his hand. "Ouch! Avril, one of your bees just stung me!"

I went to look; Ed had managed to kill the thing, crushing it in against the wall as he had smacked at it. "That's not one of my bees," I told him. "It's a wasp. Look."

Clutching his sore finger, Ed leaned over and looked at it. So did the rest of us. "It's got yellow and black stripes," he said, in a tone that was arguing with me.

I grinned. "And that's where the similarity ends. See this insect corpse, how shiny it is, with no fur for carrying pollen, and ugly brown wings instead of pretty transparent ones? This is a yellow-jacket wasp, the thug of the insect world. It doesn't make honey."

With that, I took the roof off of the nearest hive and looked at the inside of it. Just as I had suspected, it had a brownish-gray nest, about the size of a baseball. I picked up my hive tool, which looked like a wide, short crowbar, carried the hive-roof over to the edge of the yard, and scraped the squatters off, into the grass. "Evicted!" I said.

Aaron started laughing. Ed looked outraged. Frankly, I didn't blame him.

I checked the other hives, but they had no squatters, so I put them back together.

Hamish appeared, and I said, "You've got a customer, Dr. MacDonall. Ed got stung by a wasp. There's the corpse on the wall," I said, pointing at it. "He killed his assailant."

Hamish grinned. "I would expect nothing less." He and Ed went into the house.

We all took showers before appearing at the dinner table. My mother had outdone herself yet again with homemade ravioli, whole wheat baguettes, and salads with pistachio nuts, warm goat cheese, and strawberries from Whole Foods. "Why not?" she asked, though with a rhetorical tone. "The garden won't be ready to harvest for weeks. I'm still going to use the grocery store while we're waiting."

We just laughed and ate everything. The ravioli was full of different things: mushrooms, spinach, pumpkin, butternut squash, sage, and so on. My mother had made that delicious variety of fillings, and Grandmère had wielded a hand-held, round, stamp-cutter. She had sat at the kitchen table, stamping and chatting with my parents all afternoon, watching us hard at work out the back window.

"Too bad Charlie and Zoe won't have such a nice garden," she remarked.

"Oh, I don't think they're upset about that at all," Fabian said with a grin.

"Neither do I," Grandmère agreed, "which says terrible things about his willingness to exercise and to earn his food by working directly for it. I always had at least an herb garden in windowsill pots when we lived in Paris."

Infuriatingly, the house that we had managed to acquire for Uncle Charlie and Aunt Zoe up the street, despite all of the other positive points to it (not modern, not a glass house, surveillance equipment removable, and so on), came with an odious land trust. The idiot former owner had sold that right off to the government.

Attorney O'Shea was working on undoing that, but meanwhile, no garden for them.

Jacques and Edgar weren't exactly devastated not to have to toil in the soil like we did.

"What will you do for the summer vegetables, though?" I had asked them last week. "We're about to plant our garden, and we'll share some of the harvest with you and your parents, but it will only yield so much. You ought to find another source of fresh produce."

My cousins had exchanged confused glances.

"You do know that farm stands and grocery stories have limits and less variety, don't you?"

"We do now," Edgar had said. "What do you suggest we do?"

"Well…there are at least two different things that you could do. Sophia, my writer friend, rents a plot at Auer Farm for the summer and grows her own food on it. It costs $25 for the entire season, and she can grow whatever she wants on it. She's out there every other day, weeding it, tying up her bean plants, and spraying a non-toxic soap-and-water mixture on them all to keep the insects away."

"So we would have to drive over there constantly?!" Jacques said, sounding really unhappy. "I don't have time to do all that! If it were the back yard, sure, but…"

Edgar had looked equally unimpressed with that idea.

"Another idea is to pay $600 to Holcomb Farm in Granby for the season. You will get a share of crops all summer and into the fall, but you won't get to pick what crops you get. It's just whatever they grow. The only thing you have to do is drive up there and get the food."

Edgar and Jacques brightened considerably at this idea. "Let's do it," Edgar said. "We could both contribute $300. Mom would be thrilled. She and Dad might even drive up there to get the food. They like car rides."

"Yes!" Jacques said. "I'll find this online right now." He started clicking away on his laptop.

Edgar grinned at me. "Problem solved!" He said with a devilish gleam in his eye.

Sigh…well, next year, hopefully, that damned land trust would be dealt with.

After several weeks, not only were the sculptures completed and installed, but some of the crops had grown enough to be harvested, including spinach. Spinach tastes far better as young, tender, small leaves – baby spinach, it's called in grocery stores and farmers' markets. Adult spinach, I had always thought, was terrible. It had tough stems that I would rip out rather than chew, and its leaves tasted bitter.

But that wasn't all. "This spinach tastes wonderful," Claire commented as we ate it in a salad that evening. "I don't know what it is about it…I've always loved baby spinach in salads, but it's never tasted this good before."

Fabian agreed. "Maybe it's because it's so fresh," he guessed.

Hamish looked at me and waited. He and I had just picked a big basketful of the stuff an hour earlier, and I hadn't said anything about it other than to ask him to help me do the job, and to show him how to pick it. It hadn't occurred to me to say anything until now.

"It's not just that it's so fresh," I said. "It's because packaging factories spray chlorine onto baby spinach just before they seal it into plastic bags. That keeps it from wilting longer, so that grocery stores have more time to take delivery of the product and sell it."

My parents and grandmother stopped chewing for a moment and stared at me, glanced at each other, and then kept eating. After a moment, my mother said, "That's appalling. Perhaps growing one's own food isn't such a hardship after all."

Claire and Fabian looked at each other, at their plates, and then forked some more spinach into their mouths. "Home organic gardening is worth it," Fabian said. "Everyone should do it."

"Everyone doesn't have a plot of land to do it in," Hamish said. "If the Agenda 21 Farmers get their way – and prosecuting the one who committed crimes won't stop this – most people will still be steered toward urban centers and energy-efficient, high-rise apartments."

Fabian looked glum at that thought. "You mean the ones like the buildings at Blue Back Square and the new, eco-friendly, walls of glass going up in downtown Hartford."

"Exactly."

"Do you want us to move out and go live there?" Claire asked.

"Never!" Hamish and I said together.

We all laughed.

"Stay here forever if you like. Or someday, when you have money for a place, if you want one on your own, we'll help you figure out something else. You can probably buy a place in this neighborhood when someone ages out of it, if they're not on Regenics," I told them.

"Won't they just pass it on to their children?" Fabian said. "My parents had a terrible time finding that house down the street," he recalled.

"No point in worrying about such things so far in advance," Dad said.

"You're right," Fabian said.

Grandmère smiled. "Just worry about law school and getting settled into a career first. Things will fall into place later, and they will do that more easily if you don't worry so much about them. Trust me – I've learned this from experience. Life offers so much to worry about that doing so only makes it harder, and you ought to enjoy things along the way."

Hamish smiled at her. "Spoken like someone who learned that before Regenics offered more time to learn it," he said.

"Indeed," Grandmère replied. "But I'm enjoying the extension, and all that it lets me see."

Climate change gave us a very hot summer, but not so hot that we couldn't grow food.

The problem, as it turned out, was not growing food. It was insects. They loved us.

We had to be outside a lot to weed the garden, and we were never going to use insecticides and thus kill off our bees. That would end the whole endeavor, after all. But going out to work in the garden meant slathering ourselves with all sorts of funny-smelling ointments that Hamish prescribed just to avoid becoming feasts for the insects rather than merely growing our own feast. It was a nuisance!

I had never liked doing all that, even though we could take a shower later and get rid of it.

Claire didn't like it much, either. She often forgot to put any bug repellent on, despite constant reminders by my mother and grandmother. Grandmère simply stayed in most of the time, so she wasn't being eaten alive like Claire and I were.

Fabian and Hamish always used the stuff, but they did something else that drove us all crazy: they put off showers until after dinner on days when they had to work in the garden. That meant dirty feet and the smell of bug repellent during the meal. "Clean hands and faces isn't enough," I complained to the two of them. We would be happy to put off serving dinner until after your showers," and Claire strongly agreed.

After a few dinners like that, we won the argument.

But Claire liked to go outside at random times – after breakfast, before putting on bug repellent, and after dinner, when she was showered and clear of the stuff – to wander around the garden and admire its progress. She was covered with bites.

Hamish and my mother were having a fit. Occasionally, I would get the treatment Claire got, but not nearly as much scolding. The treatment was Hamish's medicine, a special brew that stung a little at first and then quickly soothed the skin as the ointment neutralized the venom from the mosquitoes. I had a couple of spots of the stuff, which had a vaguely purple hue, but Claire had them all down her arms, legs, and up her neck.

"It's okay," she said. "I forget about the bites once the stuff is on."

But she was getting bitten a lot, Hamish said, and he was watching her for signs of any insect-borne disease. Luckily, it wasn't Lyme disease, nor the dreaded Zika, which could have caused nerve damage, but she did get chills and fever and some stiffness for a few days.

Fabian started to panic when that happened. Claire forbade him to stay home from the law firm, insisting that she was fine, well able to read and compile notes for future book projects. "I might go out in the car and take some photographs of flower gardens and farms, just to see how things are growing in this changing climate," she told him.

"You're not going anywhere for the next few days," Hamish told her. "You're going to bed with hot herbal teas, honey, and whatever spicy soups Avril cooks up. And then you're going to stop walking around the garden in flip-flops, shorts, and loose blouses." He left some aspirin and other things for my mother to give her and went with Fabian to the garage. Fabian would take him to his office and then drive to the law firm.

Dad laughed and said, "Let that be a lesson to you, young lady. Take better care of yourself."

Claire finished her breakfast and went back to her room, but insisted that she could eat meals with us at the table. She let me bring her tea after an hour or so, though, and then fell asleep after drinking half of it. "I guess I'll just have to be sick and get it over with," she muttered.

At lunchtime, my mother brought her the curried carrot soup I had made on a tray, and Claire just thanked her and ate it. "I think she's feeling a lack of energy from this mosquito-borne illness," my mother said, looking serious. "She doesn't realize how sick she is."

When he came home (brought by Ed), Hamish said that Claire would be okay. "She's right," he said, when I told him what she had said. "She'll just have to be sick and get it over with." But he went into her room with a syringe and injected her with something anyway.

She recovered after five days in bed, during which she felt achy and miserable. Grandmère was told to stay out of the sick room, no visits. Fabian responded to this illness by vigilantly chasing her with the bug-repellent for the rest of the summer morning, noon, and evening.

By then, Hamish told him, Claire's immune system was primed against any more trouble from that particular bug. "It's you younger people we have to watch out for most of all. The bugs love you. See that you put that stuff on yourself, too, or we'll start all over again with Fabian."

That was exactly what happened a week after Claire recovered. Fabian must have gotten bitten at least a few times, then. She was a great nurse to him, and insisted on learning my spicy soup recipes. "It's pretty much the same except for the vegetable choice," I told her. "You put in the olive oil and spices, cook them on low heat, add some vegetable bouillon – I like the moist paste in a jar that we keep in the fridge – then add onion slices and cubes of squash or slices of peeled carrot, cook it in broth and water, add a little Himalayan pink salt or Kosher salt, and puree it all in the pot with the stick blender. Easy."

"It is easy," Claire said, picking it right up. "Thanks! I'll try it with spinach next time."

The soup was good this time, with carrots, and it was good the next time, too.

"I wonder why we aren't a favorite with those mosquitoes too," I asked Hamish. "With Regenics, we seem younger."

"Oh, they could like us, too. Keep using that stuff," he told me. I did.

Fortunately, he and I made it through the season without getting sick.

What a nuisance! I loved the warm weather and open windows, though.

Fresh air, screens, breezes with no fossil fuel stinks – just floral scents and quiet!

It was so quiet, in fact, that I actually started to relax for a while.

I still read books and journals and news aimed at understanding the world, casting about for my next writing project, but I was taking a break, reading for fun a lot now. Claire was the one now obsessed with studying, and that was understandable. She and Fabian had careers to prepare for. Accordingly, they both went downtown to watch some real-life legal proceedings.

It was natural that they wanted to prove themselves and achieve something, and good that they knew what that would be. They were enjoying it, too. Law school would start in the fall, and they would be going to the schools that they had hoped to attend: Yale for Fabian, and the University of Connecticut School of Law for Claire.

After watching the proceedings of the civil and criminal courts in Hartford for a few days, Fabian mused over lunch, "I wonder which I would rather spend my law career doing: trial-level court appearances, or appellate ones."

Claire looked at him, nonplussed; she wasn't going to court. She would write and research.

I spoke up. "You'll likely be doing a little of both, and by 'a little' I mean just that, due to the amount of necessary and unavoidable preparation involved. But you should know that the trial level is the rock'n'roll while the appellate level is the waltz, because trials deal with fact, which is all hashed out by the time you get to the appeal, and then it's all law, and therefore theory. Here, we are seeing both, but it feels like a waltz. The Justices do that on purpose, though, to make sure that they set a reliable legal precedent for future cases."

Fabian took that in. "So you're saying that most of the time, I won't be in court."

"Nope. I mean, you've got it, you won't be on stage, performing, much."

Our thoughts soon turned back to The Hague. We kept watching the website for the International Criminal Court, so we knew when the Prosecutor had gone to the Pre-Trial Chamber to request permission to investigate the Farmers, and we knew that it had been granted.

Once she was ready to proceed with the case, I intended to go there and watch, but this time by plane. We would book a commercial flight, with Ed, Aaron, and Lionel in tow. They weren't happy about the arrangement (they believed it wasn't secure enough for us), but they went along with it. "We're not going to live in fear," Hamish told them.

Claire heard almost immediately about her deposition: it would be in August, just before law school started. Excellent; she would be done with that before the academic year began, ready to move on and focus on her studies.

The 4th of July celebrations ended up reminding us of the case. We had a family party with Aunt Zoe, Uncle Charlie, Jacques, and Edgar invited, plus Jason and his parents. With Aaron and Ed present, the Lausanne group was almost complete, with the exceptions of Fiona and William. We were the American contingent.

A feast was in order, so I made a blackberry-raspberry-blueberry pie and homemade whipped cream, complete with some of the honey from my hives in the cream. Aunt Zoe made crab cakes and turkey burgers. My mother made all sorts of condiments, side dishes, and a huge salad. Claire made fresh rolls that smelled so good they made us inhale them deeply and count the last couple of hours until it was time to eat them.

Everyone enjoyed the feast, and then we tuned in to PBS's "A Capitol Fourth" to watch fireworks on the National Mall. The usual overhead shots of the national monuments were shown throughout, and Tom Bergeron was the emcee. Pop stars, Broadway performers, and the odd opera-trained singer sang the national anthem, the national hymn, Woody Guthrie's "This Land is Our Land" – and so on.

But when Bergeron launched into his teleprompter-fueled adulation of the greatest nation on Earth, Claire jumped up and started cleaning up the mess, grabbing several now-empty dishes. We had eaten buffet-style in the living room. "Don't do that now," Aunt Zoe protested. "Sit down and enjoy the show!"

"I don't want to listen to this speech," she said, and continued walking into the kitchen.

I grabbed several dishes and followed her. Bergeron was still holding forth, and I thought I knew why Claire didn't want to hear any of this. When I caught up with her, she confirmed my suspicions.

"Unless and until the International Criminal Court successfully prosecutes the Farmers and our nation somehow gets fixed – and it is broken – I don't want to hear such nonsense. My parents and lots of other people are dead because our once-great nation is broken. It just amazes me that anyone can go on TV and speechify like that now. Our financial system is holding us all hostage to covert terrorism, controlling the military, and since no one is awake to that, they're all on that lawn, oohing and aahing over the show!" With that, she rinsed a stack of dishes and loaded them into the dishwasher.

I rinsed mine and said, "I thought that was what you were thinking, so I followed you."

She smiled. "And you don't like leaving a mess for hours."

I grinned. "And I don't like leaving the mess for later, yes. Do you still enjoy the singing?"

"Oh yeah, I still enjoy that part. I'm still an American, and I love our music. I just don't appreciate sycophantic swooning. I can't wait to see this show again a couple of years from now, when this country is repaired…and I hope other countries benefit from the case, too."

Claire's deposition took place in the den, with Fabian present for moral support. The rest of us had waited in the kitchen. The I.C.C. attorneys who came to do the deposition were some of the familiar Dutch, Belgian, and Luxembourger faces from our visit. They brought a white backdrop to unfurl behind Claire for the recording. That would make it impossible to tell where it had been done.

That was it: forty-five minutes of a closed session, and she was done. Claire was pleased.

Autumn came, and law school started for Claire and Fabian.

Fabian drove down to New Haven daily to attend Yale Law School. He was determined to be an international patent and corporate attorney. We were all sure that he would succeed at it. He had just the right personality and brainstem type to make it in that area of legal practice.

Claire was very happy at the University of Connecticut School of Law, and she enjoyed its beautiful old – and new – gothic architecture, its first-rate professors, and its library. She took all of the basic, One-L courses and plotted her thesis paper. She also did some outside reading because she was so eager to learn about everything. When the academic year was up, she entered the write-on competition and made it onto the *Connecticut Journal of International Law*.

Fabian was invited to join the *Yale Journal of International Law* without having to go through that. Yale didn't hold competitions for any but its flagship journal, so that was that. Regardless, just like Claire, he would have to spend his second year doing the grunt-work of bluebooking every citation in every article that it published.

"I remember doing that," I said. I did not add that I was glad that was over for me.

Hamish took care of that. "And you're glad it's behind you, aren't you?" he asked, grinning.

I swatted him playfully. "Don't say that around them!"

Hamish and I took care of the bulk of the next spring planting because our assistants were buried in year-end exams and a write-on competition. I followed Claire's layout plan from the previous year, with one or two variations in planting choices. They could get back to hard labor in the garden when school got out, I told them, smiling.

While we were busy with all of this, the Prosecutor for the International Criminal Court wrapped up her investigation of the case. She had to verify everything that we had handed over, after all. We were surprised that it was finished so soon after that, but it was.

With that, the Prosecutor filed the case with the Court.

Now the problem was to round up the Farmers. They weren't all Americans.

They were from many other developed, wealthy nations also.

It wasn't, therefore, entirely up to the United States to do this.

What if the Farmers managed to hide, escape, or otherwise evade arrest, we wondered?

Claire sat at dinner in June thinking about this. "Where would they hide?"

"Who knows? There's always someplace, somewhere, isn't there?" I thought aloud.

Fabian added, "Maybe a special forces group could kidnap them."

Hamish said, "Blackout is full of special forces. But the U.S. government will be cooperating with the I.C.C. as Blackout makes the arrests. It won't have to kidnap them. It will simply be a shock to those monsters when they get arrested. Those Farmers are going to court."

We looked at him. "What do you know?" I asked.

"I know that we are invited on another corporate retreat, as a thank-you for last year's nanobotic solution to the plastic pollution and radiation contamination. What the Farmers don't know is that that retreat will be their last one."

"Excellent. We shall have ringside seats to their arrest," I said. "Shall we arrange flights to The Hague when we know the date?"

Hamish grinned. "We will have the opportunity to see the arrests in person, but we'll have to go home, book our flights, and then go separately. We'll each be armed with our own nanite guns during the arrest. Just sit quietly and watch, and don't show the weapons. Blackout Security will know exactly who to arrest. They won't touch us."

"Are you sure they won't just come in shooting, complete with night vision goggles on, as when they got bin Laden?" I had to ask.

"Aye, I'm sure," Hamish said. "The Farmers, unlike that guy, have no idea that they're even being hunted. They're just that arrogant."

Claire was listening over her strawberry-orange tart, wide-eyed. "We're going to the trial?"

I smiled. "Yes. We are going to the trial – at least, as much of it as we can attend before it's time to return for the next academic year of law school. I'm going to book our return date tickets for then, regardless of how long that trial takes. Those Farmers have taken enough already without wasting any more time in anyone else's lives. We'll find out what happens, regardless. But," I said, as Fabian and Claire both looked uncertain, "there's always the possibility that the summer may be sufficient to process this case. You may get back to school having seen it all."

My mother and father looked at each other, eyes wide with anticipation.

"We're going too," my mother said.

"Yes – this is history in the making. As a lawyer, I couldn't miss this," Dad agreed.

We looked at Grandmère. "Do you want to come?" I asked her.

She thought for a moment, and then said, "Non. I'll watch it from here and feed the cats."

We checked the dates of the hunting trip invitation: June 15th to June 19th.

"So they'll be gone to The Hague by the 19th," I said, thinking aloud. "Let's book the tickets for the 20th."

"Better make it the 24th," Hamish said. "Too obvious, otherwise."

"You're right," I said. We checked the academic calendars of Yale and UConn law schools next. Late August. We would have to be back by the 24th of that month, then. "So, we'll have two months for our trip to The Hague," I mused.

"Plenty of time," Dad said.

"We'll wait until this week's dinner with Charlie and Zoe," my mother said, "and then we'll ask them to come here and stay with you over the summer, Maman."

Grandmère smiled. "I would prefer that to moving again."

"Jacques and Edgar will have some time to themselves at home, then." My mother smiled.

"Jacques might introduce us to a girl over the summer, who knows?" Grandmère mused.

We all looked at her. "What do you know, Grandmère?" I asked.

"Nothing," she said. "But I have overheard him and Jason talking about meeting someone via an online gaming activity, or whatever they call it. A girl with purple streaks in her long black hair, heavy eye makeup, and…what do you call it? Goth attire?"

Claire laughed. "That sounds more like a girl for Jason. Are you sure it's Jacques?"

"Oh yes. Jason has met a girl with blue hair."

We all laughed.

"Does she recycle and code?" Hamish asked, doubling down while he had the chance.

"Of course," Grandmère said, without missing a beat. "So does Jacques' new girlfriend. Her name is Arachne. I think it means "spider". She's Greek on her mother's side. She's coming to dinner next week, so you'll meet her then." She gave an impish grin as she announced this.

"You don't seem to care about the purple hair," I commented, smiling.

"After all of the death and destruction I've seen, I don't care. I just want to see people be happy and not alone. I'm glad he's found someone, and I hope she's nice. I hope Edgar finds someone too, but that may take longer." Grandmère was a classic elder, wise and accepting.

Chapter 32

A Backfired Hunting Invitation

The Molech Group had invited us to go on a deer hunting trip. That meant Hamish, me, Claire, and Fabian, as our group was now familiar to those Farmers from the retreat in Miami.

The deer hunting trip was to be at an exclusive, privately owned resort in upstate New York, north of Saranac, almost at the Canadian border. The Molech monsters even sent a link to their website, www.TheMolechBullHideout.org, so that we could peruse their gallery of photographs.

It was nice, that was for sure. Even nicer, or so they thought, they offered us a ride to it.

Hamish had politely told them that we would be getting ourselves there. A Blackout helicopter would be taking us there, and it would be marked as if it belonged to us. Blackout was taking care of the details. All I knew was that it was plain black.

As we prepared to leave, we decided not to discuss with the family the facts that Blackout Security was gearing up to make a wave of arrests and transports with us up close and personally witnessing it all. After we saw it all, we would also have to make our own fast getaway.

Only the four of us knew that much. We packed nervously, but with a sense of anticipation.

Meanwhile, we had to meet Jacques' new girlfriend while discretely preventing her from toting an unsecured iPhone or other such surveillance leak into our home. The idea was not to tip her off if she proved to be careless or a spy, nor to offend her or freak her out if she proved merely to be not awake to such threats.

One last family dinner of being close-mouthed about secrets before we could talk freely…

I could hardly wait to be able to stop being careful about what I revealed to my own family.

At least my parents knew what was going on. Grandmère likely knew, but was playing dumb. Either that, or she was playing along with our efforts to keep quiet about this. It was my aunt and uncle and other cousins whom we were leaving in the dark; the fewer people who knew the details about our trip, the better.

For now, we focused on meeting Jacques' new girlfriend, Arachne.

Her name was hilarious, and Claire and I had started laughing quietly to ourselves more than once about it. "What are you thinking about? What's so funny?" she had asked me as I had flipped through a recipe book, planning the dinner party in which we would meet her.

"Arachne's name, unfortunately," I told her. "I'm hoping to finish laughing it up before I meet her, so that I can behave politely by then. She's probably fed up with nonsense over that name, and it is kind of pretty if you can think of spiders as both elegant and powerful."

Claire grinned from ear to ear. "Agreed. I've been doing the same thing – laughing it up and talking myself out of laughing. That elegance and power idea is the best one yet for that."

"Huh. In that case, I'd better focus on it some more." I settled on a vegetable purée soup recipe and moved on to the risotto book, looking for something good in it.

Claire said, "I'll make a cake. It's really nice that Jacques found someone."

I looked up. "Yes, it is. I was beginning to think that neither him nor Edgar would find anyone after this damned Cull. I look at people who have lost family members, like you, and then at people who need to find some for their futures, like my cousins, and feel bad. I'm really glad you and Fabian have each other. And I know you miss your parents terribly, but I'm also really glad we have you, and that we got you away from that danger zone in time."

She suddenly hugged me. "You didn't let me go back there."

"True. And neither did your parents." Claire's mother had sent her the family jewels and photographs, along with a note to stay with us. She had sensed the danger coming.

"Do you happen to know about Arachne's family background?" I asked, pleased that the urge to laugh at the name had not made itself felt this time.

Claire stepped back and considered that. "Um…I know that her mother died in a car crash when she was eleven, and her father raised her with an aunt. I think they're both still alive."

Interesting. "Do they live around here?"

"I think so."

Fabian came into the kitchen just then, toting a stack of books. He kissed Claire, said "Hi" to me, and then told us, "Jacques said that she – Arachne – lives with her family in a house that faces Elizabeth Park. They met in the rose garden there when he and Jason were looking at the recycling operations for the Pond House restaurant."

"What else do you know about her?" Claire asked him.

"I don't know!" Fabian seemed flustered.

"Don't be such a typical guy right now – give us some details!" Claire said, laughing.

He thought about it. "She's Greek on her father's side…"

"What a shock," I said. "Come on, tell us something not obvious."

"Her aunt is a great cook…complains about the lack of availability of certain ingredients now…her dad worked for the town of West Hartford for years, helping maintain and update its infrastructure. That's what he's been working on all during the Cull: upgrading it."

"Now that's interesting," I said, with Claire nodding in agreement. "No doubt that's why they didn't get killed in the Cull."

Fabian did a double-take. "I hadn't thought about that."

"Of course not," I said. "You're busy studying and getting onto a law review. By necessity, your head is in the law clouds, not as focused on your outside surroundings for now."

He smiled. "I should have caught on to that anyway."

So much for being charitable, I thought.

The next evening, when Arachne and Jacques arrived at our house (shortly after Edgar and my aunt and uncle had gotten settled), Hamish did a double-take. "We've met before!" he said. "I vaccinated you and your family, slowly, over a period of months at my office in Avon."

Arachne stepped forward and shook his hand. "Yes! I remember you, Dr. MacDonall. You were the nicest doctor I've ever had for any injection – nice and slow, with as little stress and pain as I've ever felt."

"Thank you!" Hamish said, smiling. "And please, call me Hamish."

I smiled and greeted her. "It's really nice to meet you. I love the purple streaks in your hair. That's something I've always liked but never done…but I've thought about it often," I added.

She looked at me, considering that, and then said, "I actually believe you."

I grinned. "Good, because I may ask you for more details about that at some point."

Playing around with my appearance was something for later, when life was boring, though.

Then Arachne did something that surprised us. She held out her iPhone to Hamish and said, "Here, scan this and tell me what you make of it." She was grinning like a cat with a secret.

Intrigued, he took it and brought out a hand-held nano-detection and scanning device. It was another invention of his, needless to say. After a couple of minutes of study, he looked very impressed. "No surveillance threats! How did you do this?" he asked.

Arachne took her device back. "Thank you! You're the first person to ask how I did it, rather than who I got to do it for me," she said, looking delighted.

"Well, Jacques did say that you know how to code," he said, still waiting for the explanation.

"That's it – I hacked into it with that two-thumb action that my generation gets so much flack for," she said. "It's completely cut off from the Cloud, and I've tapped into a solar energy program to keep its battery constantly charged so that I don't have to send it in to the corporation and expose all my personal data to collection by some nosy entity or other thief."

"Awesome, isn't she?" Jacques said rhetorically, grinning from ear to ear at all of us.

We all nodded and grinned back.

Grandmère smiled and said, "You'll fit in very nicely here."

We adjourned to the living room to chat, and soon were happily discussing police surveillance states, financial terrorism, and other issues about personal security. Arachne and Jacques clearly spent a lot of their time together analyzing these issues, working on their computers and hand-held devices, and were both awake to the risks associated with a life online.

Excellent.

The conversation turned to the problem of the national debt, and how debt slavery was such a problem that college educations had become appallingly difficult to afford for so many.

"The Farmers," and we had told Arachne what that word meant to us all, "want to control who has access to information and opportunities," I said. "The damned Federal Reserve System is what enables it all. It's got to go, but that's easier said than done."

"And our currency is created by them," Claire said, looking fierce.

"Them?" Edgar asked.

"Banksters. They run the Fed. Everything is done behind the curtain by those wizards," she replied. "If we could get rid of the Fed and have our currency be created by the United States government, we could get rid of the national debt."

Fabian added, "That would make it a lot easier to pay for the cost of living, plus access a college education, because the costs wouldn't balloon astronomically to pay for fractional banking and associated Ponzi schemes. Ponzi schemes are alive and well, just not out in the open." He and Claire had been studying hard plus doing some outside reading on finance.

"I wrote my case note on this for the write-on competition," Claire said, grinning.

"You did?" I said, impressed. "Cool!"

"And we have you to thank for a lot of the research material," she added.

I thought about that for a moment. "Oh yeah…I did give you a few books to read that led in that direction."

Edgar asked about the concept of community currency. "Why wouldn't that take care of it?"

"It would not be nationally recognized, so it would only help a few people. Also, it could not cover debts outside of the community, and no community can exist in completely financially isolated circumstances," I replied.

"I see."

That pretty much exhausted that topic.

Dinner and dessert went well. Arachne had brought some Greek baklava that she said she and her aunt had made together, which we all enjoyed with tea and Claire's rose-pistachio cake. "This is delectable," Arachne said, eating the cake. "I've never tasted anything like it."

"Thank you," Claire said. "My mother created that recipe."

It looked as though we were all going to enjoy getting to know Arachne.

Once the door had closed on the guests for the night, however, Claire and I went straight upstairs to pack for our hunting trip.

"What do we pack for a hunting trip when we have no intention of hunting wildlife?" she asked, sounding lost and confused over our task.

I just said, "Nanite guns, for hunting other prey."

She laughed. "Good thing we've practiced using those."

We pulled out the suitcases and tossed in toiletries, nightgowns, pajamas, and a few days' worth of casual outfits, plus a couple of dresses, rolled to avoid wrinkles. To tell the truth, we really didn't care what the Farmers thought of our outfits at this point. All we wanted to do was keep them distracted enough to relax and stay put until the Blackout Security team came to arrest them all and transport them to hell on Earth.

We smelled firewood burning as we got out of the helicopter.

The hunting lodge was beautiful, with individual cabins for every guest or couple of guests. Each one, plus the palatial main house, had an exterior of granite stone with tree-trunk door and window frames. The trunks looked like cherry, which was varnished to a high, glossy shine. The door was also cherry, with carved panels depicting bears, wolves, foxes, rabbits, pheasants, turkeys, and so on. The wrought-iron lock and door handles were huge, but gave way easily in my small hand as I turned the one on the right.

Wood-framed walls and vaulted ceilings greeted us as we entered the main house. The walls were white plaster. The floor was more granite – huge rocks, not smooth slabs, as with kitchen countertops, though I could see some of that by the wet bar. A bartender stood on duty behind it.

The firewood scent was stronger in here, and we all glanced to the right at the enormous fireplace and roaring flames in it, basking in the warmth that emanated from them. So it was a fire, I thought to myself. Despite the huge expense of firewood, they had it, and from the pile next to the fireplace, it was clear that they intended to burn it for the duration of the trip.

It was early spring, still chilly at night, but most of the world got by with solar and wind, or hydroelectricity if near water, or even hydrogen fuel cells. Not wood. No…only the wealthiest could pay those prices, which were deliberately kept high to discourage the use of wood as an energy source. This was conspicuous consumption, no matter how good it smelled.

"I remember that smell from my childhood," Hamish said, inhaling the pine.

"Me too," I said. "Dad used to go out with a chainsaw sometimes with his friends. He liked to cut firewood, and before the basement was finished, he liked to make furniture down there. He made all of our bookcases."

Aaron and Ed glanced at us as I said this. There were some things that they hadn't known, things that a background check wouldn't necessarily reveal.

"My father went with him a few times," Fabian said.

"My father liked to burn firewood when he was baking bread," Claire said. She sniffed the air, then glared momentarily at our hosts, who had just heard us enter the huge hall and were coming toward us. She quickly switched to a smile a moment later, when they saw her.

This promised to be an interesting weekend.

As it turned out, the wood-burning activity we smelled was just for the scent, a bit of gourmet cooking, and a few fireplaces. It was more about ambience than a steady supply of energy for the lodge.

Instead, Carlisle informed us, geothermal energy was the main power source.

Fabian and Claire were fascinated, and Claire immediately started asking questions about it. "How close do you have to be to a volcano to make this work?" was her first one, and it went on from there.

"Not that close, though it does help," our host told her with a smile. "We are building infrastructure for cities and towns using geothermal energy simply by drilling down into the Earth's crust for it, and then proceeding with the underground delivery structure."

He introduced us to his sons, who had studied engineering and business, at M.I.T. and the Wharton School, respectively. Of course they had, I thought to myself with a smile. The sons looked pleasant enough. I guessed that they would be calling for a ride out of here, separately from their father.

On the 20th of June, the I.C.C. finally made its move, but the night before, we didn't know that the wait was almost over, nor how this would all be pulled off. It didn't feel quite real, but we were all on edge, excited yet terrified by it all.

We later found out that Blackout Security had guaranteed the safety of any judge who would issue the arrest warrants for the Farmers. Accordingly, one had. He was a Federal judge at his summer house at Saranac Lake, by the name of Ethan Harlan Baker. He had read the warrants in a state of shock, taken a swig of Scotch, and signed them all, rapidly.

These were sealed warrants which had the added dividend of maintaining the element of surprise. Once signed and issued, all assets of the Farmers were frozen, further impairing their ability to flee, should word leak out that they were being sought by authorities. These assets had been immediately placed by the I.C.C. into the Trust Fund for Victims, to be held there until the conclusion of the trial.

While we waited, all we knew was that the Farmers were to be taken into custody, flown to The Hague, and held there until the trial began, and throughout it. They would not be allowed out on their own recognizance. They didn't deserve any such consideration.

It was early evening, dinner was over, and we were all sitting in the main house, drinking.

The Farmers were drinking hard liquor. We were enjoying fruit purées with a touch of liqueur, vermouth, rum, or whatever took the edge off the wait without actually making us drunk. Thus far, it was working, except for the fact that the waiting and wondering was getting to us. We had managed to maintain our poker faces for days now. The Florida trip had trained us.

Spades was fooling around with his iPhone.

"What're you looking up, Spades?" Enright asked, sipping his vodka on the rocks.

"News," he said, still skimming through the feed with his thumb.

"Anything significant?" Enright asked, eating his olive.

"No…wait! Yes – the U.S. Senate has ratified the Rome Statute. It did that over a year ago."

Enright almost choked. "They what?!"

"The Rome Statute – that document for the establishment and governance of the International Criminal Court, you dope!" Spades seemed totally unconcerned, as if this couldn't possibly affect him.

I watched him, puzzled. He owned Tacttag – how could it not? He was responsible for its actions. Oh well. We would find out about such details later.

Enright had gotten up and was talking to Bosch and Carlisle, who were over by the bar. Hushed tones, conspiratorial whispers, and concerned faces debated this development.

Would the arrests start now? I felt in my pocket for the nanite gun. It was there.

Dinner was announced, so we went to eat, listening to our hosts talk of a mother bear and her cubs that had been stalked and killed that afternoon. They seemed to be studiously avoiding discussion of political developments, but they looked unsettled by them. No one was smiling.

The evening was a tense one for us.

The next day, we watched and listened, hoping that we merely seemed like the newcomers to hunting that we were. A picnic was arranged by the lake, and birdshot rifles were provided. We declined to kill any birds, though, and just watched in distaste.

"None of you seem to like hunting," Enright said to me at one point.

I gave him a humorless smile. "True. We were invited to visit with you, so we came."

"I see." He looked nonplussed. Little did he know that he was our prey, and that, as far as Farmers were concerned, we liked hunting just fine, given the right prey.

"Haven't you had non-hunter guests before who merely came to hang out with you?"

"Oh yes, we have," he replied. "Plenty of them. Don't worry. It's fine." With that, he smiled politely and poured me and Claire some more Sangria.

The afternoon was spent sitting around the hunting lodge, reading, but we couldn't focus.

Dinner was a buffet of all sorts of unfairly killed fowl: duck, pheasant, and so on.

We ate it, but barely tasted it. The waiting was maddening. Our hosts seemed to be waiting for something, making tense, forced conversation with us. The trouble was that, once Hamish had updated them on the progress of his plastic and radiation gathering nanite swarms, we had no further business to discuss.

I had chalked it up, in conversation, to the fact that Aspies don't chat socially by nature. "We can go on and on about whatever we are researching, if you like," I had offered that first evening, with a wry grin.

And so, with a condescending smile, Cantilever and Enright had gotten me going doing just that. But I was nervous, and I ended up describing some of the most fun research projects I had engaged in throughout my life, which meant that many were years in the past. For example, I had talked about a paper on outer space law, which dealt with orbital debris, and space junk that falls back to Earth and triggers international arbitration.

The smiles became less condescending as my audience worked to follow what I was saying.

When I had exhausted that topic, which was suitably fascinating while being removed from our direct experience, I said, "Your turn. Tell me about what you like to read and learn about."

Some awkward smiles were exchanged, and then our hosts had to cast about for answers. It was intriguing to watch them try to come up with an honest answer about anything, and telling a guest what they liked to read seemed like a subject that ought to make no difference to any scheme that they might be cooking up, one way or the other.

They treated me to a short litany of authors' works, which included murder mystery writers, horror, Mark Twain, and even Machiavelli. I grinned when they threw that one in. So did they.

Just as the conversation seemed to be as a stalemate, we heard some aircraft overhead. It was flying low, and there was no mistake about it: it was definitely coming in for a landing. Please be Blackout Security ending this terminal visit, I thought to myself.

It was.

Hamish nodded to me from across the room, smiled, and put his hand in his pocket.

It was the signal we had agreed upon.

His phone had vibrated in a sequence that Blackout had pre-programmed, and his hand had gone to his nanite gun. Claire and Fabian noticed, and their hands went into their pockets. I did the same, moving as if to check my pocket watch.

"What's that?" Bosch asked, putting his martini on the mantelpiece. "We didn't order any transport out of here. We're not supposed to be disturbed all week."

Claire gave her best impression of a diabolical grin. "The special agents of the United States Alphabet Soup are coming to arrest you," she said, pointing her nanite gun at the Farmers.

"What?" Cantilever looked nonplussed.

"Actually, Claire, it's mostly Blackout agents, not the various acronym agencies of the U.S. government, though there may be a few of those as observers," I told her. "The United States let itself devolve into anarchy, above its own laws, so it's not qualified to make these arrests. Blackout Security's people still care about our Constitution, so they're doing this. They want it restored, and this ought to help achieve that."

"Blackout Security?!" Cantilever shouted, outraged. "We have our own security. They can't get in here," he added.

"They're already in here," Hamish said, sipping his whiskey and checking his nanite gun.

Cantilever eyed it skeptically. "We even have some Blackout agents working for us."

"That's what you think," Hamish said with a smile. They were spies. Some bright lights shone outside, and several helicopter rotors could be heard.

Cantilever looked stunned. He looked outside in time to see hundreds of men in black fatigues moving toward every building in the complex. Then he turned to look at us again, and pulled out a gun – the kind that fired flesh-ripping bullets. "I'm not going anywhere," he said.

I answered him with a mirthless grin and fired my nanite gun at him.

He collapsed to the ground, and pissed his pants.

Bosch had tried to shoot Hamish, but Hamish had been quicker on the draw, and now he too was writhing on the floor of the huge hall, right in front of the roaring fireplace that he had been basking in the heat of just moments earlier.

I coolly stepped over to him, flipped him onto his stomach, slapped a pair of handcuffs onto his wrists, and then reversed the nanite feed into my gun. Bosch stopped writhing at once and rolled over to glower at me.

Hamish retracted the nanites that I had put into Cantilever into his own gun.

"Blackout has already had plastic put over the seats on the plane," I announced, still grinning.

Claire appeared next to me. "Good one, Avril." She had shot Bane.

"Thanks. Also, good thing it was you and not me that shot him. I would have tortured him some more. I saw the video in which he said that he chose the targets in the Philadelphia area."

The Farmers were off to judgment at the International Criminal Court. Hurray, I thought to myself. They certainly hadn't shed any tears over anyone else's demise. It would be asinine to cry over that possibility.

Fabian and Claire each managed to fire off a shot each of their nanites into Winkle and Dillion before the Blackout agents burst through the doors and took over. One of the agents told them that they would have to retract the nanites, and that was a mere two minutes after they had gone into their targets. With a slight sigh, Claire did so, and Fabian followed suit with no expression on his face.

They did look grimly satisfied, though.

All in all, it was a successful trip. The hunting invitation had backfired, and it was the Farmers who had become the hunted. That was eminently satisfying.

Blackout Security had a helicopter waiting to take us all home: me, Hamish, Claire, Fabian, Aaron, and Ed. As we boarded and put on our headphones, the pilot said to us, "The U.N. Security Council has timed a declaration that it wants Farmers around the globe prosecuted for war crimes, crimes against humanity, and genocide with these arrests. It is on."

We gave him the thumbs up sign, and he took off.

When we got home, there was a pleasant surprise on television.

"Quick, come hear this!" my mother said, rushing us all to the living room.

The newscaster was delivering a report from the steps of Capitol Hill. "In a stunning but happy development, Congress announced that the 29th Amendment had passed this afternoon as the state of South Carolina became the latest to ratify it. South Carolina is the thirty-eighth state to do so, thus making it law." She looked delighted as she said this, so I went to the kitchen computer and looked her up.

Her name was Elise Cantrell, and she was in her early thirties. She had long, dark brown hair, which she typically wore parted on one side and loose, and sharp green eyes. She always kept a professional smile on her face, and was careful not to have that smile when bearing bad or sad tidings, as many newscasters often forgot to dispense with at such times.

A recent graduate of Georgetown University Law School, and a seasoned journalist, she had traveled around the nation during the time leading up the Cull, and managed to elude capture during it. Since my unsanitized history had been released, she had corroborated everything in it with tales of her own experiences. "I do not know who wrote *Vaccine: The Cull,* but everything in it is true," she had said on *NPR, 60 Minutes,* and any other news show that would hear her. There were many.

But back to the present; Ms. Cantrell was talking about the latest Constitutional Amendment some more. "Lawsuits are currently being prepared by environmental and independent food-growing groups to challenge the land trusts that have forced many Americans to forego growing their own food on their own property."

She paused, then continued, "For the immediate future, this is expected to help homeowners only. Those who rent face a tougher fight, but we can expect renters to bring suit, too, especially as libertarian-minded landowners and anyone else in sympathy with aspiring organic and other small growers choose to assist them by joining in these suits."

There was more.

She added, "In a stunning development, the United States Supreme Court ruled that, in light of this new Amendment, fracking is now illegal. This was a special judgment of the Court, issued at the request of Congress in the wake of the passage of the 29th Amendment. This is a day for the history books."

Our politicians seemed to have lost their fear of the Farmers. Excellent.

Chapter 33

Not One Once-ler Among Them

Once the news report was over, Hamish grabbed our bags and carried them upstairs, insisting that I come with him right away. Curious, I followed him to our room.

Once inside, he turned to me with an evil grin on his face, turned on our laptop, and showed me a live feed of what was going on. He had let loose the nanobotic audio-visual swarm again, and so we tuned in.

The Farmers had been taken aboard a Blackout Security jet, accompanied by Blackout agents and various U.S. alphabet-federal agents. It was headed straight for The Hague, where they would be handed over to the jailors of the International Criminal Court. That probably meant Dutch authorities, since they were on the scene.

Not surprisingly, we had not been invited to go along for the ride. That was fine. But we did so want to hear and see what went on aboard that jet. We couldn't resist the urge to engage in digital voyeurism.

We had to know what the Farmers would say on their ill-fated plane ride.

Oh, we'll put this New World Order underwater, all right! Off to The Hague to let the International Criminal Court (ICC) deal with you Banksters, Hedge Fundsters, and other Farmers, I thought gleefully. I was feeling a bit euphoric now that it was really happening.

I hoped the guards would plie them with drinks of any and all kinds just to fill up their bladders, then strike. Shoot the nanites into them if they give any trouble at all. Threaten to do so, warning them that they'll pee themselves if they get shot. That was just fantasy, though.

We'd soon see if they actually tried anything in those overpriced clothes that they wore. They are, after all, a bunch of soft, spoiled assholes who don't like to exert themselves. Most, if not all, of them have been born with silver spoons in their mouths. "That's an added advantage," I observed to Hamish as we watched.

After about a minute or two of watching, though, it got dull. The captives were pretty quiet, and there were still a few hours left on their flight to The Hague. "Could we watch it from the beginning," I asked, "or would that interfere with the recording process?"

"No, that's no problem," Hamish said, with a click of the mouse. "You're right; the most interesting stuff must have happened a lot earlier in the flight." He found the beginning of the action and let the recording play.

"You know," one agent was telling the Farmers, "you could have just waited for the inevitable evolution – it was imminent – of bacterial resistance to antibiotics. But no…scratch that…you wanted to manipulate the deaths to ensure your own survival. You didn't want random survivals of humans, as in natural selection. You wanted engineered survivals – your own. Well, you got it, at least for now." She concluded on that note with an evil grin.

Bosch glared at her. "You creepy bitch! We had every right to save ourselves. We were doing the world a favor by saving it this way. Why shouldn't we save ourselves after figuring out what had to be done?!"

She shot back at them, "Not by killing other people, you didn't!"

As I listened to the excuses and entitlements of the Farmers, a slow, cold feeling swept through me, like the cold spots of ghosts. It was sickening. They were busy justifying the means by which they had reduced the human population of the Earth, the genocide of the Cull.

It was horrifying to see that they were right, but I'd be damned if I would ever tell them that. Humans are a wonderful, diverse, fascinating lot, and yet…too much of anything was chaos and even hell, cacophony rather than music.

The fact remained: billions were dead – murdered – plus millions more. The pendulum must be swung back for balance to return. It was like the checkbook of karma, and of justice for those who were dead, denied the benefit of an Earth that was no longer pressured by too many of its dominant species.

Once started, the Farmers couldn't seem to stop themselves from talking. Enright, Cantilever, Carlisle, Bosch, Bane, and Uberfein were all talking at once, it seemed. Only Spades was quiet, sober for a change, confused, and in shock.

Some of them had law degrees, I remarked to Hamish, so one would expect them to keep cooler heads than to just admit to everything. Hamish said that the Farmers must sense that all bets were off and all was lost.

"Those people were doomed to a bloodbath, complete with suicides and cannibalism. It would have been a barbaric war, fought on desperate, base instincts. We had to stop it," Bosch was saying. He looked smug and self-righteous, which was quite a feat for someone who was likely doomed never to enjoy its spoils.

"You hastened it. You never gave those 6.8 billion human beings – people – a chance to even know to fight back. You committed genocide via stealth and deception, with ruthless efficiency, all so that you would guarantee that you yourself would be one of those alive afterward to enjoy living on a planet that could provide enough for those who remained."

This was from a Blackout agent with silver hair in a stiff, sleek cut, brushed sharply back. He looked like an anthropomorphized wolf to me, but the effect was somehow reassuring. I reminded myself that these people were ex-military, and ultimately loyal to the terms of the U.S. Constitution as the Founders had intended it to be followed, not the travesty that the Farmers' prostituted, pestituted, and pressituted attorneys, employee-scientists, and lobbyists treated it.

"An open resource war was imminent, right at home. There was no reason to wait." This pronouncement came from Uberfein. Damn – I was glad that Hamish had flown those P53-protein-ripping nanites up his nose the year before last! The fact that he would be punished was much better satisfaction than that had offered. He was the only Farmer we had known the identity of until after the Cull.

"You didn't know that it was so immediately upon us. It could have been farther off, and the people you murdered could have enjoyed a few more good years. You pre-empted that." The woman Bosch had called a bitch said this. She wore her dark hair in a sloppy ponytail, which make her tactical communications gear look like more wisps of hair.

"So what?! It was coming. Many of them had been warned, and advised not to have children, but they selfishly did so anyway, dooming them to a foreshortened, horrific future, whether last year or a few years from now." That was rich coming from Enright, who had been applying for a license to have another baby.

"So what right back. You used your advantages of money and other resources for full control and direction of a covert resource war. You let teenagers and wives get raped in front of their families, babies and elderly people get thrown around, pets have their necks broken in front of children, and simply erased them all from existence. It almost worked, except for the fact that a record exists of that." Another female agent, with straight, blond, chin-length hair that was cut in a sharply ending fringe around her head, and with a fierce, hawk-like glare, said this.

Bane looked alarmed about the record, but said, "Better them than us. And the pets would have starved to death if they had been set free, and disrupted the ecosystem in the wild."

"And what about the migrants from Central and South America and the Middle East?" The silver-haired agent asked. "What about the refugee camp corporations that American money set up – private sector money – to wall up the people who fled conflict in Syria and Iraq and elsewhere in that part of the world? Once in, the idea was to never, ever let them out – to let them all rot out the remainder of their lives in there. What have you to say about that?" I was glad it was being said it, horrible or not, so that it would be on record.

"Damned right they wouldn't be allowed out! Jordan could not afford it, and neither could Turkey, and ultimately neither could Europe! Keep them in there, not using their host nations' jobs up, not putting pressure on the health care and education systems, food supply, and whatever else. Let them in and make them comfortable, and more and more will just come in. Relocating the entire population of a collapsed society puts more pressure on the place that has to absorb them than it can bear." Carlisle had taken this question.

"So what then, you just kill them off?"

"It does save a lot of resources and aggravation," he replied.

"Wow."

"Don't 'wow' us," Carlisle said. "We had to preserve what was left of the ecosystem, not just let huge numbers of our species eat it."

"Bullshit! You have been chopping down the forests as if they are infinite for the past year. You can't plant trees and then expect them to grow fast enough to keep that going. It's over. You would rape the planet of everything that's here just for a bit of temporary wealth," the woman with the ponytail said.

"What're you, the goddamned Lorax?!"

"Yeah, and proud of it. Not one of you is even fit to be called the Once-ler. You're all a bunch of genocidal maniacs, Anti-Christ megalomaniacs, or whatever label history has the pleasure of pinning on you."

"Whatever. You're here too because of that war."

"We're not the ones who perpetrated it. You were going to let several of our relatives die in this Cull. Now you can hang around and eat disappointing food with no view and be bored for your scientifically lengthened lives. Enjoy what you have wrought." The silver-haired wolf looked ready to turn away, but Carlisle wasn't ready to end the conversation just yet.

"There was a saying that it was unknown what World War III would be fought with, but that because of it, World War IV would be fought with sticks and stones. You can thank us for changing that."

"We can credit you with changing that," the wolfish agent said, "but genocidal maniacs should never be thanked. They should be prosecuted, and you will be."

"You've never been to war. I have," Bane said. "You've never seen how desperate a crowd can get. They lose all civility, all humanity, as they claw each other apart just to survive. When I was in Prince Abdul's palace, we ran out of food, they cut off the water lines, and the air conditioning failed. People were talking about eating whoever died first, Islam be damned."

That produced a chorus of "We're all war veterans, you idiots! We're the ones you couldn't buy!" Awesome, I thought, grinning. Too many people in the military were used as tools of the Farmers. The Blackout agents had a few more things to say while they had the chance, it seemed, because they let the conversation continue.

"You call getting kidnapped and held in a war zone 'going to war'?! That's ridiculous." Another agent had spoken up, and he looked suspiciously like Alan Myer Adams, the head of Blackout Security. He was in his sixties, just starting to go un-gray thanks to Hamish's Regenics formula, a tall, powerfully-built guy with thick, spiky hair and steel-gray eyes.

Adams went on, "You weren't strategizing about anything. You were held for ransom and extracted. You should never have visited a sheik in southwestern Saudi Arabia. No wonder those Yemenis attacked that prince's compound." This was an incident that had taken place several years earlier. Bane had regaled everyone he could with tales of holding out against the siege until help arrived when we were in Florida.

"Whatever," Bane said. "We prevented billions of people from acting the way that the people who died of Zyklon B poisoning died, only they would have died a bit more slowly. They would have climbed over each other, crushing one another, breaking each other's bones, cutting off their air supply, raping and killing each other to get at the last scraps of food as they starved through a famine and died anyway."

"So you preempted that struggle, arranging for their deaths on a massive scale."

"Exactly."

"So you admit it: you didn't merely win the resource war against jihadist lunatics who swore to out-reproduce everyone else. You went farther, and decimated other people, including those who were other U.S. citizens. You committed treason, genocide, and crimes against humanity all rolled into one scheme. That is why you are going to The Hague."

Cantilever spoke up next. He sounded like he was reciting an epitaph.

"The Earth is finite, not infinite. That is a cold, miserable fact. Just think of Alan Turing when he and his secret team broke Enigma, the Nazi code machine. They had to pick and choose which messages to act on, and be the monsters who let people on their own side die. All that to win the war and stop it 2 years sooner, which saved 14 million people in the end. Saving anyone means harsh decisions, and being thought of as horrible. It is either that, or be so soft-hearted that you get overwhelmed with hordes of desperate people."

"Well, you've been so effective that you all succeeded, just not brilliantly."

"How so?" Bane asked, momentarily puzzled. "We did succeed. It was brilliant."

"No. Not brilliant – you got caught. Murderers tend to get caught, and you guys did."

He glared.

"Oh, and another thing," Adams said. "Tacttag is not going to be editing autistic people out of existence. There will still be people with Asperger's, people with autism, and parents who gambled at the biological casino of natural reproduction and went away less than delighted with the prizes that they reaped from it. That's what's healthy for the overall human gene pool, and I don't care who doesn't like it. I am a person with Asperger's, and I won't step aside and let anyone edit us out, silence us, or shunt us aside. All you wanted Aspies around for was our inventions and for Regenics. You wanted to use us for those, but then delete us from the species. What would you do when the next problem came along, with no future innovators?"

Bane, Bosch and the others glared at Adams some more.

As for Hamish and me, we sat gaping at the computer screen. Adams was one of us!

This plane ride was suddenly feeling less sickening and more fun. The ice inside my chest was starting to melt a bit. It would likely make itself felt now and then and ever after, but at least I had done something about what caused it.

There was only one thing that spoiled the overall fun: Spades. I suspected that he wished for a drink, but he obviously wouldn't be getting one. Not on this trip. He had said nothing throughout the entire diatribe, but he had listened to it all. As the nanobotic cameras showed his face, his expression got progressively more shocked and appalled. He really looked like someone who had not been in on the planning of the Cull, nor its execution.

I hoped that, if so, he would not share the same fate as the other Farmers.

Farmer he may have been, but that situation could be inherited rather than earned.

How ironic. Inheritance of money and power was not an automatic determinant of evil.

Hamish had another surprise, and another, and another: they were recordings of the plane rides to Hell – er, to the Hague – for Farmers from other nations, and for the military leaders and a few politicians, both sitting and former office holders, who had been arrested.

We watched as generals who had been surprised on vacation or at home were carted and flown away, and realized that these were the faces of the orchestrators of the Cull. They had devised and carried out the logistics of it all. They had had scientists develop bioweapons, and then killed those scientists. They had ordered the deaths of private citizens using those bioweapons – the vaccines with the cancer-inducing nanites – and then whittled the cohort of murderers down to fewer and fewer as the Cull had progressed, until the genocide was done.

Now it was their turn to face the fire, proverbial though we expected it to be.

Revolution was exactly what we got.

Our own government, having rid itself of the Farmers, remade itself even before any trial.

At least a century of regulations tacked on to statutes and codes had weakened our laws.

It was time to throw out the mess and write a newer, simpler set of laws to live by, laws to tax by, laws to bank by, laws to employ by – laws to do whatever by. Less always being more, our Congress and new President of the United States hired a small army of law and science professors to assist them with this process.

Big government was being pared down.

We would continue to have a meritocracy in education and in professional life.

Banking would be boring, with commercial and investment aspects separated by law.

There was talk of a new United Nations treaty to make that permanent and global.

Water access was nationalized in many nations, including the United States.

This was a huge change, because suddenly water use prices dropped, access by private citizens was easier, and bottling companies were unable to sustain their wasteful business model of drawing down aquifers and churning out plastic bottles.

Next, plastic bottles were banned, to be replaced by glass, and damn the marketing studies. The marketing studies proved to be nothing but lies anyway, aimed at perpetuating a system that had enabled corporations to cram more advertising onto their labels. It was back to glass bottles.

All of this was in response to the new constitutional amendment that put the ecosystem first.

Transparency ruled, and everything was shown with the help of not only the media but also legions of non-governmental organizations (NGOs). I was amazed that so many had survived the Cull, until the NGO members themselves began to share their personal stories.

60 Minutes and other news shows were having a wonderful time mining a seemingly endless supply of material as they encouraged everyone to tell their stories.

Hamish and I watched it one evening when Grandmère and my parents were over at Aunt Zoe and Uncle Charlie's house. They had gone there after dinner to play Scrabble and chat. Claire and Fabian were studying in the attic, which they taken over as their library.

"Apparently, we aren't the only ones who were able to evade the machines of the Cull," I said to Hamish as we watched yet another episode of the news show. It was all NGOs, all the time: Human Rights Watch, Rainforest Rescue, Food & Water Watch, the Polaris Institute, and No Peace Without Justice each had someone interviewed.

Hamish told me, "A lot of their members didn't, but the NGO's survived anyway."

I looked at him. "Did Blackout Security help?"

"Aye." He looked pleased with himself.

"Did you have to spend much time arranging it?"

"No. And I wasn't the only one. A lot of us, in what used to be thriving democracies and civil societies, kept in touch through Blackout after we left the military. We knew how to stay off the grid, so we used that advantage to help the groups that would be able to put civil societies back together after the collapse. That way, there could actually be a recovery, as we're seeing now."

Wow. I had always known, thanks to the many hints that my husband dropped, that he was involved with something on a grand and covert scale, and now I had confirmation of its scope and capacity. "Cool. I'm glad you're my husband," I said. "I just had to say that again."

He kissed me, squeezed me up against his side as we sat on the sofa, and we watched the interviews until the show was over. But the fact that the episode was over did not mean that the revolution was over.

There was still the matter of the system on which the banksters and other Farmers had wreaked such havoc. It was an old one, unfortunately, a Ponzi scheme that predated its moniker by several centuries, harking back to the fraudulent money creation by the goldsmiths who had engaged in fractional reserve banking.

All that meant was that they had issued loans based on their reserves of gold – many times over. In other words, they had repeatedly lent out money on paper to different people, all at the same time, betting against the exact same standard, the gold in their vaults. It was the original privately owned and operated casino scheme, and the house always won because people didn't all try to redeem their gold at once. Not only that, most people were kept perpetually in debt, so they didn't have gold to redeem.

This was what happened when the government did not create money.

This was what happened when banks were allowed to do that.

That ought to be stopped, and with the round-up of the Farmers, now was the time to do it.

Incredibly, another Constitutional Amendment was proposed, one that closed the loophole in the original document. The U.S. Constitution had, in Article One, Section Eight, granted to Congress the power to coin money, regulate the value of it, and to levy and collect taxes. It had not, however, granted it the power to create the money itself.

Two U.S. presidents had been assassinated after making moves to address this loophole: Abraham Lincoln and William McKinley. The reasons for their assassinations had been obfuscated and hushed up.

No more. The very next evening, we got another surprise, albeit a most welcome one: a special news hour was devoted to this. All major news networks cancelled their regular programming and instead tuned in to C-SPAN to watch an historic announcement.

Senator Amy LaRosse (the same one who had once been nearly choked to death on the Senate floor over the Nae-Née population policy during debates over it), a Democrat, along with U.S. Representative Jeffrey Coxey Jacobs, another Democrat, teamed up to propose the next Amendment to the Constitution. She was from Louisiana, now largely underwater. He was from Pennsylvania, still mostly above sea level.

"This time," Jacobs stated, "we will not have another Glass-Steagall Act that addresses the damage done by the merging of commercial and investment banking, requiring those two functions to divorce, only to have it all come to nothing decades later when they are allowed to remarry. That is what the Gramm-Leach-Bliley Act did. This Amendment, if passed, will embed into our Constitution the right of our government to create money."

Senator LaRosse spoke next. "This, if passed, will be the thirtieth Amendment to the U.S. Constitution." With that, she introduced it, reading off the text as a pre-released, virtual copy was shown on the television screen next to her.

Amendment XXX [2018]

The power to create the official national money supply in all its forms shall be reserved to the Congress of the United States.

We stared at the screen, nonplussed, expecting more, but that was it.

I thought about that for a moment. There were many Amendments to the U.S. Constitution that did not have sections, but operated on succinct sentences. Clearly, this was what was needed in this instance.

Even more startling than the terseness of the proposed Amendment was the speed with which it made the rounds to the nation's legislatures. State after state, fed up with the antics and machinations of the Federal Reserve Board – an entity that was only federal in name, as a slap-in-our-faces fraud that had lasted for over one hundred years – voted to ratify it.

It was law within two months (we spent the summer focused on other things, of course).

As we saw the text of the Amendment on our television screens for the next several weeks, Hamish and the others caught me laughing quietly to myself several times.

"What's so funny?" Fabian finally asked.

"It's the choice of words in the Amendment," I told him. "Take THAT, Federal Reserve Board! Now our money will actually be federal, unlike when the banksters conjured it into existence and manipulated it."

"Huh." Fabian took this in.

Claire said, "Hopefully, it will all be properly backed up by something tangible this time."

"Indeed," I said. "Silver might work. *The Wonderful Wizard of Oz* was given its name for ounces of silver – the abbreviated form of the word 'ounces' – 'oz.'."

Hamish looked up from his laptop, startled. "Really?"

"Yes. Our national fairy tale was a metaphor for banksters. Follow the Yellow Brick Road of gold to the greenback city and unseat the Wicked Farmers of the East and the West. They represented banksters, corporatists, and their political minions, all rolled into two evil sisters."

"Wow. I'll have to read that again," he said.

And so he did, starting that evening. He didn't read fiction often, unless I was writing it, because he knew that I liked to work political, social, economic, and ecological issues into it. Let's face it, people felt like it was work to read nonfiction, so when I researched and wrote my own books, I packaged it, much as L. Frank Baum had done, in fiction.

That was the only reason why Hamish would read fiction – if it taught him about reality.

Well, good for him, but I needed to relax, so I read some fiction that, as far as I was aware, was just that. We sat up in bed for a few hours, reading happily.

The day after ratification of the Thirtieth Amendment, the news was full of excitement.

The United States Treasury had called in its bonds and all other securities, paying them all off in book-entry form, i.e. with the click of a mouse on its very own Dark Net computer. In other words, it had issued fiat money, bought its debt back from the banksters, both domestic and foreign, and voided them out. Good riddance!

Now there was talk of repealing the Sixteenth Amendment, the one that had instituted the federal income tax. With the creation of currency now in the power of the federal government, an income tax would not be necessary. That would mean another Amendment...

Meanwhile, the dream team of LaRosse-Jacobs introduced a bill for the stock market. It was called the LaRosse-Jacobs Bill, and it aimed to impose a tax of 0.04 percent on each and every derivatives trade, plus a general tax of 0.01 percent on all others. The reason behind this proposal was to bring them all out from behind the metaphoric curtain that the wizards of Wall Street had been operating behind.

Transparency won the argument. The LaRosse-Jacobs Act was passed in just four hours.

We were rapidly busy with packing and leaving on our next trip. Travel arrangements were made, plane tickets bought, and hotel rooms booked. We were in a hurry, too. Grandmère would stay home, but the rest of us – myself, Hamish, my parents, Claire, and Fabian – were going on a trip almost immediately, escorted, as usual, by Aaron and Ed.

We would miss the confirmation hearings for the Farmers and other defendants, but we would be in The Hague in time for the trial of the millennium.

Chapter 34

Putting the New World Order Underwater

What one noticed first about the International Criminal Court was the whiteness.

Everything about it was blindingly, stunningly…white.

It was a modern building, designed with clean, plain, simple lines inside and out.

Of course it was. It had been designed by a Scandinavian firm called Schmidt Hammer Lassen Architects. They usually favored such designs. It was beautiful, just not the sort of beauty that I would settle into easily. It felt cold. Of course, that was what made it ideal for criminal proceedings.

Inside the courtroom was a white wall, in front of which sat the Judges, who had a long, plain, white bench in front of them. The carpet gave a vague sense of relief from the whiteness by being off-white, but the walls were white, as were the gallery areas, high up on either side of the courtroom, and the tables and seats for the Prosecutor, defendants, and their attorneys.

The only relief to be had from the whiteness came from the windows behind that white wall, which was set just inside the room. The windows were part of the exterior of the building, which was a solar energy absorption system. Outside of those windows, all was green – leaves, grass, and gardens. We could even see a bit of blue sky above. In winter, it must have been stark.

We watched it all from the viewing gallery above. There was one on each side.

Each of the participants in the trial had a computer monitor in front of them. These were used for translations, video clips, document viewing, and so on. The point was to make sure that everyone involved understood every aspect of what was happening…and happening to them, in the cases of the defendants.

The whiteness was unsettling to those of us who didn't like modern art and architecture, with its sparseness and lack of decoration or other distraction to focus on during the proceedings. That sparseness must have been far more unsettling to those who were on trial, a stark reminder of the surroundings they could expect to dwell in if, as everyone expected, they were convicted of the crimes that they were being tried for.

We had just gotten settled into the viewing gallery when we heard a familiar pair of voices.

"Hallo, Hamish! Hallo, Avril!" they said, sounding fit to burst into laughter.

We turned around, stunned. "Fiona! William!"

"Surprise!" she said, grinning from ear to ear.

We all hugged and kissed each other, and then Fiona said, "We came to testify."

"Testify?" Hamish asked, sounding confused.

"Aye," William said. "We saw some people being rounded up and roughly herded onto trucks in the days before you picked us up. If they want our testimony, they can have it."

"Oh, aye…so you're on the list to tell the court about that?"" Hamish asked, taken aback. We had known that they had seen something, but had had no idea that they would come to the trial or ever share what they had seen. We weren't even sure how conclusive whatever they had seen was, but apparently it was damning enough.

I guess I had just gotten too used to our nanobot swarms and their recordings. Those were golden as far as evidence went. Nothing could tell more, nor do it quite so definitively. And yet…a human being recounting a tale was another kind of evidence. Emotional testimony was very powerful, too.

That was why Claire's deposition had been taken: to be shown at this trial.

"We didn't want to worry you," Fiona said. "We knew that Claire's testimony would be included," and here she gave Claire a squeeze, "so we wanted to come anyway. Then we realized that we ought to share what we saw with the court, even though we didn't see any injections or murders or cremations. Rounding private citizens up, household by household, ought to count."

"Yes, it certainly ought to," I said. "It's right out of the Nazi playbook. Definitely tell."

We sat back and watched the defendants being led in. It took a while.

There were an awful lot of them, and not just from the United States. There were British and Dutch banksters and hedge fundsters, and more from Luxembourg, Russian business tycoons and other plutocrats, Chinese oligarchs, Japanese corporatists, a few Arab oil magnates and agribusiness leaders who grew food in Africa for citizens of Arab nations while Africans starved, Brazilian mining corporatists who drove and starved uncontacted tribespeople out of their homelands, and so on and on.

In all, there were over four hundred Farmers standing…well, sitting, trial. Actually, the Farmers were roughly half of the group of defendants. Generals and politicians rounded it out.

I glanced across the room at the people in the other viewing gallery and stared. Jacob Uberfein was up there, as was his mother. I started looking around and realized that the other people on either side of the courtroom, looking down on the proceedings from the opposite gallery, were relatives of the defendants. The witnesses were sitting on our side.

The charges were read out, followed by a list of definitions of war crimes, genocide, and crimes against humanity. This was all familiar to me, and to Dad, Claire, and Fabian, but it was important that everyone present, especially the accused, understand it all fully.

That done, what would likely prove to be the trial of the millennium commenced.

It would be conducted in English. The Court had two working languages, English and French, but the majority of the defendants spoke English as their first language, hence the decision to operate in that one.

I looked at the judges. From reading the Rome Statute, I had expected to see three judges, but there were five of them, and they were from nations around the world, all celebrities in their fields. These judges were from Chile, Canada, India,

Belgium, and Ghana. There were three women and two men; the men were from Canada and India. They each wore sapphire-blue robes.

As I looked at them, getting used to their faces and memorizing their names, demeanors, and whatever else I could discern, I did a double-take: the judge from Belgium was almost a caricature. She had been in her twenties during the nineteen-eighties, I had read online, and while attending law school and into her early legal career, she had been the lead singer in a band. She had stopped singing shortly after her thirty-first birthday, but retained the hairstyle of her youth, which was still naturally blonde. Her hair resembled that of Madonna's in that same decade, parted on the side, wavy-to-curly, and as I too had been a teenager then, I liked it. Of course, I also liked quirks, and this judge exhibited some. Her name was Judge Amélie Van den Herne.

The other judges were named Judge Justin Bellemare (Canada), Judge Rosa Consuela Belmar (Chile), Judge Narayan Ramana (India), and Judge Thema Asamoah (Ghana).

A Deputy Prosecutor by the name of Annalise Chloé Valois, from France, was present.

Prosecutor Aminata Diouf began.

"May it please the Court. We have video of people being thrown into volcanoes and highly acidic, boiling volcanic water," the Prosecutor informed the Court. "Hopefully – and this is appalling to have to say – they were thrown in there after they were dead. From what we understand of the method of killing them, it is possible that some might not yet have been dead when they were incinerated."

"People were incinerated in crematoria which included natural volcanic spots around the planet, plus mobile ones in the forms of ships and trailers. Either way, the purpose was to obscure evidence, and were it not for nanobotic videographers, we would have no record of this – no proof with which to vindicate the victims. Even their extended families were eradicated."

"As if that weren't enough – as if it weren't enough to ensure that no one would come around looking for their missing relatives – their murderers were promptly murdered as well. This plan was all about ensuring that no witnesses remained to report the crimes, nor to be questioned."

"Why did they do all this? What was their motive?" The Prosecutor was taking her time laying out the case, but she was doing it carefully and precisely.

We all listened, with rapt attention, as the charges were laid out.

"It was a covert resource war. Despite meetings with their nations' leaders aimed at strengthening the finances of their respective countries, the defendants – bankers, hedge fund managers, and corporate leaders – were actually traitors to their people. They served only themselves. They sought only to enrich themselves, exactly as the pirates of the seventeenth and eighteenth centuries did. These financial pirates have no loyalty to anyone but themselves."

"That was really what their crimes were expected to accomplish: to monopolize the Earth's natural resources by maintaining an exclusive playing field with little or no competition, eliminating it by any means possible."

"To eliminate it, and to reset a maxed out financial credit bubble worldwide, they committed genocide, crimes against humanity, war crimes, and crimes of aggression. When their covert financial schemes of creating fiat money – which is really just imaginary, fictitious, conjured money – proved insufficient, these wizards of Wall Street and elsewhere around the globe moved on to overt plans."

"Committing financial terrorism, they first swindled people into debt slavery via home loans, credit cards, farm loans, student loans, automotive loans, and any other sort of loan that could be created. These debt traps were inescapable in a crashed economy, which these wizards had crashed themselves. They caused defaults, bankruptcies, foreclosures, and homelessness."

"They destroyed pension funds and other safety nets and then dipped into private citizens' savings and checking accounts to cover up the shortfall. With people's safety nets wiped out, the defendants saw that there was nothing left to take. Now they had masses of people who were desperate with no way to sustain themselves in a world of shrinking resources, dwindling space, and no hope. They suddenly feared the masses, who, if history was any teacher to them, had suddenly become dangerous."

"What to do then, after all that damage was done? People in every nation were without a future, and there were too many for the Earth to reasonably take care of. Even those who would not have children and thus not have the expense of raising them faced a future in which earning their way to a comfortable, happy existence of independence, self-respect, and good health was an impossibility."

"Well, the defendants decided, the solution was simple: reduce their numbers. Trick them into thinking that their governments had their best interests in mind. Lie to them; tell them that they needed protection against an imaginary super-virus, super-bacteria, or other plague. Why wouldn't the public believe them? After all, antibiotics had been overused and were losing their effectiveness. A bogus vaccine was created, one which actually made people sick, by infecting them with multiple viruses, by crashing their immune systems, and via a nanite which broke the cancer tumor suppressor proteins in their DNA."

"Next, the plan called for duping the United Nations into doing their bidding. The U.N. was only too happy to help, operating under the erroneous impression that it was saving people from terrible illnesses. All the while, the personal data of each individual was recorded, monitored, and manipulated. The most important strategy in this resource war was to wage it in such a way as to give their opponents no idea that it was a war until they were about to die. By then, it was far too late to fight back. It was the perfect surveillance plot, one worthy of George Orwell combined with Niccolò Machiavelli."

"Wars have always been about money and resources. We have just endured a resource war on a scale never seen before in all of human history, covert though it was. I shall prove it to the Court with a massive collection of evidence that was gathered from computers around the globe, and via nanobotic swarms of audio and visual recorders."

With that, the Prosecutor proceeded to show the Court and the viewers in the gallery the evidence that we had presented to her. It took several weeks, and it was difficult to watch. I often stared at the floor, or watched the faces of the people assembled in the courtroom below, as did Claire and the others.

The defendants still looked amazed that all of it had been acquired and turned over.

They had obviously and arrogantly never, ever expected to be caught in their crimes.

The Judges looked astonished, both when it all got underway, and throughout the trial.

They clearly believed and understood what they were seeing and hearing, but were shocked and amazed beyond expectation that it was actually real. One really and truly couldn't blame them. It was so unprecedented, after all. The Farmers had outdone Hitler, Genghis Khan, Winston Churchill, Pizarro, Ivan the Terrible, Uday Hussein, or any other of history's monsters.

One face among the defendants looked different: that of Jackson Lionel Spades. He looked sickened, shocked, appalled, mortified, offended…and he physically recoiled from his co-defendants. Once, he even threw up in the garbage can next to the table where he sat.

I could see that the Judges and Prosecutor were watching him, assessing him.

This court operated according to civil law, not common law, so it had no jury.

It was all up to the Judges to decide the fate of each and every defendant.

I realized that Spades' future depended on whether or not these jurists understood what sort of person he was – that he had not wanted any of this, known or understood what was happening, nor given his consent to the plan.

He did get his chance to make a statement to that effect, and was teary and horrified.

I believed him, and I think they did also.

Claire said that she did.

It probably helped that, among the video evidence shown, was included the Molech Group meeting that Hamish had attended. The Judges and everyone else observed what the other Farmers had said about Spades not knowing the truth as he drunk himself to sleep and nodded off, never aware that a real victim was being burned to death in that bronze bull.

When Spades watched that video, he actually started to sob quietly.

Watching the others, however, was another story.

They looked outraged that we were able to watch them, as if we had watched them on the toilet or something. They acted like we had all invaded their privacy. Well, too damned bad! Privacy was for people who weren't committing murder.

Privacy was not for treasonous monsters.

The Judges faces looked nauseated as they studied the countenances before them.

I looked around at my family to see how they were reacting.

My mother broke her gaze from a hospital scene to look at the defendants, and then saw me looking at her. She raised her eyebrows briefly as she made eye contact with me, shook her head in the direction of the defendants, and continued watching.

Fabian glanced at me, looking grave, and his eyes returned to the courtroom scene.

Dad shared a deadpan but also hardened look with me as we looked up at each other for a moment, then went back to watching.

Hamish and I kept sharing glances of, well, a sense of closure. It felt like a satisfying conclusion to be able to share with the International Criminal Court the evidence that we had gathered for so long. It felt like we had taken the right action with it after sitting on it, watching for the correct moment to hand it over, and for the right venue. We had found it.

Claire looked like she was eating it all up voraciously. I knew that she was finding closure in her own way, a kind of closure that so many family members of so many billions of genocide victims were to be denied due to having been culled themselves, or that they would get as soon as they got the news of what was transpiring here.

The world would get this news shortly, but we were getting it live and in person.

Claire's face, despite the fact that an Aspie's emotions showed mostly through her eyes, revealed much. She was finding some significant sense of healing and closure from all this. She was lapping it up with fascination and pleasure.

She later told me that she felt better about her parents' murders because of this trial.

And why not? Something definitive, something that history would record, was being done.

Witnesses' statements were played, including survivors like Claire who had lost their families, and Blackout Security agents who had infiltrated the hedge funds of the Cayman Islands. Those were held by American, British, Dutch, and other Farmers. It was pretty funny when that testimony was given to see the outrage on the defendants' faces as all of their secret dealings were revealed.

We saw the plans of the Tacttag, the DNA editing company, to eradicate Asperger's, other forms of autism, and physical genetic abnormalities. The Prosecutor was particular concerned with the effort to tamper with human DNA to such an extent as to preempt people with Asperger's from even existing. Spades again looked stunned, and gave Bosch a long, steady glare. Bosch glared back, actually rolled his eyes, and looked away.

"This is a prima facie example of an effort to eradicate members of a group," Prosecutor Diouf said. "Throughout history, people with Asperger's have shown themselves to be independent and highly intelligent, innovative and inventive, and therein lay the threat to the defendants' ability to continue their criminal pattern. This was their motive for eliminating people on the autism spectrum: to ensure that they would have far less chance of being spotted. Well…you have been spotted nonetheless, by people both on and off of the spectrum."

Hamish was called to testify as an expert witness, to explain how the vaccine had worked.

"The vaccine relied partly on the nanites in the serum, which consisted of groups of 10 microscopic robots. These nanobots, as they are called, sought out the human cancer tumor suppressor protein known as PK53, and broke them on the DNA and RNA chains as they encountered them."

Hamish paused for a moment to let that sink in with the Court.

The Judges looked rapt and appalled, but said nothing.

Hamish continued, "The rest of the strategy was to crash the human immune system by hitting it with too many vaccines at once – forty, to be specific. The human immune system, when properly vaccinated, receives only one every few weeks. Even a triple vaccine causes more harm than good, delivering a shock to the system instead of a benefit. What this vaccine did was medically reprehensible, not merely unethical."

Prosecutor Diouf asked him, "Was there anything else we should know about that serum?"

"Yes," Hamish said, not sparing a glance for the defendants. Likely, he didn't want to get distracted from his points by making eye contact with them. "The serum was developed using monkey viruses, which were guaranteed to cause cancer within a very short time in any other humanoid species. Normally, it takes about eight days for this zoonotic effect to occur, but this serum accelerated the process to anywhere from a day or two to mere hours, depending on the medical background of the person injected with it."

Without asking Hamish to leave the witness stand, Ms. Diouf proceeded to show the forensic evidence that Blackout Security had amassed from farmlands around the world. It was bone dust and bone fragments, all human. The victims of the Cull were fertilizing the food supply.

She asked Hamish to explain the evidence to the Court.

He did so, mentioning the fact that crematoria never completely burn every trace away.

"There are always some bone fragments left, even hours later," he told the Court.

"Thank you, Dr. MacDonall. No further questions." Even Ms. Diouf looked stunned.

The defense attorney for Dillion and the other Tacttag defendants had no questions.

Hamish stepped off the witness stand and at last made eye contact with the defendants.

They looked livid. He had betrayed them. Hamish looked calm and relieved.

It was really the video footage from the secret Molech Group meeting that Hamish had attended in Florida that did the most damage, because it definitively proved intent to commit the crimes that the Farmers were accused of. All of the documents that Jason had mined the Dark Net for had backed that up, but being able to hear them say it – saying that they had done what they were accused of and done it deliberately – sealed their fate.

I had to keep a straight face, or it might have seemed as if I were laughing at the crime. What was so amusing was the fact that those Farmers had actually thought that they were welcoming another monster into their midst, when in fact he had been spying on them.

The Prosecutor was very fair in the presentation in that she showed the entire video, complete with Spades drunk and unaware that someone was actually burning to death inside that bronze bull, and that the other Farmers were not telling him about that, nor about the crimes being committed. Clearly, Spades' fate would not be the same as the others.

Hamish rejoined me in the viewing gallery, and I was quite frankly relieved to have him back up there with me. I had half-expected someone to try to shoot him while he was on the witness stand. (Hamish later informed me that Blackout Security was all over the place throughout the trial to ensure that no such thing happened.)

When it came time to sum up the assessment of the collective and individual guilt of the Farmers – and their joint and several liability, as we in the legal profession call it – plus that of the military leaders who had arranged for the commission of the crimes of the Cull, the Prosecutor reviewed the legal standards at bar:

"The military leaders who arranged for mobile combat-ready units to travel the globe, with crematoria that operated both on land with tractor-trailer trucks and on the seas with converted cruise ships, bear direct responsibility for what was done. It has been shown that they not only should have known what was being done and how it was being done, but that they did know."

She continued, "As for the civilian defendants, who are bankers, hedge fund managers, and corporate owners and directors, a higher standard of guilt must be demonstrated. That has been done. The civilian defendants have been shown to have had an actual, constructive knowledge of the crimes committed. They planned the crimes, in great detail, with the express purpose of reducing the overall human population using a toxic serum disguised as a vaccine, complete with a nanite that would ensure the demise of anyone injected with it."

"One defendant among them stands out as not having known what was happening, though he should have checked and found out: Lionel Spades. As the C.E.O. and owner of Tacttag, he should have discovered what his company was doing. Fortunately, it is not too late to stop it, but that is not because of any effort he made."

"This brings up another point: the element of intoxication in the commission of a crime. It is one thing to know that one is about to commit a war crime, to participate in genocide, and to make oneself drunk just before carrying out the crime in order to numb oneself to the horror of the act. When that is done, it is done knowingly, as a shield to the emotional impact of the deed. This is no excuse, and it is what many of the military leaders around the world did."

"However, when one is an alcoholic, addicted to intoxicating liquors, and lives in a state of constant inebriation, it is different. An individual who is intoxicated habitually, someone whose mental capacity is impaired not because he or she seeks to distract him or herself from awareness of an illegal act, someone who is simply never aware of everything that is taking place around him or herself, does not have the mens rea – the guilty mind – that must be shown for this court to convict." She was indirectly advising the Judges not to punish Spades too severely.

The Prosecutor reviewed the Rome Statute for the record. It was quite the litany:

"The defendants have in fact committed genocide, war crimes, crimes against humanity, and crimes of aggression, as defined by the treaty that governs this Court. Rapes, murders, the targeting of specific groups, the confiscation and destruction of property, extermination, forcible transfers of populations, causing serious bodily or mental harm to members of the group, deliberately inflicting on the group conditions of life calculated to bring about its physical destruction in whole or in part, imprisonment or other severe deprivation of physical liberty in violation of fundamental rules of international law, torture, including biological experiments, enforced disappearance of persons, other inhumane acts of a similar character intentionally causing great suffering, or serious injury to body or to mental or physical health, making improper use of a flag of truce, of the flag or of the military insignia and uniform of the enemy or of the United Nations, as well as of the distinctive emblems of the Geneva Conventions, resulting in death or serious personal injury, the transfer, directly or indirectly, by the Occupying Power of parts of its own civilian population into the territory it occupies, or the deportation or transfer of all or parts of the population of the occupied territory within or outside this territory, subjecting persons who are in the power of an adverse party to physical mutilation or to medical or scientific experiments of any kind which are neither justified by the medical, dental or hospital treatment of the person concerned nor carried out in his or her interest, and which cause death to or seriously endanger the health of such person or persons, pillaging a town or place, even when taken by assault, employing poison or poisoned weapons, employing asphyxiating, poisonous or other gases, and all analogous liquids, materials or devices, committing outrages upon personal dignity, in particular humiliating and degrading treatment, utilizing the presence of a civilian or other protected person to render certain points, areas or military forces immune from military operations; intentionally using starvation of civilians as a method of warfare by depriving them of objects indispensable to their survival, including willfully impeding relief supplies as provided for under the Geneva Conventions."

The Prosecutor asked the Judges to convict the Farmers and generals, and sat down.

The Farmers were defiant. One of their defense attorneys allowed Bosch to make a statement.

Bosch said, "The vaccine policy and what was in that serum solved a problem that had been plaguing humankind since the Industrial Revolution: technological advances were using up the Earth's resources, enabling a quarter of our species to live in comfort and cleanliness while the rest lived in squalor without enough to eat, drink, or wear or live in."

One of the Judges, Ramana, observed that if a paleoforensicist ever studied our planet eons from now, no natural explanation for the sudden, dramatic drop in the human population would be found. Only an artificial reduction in our numbers could account for what had happened. Therefore, even to someone in the far distant future, whether from our own planet or another, it would be obvious that a crime on a massive scale had been committed.

The Judges all looked revolted. Judge Van den Herne said, "It really is time for another revolution – one that stops you all from putting any more of your genocidal plans into action, or benefitting from them." They retired to their chambers to consider their ruling.

Claire's worries that the trial would extend past the time when we would have to return home in time for the fall semester proved unfounded in the end. The trial wrapped up in mid-August, and sentencing came eight days later: verdict on a Friday, sentence the next Tuesday. It was a relief there would be closure here, and that we would not have to wait and see the result later.

The Judges had a lot of charges to adjudicate when they called the Court to order.

They also had a series of recommendations for the United Nations to manage.

The Secretary-General of the U.N. was there to receive them.

Democracy would be restored, with the Nae-Née policy kept. The purpose behind that was to prevent humanity's numbers from increasing right back up to their previously unsustainable numbers. But…no more New World Order. Martial law was to be over – everywhere.

Tax codes must be thrown out and rewritten, with a law passed that acknowledged how they could be abused. "Tax codes are made obsolete once replete with regulations, addenda, and whatever other complexities grant banksters and other thieves a plethora of loopholes."

In addition, the Court aimed to put a stop to lobbyists and corporate control of politicians. "Money must not grant one a greater voice in the political process," the Belgian judge said.

The International Monetary Fund and the World Trade Organization, which gave the banksters global reach, were to be disbanded. Think tanks would take their place, without the ability to influence or pressure any nation from pursuing ecologically responsible policies.

The United Nations Environmental Programme should be relocated from Nairobi, Kenya to Montreal, Canada, a place where it will not be ignored, where it would not be sidelined, and where it would be effective. That was why it had been located in Kenya. No more!

International trade should be conducted via Bitcoin. A global currency could also be created for people who were not online, but its value would be regulated via the decentralized, egalitarian system of the Bitcoin computer experts.

Police would continue to have all of their interactions recorded, and each candidate for a police force must go through rigorous psychological screening to keep those with bullying tendencies and poor judgment out. The police would not have extra toys to play with – just one pistol, a night-stick, and a taser.

Citizens might be armed if they so choose, but their weapons shall be locked up outside their homes, just as the Swiss kept theirs. These weapons must be kept a short distance away, under combination lock or other lock and key. Background checks must be completed before any gun purchase. Guns collections shall be forbidden. Each gun owner must complete a psychological screening as well. No loopholes!

This was a separate document, announced in the Judgment of the Court, but not fully read in the sentencing because of the level of detail it included. What we heard at sentencing was a bit more to the point about the fate of the Farmers.

Judge Bellemare opened his remarks with this statement: "What motivates criminal behavior, aside from intent? It would be a sense of entitlement combined with a dose of self-pity – an often lethal combination, when acted upon."

He went on, "We are, none of us, more entitled than another. We have been an arrogant, selfish, and thoughtless species for so long that we have nearly killed the planet's ecosystems, even though they did not evolve solely for the use of humans. That attitude must change."

"You have been called 'Farmers' in an anonymous history on the Internet. This case has borne out that version of history as the truth. History books will have to be rewritten to reflect this." Judge Bellemare paused for a moment.

Then he went on: "You are what that moniker brands you as: Farmers who view the rest of the world, both human and other species alike and all of the planet's resources, as a crop for you and you alone to manipulate and profit from. You imagined yourselves to be exempt from all morality, ethics, or duty to share with others. This Court is here to tell you that you are not."

"You expected to get away with eliminating those whom you deemed 'excess' humans in order to continue to enjoy as many resources as you could grab, and then some. There is no right to do this. You declared that there was no human right to food, water, or clean air – nor to privacy when that got in the way of your quest for total control of resources."

"You couched your view that there was no such right to the basic needs of life in legalese, claiming that corporations were people. There is no such right. A corporation is a legal fiction designed to enable a business to function, not a license to steal from everyone else."

"You preempted the human right to fight for one's own existence by stealthily killing off people whom you deemed mere excess, and thus you played God."

"The first part of the sentence that this Court pronounces upon you will be to take that which you have demonstrated to hold most precious of all: your financial assets. These will be confiscated and distributed among the survivors of the genocide you perpetrated. They have been identified, and some of them have traveled to The Hague to testify during this trial."

The Farmers looked as though nothing worse could ever happen to them when they heard this. So did their families; many of them would never inherit the billions of currency units that they had grown up expecting would eventually be theirs. Whatever wealth those relatives already held in their own name was all that they would ever get.

There was more, of course; the Farmers and generals could not expect to go free.

"This court sentences you to life in prison, to be served in the Faroe Islands."

We sat in the viewing gallery, stunned for a moment.

The Faroe Islands were a Danish territory in the still-frigid waters north of Scotland and east southeast of Iceland, just a few latitudinal degrees south of the Arctic Circle. Not much went on there. The population was sparse, rural, and pastoral. The Farmers would have no Internet to relieve their boredom, and their food would likely be bland. Escape would be difficult.

Of course, with today's travel technologies, even Napoleon's St. Helena prison would be reachable and escapable, but this sounded like a viable penal plan for the Farmers. All things considered, it would have to do.

The Judge wasn't quite finished. He had some special words for Spades.

"Mr. Spades, you are a different kind of Farmer. You were not aware of things that you should have been aware of. You had a duty to make yourself aware of what was going on around you. Instead, you chose to drown yourself in alcohol."

Spades looked confused and apprehensive as he listened to this pronouncement. I suspected he agreed with that assessment but wondered where the judge was going with this.

The judge continued, "However, this Court finds that when you did find out the truth – at this trial and no sooner – your sense of morality was intact. You were appalled beyond your capacity to accept what you found out. For that, your sentence will differ from the other Farmers."

We all waited to see what this would mean.

After a minor pause for dramatic effect, the judge went on, "You, Lionel Jackson Spades, are hereby sentenced to two years in prison, to be served in The Hague, after which you may go free. You must give up twenty percent of your assets to fund educational programs that benefit people on the autism spectrum. You must also make a showing, by quarterly reports, that you are staying sober, and your corporation must not conduct unethical genetic engineering. This means not editing embryos, sperm, or ova against the autism spectrum."

Spades looked like someone who had been given a new lease on life. He would be going back to his wife, and back to his life. The catch for him would likely be to stay sober. The rest he seemed to look forward to. He actually seemed pleased.

Not all Farmers were evil. Some were simply born into being Farmers, I mused.

I looked at Claire. She turned to look at me, and she looked both shocked and pleased.

Notably, the judge had not made any directives against genetic editing altogether. The fact remained that genetic editing was one of the few weapons that scientists had against bacterial resistance to antibiotics, which were failing after several decades of overuse. Judges had to be careful not to overreach with their authority. They knew law, but they were not science experts.

We turned back to the courtroom. Judge Van den Herne had something else to say.

There was to be an extra hook to the Farmers' fate: they would be guarded by the surviving relatives of people who had been murdered during the Cull. These guards lived and worked at the I.C.C. in The Hague, and they had volunteered to go to the Faroe Islands with the prisoners.

The Farmers were led away in chains by the guards.

Dad remarked, a tone of approval in his voice, "When the 9/11 suspects were rounded up and sent to Guantanamo, I was disgusted that they would be in a nice, warm, tropical climate. Why wasn't there some iceberg made available for that?! Well, this time, with convicted genocidal maniacs, there will be one. Très bien."

We all grinned at him in approval of his little joke, serious as it was.

As we walked out of the building and headed out into the sunshine, moving in silent agreement toward a restaurant that we had become accustomed to eating in, we unconsciously separated into pairs. Dad and Hamish were talking about the legal and scientific details of the case, explaining to each other the parts of it that each found unclear, seeing as they worked in different fields. Claire and Fabian walked ahead of them, looking alternately happy and stunned.

I watched them as I walked with my mother. Claire had closure, but it wasn't quite enough.

"Mommy," I said quietly, "it's safe now to find a psychiatrist or psychologist for Claire."

She turned to me, startled, then said, "Yes! It is."

"Can you help choose one? That's your area of expertise as a nurse."

She smiled. "Yes.

We arrived at the restaurant and went inside, and I felt a sense closure, too.

Chapter 35

The Guidestones Again

So, with the human population of the Earth vastly reduced and Nae-Née continued, what could we reasonably expect for our species' future? Could we expect it to stay motivated to provide food and other necessities for itself?

We didn't all have Regenics, after all. We weren't all going to extend our own lifespans.

A true utopian society would offer Regenics to any and all who wanted it.

Those who wanted it could have it, and those who did not would be left to age.

It ought to be kept in mind that Regenics merely postponed that aging, and by a lot, but it didn't pre-empt it. Physical deterioration from aging and death would still affect everyone at some point. But...to put it off and have time to observe more of history and experience more of life...that was the draw of Regenics.

The advice of the Georgia Guidestones, meant to be taken after an apocalypse of some sort, was now more relevant than ever. That apocalypse, however artificially wrought, had indeed come to pass. Our planet's ecosystems were reduced in their capacity to support life, and the Sixth Mass Extinction of the Earth was still in progress. Species were still ceasing to exist.

Yes, there were fewer humans to put pressure on all of that.

Remove the limitations of the Nae-Née policy with its check on population growth, and that benefit would cease. It wasn't likely that any government would do that.

The legislative branch of the United States, both the Senate and Congress, decided to pass an Act of Nae-Née making the population policy a permanent one. The President of the United States signed it into law. Their reasoning was sound: it emphasized that democracy fails when a society is overpopulated because the preservation of democracy runs on money and the availability of sufficient land and other resources to ensure the comfort and security of all.

That comfort and security is found in a healthy ecosystem that is capable of producing enough for all species, human and others alike. Take that away, and you take democracy away. Human overpopulation doesn't merely threaten that – it destroys it. Eco-stability means eco-security in a post-collapse world, and that lesson had been learned.

Funny that it was learned now, after the Cull. There had to be more to it...

The "more" to it was that the lobbyists of the Farmers were no longer buying and plaguing the members of our government. How delightful! It wasn't the entire answer to the problem, but it was a giant step toward it.

There was another thing on our list of things to do, one which was growing shorter and shorter, and Jason took care of that. He infected the N.S.A.'s tool of treason, that warrantless cyber-snoop program that targeted its own citizens called Model Citizen, with a virus. Within hours of the verdict of the International Criminal Court, Model Citizen had been crashed – permanently.

I doubted that we would be discovered and retaliated against after Jason had purged the N.S.A. computers of their ill-gotten data. He had then fried Model Citizen and the rest of the unconstitutional network. But, as Benjamin Franklin had said, "Three may keep a secret, if two of them are dead." Well, we would just have to take our chances, because we weren't in the business of killing anyone, thank you very much.

What to do then? Live our lives, I supposed. Live them, while remaining watchful and vigilant. More Farmers could always come into existence to threaten the new peace. It was human nature for that to happen. Fortunately, it was also human nature to push back against it. Free at last…

However, there were other constraints on individual freedoms that were unnecessary and intolerable, such as that on travel and on the enjoyment of Nature. Why should we all be forbidden to enter the Wildlands?!

We were soon to have a One World Government, just as the Guidestones recommended, and as the United Nations Agenda for the 21st century had prescribed. The United Nations was meeting in Manhattan to discuss the workings of this modern-day Leviathan. I hoped that it would be the kind of Leviathan that did not need endless – or any – war to function.

It was a New World Order that had forced us to sacrifice far too much of our liberty in order to safeguard our security…and most people hadn't even known it.

People everywhere would have to stay awake to that and maintain constant vigilance about their liberty. People everywhere must be less concerned about security from now on, because the price of that security had been liberty, the free flow of information in the public domain, transparency of government, and ultimately, our right to live at all. We should not cede so much.

There are some unpleasantly inescapable facts to be noted in all of this: One, that whenever ANY species, including our own, reproduces unchecked, it will ultimately decimate its ecosystem; Two, that those who made the decision to reduce our numbers by stealth in order to save our ecosystem for their own benefit have committed the worst crime against humanity ever known; Three, that democracies cannot survive human overpopulation.

Chapter 36

A Send-Off for the Farmers

It was some weeks before the preparations for the sentence handed down to the Farmers were complete. At last, in early October, all was ready in the Faroe Islands.

It should be noted, however, that there was the sentence decreed by the International Criminal Court, and the sentence that was actually carried out by those charged with doing so.

We didn't watch the recordings from our nanobotic camera swarm until much later.

The recordings only showed sights and sounds – not what the Farmers thought or felt.

Bosch glanced around as they were led to the waiting ship, which was docked at the quay.

On the outside, it looked like a cruise ship, but somehow, he knew it would be anything but luxurious on the inside.

The guards nudged anyone who didn't keep moving, but not roughly. Cameras were trained on this long line of convicts. The media wasn't about to pass up the story of the century. Members of the general public had turned out as well, and were armed with iPhones, digital cameras, and all sorts of other recording devices.

The convicts could hear shouts in various languages, all in hostile tones…and that was putting it mildly. These were the surviving relatives of those who had been murdered in the Cull, as were the guards who were herding them up the gangplank.

Bosch was about halfway down the procession of prisoners, so it took several minutes just to walk from the bus to the ship, as they were moving single-file. There were two guards for each convict, just to ensure that no one could escape. Thorough, he thought to himself.

The gangplank led to one of the upper decks, but there were a couple more decks above.

When he reached the top, Bosch looked back at the shore and at the crowd, keeping his face impassive. This would likely be his last chance to see the free world.

Little did he know…

…but he found out shortly.

The guards weren't about to let anyone dawdle and slow the procession down. He was nudged forward, inside the ship, and hustled to a darkened stairwell.

He couldn't see where he was going, but it went down, down, down, and everyone was moving in a hurry. It was confusing; he couldn't see around anyone. The Japanese hedge fund owner, Takata, kept stumbling backwards into him and apologizing, trying to bow to him. The Saudi bank director, Al-Sayah, nearly fell over his dishdashah a couple of times.

At last, they stopped descending into the darkness.

Bosch was propelled roughly ahead of Al-Sayah, hot on the heels of Takata, by his pair of guards, and then they were just gone. He blinked in the sudden brightness of what proved to be a huge, cavernous room as lights came on far above them all.

More people were rapidly joining him, pressing him deeper into the room.

The room smelled oddly like a toilet, and he wondered why.

Bosch looked up as his eyes adjusted and gasped to himself: the guards were way up above the room he was in, in another one that overlooked it, behind a large glass panel.

Suddenly, he understood, and felt as if his insides had turned to ice…and liquid.

He realized, to his horror, that he had lost control of his bowels, and that that was the stench that he had puzzled over moments earlier. Clearly, the others who had arrived a few moments ahead of him had realized what this ship was, and soiled themselves just before Bosch had.

Takata had not, of course. The little Japanese man stood in his gray jumpsuit, stoic and resigned. So typically Japanese. Bosch couldn't decide whether to envy or disdain him.

It didn't matter. His attention was quickly occupied with other things.

Once everyone was inside, the door was slammed and a lock slid loudly into place.

Bosch abruptly realized that no one had thought to band together and rush the door before it closed, refusing entry to the rest of the convicts, to attempt to leave before it was too late.

He and everyone else in this group had been too stunned, confused, scared, or resigned to fight. Perhaps they were just too self-interested to coordinate any resistance if it might mean that others could have avoided being locked into this room but not them. If they couldn't escape, why help others to escape? He knew the mindset; it was his own.

There was a sound of static, and then he heard voices.

The guards had turned on the sound system in their box high above the convicts.

They weren't talking directly to their charges, however.

They were simply allowing the convicts to hear their conversation. It was deliberate.

Bosch stared upwards, unable to stop himself from giving them the satisfaction of having his undivided attention.

The guards were busy doing two things: keeping track of their progress while the captain was piloting the ship out from the docks, up the zee, and through the canals out to sea, and talking with a twisted sense of macabre theater.

That second activity was definitely for the prisoners' benefit.

The observation deck was huge. It ran all around the top of the room, with microphones trained on its occupants every few feet. There was no chance that the prisoners would miss a word of what was said, and that was the point.

The captain and crew on the speakers as well, invisible from the bridge, coordinating the performance with the guards. Clearly, the idea was for the prisoners to hear it all, whatever that turned out to be.

"So," said a guard in English, "which one do you think is our Hitler, which Himmler, Goering, and so on? Do we have a Heydrich here as well?"

Takata told him that guards who spoke Japanese were saying he resembled Tojo.

Perfect. They were to be mocked all the way to prison.

If they were actually going to a prison.

That was another thing that was occupying everyone's attention.

Bosch had abandoned all hope once he saw the inside of this room, but he could tell that some of the others were still clinging to the desperate hope that they would be dropped off at the end of a very uncomfortable and unpleasant ride. Poor bastards, he thought.

Or not. Perhaps it was better to live a little longer in denial.

Welcome to the State of Denial, he thought hysterically.

Now he was making dumb jokes to himself. Perfect. Just perfect…

So this was how it had been for the victims of the Cull, both before any vaccinations had started, when they thought that the Earth could accommodate 10 billion or so humans if they all had to fit into a territory the size of Texas, and during it, right up to the last moment before the flames were turned on.

Except…the victims of the Cull had been asleep first.

He wondered whether or not the guards would extend that same consideration to him and the others. Quite possibly not. Why would they? Bosch and the others had known all along what was happening, whereas the Cull victims had been kept in ignorance for as long as possible.

No, his fate and that of the others would likely match how much they had known.

These guards were doing their best to make this punishment fit the crime.

Cruel and unusual punishment this may be, but this was an unusual circumstance.

The ship was passing through the canals, and the guards were turning back and forth to look out the windows as it moved through the dykes. They kept watching the prisoners, alternating between views.

And they hadn't even had to buy a ticket to this show, Bosch noted.

Odd how acute one's observations got when one was hyper and overstimulated, he thought.

His feet hurt from standing on the cold floor. The prisoners' shoes were not padded at all, so he was getting a backache from standing in them for a long time. Somehow, he doubted that that would go on long enough to be much of a problem. He doubted that he would have a chance to clean himself, too. His hands were cuffed, and his legs in irons, just like the others'.

The ship seemed to be at a standstill, but rising. They must be moving through the canals.

Sure enough, after this had gone on for about half an hour, they moved, only to repeat this process a few more times.

High above, the guards appeared to be lounging on benches along either side of the observation deck, perversely relaxing on what Bosch sourly assumed were padded with cushions. They had to be. The guards were leaning over, spacing out as they rested their elbows on the ledges just inside the glass, eyes trained on their charges.

It wasn't as though they had to do any real work at this point. It was just a ride for them now.

After about four hours – and Bosch knew this from the fact that he knew that how long it took to fill up each level of the canals after the dykes closed behind the ship, and that there were eight levels of them – the ship seemed to be moving out to sea.

Yes…definitely out to sea. The captain had said so to the guards, who were all behaving differently now. They had gotten to their feet, and were milling about, glancing from the area at the front of the ship and back down again at the prisoners.

Bosch looked that way, and realized that a group of guards were standing in front of a control panel, checking the equipment.

That equipment was not for piloting the ship. It was for operating this room.

Now it was really time to get down to business.

The guards were all standing up, facing down into the room, looking at the faces below them. They were taking a good long look at each one, and enjoying it.

Bosch decided not to give anyone the satisfaction of making eye contact, but found it was impossible not to do so. Damn…what was it that Avril had said at the hunting lodge? Aspies were experts at not making eye contact, because it felt like an invasion of personal space. It was not natural for them to make eye contact, but to look away while still observing everything around them.

He envied her that trait now.

Several guards managed to lock in gleeful, mocking stares as he looked up at them.

He hated them. He knew that the feeling was mutual, but it didn't decrease his rage.

He had planned and schemed and organized to avoid ever being in this situation, and now here he was, defeated.

Bosch and the others were in the guards' hands now, and anything could happen.

And then it did.

The tops of the walls on the sides of the room began to move downwards, blocking out the light. Everyone stopped talking in the room, but not outside. However, the speakers were above those panels, so the guards' voices got fainter as the mechanism ground the upper wall panels into place with dull, rasping thud.

He was aware of a dry feeling in his throat, so dry that it hurt, and he realized that he was hyperventilating.

Bosch heard grown men around him sobbing like babies, and someone else shit his pants.

He wondered if it were Takata after all. It had to be; he had held out the longest.

All light was gone, and then suddenly it was back.

That light was coming from flames.

They were slow at first, just to light the room up, and then they were turned up to a roar.

Al-Sayah's dishdashah caught fire as he stood at the edge of the crematorium – yes, it was now obvious what this room was – and he screamed and stamped at it.

Don't bother, Bosch thought.

The others were gasping and choking, and then screaming as holes opened up in the floor here and there, right where they were all standing.

They pushed and shoved to get out of the way of the shooting flames, mad with panic, all sense of decency or consideration for others lost (had they every really had any?), falling into other infernos.

It was like being inside a volcano without lava. There was nowhere to go.

The flames were fired steadily upwards and from the perimeter of the room simultaneously.

Bosch passed out, falling head first into one of the pillars of flame, and knew no more.

It was over for Bosch and the other prisoners far too soon, the guards all thought.

They could not have stayed conscious for long, another said.

Damn!

Well, at least they wouldn't live to enjoy what they had wrought.

Those smug bastards were gone, incinerated.

The guards who controlled the incinerator shut it down after about an hour, opened the panels, and turned on the sifter mechanism. Chains and manacles – and bone fragments – were all that remained, and they were only somewhat recognizable, and that was because distorted metal was more durable that bone and cloth. Flesh, of course, had melted away completely.

The guards sifted the ashes of the Farmers into the ocean, to feed what fish still dwelled there, and turned the ship toward home, their job done, to face the authorities.

It was time to get on with the job of living.

If that meant living with a penalty for exacting revenge, so be it.

Chapter 37

Brave, New, and Underwater

We had gone out for a drive in the country, visiting the farm stores of various towns. We had apple cider, cider donuts, fresh popcorn, and other treats. The air smelled good – cooler than the intense heat of summer, but not as cool as we couldn't stop expecting autumn air to feel.

The world felt both strange and settled.

We had seen to it, as best we could, that something was done about the crimes that we were aware of, and that transparency was achieved in the process. I hoped it was enough to those on the receiving end, because nothing else would ever give anyone more closure than that.

The Farmers would miss out on reaping the benefits of that rush to balance accounts.

For that, an account with them had been settled.

I didn't realize just how settled it was until we got home.

It was all over the news, and the reporters who delivered the story seemed…pleased.

They had slight smiles on their faces, and uplifted tones in their voices.

A case in point was airing that evening, and Claire stared at the newscaster, a middle-aged man broadcasting from New York City, with a mixture of elation, shock, and disapproval. It was impossible not to second those sentiments when I considered what was behind them: pleasure at the delivery of justice, astonishment, and a moral compass kicking in despite it all.

"In a shocking turn of events," the newscaster announced, "the ship onto which the defendants of what is now being called the Human Population Cull case were herded not onto an ordinary transport ship, but onto one of the cremation ships that was used during the genocide that they arranged. Once on board, the ship was brought out to sea, the upper doors closed on the prisoners as they all stood in a crowd below the viewing chamber, and the flames turned on. From all accounts that we can verify, the defendants were then burned alive, with none of the anaesthesia that put their victims to sleep first."

We all stared at the TV in shock.

The newscaster continued, "When the deed was done, the ship turned around and returned to the dykes at The Hague, and the guards, many of whom had lost family and friends to the crimes against humanity that their victims had perpetrated, turned themselves in to authorities there. The guards expressed no remorse, only a willingness to accept life in prison in exchange for having carried out a justice that the laws of the International Criminal Court could not."

That was it.

We sat in the living room together, gaping at the television as if expecting it to provide more information, but there was no more. Why should there be? There would be no more for so many. It was all over.

It was time to get on with our lives.

In a year and a half, Spades and his wife could get on with theirs.

I thought of them, spending that year in The Hague, him in prison, and her in a hotel room.

They would have supervised visits, and then he would go home.

I wondered if he would take a drink again, or if he would be able to keep sober.

That was the very least that he could do.

We shut off the TV and went up to bed.

None of us – not my parents, not my grandmother, not Claire and Fabian, and not Hamish or I – felt like sitting around together and enjoying each other's company like we did on ordinary evenings.

This one was too extraordinary. We needed to relax and think about it quietly. It was a lot to comprehend and accept. The Farmers were gone. The Cull was addressed.

Nae-Née would continue to keep human numbers from overwhelming the ecosystem again. Life would go on for those of us who were still here. What that life would be like would be very different, but we were adjusting to it.

In the days that followed, the live cremation of the Farmers was all that was on the news.

People everywhere were stunned by it. Statements were fired off from the International Criminal Court, the United Nations Secretariat, the U.N. Security Council, and even Blackwater Security about, each denying any association with the guards who had killed the prisoners.

The guards and crew of that crematorium ship numbered sixty-four in total. They were almost all male, except for eight women. They were in their forties, except for the captain, engineer, first mate, and warden. They were in their fifties and sixties.

No proof could be found that anyone other than those guards had had any role in the planning or enabling of the act, and none was forthcoming anyway. The guards, for their part, defiantly insisted that they had done this of their own accord, acting out of revenge, and said that they now expected and accepted a lifetime in that prison in the Faroe Islands.

But the people in the Faroe Islands refused to accept them.

Eventually, a prison was set up in the Azores, a group of islands controlled by Portugal. A good portion of those islands were still well above sea level, so there was plenty of room for the lot of them. It was more of a scenic farm than a prison, complete with a library. Their biggest punishment would consist of having to produce their own food and clothing, it seemed.

For that, the world seemed to have nothing to say. The rest of the world had to do that, too.

The next big news in the United States was the abolition of the Federal Reserve Board.

The Fed had grown to a monster with twelve government-owned and operated banks around the nations, all overseen by a Board of Governors and chaired by someone appointed by the President of the United States…to a term of

14 years. That person typically had ties to the banksters of Wall Street, which was seen by many as a conflict of interest more than a job qualification.

The law that made this so, which Congress passed and the President signed, was named for the economists whose ideas had been adopted for it: it was the Greco-Brown Act.

Similar laws were being enacted in nations around the world.

Why do this? To make inflation and ballooning debts impossible to repeat, that was why.

People were exhausted and fed up with the Fed, with debt, and with fear in general.

It was time to live calmly again, and to find a little happiness in this strange new world.

A week later, Hamish brought something home to show us.

"Look at this," he with a smile, and put some paper in my hand.

It was U.S. currency, redone. It felt the same in weight as a stack of bills had felt before, but it was all different. The size of each denomination was slightly different, plus it had Braille dots for the blind. Excellent – they wouldn't have to just trust sighted cashiers or other sighted people to honestly make change for them.

Most importantly, it no longer said "Federal Reserve Note" on any denomination.

Instead, it said "United States Currency" across the tops of the fronts, and across the tops of the backs, which were green (still "greenbacks", we were pleased to observe), it read "Created by the United States of America". Gone were the irrelevant words "In God We Trust" – another welcome change. Since when had any fictitious entity granted money anyway?! Never.

Hamish had brought some ones, fives, tens, twenties, fifties, and one hundred-dollar bills. George Washington, Abraham Lincoln, Alexander Hamilton, Harriet Tubman, Ulysses S. Grant, and Benjamin Franklin, respectively, graced them.

As far as I could see, the Crane paper company still made our money. There was no reason to change that. Red and blue fibers showed here and there in the thick, durable paper. This stuff would last a good long time, and the U.S. Treasury had not had to retool its entire printing process. That was a good thing.

The designs on the bills still reflected the Masonic past of the Founders of our nation, including symbols such as a pyramid with an eye. I hoped that the meaning had changed from a surveillance state watching us to the reverse, but constant vigilance and verification would always be necessary on the people's part to safeguard that.

A woman in ancient Greek robes also graced the notes.

She represented Liberty, and she was staring right back at that eye.

Good. Perhaps that meant exactly what I was wishing it to mean.

Chapter 38

Nae-Née Forever

Hamish and I were at home, working in the yard.

He was pushing our human-powered, "green" lawn mower. I was checking the apiary.

Our yard was green, all right – green with energy efficiency and eco-friendliness, and beautiful. The funny thing about that was that we had made it green on our own, before it was ever required, and more stringently so than the law had required.

It was also off the surveillance grid. At last, that was not illegal.

A milk truck pulled up to our driveway, and Aaron and Ed came out of the guardhouse to meet it. The truck was red, with an old-fashioned sign painted across it: Tulmeadow Dairy. It had a cute cow on the side, accompanied by a smaller face, which was of a goat.

The farm delivered fresh goat cheese whenever we wanted it, which wasn't every week, and six fresh glass bottles of milk brimming with cream on top. The bottles arrived in a wooden crate with a grid of metal rungs. It looked just like something out of an old movie, and my parents loved it. They said it was exactly as it had been when they were kids in France.

Claire and Fabian and I were delighted with it. Claire and I would immediately skim off the cream and save it to ladle over berries and cakes. I went inside to meet Aaron with the milk bottles, and she and I did that right away. My mother had just brought some fruit back from the nearby orchard, so we would eat some of that for dessert.

Hamish's nanobotic swarms were quietly cleaning the oceans and the air.

It would take years, possibly decades, to show progress in repairing that damage that humans had done to the Earth's bank account since the Industrial Revolution had begun, but it was a start. Studies showed that it was working, and that further additions of toxins to the ecosystem had been halted.

The ghosts didn't disturb Hamish anymore, another welcome change.

Without the banksters, hedge fundsters, and their cronies to worry about, the U.S. government had enjoyed having nothing in the way of making the economy healthy. It was a relief to know that banks wouldn't be bricking themselves up again anytime soon.

But there was a lesson to be learned from all of this: whether our financial system was managed by honest bankers or lying, gambling-addicted banksters, it was a virtual system, and subject to manipulation, which could either benefit us or destroy us.

That wasn't the entire lesson, of course. The other side of the proverbial coin was that the Earth's Bank Account was NOT virtual. It was real, and could only be pushed so far before it refused to yield any more. We had won…and yet it was a draw. We had to live in a world of limited choices. We couldn't just do and have everything we wanted, or we would kill ourselves and our planet, propagating until we destroyed our own habitat. We had almost done that. Damn! I hated the fact that it was the Farmers' crimes that had bought us more time and hope.

Thomas Robert Malthus, the eighteenth-century population and demographics economist, had been right all along. Humans will reproduce more when unchecked by disease, famine, or war. Give them peace and health, and soon they will be overpopulated, with a booming economy. But not for long: wait a bit longer, and those checks will come back into play, brought by those very same conditions. Sex had to be kept disconnected from reproduction.

The Earth had had its resource war, with some plague and famine mixed in, felt in various parts of societies and in all regions of the planet. Our numbers were down to half a billion. The ecosystem could no longer support 2 billion humans after what 8 billion had done. They had used up non-renewable resource. If our numbers weren't kept where they were, we would start that vicious cycle right back up again, and decimate everything to the state of Rapa Nui.

Thus, Nae-Née and the population policy continued to be the law of the planet.

The Earth could not give anyone all of the freedom that they wanted. It was finite, and that was at last recognized by all, however unwelcome and inconvenient that truth was to accept. The weather patterns had changed, land masses had shrunk, and temperatures were more intense, be they colder or warmer.

We had enough food and water, it was clean, and we were not restricted in our daily lives. We could use whatever appliances and however much water we chose without the threat of it being shut off. Surveillance was back down to pre-Cull levels again.

Societies everywhere had been completely restructured, even if many old ways continued.

Still, it was not complete freedom – not a complete return to the old laws.

It was close, but our government now followed the post-apocalyptic advice of the Georgia Guidestones right along with the U.S. Constitution, and adhered to the United Nations treaties, and the Courts in The Hague.

It felt like every person for herself, or himself, and only if they could enforce their own will. That took resources in the form of money or goods or land – or all three, plus foresight. The price of liberty was, and always would be, constant vigilance. Even libertarianism had limits.

For those of us who had survived this far, I wondered what we had gained.

Perhaps it would be the opportunity, ultimately, to be the last to starve.

Those of the Farmers' heirs who had had their money separate from their parents' accounts were still active, scrambling to mine and use the last of whatever resources they could access and control. They still had not shown any sign of devising any viable plan – nor of even contemplating one – for developing alternatives to those resources. What did they intend to do once those things were exhausted? Would they finally have to face that fact that all things end, even the human species' wealthiest and most powerful individuals?

When that finally happened, there would likely be more trouble, and more conflict.

That outcome remained to be seen, however, and I was glad that it was not yet. Life would go on and show us its own outcomes in its own good time. The Earth's temperatures were still rising, along with sea levels. The amount of land would be about as much as there had been for the dinosaurs…and then what? What would become of humans? Would life be comfortable enough to go with, or merely grim, nasty, hot, and sharply limited?

Yes. It would be. Nothing lasts forever. Not even extended life spans.

That night, something else happened: a late-night comedian reappeared on television.

I flipped channels, checking the other major networks for his competitors.

They too were on, cracking jokes and making witty remarks.

I suddenly realized what was so remarkable about that: they hadn't been on for over a year.

They had not been seen or heard because democracy and liberty had been suspended.

Now they were back, as irreverent and uproarious as ever.

They were even making comments about the Cull, the Farmers, and the I.C.C.

They were telling the truth with wry, witty, reckless abandon.

The court jesters were back, mocking the politically powerful, past and present.

They were being, as Mark Twain had said, the defenders of democracy.

He had also said that "it is better to be popular than right." Perhaps he was being ironic?

Whatever the case may have been, this was wonderful.

It was a sign of hope, and hope is always good.

Hope is popular, too, and that is okay.

Acknowledgements

It is first and foremost to my parents that these acknowledgments are made.

They have enabled me to work in peace while encouraging me in my writing career and cheering me on as I have proceeded with it.

They patiently hear my ideas and give useful feedback.

My mother, Carole B.C. Fox, patiently edited this manuscript.

David D. Haines, Ph.D. in immunology, offered the same things.

Sarah D. FitzGerald, who appears in this novel and the previous one as Sophia, is another patient listener. She smiles and offers her assessment of my endless litanies of plots, character backstory, and other details without complaint. She has offered some clever analyses, too.

Lou Bottali, my cousin and an engineer, helpfully discussed alternate fuel sources with me.

Paul R. Ehrlich, the famous author of *The Population Bomb*, wrote me some kind words of encouragement in an e-mail, paid me the great compliment of buying a copy of the first *Nae-Née* novel, and surprised me with an autographed copy of *The Dominant Animal: Human Evolution & the Environment*, which he co-authored with his wife, Anne H. Ehrlich.

The fact that an authority on human overpopulation and its consequences would interact with an author who wrote to him out of nowhere, asking him about the negative response that comes with discussing this inflammatory topic, and reply to me personally, is deeply appreciated.

About the Author

Stephanie C. Fox, J.D. is a historian, lawyer, author, editor, and publisher. She is a graduate of William Smith College and of the University of Connecticut School of Law. She runs an editing service called **QueenBeeEdit**, found at www.queenbeeedit.com, which caters to politicians, scientists, and others.

Her imprint is **QueenBeeBooks**.

Stephanie lives in Connecticut, and has written about other topics, including Asperger's, the global financial meltdown, and travelogues of a trip to Kuwait and a trip to Hawai'i.

Her areas of interest include – but are not limited to –history, biographies, women's studies, science fiction, human overpopulation, ecosystems collapse, environmental law, international relations, Asperger's, and cats.

Stephanie has spent time in Manhattan, Hawai'i, France, England, and Venice. She loves cats and worries about the future of our planet.

About the Illustrator

Steve Palmerton is a graduate of the Art Institute of California in Orange County, where he studied Character Designs, Illustration, Background Designs, 2D-3D Concepts, and Concept Art. He specializes in science fiction art, and his portfolio may be viewed at https://www.artstation.com/artist/chelectonus.

He writes: "I excel at creating worlds and exciting places. Bringing interesting shapes to the canvas is what I am passionate about."